THE ME

THE MERITOCRACY QUARTET

JEFFREY LEWIS

First published in Great Britain in 2011 by
HAUS PUBLISHING LTD.
70 Cadogan Place, London SW1X 9AH
www.hauspublishing.com

Copyright © 2011 Jeffrey Lewis
First published in the United States in four volumes by Other Press LLC

ISBN 978 0 907822 77 6

Typeset in Garamond by MacGuru Ltd
info@macguru.org.uk

Printed and bound by CPI Group (UK) Ltd, Croydon, CR0 4YY

A CIP catalogue for this book is available from the British Library

CONDITIONS OF SALE
All rights reserved. No part of this publication may be reproduced, stored in a retrieval system, or transmitted in any form or by any means, electronic, mechanical, photocopying, recording or otherwise, without the prior permission of the publisher.

This book is sold subject to the condition that it shall not, by way of trade or otherwise, be lent, re-sold, hired out or otherwise circulated without the publisher's prior consent in any form of binding or cover other than that in which it is published and without a similar condition including this condition being imposed on the subsequent purchase.

Contents

Foreword / vii

Meritocracy: A Love Story / 1
The Conference of the Birds / 163
Theme Song for an Old Show / 407
Adam the King / 563

Foreword

When I started writing these books, I didn't know how many of them there would be. Four was probably always the most likely number, but it could have been three or five. What determined me, I think, was some combination of my old fondness for Durrell's *Alexandria Quartet*, or in particular the perfume of its name, and the fact that I could squeeze four decades out of the stories I had to write. The most inauthentic of determinants, but then, that's how determinants are. Already I feel the danger of rewriting or over-writing what I've written in the texts. From *Theme Song for an Old Show:*

"I had in mind to write a kind of 'meritocracy' series, novels that would chart the progress of my generation, or anyway the narrow slice of it that I knew well. The first book, in retrospect, came easily enough. Nothing ever comes easily, but I had a story to tell that was clear and seemed true enough, and I had feeling to put into it that had never gone away. It was the story of my hero in college, Harry Nolan, who might have been president of the country one day, and his wife Sascha Maclaren on whom I had a crush. My sixties book, so to speak. The sixties. The seventies. The eighties. The nineties. A book for each decade, a neat quartet, about the best and the brightest and what happened to them, or us. Something you weren't going to see on TV or in the movies. Something, I told myself, that you might not even read in someone else's book. The novel as sociology? A dirty job but somebody's got to do it?

Maybe so or maybe not. But also Forster's thing about if you had to choose between your country and your friends, would you have the courage to choose your friends? Not that in my case courage was involved. Rather, more, the imagination of courage: *if* I had to choose, which would it be?"

I am grateful for this all-in-one edition because it may allow readers to see more easily my intention in writing these four books. It feels like bringing together the members of my family for a photograph where resemblances and contrasts, and perhaps even evolution, can be found.

Jeffrey Lewis
January 2011

MERITOCRACY

A Love Story

1

It was six hours from Boston to where we were going. It rained from Augusta to Belfast, and then along the coast road there were patches of fog. After Bucksport we turned off Route 1 and the road became narrow and roughly repaired and it rollercoastered up and down the hilly country. We passed a blueberry packing plant lit like an all-night truck stop and closed garages and repair shops and empty black farmland, and I began to feel a cool unease in my throat and in the tips of my fingers, not for the passing scene but for the fact that we were getting closer. Just as now, half a lifetime later, when the potholed road and astral blueberry plant dot my memory like so many fossils from an otherwise eroded landscape, I feel on beginning to tell this story a sense of trespass, as if what happened that weekend is none of my business, and never was.

I didn't own a car then. I had no money. I was a scholarship kid from Rochester and I'd never been to Maine and my ideas of it were taken from old ViewMasters. Three of us drove up in the metallic blue F-85 Cutlass convertible that Teddy's parents had given him, on no particular occasion, no birthday, not even a B+ on a Milton paper, sometime in his junior year. Cord lay across the backseat with his face in his balled-up Shetland sweater as if it were a roadtrip back from Vassar. In the argot of the time it was road shortener that had put him in this state, road shortener meaning beer. I wonder sometimes what happens to clever slang, whether literature becomes its museum or it just gets buried in the ground like the ruins of cities, awaiting chance rediscovery by the next generation of sarcastic kids. "Road shortener" I haven't heard in decades. Cord roused himself mainly to piss, or to provide sudsy tour-guide commentary, about lobster stands and the locales of failed trysts and the size of a full-grown monster moose and about the place we were going, where his family had their compound, that it was called Clements Cove, or Clement's Cove, or Clements' Cove, the locals had been fighting over the apostrophe for a hundred fifty years, long after the last of the Clements or Clementses were gone from the coast. This was the weekend past Labor Day, in the summer of our graduation, in 1966. Harry and Sascha had been married in June. They were driving up separately, and had gone to Bangor to pick up Adam Bloch, who took the bus. Harry was going in the army in a week. He wasn't even in ROTC. He was going as a grunt to Vietnam and this was the weekend we were sending him away.

All the rest of us had deferments, me to teach in Greece, Teddy for the Peace Corps, Cord for business school, Adam Bloch for grad school in economics. The normal run of things. Johnson was still president and there were still deferments to be had.

Everyone had an opinion as to why Harry was going to Vietnam, and I did too, but I never believed that I could get it all. My shortest version said Harry's father was the three-term senator from California and Harry was headed for politics and he knew it and the wisdom of the time was that if you wanted to go into politics you had to go in the service. It kept you alive anyway. If you dodged it you were dead. But the common phrase you always heard about Harry Nolan was what a crazy guy he was, and I was sure there was something more than politics to his decision, something macho or jocky, or one of those things we didn't talk about much because to talk about them was risking to kill them, duty or honor or whatever else. Better to leave it as Cord once said, that Harry'd rather have got himself shot at than go to graduate school. But none of us thought we knew it all, for instance how to figure Sascha, who hated his going, who would have gone in the Peace Corps with him, who married him regardless and in defiance. So maybe it came back, ninety percent anyway, to electoral viability, to the old man's advice. In the summer of 1966 it was still a little early to be way against the war, at least where we were. It was more something to be negotiated around, or if you were already in ROTC to be embraced with gritted teeth, or if you were Harry to say what the hell.

Teddy, I suppose, was one of a type who used to roam the east coast like wildebeests on the Serengeti, Greenwich, St. Grottlesex, his father big in advertising, a skinny guy with skinny tortoise shell glasses, silky dark hair, choirboy nose and lips and a neat backward part, someone you could imagine getting the epithet "fast" added to his name, like the guy who married Tricia Nixon, Fast Eddie whoever, forgotten now but there was a time around Harvard Law School and in *People* magazine when he was considered a fairly big cheese.

Teddy got us to Clements Cove in five hours instead of six. We stepped out of the fetid Cutlass into a moonless night so radiant it woke up even Cord. I was a city boy, unused to seeing a hundred thousand stars, and I wandered around like a dazed dimwit until Cord said something like, "They got these things in New York?" "I know you think all Jews come from New York, but I actually grew up in Rochester." "In't that New

York?" Ah yes, the old New York City/New York State conflation, cracker fucknose, I didn't say, because I didn't think of it but also letting Cord have the last word made me feel comradely. These were Harry's friends long before mine, his old, old friends, prep school and deb parties and summer places, and relative to all that I was still a new guy, roots no deeper than the spring grass. We unloaded the trunk. We were parked on a sloping gravelly patch by Harry's old black Aston Martin. A few lights on here and there in the house. I couldn't tell much about the place, but that it was shingled and close by the water. I could hear the lapping of the bay. There were still a few mosquitoes and I waved them away, but no one else bothered.

A yellow bug light hung outside the kitchen door like the entrance to a quarantine area. Bloch was in the kitchen. "Can I help?" "Here, let me get that." "Any more out there?" Jesus, Bloch. His too-ready smile, his too-eager offers, his too-thick eyebrows. Can't you see we're grown men, we've got one bag apiece, no one said, because it was a weekend and he was Harry's latest find and we respected it and anyway you didn't cut people like Bloch directly, you cut them by looking past them, thanks anyway, got it covered.

Or it's possible Cord and Teddy didn't even notice that Bloch was annoying, maybe it was only me. What was Bloch doing here anyway? He wasn't my friend, he wasn't part of us, he was only Harry's friend. But of course Harry was the one going away. And without Harry I wouldn't have been here either. I wouldn't have known Cord or Teddy, I would have had different roommates entirely. And Sascha. Would I ever have heard her say my name, would I have more than seen her across a room or street, if not for Harry?

The main room was long with ceiling beams thicker than

railway ties and an overscale stone fireplace that looked like the entrance to a cave. In all it resembled a ski lodge where somebody had gone through and taken out all the alpine motifs and replaced them with carved boats and nautical charts.

In front of the fireplace sprawled an ancient couch you could get lost in, deep-cushioned, floral-patterned, and Sascha was there, her knees up, Harry's crewcut head wedged against her, the rest of him across the couch like a dead guy. They were so loose-limbed, that was the thing. Or one of the things, anyway. Along with her dark restless hair, almost like a banner flying her name. And the embers of awareness in the center of her star-blue eyes, that seemed to say the world hadn't crushed her just when the world seemed to think it had. Her full lips, the slightly downturned corners of her mouth, a melancholy look, sleepless, complicated, a little bit cunning; a look of many cups of coffee, and somehow, always, injury without a mark. If her look was aristocratic, it was also not quite American, not all of it anyway. I hated superlatives then. They used to sound so stupid. But Sascha was my superlative. And Harry was my friend, and I was supposed to be his.

They didn't get up. Harry waved at us with a vague sweep of his hand, as though making fun of how little effort he would expend to greet us, how relaxed he was, how sweet life was this night. They'd started a fire, though the evening was only a little cool. The lights were out and the fire made shadow puppet play of their faces. Sascha smiled our way. She too waved, opening and shutting her fingers, and her brief smile was enough to lift the downturned corners of her mouth. I saw that much anyway, even if as a matter of self-preservation I was trying not to focus upon her too directly, was daring myself to see her as no more than a figure in a landscape.

We said a few things. It was mostly Cord who said them. Had they found something to eat? Were they warm enough? What time had they got here? Had they hit the construction on the bridge over the Kennebec? It was his family's place, his family's photos on the tables, and he had a southern way about him that was half gracious and half fussy, as he made his way around the room throwing switches and checking on the mice and whether the caretaker Everett had been into the Johnny Walker again. Cord's family were cotton farmers from Tennessee, which maybe meant plantation owners once, but they'd been sending their towhead boys north for Yankee schooling for enough years that there was an athletic trophy at Yale named after one of them and this compound had made its way into the family holdings. Cord had a faint, almost breathless voice, he spoke rapidly, he was by turns kind, malicious, and clowny, and it was sometimes hard to know which he was being because it was so hard to hear him. Long-limbed and big-handed, with stubbornly turned-up Nordic features, he seemed like one in whom the instinct to be just a big old farmboy, even after centuries of refinements and "good matches," had refused entirely to die. Cord was in every social grace sanded at least as smooth as Teddy, but take away the J. Press and cordovans and you could almost see a ghost draped over a plough.

It wasn't for me alone that Harry and Sascha were like a force field. Cord too, and Teddy, and Adam Bloch. All of us who were there that weekend, at one time or another, though Cord and Teddy wore their admiration lightly, more like peers of the realm. When I was in a room I was conscious of a part of me aimed in their direction, no matter which way I was facing. If they were apart, I was bifurcated, like an isosceles triangle. If I left the room, to go upstairs because Cord was going to show me where my room was, I felt a part of me tugging, left behind, like a character's foot in a cartoon mired in glue or pitch. These feelings diminished when I was away from them, though one or the other of them often came to my mind. I always felt the next time I saw them I wouldn't be so in their thrall. But it inevitably happened again, with as little as Harry's wave, as little as Sascha's complicated smile, which this night I was doing my best to avoid.

And beyond our little group I knew there must be others, in our class at Yale or Sascha's at Radcliffe or in Maine or Nantucket or New York or Virginia who loved the one or the other or both, or talked about how much they admired them when they too loved. I was a partisan, of course, a cheerleader of sorts, but why not? At the time I felt lucky to be close. It made my life make a kind of sense, just as two vectors aimed at the same point create the feeling we call fate.

Harry asked if we'd brought any beer and Cord said yes there was Carlings he'd put in the fridge but when Harry lifted his head off Sascha's lap she said "Don't go" and put her hand on him to stop him. Her voice was quiet then and frightened and sweet, a tiny diminished voice I'd never heard before. But in moments, after he kissed her lightly—just her lower lip he kissed—she let him go and he got up and that was the end of it, the end of her mocking herself on account of her fears or whatever it was. Cord and Sascha, who'd known one another longer than Harry had known her, because Sascha's sister Maisie had gone out with Cord's brother's roommate at Hotchkiss, chattered about Maisie wanting to transfer from Sarah Lawrence but she didn't know where, maybe Berkeley, get away from it all. Soon Harry was back and he and Sascha were as before and they drank a beer together. They were the last to come upstairs.

All of us slept up there, in a fairyland warren of rooms where the kids of Cord's family had been growing up for sixty years. My narrow bed was made up with a quilt and it creaked. There were camp pictures on the walls, all girls, and a yearbook from the Ethel Walker School on the painted bedside table. Outside was the dark of the bay, the starlight barely sprinkling it. For a long time I couldn't sleep because I was hearing Sascha's voice when she said "Don't go."

Teddy was the first up the next day and he'd found some eggs in the fridge and was making some weird egg dish that required putting the eggs in the oven with cheese on top of them. Shirred eggs à la something or other. He was darting around the country kitchen, he'd awakened with such a surplus of nervous energy it was as if he could have fried the eggs himself without a stove. I stood around and watched him a few minutes and went outside.

It was a gray morning that was cooler than the night before. The tide was coming in but it wasn't yet here, and I looked out on a landscape of mussel shells and black ooze, then the gray water looking cold and choppy beyond. The cove was cut deep and angular. On its far shore there were woods, a log cabin and a shingle cottage with a screened-in porch, a faded pier. Just outside the cove two bare islands sat, or maybe they were one when the tide was low. A rickety marker stuck out of the flank of one of them, tentative, annoying, like something a picador would stick in a bull. Cord's house was set right by the water. It too had a pier, which sagged then regained a little of its composure toward the end of it, like one of those hand bridges you see in *National Geographic* movies of Asia. The house itself sat on a shelf of rock, and at first I thought it looked brave and lonely, with its mottled brown shingles, but actually it wasn't so alone, this was a compound after all, and there were two more dark shingled houses visible through the spruce. They didn't look as big as Cord's. They belonged to other Elliotts, and then there was another shingled structure that looked like a shed. All this took money, I thought. The effect was not achieved without money, money as weathered as the shingles.

When I went back inside Harry was downstairs. He was in a white T-shirt and unshaved and he looked enough like Stanley Kowalski to give Brando fans pause. Harry was not one who'd ever bought into the idea of Ivy, or preppie for that matter when his parents sent him out of California to St. Paul's. Teddy still rode him about the surfboard he'd sent east and insisted on mounting like a dead shark over his bed. Harry was someone who wore anything his mother or a girlfriend bought for him, and now he'd married a woman who didn't shop at all. He was pretty much always down to a T-shirt and cutoffs, though occasionally a worn Lacoste would appear with the alligator falling off it. In a sense he was someone who didn't need clothes anyway. He had a thick neck and his jaw jutted and his forehead overhung his eyes, putting them in shadows. His body was something machine nouns stuck to, dynamo, turbine, Pratt-Whitney engine. He had hairy legs, his crewcut was pure Beach Boys, and in short he looked nothing like a Yale guy or even an eastern guy, he looked like a pure California guy, who'd only gone east because he'd been caught screwing the chaplain's daughter at Thacher, or maybe the thing about the chaplain's daughter was true but there was also noblesse oblige in there somewhere, even in California you went east to school if you were old money enough and didn't want to wind up a provincial moron. His full name, after all, was Harry St.

Christopher Nolan, the "St. Christopher" in grateful remembrance of a San Francisco department store fortune on his mother's side without which his father's rise in politics would have been as unlikely as Jack's on the beanstalk. So Harry had pedigree, even if he looked like a Marine recruit from Pismo Beach and talked with a soft twang, like a guy who missed the beach every day the surf was up.

"Hey." Now there was a word that Harry used a lot. A lot of the time it was the only word he used. It expressed acknowledgment. Everything else was optional. Usually friendly enough, that "Hey," but sometimes withheld, sometimes impatient, sometimes ridiculing, as though what really was meant was "Hey asshole" but he'd left off the rest of the sentence. "Hey Louie." That was me, that was good morning, that was how've you been since the wedding or whenever it was I last saw you. Harry sometimes forgot. Not the way most people forget such things, out of self-absorption, with Harry it was more like he'd been overabsorbed by the world. He remembered big emotions, he remembered bright divides, he remembered if somebody'd been a good guy or asshole. And he remembered—which I did not—jokes.

We ate our eggs standing up. Teddy had put in so much paprika he could have scorched the Hapsburg Empire. He seemed to think if it was good for deviled eggs, it would be good for whatever he was making. Nobody said anything. Teddy finally said how unbelievably fabulous he thought they were and we could just shove it if we didn't think so too, and in a pissy move was about to dump all the uneaten ones in the garbage, when Bloch walked in, wearing clothes too pressed for the country, his smile pleasant-enough now, face scrubbed. Neat. Bloch was always neat.

Teddy offered Adam breakfast. Would he like some shirred eggs, he could be the judge, he could be the neutral party, because some people thought they were less than fine. Bloch wasn't sure which way to flop on this. The one thing he knew for certain was that he didn't want to alienate anyone and that in this circumstance he could be considered the butt of a joke but on the other hand maybe it was good-natured and if he didn't play it that way everyone would think he was a flamer. He ate the eggs. Um good, Cord said. Fuck you, let Adam judge, Teddy said. I said nothing. I suppose I felt too close to Bloch's position. He took another bite. Not bad, he said. Pretty good, he said, and the rest of us managed not to laugh because we were so well brought up, but Bloch wasn't sure.

He mopped his plate clean with his toast. Maybe he really was just telling the truth, but Harry threw his out as soon as Teddy was gone and slugged orange juice to get the taste out and I did too. We passed the orange juice carton back and forth. Harry asked me how my summer had been. I felt again the warmth in the back of my neck and in my shoulders as though it were the gaze of the sun on me. I told him I'd been in Europe. Bumming around, got as far as Rome. Then came back to make some money because I was going away again in October. You lazy fuck, he said. Sascha walked in. She was wearing a man's shirt and her restless hair was pulled back by something. Before I could help it I'd looked at her. Not a half-look, unfocused, with others in the frame. I'd looked at her, and knew that I was still in love.

2

The year George W. Bush and Al Gore ran for president, it seemed like the whole country was clicking its tongue about them. The boys of privilege, the smirk and the lame, and everywhere the implication (if not the accusation) that this was the best our generation could produce, or at least that our elite could produce, our golden guys, who got into Yale or wherever and their mamas were pretty and they were pampered and raised up enough that their heads were over the clouds a little, so that they could see what was up better than the rest of us anyway, and to boot they were good-looking because their mamas were, and they had the money to get there. These. Ours. Mine. Another best and brightest story of going down in flames, the late-night comedians getting in theirs, a candidate whose most radical idea was abolishing the estate tax so that the rich could stay rich forever. And what did I think about it all? Mostly that the story was true, true as far as it went. But also I thought: *It ought to be Harry Nolan up there.*

One night I even dreamed of George Bush, in a moment of candor or nostalgia or even sweetness, saying the same thing. *It ought to be Harry Nolan up there, he's the one, he's a good man.* The way W. says "good man."

Bush was two classes behind us at Yale. He was in DKE. Harry was in DKE and he knew George pretty well and he liked him well enough, thought he was an okay guy anyway. But George idolized Harry. I know this because I saw it. George was in our rooms quite often in our senior year. I wasn't his friend but I knew who he was, mostly because Yale was like that then, you knew who was the son of somebody famous, and even then Bush the father was big in the Republican Party, running for the Senate or rising at the R.N.C., something like that. Like Harry, George was the son of somebody. They must have spotted each other on that basis alone from a half-mile off. That and DKE and the fact they were both preppies from the west. But Harry wouldn't have cared, he would simply have been aware, whereas with George I wouldn't know. All I knew was that he idolized Harry, that he would stand around our room silent in a varsity jacket with other DKEs watching Harry swat a squash ball against the wall or listening to his jokes or waiting on him to say any damned thing at all.

There were people who resented Harry Nolan, denigrated his athleticism, suspected his charm, denied his intelligence, thought the whole thing about him was a privileged brew of cult and hype; who hated California, hated jocky DKE though Harry hardly ever went over there, hated all the girls he screwed and that after screwing them he wound up with the Number One Girl of them all. It enraged them that more than anyone they knew or had heard of Harry Nolan was likely to wind up president of the country someday. They thought a person you could say that about, that he could or would be president, had to be a phony and a shallow piece of shit. But these, the haters, weren't many. He was too funny, too self-mocking, too wide-open and unadorned. And he was one of those, in a class of a thousand, a college of four thousand, a university of ten thousand, everyone seemed to have heard of him. I probably could have counted a hundred people who knew me by my first name. Judging by the people who were always asking me about Harry, twenty times that number must have known him, because he'd drunk with them or driven them in his Aston or commiserated with them about one bit of horseshit or another or loaned them money or just because they did. If he crossed your path, you probably thought he liked you, and from that dared let escape the truth that preceded it and drove it, that your life's vote was his for the asking.

From our time at Yale there were a lot of guys who made it in politics. John Kerry who started prepping his run at the White House thirty years ago was in our class, and George Pataki of New York was the class after. And some Whitman in our class married Christie Todd to make Christie Todd Whitman, and of course there was Bush. And Joe Lieberman was two classes ahead of us, and John Ashcroft. At Harvard at the same time was Weld of Massachusetts, and Gore. And what year was it that Bill and Hillary entered Yale Law? I've never done the math. But it seems like a lot. The cream rising to the top, and then what?

Harry Nolan's name is not among them.

But getting back to Bush. Bush with his many flaws. My political views are perhaps what you'd expect, of a guy of a certain age, screenwriter, TV, briefly lawyer, bummed around, California, Europe, New York, an intellectual of sorts, a manqué of sorts. That is to say, I blame, I stew, I patronize, I write letters to the editor in my head, I cringe and take cheap shots and sometimes I despair. And yet, this evening in my chair, as for a little while I neglect his policies and remember the man, I'm having warmer feelings for George. He lies too much, of course. Clinton lied about sex but W. lies about virtually everything else, like a less-than-stellar candidate for mayor of Sheboygan.

But the way he tries to keep his head up, slightly stiff and meaningful, as if he's maybe afraid he isn't quite tall enough. Or for that matter the little thrusting of his chest when he thinks he's being filmed, when he's walking "official," like a stripper with new tits she's actually quite proud of. He seems, I suppose, such a simple, unguarded example of the way life challenges us all on an ongoing basis. A bit of dignity, perhaps. I keep thinking that might be what I'm seeing, growing, gaining firmness and fixity, out of the petulance and self-satisfaction. Or competing with them, anyway. Living side by side, peaceful coexistence. A boy who's trying, harder at times, less hard at others, to become a man.

It's just that he makes me think of Harry.

We used to say "good man," too. Harry did, a lot.

3

The cove wasn't a proper place for the Elliotts to keep their boat because of the mud at low tide, so we drove over to Bucks Harbor all stuffed into the F-85. Bucks Harbor was a pretty little cup of land almost stoppered by a dark green islet of spruce and pine that lay in the middle of its water. There was a tennis court with a falling-down fence and a low yacht club in the arts-and-crafts style and people from Philadelphia mostly were said (by Cord) to go there in the summer. Nice people, whitebread people, Protestant and Republican, they raced their sixteen-foot boats there and trained their kids to race their sixteen-foot boats and enjoyed the sweetness of life without the cares of time, long August days, but they were gone now. Bucks Harbor also had, up the shady road from the water, a general store, a white church, and Condon's garage, the last of which appeared, folksily drawn with its proprietor old man Condon, in a children's book by Robert McCloskey about a girl who lost a tooth. In the general store we bought sandwiches and drinks for our picnic.

There had been a hurricane warning the week before Labor Day and because of it many boats had been pulled and there were few in the water now. The Elliotts owned a Concordia but that had been pulled. On their mooring now was an aluminum skiff thirteen feet long with an outboard. We rowed out to it, half of us at a time, in a yacht club dinghy. I felt like a girl because I wasn't sure how to row even a rowboat and because it was Sascha who rowed Bloch and me and the bags of food out there. She had an easy, powerful stroke, her back arched, her slender arms supple and rhythmic, and we glided along in silence. Bloch was even more of a girl than I because he was afraid of the water and wore a life jacket, which he'd donned casually as though it were no big deal. Or this was how I thought about it anyway, as I sat there and was rowed like a young prince. I'd seldom been on salt water and the white curls of spray out past the islet gave me pause, but I wasn't going to wear a life jacket.

We were going to take the skiff out to one of the islands. The outboard was rust-old and cranky and Cord had to suck the gas out of the fuel line to prime it. He said it was that way when it was cold. The skiff was a tight fit for the six of us. It made for camaraderie, or at least something you could have taken a picture of and called camaraderie, standing up on the bow looking down at shivering smiles, but no one had a camera.

We came around the islet toward the harbor bell and the wind from down the Reach hit us and the flat aluminum hull banged on the water. Cord stood up in the stern and steered, his jaw a little into the wind as if he was auditioning for a shirt company's ad campaign. Sascha sat in the bottom of the boat in a green hooded sweatshirt with her knees up and Harry sat beside her holding a beer. Teddy hung over the bow like an overstimulated six-year-old claiming to be looking for porpoises. He was getting soaked and his glasses were covered with spray but in a few minutes the porpoises came. There were three of them and they kept alongside of us and I felt like a city boy again because it seemed like such a miracle to me. They were small, gray porpoises and each time they dove they came up on the other side of us and at another angle, as if we were the center of a Minoan mosaic they were filling in. Then they were gone altogether. Teddy whapped the side of the boat with the flat of his hand, exhorted us with more sincerity than he sometimes showed in a month. "Come on. Everybody! Come *on*! They like that." So we all started doing it, even Sascha, whapping the aluminum sides as if they were drums and Cord cut the engine so the porpoises could hear our whapping better and wouldn't be frightened off.

But the porpoises didn't come back. It was a day the wind blew early, the sky was the creamy bright blue of a fifties convertible, and all along the waterline in every direction were the low wooded shapes of islands with the tide marks on their rocks.

The place we were going was called Crab Island, which was supposed to be on account of its shape but I couldn't see it. All I could see were trees here and there, trees everywhere really, and a couple of spindly points of land and a short pebbly beach. People went there for picnics because of the beach, Cord said, they'd been going there forever for picnics and the owner didn't mind. Turned out the owner was one of Sascha's uncles, Uncle James who bought islands. He had so many islands that he didn't visit them and they were left wild. The day was warming up, though the sun was pale now and beginning to be hazed over. There were rocks in the water as we approached the beach and we were all supposed to lean over the side and look out for them and Adam Bloch made a big officious deal of looking out for them but didn't see any. Cord cut the outboard. We could see the bottom now. Harry jumped into the dark water, which swallowed him to his waist. He yelped facetiously for how frigid it was and pulled us ashore.

Sascha held her moccasins and slipped down into the ankle-deep water. There was something so easy and natural about her she very nearly left nothing to describe. A man is badly advised to want to describe a cloud or a god. Sascha had the gift of seeming to occupy only the space that belonged to her, only the parts of life she needed. Whereas I for example seemed in my damning comparison always to be leaping out of myself, stretching even when I didn't need to, involuntarily, and Cord, too, with his manners and whole sentences and Teddy with his jumpy Connecticut sarcasm. Sascha had shadows, but they were sharp and real, as sharp and real as she was. Maybe she was just too rich to bother putting on a show. She was not a theatrical person, she was one who would take in a performance, not give it. Yet Cord was rich, and Teddy was rich, by any ordinary mortal's standard. Or we all were, if you stopped and looked at the world. She seemed, walking ashore, walking the beach in her bare feet looking down, not just rich but a little fatigued by it, by all that surrounded her, and so she was left without the means to make anything up.

Late adolescent scales of judgment, full of bright lines. And where did Harry fit? He walked beside her on the beach and there was nothing wrong with the picture. He walked like a consort of an end-of-the-world perfection, like Indian gods both of them, like Shiva with Parvati.

Or am I bringing up old insanities now, do I give myself-that-used-to-be away?

I was eager to be liked and they weren't. Maybe that's all it was.

We had our picnic on the beach. Bloch sat on his life jacket and absorbed potshots from Teddy for needing his ass to be comfy. We ate sandwiches and cookies and finished most of the beer. Sascha drank a canned ice tea. As if she weren't there, as if he'd landed for a moment in a different weekend, Harry got onto a riff about Willie McCovey. "The highest slugging percentage in the majors." "McCovey's a maniac." "McCovey's a god." "No disrespect to Mays, Mays is Mays. But it's McCovey you want in the clutch." A San Francisco monologue, punctured only by Teddy who was a Yankees and Mantle guy, but the Yankees weren't in it that September and the Giants were. McCovey, Mays, and Marichal. Marichal, McCovey, and Mays. "And don't forget a little name like Jim Ray Hart." Jim Ray who? We were like seals sunning ourselves. Once or twice on the way over we'd seen lobster boats in the distance, but now there were no boats out.

It is a day the Lord hath made. Cord was always saying that. Sometimes sardonic, sometimes enthused. And as for Sascha and Harry, on short time together, you could look at them and almost forget that it was going to happen. Why should it? The breeze was sweet against her hair. Harry had his Giants in the race. And anyway it wasn't quite the end of the string yet, Harry didn't have to be in Oakland until Friday and on Monday they would leave Clements Cove and drive farther along the coast to her family house on Mount Desert, where they would spend their last days alone. Sascha wasn't teary or morose, they didn't seem to have to be with each other every moment, they didn't even have that much to say to each other. They were simply there, as if it would always be that way until it wasn't.

On the other side of the island, Cord said, there was an old schooner whose owner had beached and burnt it there, and Harry wanted to see it. Sascha and I stayed behind while the others went.

I've told you that I loved her, but not that I had never done anything about it. I had been to their wedding. I had watched it all happen. I had watched it all happen all the way. And that wasn't going to change now. She had a book with her, something I didn't expect, an old best-seller with the dust jacket missing, the kind she might have found on a painted shelf in the room where they were staying. I tried again to look at her as little as possible, or anyway not so often that she'd notice. When I was with Sascha alone I felt myself turning at angles, as though to leave so thin a side of me turned to her that I wouldn't be seen, as though all of me was a private part to be covered up. She said something about it getting warm out. The others weren't back. She got up and took her sweatshirt off and laid the book on it. Sascha's voice was small like her mouth. She wasted few words, and what she said was unadorned. She said that she was going to take a walk.

Really, her words were like Shaker furniture. And what seemed like an afterthought, her asking me to come along.

We had been friends. When there were things about Harry, she had sometimes told me, "Louie, I want him to come with me to Cyprus this summer," "Louie, I have no idea what to get him for his birthday." Though I don't think she ever used me that way, telling me something she hoped would get back to him. She was too direct for that, as direct as a pole, really. I relegated myself to being her friend, kind, thoughtful, occasionally witty, the kinds of things that as a friend I could be. It let me see her anyway. It let me hear her voice addressed to me. What else could I do? And it kept me loyal to him, though my heart was not. My heart was in a turmoil; I accused myself all the time.

She put on her moccasins to walk. She was wearing the same

men's shirt from yesterday. We walked along the beach and then onto a narrow path that climbed into the woods. It seemed like a path that rounded the island, staying just above the shore, and it was overgrown and rooted. I walked ahead of her, felt for a moment as if I were leading her. Somewhere in the woods she said to me, "Louie, do you think Harry's going to die?"

The kind of words that carry omen in them, but with Sascha they came out simply inquisitive. Did I have an opinion on this interesting topic?

"No," I said. "No, I don't. He'll probably fill sandbags for a year."

"I know there's a friend of his father. They want to make him a cameraman."

"Then he'll do that." Which, I felt, might put an end to it. A decent end, clarifying and reassuring. But I also felt a need to be the hero of the scene, so I added, "Harry's pretty tough. He loves you too much to get himself killed." Which as soon as I said it sounded trite and sentimental in the salt air of the island, to me at least, but maybe not to her.

"I hope so. You don't think he's just being a selfish jerk, do you, Louie?"

"No. You totally come first with him."

"Then I'm being the selfish jerk," she said.

"I wouldn't bet on that," I said, and her troubled eyes shot my way, like a bird landing on a branch.

"But Louie," she said, and in my fear of her I began to think she was playing with me, the way a parent keeps a baby going by calling its name. "Is any of it honest?"

"In what way? What do you mean?"

She'd picked up a stick and was lightly dragging the tip of it over the moss. "I don't know what I mean. Do you?"

I should have said no, of course I don't, how could I? But I felt honored by her asking, a sort of opportunity, as if a rabbi of Lublin had been invited to the king's court to talk about the stars. I asked, "Is it an honest reason for going? Is that what you're asking?"

"I guess. Yes. I think so."

"How could I know? I'm not even sure what his reason is."

"I'm not either. Isn't that the pits? I'm the wife."

"What does he say?"

"We don't talk about it anymore."

We walked along the path, came to a rivulet and crossed over.

You know what a wise man is? A boy who has no better way to be accepted. I gathered my words as if they were a precious harvest.

"I guess the distinction would be if he's going because he believes it's his duty, or because he believes he has to be seen to be doing his duty."

"That's it," she said. "That's right." Though it wasn't like she said it with enthusiasm. She said it looking at the ground.

"I don't know," I said.

"I think you do. Louie, why do you diminish yourself?"

"Do I?"

"I think you do—maybe not always."

"About this, really, I don't know."

"I think the world's setting a trap for him and he's too something to avoid it."

"But what's the something?" I said, and although I still hadn't looked her way, I smiled sardonically, for the pleasure of our talk, the sound of her voice and my voice intertwined, her words wanting mine.

"You tell me," Sascha said, about the something. "Please. Just tell me. Even if it's not right, I want to think I understand."

"It's always two things with him," I said.

"But it's always one thing more than the other," she said.

We eventually came to where the others were poring over the burnt carcass of the schooner. There was hardly any of it left. It was split apart. It had been there forty years. People had stolen everything. It looked like dinosaur bones but it made Harry happy, he loved old wrecked things, maybe because he was from California where things were too new to be wrecked. Or that's too easy. I don't know. But when we got there Sascha came up to him, and he put an arm around her acceptingly, and she kissed him in an easy kind of way.

A little later we were back on the beach, skipping stones, hanging out. Sascha was lousy at skipping stones, and Harry was telling her to keep her arm down, to do it sidearm, but still her arm for this was weak, until at last she got one off, a little white stone that piddled on, five times, six times, it splashed and disappeared, and Harry winked at her and the rest of us said what a really good one it was.

"Why are you going?" Sascha asked. "Really."

She was looking for another stone.

"Going where?" Harry said, which he knew was not going to make it, since he added, "In the army?"

I thought it was odd, like a door flung open when there was no breeze for it. Didn't she mind that we were all there? It was as if she must want our help.

"Is it honor or hypocrisy?"

"Don't know what you're talking about."

"You do too."

Harry skipped another stone, he skipped it hard this time,

a slatey jagged thing, and it banged nine or ten times on the water.

"For a lot of reasons. For one thing there's a draft in this country."

"You could get a deferment."

"A deferment's a deferment. You still have to do it later."

"Is that true?"

"Unless you want to keep doing stupid things until you're twenty-six," Teddy said.

"Harry. Really. I need to know."

"Whether it's honor or hypocrisy? Hypocrisy, obviously." He laughed like a horse and picked up a rock that was more like a boulder, that wasn't even flat, and he threw it at the water and it sank. "Fuck... I mean, what do you even mean, Sascha? Really."

"Maybe they're the wrong words. Louie said it better. Louie, what did you say?"

Sascha being someone who didn't notice the spots she put other people in. Either she was too honest for it or she had never had to deal with consequences.

But in the end I didn't have to answer that one because once Harry's eyebrows knitted together and he felt challenged and sneak-attacked, he didn't hear much else but his own thunder.

"There's a draft in this country! Everyone's supposed to serve. These guys feel it too, they're doing something, for chrissake. Everyone does something. So this is what I'm doing. And do politics play a part in that? I have no idea. What can I tell you? Shooting guns is fun. I like shooting guns, I like camping out, I liked the Boy Scouts. Is that hypocrisy? What's hypocrisy?"

"Okay. Alright," she said, and it seemed like she had retreated.

But we all knew he had told her nothing, and I had the sick feeling that something I said only to win her approval and not even because I thought it was true, though it might have been true, had colored the afternoon.

We quieted down and finished whatever beer was left and then everyone snoozed for a little while or tried to. When I woke up, Bloch was sitting on his life jacket. He was staring toward where the bay opened wide to the southwest. Down there somewhere was Rockland. Cord had pointed it out, even if we couldn't exactly see it, and beyond Rockland the ocean. But all that was out there now was a fluffy low strip over the ocean the color of dirty snow.

"Is that coming our way?" I said.

"I don't know," he said.

"Is it fog?" I said.

"I don't know," he said.

But it was fog. I woke up Cord finally. I didn't want to be alarmist. But the fog was almost on us by then. Though we weren't going in its direction, it seemed like it would soon overtake us. That's what I guessed anyway, and it did.

We gathered our things together. The fog was such that we could barely see to where the boat was beached. Cord said once it was on us it could stay awhile. We didn't want to be stuck overnight on the island in the fog, so we left.

The thing about the fog was that we seemed so alone in it. It was as if the islands, the sky, the trees, the mainland across the bay, had simply deserted us. All at once they counted in the calculation of what was at some sharply discounted fraction, the exact number indeterminate, what you might use to count silent shades. We could have been in a play, six people stuck with our own footprints and voices.

And the other thing about it was that it distracted us from what had gone before. I felt the taint of my impure thoughts begin to dissolve in it. Though Harry was still quiet, ruminating, and I wondered what he was ruminating.

The feeble grinding of the three-horse outboard seemed tremendous now. For good measure, every minute or two I squeezed a foghorn that was about the size of a bicycle horn. It was a little like sending radio signals out into the cosmos. No boats honked us back. We really were alone.

Sascha sat in the bottom of the boat and tried to read her book. With his life jacket on and his blank, fixed expression Bloch looked like a soldier in a landing craft on D-Day. We went on this way for a time that became as hard to judge as distance. We distrusted Bloch's watch because it said only thirty minutes. Cord steered our little ship of fools, Teddy read out compass readings in ironic tones, Harry rubbed Sascha's feet to keep them warm.

I imagined it was only myself who had begun to wonder if we were going around in circles or if Teddy was sufficiently sober to read the compass or if the fog was ever going to lift or was it rather a half-assed clammy sign of evil out of a third-rate horror movie. Myself and Bloch, I imagined, but I didn't really include Bloch. He was like the second Jew aboard. I was the Jew in this boat. He was one too many Jews.

And where had he come from anyway? Pittsburgh, but where was that? Nowhere, out there somewhere, worse than Rochester even, at least if you were a Jew. The Mellons and the Pirates came from Pittsburgh, but who else? All the snob in me rallied against Bloch. Harry had met him in the Political Union. Harry had thought he was a really smart guy, an economics guy. Harry soaked up economics from Bloch the way he'd once in our freshman year soaked up Descartes and Leibniz and Kant from me. Harry could see the role of Bloch, the need for Bloch, in future Nolan administrations, in future Nolan campaigns. You needed economic plans if you were going where Harry was going, and he was already getting prepared. Or that was my interpretation anyway, which left room for Harry not really to like Bloch, but rather simply to use him. I liked this because it meant Bloch wasn't supplanting me, he was practical, or he was no more than another from the charmed array that populated all the perimeters of Harry's life, but I was family. Something like that. It's pathetic, isn't it, or sad? Envy so soon after innocence. But Harry liked Bloch, for whatever reasons, his brain or plodding loyalty. And when he turned down all the senior societies, when he turned down Bones and Keys and Wolf's Head, Harry told them about Bloch. He told them about me too, and in some ways I was a more likely choice, I was on the paper, I wrote odd little occasional columns, had a story or two in the *Lit*, if I wasn't exactly clubbable at least I dressed and talked okay. But they didn't want me or Bloch. They wanted Harry.

The land coalesced dour and looming out of the dirty white vapor just as the metallic screeching on the boat bottom began. There was no moment we could have avoided it. We slid and scraped over whatever we'd hit until we came to a hard stop. By then we were listing badly. I was sure we were going to sink. Visions of *Titanic. Andrea Doria*, *Lusitania*, *Morro Castle*, every other ship I'd ever heard of that sank. A lot of fucks and holy fucks and holy fucking shits.

It was hard to move around in the boat, because of the list and because there were already too many of us. We crawled around the bottom as best we could inspecting for leaks and when we didn't find any Teddy shouted only semifacetiously in praise of metal boats.

We could see now that the ledge was part of a larger piece of land. "Look at this! Shit!" Teddy screamed. "We hit a whole frigging island!" We climbed out one by one onto the slippery barnacled rocks, the water lapping over our feet until we scrambled to higher ground. But Cord had an epiphany. This was Two Bush Island we had hit. It had more than two bushes on it, even the microscopic bit of it we could see, but Cord said he recognized the shape of the ledge and the rise of the land into the cloud. And from Two Bush he knew the bearing to the Bucks Harbor bell, north northwest, fifteen or seventeen degrees. So we slid on the lichen and pushed, all of us including Sascha, each with two hands on the boat like a tug-of-war, and it slipped off the rocks and we were off again, our merry little band, our beautifully screwed-up day's outing that was beautiful once again. North northwest, fifteen or seventeen degrees, we followed Cord's remembered bearing on the compass, none of us quite believing him now, because he'd hit a whole island, hadn't he? The fog was still on us, the wind was light, the outboard coughed and sputtered; we began—or perhaps was it only Bloch and myself?—to feel more like refugees than adventurers, escaping oppression somewhere or making our way from a shipwreck; but Bloch's watch didn't lie this time, and after half an hour we could hear the flat clanking of the harbor bell.

Cord let out a rebel yell signifying victory over his enemies. He steered us right for the bell. Teddy shouted he was going to hit the goddamn thing, given the talent he'd shown for hitting goddamn things. The bell got loud as a church bell. We couldn't see it till we were almost on it, and its size, tilting in the water, surprised me. It was a big red bobbing steel platform, round and about the size of a small truck if the truck was tipped up vertically.

It was painted red and marked in three foot letters "BH."

The bell itself and its hammer were enclosed in bars and around the bars was a narrow perimeter, like the outer edge of a tiny carousel, where a man could stand. With each wave the bell dipped and rose, and it was this motion that caused the hammer to strike. As it loomed Harry seemed to know what he was about to do. "Hey, get in there," he yelled at Cord, "why are you such a lame southern chickenshit?"

Cord then cut the bell so close that we could touch it, and when he did that Harry crouched like a guy going to do a movie stunt, jump from a train or across buildings, and he broad-jumped at the rolling platform. By all rights he should have fallen in the water, but for a big guy he was monkey-agile, and he clung to the bars around the bell and managed to scramble and pull himself up.

He looked fierce and brave then, like a kid who had climbed a mountain. Except the mountain was dipping and rolling and Harry was holding on and the rest of us cheered and laughed in comradely fashion except Sascha, who covered her eyes. "What are you all doing?" she cried, then she saw that it was pathetic and hopeless. Cord spun the boat around the bell. Harry rained emasculating epithets on Teddy until he jumped too, but his foot slipped away and Harry had to nearly yank his arm off to save him from the bay. Now there were two of them and Cord was crazy-eager to be next, but being endlessly polite to start with and the more so the more he drank, he asked if I cared to go first. If either Bloch or I cared to go first. Well, get bent regarding that part, Cord, I certainly didn't *care* to go, I didn't say, but on the other hand it didn't look totally impossible. The others had managed it, so why couldn't I, I didn't have a limp or a heart murmur or any other IV-F excuse. Mostly I wanted to show I wasn't Bloch, who said no thanks as if he were passing up a refill of white wine, so Cord drew the skiff close again and Harry held out a bracing arm and I leapt. My ankle caught the side of the boat and I stumbled but Harry got me up there.

Cord was next. The bell dipped with the weight of all of us and now the waves of icy gray water soaked our legs. We clung to the bars and screamed like fools. I'm ashamed to say how proud I felt then. Not ashamed for what we had done, for being so appallingly young, but rather for scarcely feeling young at all, for finding youth in one fleeting moment. The others had had their fill of it, as much being young as anyone could want, and now, with Harry especially, when he did something like this it was more like a reminder, like the last times you make love to a woman. It was there but was almost gone. I felt young for once in my life.

And if I slipped and fell in the sea? If a big wave came? If we were too much weight? Then my sturdy friends, my brave friends, would save me. Or we'd all go down together and there'd be a piece in *The Times* and people would be able to see who I went down with, and somewhere there would be a plaque and maybe someone would remember. Bloch. Bloch would remember. Sascha would think we'd all been idiots, even the one she loved.

The fact was that I wasn't really afraid.

We were all fierce for a few moments. A kind of overcoming.

The bleak fog was everywhere and we could barely see ten feet.

Sascha moved the boat easily. It bobbed in and out of the fog like a quick and leery fighter. Harry was the first to have had enough or maybe he could see that Sascha was ticked. The boys had been boys long enough. Though it's a little odd, I suppose, how much we counted her one of us that afternoon. We kept saying fuck or whatever else our limited vernacular allowed. Teddy was as snide as ever. Nobody tried to be better than we were, except me, I suppose, who always did, a little bit. And Bloch.

And Sascha? She had no need to put on airs for boys. She had no airs.

She backed the stern of the skiff up to the bell, dumped it into idle and held on, as one by one we clambered back into the skiff. Bloch said he was sorry he forgot his camera. Sascha noticed that my ankle was bleeding. It was actually bleeding rather profusely, I must have scraped it on the jump but with the lashing salt water and adrenalin hadn't noticed. My friends made a fuss of it. Cord yanked a bucket of salt water from the bay to rinse it off, Harry offered a sock that he said wasn't too totally filthy though it looked otherwise, and I tied the sock around my ankle, a rough tourniquet, a kid's red badge of courage.

From the bell it was easy to feel our way around the islet and into the harbor. Finally we heard other foghorns. Lobster boats on their way to gas up. By the time we were on the mooring, the fog had lifted. Or rather, it had withdrawn. We could still see it, around the islet, south on the Reach, like some white bird of prey of extraordinary wingspan, waiting to return. Where we were, all that remained were bits of white cotton candy flying low. The sun was warm.

4

This idea I've kept, that Harry Nolan would have been or could have been or should have been. I know that objectively it's absurd. That in a country of two hundred eighty million people I should fix on one and say he was it. That he would be the hero, the redeemer, that he would win big.

And my reasons, arguably no more than snobbish and personal, crying out by association that I am or was or might have been someone too. Might have been close to someone anyway. Might have been around to tell the tale.

And the buttresses, the building blocks of my idea, these too could be ridiculed, could be found passé, prejudiced, naive; part of the problem and not the solution, isn't that what they say? Class warfare that wasn't really class warfare. For I had no class, I never did, all I had was aspiration.

Harry had drive, connections, money, wit, looks, humility and curiosity, and he was a fearless fuck. He didn't really have ideas but he knew them when he saw them.

And luck? Was he a lucky bastard too? He seemed to be.

But now let's pick him apart. Now let's see. This privilege business. Bush the current example, with his overrich Texas shtick to hide the generations of Greenwich. If people took to Bush, was it because of his privilege, or because he learned so well to hide it? And on a not-unrelated topic, how can you tell anything from someone so young, it's like picking a colt when he's six weeks old, maybe or maybe not, what will life bring, moral courage or shit, it could be any damn thing, screw the bloodlines. And going back to Yale, Harvard and Yale, aren't they the problem too, all these guys, all these leaders that often enough don't lead? Didn't they learn it all there?

Give us a man of the people, who worked summers and after school and went to Missoula State and law school at night and married his high school sweetheart and divorced. Give us a Baptist, give us a Methodist or a Catholic even; but God save us from Episcopalians and their right to rule.

And the ones who sing their praises, the ones who are so impressed, can't they see down the pike, can't they see the world for how big it is, and the need for brave hearts?

Kerry in our freshman year went around with shirts monogrammed JFK, in case anyone couldn't guess where he was headed.

Even Clinton. Even Clinton went to Yale Law. The courtship. Hillary. The TV movie crying out to be made.

So this is where the thesis of the man of the people falls down. By the 1960s the Ivy League schools were like vacuum cleaners of the nation's talent. They swooped into the smallest towns. They cleaned out whole states. All that was left when they were gone were guys who could make money. The third best thing in life. The merchant class. The grubs. The ones who didn't know there was anything but, and if late in life they were called to do their bit, if some Republican somewhere finally rewarded their patient contributions, they brought their blinders with them, and their anxiety, if not their bitterness. For they were most of them anxious by then, anxious about money and position and some bigger boss's foot always on them, and blinded by suspicions. Commies? Fuck 'em. Cubans? Fuck 'em. Your black man? Fuck 'em. Cunts? Fuck 'em. Chinks fuck 'em, Frogs fuck 'em, fucking intellectual Jews fuck 'em, Arabs fuck 'em, gooks geeks and slopes fuck 'em. Basically, fuck 'em all.

Not that I'm taking a position here. Not that I don't see the zircon charm in a little country club prejudice.

All I'm bearing witness to is that sometime postwar our nation culled a leadership class and concentrated it in a few schools. If you didn't get in, you probably had to work for a living. If you got in you might still have to work, but maybe not. You might get to teach. You might get to see your spirit soar. You might turn into a preposterous old queen. You might write, take drugs, eat shit and die. Or you might, if ten other things turned out right, get to lead.

So let's narrow the field. It wasn't Harry against two hundred million. It was Harry against, say, several thousand. Many of whom were rich and driven, a few of whom were fearless, some of whom were connected, witty, curious, humble, good-looking, and/or lucky. And how many were all of these? I don't really know.

☙

Harry's plan for getting there. One. Enlist in the military. Two. Go to law school at Stanford or Boalt Hall. Three. Do public policy law a couple of years and run for Congress in a decently safe Bay Area district (one or another was always coming along). Four. Serve in the House until his father retired from the Senate. Five. Do *not* immediately run for his father's seat because that would smack of nepotism and maybe turn people away, *but*. . . Six. Run for the other Senate seat the next year it came available, by which time the nostalgia for Nolan, the memories of the white fox, would be burning bright and Harry would be the obvious beneficiary. Seven. On from there.

This was not a plan Harry came up with himself. One of Senator Nolan's advisors proposed it to him on a Christmas ski vacation in Mammoth. But Harry was quite proud of it, in a cynical, joshing way. "Hey Louie, I've got a plan. Kerry's got a plan, so I've got a plan."

He laid it out for me in Yorky Yorkside's coffee shop on York in low conspiratorial tones.

"I want to know what position I might hope for in a future Nolan administration," I said.

"What do you have in mind, son?"

"Court Jew?"

But overall, none of it was a joke.

☙

The origins of the meritocracy:

One. In the Depression, and its legacy that the rich were to blame, and that smart people in government could bring us out of it.

Two. In the War, and the rising democratic expectations of those who fought and won it.

Three. In the Cold War, and Sputnik, and the felt need that we would have to harness every bit of the nation's native talent in order to defeat the insidious enemy.

Four. In the College Board exams, that gave the elite colleges a way to pick the most promising from the most obscure high schools across the country.

Five. In the goodwill of people like Inslee Clark, Yale's admissions director who wore his pink-cheeked white shoe preppiness like camouflage, who made it his calling to bring Yale into the new democratic age.

Six. In the traditional ruling class fear, particularly strong in the United States where so many rough-edged guys got the ruling class going, that if they didn't get some new blood in there soon the whole thing would go to pot.

Seven. In the Holocaust, though it wasn't called that then, but anyway a slight softening of the contours of traditional anti-Semitism, in the guilty aftermath of catastrophe.

5

For thousands of days Shiva was united with Parvati, and that contact transmitted a tremor to the earth.

—Roberto Calasso

Stasis. Hanging out. The dance of nothingness. Afternoon.

We were back at the house by three o'clock. At the Bucks Harbor Marine they were saying there were still mackerel around. They weren't running exactly, but they were around, and the "around" made them sound like a legend, a vague presence, a school of ghosts. Cord wanted to go get some and he dug poles with rusted mackerel jigs on them out of a cobwebbed corner of the shed. The day was mellow now. The sun came and went but the mosquitoes mostly stayed. Cord took Teddy and Bloch with him. There were some rocks to the south of the cove and that's where they were going. I stayed behind. Harry and Sascha went into their room and closed the door.

I re-bandaged my ankle with gauze and then I read awhile, feeling proprietary, in an armchair downstairs. Some years-old magazine about Life in Maine, with twelve tips on what to do with a pumpkin and getting your gun ready for hunting season. And L. L. Bean ads in black and white. They had fewer items then; boots, waders, chamois shirts. Remember the *Whole Earth Catalog*? This was before the *Whole Earth Catalog*. The big room downstairs faced the water, but the windows looking onto it were narrow and wouldn't open. I guessed it was to keep the winter out, no compromise with the howling winter, every little bit helps. On the mantel were carved boats signed "P. Elliott, 1934," and there were two lamps made out of liquor bottles on a desk that had birch logs for legs. I was beginning to feel at home in my genteel snooping around. In a corner on a table I found a photo of a girl I knew to be Cord's sister, in the sash and crown of a beauty queen, kissing Elvis Presley on the cheek. He wasn't kissing her, she was kissing him. She must have been standing on a step or a platform because he was looking slightly up at her. She was Miss Memphis County Fair or something similar and he was so young he wasn't famous yet, bright eyes and cheeks and the trace of a smirk, playing the county fair, and Cord's sister was making his day.

At first I wasn't aware what went on upstairs. It started like occasional gunfire, a voice raised here or there. "Your father." "Shut up!" "Always your father!" They must have been moving around, a door opened, and for a little while I heard more. "This is crazy. Would you fucking calm down?" "Don't talk to me! Just go away!" "I'm going! I'm going soon enough!" "Go rattle your sabers with somebody else, I don't care!" Their voices parched in a way that I didn't know them. I gave up any pretense of going about my business, which is to say my downstairs poking around, and strained my ears toward the stairs. Another lull. A door. Harry pacing in the upstairs corridor, into the bathroom, out of the bathroom. "You knew what I was doing all along!" "I didn't know you'd be this *stu*pid about it!" "You're the one that's stupid!" My heart being bounced like a ball. "You idiot! I'm afraid!" "Oh, the sympathy vote!" "Fuck you." "Fuck yourself." These being some of the things that were said by the ones I loved, who sounded mortal enough then.

If Harry and Sascha had a fight. If Shiva and Parvati had a fight. The real fight would be in silence. He said, she said, so on. These are the things great lovers say their fights are about, or that people like me overhear and report and analyze, but really the fight has no words, as the deep of the ocean has no words. Or anyway it was something close to this I told myself and half-believed, as Harry tramped down the stairs past me, muttering "Hey Louie" softly, his eyes rimmed with red.

He pushed the screen door open with his foot and went outside. I waited what I imagined was a respectful moment, a moment that would suggest no urgent curiosity on my part, then went out to see. He had the hood of the Aston Martin up and was tinkering underneath it with a wrench and a screwdriver and a dirty rag that he laid on the fender to protect the paint job the way mechanics do. I approached him and he said "Hey Louie" again, as if he'd forgotten he'd just said it, in a flat tone, and he didn't look up.

It seemed more manly to me not to have overheard them, and not to admit it even if I had. Though how could Harry have thought I had not? Or was I only learning a first lesson in weekend houseguest politesse?

"What are you doing?" I asked. Cleaning the plugs, setting the timing, something like that. Harry was always doing something to his Aston Martin, so it made as convenient an excuse for him as for me. It was a pretty bad car. You hear Aston Martin, you think hundreds of thousands of dollars or even back then tens of thousands. But I never thought it cost that much. He'd bought it in Paris off a guy he met at American Express and had it shipped back. It often didn't run, which Teddy explained by the fact that Harry worked on it. Harry was always threatening never to give Teddy a ride in it again.

But he liked to give people rides. In fact he liked to lend his car out. Which maybe was why it was always broken. He asked me why I hadn't gone fishing with the others.

I shrugged. My ankle, and anyway I didn't feel like it.

Then he told a mackerel joke, which of course was also a pussy joke, though I don't remember it now. And about the flesh of mackerel, he was onto mackerel now, it wasn't always salty and gamy, not if you cooked it fast, he said, if you cooked it an hour after you caught it, the flesh was sweet and delicious. I said fuck the mackerel, we were getting lobsters later. The rims of his eyes were still swollen with anger but I didn't say anything about it.

All this time he didn't look up. He grabbed his screwdriver and did something jagged with it and cursed.

If Harry and Sascha had a fight. If Shiva and Parvati had a fight. There would be a moment when she would appear less magnificent to him. For a moment in his anger he would fuck a cow if it was around. But she would see this and scorn him on account of it, and in her scorn he would see her magnificence return, and be overcome with remorse and desire.

"Louie, you know what, buddy? I *am* a hypocrite."

"What?"

He started changing the oil. Something else to do.

"And you know what else? You were right."

"About what?"

"What you said."

"What did I say?"

"To Sascha. When you're doing your duty as opposed to doing it so other people will think so. I can see that," he said.

And I thought what a simple pure mind his was and what a

patronizing shit I was in ways, unlike Harry, that I didn't know how to say.

"I don't know," I said.

"You don't have to get yourself shot at. That's not what I'm saying. I'm talking about me, what a pompous jerk I am."

If Harry and Sascha had a fight. If Shiva and Parvati had a fight. They would have to work it out. He with no choice but to start over. The grin. The wit. The gesture. The capacity to bet it all, to say fuck you not to her but to the universe; or to give that impression, to let her think that, to be a little sly. While she's not sure. She's charmed but wary. Her memory warns her but it's growing dim. The scene goes on, as structured as a ritual dance.

Harry's under the car now, unscrewing the oil plug, his hairy legs sticking out. I'm still hanging around. The conversation reaches a dead end. How can I talk about getting a deferment when he's going to the war in a week? And Sascha told him everything I said and he wasn't even pissed. He's praising me! What the fuck for? So now we're talking about Ft. Ord, which is where he will be going. It's in California somewhere, of course, but I don't have a clear geographic fix on it. Harry really loves California. He talks about climbing in the Sierras. From Ft. Ord, if he has weekend leave, he'll get back up there, he'll drive all night, he'll hike around. Now he comes out from under the car pulling the pan with the dirty oil after him. It can't be a very good car because he changes the oil often and it's sludgy black in the pan. He complains about this. The engine's a piece of shit and will have to be rebuilt, he says.

The bottoms of his eyes are still red and all the while that we talk about the car and the guy in Los Gatos who rebuilds sports car engines and Ft. Ord and the future and never once mention Vietnam, I'm ashamed because some part of me is starting to act up again, the part that was never content with the peace I made, the rebel part, like some guys in the hills wondering what the news from the city really meant. That is to say, their fighting again. That is to say, Harry going away. Judas thoughts or brave thoughts, depending whose life you believed in, whose was the main narrative line. Rebels dream about cracks in the kingdom. They wait and have no pity for those they love.

Not that the rebel was strong in me. I felt faint stirrings, not much more. Mostly I was a loyal subject. A flag waver, a guy you could count on, a bit player who knows his part.

But it made me a little slow with Harry, as though I was thinking twice. And who was the innocent one here, I with my rare love for him or he who didn't seem to recognize all my pathetic contradictions? Maybe both of us were. He started putting his tools away. His hands were black with grease and there were smudge marks on his face. The kitchen screen door scraped and banged. God how loud it sounded then, as if it were the only sound on earth. Harry looked her way, got nothing back. I also looked, feeling a tightness, gray fear, in my neck.

She walked in our direction with no more expression than a sock doll. Two eyes a nose a slightly downturned mouth, and dark restless hair, as if there was Jewish blood in there somewhere, though if there was, none of us knew where. Did I tell you she was going to medical school? In January she was starting science courses so that she could get into med school the year following. It's I suppose why I'd been surprised to see her with a summer novel. She'd brought a biology book up with her, as thick as the Boston phone book. Though again, she was an omnivorous reader, one of those pre-Raphaelite beauties, otherwise restless, who would sit still for books, Gide, Proust, Pushkin, Italian novelists, Germans.

Harry looked her way again and his eyes asked, What the fuck?

What the fuck nothing you fuck. Don't you know the word nothing? Nothing is nothing. You don't exist.

She walked to the car. There was something she wanted to get out of it.

Harry went back to his screwdriver and wrench. All his little instruments, lined up in a row, as though they would offer some kind of protection, some recourse, in case this turned out badly.

She got her biology book off the floor on the passenger side. What it was doing there I didn't know, since it had been downstairs in the morning. Or maybe it was a two-volume set.

He whispered through his teeth, as she slammed the door, "You asshole." By which I guess he meant you wouldn't be out here if you didn't love me, admit it, you skinny bitch.

He caught her in a sidelong glance and she turned and whacked his head with the book.

She got in a pretty fair shot, almost a cartoon shot, the flat of the cover as if making an exclamatory THWACK! right on the side of his crewcut.

I knew it was over then. I knew they'd be in bed in an hour and they were.

The rebels who dreamed of an independent me, a day when King Louie would seize the throne, retreated to their mountain caves where they belonged.

It was past six o'clock and if you were upstairs you could hear Parvati's tender defeated moans, when the fishermen came home from the sea. None of them had caught anything but Bloch, who had two skinny mackerel on a string.

6

Where am I now? Far away from all of this. Most of a continent away. Much of a lifetime away.

Have I learned anything at all in the meantime? Of course. The cost of living and the scores of games and more names for things than there really are things. The limits of irony. The limits of very nearly everything except love, and maybe the limits of love too.

Interior exterior I've written a lot of scenes. How many of them do I still believe in? Or really, did I ever believe in?

And yet I seem to believe in these, the scenes of my youth, improbable, naive. I believe in their beauty, oddly enough, at a time when beauty is derided, denied, relegated by right-thinking people to the kitsch dreams of simpletons and fools. Beauty is not trusted, and I suppose that's right. Beauty can never be trusted, which is part of why it's beautiful. And nobility, the evil twin's twin? We don't carry that stuff anymore. Maybe we could special-order it.

I was scarcely a man in 1966. Did I tell you my father had gone away? My father had gone away long before and I suppose that I was looking for him. And then Harry Nolan came along.

Sons of disappeared fathers, unite. There are still men out there to believe in, or if you're too wounded, to betray.

Not that any of that matters. Time passes, and none of our fathers are good enough, and then they're all we have.

Meritocracy

☙

Things that were never so about Harry and Sascha in relation to me.

That I ever told her that I loved her.

That either of them knew. Or if they knew, they didn't care, not too much anyway, because people were supposed to love them. They didn't go out of their way to seek it but it was kind of inevitable, the same as trust funds were inevitable or someone to write a letter for them, someone who knew someone, no matter what it was they wanted or where they were going; and if they thought about it too much every time it happened, it could throw them off, make them a little crazy.

They'd known each other three years. During that time they'd been back and forth between Cambridge and New Haven. Sascha often stayed in our rooms, but Yale still had rules with the archaic-poetic name, parietals, which boiled down meant no girls overnight, so they had to be sort-of careful. A couple of times they broke up. When she wasn't around, Harry was an aficionado of townies and streetmeat. He could be walking back from the library and arrive with four girls at our place. He was always getting laid, he got laid more than anyone I knew. Most of us didn't get laid at all. But none of it meant anything when it came to her. He could rest his head on any part of her and read a book and be content. He worshiped her. He did what she said.

Flashback interior exterior series of shots New York day night June. The wedding, the events leading up to it.

A cattle call for aristocrats. Ambassadors to here and there (Sascha's father had been ambassador to Italy), foundation types (Sascha's father had also been head of the Carnegie

Endowment), bankers from Chase, investment bankers from Brown Brothers, lawyers from Debevoise, doctors from Columbia P & S (Sascha's uncle was head of cardiac surgery), cold warrior types, philanthropists, women who painted or had galleries or gardened, a few dames and drones and polo players and people who were plain rich.

And that's not yet counting the California contingent, the Nolans and St. Christophers, who were this and that in San Francisco, who were said to run the opera there and anything else they cared to run, and the senator himself, the white fox of the west.

Though if I could highlight any one it would be Sascha's Uncle Timothy, who wore a bowtie and covered his forehead with a sweep of thin silky hair. Uncle Timothy was an old whiteshoe CIA guy who thought up the plan of dropping extra-extra-large condoms on the Soviet Union, all of them marked "Made in USA," to demoralize the enemy. Why highlight him? No good reason, really, I just thought he was funny, like an older version of Teddy, I could see Teddy in the CIA, thinking up psy-ops, dropping the condoms, having a laugh. Maybe if it had been farther back in time. By our time the Cold War was pretty humorless, the Cuban missile crisis, Sputnik, Vietnam.

At the rehearsal dinner I made a toast. All the ushers had to. Mine was flat and labored, about how the Nolans and the Maclarens had been secretly and fatefully mis-meeting for two or three hundred years. I'd been working on it for days, until it had come to seem like one of those little square plastic puzzles where you try to get the numbers in order but two always wind up inverted. 1 2 3 4 5 6 7 8 9 10 11 12 14 13 15.

Or I thought it was lame anyway, but it got a few laughs, and afterward Sascha's mother came up to me and told me what a hoot it had been. She used that word, "hoot," that sounded so much like the forties. She had a big smile, bigger than Sascha's, especially for the size of her mouth, as though she could devour you if she wanted to, and her face was strong-boned and lined and a little bit tragic. She said my toast was the best of the night and asked if she could have a copy. From this I concluded for a minute or two that the Establishment welcomed me with open arms.

Then at the Yale Club where they were putting up the out-of-town ushers, in my sliver of a room on an airshaft, I dreamed that Sascha was in the room with me, in the narrow bed. She had her clothes on and I had on mine as though we'd just kind of fallen into this, suddenly and without preparation, but our legs were intertwined and her face was close to mine, bigger than I'd ever seen it in my life, and her smile was like her mother's smile. She touched the side of my face. She held my face. Her hand was cool. I kissed it. We kissed. Her face was so close it was like I was seeing it for once in my life, little marks, blemishes, rivulets, rises and falls, little lines on her lips, her dark hair, her dark eyes like blue coals. Her tongue, I tasted her tongue, and she smiled her mother's smile so sweetly and voraciously that I knew we'd reached an understanding of a lifetime and that it was a dream.

How could it not be a dream if Harry wasn't even mentioned? And then of course he was mentioned, in the not-mentioning of him he was there, somewhere, in the dream, hovering, telling me how right this was, he concurred a hundred percent, life had a way of coming out fairly. I woke up in a sweetness of my whole body so intense and enveloping that if I'd had an orgasm just then it would scarcely have registered. I tried to go back to the dream, refuting pale, aching reality on the grounds that the other had all the truth of my life. But there was light in the airshaft somewhere and the sweetness drained away.

There are dreams that are prophecies and there are dreams that are as close as it gets.

The wedding went off without any fool like me standing up with hoarsely voiced objections. At four in the afternoon of the nineteenth of June in Riverside Church, up by Columbia, presided over by the Reverend William Sloane Coffin, Yale's chaplain who'd been arrested in Mississippi and was the champion of so many liberal causes that the FBI would eventually put him up there with Dr. Spock among the country's top-ranked delusional misguided corrupters of youth. A lot of DKE guys showed up for the wedding, though I don't remember Bush as one of them and I doubt he was invited. The prettiest bridesmaid was Sascha's sister Maisie, who'd just turned nineteen and had astonishing red hair and Sascha's lank build and in her close orbit an "admirer," as her parents might have put it, a beautiful slender black-haired kid from Venice who was bumming around the New York art world for a year. Harry looked like a shark with gleaming teeth in his wedding suit and Sascha's skin had never looked so pale. They did it all with ironic smiles and easy grace, as though they'd already long been married. There were so many people there who seemed to have known one another forever, cousins who'd grown up together in summer places, bridesmaids who'd gone out with Cord's or Teddy's prep school roommates, people who'd all been to the same deb parties in New York or Philadelphia. I seated a lot of WASPs.

How do you feel when you lose? Some baseball wise guy must have answered that one. You feel like a loser.

Or in my case you follow the lead of Teddy Redmond for

a little while, trying to charm one or another of the bridesmaids into a drunken encounter in a closet, and failing that, when none of them even bothers to smile back at you, sensing, perhaps, your halfheartedness or the mark of the interloper in your brown eyes and uncertain carriage, you dance once with the bride, finding her face close to yours in a way utterly unlike your dream. Sascha was radiant with goodwill that day. Either that or she was great at putting it on. "Louie, are you having a *great* time?" "Louie, I'm going to introduce you to some *girls*." I stepped on her toes once and she wasn't wearing shoes and when she laughed it off I wondered if I would ever know one single thing she felt. Then, getting back to the second person, you say congrats to the groom, hug him because he hugged you first, sense his openheartedness and graciousness and decide he's a thousand times better than you, and say good-bye before the cake is cut, pleading indigestion.

The Maclarens supplied a car to ferry people back to midtown so I didn't have to take the bus in my tails. At the Yale Club I changed into my street clothes and then wandered over to Eighth Avenue. Exterior interior New York night junkies and whores. I found a girl who looked at me back and for fifteen dollars she took me to a room on Forty-eighth Street and sucked me off. I assumed she was a junkie but she didn't seem to mind what she was doing and her lips were supple and sweet and enough like Sascha's in my dream that for a few moments I was happy. When we were done a friend of the girl's came in. She was a bigger girl and I didn't know what she was doing there but she said did I know that the girl wasn't really a girl. The girl, my girl, said don't listen to the other one, she's crazy, and we left.

7

The sun moved toward evening. I never used to notice where the sun was in the sky but I noticed it then, like a slowly ticking clock. Which brings to mind that a clock is made in the sun's image and not the other way around, but a city kid has to start somewhere. You could see for miles to the southeast from Clements Cove, over the low huddled islands and the Reach and the southern bay. I checked a chart on the wall downstairs. I wanted to make what I saw official. The cabins and the dock and woods across the cove took on a gilded clarity, as though a Venetian painter had lit them up. An eagle flapped its wings in the topknot of a spruce. The flank of an open boat spread out its wavering crimson shadow on the water. Venetian light. Out there somewhere was the fog, but I couldn't see it.

We got lobsters from the Bucks Harbor Marine and dumped them in a black kettle that covered all the burners on the stove and ate them sitting on driftwood on the pebbled beach. The mosquitoes dined on us. We passed around 6–12, because Cutters hadn't been invented yet or hadn't reached Maine, but it was oily and only half-worked. Teddy in particular kept slapping away at the air or his own flesh with righteous vengeance. "Beast of the ocean! Get out of my tomalley, you beast!"

"They like that aftershave you're wearing," Cord opined.

"Fuck you, I don't wear aftershave."

"You don't wear that Skin Bracer shit? I thought you were a Mennen Skin Bracer man."

"Screw you. Jesus, these bugs!"

"Brought 'em up from the swamp in Tennessee."

"*That* I believe. Isn't that your family business? Aren't you all bug farmers?"

"They like soft Greenwich boys."

"Jesus!" Swatting at the air.

"See they don't bite Louie. New Yorkers are too tough for 'em. Too tough and mean."

My facetious rueful smile.

Harry and Sascha were becalmed now. J.b.f., just been fucked, is what used to be said and maybe still is. And I was becalmed. The approach to evening. The cold, clear country, as though the sweat of the world had been wiped from it. These friends, like figures of this landscape, who drove me up and gave everybody shit and didn't seem to mind me. And Harry and Sascha like restored monarchs, the king and queen are *back*, folks, let's give 'em a big hand! That is, together, tolerant, slightly sardonic, quiet. And easy at heart, whatever that means. Or maybe what it meant was that when Sascha's troubled heart rested in his, it truly rested. Sascha on a rock with her lobster, knees together maneuvering with a pair of pliers and one of those sterling silver pokers. She had a surgeon's way about her, deliberate and patient. Even when she cracked a claw she hardly made a sound.

What was this "troubled heart" business? What was her heart troubled about? I never really knew, and it's possible Harry didn't either, he only knew what he could do about it. Or not to be mysterious: Sascha may have been a little bored by life. By much of it anyway. She had trouble finding its primary colors. Where this started, though, and what could explain it, the determination of a cause—I don't really trust causes.

Not concerning those I've loved, anyway. Causes distract from what is. And you never hear the end of them, there's always one more, and meanwhile the one you love could choke on a bone or go blind.

Sometimes people try too hard to say something, the world becomes clotted in their minds and takes on unreal shapes. We were quiet so long that Bloch must have thought it was his fault we were quiet, or his obligation as the witty, intelligent, serious guest to do something about it. Am I being too rough with Bloch? Am I importing what I felt then into what I feel now? Sometimes like a CD in skip mode I tell this story and the years collapse, as if they never were.

A fault, an error, or simply a fate?

What gives me the strength to go back, I suppose, is that I've never entirely left, like one who still wears the clothes, the styles, of his youth, who parts his hair as hair was parted then. Which by the way I think is a not-ungallant thing, loyal in a way, a not-unmanly thing.

Bloch asked Harry if he knew where he was going to be sent. He was a little earnest when he said it, not enough to be cloying, but enough to let everybody know that he'd been mulling what had been said before, that he was sincere and concerned about it.

Harry said Ft. Ord but Bloch said he meant after basic, did Harry know where he was going after that.

Harry said he didn't know.

Bloch could have shut up then. He could tell from our faces, mine and Cord's anyway, which were set in a way to endure discomfort, that we wanted him to, that enough was enough, that we'd gone this way already and what was the point. I felt again as though the conversation was headed where I had no right to be, where I'd already trespassed once and gotten away with it. But Bloch plowed on, saying he'd heard, he'd read, it wasn't necessarily Vietnam you got sent to, only a certain percentage got sent to Vietnam, it could be Germany, he said.

"Maybe," Harry said.

"Maybe they'll send you to Heidelberg and you can duel," Teddy said.

"That's stupid," Cord said.

But we couldn't get off it now, we went around in circles as if some experimental scientist in a funny hat had hypnotized us, until Sascha said, "He's going to Vietnam. Of course he is."

"What about being a cameraman?" I asked, and when Harry only shrugged I went on as if I was bundling the conversation into the back seat of a car to drive it out of town, about how they'd probably have him filling sandbags for a year.

"That's what Calvert did," Cord said, and enough of us nodded sagely.

But Bloch seemed still to want to get to the bottom of something.

"It's a colonial war," he said. "They shouldn't have a draft for a colonial war."

"I volunteered," Harry said.

"But would you have if there wasn't a draft?"

Harry paused and sucked on his lobster shell. "Maybe," he said.

"But if there was no draft, even if you were going into politics, you wouldn't have to. It's the draft that makes it necessary."

"So fucking what?" Teddy said.

"So, are you going? Are any of us, but him?" Bloch must have known he'd said more than he wanted to. He didn't want to be hated, after all. He wanted to be liked, for his acuity, his sensitivity to undercurrent, and in the end, his reasoned sympathy. Whereas I thought, just then, how brilliant do you have to be to say there's a gorilla in the house when everyone already smells it. "I mean, that's not the point anyway," Bloch said. "I just think it's going to come out badly, having a draft to fight a colonial war."

Which finally got out of Teddy, "What's this colonial war shit? We're fighting communism, for chrissake."

But Bloch had had enough. His dark eyes had a dull hurt in them, as if he'd come up once again against the inevitable obstacle, the monolithic sheer stupidity, that had somehow continued to confront him, the honest broker of blunt reason, at every turn of his life.

"I'm sorry I brought it up," Bloch said.

Are you really, I thought, you self-pitying passive-aggressive piece of shit. The truth was that the better Bloch's points were, the more I feared him then. I wanted to make a better point than he did, I wanted to make a point that would shut him up. A showdown of the intellectuals, of the meritocrats, only one comes out alive. But Bloch had already shut himself up.

And wasn't it also true of Bloch that he used ideas to advance himself and not the ideas themselves? As had I twice already today, with Sascha on the island, with Harry at the car. Couldn't I be cursed by association? Better, like a liberal after the war issuing an anticommunist denunciation, to draw the bright line between us, his side, my side, my side being our side, our little band whatever it stood for.

But as I say, Bloch had already shut himself up, so what could I say?

"Aren't you going to finish those feelers, Adam?" Harry said, and when Bloch shook his head, Harry sucked them clean.

We washed our hands in the salt water that lapped on the pebbles by our feet and Cord brought down one of the bags the lobsters came in and we dumped our carcasses in it. When he brought the bag he also brought a football. No white stripes, no NFL endorsements. From the lacing it looked prewar. Cord could throw a football easily and with accuracy thirty yards and sometimes thirty-five. He was Yale's third-string quarterback our sophomore year but the guys ahead of him were better and he saw no way up and he took an interest about the same time in a girl at Sweetbriar, which was a hard weekend trip, and a smaller interest in the English metaphysical poets, and so he quit. His name wasn't going to be added to the Elliotts of Yale athletic fame but he was still a pretty fair athlete, and when it came to touch football he was competitive as hell.

He must have brought out the football as a way of changing the subject, the way the hostess of a dinner party would if a guest started talking about new foods that cause cancer. He didn't ask if anybody wanted to play, he just chose up sides.

We played on the beach. A fall meant cuts from the mussel shells, but no one fell. Basically it was Harry against Cord, Cord who loved to beat Harry and Harry who hated to lose to Cord, who he referred to as the winged wonder.

The rest of us were bit players, though I could run a little bit and my hands were not bad and Teddy was a swirl of gangly moves.

We were losing the sun. It got hard to see the ball. But the game seemed to loosen us up. It wasn't that we wanted to forget that Harry was going away, it was more that we couldn't forget. Talking about it just seemed to make lies of it. Witness just before, and don't even mention Bloch, just observe the generic principle. You're going to say something to make things better, to put it all in perspective, to make a joke of it, but what you say actually is something to make you look good, make you look like the sage or the wit or the compassionate one, the number-one guy. Well screw you bullshit shut up and leave it alone. It wasn't a joke and we couldn't make it better, or that's what we thought anyway. Or it's what I thought "we" thought, drawing the circle again close to my heart. We couldn't make it better, so we played touch football instead.

I caught one of the winged wonder's bombs and our side went up a touchdown as the sun got fat and squat in the western sky behind us. We were playing until it was gone. You couldn't tell with Harry sometimes whether he was angry or facetious, he was a deadpan kind of guy, his jokes were always flat and smileless and you had to figure out if the punchline had come yet because he never let you know, but (as I said) he hated to lose to Cord, mostly because of Cord's unbearable crowing when he won. So Harry marched his little squad back down the beach, two-minute drill precision, short passes to Teddy, three complete and a first. Sascha was our pass rusher who chased Harry around like a fool, both of them laughing, Harry feinting and dodging. He always got his pass off and afterward she always pushed him.

Our goal being the invisible line between Cord's sweatshirt and my sweater. As they got closer there was less room for Teddy to run and we held them better. Finally it was fourth down and they needed a completion for a first and only a spreading pencil-line of pink still showed in the west. Cord was yelling "Sundown! Sundown!" It was making Harry crazy. They broke their huddle and did a three-man team's version of lining up. Bloch hiked, but instead of putting his arms together to block he ducked back and took a handoff from Harry, who darted away from Sascha and was open by five yards in the end zone. Teddy had gone deep and Cord though long-limbed and quick couldn't cover both. We didn't even think Bloch could pass a football. But of course anybody can, a little bit at least, and all he had to do was lob it anywhere in Harry's direction. I started toward Harry. I was going to be way too late but then I saw Bloch hesitating, his eyes darting between Harry and the hole I'd left behind. Harry yelled for the ball and waved his arms like a guy on a desert island at the first passing ship in years but Bloch decided to run. It was only those few yards, after all. He wasn't that slow and he ran easily around Sascha, to the left, toward the goal line where I had been. I darted back and nailed him with two hands front and back while he was still a couple of feet short. Feeling vengeance on all fronts, his sweaty solidity, his hard breath, feeling like I'd nabbed one of the Beagle Boys—and getting ready for my picture in the *Duckburg Gazette*?

Bloch looked surprised, as though to ask where the hell I'd come from, I who was going the other way the last time he'd looked. Cord whooped like the Grays had won the war. Sascha didn't know what had happened except the sun was down and the game was over and she was glad of it. Harry glowered. He said to Bloch, "I was wide open, Adam."

"Sorry," Bloch said.

"The play was, you pass."

"I saw this hole. Sorry."

"What hole? Shit."

"I thought. I don't know. I don't know what I was thinking," Bloch said. "Sorry."

He'd been afraid to throw a bad pass, which made running look like a better bet. We all knew it, but he couldn't say it, it was like a stone in his throat.

Harry yelled at Cord, "Hey, winged wonder—you're a lucky fuck!" He seemed annoyed only at Bloch, and a guilty pleasure grazed me, as though I was nine years old and had gotten a kid who had it coming in trouble.

We all went inside. Bloch held his head high and didn't say anything, but his neck looked stiff.

8

Scenes I never saw. The legendary, sort of, Harry Nolan.

Harry in Mississippi, in the middle of the fall term, in October of 1963, in a room in the jailhouse in Hattiesburg, telling Allard Lowenstein off.

Lowenstein being the guy who'd got him down there in the first place. Al is in the history books now, a small white figure in glasses somewhere at the back of the civil rights movement, and maybe there's even been a movie about him because years later one of his disciples shot him dead. He came to Yale in the fall of sixty-three, one of those early Pied Piper activists of the sixties, recruiting volunteers for a cause of his own invention, a "Freedom Vote" in Mississippi. Harry heard him speak in the Political Union and went out for coffee with him after. What was said about Lowenstein at the time made him seem like an adult version of Adam Bloch. That is, in the parlance and character analysis of the era, he was either a weenie, a flamer, a tubesteak, or all three. But according to Harry he was kind of a fearless bastard.

And this thing he'd thought up, the Freedom Vote, was clever and brave in a way that things seldom manage to be at the same time. The Negroes, who weren't being allowed to register, would get to vote in a mock election instead. It was to be an exercise in confidence building, in consciousness-raising, and publicity, and the role of the white students from the north was to solicit the Negroes to vote in it and simply by being there to draw the nation's attention to the effort.

The setting and the sentences are lost to me, but when Harry came from talking to Allard Lowenstein he used the word "justice." I remember it for how odd it sounded, that word with its granite finality being applied to something in our everyday lives, rather than as a concept out of Plato or some other thin paperback. Probably he used the word several times. Justice. Justice. Justice. A word that even today when I hear it as the last name of someone, the ballplayer Dave Justice or a guy I knew from law school, Bob Justice, who wound up a judge in Indiana, Justice Justice, seems out of proportion, dramatic, solitary. The scales. The blindfold. The bearer of vast hopes.

The civil rights workers, the three from the north, hadn't been murdered yet.

Harry decided he was going to Mississippi. Cord had a southerner's sort of objection. In the end he thought it wasn't courteous. Harry said oh no, it was going to be incredibly courteous, people were going to be sitting around drinking mint juleps with each other, it was going to be unbelievably fucking courteous. Fuck you, Cord said with impeccable courtesy, northern piece of shit troublemaker, but if Harry was stopping in Memphis he could stay with Cord's family.

One thing more I remember: the incongruity, the leap, of it being Harry who was going down there. He was pledging DKE. He was a quasi-jock, not some wonk from Bronx Science. He was a Democrat because his father was a Democrat, but his father wasn't a raging leftie, he was the sort of Democrat who was a confidant of JFK and a good pal of Douglas Aircraft, of old Don Douglas himself. It was said there'd never been a defense bill Senator Hal Nolan disliked. Harry wasn't standing in his father's tradition to go to Mississippi, he was running way ahead of it, he was staking out fresh ground.

But he went, while the rest of us wrote papers about this and that and dreamed lurid dreams of Dartmouth weekend.

In his laconic, Gary Cooper version of it, Harry had a run-of-the-mill time there. He walked the auburn dirt roads and knocked on the tin and paper shacks like a tourist of misery, and passed out dummy ballots and tried to get the sharecroppers who were often scared out of their drawers to listen to or even look at him. He was called a nigger-lover in various tones of voice, had a shotgun waved in his direction by a skinny shit in a truck, tried unsuccessfully to charm the Hattiesburg police, got arrested and dumped in jail.

But the scene I care to remember, I can't precisely, because when he came back he only alluded to it. It's the one that could have happened to Harry Nolan alone, and it doesn't make him a hero, it only gives a glimpse of where for a moment he was. He's in the Hattiesburg drunk tank and it's not really too bad with eight people in it. The food's pathetic and you piss in tin cans but there's camaraderie and a dumb pride and less fear than on the open roads where you were never sure about the next pickup truck. Lowenstein shows up. After a peptalk to all, he wants to speak with Harry. He persuades the chief of police to give them a room, which isn't so hard since the chief looks forward to listening in.

Allard says to Harry, "Have you told your father?"

Harry says to Allard, "What, that I'm down here? I've told him. He doesn't know I'm in jail, I don't think."

Allard says to Harry, "See but this is it, this is our good shot."

"What's our good shot?" Harry asks.

"'Senator Nolan's son arrested.' That's news. That's drama. What's the senator going to do?"

"You let that out, you lean on that, Al, and you're dead."

"Excuse me?"

"You won't use my father like that. You won't use me against my father like that. Try it and I'll tell every reporter in the county about this conversation. And I'll have Chief Lardass outside the door to confirm it, Al."

So maybe the dialogue's compressed and a tad on the snappy side but something like that was said. I knew it because he told us he went down there on condition he be treated like everyone else and his father not be involved. I knew it further because it's what Harry alluded to, that Lowenstein approached him with a publicity angle. And the story never came out. No one even reported that Senator Nolan's son was down there.

Harry in Millbrook, N.Y. at the Hitchcock estate, dropping acid with Leary and Alpert.

This was in the spring of sixty-four and it's possible the phrase "dropping acid" hadn't been invented yet. Leary and Alpert had been booted out of Harvard on account of their experiments but some rich kid had given them his house in Dutchess County to carry on. Harry was taking a psychology course in fear and courage from a guy named Webber, and this Webber was a protohipster who grew outsized sideburns for the time and flew a plane.

Webber was a pal of Leary and Alpert's and made weekend flights to Millbrook. He invited his students to come along. He made it seem that if you were the kind of person to be taking a course in fear and courage in the first place, this was a thing you wouldn't want to miss.

Most of Webber's students declined for no better reason than that they secretly didn't want to be flying on any plane that he was piloting. Very reasonable, thought Harry, but he went anyway. It's been written in books what happened those weekends in Millbrook, but it's been so many years since I read any of them that I've forgotten. Who was fucking who if anybody, whether there were experiments that felt like science or just everybody getting high. I don't have a bibliography. But I do know the phrase "bad trip" had been invented by then, because Harry talked about a poor guy who'd had one and embraced a cow the way Nietzsche embraced a horse when he had gone crazy from syphilis. Harry did not. He saw colors and stars and galaxies and flew around and he told us he ran into Sascha in deep space. We thought he might be going insane. Our blessed bourgeois perspective, which I still sort of love and have hardly the will to escape. But Harry wasn't going insane, he was just having little epiphanies that we were not, seeing the world inside out, and having some fun while he was at it. As best I can remember he spared us the word "profound." But he wanted me in particular to come, "Hey Louie—it's right in your strike zone, it's philosophical," he thought it would loosen me up and do me some good, and when I passed he called me a pussy. After three weeks he quit going down there. Sascha made him. Her egoism again, her stirring will, her defiance, of as much of life as she needed to defy. When he was in Millbrook he wasn't with her. And she knew Leary a little from Harvard and detested him and wouldn't go there herself. She got afraid for Harry, not because she knew much about LSD—none of us did, except through him, and he was so understated about whatever he did that we never got that full reverent sense of its phantasmagoric properties that a few years later everyone in the world sported like this year's T-shirt—she just figured if Leary was promoting it, it had to be no good.

It was as easy for Harry to stop going to Millbrook as to start. He was probably the least addictive personality I'd ever known. His only addiction that I ever saw was for Sascha. So why do I mention any of this? To show my friend in one more vanguard, as if being first in so many things meant he must have been a born leader? Maybe, probably, in part. To show his adventuresomeness? Also that. I admired it, envied it, couldn't hope to match it. When I heard something new that Harry had done it was as if I could feel my bones and heart and knew they were not as strong as his. To paraphrase something I once heard a TV preacher say about Jews and money, he took more chances before the rest of us got out of bed in the morning than we did all day long.

On the other hand, Harry wasn't one of those guys, "You know me, I'll try anything once." He had a conservative bent, he ignored or kept away from stuff that was stupid, bad taste, or boring, and it's possible that innate upperclass sense of what passed and what didn't would one day save his electoral possibilities. You could never imagine Harry getting caught in a vice trap, or people thinking he was un-American for sampling a few pharmaceuticals. He would charm his way out of it, laugh his opponents into a corner. He could out-American mostly everybody, with his crewcut, his beachy twang, his dimpled chin and effortless affability. But he was counterphobic, if I understand that word correctly. That's mainly, I think, what I'm trying to remember about him here. He was the biggest counterphobe I'd met. Since he couldn't bear to be beholden to it, fear became his ultimate guide, his ticket to freedom. When he felt it, he went in the direction that made it stronger, until whatever it was telling him he was afraid of was so close up, so overblown, it looked like a joke, like a big fish's mouth, yawning, white teeth filed, big fish's toothpaste smile, in a cartoon.

Harry in the Political Union making a definitive statement in front of his father.

The punchline first. Harry got up in front of about three hundred people after his father had delivered some starchy speech about our obligations to our neighbors in Latin America, and mooned the room.

But there was more to it than that. It was actually, from a debating point of view, a shot through the heart. In the Political Union they were often resolving some dubious proposition and arguing it in an arch and languid manner as they must have imagined was done by the debating societies of the only place Yale guys felt inferior to, Oxford. The night that Senator Nolan spoke he stayed on for the debate, which was something like, "Resolved, symbolic speech deserves free speech protection under the Constitution."

So what was a boy to do if he had the affirmative on that proposition, but get up there, yank at his belt, let his pants drop down, show his buns to all concerned, and get out of there without uttering a word?

If that wasn't symbolic speech, what was?

And if they laughed? Shouldn't laughter always be protected?

Case closed ipso facto Q.E.D. habeas corpus delecti.

There were those that night who swore that Harry had a bulldog tatooed on his ass. But I'd seen Harry drop trou a score of times and never saw a bulldog, so if it was there it had to be a decal. George Shultz, on the other hand. Remember him? Secretary of State under Reagan. George Shultz went to Princeton and was said to have a tiger on his ass, and as far as I know he never even bothered to deny it.

Styles of the times. Teddy dropped trou once in a while, and so did Cord, and even I did a couple of times, mostly to show I knew how. But with Harry it was a kind of passion. It really was his free speech. Defiant, funny, friendly, gross. When he was asked about his son's performance in the debate, Senator Nolan said that it was succinct and persuasive. The judges had less of a sense of humor and disqualified him.

This was in the winter of our senior year. And did Senator Nolan have another conversation with his son that night or the next? In which the subject of his service came up? In which he was reminded what was necessary and what could be done and who could be called and that there were a lot of things you could do in the military, you could do intelligence, you could learn film, or read the news on the radio, or write propaganda leaflets. You could hook up with A.I.D. You could work on psy-ops. You could win hearts and minds. You could get into the Air National Guard and keep the skies of Texas safe from the Vietcong air force. You could march around the 94th Street Armory on the weekend. You didn't have to get shot at.

Scenes I never saw. That require reconstruction, guesswork, sympathy.

Do I have such sympathy, or is it only a trickle, enough to identify and feel self-satisfied about, enough to serve my own purposes? It's why, of course, I admire Harry to this day. With him sympathy would be no question. It flowed out of him like a big river. In my mind, at least. The legendary, sort of, Harry Nolan.

༶

Harry as my friend, a primer, in images.

He was like Alexander and I was like his Aristotle. I tutored him here and there, I stayed up late with him, listening, reading his papers that had knit up his brow at three in the morning and making suggestions. It was amazing to me how much he trusted me, as if I really had some answers, and after awhile with him I always came away half-accepting that I had. On this purely intellectual playing field we believed in one another, like a prince-and-his-tutor tag team. I realized Harry had a strong mind, he was thinking all the time but he was quiet about it and not quite sure. And he was impatient with it. He liked to drive fast and his mind was like his car.

He was like America, and I was like a small convenient client state, maybe Israel. America loved me because I would do its bidding but also because I aspired to be like it, I really appreciated America, I saw its greatness, I was not one of those creepy little states that only wanted to take it to the cleaners. And America in turn protected me, lavished favors on me, spoke highly of me to the world.

He was godfather, I was consiglieri. He was chief, I was on the war council, patient, considered, cautious.

I was a mascot, of irregularity, proof of the ruling class's broad, generous reach. Mascots are often funny-looking, or anyway odd. Yale's bulldog. Tigers with funny smiles or birds with big feet and beaks.

I was the kid, still with a lot to learn.

I was Louie, a nickname, a baptized one.

The fact is it was only blind luck that I roomed with Harry at all. The rooms Harry, Cord, and Teddy were to live in sophomore year had a fire in them in August. Painters, cigarettes, turpentine. So they had no place to live and I had too big a place because my intended roommate decided he was lonesome for Texas and transferred to Rice. It was really the dean who put us together.

Although I suppose, after a little while, it was Harry, with his democratic impulse, who wanted me there. His democratic impulse: one part love, openness, optimism, his sense of justice; one part egoism, narcissism, ambition.

The sound of Harry as friend, "Hey Louie, come on, let's go," "Hey Louie, you asleep?" "Louie, you douche," "Louie, you fuck," "This is my friend, this is Louie." The world's tit-for-tat, like its laws of gravity, for a few moments suspended.

ఌ

Possible flaw (observed long ago) in the meritocratic theory:

That those who were raised up and given their big chance would have only their own interests at heart, that cleverness was no guarantee of character, that they'd give nothing back.

ఌ

Harry as my friend, a primer, one more image:

He was the guy and I was the guy who had to be there so there'd be somebody someday to tell the guy's story.

9

It was the last night of the fair in Blue Hill. Cord wanted to show it to us because it was an old fair and the one where Wilbur the pig was headed in *Charlotte's Web* and it was a place for fried dough. There was something wrong with the Aston Martin. Harry said he thought it was the oil pump and he didn't want to run it till Monday, so we drove over there packed again into the F-85. It was about a half-hour drive.

The fair was a lake of colored lights in the country, sitting under the black shadow of the hill. It was stock car night and the race and rage of the cars filled the grandstand and the narrow lanes of food concessions and carny games with an incessant metallic groaning. The crowds flowed like fleshy lava through the lanes, people who worked all week or stayed home all week, people who'd been brought out for the first time in a month, people from "homes" and asylums, people from halfway houses, inland people, poor people, ordinary people, people fat on the fried dough of their whole lives, kids, babies, pregnant wives. Teddy kept an eye out for free girls, but the pickings were slimmer than a starving Armenian, to quote one of the barkers who caught Teddy's roving glance. We got jostled by the crowd. We were a little crowd ourselves, meandering, leaning, getting lost from one another. There was a dithyrambic energy to the night. We ate ourselves silly when we were already stuffed, as though this was going to be the last pig-out of our lives. Fried dough, cotton candy, fries, onions, custard. We walked around with food in our hands like two-fisted gunmen. "No really, can ptomaine get you out of the army?" Teddy asked. "I mean, if it was a *really* serious case. Like if it lasted for three months or something." The evening turned cooler. Sascha wrapped herself in her sweatshirt and put her hands inside her sleeves. We lost about nineteen times trying to knock down three milk bottles and Sascha didn't want the prize anyway. What was she going to do with a plush zebra the size of a golden retriever?

Or for that matter a Baltimore Orioles hat, but she won that one on her own, at a pitching cage where you were supposed to guess the speed of your own throw. The rest of us were off by miles, always high. But Sascha guessed low. She threw an awkward slow girlish lob that barely got to the back of the net. Twenty-two miles an hour. On the button. She didn't giggle when she won. She didn't even smile. She had the brave, slightly perplexed, slightly embarrassed look of someone who'd just saved somebody's life. It was the only thing any of us won all night. The barker talked to her in the third person. What would the little lady like? He had a kind of bemused leer, and the sly, unshaven look of porn stars of a decade later. He asked all the rest of us weren't we ashamed, the little lady was the only one to win in an hour, who was going to step up and save the honor of the male race? Sascha had her choice of any hat on the top row, all the big league hats. She asked for the one that had the little bird on it, the oriole, with the orange wing.

She loved the color orange. An oriole's wing, a breadbox that was orange. In Cambridge she had an orange jeep. Anything else about her? While we're on the subject? Of her, her greatness, her winning ways, her lack of smiles. She always used too few words, and her voice was low and hard to hear sometimes. Her breasts were small. She wore mostly men's shirts. She knew things were easy for her and that she was patronized often, but she didn't blame people, she didn't think it was their fault that she was pretty and connected and rich. She believed that people exaggerated her gifts. She believed her real gift was something careful, patient and small, that few people ever saw. I could go on. I could get sidetracked. Her little brother who was thirteen. Maisie her sister. Her family were her best friends. At Harvard women crowded around her but she stayed aloof. And why did she love Harry? She told me once she didn't know why. I thought it was the first lie she'd ever told me, but maybe it wasn't.

His sweetness, maybe. His suitability. Mirror of her soul. A leonine sweetness, found at the heart of a roar, and not really a sweetness at all. A fearful symmetry.

Who the fuck knew. If you try harder do you think you'll discover it? Do you think trying harder is the key to the universe? You meliorist, you capitalist, you dull Johnny, is what being around Sascha made a boy think.

The fair with its country poor and cheap thrills had the odd effect of relaxing me, as if I were somehow closer to home, as if we were all proletarians now. I became aware of having been in a kind of slump with my friends, wary, unfunny, like a kid at a new school who doesn't know yet what to say, but away from the summer house, away from the rich people's weekend, the slump dissipated and I was for a little while wry and whimsical and quietly sarcastic, which was my version of funny. I could make a symphony of the word nice, a dozen tones, a dozen meanings, a dozen ways to raise an eyebrow, a thousand variations on a theme. The popcorn guy who picks his nose before filling Teddy's bag. Nice. The rubber worm that Cord won for only eleven dollars of SkeeBall. Nice. My own cotton candy mustache, that I didn't know I had until I saw it, as big and fat as a whore's mouth in a German expressionist's dream, in the fun-house mirror. Really nice. I never felt happier than when I could direct my friends' attention with some monosyllabic comment, and I played the comment and their laugh over and over again like a needle stuck in the turntable of my mind.

The rides flanked a wider, muddy promenade. A rickety ferris wheel, carny lights, thick electrical cords snaking the ground, things that went round and things that went up and down. Cord spotted three chone. "Chone" was a word that year. A hundred words for girl. The girls had round faces and cute hair and one of them wore a UMaine zipper jacket. They were going on the bumper cars, so that's where we went. Sascha found the naked chase amusing. Harry looked edgy, as though the presence of these girls might somehow slant the conversation in the direction of his talent for streetmeat. He said nothing to the girls. He paid extra attention to Sascha. Like Claude Rains in *Casablanca* he was shocked, shocked. By now Teddy had gotten their names. Maureen and Annie and Jackie. Catholic girls, French-Canadian, a couple of them anyway, with broad local accents that lacked r's. I felt stupid chasing girls when Sascha was around. She would see what a revelation I was, me of the wise and judicious and sensitive demeanor with which I'd so often plied her. But she looked mostly wry. So this is what boys do.

It was a small rink for the bumper cars, the kind that could be packed and unpacked at every step on the carny tour, with faded hand-lettered one-way signs that everyone ignored. There were kids and dads on the ride, a couple of boyfriends and girlfriends, and an obese guy who let his hand dangle on the glassy metal floor as though this were very cool. And we slummers of the ruling class, and the girls. A simple seduction. You beat the shit out of the girl's car with yours as often as you could. Maybe the first seduction to be learned in country America, even the eight-year-old boys were bashing the cars of the eight-year-old girls. Sascha looked slightly surprised, as she had a tendency to look whenever she did something that ordinary people did, as if she didn't know quite how but was game to learn. I didn't see her smack into anybody hard. She was playing a polite game, and when the cars stopped she left.

The rest of us stayed on, even Bloch, though who was his chone?

The cars went around again, in a dance of sparks and ozone. It was becoming apparent that Jackie, the one in the zipper jacket, was mine. I bumped Jackie a couple of times to show my interest. It was a very small interest, and she may have seen it. One of the times around I could see Sascha across the promenade. I saw the back of the cap that she still wore and she seemed to walk slowly, beyond the crowd. There was a bench in the scruffy grass. I missed whatever happened next because I was going the wrong way but when I came back around she was sitting on the bench, her face mottled by the colors from a strand of high overhead lights. For a moment I only watched her. She got off the bench and sat in the scruffy grass. It seemed inexplicable, why she moved from the bench to the grass, and then she was lost to me again and when I came back around I could see she was pulling out grass and rubbing it on her face, as though to cool it, for the tactile sensation, or who knew why. What it reminded me of was a dog eating grass when it's sick. Yet so beautiful, she was so beautiful, sitting in the darkened patch alone.

Again I went around like a kid on a merry-go-round, Jackie bumped me lightly and snickered my way and I hated her for it.

Then I thought I saw Sascha crying. I could have been wrong. The colored lights made puddled reflections in her eyes. She didn't touch her eyes. She sat and rubbed the grass across her mouth. Harry saw it too. He got out of his car and slid across the slick floor, dodging and kicking at the other cars, the operator yelling curses at him.

All of this to me was like a movie with many frames missing. The next I saw he was sitting beside her in the grass. His legs were crossed. It looked like he was speaking, and then she lowered her head toward him. He took off her hat and held it in his hand. They sat there a long while without speaking, like figures in a sad billboard.

And then we were all leaving the fair. Teddy and Cord had made their case to Annie and Maureen. The girls wanted to go to a roadhouse, or anyway Annie and Maureen did, and they seemed to be in charge. Jackie was more the follower, the quiet one, content to do whatever, to be along. There was some talk of taking the rest of us back to Clements Cove and then meeting up with them. The talk about car arrangements soon got complicated, the way those conversations always seemed to.

But Sascha was revived by the idea of a roadhouse. She wanted to go. Mostly, I think, she wanted distraction, and watching Cord and Teddy work on "chone" must have seemed like a distraction.

And plain, quiet Jackie and I, were we an item too? It occurred to me maybe Sascha thought Jackie was the right sort of girl for me. Not as great a girl, perhaps, as I might have wanted but one who fit into the scheme of things, and as for my painful self-inflation well I'd just have to live with it.

We walked out of the fair and into the parking lot, which was in a muddy, tracked-up field. The girls gave us directions and waved us off. Their car was parked out on the road.

We continued walking toward the F-85. I was beside Sascha and for no seeming reason she took my hand. Her other hand was in Harry's. The three of us walked along. Her palm was dry and warm. For a moment I felt like we were in *Jules and Jim* but then I struggled with my sweet curdled silly and dishonest self, my self that placed myself in films. She liked me. They liked me. That was enough. God bless their union, or whatever pious people might say. Harry said, "I really want to get drunk tonight."

"I do too," Sascha said, and let my hand go.

10

Scenes that never were.

Turgid arguments over the correctness of the draft. Spirited arguments over the correctness of the draft. Hatching plans to go to Canada or underground or join some radical group.

Cooking up this thing that Al Gore had, where he was against the war but he was even more against having some poor kid from his draft board go in his place. A neat package, morality and viability retained in a deft stroke.

But Gore was later. Gore was in a tougher spot. Harry didn't really hate the war until he got to Ft. Ord.

And I'm unfair to Gore. I don't know the guy. I don't know if he cooked it up or not. I only know that Harry did not.

Another scene that never was. Harry telling me that he knew that I loved Sascha and that it was okay and that he was sorry, and gripping my shoulder shaking it slightly or the back of my neck in a way meant to help me move on. Because what else could I do but move me on?

Another: Harry telling Sascha about all the townies he had his way with. Yeah sure, he was just about to. But I almost did. During junior year, when they broke up for awhile. I thought he was being unfair to her and I thought she should know. Telling, ingratiating, angling. Maybe all of those, and maybe worse. But of course I didn't. They were back together again before I could, and anyway I never would have. Oedipal terror. Respect. Love.

No Judas here. No Judas on this boy's watch. If there was one thing out of a trillion I would steer my life to avoid, wouldn't it be that?

Iago Cassius Judas Shylock Caliban all that's turned out badly. I flirt, I fly from it. Envy and despair.

Though that was also the time I came closest to making a pass at her. We were at the train station. She was going back to Boston. We were up on the platform, on one of the cold benches, the white cyclopean eye of the train already distantly down the track. The politenesses of the well-brought-up. "Louie, thanks for taking me to the train." Nada, nada. "Thanks for everything, really. This was a mess, wasn't it, Louie?" "I guess it was." The train's eye had reached the start of the platform. We could hear its bell and its diesel rumbling. I looked its way, past her, and she did, and I grabbed the handle of her bag. She was wearing an old bomber jacket, some uncle's real one, and she turned back to look at me when I didn't expect her to at all. I looked at her as though to ask, why is this, why are you doing this, why are your star-blue eyes on mine when the train is coming down the track, and I cocked my head slightly, and my lips parted slightly, and I composed a friendly sympathetic noncommittal smile but I could have tried to kiss her then. The train bell clanged again, louder now, more insistent, like a dinner bell rung by a bored and angry cook, and she turned because it was time or maybe because she'd seen my funny look. The next day Harry was in his Aston Martin on his way to Boston.

More scenes that never were. Harry being a prophet, seeing two years ahead, the dirty colonial war like a knife to our hearts, like a mirror to our bowels, we who thought little before killing, we who built all these bombs and planes in clean factories, we with our cockeyed myopic ideas of the world, our Manichaean ideas, our blacks and our whites and our swaggering fat murderous ways. Harry being a prophet, seeing thirty years ahead, the Clinton years, America the placid, spreading her bounteous dominion, still ripping up a few markets, still decimating a few native peoples, but if you'd asked the people themselves, asked them in Hanoi, asked them in Pleiku or Ho Chi Minh City, they'd have told you about America the land of freedom and movie stars and their relatives in Orange County who were sad but sending money back, and then. . . and then. . . the planes flying into buildings and the guy with the broken grin who used to watch Harry batting handballs around leading America back to war. America in peace and war, but mostly war.

But Harry was no more a prophet than he was a historian. In his administration he would have planned to have both, a Secretary of Prophecy and a Secretary of History and they would have sat across from one another and glared at each other and canceled each other out, all but a tiny residue, which Harry would have lifted off the table with his fingers like grains of salt and licked and gained wisdom from. What an administration it would have been, like the best of the *Wizard of Oz* and Mr. Smith Does D.C. An administration with no chip on its shoulder.

Another scene that never was, this one arch and melodramatic as the players themselves were not. Sascha telling him not to go into politics because it was a dirty game and it would take him from her and they had each other and maybe that wasn't enough but if they lost that they'd have nothing at all.

And Harry saying what would he do then, what else could he do, which she had no answer to so they'd make love instead.

And then she would dream of Harry as a sculptor or Harry as a college professor or Harry sailing around the world in an open boat and none of them made any sense except maybe the sailing around the world but he would do that after, after he was president or whatever he would be, his beard would be white and their kid would be grown.

Did Sascha secretly love power? I never knew. But if I'd had to guess, no. She dreamed of amelioration, by whatever means.

Another scene that never was. Harry blaming the war on Johnson. Everyone blamed the war on bumbling hayseed Johnson. Kennedy had gotten us in but Kennedy would have got us out. Johnson wasn't smooth enough or clever enough or enough at home in the world. He didn't know a fucking thing about communists except what he was told. Everyone said that or thought that about Johnson, everyone I knew anyway. But I never heard Harry say it.

Anticolonialism anti-imperialism third world developing world national liberation. Harry read about those things, but he didn't talk about them. He was still mulling. He hadn't decided.

Anything else, or do we quit while we're ahead?

Harry at *Dr. Strangelove* the first night it came to New Haven, in the Roger Sherman Theatre in the second row because the place was thronged, and we all laughed our asses off and did Peter Sellers all the way home. But Harry didn't laugh at all. The rest of us living under our comfortable if slightly scratchy nihilist blankets, with our thin pillows of irony to give us rest. But Harry didn't, couldn't, live that way.

A naif, then? A big strong know-nothing naif out of

California, as naive and clean as fresh grass, who didn't want the whole human race to be annihilated and really thought, sometime, somehow, that he could, he would, do something about it? Another scene that never was, when he told me this, in grave sincerity, while we were walking home from the gym. He told me things in grave sincerity from time to time and sometimes when we were walking from the gym, but never that.

Then why mention it at all and where does all this come from? Maybe it's but an article of faith, maybe it's a convenient narrative trick. I'm not allowed to rely on dreams, am I? Yet I dream of Harry on Chapel Street, marching on a Sunday with a ragtag bunch of lefties with whom otherwise he had little in common, in favor of nuclear reductions or a nuclear freeze or nuclear nonproliferation or something, a placard in his hands, his voice raised, the local TV capturing it or not. A dream, not a memory.

Scenes that never were. Harry acting like something was a crisis, Harry in "crisis mode," if what is meant by that is acting like an asshole because something's gone wrong. Harry getting sentimental about anything at all. Harry without an edge. Harry looking awkward on his feet.

Harry loving anyone but Sascha. Harry doubting that he loved Sascha, or doubting that he had the ability to love, or that he knew what love was, or that love existed. He didn't take things like that apart. He was too simple for that. His heart wasn't broken.

Harry pissing on someone's grave. Though it's what we said we would do, in a drunken stupor in the Heidelberg bar. If one of us died, at the funeral the others would piss on his grave. A silly solemn college kid pledge, and it had to be at the funeral.

You couldn't just wait to do it at night, and best of all, the preferred option, was on the open grave, before the dirt was on, so you could really water it well. But none of us had died.

Harry in drag. He didn't do drag.

Harry stoned. There wasn't really any marijuana around yet. Not at Yale, not in the towers of the meritocracy.

Harry in despair. For what? Why?

☙

Did I love her so much that in a secret part of my bones I wanted Harry to go to Vietnam and get killed so that I could have her for myself? No. No I did not.

Did I love her so little that in a secret part of my bones I wanted Harry to go to Vietnam and get killed so that I could have her for myself? No. No I did not.

Did I have a clue as to what love is? Probably not.

Did I or could I analyze it take it apart put all the parts on the table and name them and oil them and see how they fitted together and make a chart for future purposes? No.

Was I smart enough to realize that might not have been the way to go about it anyway? Maybe. I don't know. Probably not.

Did I have this oceanic, obsessive feeling? Yes.

Was tenderness a part of this feeling? Yes.

Was compassion a part of it? I can't say.

Were aggression, regression, a vast laying waste of the whole universe, violence, taking, theft, cruelty, cunning and stupidity combined, a part of it? Yes.

Was guilt a part of it? Yes.

Did I love her as an extension of my love for Harry? No. Possibly.

I'm not sure.

Did I love her more than I loved Harry? I don't know.

Did I have fantasies that it was I who had introduced them to each other, that my love for her had pre-existed Harry's, but I'd kept it quiet, waiting my chance? Yes. And in the meantime he jumped in with both feet the way he always did everything and she responded and it was all there, done, a fait accompli, and I was gracious because it was meant to be? Yes. But did I still remember, in my fantasy, how it might have been otherwise? Yes. Did I invoke justice in my fantasy? Yes, and when I did I hated it and chased it away. Being, even in fantasy, insufficiently fantastical, or insufficiently obscene, to think justice had a role.

There is no justice in love. Forget how bad the schools are, it's the one thing we're always taught young.

And yet, it was the most just thing in the world that Harry and Sascha were together. Anyone could see it. It was the first thing people felt. The second being some version of his destiny, unless they knew him before they knew Sascha in which case it would be the other way around. One-two, two-one, either way.

The kernel of truth in my fantasy: I saw Sascha sitting in Sterling Library, reading a book, while I was working there, before I knew anything about her and Harry. They'd just met, through a cousin of hers in Cambridge who'd known Harry at prep school. He'd talked about her, hey Louie I met someone, this could be the one, those things that are such clichés but nobody ever comes up with really a better way to say them, and he talked about her looking French or Italian, but I still didn't know what she looked like. Then there was this girl sitting in the library, at one of the long tables, with her knees up, with dark hair and eyes like blue coals and a pencil, left-handed, and a mouth that turned slightly down at the corners and something erotic in her lanky, athletic indifference. I looked at her. Probably I stared.

A little later Harry came in and sat down beside her. This also felt like destiny. And as well it gave my soul proof that I didn't love her just because she was rich or because of her family or because Harry loved her. I loved her, in a sense, before I knew a thing about her.

☙

One possible rebuttal to the supposed flaw in the meritocratic theory: even if the clever kids chosen for advancement were predominantly selfish, they would wind up helping others by helping themselves, exemplary players in the capitalist drama.

A second, more charitable, rebuttal to the supposed flaw in the meritocratic theory: clever kids weren't any more selfish than anyone else. If anything, they were more sensitive—and so more amenable to being inspired by the liberal canon, to the point where they could not only recognize superior character but have the imagination even to follow it, to put their cleverness into its service.

And anyway the meritocracy didn't want only the clever ones. It wanted the eagle scouts and the artists and the beautiful and anyone else who had *something* and maybe not the very rich per se but the buttressing, and very occasionally the grace, that all the money seemed to promise to buy.

☙

Class Poet Louie. Sascha called me that. And it was true, I was. A couple of poems, a prize. A giddy starlet's surprise, not entirely disingenuous. I felt I'd finally brought something home. A varsity letter, a merit badge. Something to put up on the scoreboard, Louie's contribution, March of senior year, at last. And would people see my talent now, the concealed burning of my heart? "Class Poet Louie." A joke in almost every way, because who gives a fuck who a "class poet" is, but on the flip side, Robert Penn Warren was the judge and Sascha seemed to think it was something. "Class Poet Louie." Her phrase, her greeting, the words champagne light and teasing on her softening lips. For a couple of weeks anyway. She wanted to know what my "class poem," to be delivered on "class day" in front of everybody, would be about. I never told her that, disguised in a hundred ways, it was of course about her.

11

We hit a few patches of fog but not many. The roadhouse was back on Route 1, not a real log cabin but built to look like one, with log siding and the logs overlapping in the joints like tightly folded hands. A single streetlamp on a phone pole bathed the trucks and beat-up sedans in the parking lot with a milky thin light. The whole place hovered between the authentic and the banal. A large Narragansett sign hung over the door like an assertion of provincial propriety while the national beers, Schlitz and Carlings, were consigned to twinkling in the narrow windows. The bar itself was a sea of lumberjack shirts and flannel shirts and T-shirts. As we walked in Cord made an anthropological observation about "Deer Isle smiles," where the locals' pants hung so low you could see the crack of their ass, and a jukebox five years behind the times played lyrics I'd rather have forgotten. It's my party and I'll cry if I want to. The girl who sang that went to Sarah Lawrence and people were always claiming to have fucked her. Calumnies and lies. In my analysis of the universe the human population would soon be down to zero, since all the people who said they were getting laid never actually were.

The girls had got there before us and had put two tables together in back. They ordered drinks with fruit juice in them and talked for ten minutes about their fake IDs. We were all twenty-one by then and around New Haven it seldom mattered anyway, a trip to the local package store was more a rite of passage into a universe of winks and nods than anything else, but Teddy paid a lot of earnest interest to Maureen's tale of having a friend who worked at the phone company where they had a Xerox machine and the tricks they were able to accomplish on her friend's breaks. She showed us her ID for the third time. A lot of talk about Xerox machines then, ending in Teddy bringing in his uncle who bought stock in the company when it was still something called Haloid and it went up six hundred times.

Thereby playing the inevitable but no less shameful for its inevitability money card that I was sure would come to a bad end somewhere, but the girls didn't seem to mind. If anything it spurred them on. Jackie replied that she had an uncle at Bangor Hydro and he bought shares in that and that went up too. Maybe not six hundred percent but it went up.

I thought of pointing out the difference between six hundred times and six hundred percent but I didn't want to sound like a pedant sweating the details.

Especially not on top of the preppie-pink-shirt-J.Press-maybe-you-didn't-previously-notice-but-we're-so-far-above-you-we-could-spit-and-the-spit-would-evaporate-before-it-landed-on-your-heads dynamic that already seemed to be the alpha male weapon by default if not of choice around our two wobbly tables.

More than a little bit, I'm sure, when I start ladling out the irony, I'm reimagining these moments through Sascha's eyes. Even then I was pathetically sensitive to how she must have seen them. Did it make her more lonely? Did she even care? Sascha and Harry were hanging back like psychology majors doing the required field research for a course. And Adam Bloch was having a quiet night. He was acting as if he didn't want to make any more a fool of himself than he already had. Which wasn't so much, really, but he must have thought it was.

I was glad Sascha was drinking more, maybe she wouldn't notice as much. I drank a couple of gin-and-tonics quickly. Everyone else went through a couple as well, except for Bloch, who nursed a beer.

And as for the girls? Were backseat liaisons in the cards for us out-of-town princes that night?

The fact is, was, that preppies weren't really noted as cocksmen, to use a phrase that must have had more synonyms in Ivy vernacular than any other. It was true that preppies tended to get the cute preppie girls and made beautiful couples with them at Fence Club or in parking lot B on football weekends but by and large when it came to intersecting with the general female population in hopes of getting some, they were duds, a little on the slow side, encumbered by all the baggage of accents and manners and non-experience, and overall a little English, if what you could mean by that was horny enough but shy. The rumor was that preppies grew up to be insurance executives and in a few instances homos and their cute preppie girlfriends grew up to be wives who shopped at Hammacher Schlemmer.

Harry on the other hand was a born cocksman. No eastern effete etiolation of the organ through guilt and too-careful breeding for him. And even I, despite all my desperate young Werther-ing in the direction of Sascha, had a certain potential in that area, in that I was shameless in the lies I could tell. Or at least I felt I could tell them. I hadn't often had the chance.

The problem, which I may have alluded to, was that Teddy and Cord, not to mention Harry, were by any culturally agreed-upon standard better looking than myself, and girls looked their way first. And they were rich and had other attributes. I am only expressing a wish, or a fantasy, which I held to dearly at age twenty-one, that if I didn't get Sascha, in the long run, as a kind of velvety consolation prize, I would get laid rather a lot.

And as for Teddy and Cord, they would or would not. Teddy could have turned out queer. Not a big chance, but some chance. We all vaguely sensed this, in the nervous unease he felt in his skin, as if he was always playing some game that he didn't entirely like. He turned certain situations caustic. Like he didn't have to mention the Haloid stock to Maureen. He was smart enough, he knew how obnoxious it would sound. But he was playing the game of being obnoxious, topping it all like an overrich dessert with cynical gloss. And Cord was too much a gentleman to be a cocksman. He was wonderful, he was charming, girls liked him and he liked them. But Cord was our Jimmy Carter who would tell them he had lust in his heart. He was, oddly, a kind of poet. If he'd had his chance at the Fireside Inn, he would probably have taken Annie out to the car and read her Marlowe, Christopher not Philip.

Also Cord was streaked with an indelible loyalty. To Harry, to Teddy, even to me. He would never steal a girl from any of us, or anybody else whose hand he'd ever shaken, and what kind of cocksman could you say that about?

But I love the concept. The three of us trying to get laid in our half-assed way, even on the weekend we were sending Harry away, even with Harry and Sascha sitting there.

But what else were we going to do? It was Saturday night and we were somewhere. Late adolescent boys fanning the flames of their last campfires.

Should we not have tried at all? Should we have been home with pipes and Monopoly games and earnest girlfriends we were trying to make a go with? I had my earnest love, sitting right across the table.

We got drunker and the girls wanted to know why we were here and Cord said it was because we were seeing Harry off into the service.

"Which service?" Maureen said.

"The Army," Harry said.

"My brother's in the Marines," she said. "Were you drafted?"

"Unh-uh. Enlisted."

"My brother was going to be drafted. So that's why he went in the Marines. Were you going to be drafted?" she asked.

"I don't know. Probably."

"My brother said at least if you enlist, you get your choice of some things."

"I guess that's so."

"But you have to be in three years instead of two."

"What's your brother doing?" Harry asked, and she told him about the Signal Corps and Camp Lejeune and how he might be home for Christmas, they were all hoping, and then Annie said her boyfriend was drafted in the Army, her old boyfriend from high school, and Harry asked her things about him too, where he was and what he was doing, and so the conversation became not about seduction, it lost its feints and jabs, it was about the things that were on their minds—in other words, it was seduction itself.

"So when you enlisted, what did you choose that you wanted to do?" Jackie asked.

"Nothing," Harry said.

Sascha sat there and didn't mind that he was the center of attention again.

His blue eyes hooded under his brow, his easy twang, his

actual interest. He spoke so easily with them that the rest of us sitting there could almost imagine he was doing it to correct us, to show us how you talked to working-class girls or anybody else.

But he wasn't doing that. It was simpler than that.

"And where are you going?" Maureen asked Teddy.

"The Peace Corps."

"And you?"

"Business school," Cord said.

"And you?"

"I'm going to teach."

"And. . ."

"Grad school," said Adam Bloch.

It felt like the whole class telling about their summer vacation, but at the end of it the girls looked more troubled than enlightened. "I thought everybody had to go in the service," Maureen said, in a voice that hurt slightly.

"They do," Cord said, "but not right away."

"And not if they get to be twenty-six," Teddy said.

But twenty-six seemed impossibly far away.

Annie changed the subject back to Harry. "So you didn't ask for, like *any*thing? I thought they gave you a questionnaire or something."

"I guess I like shooting people," Harry said.

"No. Really."

"I don't know."

"You'd be a good captain. You know, like an officer," Maureen said.

"No, you know what? You want to know really? This is all bullshit. I'm doing this for a really stupid reason."

It was then I realized he'd been drinking steadily, not a huge amount but not a little either. He'd told Sascha he wanted to get really drunk and he was anyway on his way. "If I told you I was going in the service because it was my duty, to serve the country, you'd say, good, right? But if I told you I was doing it so other people would see that I was doing my duty, so they wouldn't criticize me for not doing it, so they'd like me better, so they'd even vote for me if I was running for something— I mean, would *you* vote for me if that's what I was doing? I wouldn't. I wouldn't want a leader like that, a leader who thought that way. He wouldn't deserve it. He's the wrong guy."

The waitress delivered another round, the ritual that stops all barroom riffs cold, as money is fished for, who gets what is sorted out, bare fleshy arms stretch across tables and get in the way of faces. And then–

"But if you have to go anyway, what's the difference?" said Maureen, who was urgent, who really meant it, who was trying to save him now.

Harry's eyes sparked as he swung his head through the arc of light from the overhead. "Have to? Have to? Do these guys *have* to?"

Maureen was grazed. "So you don't feel any obligation at all to go in?"

"Yeah, no, I actually do. I do feel that. But that's only part. I don't want to get that part dirty."

"Everything's a little dirty," I said, thinking I was helping out.

"'The fuck asked you? Jesus Christ!" He glared at me as if he would murder me and the table quieted down. Harry pulled at his new gin and then he said in a low disgusted voice, "Fuck it. I'm not going."

Maureen was probably the only one at the table to take

those words seriously. "You already enlisted. How can you get out of it?"

"His father's a senator," Teddy said.

"He is? Really?" Annie said.

"I'm more cynical than they are," Harry said. "They're at least doing something they believe in. I'm doing something so that people will think I'm doing something I believe in, so I can do something else."

"You like the idea of the Army," Cord said.

"Fuck it. Let Louie go in his place," Teddy said, and I wondered where that came from.

Harry sat back, closer to Sascha. His words left an echoey space that we didn't know how to fill. The girls shifted in their chairs and said a few words to one another in lowered tones. We knew we were losing them before they were lost, it was too uncomfortable for all of us now, and they took the last long sips of their drinks, fond and final, and got up to leave. They wanted to give us their phone number, they said. They wanted us to call them up. Teddy gallantly tried to explain how that could be difficult, since we didn't really live in Maine and wouldn't really be back, so maybe it would be better if they wanted to know us better to get to know us better that night.

But his heart wasn't in it. For a moment only Harry's was. Cord came back, Cord could call them, he said, and he was grinning then, and none of us knew why after what he'd said before.

The girls said their good-byes more to Harry than to the rest of us and then they were gone. He was still grinning as though to say what losers we were and how he could have shown us how to do this correctly with two hands tied behind his back and his cock in a brace but not, unfortunately, with his beloved bride sitting next to him.

For the moment his melancholy, his anger, his new resolve, were gone, a squall that came and went. When he was drunk, his moods were like rockets.

It was later still that the rest of us realized why we'd picked up the girls. It was to avoid, one, melancholy, two, sentimental recountings of past exploits, three, lies about the immediate future, and four, fear. All of them crept back at us as soon as we were drunk enough and alone.

Even I opened my mouth, with the longish story about the first time I saw any of these guys, when they busted through the firedoors of my freshman room chasing a rat with a pair of squash racquets, and what total preppie assholes my freshman roommates who were from the midwest and Texas and I thought they were and how we sent over a delegation demanding reparations on the firedoor, which the building inspector had blamed on us, and I expected they would have forgotten this, and they had. And later that year, when I was doing my bursary job in the library, how I'd helped Harry through Leibniz and Kant when I didn't know the first thing about either one of them except that they were the better sort of dead Germans. The best of all possible worlds, yeah right. The joke being on me, I supposed. Was that the point of it all? Or was the point that I could finally say to them I'd once hated them?

Harry had looked at me with murderous eyes and that was frightening but normal. But what Teddy said, I still wondered what that was about and maybe was trying to assuage it, to pass it off or pretend it hadn't been said.

Nostalgia night continued. Names of flamers, good guys, weenies, saints, tubesteaks, townies, thieves, bookies, hangers-on, various faculty and their notable perversions, were dredged up and polished like family silver recovered from a shipwreck.

Only the last names, always the last names.

But things that had been funny were no longer quite as funny. We could feel this. We began to feel older. We began to feel as if we were living in the past, which was of course the whole point of it, to live in the past a little while longer, but it's one of those things you only become aware of the moment you've turned away, and when we turned, what did we see?

It got blurry. Whatever was out there was like the fog.

We laughed about standing on the bell.

I wished Bloch too would drink but he nursed his Schlitz.

I wished Harry would say anything at all, because he was quiet again and what if he still believed those things he'd proclaimed?

And then Sascha said, "I don't believe this is happening." She hadn't said anything at all until then.

Nobody, not even Harry, asked her what it was she didn't believe was happening. We sat there quietly as if a seer had spoken.

"We shouldn't have gotten married. Why did we? We shouldn't have. This is ridiculous. How could I have been this stupid? How could we have been this stupid?" She was speaking in a low voice with little inflection, in sentences so short it seemed like each one was separate, considered, a whole thought, a whole wound. "None of this is necessary. You don't have to go. I don't have to be here. None of us has to. Vietnam doesn't even exist. It's an optical illusion. The army's an optical illusion. Why didn't we see it before? This is so stupid. We're so far behind. I stopped reading the papers. You know why?

Because there was nothing about mirages in them. Why is that? It's so stupid. Really. Don't you agree?"

I don't know if Harry even cleared his throat, and then she said, still in a low voice with little inflection, "Of course you don't. You never agree with me. Nobody does anymore. I see all these mirages. But why? Why did we get married if it was an optical illusion? You think. . . I don't know what. . . but I'm going to study it in med school. It's in organic chemistry. Really it is. Organic mirages. They come and go in the morning."

I remember all these words she said. Well, maybe I've reconstructed a few.

It was all she said then. Really it was like the pythoness of Delphi or something. But she didn't get excited at all. She was speaking to Harry as if they were having a normal conversation, and I'm sure she was answering somehow what he said before, but the connection seemed clouded, obscure.

He didn't seem surprised.

Maybe it was because we'd all drunk so much. Four or five rounds except for Bloch with his Schlitz.

A little later we stumbled out of the bar. "I'm not going," Harry said again when we were outside. But there was neither affect to it nor context and no one asked him what he meant or where it was he wasn't going, so it just hung there and we didn't know. It was like a cold that had come back.

Bloch offered to drive because he was the only one sober. The night had gotten warmer instead of cooler and the parking lot smelled of marsh and diesel. It may have been two in the morning. The streetlamp over the parking lot was lost in blips of mist but the road was clear. Cord had the keys and was going to drive himself but Bloch asked again. It was like he'd saved himself, the sage, the designated driver, boring work but somebody had to do it, and why not he who'd humiliated himself playing touch football and wasn't even worthy of getting shot down by a bunch of townies from Bangor? A little act of redemption. Bloch had been saving himself for this, nursing his Schlitz, and anyway it made sense.

Cord gave him directions, which were to go a long distance down 15 past Blue Hill and when he got to a "T" take a right and wake Cord up.

We arranged ourselves back into the F-85, Cord and Teddy and I in back and Sascha between Bloch and Harry.

We went a little ways down Route 1 and then we turned onto the other road and we all fell asleep but Bloch. The road rollercoasted up and down the way it had the night before and it lulled me almost as if we were on a train. Sascha is a little crazy, is what I thought in a sort of dream, Sascha is a little mad or at least very much drunk and why not, I loved her for it, I loved her being a little teched, mad like Ophelia. In my dream I preferred it to very much drunk, more cosmic than very much drunk, more potent yet more fragile. Sascha with her restless hair and low, even voice, in the seat just in front of me, which when I thought it or dreamed it caused me to open my eyes, but I could no longer see her head because she'd put it in Harry's lap. I dozed again thinking of Harry and Leibniz and the best of all possible worlds, not that the world itself was that way, but the beauty of the words which for a moment made it almost so, and Harry looking at me with murderous eyes when I'd only tried to help. Everything's a little dirty. It's true, it's true, I pleaded in my dream. How inarguable is that, even Leibniz wouldn't argue with that, but Harry knew what he knew and he had a wish to be clean. Then I felt Cord who was next to me leaning forward and I heard him say in a gin-drenched but polite tone, "Don't put your brights on. It's better without the brights," and I felt uneasy and opened my eyes because I knew those words meant the fog was back.

Bloch had slowed down. He had both hands near the top of the wheel like they teach you in driving school, ten before two, ten after ten, and his shoulders looked rigid and I caught his hawk-like eyes in the rearview. The fog swept by us and for a little while it was gone and Bloch put his brights back on and the road opened up and then we went into it again. I was drunk but not so drunk as not to pay attention. It became like a contest between us and the fog to get us home, and I didn't trust Bloch though I saw he was doing his best.

We went past the fair that was dark now and the hill and Blue Hill village with its gas station and shuttered storefronts and church in the New England style like a ghost in the dark, and in none of those places was there any fog so I dozed off again.

I dreamed sweetly again, Harry had gone off to the war after all but now he was home and we were all singing with preposterous grand enthusiasm *The Battle Cry of Freedom* or at least the part when Johnny comes marching home again, hurrah, hurrah, a song he told me once he'd loved as a boy, and when I awoke it was because the car seemed to have shifted somehow. I heard Bloch say "deer," but I didn't see a deer, he yanked the wheel back too late from the other way that he'd already yanked it and we were off the road hitting a rock that blasted a tire and we flipped but didn't go over and then all I saw was the boulder ahead of us.

12

It was like a wonderment at first. So this is what something like this is, so this is what this is. A crash, this is a crash, we're already off the road. It was all going to happen too fast. There wasn't time to shout.

Teddy and Cord woke up soupy and dazed but trying to brace themselves and Teddy tried to curl himself and I felt myself between them and saw the tops of Bloch's fingers yanking the wheel one more time but either the car had left the ground or it was too close and it hit the boulder almost dead on.

In the backseat we were thrown forward against the front seats. We were debris, gravitation had no pull. I couldn't see Harry or Sascha. I don't remember any pain. The engine caught fire. I was conscious. Now I heard Harry shouting shit and Jesus and pushing against the door that wouldn't open. I still couldn't see Sascha but I heard him say her name. He was ramming the door with his shoulder and cradling her head with one hand but then it seemed that he let her go so that he could ram the door with all of his force.

Teddy managed to twist around and get one of the zippers to the rear window open and I twisted around and got the other, then we launched ourselves one at a time through the narrow passage as if we were triplets being born and slid down the trunk onto the ground. Cord's face was streaked with blood but I couldn't see from where. We went around the car. Teddy helped Bloch out the driver side while Cord and I pulled on the passenger door as Harry kicked it and shouldered it until finally it creaked open.

I saw Sascha then. One side of her face was bloody. She wasn't conscious. Harry got under her arms as if lifting a child and eased her from the car and I took her legs, which were warm and still and as normal as sleep, and we put her down on the ground. But the engine was still flaming, so we lifted her a second time to move her farther from the car. We all moved farther from the car.

All this time I felt nothing but the need to stay alive, like something that's always on but you never hear, an electric current or a rain when it's rained for days, pouring down now, the need for all of us to stay alive.

Harry knelt down over her, put his face close to hers and his hands on her cheeks and throat and breathed into her mouth or kissed her, I wasn't sure. I couldn't see her face. What had happened began to dawn on me but all of it had already dawned on him.

She must have still been sleeping and he was sleeping and maybe the bumps of going off the road had begun to awaken them but not enough. When we hit the great rock her head went into the dashboard, into the glove compartment or the vent knobs. Dashboards were metal then.

Teddy and I ran to the road. In back of us the flames from the car reached higher. In the fog they glowed, their light diffuse, like a fire inside a tent.

I thought to myself it will set the woods on fire but then I remembered it wasn't in a woods it was in a scrubby field with rocks and I asked myself if scrubby fields with rocks caught on fire and I didn't know the answer.

It was then I became so afraid for Sascha I had trouble getting a breath.

Teddy wavered like a pendulum and waited for a car. I shouted that we should move Sascha still farther from the car. One of the few times I ever told Harry what to do. He lifted her up, alone this time, like a man with his bride in a movie when she is young and dying. He brought her toward the road and laid her down again. She was breathing, he said, and then he said it again.

He had blood on his arms and face. Cord ran up the road looking for a house and Teddy went the other direction. It was almost three o'clock, but I'm not sure I knew it or thought of it or of how slim were the chances of a car. None of us talked, except to shout at the world for help, and that we were here, and was there anyone around.

The gas tank went off with a rupturing thud and the car burned brighter and higher but the blueberry scrub didn't catch. I began to feel a stinging on my face. I touched around and there was blood coming from my hairline.

Bloch was also around, in a daze, saying again that there had been a deer, he had seen a deer. I didn't say I hadn't seen it. I didn't say anything.

We could hear Teddy and Cord shouting, their voices like cotton in the fog, and then Cord seemed to shout louder so that he cut through the fog and maybe there was a second sound, of another voice or an engine's mutter, and I strained for the rhythm of a conversation, a back-and-forth of human voices or a car door cracking open. Now the fog in Cord's direction brightened like a thinning cloud with the sun behind it, swirled and confusing, and through it, as if our solar system had gained a second sun, came two beams of light. A pickup truck approached us.

There were a guy and his girl and the stuffed poodle they'd won at the fair in front and Cord jumped down from the truck bed. Teddy came running from the other way. I don't know if we'd all turned sober by then or were too drunk to know the difference. The guy and the girl looked like they'd been out screwing, there was grass in her hair and she looked swollen and his eyes were sweet and tired but he was a big guy and quick to help. He did some mechanics to get the passenger door to open and Harry laid Sascha on the seat and crouched down beside her in the space where you put your legs. The rest of us scrambled into the truck bed with the girl. The big guy climbed back behind the wheel, double-clutched in a show of ragged determination, made a U-turn in the fog, and we went off toward Blue Hill where they had the hospital. The car was still burning in the field.

He drove fast. We sat with our backs against the side of the truck bed and the fog flew past us like dreams. The girl sat in a corner, holding her prize from the fair between her legs as if she was afraid it would blow away. Bloch was across from us, so sober and unblinking he might have been in shock.

Though it was one of the things about Bloch, that he seldom blinked. He could out-stare anybody. I prayed every second that Sascha was still alive. Every second, that is, that I wasn't cursing my inability to pray, the words seeming false and belated in my life, like who would believe me now.

In Blue Hill the fog was gone. The hospital seemed nearly shut. A pair of hundred watt bulbs were on where the sign said Emergency. The big guy honked mercilessly and Teddy ran inside bringing back two big-hipped nurses with a gurney. Everything seemed slow motion but I don't suppose it was.

The rest of us got out of the truck bed. I heard Harry say,

to one of the nurses, that she was alive, that she'd hit her head.

I saw her then, as the nurses and a male attendant who also came out moved her onto the tray. Harry had put a towel from the car to the left side of her face, but around the towel her face looked dark, looked black-and-blue perhaps. She was as still as sleep, her eyes were shut. The male attendant laid a blanket over her.

I thought, as they wheeled her in, that she could have been going to have a baby.

But why did I think that? Harry's baby? Harry who was beside her, who followed the gurney as though he were a boy racing to keep up with a lover's departing train.

It was a country hospital and it was late at night and calls had to be made. We were the only emergency patients. There were cots and the nurses had been dozing on them. It was almost like a motel where you arrive late and wake up the attendant to ask for a room. They wheeled Sascha through white doors and down a corridor. Harry remained by her side. I heard one of the nurses phone the surgeon. Her accent was flat and heavy. A car crash and a girl with a head injury and how long and the phrase "fifteen minutes." The surgeon would have to drive over. More time, more waiting, the loss of all context. I couldn't tell how long fifteen minutes was. It could have been all the time there ever was. The nurse called the sheriff and the fire department. She cupped the phone and asked Cord where the car was but he wasn't sure. I went out and got the guy from the pickup truck and he told her, such-and-such miles, so-and-so's farm. The room we were in was a boxy, fluorescent-bathed space with plastic chairs in addition to the cots. Not much medical equipment around; posters on the wall concerning poison ivy and measles. All of us kept looking through the small windows of the white swinging doors but there was nothing down there but corridor. The other of the two husky nurses began to examine us by turns, asking us to lie on one of the cots while she probed with a portable light and cotton swabs. We were told there was a doctor in attendance but he was with Sascha. I kept looking at the clock until fifteen minutes were gone. There was nothing wrong with any of us but bruises and cuts, and Bloch had the least of all. It was kind of a miracle, the nurse said. Bloch said that he'd been wearing a seat belt. We looked at him strangely. "Were *you*?" he asked lamely, of Teddy, of Cord, of any of us. "No," Cord said, and Bloch didn't know what more to say, he nodded and put his hands in his pockets.

The surgeon arrived. By now I knew the time too well: twenty-two minutes had passed. The surgeon drove an MG which he parked in front. He was a horn-rimmed kind of guy who must have moved here from somewhere, thinning hair, small nose. He went past us in our piteous irrelevance and took both the nurses with him, through the doors, down the corridor, off to the left somewhere where Sascha was. All of this, at last, in a hurry.

We waited. Harry didn't come out. The sheriff's deputy arrived, a guy in his twenties, brown uniform, sunken cheeks, watery eyes, poor complexion. It was both relief and an irritation to have him there, in that we hated to look down the corridor nor could we bear not to for more than a few seconds.

The deputy had his pad out and asked each of us some questions but he didn't take us one by one. We all stood around him like a basketball team with its coach. He wanted to know where we were going and how fast and where we'd been, our whole night, and was there liquor in the car and who was driving. Bloch said he was driving. The sheriff looked at his license and asked him if he'd had any alcoholic beverage to drink. Bloch said about three-quarters of one beer, and then—too much? was it always too much with Bloch?—that he was driving because he was the sober one. The deputy asked him how the accident happened. Bloch said, "I don't know. We were in fog and I saw a deer, so I swerved, I don't know. I swerved too far so I swerved back."

"Did you hit the deer?"

"No. I missed the deer."

"Did you know," the deputy said, "maybe not where you come from, but up here, when somebody has a crash and they say they swerved to miss a deer, it's usually believed that's a story to cover they were intoxicated."

"But I wasn't," Bloch said. "I only had three-quarters of a beer," and Teddy chipped in that that was so, and I did also, and Cord said he gave Bloch the keys because he knew he'd had less than one beer total.

Bloch offered to take a test. But he was acting sober and the deputy asked him to exhale and he smelled Bloch's breath and that was the end of that part of it.

Meanwhile Harry had not come out, nor either of the nurses.

The deputy wanted one of us to accompany him to the scene of the wreck, so Cord went with him. The wait became so unbearable it took on personality, like being strangled by someone you know.

And as I waited I began to thaw, began to have feeling again, and it dawned on my slow mind what "traumatized" meant. I, I was traumatized, self-anesthetized, and the anesthesia was wearing off. Sascha. Her name sibilant and soft, like furnishings in old homes. What was Sascha feeling? Her mind. Did Sascha's mind still exist? I felt the possibility like a flicker, then like a flash. Her injury. Was she in pain? Could Sascha live with pain?

In a weird jujitsu of feeling I could more easily imagine Sascha dead than in pain, because if she were dead, death not being real to me, it seemed a short jump back to life, but pain was just what it was.

I knew what pain was. Sascha in pain, Sascha in life, Sascha down the hall out of sight with strange men and women working over her and Harry for once in the span of my knowing him as helpless as a child.

Bloch sat in one of the plastic chairs with his hands folded, leaning forward, little Band-Aids on his hands, one ear, his chin.

Teddy and I stood around. I had a bandage on my forehead and he had something on his arm.

Life reduced to dazed, stripped moments, all that had gone before erased, history restarted on a bleak and ugly page.

We stayed quiet, even Teddy, who always had something to say. Were we strangers, after all?

In the silence I rehearsed words to say to Bloch, rehearsed them until they were sanded clean of my feelings, until what was left was something smooth and fraught, like a careful piece of work. I'm not sure I meant to say any of them, but then the waiting got too long. "You know, Adam, I kind of had my eyes open. I didn't see it."

He looked at me oddly, as though that was the oddest thing to say.

"The deer. I didn't see it," I repeated.

"Were you awake?"

"At the end. When you were losing control I was."

"It was there," he said.

"I didn't say it wasn't. I just. . ."

"It's why I swerved."

I could tell nothing about what Bloch was feeling then. He was like something that had petrified.

"So you were wearing a seat belt," I said finally.

"Yes."

"It's a good thing," I said. "Lucky thing."

"Was it?" he said.

Then we were quiet and I looked again through the swinging doors. Nothing more was down there than had been there before.

Teddy was looking at the pictures of poison ivy and poison oak and poison sumac on the wall. He was avoiding Bloch's glance, which I could see and it was pleading. And he was also, I thought, avoiding mine.

Bloch shuddered like a machine coming apart. Then he said to Teddy, or to both of us but he was looking Teddy's way, or maybe mostly to himself, "I was going to tell them they could put their seat belts on, too. I was trying to think of a funny way to say it. The captain has turned on the Fasten Seat Belt sign. Or offhand, like seat belts are in there somewhere if you want them, there's a little fog. You know. So they wouldn't think I was a flamer. So they wouldn't think I didn't know how to drive. Or I was bossing them around about something really stupid."

"You're a considerate fuck, aren't you," Teddy said.

13

My guilty secret about Bloch: I believed he was me. In some part of me each thing I ever saw Bloch do, each way he looked, what he said or failed to say, his crooked humor, his striving, his wish for validation, all me. I could see me taking the keys from Cord. I could see my humiliation at the goal line. I could imagine saying too many things and not knowing when to stop. I could imagine my hands on the wheel. I could imagine nursing a single beer. I could imagine the fog and not saying I didn't know how to drive in fog and putting on my seat belt and thinking that others should but not telling them so they wouldn't think I was an asshole. I could imagine myself frozen in fear. I could imagine my shoulders hunched. I could imagine all of these things more easily than I could imagine being anything like Harry. I could imagine my entire self as dull clay, yet a tremendous dream to be a hero. Grandiose fantasies of me, and a dull unblinking look, as though to ask how did I get here.

Scenes that never were. Bloch telling a joke. Bloch moving in a way that was graceful or natural. Bloch losing his temper or saying an unkind word or doing anything uncontrolled.

Are my characters getting away from me? Are they running into the ground?

Scenes that never were. Bloch giving up on himself. Bloch letting go.

Not this and not that. The sculptor chips away.

I could imagine seeing the deer. I could imagine the dark unfamiliar road, and my hands tightening. I could imagine the futility of my headlights, lighting up the clouds. I could imagine the deer, tremendous, bright, and leaping in front of me. I could imagine turning the wheel as if I were in snow in Rochester in January and I was sixteen years old and had been told if you skid to turn the wheel in the direction of the skid but it was so hard to believe, so counterintuitive, so full of a dangerous dare. I could imagine the deer dissolving in the fog but too late because I had turned too far. I could imagine still believing in the deer, still clinging to the deer.

But the deer was the light and the fog and I could imagine knowing this, somewhere in my dense soul.

I could imagine swearing never to admit it or think it for a very long while.

I could imagine turning the wheel back and bumping off the road and having no control at all.

I could imagine myself in my incompetence and helplessness and rage hurting her, hurting all of us, being the one, wrecking Teddy's car, wrecking it all. I could imagine fucking up, and thinking of it that way, Bloch, you've fucked up now, Louie, you've fucked up now.

I could imagine my light-headedness. I could imagine wandering around and not knowing what came next in the world.

I could imagine being still behind the wheel and seeing Sascha's crushed face, what I had done, what the car had done, what the deer had done.

I could imagine wanting to cry, but not crying. Stiff upper lip, Adam. Stiff upper lip, Lou.

Isn't that how it's said in wartime films? Isn't that how men behave?

Years later I would feel the same about Nixon. When they were kicking Nixon around I would say to myself there's a lot of Nixon in me. I said that to Cord once, I thought it would astonish him. He said to me, "There's a little of Nixon in all of us. It's how he got elected." And he said: "But Nixon is all Nixon all the time, and you're not."

Proof that friends have wisdom, that you learn things from friends. Which as it happens is what I believed with my whole heart in the summer of 1966. I think we all did, as if in a Mafia movie where the first act they're all friends, and the first act never ends.

Third acts were only a hypothesis, distant and bloodless, like rumors of war.

No, I wasn't Bloch. But I felt as bad and as guilty as Bloch. Or maybe I didn't. Maybe I couldn't. Tend your own garden, Louie. Don't go looking for others' troubles. Harry might have said that, if the mood had hit him that way. The exact advice he would never have taken from anybody. He who was headed in the opposite direction from me, from Bloch. But we were together in the car that night. No, I wasn't Bloch. What he felt, the depths of what he felt, would be, on calm and measured authorial reassessment, obscene for me to assert, claim, announce, colonize, presume or for that matter a dozen other verbs. It is what it was. Imagination.

Scenes that never were. Bloch in the emergency room while we waited, coming up to Teddy or me with a broken heart. Bloch shouting or screaming. Bloch looking through those narrow windows, down into the empty corridor.

And another: any of us, myself, or Cord, or Teddy, saying to Harry, ever: you shouldn't have invited Bloch. You shouldn't have incorporated him, made him your friend, gone that mile too far. A tragic mistake, we never said. An overreaching, we never said. And if you hadn't. . .

☙

Meritocracy vs. democracy.

At the heart of democracy is equality for all, but in its operation is equal opportunity for all.

At the heart of meritocracy is equal opportunity for all, but in its operation is a picking and choosing, of those most worthy to advance.

Meritocracy is proud of its efficiency, its shrewd use of resources, its modernity, its fairness, its wisdom.

But democracy scorns such "advancement." What good is it? A man who is clever may become rich and enrich the nation, but he has no better chance of solving the existential riddle than a slow, plodding man. No better chance of behaving well in a car crash. No better chance of behaving well when pain and horror are let loose, when charity might be found or lost.

Meritocracy knows it has an answer to this, but it cannot think of it, or is afraid to say.

14

The three of us and Bloch. Or a stranger, a visitor, I suppose would have said the four of us, as a Venutian on late night TV would say earthlings, not Americans, Russians, Mexicans. No more words. The only time any of us said anything was when the terror of the silence got so big it filled every crack in the room, and we spoke to get a little space back to breathe. "The fuck they doing?" "The guy's good. He's from Mass. General." "There's some coffee."

More than an hour went by. Cord returned with the deputy, who seemed to have become his pal, or his worried guardian. "Anything?" Curt looks. "Harry's still in there." The deputy got Cord a cup of water from the cooler. Then he stood around with the rest of us like we were still his old team, until a call came in and he left.

At the end of the corridor we could see there was a second corridor to the left. It led to the operating room, but also offices and lockers. Harry was there, in one of the offices, out of sight. Everything I can say about him now was from what he told us later. He had phoned New York and Sascha's father had in turn awakened her uncle, the one who was the heart surgeon at Columbia, and the uncle had spoken with the surgeon in Blue Hill and from all that was said Harry knew that the situation was grave, there was no question of moving her further, to Bangor or Boston, not for now anyway, there wasn't the time, there was no stability, the surgeon would have to go in now.

These were things the surgeon had also told Harry directly, but when he heard them repeated on the phone between doctors he knew they were true, or anyway as true as the surgeon could represent them. The surgeon turned from peremptory and self-important to attentive and comradely after he learned who Sascha was and who they all were. Impressed by the Maclaren name, knew somebody who was somebody who knew somebody, and so it went even in the corridors of life and death. Harry disliked the man but Sascha's uncle said he seemed okay and his credentials were first-rate, better than you could have hoped for. Harry remained on the phone a little while, after the surgeon went in to do his work, and the uncle kept talking, about this and that, protocols and indications, which was a good thing, Harry thought, although he had trouble taking in the words. A good thing because Harry and Sascha's father were two men separated by a wire, Harry could imagine the plunge of the Maclarens' happiness and hopes more easily than he could imagine his own but he could say nothing about it that didn't sound ridiculous, nor could Sascha's father.

Harry, alone now, tried to will the phrase "head injury" into a shape he could understand, that images, thoughts, and hopes could adhere to like messages on a kiosk. If the doctor had meant something more serious would he not have used a more complicated phrase, but "head injury" was what he used. Even with Sascha's uncle he said "head injury," though he used other words as well.

Harry didn't believe what he was thinking any more than he believed in spring training dreams. But he did, for a few moments, believe in his own dumb will. It was what other people always saw in him and he had never had much time for it himself, but it was all he had now. He could will "head injury" to be less than what it was. He could will "head injury" to be as benign as it sounded. Stitching, patches, scars, a little cosmetic surgery, unhappiness but life. You can't take someone like Sascha away. It's preposterous, it's unprepared for, there must be an appeal from this somewhere. A mistake has been made, like an error in celestial addition. But if we shut our eyes really really really hard. . .

Is this Harry, so desperate, so forlorn? Twenty-two years old. Sascha, also, twenty-two years old.

Is it old or young?

Depends, I guess.

He willed the surgeon's hands and her protoplasm and her skin, healing up like a film running backward.

He willed her to pull through and to be fed an incredible amount of drugs so that her pain would be less but at last she would open her eyes and she'd be weak and her skin sallow and she'd hate food for awhile because of the drugs but others would come, her family, everyone would wait outside or come in for a few minutes at most on account of her weakness, but or until eventually when she would sip something, her lips would be moist and the IV would become obsolete and she'd watch a few minutes of TV before drifting off. That would be great, that would be everything he could wish for.

But no one came out.

He thought about Sascha's sister, Maisie, coming to visit, and her beautiful little brother.

And then what seemed a long time, as long as to cross a desert, all he could think about was the time he'd stood her up. They'd just met, this was in Cambridge, a complicated story with exculpatory factors but what it came down to when you rubbed away all the sly and pliant arguments for the defense was that Teddy had tickets to a Red Sox game. Yes, their plans (Harry and Sascha's) had been tentative, yes, he left a message. But her bristling rage. That's what he remembered. Her rage with the word *bristling* attached to it, compounded of her heart's opening to him and her hurt and her absolute conviction that once things are so far wrong they can never be made right, an omen, conclusive evidence, and her need to blame someone more than herself because she already blamed herself too much, for being in this fix, for liking the jocky bastard with his no-good western ways, for falling in love in a way no better than any other cliché. He showed up at six o'clock at her dorm, after the Red Sox had lost to the Yankees, and she was throwing stuff at him, phone books, she threw a phone book. That's what he kept remembering, not how they'd make love later in the bushes of the observatory.

Sascha wronged. What a concept. He almost laughed.

And then, as if on account of it, he had to believe in immortality. Not out of weakness, it seemed, but obviousness, a sort of *force majeure*, in which sometimes you give up and go with it like you're still on LSD, all manner of shit flying around including the truth if you can only find it.

Latch onto Sascha. If anybody can't die, she can't. Not with a bristling rage like that. Goddess Parvati dark-haired girl.

In her blood, in her corpuscles, this is where the battle is fought, house-to-house, hand-to-hand. Here Sascha wins. The territory of Sascha is inviolable. The territory of Sascha is immortal. There's a flag, there's *élan vital*, there's a song. They give up territory but they win it back. Valiant soldiers who sing her song and he, Harry, is one of them. He would die for her, for any and every inch of her.

Though later, when he told me these things, Harry also said

that metaphors of war are horseshit. He wrote this to me from Ft. Ord. I thought it was so brilliant and I wondered if he'd heard it or read it. Metaphors of war are wrong for everything but war, he wrote. Everything else they mess up, they turn complication into this-or-that, one thing or the other, enemies.

Sascha was not an enemy of death. She would win finally in transcendence. There would be realms where he would find her, big realms, not little dinky ones like this room with a desk and a phone and a chart of what makes a person obese according to the Department of Agriculture. Harry went, while he waited for Sascha, from a psychologist's point of view, insane.

Realms of being that he'd only read about, he believed in. And then he came back, like a tumble at the end of a trip, with a headache and the headache's name was Adam Bloch.

He felt he shouldn't hate Bloch, for eminently practical reasons, because if he hated Bloch and it was not just, God might take it out on Sascha. He wanted to do nothing to alienate God. He wanted to be the best little boy he could be. Instead he blamed himself, for getting drunk, for letting her get drunk, for falling asleep, for not waking up. Where had his hand been? His hand could have saved her this. Why did he not always sleep with his hand on her face? Where had he been in his dreams to neglect it? An argument, a pledge, against dreams, ever, they're too dangerous to life. How could he have left her so, it was worse than going to that Red Sox-Yankees game.

But he knew Bloch had caused the crash. Lame evil weenie flamer who stares at you and doesn't even blink. Who couldn't save somebody's life, who couldn't even bring people home safe, who didn't even drink.

He tried so hard not to blame Bloch, for Sascha, for superstition or faith.

When the surgeon came out it was possible to know from his expression what had happened. Harry saw it but refused to accept it, because what if the surgeon was a man of head-fakes and feints and drama, or what would it mean if Harry plain guessed wrong, if he guessed his bride had died and she had not? He felt, somehow, that would be a crime. The surgeon's eyes making a point of not looking away. Pulling his cap off, rubbing his nose with his sleeve. "It was a serious head injury. We were unable to revive her, or help her." Harry heard the downward flow of the words.

He had never imagined that this small office with its metal desk and obesity chart would take on dimensions so definite in his life. The fluorescent light felt like the light of the whole world, thin and with a hum.

The surgeon's name was Cairns. He introduced himself, which he had done once before but it seemed forgotten. He said how sorry he was. Harry heard something kindly in his voice. He went in to see her. His life was changed now. He knew this. Nothing else but this could have changed it. He kissed her face many times and held his cheek next to her cheek and imagined that she was smiling at him in a way that was sweet and overwhelming.

He lingered in the sweetness. The son they would not have. And her thoughts, what happened to them now, where did they go?

Lingering awhile. Let them say something, the hospital people, if he wasn't supposed to stay. Let them bring words in here, where they didn't belong.

Extinction. What sort of word is that?

Her cheek was cool.

Harry made a mental note to ask the doctor about her pain,

what sort of pain she had had, and for a moment making such a mental note gave him strength, like an early sign that life would go on. But he soon forgot the mental note.

He didn't want life to go on.

It seemed like no one would come in to disturb him. He touched her legs, her feet, he pushed back her matted hair. He kissed her wound, where the surgeon had worked and left it dark and like a small worksite, a place of excavation.

Then one of the nurses came in, her white uniform like a badge of the world as it is, ongoing, time-deceived, and he went out to call New York and tell them.

It was the other nurse who informed the three of us. Teddy yelled "Shit!" and spun around. Cord hung his head, said a halfway audible prayer, his lips moving, his eyes squinted close to shut.

I don't know that I said anything at all. Nothing you could mark down, say was behavior. I felt inadequate to life. Both my parents were alive. I didn't know the laws of grief. What it would be, whatever it would be. The only thing I could compare it to was so stupid, but when I heard that Kennedy had died. Not when he was shot, but that little while afterward, when everybody was still hoping and then we heard.

I suppose I kept my counsel. I was afraid to speak, knew it would just be show. I waited for the next thing to happen.

Bloch started to walk away. I hadn't looked at him until then. He had a stumped, bewildered expression, someone who had caught the wrong train or a scientist with an experiment gone awry. I saw him blink. Now there was something. It was a slow blink, almost controlled, and he tried to look at all three of us, in succession, almost the way they must teach you in salesman school, get everybody in the room. But he was trying harder than that. He was trying hard to be real now. What could he say? He'd ruined his life. He'd crossed one of the only lines. "Tell Harry I'm sorry, okay?"

We could have said something. Any one of us could have but we didn't. We were pretending it was too hard, as if no words could suffice for the vast disappointment we felt. We glared, or looked away. What self-righteous bitches we were, but it was also true, in part, that we couldn't help ourselves. We had to do something. We could have hit him, but we didn't do that. A whiff of violence floated in the antiseptic air.

Bloch saw our contempt for what it was or pretended to be and said, "You want me to go kill myself. You want me to go jump in the river."

"There's no river out there," Cord said. "It's a bay."

"I get the idea. You don't have to be sarcastic." It was the only time I'd ever seen Bloch's eyes bright. Incandescent with crazy guy fearlessness. "I get the idea," he said again. "How about electricity? Would that be better? Electrocute myself? Slit my wrists? Get myself run over?"

"Adam, come on," I said. Then I said, "Nobody wants you to kill yourself, Adam," but what I really meant was that no one wanted the problems of it. About the rest I wasn't sure, I couldn't think.

"Thanks," Bloch said. "Thank you very much."

Were we utterly powerless in the face of Sascha's death? I think Bloch knew we were, but felt more powerless still. What destiny could he take charge of now? What transformation of self effect? The logic, the harsh, stilted rhetoric, of death.

"Where are you going, Adam?" Teddy said.

He was walking out of the hospital.

We looked at each other when he was gone, fleeting glances, but they showed no guilt.

A little later Harry came in through the white doors. His face was still not bandaged or washed. Marked with his blood or hers. We crowded around him and embraced him. He seemed then like a man who'd been pointing, looking, guarding, all his life in the wrong direction, and now he'd been called from another. Like a gun emplacement facing the sea, and then the enemy attacks by land. I felt an odd, light sensation, as if a wind was lifting me up.

"Where's Bloch?" he said.

"Out," I said. "He's in pretty bad shape. He's a little crazy."

"He said he was sorry," Teddy said.

15

Sascha. Outline of her, a little later in life. A doctor. In the field. In Lebanon or the hinterlands of New Mexico. Somebody Oriana Fallaci might have written about. Compassion and a certain hardiness, even resilience as if she'd grown up to be, surprise surprise, some species of beautiful weed, surviving drought and fire, indestructible. One who never watched TV.

Would their marriage have survived? All the marriages from that time, all the ones I ever heard of anyway, seem not to have. The wear-and-tear, the rough roads of all those years. Yet I can see them breaking up and getting together again. Getting married not two times but three. Something crazy, slightly mythic. Something that wouldn't keep him from getting elected because people would see what a miracle it was. Her work would keep her apart but bring glory and a touch of morality to them both. Someone taking on the heart of the world.

Sascha. Outline of her in middle age, in late middle age, as the third millennium of the Christian era begins. Her hair mostly white but still flying, and her eyebrows dark in dramatic contrast. Still in the field, here or there. Doctors Without Borders, maybe. A couple of kids, the girl at Harvard the boy off in South America somewhere. A couple weeks of Maine in the summer, where she's begun to sculpt. A more cheerful sort than she was; gives a lot of money away.

And if the White House thing really happened?

It feels a little kitschy but I'll get there. Not Jackie Eleanor Laura Ladybird Hillary, surely not Pat nor the others. Wretched job, best to ignore it but you can't. Embrace the capacity to do good, do what you can anyway. Forget the cheerleading, just the example. A little clinic somewhere in D.C. Every day to the office. Poor kids, kids with AIDS, bloated mothers, gunshot wounds. The run of the mill. And a TV show? *E.R.* meets the White House?

Thirty-five years have passed and I remember her preciousness, her promise, her quiet, and yet the great galloping stride of her life.

The thought of her babies. Fat and ugly, born with a crewcut. How beautiful they would have been.

೭ಾ

Am I exploiting my friends, dragging the gold out of their teeth?

Pitiless world, this meritocracy. More like a stampede, souls climbing over one another to be the first to die, capitalism's neatest, most efficient trick yet.

My friends were beautiful and I was sly, for it's I who write all this down.

Although how sly will I seem if my book sits in the second drawer from the bottom, where like a half-built bridge it currently resides, until I die and the desk is sold in the garage sale whereupon a lot of papers will have to go. Or do I presume to say. . . *estate* sale?

Then would I be a martyr, as much as they? They would still be beautiful. They would still give hope. But I would have failed them and failed myself and in the name of what?

I could have had a job all this time I've spent in my room. I could have been making good money. Lawyer, producer, scriptwriter, guy on the phone. I've done that stuff, I know how it goes. I could have been in the world, hurly-burly, getting laid.

Setting aside my friends for the moment, I seem to wish to be the poet of something that may not deserve it. Meritocracy. Hardly a poetic word. Neologisms seldom are.

Or, in a more considered view: the lives of those who deserved it all and didn't get it.

And the shouting of the Robespierres, why the fuck did they deserve it all in the first place, what romantic hooey is that, rose-tinted and touched with consumption, they *had* it all and *earned* nothing.

From the bitter ashes comes something glorious, and it's not wrapped in a flag.

Sascha. Outlines. The origins of my love for, or if you will, obsession with, her. A steady mind. A sturdy but turbulent heart.

The best are bright but not the brightest. The brightest are like those halogen headlights in cars, so bright with their silver-white light they make it harder for anyone else to see.

Big two-hearted rivers are what we need, the pledge of the words if not the story.

Sascha. Outlines of grief. I grieve, you grieve, we all fall down.

❧

A plot alternative, a plot possibility.

On account of Sascha's death, a brilliant career is derailed, Harry grows into the ways of the times, marches, black churches, a place in Vermont, he drops acid one hundred and seventy-eight days in a row but it does him little harm and a few years later he founds an ice cream factory or a fish farm and just when you think his political days are behind him, twenty years late, out of the ashes comes a candidacy, backed by all that ice cream money, which is fifty times what his inheritance ever was, and then, and then. . . colon cancer?

A reversal on Forrest Gump, here a brilliant guy brought down. No fat-bellied Middle American platitudes that the '60s were our misfortune. Like a forty-four caliber hollow-tipped bullet through the heart of the comfortable revisionism and out the other side comes the man who could lead us all.

And Bush, who had his nose in the air like a priss over Bill Clinton, cringes when he sees who's coming. The jig is up, in a certain way. The prissy probity gives way to a nervous grin.

But I feel I have no right to say more than what happened. Or more truthfully, I'm scared to.

༒

We fall from grace early, we products of the great American meritocracy. I'm sure I half-forget how snobbish we were, how ambitious, how unfair, our lack of mercy and dumb labels and casual little crudities. Our short-sightedness, too. We were nearly blind.

But compared to today, when perhaps we see more but all the colors are gray?

16

Harry sat on the gurney with his legs dangling down, so oblivious to the nurses attending to his cuts they could have stitched his lips shut and he might not have noticed. The rest of us stood around in the bath of fluorescent light like the accident victims we were. I felt a growing nausea, for the altered, cramped dimensions of things. I felt claustrophobic, as if Sascha and Harry had been holding the tent of the world up and now it was fallen down in suffocating shreds. None of us said anything. The surgeon, Cairns, came through, with his head down and papers in his hand, grimacing, in a hurry to get to a desk. The wall clock said a quarter to seven, a colorless dawn mounted the storm-streaked windows. The nurses were done with Harry. He hardly seemed to notice. He still sat there, and then Bloch came back.

He shut the door with such quiet exactitude it seemed to bring even more attention to himself, to how hard he was trying not to disturb. He looked almost serene, as though he'd gone out and given himself a good talking-to. I caught Harry's look. Studied neutrality. He told me later he dreaded to hear Bloch's voice then, he thought he should just walk out.

But for myself, I began to feel something like pity for Bloch. He seemed like an old tragic actor wearing too much makeup. The Great Bloch, Bloch the Magnificent. Probably what I felt was a lot less than pity; more like a generalized inclination, if "a" and "b" and "c" were so, to cut the guy a little slack.

Pity being way over my head, pity being something a kid read about and never quite understood. But I saw it then in Cord too. Mixed with a little bit of gristly fear that Bloch might have gone over some sort of cliff and we didn't want our hands on it.

Bloch rolled his lips together. His hands were in the pockets of his jacket. He came up to Harry, unblinking, maybe hoping or half-expecting Harry to say something first, but he didn't.

Bloch seemed defenseless then. Throwing his dirtbag self on the mercy of the court.

And what if there had been a deer? This idea dawned on me. Maybe I hadn't seen everything. Maybe it had been there darting and leaping, at an angle or a depth in the fog I couldn't see, and Bloch swerved because he had to swerve because it was worse if you hit the deer.

I still didn't think there'd been a deer, but I wasn't sure now.

"If there was something in the world I could do to change this. . ." His words felt rehearsed, yet there was hoarse, groaning feeling in them.

"Me too," Harry said.

"I told Louie. I told these guys. I can barely speak. . ."

Harry nodded.

"I'm so sorry," Bloch said.

But he didn't back off or bow his head. Instead he stared at Harry, and he still didn't blink.

"Please don't stare at me," Harry said. "I'm not a freak."

"I'm not either."

"Nobody said you were," I said.

"Why would they have to?"

"Oh come on, Adam," Teddy said. "Self-pity's not the thing right now."

"Self-pity? *Me?*"

"No, not you," Cord said. He spoke so softly it seemed at first the inflection of his courtesy, but it was really his desperation.

"We're just trying to get by here," he muttered. "Nobody's blaming you."

"Of course you are," Bloch said. "Of course you are. What a joke! What hypocrisy! You're all hypocrites! This is bullshit!" Bloch broken open, his hoarseness like a wound, his secret life pouring out like dark unaerated blood. "*I* killed her? Are you saying *I* did? I had to drive you home, okay? Who asked you to get drunk? Drunk pieces of shit!"

"Adam, calm down," Teddy said.

"I *am* calm. Can't you see? I'm calm. Calm. Calm Adam Bloch, cool under pressure, all the grace in the world under pressure. So fuck you, alright? *You* calm down. I was driving in fucking fog, I saw a fucking deer, I tried to miss it, I did my fucking best, alright? That's not good enough? I didn't try to kill us all! I didn't try to kill her!"

The fluorescent hum again. The murmurs of our hearts.

Bloch shifted his weight, glared at the floor with a kind of willed focus, as if looking at Harry again was forbidden so the floor, in spite, would became his self-imposed exile.

Harry asked Cord if he had any change and we all went into our pockets, almost comically, like guys in a forties movie when a pretty girl asks for a light and they all pull out their Zippos. A quarter, a packet of pretzel sticks from the vending machine. Harry chewed through the cellophane but then he couldn't eat any of the contents and passed the packet around and we couldn't eat either.

Bloch too waved it away. Down-turned head. No thanks. Bloch's breath heaving. Harry dumping the pretzels in the trash, angrily, first crushing the packet in his fist.

"You don't even know I exist." For being so hoarse, his throat in every syllable, Bloch's voice was almost gentle now. "None of you do, not even you, Harry. Not really. I only exist so you can blame somebody. If somebody gets killed, it's Bloch who must have done it. There couldn't have been reasons. There couldn't have been a deer. It had to be the weenie flamer."

He looked at each of us again, by turns, a lawyer silently polling the jury.

"Adam, cut it out," I said.

"I loved her too, you know that? That ever occur to any of you? That's not possible, right? Adam Bloch, love somebody?"

He walked toward the door, his head down like Jacques Tati about to make a comic exit. Somehow he stuck an arm out and the door gave way, then we couldn't see him anymore.

I had a moment of almost tender wonderment. Bloch was right, it had never occurred to me, that he loved her too.

And those other things he said? What a terminal jerk, I must have thought.

You're no credit to your race, you terminal jerk, is what I must have thought.

George Washington Carver, a credit to his race. Adam Bloch, not.

But I still wondered about the deer.

We were a sea of anger and without Bloch there was no shore to lap on. My claustrophobia returned. What could anyone say to Harry? Trash Bloch a little more? Why bother. Ask Harry if he wanted something, ask if we could help in any way? What a pious crock. Not worth bothering with that either.

The heavens must be very full, because the world was so empty.

I didn't believe that Sascha was dead. Or I believed it but

only intermittently, what they say about stopped clocks, right twice a day.

We were all waiting for Harry to be the good daddy and tell us it was all alright.

But how do you comfort a good daddy? And how do you continue to believe such errant crap when the "good daddy" is struck down?

Silently, I struggled to find compassion for my friend.

And then he said he needed to make more phone calls.

Cord offered to go with him, stay with him, make some of the calls for him. But Harry didn't want that.

Of course he didn't.

In his absence we drank a little coffee and finally ate Oreos out of the vending machine. We were tired now. The hospital began to show signs of daytime life. At eight the shift would change, but by seven fifteen the nurses were sitting down more, doing their night's paperwork. My head buzzed and I ached to sleep. I was "thinking" of Sascha, which meant that I was thinking nothing at all, playing an elaborate mental hide-and-seek to keep away the feeling of her absence.

Cord asked one of the nurses where he was. She said he was in a room on the phone. Cord's forehead looked crinkled up, so I said, "It's only been fifteen minutes. Not even fifteen."

"More than fifteen," Teddy said.

"Is it?" I said, though I knew it wasn't, I'd been glancing at my watch and anyway I always knew the time.

"Just seems long," Cord said.

"It is, it's been," Teddy said.

They were sitting in a row of plastic chairs and I was standing by them, so that we wouldn't be three in a row, so that we'd be tighter than that. "Did you go to that party?" Teddy said.

His voice tailed off a little, as he remembered whatever it was he was going to say. He leaned forward and folded his hands. He was talking to Cord. "At the Field Club. Did you come down? When Deedee Winchester puked all over me?"

"You were such a gentleman," Cord said.

"Well for Christ sake."

"You didn't have to push her out of the car."

"I did *not* push her out of the car. I pushed her *head* out. So she wouldn't puke on the upholstery. Christ, you think I pushed her out of the car?"

"No Teddy, you were Mr. Chivalry."

"She barfed on my jacket, my shirt, my pants."

"She had the flu. She wasn't blotto or anything."

"The flu is no excuse for projectile vomiting in a grown female."

"Did you screw her?"

"Hell no. Jesus. . . Remember Breed Phipps, hanging from the chandelier? That was the same party."

"What was that, fourth form?"

"I don't know. Was it?"

I didn't even try to say anything. Why would I? Their lives, or their once-upon-a-time lives. Mine was nowhere to be seen.

Teddy, never looking up, as though I wasn't there, continued on about Deedee and dry cleaning bills and Breed's parents having to pay eleven hundred dollars to fix the chandelier.

I thought of telling him he was starting to sound like Noel Coward, which would have pissed him off because even we knew Noel Coward was queer, but then he said, to Cord, "Sascha was there."

"She was?"

"She came late. She came with Alison Gardiner."

"I don't remember."

"You don't remember because you were off in the bushes doing the evil deed with Veronique, you vile-minded fuck."

"Definitely not the bushes in December."

"I'd gone home. I'd come back with clean clothes. I'd never met a girl from Brearley. Supposed to be brainy, all that shit, I gave her shit for that. Tony Garrison introduced us. You know him? He was from Greenwich. He went to Hotchkiss. . . I danced with her three or four times."

"And?"

"And what? Did I put moves on her like a dirty-minded southern fuck undoubtedly would have?"

"Did you have a crush on her?"

"No. You know, I didn't. I liked her. But I was in love with somebody else at the time."

"Who?"

"Deedee Winchester."

I laughed. Funny turn, touching. But even my laughter didn't get an acknowledging glance from Teddy.

"Now it's been twenty minutes," I said.

"Maybe we should just go in there," Cord said.

"I didn't know you knew Sascha so long ago," I said to Teddy.

"It's been more like half an hour," he said to Cord. I said again, in case he hadn't heard me, "I didn't know you knew Sascha so long ago."

"Something you don't know? Amazing," Teddy said.

"What do you mean?"

"Nothing. I don't mean anything, Louie."

"Teddy can be so charming," Cord said.

"Hey, if it's twenty minutes, it's twenty minutes, Louie says so."

"Teddy, Jesus," I said.

"Did it ever occur to you, Lou, that this whole thing's your fault?"

"Actually, about every other minute," I said.

"You think I'm kidding? What was that shit, you being so fucking smart, if you go to Vietnam because you want to get elected president, you can't do that. It's not pure enough. Who asked you?"

"Nobody."

"So great, so Mr. Knows-every-fucking-thing, if you didn't say that to her, she wouldn't've gotten him upset, he wouldn't've gotten plowed. If he wasn't plowed, Bloch wouldn't've been driving."

"Teddy, shut up. You're being a total flamer," Cord said.

"That's the stupidest thing I ever heard."

"Okay. I'm not saying it was a direct cause."

But he was.

"I'm not Bloch," I said.

"Who said you were?"

"You're acting like it. You're substituting me for him."

"Don't be paranoid."

"*Me*, paranoid? Cord's right. This is bullshit."

The nurse came back to say Harry wasn't in any of the rooms. The other nurse, who heard this, said she'd seen him go outside, she thought he was looking for our other friend.

We went out to the parking lot but Harry wasn't there. The squall with Teddy lingered sullenly over us, he wasn't talking to me and I didn't know what to say to him, so Cord said, "We better split up. We better look for them." The morning was starting overcast and cold. We seemed to be the only ones around.

From the parking lot there was a road that went into the village and a dirt track that seemed like it might go to the water. Cord and I took the track. It was a crooked little track overhung with birch and spruce and posted with No Trespassing signs. At the water's edge were gravelly mud and beslimed rocks and a seascape of low tide, mottled grays, and calm. A cormorant made its low Spruce Goose takeoff from the water. Our visibility in either direction down the shore was limited by outreaches of land. Across the bay was nothing but forest and quiet shingle houses curtained by the spruce. There was no one in view anywhere, so we split up again, Cord moving north toward the village and I to the south.

A partial path snaked into the trees, but I was afraid it wouldn't continue to hug the waterline so I left it and made my way over the rocks and oozing mussel beds, my legs soaked almost to my knees and my pants like heavy flaps. I came around the first point of land and looked down the bay but there was another point directly south and the shoreline became steep and abrupt, so I had no visibility.

I scrambled over boulders, cutting my hands on the barnacles. My legs were freezing, my bandages fell off, the palms of my hands and my fingers stung from the salt water and barnacles. I felt like I was on a mission, driven by a rush of bitter resentment so profound I had scarcely felt it since my parents split apart. The fuck had Teddy been talking about? It just showed, it really did. When I loved people, it got messed up. Jesus, when I even *liked* people. And all this "we" shit I'd embellished. The boy runs shivering and alone. The "we" busted back into its atoms. All I wanted to do was find Harry. Or Bloch.

Out in deeper water I could see the staid, duck-like torso

of a lobster boat puttering out, so indifferent to the drama I'd defined for myself that I thought it floated in a parallel world. I reached the second point of land, crawled up the scruffy grass to the top of it, and then I could see, two hundred yards to the south, a rickety pier like a bridge to oblivion and at the end of it two human shapes.

It appeared as if they were sitting at the end of it, their legs dangling off, as Harry had sat on the nurses' gurney in the hospital.

Quickly I covered half the ground between us. I waved but they weren't looking my way. I kept climbing over rocks. As soon as I could I began to run.

I was almost to the pier when Harry saw me. I hadn't shouted but he turned my way. Again I waved. It seemed to make no impression on him, as if his eyes were fixed on something more distant. He again looked out into the bay. I mounted the pier. For a few moments I felt in the creaking boards under my feet a kind of overlay, of another pier, or something like a pier, possibly the Playland boardwalk on Long Island Sound near where we'd lived before upstate and my parents' divorce, and at the end of it, awaiting my tentative, halting steps. . . who? My father? My mother? Both of them in the same picture, two stars in rare conjunction, looking slightly down in my direction, as if I was just beginning to walk?

Harry got up from the damp boards on the pier, brushed off the seat of his pants. Casually he looked my way. I had trouble reading his expression at first, but that was really because he hadn't one then. A little unslept, a little hungover. Otherwise he was just Harry. As if all the sorrow, the tragedy, now resided within him, he'd swallowed them whole as the whale swallowed Jonah.

Bloch got up too. He had a bloated look and he was starting to look unshaven and he didn't look my way. I thought he was looking past me. I turned to see if Teddy or Cord were there but they were not.

Bloch was still looking past me. I thought he was crazy on account of it.

Harry said, "I forgive him."

Bloch didn't even blink.

For a moment my only feeling was the rage I'd carried from town. Bloch was standing beside Harry like a friend. There was no space between them, only inches, as though they could smell each other's breath.

I could have mouthed the words then, some formula, some piling on top of Harry's, "I forgive you too, Adam," mumbled or muttered or oddly without affect like a defendant's confession at a show trial. But Harry must have known where I'd be going.

"Wait," he said. "Wait till, you know—I can't say it, Louie. You'd have the words."

"Find it in my heart?"

"I knew you'd have the words."

But I didn't think I really did, and maybe he didn't either.

He looked so normal. He looked like nothing had happened at all but the end of a late summer idyll, a slightly wrecked weekend in the country.

I knew my rage was finished then. It had nowhere to go. The same spirit that forgave Bloch accepted me. There was not one without the other. Take it all or leave it all. I'd ridden in with Harry Nolan and I would ride out with him, or I would ride out alone. His girl, his gang of guys, his big ruling spirit, his catastrophe. If he wanted to forgive Bloch, who was I to say?

At last Bloch looked at me. "There wasn't any deer," he said, and I nodded.

༄

And later in Blue Hill we found Cord and Teddy, exhausted, on the steps of the old white church. Teddy got up when he saw me coming. He had an odd, surprised expression, as if he needed to make sure we weren't ghosts. I was a little surprised when he began to weep profusely. He puts his arms around me in particular, and his thin frame shook as he wept.

17

In one of the letters I received from Ft. Ord, Harry told me what happened with him and Bloch. Even today, when time has licensed me to carry a more jaundiced view of the world, I take what he wrote for about how it was.

He went out looking for him because like the rest of us he didn't want him on his conscience. He was prepared to lie like hell, to say anything at all, so that Bloch wouldn't do something stupid. He didn't want to have to think about Bloch anymore. That was it, really. He wished the world, or rather his mind, was clean of him. He wished, from his soul's point of view, that Bloch be extinct. But that would never happen if Bloch threw himself in front of a car or whatever else he could think of.

As well, Harry was trying to run away from Sascha. Not from her spirit, which he posited elsewhere, but her body, lying without dignity, confusing and challenging to everything he was willing himself to believe, an outrage, in some white sterilized room of the same building. It was driving him crazy.

He struggled to think instead of all the things Bloch had said in his tantrum if that's what it was. The fucking fog, the fucking deer, his fucking best. He couldn't even curse right. Bloch couldn't. Too many fuckings, too much pleading. He sounded like a bitch.

The first place Harry went looking was the bay because on reflection where else would Bloch go, Bloch who was afraid of the water, who'd worn his life jacket all day long. It took but ten minutes to find him, Bloch standing at the end of the pier as if in position for some darkly plotted version of an Olympic dive. That is to say, he was facing away from the land, with the toes of his shoes over the edge of the boards, and every little while he looked nervously down, at the slushy water or his shoes.

Which was all, grotesquely, like one of the experiments in the course on fear and courage that Harry had taken from Donald Webber, the one who flew him down to Millbrook. Yale had a new building for art and architecture then, it was the cat's pajamas of its time but it was not yet complete, so that it was possible to sneak around the scaffolding at night and climb up to the flat roof and put your feet half over the edge and stare down a hundred and fifty feet at the tops of cars and beckoning asphalt and write a paper on your findings. It was not only possible, it was required. Bloch was also taking that class, it was there that Harry met him. Bloch had been florid in the paper he wrote, he had recorded every millimeter of fear in his body, he had been a poet of fear.

But the tide was out now, and if Bloch had jumped he might have hit his head or broken a leg but he would not have drowned. Or it would not have been easy to drown, after he jumped he would still have had to want to drown, or he might have been knocked unconscious.

The water at the end of the pier covering the rocks was, by Harry's guess and depending which rock you stood on, four or five feet deep. Harry walked out on the rotting planks toward Bloch. He called so as not to scare him. Bloch said nothing but by the time Harry was close he had turned around. Now his heels were at the edge of the boards, as if keeping contact with the edge for safety's sake, or assurance of escape, the way some people will only live on the coast. Harry stayed six feet away, didn't want to crowd him.

"Hey."
"Hey."
"So. What's going on?"
"You care?"
Harry's shrug.
"You must hate me."
"Maybe."
"I want you to hate me."
"That's horseshit, Adam."

Bloch turned his back on Harry, his feet pivoting around but still working the edge.

Harry thought, he wants me to push him over, he wants me to do it for him. And he hated Bloch even more. The masochist says hit me, the sadist says no. But he hated Bloch so much then that he really wanted to do it. How hard would it be? A tap in the middle of the back and he would fall. Harry even looked up and down and around like a burglar casing a block. No one. He didn't give a shit. His caution was gone.

But then he remembered the shallowness of the water. Bloch would be standing on a rock with a couple of bruises and freezing and he'd wind up jumping in to save him.

Then he hated him that much more. "Turn around, Adam. This is pathetic."

"What is?" Still turned away.

"Your self-dramatizing shit. You can call attention to yourself as much as you want, it's not going to change anything. It's not going to make you a better person. It's not going to bring her back."

So Bloch turned around and faced him, and took a shuffling step away from the edge, and then, according to Harry, he hated Bloch still more. He hated his brown pleading eyes, his hair, the hoarseness of his voice, his thick eyebrows, the way he stood there like a round dumb stone when he was not. In fact he hated that he was smart. He hated that he had thought everything out. He hated that he wasn't afraid to jump.

Because Harry knew that now: Bloch was not afraid to hurt himself, and if he was still afraid to die, he was not afraid enough.

"I, uh. . ." Bloch fished around for words in a way that seemed at first like it wasn't real but it was. "I don't think I saw a deer." He blinked. "No, that's not right. There wasn't. There just wasn't. I'm certain of it. I wasn't falling asleep exactly. But I got confused by the fog. . . There wasn't a deer."

Harry saw that there was no more pleading in Bloch's eyes. He had given up. He was like a bag of flesh and bone. Harry didn't mean to forgive him then. It wasn't anything he tried to do. But Bloch was as good as naked. Harry felt the urge to throw clothes around him, as if he'd just been lifted from the sea, lips chattering and blue.

And he stared at Bloch so hard that the outlines of his body seemed to vibrate, then grew diffuse, as though what was Bloch and what was the world were no longer clear.

Harry wrote me that as he stared at this sack of flesh and bone, Bloch seemed to him no more nor less a part of the world than the ocean. Would Harry blame a drop of water? Would he blame a fish?

If Bloch had fault, the world had fault.

And was Harry himself a part of the world? He felt the bitter parchedness in his mouth turn to sweet plentiful saliva, as if he had a taste for Bloch, as if he was about to eat him. The carnivore loves his prey, the cannibal has his reasons.

Harry and Bloch and the fish and the carnivore and the prey and the cannibal and the cannibal's reasons and all the fault of the world swimming in the same ocean.

Harry forgave Bloch, in a sense, because he didn't want to piss himself.

Though it was really a movement of his heart as much as his mind. His heart, unspeaking, swimming in the world.

Those last words are mine, not Harry's. I apologize to him for getting fancy.

He had hated Bloch out of existence. What was left was purified, the end product of futility.

He walked toward Bloch and put his hands on his shoulders. Bloch looked at him with a kind of acceptance, beyond fear or humility, a gazelle showing her neck.

Harry was inches from Bloch, so close that Adam's face seemed like a landscape of sorrows, fought over, pitted, abandoned.

Harry, leaning forward, felt on his lips the brittleness of Bloch's dark stubble. Bloch was poised, frozen, as if for death. Harry kissed his cheek.

"You're a fucking asshole like the rest of us," Harry said.

Bloch blinked away silent tears. Harry felt their dampness on his cheek as he withdrew.

A few minutes later they were sitting side by side with their legs dangling down, looking out at the cormorants on the bay. Somewhere in there Bloch repeated what he'd said before, "I'm so sorry." Harry said nothing. The alchemy was over. He was thinking only of Sascha again. A little while later I found them.

An alternative version of Sascha's death. With her out of the way I danced with Harry. I was a terrible dancer but he swept me around the room. I dreamed this once. And in this scenario what is Bloch but the new bitch on the block?

I also dreamed that I forgave Bloch, his face was big and square, we were somewhere that was near a carousel, in a park in Italy, in a black-and-white film on a Sunday afternoon, and I felt the idiocy of not forgiving him, because here I was and here he was, and I said to him, "This is all Harry's fault. This is his miracle. If I can forgive you, that's really something." "Are you doing it because Harry made you?" Bloch said. "*Made* me? Don't be ridiculous," I said. "Then he inspired you." "I told you, it was a miracle, what more do you want from me?" And then Bloch said, "I forgive you too," and I thought that was ridiculous but very sporting of him. We bought tickets for the merry-go-round and paid in lire, of which I had a wad, and after that I didn't remember.

☙

Another alternative version of Sascha's death. She is an angel. She is my muse. She flies close over our heads.

☙

To my knowledge, Harry never mentioned again not going in the army.

18

There wasn't much in the papers. The bare details. A car crash. Where she went to school and who her parents were and her husband's name.

I don't know what was in the *Harvard Crimson*. Probably the same.

One thing about dying in a car crash when you're twenty-two and newly married is that you probably never talked about where you want to be buried. She hadn't exactly, but on the other hand they had talked about where Harry wanted to be buried if he died in the service. It was a conversation you had if you were young and sincere with each other and Harry had said California, by the Pacific, by a surfer beach. But now it was she who was dead and there was no question she would have wished to be near him, and yet her family didn't want her so far away and "alone." Harry didn't hesitate. It's where you were when you were alive that counted. Of course, we say. Of course.

There was a graveyard on Mount Desert Island near the Maclarens' summer homes. I say homes plural because several of the family had places scattered around, their estates like British colonial pink on the local maps. The graveyard was on a rocky rise near the sea. On a good day in August you might see whales breaching offshore, but this was September and the ocean was flat and empty.

The funeral was on Thursday. Harry's father's office had

made the phone calls and his induction was delayed until Tuesday. They would have given him two weeks but he didn't want it, he didn't know what he would do with the time, he wanted to get on with it.

I spent a little while with him the morning of the service. We walked along a ridge by the water. He was as solemn and measured and composed as I'd ever known him to be. But I remember the tiredness of his eyes. Harry's eyes had never been tired. He said to me, "She really loved you, you know that, Louie. She talked about you. Of all our friends."

"No, I didn't know that," I said.

"Poor fucking taste on her part, if you ask me," he said.

"Anyway she didn't *love* me," I said.

"Okay, she *liked* you. That more comfortable?"

"What did she say about me?"

Harry shrugged. "I don't know. Just things. Things she liked. She liked that you were smart. The way you talked to her. . . You know, it could have turned out like *Jules and Jim*."

"I don't think so."

"No really. She would have gone to you for stability. She needed both. She needed me but she also needed, or she would have. . . someone like you."

"You're making that up."

"She would have left you, of course."

"Yeah, of course." Sarcastic.

"Shit! Stick up for yourself! Jesus! When are you going to grow up? You had to fight me for her, you fuck!"

"I hate to lose."

"Next time you fight."

"What next time?"

"You'll have one."

We walked along the ridge.

"Just remember, you jumped on the harbor bell," he said.

"That was slightly stupid, wasn't it?" But I smiled.

"I did it. You did it."

We walked along. I kept my eyes close to the ground because I was too full of feeling to put them anyplace else.

"When do you leave for Greece?"

"A couple weeks."

"I'm not going to let this kill me. She'd kill me if I did," Harry said.

"She would," was all I said.

Then the service in a stone Episcopal chapel. Hymns and prayers and no testimonies. The interment of her ashes in the spare, lovely graveyard. Familiar faces from the wedding in June, all sensing it was about sixty years too soon for this, surprised, shaken, wounded, their chattering and laughter now become a dark mirror image of shadow and silence, like a film turned into its negative.

I had trouble listening to the words of the prayers. My mind flew off, replayed a hundred scenes, but what it did not do was think of the future.

Teddy and Cord were beside me, the three of us standing behind the white rows of chairs, lined up as if we were still the ushers at the wedding. They owned dark suits, the best I could do was gray. Adam Bloch was not there.

I watched, as much as I watched anything, the back of Harry's head. He was the one who carried the box of ashes to the gravesite.

As he did this I thought of his crewcut and of the crash and of where Adam Bloch was now, and I heard the word "God" pass through my mind like a cloud and I tried to picture

Sascha at a moment when her downturned mouth turned up but I had trouble picturing her at all and I wondered, if everyone's mind wandered like mine, who there would be to mourn her.

What is mourning? I don't think it's being sad, or any single feeling of grief. I think it's when your whole world darkens a little, as if the power supply has been cut by a certain percent, as if the universe is showing its respect.

We went to her parents' summer house afterward, a sprawling white clapboard cottage of loose-limbed charm with lawns down to the water. Sounds like a real-estate blurb but there it was. I stayed only a little while. Harry was busy with the family. We spoke briefly again, inconsequentially. I gave him the address of my school in Greece. We hugged and I felt the enormous muscular solidity of his body. He must have been twice as big around as I. He said watch your ass with the greasers. He went inside because someone was on the phone, one of Sascha's friends had gotten lost trying to find the graveyard. I said good-bye to everybody and left.

℘

From Pvt. Harry Nolan, #28299754, class 29A, Co. C-1BN-5BDE, Fort Ord, Calif., November 12, 1966:

Dear Louie,

Do NOT, if you can possibly help it, go in the Army. You will not like it.

The only saving grace of military life is that the Army seems to think it's come so far in turning me into one son-of-a-bitch of a killing machine that they've promoted me to "acting sergeant."

This is outstanding, it frees me from all details, gives me the advantages of rank, and challenges me just enough to pass the time. I'm in charge of sixty men, most of them draftees, and feelings can get rather vehement against the old Ivy League. But they're not bad guys. Really they're pretty great. One's a total ringer for Doberman.

Speaking of Ivy League, you hear anything about Brian Dowling? This guy is good. And Calvin Hill? Whoa! But I'm betting you don't get too much Yale football coverage in the Salonica newspaper. For that matter, they don't give a fuck in the SF Chronicle either.

Cord's written twice. Hates his business school classmates, but likes Wharton, even likes Philadelphia. Conceivable explanation? He's got a girl, Leslie, junior at Penn. Further details not forthcoming. You know the winged wonder is a bit of a discreet tight-mouth. He did tell me about Teddy, though. Which is good because that lazy dick hasn't written me himself. But he's officially P.C. now, he's arrived in Peru, he's assigned to some village in the Andes, and they've already managed to nearly blow up a whole mountain with dynamite. By mistake. The natives must love them. Also heard from Fred Singleton. Remember Freddy? He's already in Nam. USAID. He was asking if I was interested. I guess loanouts happen all the time. But I don't know.

As for the rest. . . And I guess you know what I'm talking about. . . I don't know, Louie. I think about her constantly. No matter what I'm doing, running, doing push-ups, ordering these clowns around, reading a book. I can't even read a book. Even getting shot at. Sometimes I wonder if I should just go get laid, maybe that would distract me for a little while. But I can't do that.

Time, they say. Time, lots of time. I guess I have lots of time. She ought to be with me now. That's my dogma. That's my one official belief. It's also all I can say about it for now.

Do you get the Herald Tribune over there? Maybe it was in there. The white fox made a speech in the Senate, questioning Westmoreland, questioning the whole thing. Go, Dad! It's a start, anyway. Just got to keep Scoop Jackson and the guys from Douglas Aircraft from pissing in his ear.

Okay, so I'm an inarticulate, slightly illiterate and uncouth fuck, but I've done my bit. Now, Louie, you write me back. I am desperate for tales of sunshine and blue water and statues with mysterious smiles. All we've got here is shitty food and talk of war. And keep your nose out of those hairy Greek armpits.

Harry

It was the first, and the only one of the four letters from Ft. Ord that I still have. It was written on an aerogram, one of those things you fold like origami and there's no envelope so the thing is lighter and cheaper. Until I pulled it out recently I hadn't seen an aerogram for years. Harry wrote with a fountain pen, in thick, squat blue strokes that were somehow like his body. A clear hand, young, and if I could speak of the four letters as a whole, his writing style was easy and fluid, as if the kinks were few from his feelings to his mind to his hand.

I was surprised to get even one letter from him. I was a lame correspondent myself. My handwriting would get crabbed and I would say only the barest things and feel that I had to copy the thing over before I sent it. His letters all reached me in Thessaloniki, where I was teaching high school kids English so they could get ahead in their world that we Americans were laboring energetically and sometimes clumsily to turn west. From my windows in the stone dormitory I could see Mount Olympus fifty miles away. Not a bad life, an easy interval on the road to law school, but the letters from Harry made my days.

As for the others, which arrived every month or so, in a rhythmed response to my own lame efforts, a common theme (aside from the one about Bloch) was how quickly Harry was turning against the war. The thing that had so exercised our weekend had nothing to do with it, was never mentioned. Too late for purity of intention. It was all politics now. Allard Lowenstein had reentered his life. Lowenstein's new project was to find a peace candidate to run against Johnson in sixty-eight. Harry lobbied him for RFK but it was too early for that big play and eventually Lowenstein settled on Gene McCarthy. I don't doubt it was Lowenstein's influence that pushed Harry so quickly to an antiwar stance. But also a lot of his recruited buddies were black, and they were quiet but if you pressed them none-too-thrilled about the war. Harry was getting a first-hand look through the reverse end of the meritocratic telescope, where it was as plain as clap in the morning (his phrase, not mine) that the same policy that made safe harbors for the "best" so we'd be there to lead and preach and invent and administer in the future put others, maybe not expendable but simply less valuable, squarely in harm's way.

Not that even I wasn't playing my sweet, cosseted part in the Cold War effort. The school where I taught was private and plaques commemorating its largest, mostly American, donors lined the administration building's front hall. Sometime early in the year, two of its patrons were exposed as CIA fronts. I wrote Harry about my contributions protecting NATO's southern flank, more in irony than anything else, but I don't think he was amused.

He was smoking marijuana by then and was the first person I heard, by at least a year, to call it dope. Always a quick study. He made it to the Sierras finally, on the long weekend at the end of his advanced firearms school. I was so happy when I read that, in the last letter I received. He hiked alone the whole time in Kings Canyon park, he caught a seventeen-inch German brown trout and decided that if Sascha were alive he would have gotten her pregnant that weekend. He didn't seem unhappy. He seemed to be playing his hand.

The letters stopped. I assumed he had bigger things on his mind.

Then, too, I might not have received a letter. There was a coup in Greece in March. The rightist colonels who took over had all the *savoir faire* of Chaplin's little dictator. They banned miniskirts, cut the hair of foreign hippies, and censored the mail coming in from abroad. They were a nasty lot, really. Fathers of my students were arrested and tortured. On the night of the coup itself an old Greek philologist at our school actually played Chaplin films to our students, who were confined by martial law to the hilltop campus overlooking the city, and he too was arrested. Then there was the young American diplomat whom we post-Ivy League teaching fellows had admired for his silky, amiable manner and the fact that he played squash every week with the king. The *New York Times* soon enough exposed him as the supposed American contact man for the coup. It seemed no matter where we went in the world in 1967 those of us who thought we were dancing on velvet saw the iron underneath.

I entered Harvard Law School in the fall. Bill Weld was in my class, and Mark Green who would lose spectacularly in a mayor's race in New York. More fodder for the mill. I thought law school would be a lot like college but it was not. No one had time to be friendly or nuts or scary or funny or anything that had any character to it anymore. My classmates with a few memorable exceptions were a stony bunch, as focused as a Zeiss lens and scarcely troubling to hide their ambitions, like a phalanx of Adam Blochs. And this was despite the collapse, the hippie-ization, of student life going on all around us. Some of this, but surprisingly little, wore off. Too many had invested too much. When Harvard College struck, it was at least roughly speaking for world peace and democracy. When the law school struck, it was because law students felt sorry for themselves, unable to study enough because of the local turmoil, and demanding pass/fail grades and no finals to ease their burdens.

The last thing I received from Harry was a postcard from Vietnam. Or it wasn't a postcard, it came in an envelope, it was a photograph the size of a postcard showing Harry filling sandbags. He had a shovel in his hand, his shirt was off, his crewcut was just as always, and he was laughing at the camera. He had a suntan and his boots were muddy. There were a couple of black guys also in the frame, leaning on their shovels and smoking cigarettes, and some sort of structure sat in the background. Nothing identified the place. On the back of the photograph he'd written, as if it were a postcard, "Hey Louie! You fucking prophet!"

When I heard, it was from Senator Nolan himself. I guess he

was going down a list. His voice was like worn-out sandpaper. "Harry always spoke highly of you."

He was on short time, eleven days to go. He came under enemy attack and died at Thong Bon Tri, near Hue, February 10, 1968, while assisting a wounded soldier to a medevac helicopter.

19

An alternative version of Harry's death. Trumpets sound, as Shiva rejoins Parvati after an unbearable absence.

Another alternative version of Harry's death. There is none. More than three decades have passed and I have no words.

20

The fall I started law school I attended a series of lectures Borges gave to the university on the craft of poetry. I remember the slow movements of the frail blind man and the hushed reverence of the crowds that filled Memorial Hall and the steady, sly cadence of his voice, breaking each phrase with a little pause, as if everything were on an equal plane of mystery and discovery. But I couldn't remember anything in particular that he said until recently someone gave me a copy of those lectures on compact disc. I've been using the CDs to go to sleep at night. I find the reediness of Borges's voice comforting, and still being a meliorist, or maybe self-improvement addict is the better phrase, I keep imagining I might learn something in my sleep. But one thought of his has kept me awake. He was referring to the familiar lines of Robert Frost, "And miles to go before I sleep, / And miles to go before I sleep," and he said everything suggested is better than anything laid down. He quoted Emerson to the effect that arguments convince nobody. And Borges said the reason this is so is that when people hear an argument, they treat it like an argument, they turn it over and weigh it and they may decide against it. Whereas for something merely hinted at there is a kind of hospitality in our imagination, we're ready to accept it.

What keeps me awake is the thought that I may have put a sort of argument not too far from my book's heart.

Would Harry Nolan have been the American president if he

had lived? I could say "of course not" and "probably not" or be preposterously optimistic and contentious on the subject, but the truth is without gravity, gone. Even if he had lived and persevered into a career, a score of things might have tripped him or turned his path. A close election loss somewhere or a brush with the law or a second wife who abhorred politics or a third who was Italian and took him off to Rome or the tilt of the country to the right while he continued left, or somehow, conceivably, a sex scandal, say, if it involved an illegitimate child—but nothing would have brought Harry Nolan down easily. If he had wanted to run in California, there are Democrats in high office who might be practicing mergers-and-acquisitions law today or be auditioning as Buddhist monks.

Though that's something else that might have stopped Harry. Becoming a Buddhist monk. Entering a monastery. Returning to Vietnam, or Cambodia, or Thailand.

It's hard to say. It's easy to list the obstacles. And yet.

I can see him up there where Bush is now. Someone who could see both sides of things. Or many sides of things, someone who could laugh at the scandal-mongers and yahoos and get away with it, who would rally the center and make it huge and yet be idiosyncratic and daring, and large-spirited in such a way that the word itself would not get used for propaganda. A president for war if need be but also a peace president, looking to the future with zesty favor, embracing the hurtling, contradictory world. A counterphobe, a guy who would run at fear and overwhelm it.

We all want a good daddy to be president. But why do we so seldom get one?

Or to put it another way, coming back to my generation.

And leaving aside for a moment the issue of Harry Nolan,

my friend Harry Nolan, my likely prejudiced presentation on his behalf. Let us say it wasn't Harry Nolan, let's say it was someone else, from the nearly sixty thousand who were killed in Vietnam, or from the scores of thousands who went to Canada or jail or into hiding or otherwise removed themselves from the circle of public possibility. It's not about sides, it's not about who owns history.

I suspect that our generation may not have produced its greatest leaders because the best of us are gone. Or many of our best, anyway. Enough to make a difference, enough to have worsened the odds. We know from other times and places that great wars do this to nations, but we scarcely think of Vietnam that way out of a reluctance to remember that it was a great, omnivorous war, it swallowed up the country. Wasn't it just a dirty little colonial war, we say, a dirty little colonial war that still dirtier resisters turned into something big? Were the casualties really so many?

Maybe not. It depends how you count, I suppose.

But I do know this. We were and probably still are a predominantly Christian country. And in a predominantly Christian country there's very little to prevent the best going first. No membrane, no web of social relations or propriety is there to catch them. All the rules are built for those who would take advantage of them, hypocrites among them but anyway lesser men, not for those who would take no advantage at all. It's like a tragic law, of self-sacrifice.

Those who fought with pure hearts and courage, on one side or the other. All those who went over the edge. All those who stuck their necks out. Don't you do it, I'll do it. Good-bye.

Ghosts, dead or alive, calling out to us from Asia or Canada or the hills of Vermont or Oregon, or the graveyards.

The tremendous promise of our generation, carelessly lost, squandered.

And the guys who do get elected, our guys but not our best guys, do their best to hold the banner up. To be worthy, in a darkened world.

The funny thing is, I believe George Bush must know what happened to Harry Nolan. He probably vaguely remembers the whole story, Harry's promise, Harry and Sascha, Sascha's death, and Harry's. But what he thinks about any of it, I cannot imagine.

Is this an argument? Or is it only a hint, after all?

❧

A cold day in March. Once again, the graveyard on Mount Desert Island. The wind bit our faces and snapped the legs of our pants. The white fox of the west was there, and Harry's mother, and his sister whom I had never met, a big-boned woman then serving in the Peace Corps in Melanesia. Sloane Coffin was there. Allard Lowenstein was there. A black guy who was out of the service now but had been with Harry somewhere along the line was there. Adam Bloch was there. Sascha's mother and father and sister and brother were there. A few guys from DKE. A hundred others whom I couldn't identify. Cord and I were there, and Teddy who got leave from the Peace Corps to attend.

Words of caution from Sloane Coffin, followed by words of grief, then words of glad thankfulness. He used the word *glory*.

The hole already dug near Sascha's low stone. The ashes under a cloth, in a box, on a table beside the makeshift podium. Sloane Coffin's thinning hair flying around. All of us freezing, our toes rigid.

A few of us had asked to speak.

Allard Lowenstein went first. He mentioned that time in Mississippi where Harry had shut him down. In his rendering Harry was more like the agonized apprentice afraid to go against his mentor but finally getting up the guts. It felt unfamiliar, oddly refracted, but then Allard recalled a time when Harry had finally gone against his father, over some bill that had money in it for the Phoenix program, which meant assassinations in Vietnam, and Harry had called up Washington from Da Nang and given his father hell. And that part felt real enough. Lowenstein never knew Sascha.

Then it was our turn, Teddy and Cord and I. We had asked to speak together, but now there was a minor hitch. We conferred with Reverend Coffin. Would it be possible to speak once the ashes were in the ground? He was not a formal person and he didn't see why not.

Senator Nolan placed the ashes of his only son in the earth. He wept openly.

Sloane Coffin read the twenty-third psalm.

I saw the whitecaps on the ocean and I thought I saw a whale, but it was as illusory as Bloch's deer.

We sang *The Battle Cry of Freedom* and everyone knew the words and it wasn't a dream this time.

Then a few others asked to speak and this went on awhile, Harry's sister Susan spoke and she was strong and funny and Sascha's mother who was unspeakably sad, and a coach from St. Paul's, and an aunt.

Until it was our turn again. Despite the cold I had begun to sweat. We meant to be short and sweet, Teddy told the crowd.

We had made this pledge, Cord said, and Harry was holding us to it.

The three of us turned around in poorly choreographed disunity and unzipped our flies. I was afraid I would not be able to piss on account of the cold, I was sweaty and my neck was stiff from embarrassment. I managed only a dribble at first, which flew back with the wind against my pants. Teddy and Cord got theirs going easily, and slowly my stream grew stronger, as I realized there was nothing left to lose. Soon all of us were watering Harry's ashes, the best we could anyway, the box and the muddy hole they sat in.

When we turned around we met horrific stares, but I felt sane and even proud.

Was there anyone on our side? Lowenstein, maybe, and a couple of the guys from DKE, whose eyes shone in recollection. I couldn't see Adam Bloch then. I didn't know where he had gone, or maybe he'd gone nowhere and I just didn't see him.

As we walked away, Senator Nolan approached me with a quizzical expression. "Symbolic speech," I said, and the white fox of the west smiled lightly through his tears.

THE CONFERENCE OF THE BIRDS

for Rick

1

The window is dirty. Soot has mottled it so that it resembles a topographical map of a region of hills. Rain has caused the soot to run in places, creating rivers or gullies. Raindrops themselves, bearers of the city's detritus, have left faint pockmarks, as though long ago a war had been fought here. Shelling. Death. Verdun. The Western Front. One's imagination could run wild. Don't. Stop. Go back. Nothing wild here. Wild is the city, the world, the wind. Here is cultivation. Here is human possibility. Go back. Stop. Gently, so that even "human possibility" is stopped, so that even stopping is stopped.

The landscape of war is deposited on the window's outside. On the pane's inside, particles of dust and faint angular streaks where some window washer years ago used a dirty squeegee. Also, dapples of grease, like settling mist, as though grease has been in the air of the place.

I reach for a scrap of torn-up newspaper. I feel the air rustle against the insides of my fingers as I extend my arm. I feel my fingertips as they land, gentle as a mosquito on skin, on the pile of newsprint squares. My thumb and two fingers pinch the top sheet, which like something hypnotized slides into their grip. Gently, cautiously, they lift the single sheet. With any less pressure it would flutter away. My right arm reaches for the bottle of window cleaner. The solution is pale, diluted, watery. One doesn't waste Windex just as one doesn't waste newspaper.

There's no need. Need is elsewhere. Need is a poem, or need has no name. Stop. Gently. Go back.

Sense my arms and legs. Look. Listen.

The muffled boogie-woogie of the taxi honks, ten stories down. The creak of floorboards as they're stepped on. No voices. No music. Somewhere the low beating of a helicopter's heart, becoming stronger, then receding. I press my finger down on the Windex pump. The flesh of my finger flattens against the concave plastic of the pump, the pump emits a snorting sound, then the splat of the cleaner on the window. I squirt again. I squirt until the entire window is laced with drips. Have I squirted too much? In my inattention did I press too hard? Stop. Don't bother. Go back. Sense my arms and legs.

Words, that's the point, everywhere words, words for everything. I drown in words. I struggle to keep my head up. Stop. Go back. Gently float as mild as Ivory soap ninety-nine and forty-four hundredths percent pure but that isn't pure enough. Why isn't it pure enough? Why does everything have to be pure? What's the point? Who says?

Stop. Go back. Sense. Look. Listen.

Nothing more.

The window cleaner dribbles down the pane, tears on a ravaged face whose sorrow I arrest with my slip of newsprint. As lightly as I can, so that I can sense the resistance of the wet glass to the paper, I make rounding motions with my arm and swirl the cleaner around the window. I continue to rub. I sense the cleaner loosening the grease, I sense the newsprint absorbing the liquefied grime. I rub but also I glide. I'm like a skater on this pane of glass.

What time is it? I lift my left wrist to look at my watch.

Twenty after seven. Only twenty minutes gone. I have to do this until nine o'clock.

I could sink into time. I could arrest time. I could cause clocks to slow.

Stop. Imagination. Go back.

Clocks are already slow.

Fuck this shit this made-up shit why am I here why don't I walk out of here?

The window sticks when I try to raise it, to bring the top window down, to make an exchange of windows. I press with the bottoms of my palms on the inside frame, my neck and jaw and shoulders tense, the window flies up on its ropes, and only then do I realize how many unnecessary muscles I've brought to bear, and begin to relax them.

The top window is divided into six panes. I will squirt them, rub them, clean them one at a time. Space can expand or contract. Time can slow or race. It's only a matter of attention, or would the psychologists call it perception? And am I spouting merely metaphor? And anyway stop, go back, gently.

I must move my attention to my arms and legs and to listening and looking.

Six panes. One pane at a time. More squares of newsprint. More squirts.

Now it's seven forty-five. Joyous thought. Am I looking at my watch again? This is easy, it seems to say, just wash the windows and don't think and I'll watch your life tick by and soon enough ... nine o'clock? The sweat under the leather strap of the watch. Its round and friendly face. Is it time to take a break? I'm almost out of paper squares. This too is reason for joy, that now I'll have to walk across the room to the stack of newspaper in the broom closet. It's like a prisoner's walk in the yard. Life is sweet. The colors of Laura's clothes her breasts the carpet Cal washing the windows next to me Bobby peeling the paper off garlic dumping bok choy in the wok Julie pretty Julie her mouth slightly open her jaw slack with woozy extended motions sanding a table leg. Joe like the Little King in his corduroy pants with the elastic waistband walking around saying nothing. I bring a section of newspaper back to my window. The paper is months old. Classified ads for boats. I ignore this, I try to ignore this, I try to ignore the other pages as well. Don't try, do.

I lift the window with pliant fingertips. I turn around and seat myself on the sill as if I'm about to eject from an aircraft and slide on my pant legs over the uneven edges of the sill until I'm outside facing back into the loft. I can see the galley, the clamp lights, the particle board furniture, Joe's miniature roses under their Gro-lites, as if I were spying into a stranger's home. I lower the window until its frame rests on my thighs, my calves dangling inside as if held ransom for my safe return. I breathe the chill night air. My abdomen tightens. I tell myself to breathe. I tell myself not to tell myself anything at all.

I begin again to wash the window. I do not focus on the color, the movement, or the humanity inside the loft. I do not focus on being ten stories up and the possibilities that if the window broke or I got stupid or a pigeon shat on my head I might fall. I focus on the topography of grime. What time is it now? Yes, I am afraid to die. Yes, I am proud to be out on this sill. I am better than earth dwellers. I am part of a merry band my heart beats lightly I cannot die not now not like this why would I?

I love life down to its atoms. When have I ever thought that before? Stop. Go back. Look at my watch don't look at my watch don't start that shit again.

But time is slow. This could go on forever. When will it be over?

I see Bobby in the galley. Slender Bobby with his curly dark hair and no smile just now as his wrist flicks the knife and the scallions go down in a chopped heap like he was a G-man riddling a pack of John Dillingers. A quarter past eight. Still three-quarters of an hour to go. I descend into the Land of Window. I tell stories of this Land. I'm tiring. I should take a break. Yes, I'll take a break. Out on this ledge I take a break. I don't wash. I look up and see that the moon is out, a half-moon, sickly, between buildings.

In the Land of Window there are mountains and streams. In the Land of Window there is paint in the corners. Send in the troops, get this thing cleaned up.

Why is everything I do accompanied by words?

What happened to my joy in possibility? So recent I could taste it but I'm totally crazy now, my mind flies around.

I forget about the paint in the corners. Or rather, I move my attention away from it.

A conscious act not an unconscious act.

Oh yeah who says I'll be the judge of that says who.

I raise the window. I gather up my stack of unused newsprint and the used, dirty squares of paper and the window cleaner and I duck back inside. I feel a measure of warmth and safety in my throat and behind my eyes.

Now the window looks beautiful. Between outside and inside a veil has been lifted.

O prideful one, O bullshit artist calm down, don't you see, calm down. Go back. You know the drill.

If you can't see the window at all, that's when you've got a window. If a bird could fly into it.

I look at my watch again. Eight thirty-five. In the loft, here and there, others sit and smoke cigarettes, their feet flat on the floor, the smoke inhaled and exhaled in easy, attenuated drafts like the coming and going of a sea on a flat beach. I could take a break again but I just took one.

I must wash a second window. I have time. There's no excuse. The thought sickens me. Wasn't one plenty? I did so well, got it so clean. You lazy swine what better have you got to do go pick up girls uptown in bars, long for girls in bars on Broadway? And yet if I am deceived? And yet if we are all deceived? We birds of desire we birds of longing dirty New York birds with doubts in our heads.

What is life worth except to be impeccable? A clean window, something more than I'd done before.

Wash the window and dirty more paper and tear more paper and rub and swirl and cleanse and dry and quiet my mind.

And then, like life or so they say, a bout of amnesia and it's almost over. Five to nine. Clean up. Put the window cleaner and the unused paper back in the broom closet. Cal does it too. I'm not alone. I'm not the first. I'm jumping no guns.

Everyone put to sleep, waking up with regret, nostalgia, forgetfulness. Waking up just before the end.

I tell myself I did it. I actually feel quite strong. The work is humble but the work is real, it is the work of waking up is it not?

Go back. Sense.

Stop all the other nonsense including the nonsense of stopping the nonsense and the nonsense of talking about the nonsense of stopping the nonsense and so on in endless recessional.

Go back. Sense.

The meeting is short. Scarcely anyone has anything to say.

We sit on pine benches or on the floor in front of them. A few lonesome, venturing voices. "I was finding it hard to sense tonight." "A lot of anger kept coming up about my sister." "I felt this sensation in my chest, like it was almost burning." Offerings of a sort, expressions of hope, of ongoingness, or fear. Joe says nothing. Joe sits in his Eames chair. His watery gray eyes moving around, avoiding people's glances. Now, dinner. A single lamb chop on a bed of greens, a shot of iced vodka. "Damn the torpedoes! Full speed ahead!" Joe's perennial toast. The pine benches in a square. Bobby and Julie serving. I throw my vodka back. It burns, a pledge, a confirmation. Are we not men, Devo said and we say it too. The bloody juice of the lamb, salty and slightly fragrant on my tongue. My teeth grind slowly, sacramentally. The flesh of the lamb gives way. I swallow and wonder how. The shadows of words even on this bench. Silence now. Plates collected, piled one on top of another with short ceramic claps. Sense. Look. Listen. Joe smoking a cigarette. Now a dozen others smoke and the smoke lingers over us all as if a reminder of the sea of air we swim in. Abdomens relax. Breathe deep. Sense. When will this silence be over? Is not enough enough? Has the vodka made me drunk?

I will be happy to be out of here. I will be happy to be out in the world. I've done as much as I can.

My ass begins to ache. Bony ass on the pine bench. My wallet in my pants doesn't help. What's it doing there, so asymmetric? I fidget. I straighten my spine. I lift my weight slightly onto my feet to give my ass a break.

Joe butts his Newport out. He has a face like a stone wall. Silence as a reminder, or a goal, or an enemy. I'd like to tear it to bits. When. When. When. Sense. Look. Listen. "That's all for tonight," Joe says, and rubs his cigarette butt around in his ashtray.

I rise. It's over. No one says another word.

At the elevator people's shoes are scattered around. It looks like a haphazard parking lot of shoes. I find my old loafers, dirty, their leather cracked and split apart. I slip them on. My feet feel like they've entered a womb.

The elevator arrives. I'll be in the first batch down. But before anyone goes anywhere, Joe shouts as if it were an afterthought, "The week between Christmas and New Year's, don't anybody fly to Rio! We're having an event!"

His voice bright and hortatory, for a moment the voice of a cheerleader.

I know the word "event." My heart sinks faster than the elevator down. We've had weekend events, working night and day from Friday evening through Sunday. But an event for an entire week?

Go back. Calm down. Sense. No one says anything in the elevator. It's one of the things, no talking till you're in the street. Things to gather and save attention. On the street we say nothing either. We walk in our separate directions.

I hate Joe now. I hate his jaunty tone. A whole week without sleep, without escape, a whole week of. . . what?

Is that what he said, a week? Or did he mean, an event *sometime during* the week, two days perhaps?

No I know what he meant. No doubt in my black heart. I can't do a whole week of this, I'll lose my mind, or isn't that the point?

Go back. Gently. Sense. Look. Listen.

Broadway. Wind whipping the trash. A few bums, a few kids. Street smells of ozone and exhaust and broken bags of garbage. I renew my conscious effort to see and this world of disorder becomes fixed and composed, as if captured in a time elapse photo. Ribbons of taxis.

I wait for the train at Broadway-Lafayette. I catch the D and ride uptown. People on the train read the paper, spread out, find warmth in hooded sweatshirts. I begin to feel superior to these ordinary lives, worried about this or that. I watch a woman with a careworn face as if to correct myself. All my life have I not found some way to feel superior to someone? Are people telling me I'm crazy? Sense. Look. Listen.

At 59th Street where I change trains there's a homeless guy on the floor who asks for change. I look at him and think of the stories of gods or holy men who've gone in disguise to test the nature of man, and for this reason alone, no other, I reach into my pants and throw a quarter at him. It lands on his leg and skitters off. It rolls on its edge on the floor until it's out of his reach. I think what the fuck, in for a penny in for a pound, and lean over and pick up the quarter and put it in his hand. The backs of my fingernails brush against the roughness of his palm. The homeless guy mutters "bless you." For a moment I hate myself with all my heart and even that feels like a lie.

I change for the IRT and continue uptown to home.

2

Joe sometimes read aloud the story of the Greek and Chinese artists. The emperor of Persia offered a contest: whoever proved themselves to be the greatest artists would win a valuable commission. A delegation came from China, another from Greece. The Chinese artists, who brought with them rich pigments, the finest brushes, rare papers, set to work at once with great skill and soon produced a magnificent painting. For vibrancy of color and delicacy of figure and line, none had seen its like. The emperor declared it to be the most beautiful work of art he had ever seen. The Persian court little doubted that the Chinese would take the prize. Meanwhile no one had seen what the Greeks were working on. All that they did, they did in secret. When at last they unveiled their achievement, people were first bewildered. It was nothing more than a cleansed and polished mirror. But when the Chinese painting was reflected in it, it appeared even more glorious and beautiful than before. It shone in perfect splendor, as did all the rest of creation. The Greeks were awarded the commission, for, declared the emperor, they had most truly held a mirror to life.

༺༻

We had no name. We were simply "the group."

༺༻

The Conference of the Birds

In *The Conference of the Birds*, a twelfth-century poem by Attar, thirty birds set out on a perilous journey to reach the mighty Simurgh, whose name means thirty birds. Is that who we were?

Starling and pet shop parakeet and sparrow and seagull and crow.

The Hoopoe, who was a guide to King Solomon, who obtained a crown of glory, was their guide, urging them on, defeating their excuses, giving them hope.

☙

Was the Hoopoe too fancy a bird for Joe? He who said he was "just another kike from Brooklyn."

☙

Sometime in July of 1974 I went on a Thursday evening to the apartment of Philip Deschayne on 13th Street in the Village. I was brought there by a friend of a college friend, a woman named Joan Dreyfus. Joan was unclear exactly what was going on in Philip's apartment, but whatever it was was vaguely "literary" and open to the public. At the time I had not expected the world to ignore me so completely. The fact that Philip wrote for the *New Yorker* enticed me. We entered a small back apartment in a townhouse. An assortment of books lay in a pile on the living room carpet, surrounded by a half-dozen people who sat in a rough circle almost in reach of them. Philip told us to pull up a chair. Thin and tall with sunken cheeks and a boyish sweep of dark hair, clear plastic prep school glasses, he had, I thought, an unusually intense gaze. He was willing to stare at a stranger. At the same time his manner was pleasant.

Others present included a guy in an ascot with a hawkish nose, a slight dark-eyed kid in his early twenties, and a girl with saucery glasses and orange frizzy hair, a face like a lollipop. At the last moment a man with the proportions if not the full size of a defensive lineman walked in, stood behind the couch, removed a trench coat. He had bulldoggy jowls and a notably immobile expression—not mean or scowling, simply immobile—that I remember at the time thinking contrasted oddly with his boyish freckles, as though you were looking at both man and boy at once. He may have been in his mid-thirties. The books were full of stories. People were free to pick them up, peruse them, and if a story struck them somehow, read it aloud. This was how things appeared to me, anyway. I couldn't tell a pattern to what was read, except that all the stories seemed "oriental." Several were humorous, others seemed quite beautiful. The entire impression the evening made was of quiet and an esthetically pleasing purity. The last story was read by the heavy-set man with the jowls and freckles, and it ended with an offer of a few dates to a needy person. Philip Deschayne then passed around a small plate of dates. I returned to his apartment the following Thursday. Joan Dreyfus did not. I presumed the stories, or the company, were not to her liking. Afterwards I began having small conversations with other participants, particularly the kid, Bobby Gelfand, a cartoonist who'd dropped out of Harvard after painting a lamppost on Mount Auburn Street with the 100 Greatest Hits from the Hundred Years' War. I remembered the painted lamppost from my time in law school, its stick-figure drollery, its stark hysteria. The second time I went to Philip Deschayne's, I read a story out loud. I didn't know why I was doing it. I liked the story. I thought it might show my good taste. I wanted to have new friends. I had chosen to be a writer, I was stuck in my room, and here seemed to be my people. After the third week, Bobby said to me that if I wanted to find out a little more, I could go to another apartment, on Charles Street, on Saturday afternoon. The second apartment belonged to Joe, the heavy-set guy who had by then made a firm impression on me for being the last to read each Thursday evening. When I arrived, Bobby and Philip were both there, as was the frizzy-haired girl, Liddie. They were each painting a section of a lime green wall with what seemed to be obsessive care. They were moving so slowly, it was as if some drug had slowed their metabolism. Joe was efficient and nonplused. There was nothing slowed about his movements. He asked me if I would like to try this. He was friendly enough. I tried to gauge if I could still come on Thursday nights to Philip's and read stories if I declined. I guessed that I could but that I would be a second-class citizen. I wanted to know what was going on, I wanted to be a part. I said sure, why not. He told me to sit in a chair and to shut my eyes and then, in a tone of voice similar to the one in which he read stories, that is to say, very clearly, very declaratively, as though making a deliberate effort to avoid imparting to his words any sort of emotional coloration, he gave me a certain mental exercise to do. He told me to repeat the exercise each morning shortly after I woke up. He told me not to reveal the exercise to anyone unless I consulted him first, because they might not know what to do with it, by which I thought he meant they might be harmed by it. When I opened my eyes, Joe told me to do my best to sense my arms and legs and look and listen, and if I became aware of being distracted, by words or pictures in my head, to go back to sensing, looking and listening. I could do this all the time, he said, day and night, but I should begin now, in the apartment, painting a section of wall. Afterwards, he said, we could talk about how it went.

❦

Four years passed.

3

Whenever I saw Bobby with Joe, I was aware of the watch. A Casio that sold at Bondy's on Division Street for eighty or ninety dollars, with a stainless steel band that reminded me of a high school ID bracelet and digital readouts as though the future had arrived and it was all about putting things in neat rectangular boxes. Both wore the same watch, but on Joe it seemed to fit, with his elasticized pants and engineer's short-sleeve shirts, whereas on Bobby's narrow wrist it looked outsized and imposed, as though he'd decided to hype his masculinity or a salesman had sold him on that idea. But Bobby was masculine enough. And one of the few certainties I felt about Joe was that he had lousy taste in clothes, Sears Roebuck taste in clothes. Bobby's Casio watch on his wrist felt to me like the black choker Julie Christie wore in a film once, to suggest she was the possession of some man.

Though Philip had a Casio, too, and I had a Seiko that I wore for awhile then put away in my drawer. We all imitated Joe in ways large and small. I told myself it was certainly not in adoration and probably not even in admiration but rather an experiment, to try to see what Joe was like, or rather, by seeing what Joe was like who hypothetically had the goods on self-discovery, to see what we were like. We were becoming Joe in order to become ourselves. Yet when I saw Bobby wearing that watch, I felt embarrassed by it. It was in such pathetic bad taste. "Just a kike from Bensonhurst." I didn't want us to be from Bensonhurst. I wanted us to be from Harvard and Yale. Although he never said it, I assumed it must be part of Joe's program to knock Harvard and Yale out of us.

For were these elite universities not part of our conditioning, too, the part that allowed us to feel special and superior and kept our minds busy with fantasies and divided us from ourselves? This much, in time, I came seriously to consider.

Though "considering," also, was not a part of what we were supposed to be doing, and anyway not all of us had gone to Harvard or Yale. Philip had gone to Harvard, and Cal Bittker, and Bobby dropped out and Ty Duncan was on the *Lampoon* there and I went to Yale, and Valerie worked at Sotheby's and fucked guys who had gone to Harvard. But most of the rest of us Joe found through an ad in the *Voice*. I never knew what the ad said. I didn't really want to know, though I imagined it must have been something like "Are you interested in understanding yourself?" Something overripe with patent medicine promise, or just bizarre and vague enough that if I'd read it myself I'd not have given it a second thought. Yet the ad attracted filings from every sort of New York life, bond salesmen and musicians and secretaries and con men. Or to go back to the old metaphor: birds of every plumage flew in through the window, the variety of birds you find in a city, not least among them quite ordinary pigeons.

I had just done my bit for Thanksgiving at Astor Liquor. As if the gleaming glass alone could stupefy me, I'd stood paralyzed in the aisle of vodka bottles for twenty minutes, taking one bottle off the shelf then another. Twice I got to the checkout counter with half a dozen bottles in my cart and turned around. To buy the cheap shit, the house brand, or only the best or something in-between. Arguments crowding my mind.

My relative poverty, my civil servant salary, the difficulty for the average consumer of telling one vodka from another but were these really average consumers and was it going in a punch or would it be drunk neat? I tried to distinguish the voices in my head. Were these mine, my mother's, my father's, Joe's? Go back, I told myself, stop, it doesn't matter, go back, sense, look. Look at these sleek bottles of vodka in their long row like soldiers. In the end I chose the best. Nothing but the best for Joe, I could not be humiliated if I bought the best, I could not disrespect. A hundred dollars of vodka, half my take-home pay. Why not? Did it not lend a touch of glory to the enterprise, didn't it mean I was in synch? I brought the vodka bottles up to the loft, removed them from the Astor Liquor shopping bag, placed them lovingly one by one on the galley counter as if they were a catch of fourteen-inch trout. Joe padded by but said nothing. He was working on something with the band saw. All right well fuck you then, if you won't even recognize my sacrifice don't you see what I've done. But he didn't, or didn't care to acknowledge, or was just making my life miserable. Sense. Look. Listen. Bobby chopping scallions. He was always here, in the loft, or so it seemed. He had a room somewhere but it must have been airless and tiny, he had even less money than I—every once in a while the *New Yorker* paid him for a couple of cartoons and he spent all the money on what? I wasn't sure but on something other than survival. Bobby chopping scallions. The day before Thanksgiving, doing all the prep. Two obscenely white Chinatown toms, stripped and humiliated prisoners, sitting trussed on the counter. I began to chop alongside him. I had often helped him, I was very nearly his apprentice in the galley, I liked the smells and the tastes and the fact I was learning something practical, so that if the whole group went to hell I'd still come out of it knowing how to boil a potato or cure a wok. Bobby had taught me how to chop with easy thrusts of my wrist so that the weight of the knife carried it through the food. With scallions this became almost effortless. No squeezing of the knife, no chops to mar the cutting board, no tensing of any muscles. Kitchen Zen, kitchen ju-jitsu, more miraculous than any late night invention by Popeel. I watched the scallions collapse into little piles of green O's and imagined, like the text of one of Bobby's recent cartoons, which had become more esoteric and less funny and salable, that "from this cook I learned how to take care of my life." Stop it, fuck it, don't be absurd if you're going to do this then do it but don't brag.

And not because bragging was wrong, it was no more wrong than anything else but it didn't get you anywhere—it was one more turn on the wheel.

Though wheels weren't our metaphor. Wheels weren't our deal.

The doorbell from down in the lobby. On the intercom a voice you might imagine coming from a happy piece of sandpaper, animated and jumping around. A woman's voice, nasal also. "I come up? What are you doing? It's Maisie." Joe buzzed her in.

A few moments later, Maisie McLaren got off the elevator, her olive-dyed suede coat, her freckles, blue eyes, round face, her red hair that if it were only longer as I remembered it would have been flying around. Her red hair that was darker than Liddie's, streaked with fire in a way unmatchable by CVS, some throwback to the highlands.

Because I was working for the moment I said nothing to her, nor she to me. Our code of courtesy, our prime rule: don't interfere with another's attention. Don't try to steal another's attention. Crappy little hello's, don't bother, don't pretend they're not little concoctions of neediness or hate. But I knew Maisie from before, not well, really, but I knew her. She was the sister of a woman I once loved and tried more than once to write about. Sascha Maclaren who died in a car crash and I never kissed her once. But she's another story, or maybe she isn't, since Maisie was a friend of Joan Dreyfus who took me to Philip Deschayne's, and so if I hadn't known Maisie and hadn't loved Sascha I could not have felt the sweet scent of scallions marking my breath like colored dye the moment she walked in. Maisie had started Sarah Lawrence but wound up at McLean's, where rich girls went for their nervous breakdowns which in her case may have had to do with Sascha, with her death, or maybe not. After McLean's she'd hung around Cambridge and got involved with a group in Somerville that was run by Joe's old teacher and came up or down with Hodgkin's disease and so she was treated for that and continued with Joe's old teacher and wound up saying, in her throaty voice with her smoker's happy cackle, that it took Hodgkin's to cure her of McLean's.

She was supposed to be better now. I'd heard something about her coming down to the city to hang around Joe for awhile. Joe who himself had beaten testicular cancer, and this was part of his legend too. The doctors had given him a pick-a-number chance, ten percent, twenty percent, but he'd chosen to understand himself or die trying and here he was years later, one ball short but breathing fire.

Joe's legend. "Just another kike from Brooklyn." The pieces Philip wrote in the *New Yorker*. "Our friend from the Pratt Institute." "Our friend Joe."

People always seemed to know one another's names. Either

that or it didn't matter and when they needed to they'd know. I say this because it wasn't as if Joe introduced Bobby to Maisie, or that Maisie introduced herself. She stuck around, took off her coat. "Need help with the food?" "Thanks. Nah." "I'm good with pumpkin. I'm good with marshmallows." "Done for today."

He slid the birds into the fridge and looked at her twice.

Bobby who had a childlike smile, a smile you could make a bet on, though I don't remember if he smiled at her then.

Joe came back from the band saw and put *The Thief of Baghdad* in the Betamax. Joe, Maisie, Bobby, myself. It being another portion of the indecipherable puzzle of ourselves that we watched Joe's television as much as we did. Before going to Joe's I hadn't watched TV since I was twelve. But here he was like a boy with his Betamax and his tapes and the biggest Sony you could then buy. And we all went along, sat around. Smoking, sharing the air, not looking at one another but rather at movies we'd seen many times before. Joe treated Bobby like a servant. If Joe wanted a bowl of ice cream, Bobby got it for him. If Joe was out of ice cream, Bobby went to the store. Even with Maisie there, Joe ordered Bobby around. "Jeeves, how 'bout some coffee?" "Jeeves, what's cooking for dinner?" "Jeeves, did you remember to buy cigarettes?" "Shit. I forgot." And Bobby would run off. All of which I understood to be part of Bobby being Joe's most promising pupil, either that or his most problematic case, the one who was so desperate he was ready for all or anything. But why, just now, in front of Maisie? Bobby who seemed as sweet as a baby yet Joe had often said, and Bobby concurred, that he was full of narcissism and loathing. "A power-mad rat." Were we not all power-mad rats? The phrase in vogue, the vernacular phrase. Why else endure such patent abasements except in hopes of grabbing the golden ring? I felt pity as much as envy for Bobby. But would Maisie understand? Maisie who'd been part of the Boston group, who sat and watched the *Thief* and seemed surprised by nothing.

The old movie with Sabu for the umpteenth time. Has umpteenth become a word yet? Hardly matters because it wasn't really the umpteenth time, more like the fifth, each Thanksgiving Joe brought it out, his favorite film, the little boy hero who just wants to have some fun after he's solved the big world's problems. Joe chattered, rooted, cheered, he was like a kid in a Saturday matinee and everytime the thief was about to get in trouble he'd shout at the screen, "Don't do it! Don't *do* it," singsongy, entirely engaged, as if the next thing he'd start biting his nails. Sabu reminded me of Bobby, his size, his sly charm, his agility. More than a few times I wondered if what drew Joe to Bobby was his resemblance to Sabu, as if in that resemblance he saw a clue to Bobby's possibilities. Joe believed in movies, more than I did, believed in Errol Flynn and Janet Gaynor and names I never knew, all from the forties and thirties, from the time when he was a kid or just before he was born, when his parents were young. As if somehow, in these dreams that must have overarched their lives, or sprung out of them by the populist alchemy of Hollywood's machine, Joe was seeking the romance of his parents' lives, or his own romance when with a kid's inevitable longing he tried to live theirs. Joe's father had a dry cleaners. Joe never talked about him.

Just as none of us talked about our parents but watched the movies of their youth and listened to the Andrews Sisters and a young Bing Crosby and Maurice Chevalier on the scores of tapes that Joe churned out on his dual-cassette deck. We seldom spoke of our parents, seldom visited them or said a kind word about them, but often relived the moments when our parents might have danced or been in love. And Joe got as much pleasure from his cassettes as from his Betamax, singing along, crooning really, like someone who'd once been afraid of the sound of his own voice but gotten over it. "Oh Rio, Rio by the sea, oh." "I'm just a lonely babe in the woods / So lady be good. . ." Though Joe loved the old Apollo too. "Gimme a pigfoot and a bottle of beer. . ."

It was as if he'd secreted a whole other part of himself, maybe the happiest part, in these movies and tunes.

I didn't understand. I couldn't understand. Why try to make words out of something that had no words?

Sense. Look. Listen.

I had to leave for a couple of hours. Work related. Downtown. The D.A.'s office. Where I worked, by the way. Assistant D.A. me. The result of Joe's prodding me to quit writing, get out of my room, get out in the world. "You ought to get a job. Quit driving yourself crazy." Offered as a suggestion, nothing more. Except for Bobby, Joe never ordered anybody to do anything, but I hated him for suggesting it. I had my ninety dollars a week from a one day gig at Columbia. But Joe thought I ought to be more "normal." In truth the D.A. was the first job I could find. Their hunger for Harvard Law grads who would work for fourteen-five, in an era, as well, when law enforcement was not always approved of in liberal quarters. I came to like my job. The shining badge just like a cop's, the other A.D.A.'s from Saint John's and Fordham with their charcoal suits and political ambitions, the general raffishness, the panorama of New York's streets hauled before me for my judgment. Then too, the fact that Philip started writing Talk of the Town pieces about *me*, "our friend the Assistant D.A."

One or two anyway. And all the while I was sensing myself or trying to, keeping words out of my head, looking, listening, in the world but not of it, as was said, as we said. At work it sometimes seemed like a sneaky trick, like fucking in the mop closet.

I played my efficient part revolving the door of Manhattan's justice until nine o'clock and returned to the loft. Maisie and Bobby and Joe were still watching movies. Now it was *Mighty Joe Young*, the old King Kong knockoff, Joe croaking in delight every time the gorilla got a good one in. Half-empty Häagen-Dazs pints sat on the table. Another evening at the loft. Joe and Bobby smoking Newports, though Maisie, after her illness, must have quit, and I didn't smoke. My badge of resistance, my guilty secret, my confession of doubt. Which got me neither the pleasure of the tobacco nor the supposed benefit of a relaxed and measured breath, even while permitting me the opportunity for second-hand smoke enough to last a lifetime. Bobby went to do the dishes from dinner. Joe asked Maisie how she'd been. She talked awhile, about finishing her chemo, the group up in Boston getting ready to buy a farm in Haverill, the apartment of her parents in New York that she'd be staying in while they were out of town. Nothing esoteric, just gossip and talk. I wasn't even sure that Joe knew that I'd known Maisie for years. When Bobby came back to the table he said the garbage disposal was screwed up. Joe grunted. "You drop a fork in it?" "Nothing," Bobby said. "Nothing's in it. I mean, I *know* it's probably jammed." "I dropped a diamond ring in a garbage disposal once," Maisie said, then Joe said, "Why don't you two go fuck?"

I don't know why I should have been so surprised. Maybe I wasn't, really.

Bobby seemed embarrassed. His tongue hung slightly loose in his mouth. He looked at Maisie more as if to apologize than anything. My drunken uncle, sorry. He liked her, of course he liked her.

Maisie looked more curious. Like why had Joe said such a thing? Did she look like she needed a fuck? Did they both?

Or maybe he didn't have any reason at all. We let it drop. No one really answered him. Joe got distracted, or pretended to be distracted, as on screen his namesake beat the ten toughest men on earth, including Primo Carnera, in a tug-of-war. Carnera, the old heavyweight champ, then tried to punch the gorilla in the face. Mighty Joe seemed more perplexed than anything by so puny a gesture, and Joe laughed and the rest of us sort-of laughed.

In a little while Joe wandered off to play with his roses. Playing with them was really what he did, he doted on them as if they were children, clipping them, if the branches were especially long, with his nail clipper, lavishing on them tiny amounts of Miracle Gro. Cultivation as play. Joe never said such words, but it was what I understood by watching him, or from those moments, more frequent in the old apartment on Charles Street than in the loft, when, perhaps on account of the breeze from an open window, the scent of the roses wafted across the rooms, infiltrating our senses, penetrating our brains, an intoxicating fog. Cultivating the human mind as play. The "work" as play. These, too.

I didn't much care for the movie and went home. The next day it was plain that Bobby and Maisie had spent the night together. They showed up together and cooked side-by-side and seemed to know each other's moves. A couple times, as rare as stolen kisses, they smiled at each other. The entire group came to dinner. Thirty of us and Maisie, which as I then supposed made us a little like the first Thanksgiving when all the Pilgrims came, when "nuclear family" was a phrase yet undreamed. We told stories. Joe read the story of the Greek and Chinese artists. My high-class vodka was rather a hit. It may have made Joe drunk enough that he started talking about his father. He said something nice about his father. He talked about his father when his mother died, standing as though the wind had hit him. And when he was done and no one knew what to say, he said, "How do people feel now? What are you sensing?" The question went around the room. Mumbles and pieties. I said it reminded me of a song but I couldn't remember which one, which sounded like a cheat but was exactly true. When it came Maisie's turn, she said, "You're a manipulative shit." "Thank you," Joe said.

The dinner Bobby prepared had enough courses for kings, but nothing about it was more delicious than the fact that he'd been cooking less than a year. And he wasn't afraid to cook with Jello, he found Jello to be a fine ingredient. Black cherry Jello, the best. On that could we not all agree? After dinner, we watched *The Thief of Baghdad*, the previous evening having been but a warm-up. Joe laughed as though he hadn't seen it in years. The little thief and his triumph, flying off on his carpet leaving the world of sighs behind. I, too, at its conclusion, had the urge to have a little fun. And I wasn't alone. I went to pee and felt the toilet door resist, a foot or shoulder against it. I waited, the door opened, and Maisie and Bobby came out together.

On cleanup I pitched in. Nearly everybody did, one of those modest mysteries of communalism among thirty birds who were each supposedly minding their own business. Dishes, floor, sink, stove, carpet. I sensed my arms and legs and looked and listened, either that or I was aware of sensing my arms and legs and looking and listening, either that or I was aware of what I imagined was me sensing my arms and legs and looking and listening. Anyway, I felt I was making up for lost ground, after a lot of not sensing.

4

A day in the life, *i.e.* the ins and outs of consciousness also known as the narcoleptic's progress, to wit, wake up, sit up, morning exercise, jump the engine, shut eyes, sense, arms, legs, open eyes, look, listen, shower, back to "sleep," dress, back to "sleep," remember to sense, Pepperidge Farm breakfast, last two Orleans, first two Milanos of new pack, back to "sleep," remember to sense, more "sleep," Broadway, Koreans, dry cleaners, back to "sleep," IRT, more "sleep," remember to sense, back to "sleep," sense, N train, sense, back to "sleep," Appearance Part 5 of Criminal Court in and for the County of New York more or less accidental workplace of more or less accidental pilgrim, back to "sleep," low level sensing, AP-5, more "sleep," Diane, beautiful lush Diane of AP-5, back to "sleep," the violet sheen of her skin, its gleam, the swishing of her legs over her stenography machine, back to "sleep," remember to sense, sense, her almond eyes, her silky hair, black, back to "sleep," sense, back to "sleep," remember to sense, more "sleep," hearing on competency of man to assist in his own defense at trial which if he's incompetent he gets remanded to a mental institution upstate, back to "sleep," low level sensing, remember to sense, the man hearing voices in his head, shrink says he's crazy, I say we all hear voices in our head, shrink says this guy can't tell the difference between the ones that are inside and outside, I say none of us can at the moment we're hearing them, judge thinks *I'm* crazy or at least pain in neck, man remanded to Mid-Hudson for sixty days evaluation, back to "sleep," remember to sense, sense, was Diane impressed by my valiant argument I wonder, "sleep," sense, more "sleep," remember to sense, back to "sleep," "sleep," more cases, more "sleep," whores, back to "sleep," gamblers, back to "sleep," is the judge getting paid off I wonder, "sleep," remember to sense, "sleep," sense, sense, back to "sleep," lunch, back to "sleep," Chinatown, more "sleep," Joe's favorite restaurant shrimp and noodles in curry sauce for a dollar sixty-five, back to "sleep," remember to sense, back to "sleep," low level sensing, back to "sleep," Diane, "sleep," AP-5, more "sleep," clean out clear out calendar, back to "sleep," sense, sense, low level sensing, remember to sense, back to "sleep," judge's Tuesday haircut, back to "sleep," joke with Diane about judge's haircut, back to "sleep," maneuver Diane into judge's chamber, "sleep," remember to sense, shut door somehow, somehow smooch Diane, back to "sleep," up against wall sort of half way against wall, her ass against wall, what if Dan comes in, Dan the court officer, what if, what if, Diane wriggles away, sitcom scene, back to "sleep," judge returns with twelve white hairs left on his head, more "sleep," sense, low level sensing, back to "sleep," AP-5 stands adjourned, thirty-seven cases, twelve plea bargains, fourteen adjournments, four dismissals, two warrants issued for non-appearance, one competency hearing, court officer declares, judge raps gavel, Diane packs up stenography machine, another day another dollar, back to "sleep," remember to sense, sense, back to "sleep," but don't go yet Diane, wait a minute Diane, wait up Diane, why not Diane, come on Diane, walk with Diane, night air, rush hour, "sleep" a little sense a little, Broome Street, Diane, at last her apartment, quickie, good, sense Diane lush Diane, good night Diane, tomorrow Diane, back to "sleep," walk, more "sleep," pride in quickie, back to "sleep," sense, north to loft, "sleep," up elevator, dread, shoes off, remember to sense, sense, sense, sense, sense, sense, back to "sleep," get out book, copy book, one hour copying book, to wit, *Maltese Falcon*, back to "sleep," remember to sense, sense, Joe padding around in his slippers, Big Ronald cutting shelves, atmosphere of Christ the carpenter, more "sleep," write, *i.e.* copy for one hour, as yesterday, as tomorrow, sense, become Hammett, sense my hand that writes Hammett, sense, back to "sleep."

All of this, I suppose, the sense of all my days passing thus, reminded me of nothing so much as a certain John Held woodcut from the twenties that Bobby showed me once, a favorite of his, a map of America marked everywhere, like a ditto machine gone crazy, HOT DOG HOT DOG HOT DOG HOT DOG ORANGE DRINK HOT DOG BOOTLEGGER BOOTLEGGER BOOTLEGGER RUMRUNNER RUMRUNNER RUMRUNNER HOT DOG HOT DOG GAS STATION HOT DOG ORANGE DRINK GAS STATION RUMRUNNER HOT DOG HOT DOG.

Bobby loved rawness. "'Twas Christmas in the Pest House." Another Held, another Bobby favorite. Bobby of the sunny grin, boyish, gentle soul.

And "sleep?" "Sleep" meant not sensing. "Sleep" meant not self-remembering. "Sleep" meant forgetting that one day we die. Passing one's life in sleep. Not knowing one was ever alive. What can be done if you don't even know you're alive?

Or that was the theory anyway or the theory as I understood it. Or what was put out as theory. "Those that have ears to hear . . ." Another phrase.

As for my copying *The Maltese Falcon*, Joe was apprenticing me to Hammett. Again, my understanding only. Nobody ever told me such things, least of all Joe. In one of our first talks I had said to him that I was a writer. For writers he held what seemed a bemused contempt, as if you'd do better to be a carpenter or farmer, not messing around in your own delusions, eager to foist your power-mad schemes on others. The only writers Joe seemed to appreciate were sci-fi guys like Dick or hard-boiled detectives. Those and the old mystics, the stories from Philip's apartment. Thus, Hammett. If I wanted to be a writer, apprentice me to the best, or at least someone worth a few laughs. Or journalism. Somehow, journalism passed Joe's smell test as well. Just the facts, ma'am.

And so I copied *The Maltese Falcon* an hour a day, telling myself that if I were Japanese and wished to be a potter I'd mix clay for years before touching a wheel, if I wished to be a painter I'd clean brushes. I sensed my hand copying each word. I held the pencil with so light a grip that the tips of my fingers felt round and whole. I touched the point of the pencil to the page as if I were landing an airplane on an eggshell. I sensed my hand and looked at the page and listened to the band saw and the fretting in the shop and distant taxis and the still air between, all so that the words, Hammett's words, might not appear as subvocalizations in my head but rather go directly through my hand to the notebook, felt, understood, unshadowed.

It was impossible. My eyes could not apprehend, my hand could not write, without the words sounding-off like muffled echoes, mocking my effort.

Go back. Gently. Sense. The pencil in my hand, each finger swimming in air. The pencil itself leaving its sharpness behind on the paper, a dribble, a stain, life.

Now the pencil grows dull with the losses of its own stuff but at another angle due to the exact same attritions it's become sharp. I turn the pencil. Sense. Listen. My mind my desire in the end not sturdy enough to resist the slyness of the language: I am writing these words, am I not? I am writing these words of the man from Tacoma who was walking down the street on an ordinary day when a beam fell off a building and nearly killed him. The man, I write, then disappeared from Tacoma without a trace, left a wife and happy family behind. Years later, I write, Spade found him in Spokane with new wife and kids. Because, I write, when life ceased to be ordinary and predictable, the man ceased to be ordinary and predictable. When life became steady again, he became steady again. All this I write. Is it really so big a deal that I am not the first to write it? What is writing, after all?

Contentment with small things. I wrote *The Maltese Falcon*. I was an apprentice to greatness.

Though left to my own devices I might have picked Proust. Joe who may never have heard of Proust would, I was quite sure, not have approved. Too fey for a kike from Bensonhurst, too whatever else. *What was this bullshit?*

Go back. Gently. Sense.

I write single-spaced in a composition book. When I fill the composition book I begin another. I am like a medieval scribe.

And when I am done and putting away my composition book, Joe half-waddles by in his corduroy pants and asks if I feel like some chow, he's throwing something in the wok.

Joe's watery eyes, his bulldog frame. As an architect he'd built power plants and sports stadiums. Well, fair enough.

He no longer practiced. He'd quit when he got cancer. Threw it all into the Self, the building and saving of Selves, his own first of all. His teacher some daffy Jew painter, or that was the guy's affect anyway, who painted butterflies and bees and who spoke like South Amboy and had studied with somebody who was somebody and seen Gurdjieff passing through or by.

Though we weren't Gurdjieff people. Or at least Joe never said we were. We had no self-description. Unless we were beggars, mongrels of the spiritual. Gurdjieff-Sufi-Buddhist-Hindu-Jew-New York-mutt the glory the secret sinew of our city.

Sufi mostly? Gurdjieff?

How could I know? Were the two the same?

I loved the poetry. I loved that Joe taught at Pratt now. I loved the power. I loved the straight or crooked line, and that Joe cooked with garlic and meat.

No vegetarian this boy. Yet there was a delicacy to Joe with food. His supple wrist when he flicked the spatula. His fingers, thick and muscular, yet supple; his thumb, gripping the strainer, the peanut oil dribbling down, spattering the wok. Joe cooked with noise, and taught Bobby how to cook with noise.

Dinner on glossed blue Arabia plates on the long particle board table trimmed with cherry. Joe made everything himself, his furniture, his food. Though the loft itself was a work in progress. Ty Duncan had bought it for him, or loaned him the money on negligible terms, part of Ty's winnings when the *Lampoon* went national. We who were as establishment as we were subversive, like a secret cell in an officer corps. Joe had only moved in in September, which I was sure was part of what the "event" after Christmas was about. Getting the loft into shape, finishing the painting, finishing the ceiling and floors. Cheap labor, so went my line. Though it was Joe's position, one of those "positions" he occasionally took, with volubility and an air of certainty as if you could almost hear the quotation marks, that he had no need for so large a loft and only bought it so that we could work on ourselves and it was slower and more expensive to have us work while sensing than to call in a crew of Puerto Rican painters.

Was Joe a bully? Was Joe insecure?

He turned on the TV. Avoiding all the news, local or national, landing on an old John Wayne picture. Joe styling himself rather after the moguls, of Hollywood not Delhi, films in his vocabulary overleaping even movies and becoming directly, inevitably, "pictures." He'd seen this one before. He'd seen everything before, or everything in Technicolor anyway.

Me doing my silent bit by setting the table putting the utensils out. When I was with Joe it was easy to sense. His voice, his skin, his characteristic clothes, his glance so often averted as if he were afraid it might burn you, all of these seeming to radiate remembrance.

Though if I'd simply seen him in the street, a man hardly tall, minding his own business? It was easy, as well, to fantasize. Joe without doing or saying anything to or about me, just sitting there thick and sturdy shoveling rice and pork into his mouth his bowl up to his lips like a bib, watching an old western, two shoes off his thick feet, his black socks on the table, evoked in me a sense of being small beyond compare, awash in everything I'd ever felt for my father, teachers, big kids, cops, bosses, building inspectors, driving instructors, the famous, the rich, anyone else in whose shadow I ever fell who looked like they could or might cut my balls off. Or forget the balls, forget psychology forget even evolutionary biology. Somewhere in the thick folds of our secrecy we were talking about eternity.

Joe asked if I wanted seconds and helped himself. I had little to say. I took a little more. Words dried up in my throat. I kept waiting for some to appear that I hadn't rehearsed. Only these had a chance, only these were so-called real. The live wire of speech. Had I not a spontaneous bone in my body? I felt embarrassed, poor, without resource. Joe cackled at something on the screen. I poured the coffee into mugs, poured the half-and-half. No sugar for either of us because that's how Joe liked it. Joe smoked a couple of Newports. I felt embarrassed letting him smoke alone. Would he note my lack of conviviality? A small personality, one whom the grander gestures escaped.

Being there. The two of us as though watching John Wayne was an interesting thing to do. Though, wasn't it? What was uninteresting about it? Wasn't it more or less as interesting as anything else on the face of the universe, given all the givens? Some turned loaves into fishes, others turned our perceptions of loaves and fishes. Which miracle was greater, or weren't they just the same? Another Joe line. He had any number of them, and enough of them, at their moment of application, seemed to comfort, cure, salve.

My peripheral vision widened. My resentment of him melted away.

Joe as ample Jewish mother?

As soon as I put any of it into words it was gone.

Meeting at 7:30. I got out and arranged the benches. In came the troops silent and grim. Shoes by the door. Does anybody have anything they want to talk about? Tuesday, the no-work night, the talk-about-stuff night. The night you would almost think it was therapy. But everyone here was here because they were dissatisfied with therapy, or didn't believe in it to start. Therapy was ground transportation; here we would fly. Philip, Bobby, Cal Bittker, Ty, Valerie, myself, Liddie, Big Ronald, a half-dozen other birds, one half the entire group. And Maisie.

The quiet of the sea before the swells come in. Stingy bastards, hoarding the fragments of our ruined personalities, when there was a whole world that could be talked about. Cigarettes and straightened spines and wiggles on the benches and finally Bobby, about the job he got at *Harper's*, offering it up to Joe like a fatted lamb for acceptance or contempt. Not the job itself but the words, were they real, was there any "I" behind them, or were they all just another part of some endless mechanical program, conditioned, habituated, sleep-walking, sleep-talking? The room placing its bets and waiting, or rather I imagined the room betting and waiting, hushed audience before a curtain, while I myself snuck away, into a rushing tide of subvocalizations having to do with Bobby's article, now it was an article he was writing, he could do anything, this boy, cook, clean, fetch, draw, write articles. The article being about paranoia and cooking, which sounded like a joke but who knew what Bobby would write, it would probably be weird and wonderful.

Without thanking Joe directly, Bobby noted that if Joe hadn't turned him into a cook and general houseboy he could never have sold this article.

Joe nodded in noncommittal fashion, as if stepping gingerly in a field of words that must be booby-trapped, with bits of confession, flattery and gratitude all looking almost alike; but he seemed pleased with his handiwork. "I told you! I told you!"

An appropriate-enough title, I thought. Cooking and Paranoia. Joe had contempt for me—what other conclusion to draw? Why should I alone be starved? Which was to say that Bobby was getting paid for articles when the only thing Joe told me was to quit writing. Not that I wanted to write articles, but wasn't it a start? I sat there, black tar bubbling up in my throat, and would I dare to say what it was while it still tasted fresh and oozy, I who at the moment could recall hardly one thing in my life I'd ever said that was truly dangerous, that I knew in advance would make me sound ridiculous. Blurt out your life, here and now, why not—I managed to think for a moment before the words all but blotted out the thought— what more can you lose, have you not already lost everything? What else could this group be about, if it is not the club of those who lost everything?

Lost everything or gave everything up or was there really any difference?

Bobby talked about the shitty pay he'd be getting from *Harper's* and Joe, who was a practical man as well as an impractical one, counseled him to do a good job this time and make up for it next time which sounded to me fatuous and true at once and Bobby nodded and said, "Right." Bobby and Joe. My despair at perfect marriages. A prayer of the wounded, flushing my face and heating my eyes. I said, without hearing the words until they were in the air, "I'm feeling . . . a little envious."

Joe's watery eyes swept my way, his thick neck like a gun turret.

My vision widened, my mouth dried up.

"Oh? Of who?" His voice unexpectedly soft, as if cosseting something precious.

"Bobby," I said, feeling I'd said something right for once, already forming the words of self-congratulation that would send me back to sleep.

"You're envious of *him*... He's envious of *you*?" Joe's delighted whoop. Though who else could I have been meaning, was Joe playacting or was he dense? "Why are you envious of Jeeves?"

Joe's eyes ticked back and forth between us.

"All the usual suspects, I guess."

"Guess you'll just have to suffer," Joe said, with an offhand fierceness, even glee, to show he was unimpressed. Then, in a more modulated tone, as though he'd just mulled it over and his conclusion was the same, he repeated, "Guess you'll just have to suffer."

Suffering being another one of those things that Joe talked about, but, unlike many others who wrapped themselves around this endlessly fascinating topic, with neither sentimentality nor blame, like a Zen master's stick. "Suffer" meant don't act like a baby and don't waste my time. "Suffer" meant you've got to be kidding. But it also meant, in some deeper register whose resonance I faintly caught, self-remembrance, the only escape, the only honorable way. Joe smothered the ways and means of the everyday world in a relentless, suffocating irony, yet he seemed also to get a nostalgic pleasure from them, in the Japanese fashion, nostalgia for the evanescent.

Was I part of the floating world or a dead weight? Joe's attention snapped back to Bobby. I felt like I'd dared everything for nothing.

"How do you feel? You've got a secret envier."

"Flabbergasted," Bobby said.

"What does that mean?"

"A little bit flabber, a little bit gassed."

While they were talking about something I said, neither was looking my way. I was like the rabbit that got the greyhounds going and then disappeared.

"Where are you right now?" Joe asked him.

"A little bit behind myself," Bobby said. "In the woods."

"Cold and dark in the woods?"

"Yes."

"Try stepping forward. Can you? Can you step forward a couple steps?"

"Yes."

"Did you?"

"Yes."

"Still in the woods?"

"No."

"Catch up with yourself?"

"Yes."

"Any little shadows?"

"Can't see any."

"Feel better?"

"Uh-huh."

"Just stay there then. Just enjoy it for a little while."

Joe's cosseting voice again, wrapping up Bobby like an infant.

I had no idea what they were talking about. I was utterly lost, in whatever woods Joe was referring to or some other woods or in no woods altogether. For a moment my envy, my resentment, my sarcasm, all evaporated, as if in conformity to some newly discovered law of physics purporting to describe envy's inability to survive too great a distance between the envious and envied. Bobby and Joe sat there like two guys on a walkie-talkie in the darkness. The rest of us dead quiet. Fragments of words, half-phrases, kicked around my head like incomplete crosswords. Mostly quiet; fires tamped down. All I felt was the luck of being on a journey to the unknown, even in steerage.

Maisie stifled a giggle.

5

"Why do you have to be a *young* writer?" Joe asked me once. "Why can't you be an *old* writer?"

☙

Biographical explanations for why they came to the group.

Cal, because his whole life had been money and music, one of those kids from Park Avenue who play Carnegie Hall when they're fifteen and where do you go from that? Because his father, a furrier, the "king of sable," lost all the money one day? Because his music depended entirely on precision, it gloried in its precision, advertised its precision, but one day in secret Cal discovered that nothing in the world was precise?

Liddie, because the Church had disappointed her, she might have been a nun but she liked to fuck? Because for a long time no one wanted to fuck her?

Valerie, because something weird's expected of you when you grow up near that UFO highway in New Mexico and you're crackerjack smart to boot? Because she slept with Carlos Castenada, more or less at the height of his fame, and realized what a blowhard he was? Because she really, really, really wanted to be the best little girl in the world?

Big Ronald, because you never knew with these Okies, they're slyer than you think? Because, bouncing off a divorce, he liked the anti-family, the loose women, the lack of stupid questions? Because his favorite uncle had been a preacher, and what that had to do with it he wasn't sure, but he thought something, something about love, something about things you don't really talk about, not in Tulsa anyway—and was this a question too?

Philip, because his father was a communist or accused of being a communist and it was all sort of an embarrassment and an inconvenience and a blotch on the family escutcheon and it made childhood hard and confusing and what could be more opposite to being a communist but at the same time sort of the same (in its social aspects, its *cogniscenti* aspects) than this? Because he had a tender, spiritual nature that hoped for the best for the world? Because he had all this anger bottled up, and after shrinks and liberal Episcopal bishops and drugs and repressed sex and sitting in his bathtub many, many hours he still had it?

Ty, because he won the lottery with the *Lampoon* and he wasn't the type to splurge? Or because he was precisely the type to splurge, to bet it all, to believe in nothing or all of it? Because the inside of his mind, as he once described it, tasted as dry as the stuff inside a pencil sharpener, and he was desperate for a cool drink? Because the professional cynic with his chewed-up pipe stem, more than most, needs something?

Maisie, because she'd gone through too many shrinks and they'd all more or less fallen in love with her—with her or her money or family—so she didn't trust them anymore? Because of McLean's? Because of Hodgkin's?

Bobby, because he came from Shaker Heights which was almost like coming from Great Neck and if you were from Shaker Heights and were a light spirit afoot in the world you were supposed to do something about it, make your statement, make your escape, fly away? Because when he was seven years old his mother lay on the chaise by the pool and loosened her swimsuit strap and had Bobby slather her back with suntan lotion?

I could go on. There were thirty of us, after all. Thirty-one, including Maisie. Or also we could take a closer look, zoom in, more a shrink's-eye view, Maisie's this-and-that, Bobby's this-and-that, Philip's this-and-that.

Would it help? Would it explain?

For a long time, biographies seemed like lies, stories we told ourselves to avoid the fact that when it came to what we were doing, we all had the same story.

We were here. We had got here. Where did we go from here?

༄

At a meeting once I tried to explain why I had begun to write. I said it was because it beat getting a job, but that didn't sound right. I said it was to be the best, because I had to be the best, but that didn't sound right. I said because you could live and explain life to yourself as you went, you could chew it all, the flavor would last longer, it wouldn't be over so soon, but that didn't sound right. I said it was to be famous and get girls, but that didn't sound right. I said it was for immortality, but that didn't sound right. I said maybe it was just because I liked the sounds of words, I liked hearing them in my head, phrases, little speeches, they reassured me somehow, comforted me, made me feel brave in a weird way, I didn't know who else could have so many words in their head, crowded in there, packed, chockablock, and wasn't that a sign? But that didn't sound right, and I said so. I said none of them sounded right. My voice was gruff.

"Why are you telling me this?" Joe asked.
"I don't know. I'm not sure."
"Are you writing now?"
"Just the hour a day, copying."
"What are you tasting now?"
"My saliva. It's sweet."
"Do you hate me for taking your misery away?"
"Yes. I do."

☙

Bobby: wren.
Philip: robin.
Cal: hawk.
Valerie: crow.
Ty: scarlet tanager.
Liddie: flamingo.
Big Ronald: mockingbird.
Maisie: oriole.

☙

A list I wrote once. Are the birds less than rare, the choices a bit obvious? As little as I knew about people, I knew less about birds.

My friends: was I right even one time?

☙

Joe, on one occasion, on the value of the "work."
"I can't tell you what it is. If I could tell you, I would. But

nobody can do that for someone else. You have to find it for yourselves.

"What value does it have for *you*? Really, you should be asking yourselves that.

"If it doesn't have any value for you, why be here? Aren't there pleasanter things you could be doing?"

6

The *Bird Guide*. Almost on the periphery, yet a full picture of whatever it is I'm picturing (or *us*; is it *us?*) cannot be had without it. The *Bird Guide*, our magazine. Or really, it was Philip's magazine, and Cal's, and Bobby's, and after I was around for awhile, a little bit mine. We published it twice a year with a black-and-white cover out of Philip's narrow *New Yorker* office, where boxes of old copies were stacked up along with old railroad timetables and leads for "Talk of the Town" stories. It cost sixty-five cents, or as was said from the first issue, "still only sixty-five cents." Inflationary times. Its subscribers included the *New Yorker*'s editor Shawn, most of Cal Bittker's East Side relatives, Andy Warhol, a few public libraries, some publishing types, the New York City Police Department's Public Information Office, and a miscellany of wise souls and oddballs who saw it at the half-dozen newsstands where we managed to display it, the 72nd Street IRT subway station, the bookstore on Spring Street, the Gotham, and the one on Eighth Street. "The best zip codes in the business," total circulation four hundred fifty.

You could call it a cult magazine, but we never did. It already existed when I first went to Philip's apartment, and it was funnier then than it was later. It published Bobby's explosive cartoons featuring Mister All-Electric Kitchen and others, snippets of the Sufi stories that were read at Philip's on Thursday evenings, musical scores by Cal and his composer pals, various articles that Shawn had commissioned for the *New Yorker* but subsequently found too bloody or flaky, pieces by non-professional writers about things they had a peculiar passion for, famously bad cars or gardening in the Shetland Islands *circa* 1935, and police photos. When Joe came along, in my view, the *Bird Guide* started downhill. As Philip grew more serious about the group, the magazine lost some of its cockeyed irony. We published more articles that seemed to have a point, even some with a self-helpy flavor. I felt like I'd been born after the Golden Age. Though not entirely—and this I attributed to Joe seldom paying the magazine much mind. We still published such esoterica as the classification of male and female sexual organs in the work of Sir Richard Burton (the "crowbar," the "importunate," the "vast one") and reviews of Memphis barbecue joints written by a famous pornographer while he was on trial there for obscenity.

On the evening of the *New Yorker*'s 1978 Christmas party, we were moving the *Bird Guide* out of Philip's office and into our new, plainly more ample quarters in Joe's loft. I had regrets about moving at all. Like a rebellious girl from a good family, part of the *Bird Guide*'s seduction of me was how comfortably it still rested in the *New Yorker*'s staid old bosom. We were the anti-*New Yorker*, the camp-following devourer of its rejects, the little engine that could when the great big one couldn't or wouldn't. But would we still be any of those things once we were gone from the eighteenth floor? The lore of the *New Yorker*'s offices, the eighteenth floor, the nineteenth floor, the faded paint and file cabinets everywhere and old maps on the wall, the utter lack of a decorator's hand, the aura of a place where things had been piling up for fifty years and no one spoke much above Shawn's whisper—mere contiguity to these left me with a feeling of being somehow part of a world, the way copying Hammett everyday made me feel somehow tough and writerly. Maybe the janitors felt the same. Even the surly girl at the eighteenth floor reception who grudgingly buzzed us in was writing a novel as she sat there. Did she too feel that she was *New Yorker* material, and if she wasn't was it only because she was too good for it? Were we interlopers in her eyes, competition? With a chip on a shy shoulder, I sat on the gritty old Khorassan in Philip's office emptying the contents of the *Bird Guide*'s file cabinet into boxes, a melancholy exercise, not least because three or four boxes would hold all there was of it. Bobby sorted out expired subscriptions. Philip was off making the punch for the Christmas party, a duty which might have fallen on him or which he could conceivably have sought; he said he was mixing up a doozy. It being his feeling, generally speaking, that the *New Yorker* staff were a decent bunch but unwholesomely reserved such that an overdose of alcohol once a year could be hoped to be more tonic than fatal. A Fishhouse punch, all rum and vodka and a touch of sherbet to hide the implications, once concocted at the Union League in Philadelphia or someplace like that. Philip had ancestors who ran in such circles, before the later generations turned lefty. I was feeling, too, a little like Cinderella uninvited to the ball—or worse, missing her last fucking chance for the ball since next year we'd be downtown in our new digs—when Philip, turned out like some Ivy League P.T. Barnum with a carnation in his blazer, poked his head in to say we could come to the party if we wanted, if it wouldn't be too boring, Renata Adler'd brought three or four Belgians so if there were Belgians why not us?

In the corridor Philip was ladling out the punch and Bobby knew all the cartoonists, leaving me to my own devices. There were maybe fifty people mingling around in shirtsleeves, workshirts, the occasional old J. Press tweed, plastic cups were piling up on the file cabinets. I sipped my Fishhouse punch like all the rest and realized that the din was gaining. I struggled to keep my bearings. People looked at me as though wondering who I was and how I got there. I had the right clothes but the wrong face. I felt a certain melancholy resignation that an opportunity, once cherished, was slipping away. Could I not speak to someone, say one thing? It was I who was sensing myself, after all, I who was leading a secret life stiffened with peculiar insight and hope that these ordinary souls had no clue of, it was I who was rich in my poverty, so why was I still so scared? Even to tell them I was an Assistant D.A. And not any Assistant D.A. but *our friend* the Assistant D.A. The more I sipped my second glass of punch, the more my worlds seemed to collide. Which one was the dream? I would probably have left without a word to a soul if Bobby hadn't pushed by and introduced me to a cartoonist pal of his, a sweet-seeming man half as woolly as his characters who in the accelerating turnover, propelled by the punch, in turn introduced me to a film critic with mousy hair and librarian glasses whose reviews were celebrated at the time. She too had been drinking the punch. So had everybody. The room was getting loud.

I told her I was a friend of Philip's.

Philip would have a lot to answer for in the morning, she said agreeably enough.

I said I worked on the *Bird Guide*, and did she know what that was?

"Of course I know."

"But you don't subscribe."

"No."

"Would you like to subscribe?"

"Actually, no. Why would I want to subscribe? I don't understand what it's about."

She seemed annoyed by the whole subject, as though it had been an irritant for some time.

"Do things you don't understand irritate you?" I asked.

"Well what's the point, really? Really, what's the point?"

"Would you like me to show you the point?"

"It's all so shapeless. Maybe *that's* the problem, it's shapeless. It doesn't have a shape."

"Do you think the world has a shape?"

"Maybe not. But magazines should. All the more so if the world doesn't."

"Why don't we go to Philip's office and I'll get out a copy and I'll show you the point," I said.

"It's the shape," she said.

"Oh, so now it's the shape."

"It has no shape."

"Then let's go to Philip's office and I'll show you the shape."

And so we went to Philip's office. She continued to sip from her plastic cup and to complain about Philip's malicious punch. What's happened to him, she wanted to know, he's gone off some deep end.

"Bad company," I said.

"I didn't mean you. I wasn't accusing you."

"And I'm not accusing you," I said.

I showed her the *Bird Guide* that was mostly about smoking. "This is our smoking issue," I said.

I laid out the magazine on Philip's oak desk, pulled the chain on his banker's light and showed the pages under its yellow-green glare.

"You see, it's in favor of smoking. It says smoking's good for you."

"But that's ridiculous, it isn't," she said.

"But neither's that harsh, puritanical, self-righteous put-down of smokers that everybody's into now. It's just a way of people scoring points on others, it's hatred, it's aggression."

"You're telling people to go kill themselves!"

"We're just telling people to relax, life's not as bad as it seems. Unless, of course, it's worse."

"I've been trying to quit for three years."

"I don't smoke myself."

"There's no point to this."

"But at least there's a shape. You can see the shape, at least."

"What's the point?"

"I can't say."

"Well if *you* can't even say. . ."

"I thought we were talking about shape."

"*And* points."

"I can show you. Here it is."

"What's *this*? What's *this*?"

She was looking at another article now.

"*Labial beauty?*"

"Some people are interested in that."

"So what? So *what*? It's not even obscene. At least if it were obscene. . ."

"I'm not defending every article. But you can see the point."

"It's *stupid*."

"It is. Agreed."

"Well then. . ."

"If you're so stupid that you think nothing in the world's ever allowed to be stupid"—I said—"or at least not in your hallowed corridors, nothing stupid allowed on the eighteenth floor. . . You're narrow-minded, Miss _____. There's no room for stupidity in your universe, when in fact in the real world stupidity's all over the place. We of the *Bird Guide* are getting a handle on it at least."

"I'm certainly not narrow-minded."

"You are so narrow-minded that you know what? We're sick of your condescending patronizing glances every time you walk by our door—we're moving out of here! We're moving to freer territory."

"I didn't say you should do that."

"What do you think all these boxes are about?"

"So you were moving out *already*!"

"And you know what else, you know what else, you're so narrow-minded? I was going to let you give me a blowjob, but now I'm not."

"I think I want to get more punch," she said.

"I realize I may have blown my chance to send you my movie reviews," I said as she stepped out the door, "but my cock says no and I back it up!"

So much for networking, which may, by the way, have been a new word that year. So much, as well, for *bien pensant*'s take on the *Bird Guide*, and by extension, for sure, our little rogue band.

Better to keep your mouth shut.

But why?

It wasn't so bad, to be a scoundrel, to feel so young, I who had never really felt young even when I was.

To whom does the future belong, after all?

In the world, but not of it. Give them a taste of this or that.

I felt for a moment like a man who'd cut off the bridge he was standing on.

And was I proud of it, yes or no?

Stop. Go back. Gently. Sense yourself. Are you there at all?

Later we went downtown in a cab together, Philip and Bobby and I. Nobody said anything.

In the meeting it was Philip who spoke. I tried to sense while the room whirled away, but it was his voice alone that steadied me. Philip was the only one of us who when he had something to say in a meeting spoke in an entirely conversational tone, as though really speaking to a friend.

But weren't we all friends? Wasn't even Joe a friend?

Who is your friend if it's not one who helps you?

Go back. Don't speculate. Don't say to yourself "speculate." Sense.

The room steadied. Philip's voice, slightly reedy, flat, the cadences of his sentences like the lengths of an easy breath. "I'd say the party went well until the third punch bowl."

"Oh, how *was* the punch?" Joe asked.

"Effective. And tasty."

"Shawn there?"

"Nah. He hates parties. Or at least big parties, where he could forget somebody's name. But Galen Townsend was there."

"Oh?"

"Somebody's guest."

"And?"

"And nothing... Nothing, really. We said hello... perfectly cordial."

When Joe wished to keep a conversation floating, he lit a cigarette. The rituals of a new package. The crinkling of the cellophane.

Then, in a slightly lower register, as though abruptly the

therapist, vocal downshifting, asking Philip to dig deep: "What did you feel?"

"Nothing. Really. Nothing."

"I'll never sleep with you," Joe said.

"Good."

Philip said this a little bravely, added, "I never thought you would."

I was certain Joe would then say: you never even imagined it?

But he didn't. He let it drop.

I should put in here that it had never occurred to me that Philip was queer. Nor was the group exactly a queer-friendly place. The subject would come up from time to time and we attracted our share, but Joe mostly seemed to view homosexuality as a distraction from the work, or perhaps a disability as well, in the same way that being a writer or drug-taker, even of pot, was a disability. Carpenters were good for the work. Normal people, normal habits, were good for the work. Complications, twists, special pleadings, were just a pain in the ass. Joe viewed everything, mercilessly, in terms of its usefulness to what we were doing. In furtherance of which, he'd made a match between Philip and Liddie, the F-train girl and the Talk of the Town guy, part of his plan to "normalize" Philip, which involved, as well, the substitution of Philip's old pink plastic prep school glasses with aviator frames, the growth of a mustache and sideburns, and some serious weight gain, with the result that Philip looked less like a grown-up altar boy and more like a seventies incarnation of Teddy Roosevelt as police commissioner. In truth, I preferred the old Philip to the makeover, but Philip himself plainly went for the "new guy." If anyone from the group's early members was a true believer, it was he, or at least he cut Joe the most slack, was most resourceful in defending him against perceived slights, and seemed on the surface, anyway, the most transformed of anybody. His old writer's block was gone, he was banging out Talk stories, he no longer did drugs or spent whole mornings in the bathtub.

After the meeting, Philip, Bobby and I walked up Broadway together. A little December night air to sober up, and anyway I was feeling comradely. Though I might mention here the unspoken hierarchy that made us something other than three cheerful musketeers, and that overlay even the fact that Bobby was the group mascot and everyone loved Bobby. If somebody had diagrammed us as a corporate power chart, Joe would of course have stood at the top, with Philip his first lieutenant and Bobby under Philip and myself under Bobby, exactly in the order we'd been introduced to Joe, and with other shoots of authority stemming from Liddie, who was from "the old group." Or to put it another way: if we imagined ourselves in an esoteric group with secrets to be transmitted, these might be expected to run from Joe through Philip to Bobby then me, or to Liddie directly. Although, as was often said and was actually inscribed in the spare, wistful watercolor which I imagined was a gift from Joe's old teacher that hung on the wall in back of Joe's Eames chair, "Sometimes those that are near are far and sometimes those that are far are near."

The fact that Philip looked after Bobby and Bobby looked after me diminished not at all the admiration I felt for Philip. It equaled the fondness I felt for Bobby and far exceeded anything I felt for Joe. My problem with Joe was first that he didn't care enough for me and second his frightening, destructive vulgarity, his raw power, that had turned the heads of Philip and Bobby and converted Philip's sedate little reading group into a world-defying adventure. Or you could also say that this was Joe's allure, even to me. But getting back to Philip, whom I could love (though love was a word in dispute in the group, not that it was but what it was, Joe insisting that love could only be an action, compounded of kindness, attention and respect, or anyway that its existence could only be proved by such an action, and that the puny or morbid feelings that people usually plastered with love's label were nothing more than conditioning, habit, confusion, pathology which might or might not accompany the real thing but most often stood fatefully in the way of it) without fear. Philip was first off the finest writer I knew and yet he wrote about nothing but New York. His love stories, his historical epics, his lyric bouts with nature, were all compressed into prosy eight hundred word blocks about butcher shops and circuses and new restaurants and street fairs and the theater with the most flops on Broadway. His sentences ran like babbling brooks, running over rocks, hitting surprises, gurgling, picking up nouns, turning onto fresh vistas, ending who knew where, with some lonely first person plural somewhere looking on as in a Hudson River painting with a train, giving the whole its human dimension, its hope, its nostalgia, its curiosity. For a long time I wondered how Philip had come to know and love the city so well. He'd grown up in Berkeley and gone to Harvard from there and hadn't come to New York and the *New Yorker* until graduating from the *Crimson*. But it turned out there was a lacuna in his life. His father had been in the Berkeley physics department, a friend of Oppenheimer's, blacklisted in the fifties and fleeing to Mexico at the same time that Philip's mother had a nervous breakdown. So for three years in the fifties they'd shipped him off to friends in New York, rich Jews, old family of East Side liberals, who'd introduced him, with grace and openhandedness, to a charmed East 82nd Street life. The result being that Philip became a poet not of seventies New York but of an older, more refined, and maybe grayer thing, something like what Woody Allen aimed for in *Manhattan*, though Allen himself was a creature of New York in the seventies, singles bars on Second Avenue and cute meets in Laundromats. These things were not omitted from Philip's New York, but they didn't hold pride of place. That went to the old restaurants whose eulogies he wrote, the side street second floor restaurants, the bus routes, the toy train shops on 45th Street, the remnants of the El's, the steam heat in rent controlled buildings, and how it all got there.

We stopped on Eighth Street for takeout coffee, and when we got to Sixth Avenue Bobby kept going west. Philip and I walked north and for the first time since the meeting I remembered, as if it were something that if I paid it little enough attention, like a canker sore or a headache, might just go away, something about Philip being queer. What was it exactly that Joe said? *I'll never sleep with you?* And who was Galen Townsend? None of it, through the gauze of detachment I half-consciously tossed over it, made too much sense and in any event he was fucking Liddie now. And who cared anyway where penises were put? We had enough else to be concerned with. Mine had been in enough sleazy places.

But still. Go back. Gently. Sense. Walking side-by-side past Balducci's with my friend. The avenue all but deserted, its sidewalks anyway which were the things that in Philip's New York counted, a breeze out of the west. Walking with Philip, I felt not so much that I owned the city as that I didn't care who owned it.

Go back. Gently sense. Listen to the breeze.

"Who was Galen Townsend?" I asked.

"Oh. He was my boyfriend. Back in college."

"You had a boyfriend in college?"

"Of course." And a few steps later: "Just one more Harvard fairy."

Go back. Sense. Listen.

Would I ever say to Philip I'll never fuck you, would he ever say that to me, no of course not I don't think so but it would never happen anyway not in my lifetime not in many, of that you can be assured, of that I could be assured.

Friends walking along; Twelfth Street. Avoiding the dogshit where the sidewalk narrowed for the boxed-in trees and the garbage bags and then a gypsy cab that had been crawling down the block pulled up beside us and a black guy got out.

A smooth brown leather jacket, belted, a beard, a big guy. I thought he wanted directions.

"Are you Diane's friend?" he asked.

"Who? Diane Leeson?"

"Don't be an asshole," he said, and he started to thump me.

He was a big guy but he could have been a small guy and still killed me.

I fell to the sidewalk and hoped it wasn't in shit and he kicked me as I curled up. "Smartass! Smartass!"

It's about all he said, asshole and smartass.

I tried to sense myself as the toe of his boot found my groin and this worked in an unanticipated way, turning everything into sensation, undifferentiating the pain. For once I felt sensing myself had some immediate usefulness.

And then I saw Philip, a hapless, fallen expression on his face, as though all of this was beyond him. He shouted help and called for a cop but there wasn't a cop around and he pulled at the guy's arms but the guy at once yanked free of him, as readily as a circus strongman might pull away from the kitschy blandishments of a clown.

I saw Philip's calm rabbit eyes in the middle of his face's commotion and I was embarrassed for him, as I might have been if he was my father and if it was he, my father and not me, who was abjectly losing this fight.

As well, I saw his sideburns and cop's mustache for a moment as but a mask, tokens of an earnest enough aspiration, betrayed.

The guy rolled me over with his foot and kicked my ass and then less sportingly the back of my head and the miracle was—I sensed this miracle—that I still wasn't thinking of myself.

I caught Philip's expression again, rueful more than anything, his fear fading into something more resigned, at the moment he launched his coffee underhanded at the big guy's face.

The guy yipped like a bitten dog, swiped at his nose and cheeks with the back of his hand, but whether the coffee hurt him or was more like a wake-up call to remind him to get the hell out of here before someone in the brownstones called 911 I couldn't be sure. But he backed off, went back to the cab. Unafraid to show his face, which was a little bit bony and bearded, pockmarked with eyes like coals under heavy brows.

He must have known I'd never prosecute; even, that I had the power to call the cops off. He must have known, as well, not to hurt me badly.

Off went the gypsy cab, dragging its tailpipe banging and sparking down the potholed block like a cat with a can on its tail, in only a slightly greater hurry than on its arrival.

Saint Vincent's was only a block away. Philip lifted me up and cleaned my face of mucus and blood with the handkerchief from his blazer and when no cab came walked me slowly, like a patient a day after surgery on his first tour of the hospital sunroom, towards the Saint Vincent emergency.

I thanked him for throwing the coffee.

The least I could do, Philip said.

I explained to him why I could never prosecute, while privately reviewing whether continuing to feel up Diane in the judge's chambers was really such a wise idea.

Then, back to sensing, looking and listening. For the moment there was plenty to sense.

The place was busy for a Tuesday night. I heard a nurse say that anyway. People lined up in rows of plastic chairs like it was an unemployment office. The sicker or more assertive of us spread out over two or three seats, or rested a head on a lover's lap. One guy with a stab wound was bold enough to take occupancy of an empty gurney, but the nurse chased him off. His stab wound was pretty minor. Fluorescent lights shone down on us all like a chilly benediction.

Philip phoned Bobby, who came over with more coffee. I was going nowhere fast. The bruises on my face were complaining more angrily and something in my abdomen ached. But nothing seemed to be broken, no bones anyway.

An hour passed, then an hour-and-a-half. Bobby maliciously sketched the nurses and doctors, filling every unprinted-upon inch of the bag from the coffee shop and the napkins he found inside it. This was probably to cheer me up but could also have been to cheer himself up. I laughed a little at the cartoons but was otherwise bored. We all were. I kept telling my friends to go home. At two o'clock Bobby did. There were still at least fifteen people ahead of me. Philip fell asleep with his arms folded, like a Buddha who'd chosen to die, and I dozed off as well. I had a dream that we were in a church under attack somewhere in Europe, for some reason I thought Barcelona, or Bordeaux, and guys with black helmets and faces like rusted iron were finding us, finding Philip and me, who ran out of the church but were paralyzed as we ran, turned into pillars of salt as the rusted iron guys launched their napalm from their guns and my face screamed in the blinding white blast of wind that overtook us. I woke up with the bruises under my eyes burning and my cut lip miserably swollen. Philip got me a couple of Tylenols from the nurse but it was still going to be an hour. I felt Philip's soft concern. It would probably be an hour and a half. Philip struck up a conversation with the guy in the chair on the other side of him, a slight, dark-skinned guy in a beret. The guy's voice sounded like "the islands," even if I couldn't place which island, or at the moment exactly where any of "the islands" were. It turned out he was from Brazil and they talked about Pelé for awhile and then the guy, who said he himself was feeling malarial but it was no big deal, asked what was wrong with me.

Stupid question, he then concluded, on looking at my face. But he was rather quick to understand that this must have something to do with a woman.

Philip complained to him about the wait, or rather complained and simultaneously explained, because this guy was from São Paulo and might not know that New York was broke.

The guy said in São Paulo this was nothing, the clinic took all day.

I suggested to Philip we fuck it and leave.

"But why? I help you," the guy from São Paulo said.

It was Philip, not I, who asked him, "How?"

The guy raised his hands, showed his outstretched fingers, like a mime. "If he lets me." He looked at me benignly enough, as if he could understand my skepticism.

However doubtful I was, Philip was less so. Or maybe he just wanted to go home so anything was worth a try.

"Sure. Okay," I said, figuring if I said no thanks I'd sound like a prig, more to Philip than the guy.

Philip stood up and so did the guy from São Paulo so that I could stretch across the three plastic chairs with my face up and I sensed myself like crazy as though that would somehow make me a cooperating partner, a conscious man is a healing man, and the man put his thumbs that looked rough but were soft into my wounds in such a way that I feared infection but also felt their probing care.

Or in truth I didn't know what he was doing. I did, however, believe that in certain cases and with certain gifts or practices that spirits could trump bodies.

I believed this because I had to, because if I didn't what was I doing with my life?

The guy's eyes peered down at me on my makeshift operating table as if I were a meal he was preparing and Philip's eyes somehow looked the same, the eyes of cooks or maybe naturalists, and I remembered or thought I remembered that both of them were queer.

I felt, actually, in good hands. When the guy was done my face tingled as though I'd put an astringent aftershave on it but there was little pain. Disproving the notion of time's arrow, I was told I still had an hour or more to wait to see a doctor, even a nurse. I thanked my benefactor and we left. On the same paper that Bobby had sketched the emergency room personnel, Philip took his name and number, because the guy felt a story about himself—it turned out he came into Saint Vincent's nearly every week and laid hands on whoever would let him—might help his immigration status.

We picked up a few bandages at a late-night pharmacy on Seventh Avenue and Philip flagged me a cab. It was almost four o'clock. And what would I tell my co-workers tomorrow? Maybe I'd skip it, declare a day of world forgiveness.

Philip craned his neck avuncularly through the cab's rear window, as if I were a drunk or an out-of-towner about whom it would be best to remind the driver that he had a lot of local friends. Was there maybe a story in this South American guy, sort of the angel of Saint Vincent's, he asked.

Before in my woozy condition I could make a judgment on this, Philip added as if in afterthought: "Would you like to write it with me?"

"Sure."

"Then okay, we'll do that," he said, "why not."

The "why not" more like punctuation than interrogatory, the way Joe so often said it.

Philip's head, leaning into my cab, at that moment reminded me of a giraffe's in a zoo, benign and herbivorous, leaning over its bars for a peanut.

On the way uptown I wondered if I might have been more effusive in my response to him, more gracious. I decided not. Philip, I decided, was practicing kindness. I was practicing truth. The truth was that I was flattered and a little bit thrilled, but the truth was also that I could see that I was thrilled and I wondered why and this wondering was sobering. What difference did any of it make? Why was I still such a slave? Words in my head, but I listened to them.

7

A few of the secrets of us.

A lamp in a niche.

Chakras, yes, more or less, chakras seen through a western eye.

Sex.

Gurdjieff's intervals, Gurdjieff's octaves.

Which is to say the world and all worlds run in octaves, with intervals where the F flats and B sharps ought to be that seem to throw everything off.

Much Gurdjieff detail that seemed cockamamie and as if out of some nineteenth-century sci-fi novel about shooting for the moon and that I never understood but if it mattered, I felt, if Joe really believed this stuff, we were all in bad shape. But I didn't believe he did.

Sex.

To break free, first of all, you must break free of your parents.

We are all of us born alive up shit's creek without a paddle, or in alternative formulation also using the well-regarded article, up to our eyebrows in it.

All religions have their inner truths, and all these inner truths are the same.

People should have an aim.

Self-understanding is all.

But what is a "Self?"

What is an "I?"

We swim in a sea of air.
Breathing is all.
Lots of things are all.
Consistency as the celebrated hobgoblin of the second-rate mind.
What's wrong with a second-rate mind?
Ch'i: breath; but also, spirit.
The sermon on the mount.
Just another kike from Brooklyn.
A little Chinese mud man, lost in mountains.
Lazy. Good. Sweet.
Godzilla.
Errol Flynn.
Hot fudge sundaes.
Japanese transformers.
Vegetarianism is not all, nor is physical fitness.
Cheers for stomachs, for bellies, for good food and glowing coals.
An example of an aim, that you might write on a slip of paper and put in your wallet between your social security card and your cash machine card: always to remember that you're going to die.
Politics are irrelevant, or anyway leave public debate to those who care about it.
Leave the maintenance of the machine to those who care about it.
There will always be people who care about these, and while the world chugs on, others may slip away.
Don't gossip.
Don't argue.
If you want to understand people, mirror them.

Don't attack unless attacked.

Help others.

In whatever ways they can be helped, help them, but what is help when the ship is sinking?

The "work" may or may not be the "path."

Whatever is said about the work is only true or not true, helpful or not helpful, harmful or not harmful, depending on who says it and to whom and when and how and why.

Seek knowledge, even in China.

But it's not necessary to go to India.

In fact, it's better not to. India is vacation, India is running away.

All knowledge must be adapted to the local culture, or imagination enters.

You can't learn except from one who knows.

But if someone's a step above on the ladder, they have that much they can teach you.

To rise on the ladder you have to place someone else on your rung.

All of this is bullshit.

Philip K. Dick is "not bad," Errol Flynn is "not bad," Fred Astaire is "not bad," Sabu is "not bad," King Kong is "not bad."

"Not bad" is about as good as it gets.

You need a group to get anywhere.

Without a group to wake you up you'll fall back asleep.

Without a group you could go crazy.

Even with a group you might go crazy.

You don't have to go to Harvard.

But you need a little meanness, a little ruthlessness, and going to Harvard's proof you've got it.

The elusive "I."

The habitual, false I.

The habitual false I that one moment thinks and likes this and the next moment thinks and likes the other, that is a multiplicity of I's, very nearly infinite I's, all thinking they're the one.

Everyone wants approval all the time for everything.

Be aware of your facial muscles.

Relax your facial muscles.

Be aware of relaxing your facial muscles.

Be aware of all your muscles, be aware of relaxing all your muscles, be aware of not relaxing all your muscles.

Be aware of wanting approval all the time for everything.

Be aware of everything.

Don't change anything, just sense look and listen.

But doesn't that change everything?

Doesn't that make it possible to change everything?

Or even one little thing?

If one little thing is changed, is not everything changed?

Be greedy.

Don't be greedy.

Wake up buddy it's the real world.

It's possible to have something like an orgasm all the time.

A girl looks into a pool and sees the reflection of her lost necklace on a branch just above her head.

If something comes up, follow it.

Don't put others in double binds.

Don't project feelings about your parents onto others.

The world is our oyster.

The banality of writing any of this down.

How if said and heard in person between willing souls the same words that sound so trite on paper might touch the heart or mind, might awaken nobility, love or truth, the real things not kitsch, might stimulate self-remembrance.

Nothing is as it seems on paper.

If you can't get rid of the words in your head try counting from one to one hundred then back down to two, then up to ninety-nine then back to three then up to ninety-eight and down to four and so on up and down and back and forth constantly in your head for a month.

Become like a mirror to the world.

Li Po.

Tu Fu.

Lao Tzu.

Peking duck.

There are no secrets.

Those that have eyes to see and ears to hear.

Old stuff new stuff all the same stuff.

The secrets of pre-sand Egypt.

Freud.

What about him?

Onto something but didn't go all the way.

Transference.

The right use of sex energy.

Is what exactly?

The production of fine energies through conscious effort and attention.

Worlds within worlds.

Movies with instructional value *The Thief of Baghdad, The Razor's Edge, Kim, The Incredible Voyage, Willie Wonka and the Chocolate Factory*.

Dikr.

Aladdin's lamp.

Damn the torpedoes! Full speed ahead!

The orgasm inside your head.

Every religion has an outer shell of the faithful and an inner kernel of the knowing.

Life itself is the miracle, rendering other miracles showy and banal.

The Sufi's patched coat.

The Monkey King, the chattering mind.

Secrets best passed in riddles and tales.

☙

Biographical explanations for why they came to the group, continued. Example number eight: me.

Because I was lonely in my room. Because I knew I could never write myself out of where I found myself. Because my father left my mother and my world was fractured. Because I became a man too soon. Because my cock told me to. Because I'd go far to get close to the *New Yorker*. Because I'd gone to Brooklyn some months before going to Philip's and had seen at the Brooklyn Academy a performance by Peter Brooke's troupe of *The Parliament of the Birds* performed for free on a Persian carpet laid over a basketball court mostly for kids from Bed-Stuy bused in for the show, and this performance, at once poetic and raw, pitched to the street jocularity of the kids, made an impression of prophecy on me which when I went to Philip's apartment, and then Joe's, seemed somehow confirmed. Because I was a dissatisfied Jew. Because I was broke. Because the long time I spent as interlocutor between my father's indifferent cruelty and my mother's hurt rage exhausted me psychically and I was ready for anything. Because it was the seventies.

Because it was New York and I was looking like everybody else for the next new thing. Because there'd been too little love in my life. Because I was looking for my father. Because it would give me something someday to write about. Because God was dead.

All I can say, really, is maybe.

8

Nobody around the courthouse said anything about my pounded face. The stale air of business as usual, as if the fluorescent lights never went out, no domestic beef jokes, no wry comments about the perils of law enforcement. This was after I skipped a day. Now it was Thursday. My bruises may have failed to stand out against the local backdrop.

Or was it another glorious example of conscious healing, your alternative medicine dollars hard at work?

Diane noticed. But I didn't see her till mid-morning because she'd been assigned another courtroom for the day. She was wearing a dress of mauve angora, as if very possibly the entire flotsam of 100 Centre Street had gotten together to crown her their queen. I informed her that due to health considerations and also out of remorse for potentially compromising her professional status through my persistent and inappropriate gestures of affection in potentially revealing and quasi-public circumstances, I would be quitting the more intimate aspects of our acquaintance as of immediately. In words more or less, the way words of disengagement are always more or less. She said she knew who did this to me and he was an asshole and she was sorry. I said thanks, and we were both very cool. All of this *sotto voce* in the din of the fourth floor corridor in the middle of mamas making bail for their boys and lawyers hustling pimps and vice versa, as if we, or particularly I, were part of the human comedy after all.

But where did it all lead?

Sense look and so on be absorbed in this great consciousness all around you be a speck in the universal wonder just don't get too fancy about it. Nor too fancy about not getting too fancy, nor too plain about it, nor too plain about being plain, nor too prideful nor too critical or nothing at all. One's mind can spin like a top. One's mind can do a dervish dance all by itself. As consciously as I could I silently wished for Diane success in all her endeavors, to wit, that with her tits and stenography machine and glossy makeup and fine bones she'd one day be discovered by a complainant who would turn out to be a movie producer or publisher of *Ebony* and become some kind of star, then left it at that, went upstairs to my office, and found a slip on my metal desk, like a bit of pink propaganda dropped on the deck of an aircraft carrier, saying "M. Maclaren" called and please call her.

Hey, hi, how's it going. Maisie's throaty voice had—always had had, even when I met her when she was sixteen and even when the words themselves were no more than social boilerplate—an unlikely directness to it. Something about her voice seemed to power her forward, like one of those rocket-propelled personal vehicles the Gyro Gearlooses of the fifties were always inventing. She was going to be in Chinatown and did I want to have lunch. Well really, why wouldn't I, one o'clock, Win Lo.

The crowded downstairs place where I often went, where Joe used to go. Yelling and noodles, din and noodles, as if the noise were so essential a component of the dish that it should take over part of its name. It was a gray day and Maisie had on her long olive coat and coming down the stairs of the tiny shop she looked Irish beyond all reason. Maureen, I called out, and she knew who I meant. Her freckles, her green eyes, her round cheeky face, like a cherub they'd have to keep an eye on. There was barely room on the back of her chair for her coat. I could see it dragging on the tile floor with the used-up napkins and felt oddly sorry for it, for her, as if I could remember a moment in her life when everything was pristine. I offered to put it on one of the hooks, piled up with everybody else's, but she declined, didn't care.

We ordered whatever we ordered and for someone I didn't really know well she looked at me as if I did.

And maybe she was right. We had Sascha's death, after all. I'd been in the car when her sister died in a crash.

"Bobby and I broke up," she said, and when I said nothing because in the group when you didn't know what to say you didn't lean off balance to get words out of your mouth, she said, "He was getting to be too much."

"Oh?"

"He was attacking me."

"Oh no! Poor little defenseless Maisie? Couldn't defend herself?" Amiable and facetious, as though reminding her of the endless course in interpersonal fencing we'd been party to, reminding her as well of the tone of Joe's chiding voice.

"He kept saying he loved me," she said.

I produced a likely-enough grin but what I really felt was badly for Bobby, falling in love with one you weren't supposed to fall for. Falling in love being to start with our local version of a cardinal sin, most habitual and inevitable and delusional of human behaviors, the mother of all attachments, but being a cardinal sin didn't mean don't do it, but rather if you did it be prepared to observe the consequences.

Sin as descriptive not proscriptive. Sin as warning sign. Sin as something that could waste a lot of your time.

Or, wasting a lot of your time being the very definition of sin in a clocked world, unless of course you learned something from the waste, all rules being made to be broken.

All rules being made to be broken. . . but not all the time . . . Stop. Go back.

"He thinks I'm his mother," Maisie said, and the word "mother" must have hit a flat spot in the restaurant's roar. A guy with an off-duty cop look, mustache and a face like chuck steak, catty-corner from me, looked knowingly my way.

She's an emotional flasher, I thought, Maisie gets off on giving strangers peeks at the fleshy thighs of her secrets.

But I liked that about her, that little sexual *frisson* in her voice as her complaint hurtled past the perimeters of our tipsy little square table into the general communion of elbows and mouths: "I don't like screwing people who think I'm their mother."

"I went out with an Indian girl once," I said, "who insisted that American men only think about their mothers and baseball."

I was trying to be agreeable.

"Exactly! Exactly!" she shouted.

"But I'm surprised about Bobby."

"He's such a baby. I told him to grow up."

"And what did he say?"

"Nothing! *Nothing!* Passive-aggressive. I don't need passive-aggressive in my life right now. Which I also told him."

"Did you tell Joe?"

"Why should I?"

We slurped our noodles awhile, each of us measuring out even breaths because we knew the other one was and sensing sliding noodles down our throats as if we were eating something alive. Once you subtracted to and from, I had only forty-five minutes for lunch, and my glance was already cruising for the guy to get a check when, apropos of what could have been anything at all—we'd been talking about a book about Chinese brush strokes that her own teacher, the painter from New Jersey, was fond of quoting—Maisie asked if I'd ever been in love with her sister.

I sensed my eyes letting in less light, the room getting gray at the edges, as though viewed through an old stereopticon.

"Why do you ask?" I said.

"Don't pull that shit on me. Why do you think I asked? I asked because I want to know."

"Of course," I said, "I had a huge crush on Sascha. I thought you knew that. I thought everybody knew that by now, of the old crowd."

"Everybody loved Sascha," Maisie said, and for a moment her rhetorical wall seemed breached, revealing the rue growing quietly in the garden.

"I guess. Maybe that was so."

As if appealing to it for some unspecified relief, I stole a glance at the greasy Bulova wall clock that overlooked the room like the guardian of its good order.

"Bored? You're bored! I don't believe it!"

"Sorry. Can't piss off the judge. Just a city employee, wage-slave."

We walked through the little park, Chatham Park I think it's called, that separates the courthouse from Chinatown. A Chinese funeral band tramped through in back of us, its tone all the more mournful for its tinniness. Maisie came back to her sister, or rather to the group of us around Sascha, Harry her boyfriend who married her and then she died and then he died in Vietnam, and me and Cord and Teddy Redmond, and what surprised me in Maisie's rendition was that to her we were all the "big kids," Sascha's boyfriend and his roommates from Yale, she didn't distinguish us one from the other. I told her it had never seemed that way to me. Among Harry and Cord and Teddy, who'd known each other since prep school, I'd always felt like the outsider, the "meritocrat" who snuck in, the Jew who'd one day be thrown out. And as if I hadn't deserved to love Sascha, whom a hundred guys had loved, who'd been loved, as they used to say about beautiful girls with dark hair and star-blue eyes who were also rich and smart, "up and down the eastern seaboard;" it was an impertinence, even from afar. Though with Maisie I then corrected myself to add: it had not always felt like an impertinence. At first I loved her sister with the naive optimism of a boy taking on the world, it was only when I got close to her and could compare, the way say an amateur painter might by putting his work next to an old master's, her looks to mine, her style to mine, her family to mine, her charitableness to mine, even probably her mind to mine, that I despaired.

"What do you think about it now?" Maisie's head for a moment facing down.

"It's who I was then."

"When she died... it didn't release you?"

"It's all bullshit," I said. "I loved her, but it's all bullshit."

"No it's not," she said.

"That's what I was hoping you would say."

"You're so brainwashed," she said.

"Am I? Or am I just what they say? One person then, one person now, a thousand people in-between... I don't know anything."

"You're just chicken to say what you know," she said, and by then we were back on Centre Street.

See you. Thanks for coming. Sorry about you and Bobby.

"You're not sorry."

"I am."

"Thanks for lunch."

"Nada."

"Is the court open to the public? Can I come see you at work?"

"I can't stop you."

"Thanks a lot."

"I wouldn't stop you."

"I don't have anything to do now..."

And so it was that Maisie found a seat in the back row of Part AP-5 of Criminal Court in and for the County of New York and watched me do my civil servant wage-slave job for an afternoon.

Although twenty cases were still on the docket and the D.A. had mostly to face the judge, I never quite forgot she was there. If the lawyers approached for a whispered bench conference, I assumed she had to be bored. When I took a plea or made notations on my calendar, I imagined she might note my professionalism. In this odd little world was I not something? A performer on a two-bit stage, anyway, a man without a text.

Go back. Sense. Maisie out there somewhere with little to do of an afternoon, free, of Hodgkin's, of Bobby, one tough cookie Joe would say, who put old slang in everything the same way some men never change from the dress styles of their youth.

And when Diane, on one occasion, shuttled in and out, did she notice? The downtown Helen, cause of strife and shipwreck.

Maisie in this scenario playing Athena.

Go back. Sense. Don't let her steal your attention. Don't let anyone steal your attention. Plea bargain, issue warrants, postpone, argue, bench conference, clear the calendar, pass the time, the end of day.

And when I turned around she wasn't there. I felt a disappointment. A tree that whistles in the forest alone.

Would I always be alone?

Don't get sentimental.

Don't get grand.

Get back.

To where?

Lost.

Sense.

Maisie out in the corridor with the bailed perps and the spit on the floor, having a cigarette, waiting.

"I needed a smoke."

"It was boring."

"It wasn't."

"You weren't bored?"

"That *guy*? That one guy? Who butchered the cow in his apartment?" Her little enthusiasm lighting up the hall.

We walked uptown together. It began to snow, but so lightly it might have been bits of trash swirled by the breeze from the subway. The first bits-of-trash-snow of the season. The darkening crack of Broadway.

She said she loved to walk in the city even though she knew it was a cliché. She who'd grown up on Fifth Avenue, had known the East Side only, then been sent off to school. Summers in Maine, finally Sarah Lawrence, when she'd take the train in and poke around a little, but that was only two years, and now she was learning her native place for the first time.

I can't say that I was attracted to Maisie. Not in the low—or was it comic—way I went for my various Dianes, nor my reverent, impossible love for Maisie's sister. More a comrade than a friend, Maisie made an ineluctable presence. I liked walking with her, talking with her, she'd been away from the city so long it was as though she was from out of town, yet she was one of us without a doubt. One of the Boston cousins, the same language, the same swagger, the same odd tenderness you get from taking on the impossible. Or maybe tenderness isn't the right word, maybe it's more like exposure, like your skin's exposed to something radioactive, something that will burn.

We got up past the loft and kept walking. We were walking just to walk. The temperature was dropping. Maisie's hands in the thin pockets of her coat, her breath blue in the oncoming night, walking slightly faster than I would, setting a pace that had no purpose, businesslike without business, unless the business was to keep the cold at bay, then at Union Square she said, "Fuck it, I'm taking a cab."

"Where to?"

"Home."

"I'll take the train, then."

"You can come with me if you want. You want to come over?"

She was stopped with her hand out into Fourth Avenue, flapping like a frozen piece of fish for a cab.

Going uptown, stuffed in with the foam padding and anti-robbery plex, I had little choice but to look at her a few times anyway. Each time she looked at me back, which was not usual in the group, where theft of attention was always an issue and eyes were often the culprits. Once I thought she was looking at me with pity.

"Just tell me. The black girl who walked in. With the great body? Did you know her? You know which one I mean? She worked there."

"Why do you ask?"

"Would you stop that *shit*, that group-speak *shit*! I want to know if you're fucking her."

"The one in the dress?"

"The one in the dress, yes."

"Not anymore," I said.

"I knew it! I knew it!"

"Bobby told you."

"Told me what? He told me nothing."

"You're just psychic, then."

"I am. I am psychic."

"She was the one the guy beat me up about," I said.

"Well he can eat shit and die," Maisie said.

The Maclarens' duplex was at Fifth and 83rd, across from the museum, Jackie O. country in the argot of the *Post*. They had every sort of art and every sort of rug, yet it was a comfortable place, as though there was so much space they had the luxury of being civilized about it, even casual, anything but grand, no sensors protecting the Seurats and the Monet, no surfeit of maids scuttling around. Views over the dark mounds of the museum, the West Side beyond the trees lighting up its million eyes.

Odd to me then how little impressed I was. In college I'd been in thrall to the rich, the way scholarship boys get. But I was no longer in college and I embraced poverty now, poverty in pursuit of a goal anyway, money being energy for when you needed it and if you were awake you could always get money. Which may not have been true but there were things that I believed. I trailed Maisie from room to room like a slightly bored tourist. But she wasn't showing off, she could have cared less about any of it, it was a place to stay and she was a natural monk. Her parents were on one of those rich people tours of Antarctica, one tablespoon luxury one teaspoon adventure, and in the meantime Maisie let the maids go off, why shouldn't they have a vacation too?

A picture of Sascha on a table in a sterling frame, younger than I'd ever known her, in Brearley then, Maisie said. Maisie stopped beside me. Look. Sense. Sweet saliva on my tongue. A girl I'd never known, dark eyes, intense stare, eyebrows a little thick as if no thought had yet been given to plucking them, the beginnings of a smile. Sascha had never smiled much but she liked to be made to laugh. The girl in the picture with more hope than the one I knew. A virgin? Maybe, probably. Maisie would have been a little girl then.

We said nothing.

The two sisters are little alike, I thought.

The two sisters are much alike, I thought. Their mouths, maybe. Something defiant.

The corners of their mouths a little downturned, Jeanne Moreau-style.

We continued to say nothing until I said, "Tell me about Bobby."

"No I won't," she said. "You only want me to so you won't feel guilty. Because you know what's going to happen now."

"Do I?"

"Don't you?"

"Anyway I won't feel guilty. No matter what, I won't."

By which I meant I'd feel what I already felt, which Maisie understood, broken down into its constituent parts, the queasy stomach, the tight shoulders, the parched mouth, the hot forehead, and words in my head repeating everything I was not and did not believe and did not truly think, for instance that I was a free man and a strong man and strength and freedom were virtue and virtue is truth and my cock is hard and will not only not be but mustn't be denied, the best of all possible worlds and anyway the way things were.

This we might call guilt. These we might classify, anyway, as manifestations of the emotion. But because we don't attach to it, because we let all of it go and see where it goes and don't care and there's still this other "I" somewhere watching it, "I" the observer, "I" the sensing looking and listening guy, "I" do not feel guilt at all.

Ipso facto proved, and you ought to know it, bitch. Do you want to get fucked by a machine? Only the machine feels guilt, it's a product, a result, a mechanism. "I" am free, Maisie. "I" am free. Or anyway "I" am inchoate and a chance and chances have no feelings.

"But what *about* Bobby, then?"

"Tell me," I said.

"Why should I?"

"You yourself just said."

"What did I say? What *did* I say?"

"You are crazy."

"Of course I'm crazy. I was in McLean's."

When I kissed her, I wasn't kissing her sister. I swore I wasn't and it didn't seem like it. Her green eyes, for one thing. And the voice, and her upper arms firm and a little muscular, her skin so white, and the way she knew so much more than I did but different things from Sascha. Sascha never had reason to know much about me, I was a minor island off the coast of her life. Maisie had already shared my mind, along with thirty other birds.

We kissed a couple times more, her lips a little chapped, our saliva on them like a milky balm.

"We could do this or we could not," she said.

"I know."

We let go of each other's fingertips.

Her face grew foreign to me, exuded unfamiliar detail, a jaw, a downy lip, as if she really were some Irish girl I'd just picked up and I had a sudden urge to go home and hide. Maureen? Is your name Maureen?

My name is Maisie Maclaren and I see right through your shit. Go back. Sense. Her eyes reflecting mine and mine reflecting hers, aqueous, unstable, for a moment almost clear. Love is an action.

Love is kindness, attention, respect.

Love is nothing more.

Now somehow we were in the kitchen and I'd made her an omelet the way Bobby showed me how to make one and she'd poured me more wine from a very good bottle and I asked her about her chemo and her hair, how long it had taken to grow which I thought was a true question but she smacked me in the face.

Pity the poor fella who falls for the wrong sort of girl.

And I wasn't really falling. Not yet, anyway, not now.

"My chemo's none of your fucking asshole business," she screamed at me, as tears streamed down her face. "All right? Okay? A half an inch a month, okay? Okay? My hair."

She was pulling at her hair.

"That's how fast it grows," she screamed, "so do your arithmetic, asshole!"

When she was done screaming, she was kissing me, our cheeks and lips brined with her tears. Sex with Maisie was easy and comprehensive, it lasted as long as we wished and we came or not as we wished and we tore at each other and cried and retreated as we wished and the only fissures in "we" were the ones, for kicks, we allowed: love is an action, love is kindness attention and respect.

Yes? No?

Is "comprehensive" too cold a word for sex?

But it wasn't then.

Yes. Yes. Maisie. Sweet crazy Maisie, whose sister I'd known and loved like a troubadour's apprentice and now I was with Maisie.

Rich girl poor little et cetera with Hodgkin's and short hair and chemo, all better now Maisie.

No liberation in our bodies, but rather the truth that our bodies are with us. We lay where we fell, on a rug somewhere in one of the rooms of which there were too many and I remember on the ceiling there was a little crack like in the *Madeline* book, Maisie pointed it out to me, raised her hand towards it, as if pointing up to God, and I knew what she was talking about.

She loved that crack in the ceiling, she said, it was the only thing wrong in the whole apartment.

It was like a holy idiot, I thought without words, and I told her I thought that without words and she said she was going to tell me about Bobby because she could see I was his friend and she could see I wasn't guilty.

I who, when it was Maisie's sister I'd loved, had never kissed her once nor even tried.

But after Sascha was dead, her husband my friend who knew

I had the crush said next time I mustn't roll over, next time I should fight for love.

And ever since I'd been screwing whoever but hadn't been in love and gave up being in love but also gave up certain qualms, in keeping with the common superstition that people grow up or anyway get older.

You must be capable of taking everything. You must prove to yourself you can take everything. For if you're not capable of taking it, how can you truly give anything away?

I said to Maisie, in words more or less, yes, tell me this tale of Bobby my friend that I might hold him close to my heart, in generosity and trust.

But she must have changed her mind again because all she could tell me was that Bobby only liked to fuck her in the ass and she didn't like being fucked in the ass. "He likes fucking his mother in the ass," she said. "Can you believe that? Is that sick or what?"

"But you're not his mother," I said. "Not really."

"You're *so* literal."

"That's not all there is to it," I said.

But she turned away from me. "It's all I know."

"Why did you tell me such an ugly little thing?" I said, "I wished you'd left it at 'He keeps telling me he loves me.'" When I said it I was thinking she was going to bite my dick off but actually she cried.

"Hold me," she said, "just hold me you jerk," and I did.

9

Bobby and I, history and background.

There was no real rivalry between us. How could there be? In each area where our lives appeared to carry on in parallel, so that comparisons might be made, Bobby was way down the track, so far ahead that we might have been like two of Gurdjieff's worlds, one composed of matter so much finer than the other that the only way the one might appear in the other's perceptual universe was as a sort of shadow, a faint suggestion of its genuine self.

But for a long time I didn't see it that way. Like a nation of modest resources trying to avoid confrontation through diplomatic means, I suppressed my instincts for rivalry by developing the notion that we were complementary figures, the way they sometimes say of partners that it takes both of them to make one good man. I aspired to what I settled on as Bobby's lopsidedness, his loopy brilliance which captured the attention of Joe and Philip and the *New Yorker* and every Harvard kid who ever saw his lamppost, and he, in my jujitsu configuration of it, aspired to my normality. Bobby was one who flaked out on appointments, quit jobs, lost whatever money he had, and rubbed the skin off his knuckles as soon as the scabs from the last time he did it began to heal. None of these were considered adaptive traits for the group's spiritual mountain climbing, so Bobby strove to "grow up." Could I who paid my bills on time help Bobby to "grow up?" Could that have been in Joe's mind when he assigned me to be Bobby's assistant in the kitchen? It dawned on me only in the course of the group's slow expansion, as Joe with his ad in the *Voice* stocked us with all sorts of normal types—he interviewed every applicant and more than once mentioned how he tossed out the "crazies"—that "normality," in terms relative to Bobby or even to me, was not so hard to come by. It represented the norm, after all. Bobby was soon making friends with Big Ronald the commodities trader and Julie the receptionist at Cahill, Gordon and Greg the appliance salesman downtown whom Joe met while buying a new TV. In comparison, I with my Yale apparatus and complicated writing fantasies, the days and years spent in my room feeling superior to most of humankind, hardly qualified as a paragon of "normal." Bobby didn't need my help to grow up. At the same time, he was obviously Joe's pet project. Philip was Joe's ally and confidante, but Joe doted on Bobby.

༄

Then what did Bobby need me for at all? He didn't "need" me, but I think he liked me. And it may have been that he had a need for people to like. I was like a throwback to his past, a link to more indolent days. We shared a commitment to one of Joe's principles that others more honored in the breach, namely that one must accept nothing on faith, but only what has been proved beyond doubt to one's own satisfaction. Who was it, which Protestant theologian, said the essence of faith is doubt? Tillich? Niebuhr? Some saint of the twentieth century, some gray name from college, his modernity etched in the makeshift eternity of the trade paperback. I've forgotten so much,

I forget nearly everything, the ends of movies, the middle of books, lines of poetry which I claim to love, and the names of the people I met at dinner last week. But somehow not that phrase. Bobby reminded me of it on one of the first walks we took together. We walked, we were *flaneurs* of the spirit, aristocrats of the streets. We still talked about Kierkegaard, for God's sake. Had Joe ever heard of Kierkegaard? Those lines of Baudelaire Bobby quoted to him. Joe was not a learned man. There were moments when I felt with Bobby that we were like medieval monks, storing the learning of the ages for future generations. We were subversives in a way. Joe's theory was that too much interference of the intellect spoiled the chances of the whole Self. And moreover that the chief flaw of our age and place was the over-domination of the intellectual factor. People were thinking themselves to death. No wonder intellectuals were so unhappy. Theorizing and intellectualizing and idle talk untethered to a practice, a tradition, a group, an inner search, a body evolving self-consciousness, were useless. Yet Bobby and I kept talking, about whoever and whatever, again like medieval monks who dedicated their lives to reconciling the Church with Aristotle, trying to find points of contiguity between the group and the world, reassurances, proof.

Of course from another perspective it was Joe who was the true subversive, understanding the whole world differently from most, and Bobby and I were merely trimmers, a reactionary faction, unwilling to commit to what our eyes and ears and hearts told us was so, but which our brains, like the last of the bourgeoisie, resolutely feared.

The Chinese curse, to live in interesting times.

We stayed, week to week and year to year, because of one thing we were certain: otherwise we were doomed.

We had not come to Joe, either of us, until we were disappointed by life.

We continued placing our two dollar bets on the world, playing for the glittering prizes.

But we were seekers after all.

༄

He was the one, at the outset, who held his hand out to me. "Why don't you come over to Joe's on Saturday? You might find it interesting."

"Why? What's going on?"

"It might explain a few things."

This at a time when the Thursday evening readings at Philip's were spinning my mind like a top. They had become the highlight of my week, a point of new departure.

Bobby was pimping for Joe, I suppose you could say. But I never saw it that way. Rather, I saw Bobby as my backer, the one who must first have seen my possibilities, who tossed my hat in the ring. Not everyone from the Thursday night readings was asked to come on Saturdays. On account of Bobby I became once again a part of a privileged sector.

༄

If there was no true rivalry between Bobby and me, then there was none for the affection of Philip. A syllogism of the distracted. Philip had gotten Bobby his gigs at the *New Yorker*, the cartoons, a couple of Talk pieces, a casual in which Philip wrote the text and Bobby did the drawings. With the *Bird Guide* it was the same. It was as if Philip was grooming him in the literary world just as Joe was grooming him in the spiritual one. As above, so below. Thus my sense of contained miracle the night Philip asked me to write a Talk story with him. It was as if I'd sat in the back of the class waiting to be recognized, or on the bench, a third-string quarterback getting old—but abruptly and with scarcely an explanation in the last quarter of the Superbowl, introducing number thirty-three. . . the PA like a sonic boom, the slutty cheerleaders in a pat routine of legs and flounces.

༄

"Maisie and I got together," I said to him the next afternoon at the Sloan's on Eighth Street.

"Go for it," Bobby said. Cheerful and supportive, as if he expected anywhere he went that I would follow, even that it was part of a plan. In accord with the old dictum: you can't advance without placing someone on the step you now occupy. "Has she acted crazy yet?"

I shrugged because I didn't want to say.

"Of course, she's crazy."

"We're all crazy," I replied, feeling uncomfortably manly and full of shit, not believing any longer than it took me to hear my words, their false declarativeness, their reach for the aphoristic, that eliding Bobby's world into mine would somehow patch things up.

"Some more crazy than others. Well, bonk her for me."

Bobby was buying Häagen-Dazs for Joe. He paid with Joe's money, like a child sent to the store. I looked at him as he waited for change. No hint of anything but a resolute goodwill. No negative emotions from this boy. The beginnings of a smile, white teeth.

We came back to the loft and chopped vegetables for most of an hour. Our blades were very sharp that day.

"Don't be embarrassed," Bobby said finally.

"About what?"

"What you were just thinking," he said, but I couldn't think what that was.

☙

The provenance of the group.

The Old Painter: studied with Gurdjieff people somewhere in rural Pennsylvania, but also his mother was a Freudian shrink.

Joe: studied with the Old Painter, but also at an ashram in India, which later he called a waste of time. Both grandfathers, rabbis.

Philip: before Joe arrived at his apartment, had been involved with Sufi study groups led by a psychologist at UC Davis who was among the pioneers of "left brain/right brain" thinking, which itself, in certain circles, was held to be a Sufi idea. The psychologist himself was said to have contacts with, or have been acting at the behest or instruction of, a nine hundred-year-old dervish school in Marrakesh that had also opened a "branch" in England. Philip began the story readings in his apartment, as well as the *Bird Guide*, in furtherance of his involvement with the left brain/right brain psychologist, whom he also promoted in various articles, in the *Times* and elsewhere, into something of a national figure.

But once Joe arrived at Philip's, he took over. Sufi stories continued to be read, but with less piety and mysterious conviction, and perhaps with less poetry as well. A strain entered, but never a total break, in the relationship between Philip and the left brain/right brain psychologist.

Thus, many streams made the Ganges.

It is said the teacher finds you and not the other way around.

Sometimes I tried, with arrows, to draw this provenance in my head, searching for reassurance, reliability, the chances of truth. I may as well have been playing tic-tac-toe.

☙

Joe on self-understanding:

"Why bother?

"Really, it's worthless.

"It's the most worthless thing in the world. What can you do with it?

"That's one way of looking at it, anyway.

"You have to decide for yourself. One way or another, you have to pay for it. It doesn't come cheap. What are you willing to pay for something so worthless?

"The pearl of great price."

10

Joe loved his Christmas tree as only a kike from Brooklyn could. He shaped it with his Swiss pruners like a patient haircutter confronting an unusually shaped head, clipping tufts and outcroppings, patting and circling and standing slightly back. He fed it daily rations of soluble plant food, little sachets of pink crystals. He doted on its decoration, pulling his Eames chair up and playing Bing Crosby as he sat before it with the blank, well-fed gaze of satisfaction that men in corduroy pants more typically reserve for a crackling fire, as though Joe understood the tree lights to be nothing other than a visual avatar of fire's warmth. Joe whose take on Jesus included prominently the fact that he was a kike like himself, who moreover like himself would not have denied his kikedom even while proclaiming understandings that drove the priests and rabbis nuts. "Only a kike from Nazareth," one in a line of great saints that have appeared here and there throughout the length of human history, but more often than not below history's granite gaze, the difference with Jesus being that he was discovered or remembered, great p.r. whatever. An incarnation, as we all might be if we but knew it, if we could only discover our true selves we would be as little selfish as he, because our self would be other than the false self for which we'd been selfish. Jesus in the abstract, untethered to church, available to all, merciful and not jealous, in some singsong echo of a speech writer's dream asking not for your belief but your understanding. Jesus on the cross?

Okay for those long skinny types but Joe himself would have been too heavy for a cross. It would have taken quite a skilled carpenter of crucifixes, or quite a lot of extra nails, to hold him up there. Or in all events he would not have looked good crucified, his agony would not have got its due, his belly and arms sagging, his face disappearing in his neck, his rotundity zeroing out the cross's stern lankness. No, better if you were Joe to sit cross-legged under a bodhi tree. But it was his Christmas tree that he loved, pagan symbol, clad in the forest's moist and furry mystery, redolent of rebirth, the thing he didn't have as a kid.

Liddie and Big Ronald had gone shopping for it and come back with one ten feet tall. Joe wanted it near the TV, perhaps so that he could always have it in his sight. It was gaudy as hell by the time we were finished with it: good taste and moderation were for us like lapsed aims from another, failed universe, Joe kept exclaiming it didn't look Italian enough, or *now* it looked Italian, kept asking Liddie if it yet looked like a tree out of her Queens childhood, Liddie would nod yes or no, and the tinseling and popcorning and stringing of feathery golden boas, as if it were Mae West we were dressing, would continue. In the group, everything was a lesson, that might return us at any instant to the question of consciousness, and the tree was no exception. Joe insisted that we apply tinsel to it one strand at a time. No draping of handfuls over branches as if in the lazy arrogance of our human power we could bring silver waterfalls instantly into being, no industrialized, sleep-made Christmas tree for us. No, our tinsel would be applied with a Pre-Raphaelite, or Japanese, care, as though we were tending to a forest of bamboo, making sure it was thinned so every tree could be seen. Each strand of tinsel must have its own being. None can lie on top of any other.

This was an experiment for life, after all. This was a training to see, to be. All existence a slender reed, a tinsel strand, a chance, or nothing at all.

Saturday morning, twelve of us over at the loft, myself and Philip and Cal and Bobby and Valerie and Julie and Ty Duncan, Big Ronald, Colin Folger the saxophonist, Laura the barkeep at the topless bar on 33rd Street, and Joe. And Maisie. Somebody had brought doughnuts. Maurice Chevalier on the tape deck now, wry, slightly ridiculous and rouged, like a beautiful pedophile found out, and after Mo a Donkey Serenade and band of faux mariachis. There wasn't room around even so large a tree for all of us to crowd at once, so three or four at any one moment would approach, emissaries in motley hues, reluctant Magi, to lay on our gifts, our sacrificial offerings. All the rest of us using our eyes looking for spots that might love a strand, lifting the tinsel off its cardboard racks as patiently as monks raising a sand mandala, so that not a single strand would be lost.

Essential also to our dance that we used the same boxes of tinsel, the same cardboard racks, that we'd used the year before, and after New Year's we would again remove the tinsel from the tree strand by strand, drape each filament back on the scarecrow cardboard racks, like pants that had been pressed, and place the racks in their flimsy cardboard boxes for next year.

A strand of tinsel adheres to my pathetically pink finger. I sense its feathery embrace, sense the moisture of my finger offering it a tentative adhesion. When I move my hand, the tinsel resists, glinting slivers of wings, blown in the turbulence created by my movement. As if offering the reassurance of accompaniment, I cup my other hand beneath it, I sense the tinsel tickling my palm. I begin to hate Joe for this torture, this absurdity. Why bother with any of it where was it getting me nowhere while the world rushed by people getting ahead it's Saturday for chrissake I could be out shopping. If only I had a little money, which is Joe's fault too though I don't remember exactly how. Stop. Go back. Sense the tree the greeny whispered scent the tinsel borne aloft no fuck you pardon me excuse me but fuck you fuck the tinsel April is hardly the cruelest month the month that is the cruelest month is the month between Thanksgiving and New Year's joy drawn too tight for comfort turkeys tossed across the table domestic beefs murders and cheap toys break. The warm part of Joe, the *heimische* mothering psychologizing part, embraced the worst shit theory of the holidays, to wit that's when the worst shit comes up because that's where it lies. Suffer, you bastards, seek repentance and forgiveness because you can't help but seek them, but follow whatever comes up. Well, I am sick of it now, I am sick of all of it, I will not sense and yet I do, the more easily the more I urge myself not to. I place my tinsel on a lower branch. I sense the bending of my knees, the leaning of my torso. I extend my finger like a docking station to the branch and drop away, leaving the tinsel hung like a silent film comic on a flagpole.

I do my job! So don't ask me *how* I do it! And yet. . . And yet. . . I sense all this. I think I let it go. My rage, that is, if that's what it is, my fight, my defiance, my sadness. It floats off like the tinsel from my finger. It is lighter than air after all. My sense that Joe, too much like my secret self, is embarrassing.

Joe rails about us not having enough tinsel. If we hadn't wasted it and broken it last year, we'd have enough now. If we were conscious, if we sensed ourselves, we wouldn't break it. Now we have to go buy more tinsel and next year we'll have to buy still more, and it could go on and on, forever. Did we expect the group to go on forever? It would not go on forever, he guaranteed us that. It would go on only so long as it was useful, for the time and the place, and then it would be gone. How did we feel about that? What did we sense? Missing mom?

"Work, you bastards. Get this tree fucking decorated!" Joe's meat grinder laugh seeping more subtly into his railing, until, achieving a critical mass of infiltration, it overwhelms it and takes it prisoner.

Were we fools to take him seriously?

He meant no harm.

Zen master's stick.

Joe asked who wanted to go to the dime store for more tinsel and because I was dying to get out I said me.

He retrieved from his pocket a ten dollar bill which he managed to finger so that it folded down lengthwise like an inverted "v." I took it thinking how old-fashioned Joe was, that the provision of cash still inspired flourishes in him. Cash was king when he grew up, when his father had the dry cleaners. Or was the flourish an act too?

"So. Now we know who wants to get out of here."

I sensed myself grinning like a wooden doll, primitive, untutored, with my mouth painted red.

Up until then I'd scarcely paid attention to Maisie, Comrade Maisie my new squeeze, in the room but not of it, tinseling the tree like all the rest of us. Nor had I noticed if Bobby stole glances her way, or if like moons of attraction they came close. I knew she hadn't come close to me, not so that I sensed the heat of her or the sweet brush of her hair. That is, until I was at the elevator my toes pushing into my loafers, and I caught a sidelong glance of her olive coat, flashing and stretching out, like a forest animal waking up. "Gotta go," she said to Joe. "Gotta go uptown." We left in the elevator and I kissed her.

Her saliva as though we'd just met, foreign with coffee and cigarettes and a burnt unfamiliar taste of cinnamon, street girl in the elevator, eyes open and fluorescent-lit, her lips chapped and cool.

As though to beg the question why kiss at all, but in the street she took my hand.

O Maisie what shall we do today, shall we to Banbery Faire, or to Lamston's and buy tinsel?

A break in the weather, in the forties. Jackets loose, people in the shops, bags, bustle, Salvation Army guys, more than enough terror of the situation to go around, dear Maisie, but let us pay it no mind, shall we?

"That's *plenty* of tinsel."

"*This*?"

"Four boxes? Come on. How much are they?"

"Dollar nineteen."

"Plenty."

"Okay."

"Fuck it."

"*What*?"

"I don't want to go back there."

"You don't have to."

"Come with me."

"What about the tinsel?"

"Fuck the tinsel. Really. Let's go home. It's so nice out. You want to walk? We'll walk fast."

One reason not to go back being to test the torque of my resistance, to see how guilty I'll feel.

But why should I feel guilty at all?

"Why should you?" she said.

"I've gone through this before with you," I said.

For profaning my deepest wishes, slighting my seriousness, muddying my purpose, sullying the finery of the ragged cloak that I bring to my would-be self?

"They don't need the tinsel. He's got like what, eight boxes? The thing looks like a lamé dress. Trust me, he will *not* care."

"The devil with red hair made me do it."

The plastic air of Lamston's, as if every product on its shelves were emitting a gaseous residue of itself. Pay for tinsel with crisp ten-spot, get ass pinched by Maisie and I don't know why or if anybody saw.

Walking uptown fast, film of the city speeded up. Like two escaped convicts now, the biggest thing they hold in common their shared escape. Back to Maisie's parents' place where we can fuck on any rug. "You like to defile," I say.

"I think I do."

Reason to fuck her again.

Green eyes and freckles, green eggs and ham. "You're not my type," I say, and she says the same back to me.

"Jewish boys. I don't know."

"Fuck yourself then."

"Go take your tinsel, go, go, they're waiting."

"You said they wouldn't be."

"I lied."

Instead the phone rings and it's Bobby, who knew, he says, we'd be here.

Lying on Maisie's breastbone between her puppy ear breasts, I can hear the cadences of his words like distant calls, of departing trains or planes. Maisie chirpy and easy with him, her husky voice a slather of possibilities. Did he want to come up? What was he doing? What were *we* doing? Just goofing around. It's such a nice day. The tinsel's on hold. She's a bad influence, she's teaching me how to be bad. Sure. Okay. Why don't we just blow this popsicle stand?

Which in the end is what we did. We met him on the steps of the museum. He had on the ratty camel coat, so oversized it made him look like a waif, that he'd bought off a *kif* merchant in Cairo in the vague understanding that a British diplomat from an unspecified era had left it behind. There was no tension to the three of us together. If anything we were closer than we'd been, as if a clingy fatalism, a web spun of erotic vectors, bound us now. Three little lambs who showed no negative emotion, who let everything go. The world is our oyster, we shall not want. Bobby slipping in between us like a brother or a son. Bobby, as well, who could make us laugh just by being there, his sly smile, mustard smear on his lip, eating a hot dog, in his ratty tent of a coat.

Why had I gotten involved with Maisie at all? He must have cared for her so much more, he would have doted on her. Pity is hatred. Do not. Stop. Go back.

Her choice. Maisie's. I'd had nothing to do with it. Had I? We sat on the cold of the stone steps, runaways who were about to be runaways again, pound puppies, call the dog catcher, has anyone seen his cartoon car?

Situation without words. Pale sun filtered through the bare trees. The rivers of museumgoers, their pant legs, the hems of their coats, their shoes roughed by the winter, trickling to either side of us. As if unwittingly revealing something intimate about themselves, their lives from the knees down, neither sordid nor inspired, the workaday parts. We were laconic by then, a mystery to ourselves. "I've got a car," Maisie said, and it seemed like all that needed to be said.

Why?

Because.

It was as though for a little while we were saying to each other, without words, you matter more to me than this group, this process, this Joe and all of it. You matter to me as people matter to each other.

A rebellion that could spread like wildfire, people remembering that they were alive.

But wasn't that the whole point of the group to begin with?

It all felt like a holiday in an Italian movie where you take your girl on the streetcar to the end of the line.

Driving north on Route 9, 9J or 9 or 9W, we were seldom sure which, the old road through the Hudson River towns, Peekskill and Cornwall and Tivoli, the denuded valley of December.

Maisie's father's BMW with low number plates, a four door scooter in black, Bobby in the back seat with the tinsel that I carried with me like my lunch.

By three o'clock the sun was slanty and low. Maisie liked to drive, both hands on the wheel, as though it was all between herself and the road. She passed a lot of slow vans. I fidgeted the dial and found some mournful country station the others seemed to like. All the while finding that the faster we drove away, the easier it was to sense. As though the hardest thing about sensing looking and listening was trying to do it; if you didn't try, it happened easily enough. But then why do people pass their lives daydreaming?

I remembered Stuart Little, driving north in his little car, looking for Margalo, the bird who flew away.

Choking on the truest moments of my childhood.

I'd grown up around here, for awhile anyway. Westchester suburbs, closer to the city, but we'd drive up this way to look at the trains along the Hudson route and I'd taken this road, as well, with my mother to her parents' upstate when my father went away. We left everything behind.

Go back. Sense. For several seconds at a time my mind is like an empty mirror. I say this to myself, I become aware, in words, that my mind is blank, I rue the words, I go back. This must be a world record, no don't get grand, call it personal best, my personal best several seconds of clarity no words in my head that I'm aware of. Until once again I say it to myself and go back.

Is this not profound progress?

All you need to do is run away.

Bobby's legs up on the back seat like an odalisque. "Hear the boy talk. Hear the boy talk. Can he talk? He can talk."

"What?"

"If you do something, you think, 'I've done something,' right? Big fat whale big sack of mouth swallowing you up. 'You think you *did* something? Yeah. Sure.' What are we doing here?"

"I'm driving. You're sounding like a stoned monkey."

"My mistress speaks. I'm going to shut up."

Which he did for a little while, but he started again. Talking with his hands, but liltingly so, as if conducting an orchestra of himself, Bobby the back seat conductor. "Will the *New Yorker* buy a cartoon of the void? This is an existential question. If the *New Yorker* won't buy it, does it exist? I was thinking, if I made it really cute. A cute void. Acute void."

Trying too hard to have something to say, I said, "You know those maps from when the world was flat? And the ships fall off if they sail too far, it looks like the ship's going over a waterfall? Like that, maybe?"

But it sounded rehearsed, the air around the words controlled and organized.

Bobby a quiet odalisque.

"Make it like a pussy," Maisie offered. "A. pussy sells, b. what's this void shit if not a pussy? You don't hear women obsessing about voids."

"Was I obsessing, glorious mistress?"

"You were, a little."

"Forget voids. Forget it. Forget voids. What about. . . 'Dr. J. and his Flock, or The Cartoonist Goes Into Therapy?' Tune in next week to see how Dr. J. manages to set up what to the untrained eye appears to be a cute little family circle, eliciting from his desperately injured patients their desperate need for approval from him, which he can then, panel two, turn around, they see their transference, they're *cured*! Wow! And now it's the week after next, panel three, and having been cured, all their fears and their hatred, their insecurity, their abject longing all relegated to the harmless closet of non-attachment, they're ready to take on. . . go out and do battle. . . big action sequence . . . special effects. . . Forbidden Planet. . . panels four, five and six. . . the Void! Returned in a new secret guise. Dr. Void, doing battle with Dr. J!"

A little north of Albany, on whatever road we were on, we found a motel of cabins with electric heaters. It was already late and there was no TV and we'd been eating in the car. There was only one bed, which we knew going in, but Bobby slept on the far corner of it and Maisie I suppose maybe slept a little closer to me than to him, except when she rolled over. Did their feet touch then?

At one or two Bobby sat up like the guy in his favorite John Held cartoon of Christmas in wherever it was, the asylum, the quarantine, the "pest house," and started talking again, as though he hadn't stopped from the car. "But did you know *this*?. . . Joe's got quite a flat ass. Try drawing it sometime. What fools we be! In the course of my apprenticeship have I not gone to the store 617 times, washed 4,112 dishes, cleaned the toilet bowl eighty-seven times, taken clothes to the Laundromat thirty-one times, how did I know all this, am I a mad autistic genius? No, a simple parlor trick, I keep track of how cheap I am. A fine spiritual exercise, the very doing of it supplies you with the proof of its existence. You know what else I keep track of? How many girlfriends I had before. Three. Not including one whore in Pamplona, Spain while everybody else was running with the bulls. On this basis I could say you were my number one, my love. Oh do not quibble over the meaning of love, my love. Let us not demean ourselves with mere words. I know what I meant to you. I'm under no illusions. But in the morning I want a pancake breakfast."

I thought for a moment Bobby looked my way, plaintive, even contrite.

Maisie slept a little closer to me after that.

Rumpled and breathy, we were up early in the dark and found a diner open for the hunters.

We picked up the Taconic Parkway when we could, smooth over hill and dale, and drove south. Bobby sang a song of his own creation, a plaintive recitative, in which he seemed to be apologizing to Maisie. "Mama threw me from a high high building and I landed on your back. Can I put suntan lotion on your soul?" But she was ignoring him now. Driving, both hands on the wheel. Joe was still in his bathrobe when we arrived. I handed him the tinsel and his change. He said, "Thank you" with that old-fashioned flourish where the "k" becomes the first letter of "you," and in general acted as if we'd been gone twenty minutes. Like one of those moments where a postcard's mailed in 1948 and half a century later the post office finds it in some dubious place hiding in plain sight and delivers it with a one cent stamp.

It was a day of NFL playoffs. Maisie left but Bobby and I stayed, and we added to the overdressed tree, one strand of tinsel at a time. My eye found little places. The overcrowding seemed to dissipate. It seemed a miracle how much room there was in the world. Joe watched the football. Nothing more was said about any of it.

11

Is there something eternal to be found in each of us or is there not?

And if there is, what price shall we pay to find it?

What price shall we not pay?

Shall we not bet the farm?

And if we're not sure whether there's something eternal in us or if there's not, what shall we do then?

Shall we shut our eyes and assume the worst?

Shall we claim as beliefs things we don't believe?

How else define what's ignoble in man, except by this pitiful sleep, this endless hypocrisy?

We thirty birds were not believers but on our best days we were not ignoble either. On our best days the thought of transcendence drove us on, causing us to endure humiliation, doubt, embarrassment.

Each of us sensing that we must look like fools.

What was it about Joe that made us sense he was a good bet?

His watery eyes, his baritone voice, the easy assurance of his manner when he came to Philip's? His seeming knowledge of "groups," of Rumi, of Gurdjieff? His lineage through the Old Painter? His talent for guessing people's minds? His ability to take Julie's migraines away when no one or nothing else could, the light touch of his fingers, here, there, who could tell how or why, he did it once in the middle of a meeting, oddly like the guy from Saint Vincent's? His laugh, his imperturbability? The fact that others saw something in him?

Some turn loaves into fishes. Others turn our perceptions of loaves and fishes.

He did not hold any of us prisoner. We might have walked away.

But did any of us have a better bet for saving our skins, or if not our skins our souls, or if not our souls then something unnamable, that was nonetheless in us?

༄

That which senses, looks and listens.

That which is everywhere, so that if we sense it deeply enough the barrier of our skin seems to lessen, it's still there but it isn't so fatal, there's more and still more of us, we are everywhere, you could not kill us with a stick.

Though someday the universe may run down. Even the scientists will tell you that.

But if it runs down, will not Brahman breathe again?

In breath, out breath.

What had we to lose, really? A house in the suburbs, cars and money, assumptions, conventions, beliefs, unhappy histories with parents, the sadness of sickness without friends, sexual urges that hardly knew they were alive, that were as atrophied as everything else?

Stop. Please. Listen to me.

We were not crazy.

Quite.

Though "we" may have been the biggest myth of all.

Gurdjieff said the ways of escape were four. The way of the monk, which was the way of faith. The way of the yogi, which was the way of mind control. The way of the fakir, which was the way of physical transformation. And the way of the sly man.

☙

And whether he was right or not. And who cared whether he was right or not.
But we were in our twenties and God was dead and we were looking to make the best of it.

☙

The cult of the individual.
The curse of the individual.
The chance of the individual.
Like mountaineers roped to one another.

☙

It is possible to be an atheist. It is possible to believe in the finality of death.

☙

It is possible to believe in alchemy. It is possible to believe in any damn thing.

But don't go crazy. Go back. Look. Sense.

The world is all around us.

They say the New Age died, but we were never "New Age." Go away with your astrology and veggieism. Go away with your acid. Go away with your droopy hair, hard rock, counter cult, pop cult clichés. Go away with your touchy-feely. Go away with your tendency to blab everything.

A few good men wanted. No bullshit. A few women as well.

༄

My favorite quotation of all, the most pertinent, the one to hang on a wall, a ballplayer said it: "It's great to be young and a Giant."

༄

When will I write my Talk story with Philip, about the angel of Saint Vincent's?

When will I fuck Maisie again?

When will I be sick with envy over this and that?

When will I ever see Joe as neither good nor bad nor good nor evil nor yes nor no nor anything but that he is and I am and we are?

Love is what, say again?

Transcendence, bud.

All about transcendence.

You don't want it, don't pay your two dollars.

And the millennial edifices, the great religions, the work of the blood and piety of billions: how dare stand up to those?

We weren't standing up to them. We were sneaking into their secret heart.

☙

Say again, why Joe?

Because he was there.

Because he flattered us, or we imagined that he flattered us, that we might be there too.

Because we worried that we weren't "there."

Because once you start on something and make friends and your life gets used to its new assumptions, it's hard to leave. Even the habit of being unhabitual is hard to give up.

Or because we still believed in Santa Claus?

☙

A bird in a cage longs for freedom. It falls down and plays dead. Its owner opens its cage to remove it and the bird flies off.

Margalo, Stuart Little's love?

Not quite, perhaps, but close enough.

☙

O do not say we are alone.

12

Joe on piety:

"Don't trust the pious ones. They're full of shit. Maybe that works in some places. But not in New York. Here we muck around. Here we go down in the plumbing.

"I look at one of the pious ones, all their talk about 'enlightenment.' What I usually see is anger, hatred, fear. Unacknowledged, of course.

"Give me a good hater. That we can work with.

"And don't talk to me about 'enlightenment.' I hear that word, I want to go take a bath."

13

It was the day before Christmas, we were in my apartment, behind the robbery gates, on the narrow bed, she was on her side with her head propped on the faded corduroy pillow we'd borrowed from my writing chair, and Maisie said let's masturbate.

Her hand reached between her thighs and rested there, in the folds of the dark fabric of her skirt. "Can you do it without fantasizing?" she said.

"I can't do anything without fantasizing," I said.

"Okay, but mostly not fantasizing."

"I'll try, Maisie. Just for you."

"Really, it's better. You'll see."

"Jesus. Miss Patronizing Bitch."

"I thought you didn't know."

"But I do."

"Then take off your pants," she said, in a way that was sharp like some kitschy prison guard in a porn movie yet sweet and coaxy enough.

I took off my pants and she pulled down hers, we hadn't touched each other once.

"How should we do this?" I said.

"Are you stupid?"

"I mean, should we do it together? Should one of us go first? Should we look at each other? Are we supposed to get excited by each other, or just by the physical sensations?"

"Good questions."
"So high and mighty. So quick to fly off."
"Okay, okay, you made your point."
"I say. . . you go first."
"I say you."
"Why me?"
"Because. Men always come first."
"Is that a joke?"
"You don't have to *come*, you know. You don't have to *get off*. Didn't you ever hear of seminal retention?"
"I like to come."
"Do you use spit?"

I did use spit. But I hadn't always. Spit came with the group. "Try spit," Joe said once, not to me, but I did. And I found that spit had many virtues. It brought you close to your body, you could smell its breathy, mucousy odor on your hand, it was all-natural, it was free, it left no residue, it was slippery wet in a way that even "love oils" were not, and there was plenty of it, the more excited you became about anything, the more of it you produced. Spit in a way being emblematic of what to us masturbation was about: if you want to love others, love yourself first; practice on yourself. And if you want others to love you, don't go to them needy, go to them with a belly well-fed and a spirit bright with satisfaction. People smell neediness and run away. People are too weak to love others' weakness. Masturbation, as well, an opportunity to discover the secret workings of the flesh, the glands, the nervous system. And what else, anything else? Independence, self-reliance? The refutation of old, false shibboleths that were society's propaganda? If you jerked off dry, less tactile pleasure, fewer nerve endings, were available to you, so you were more likely to fantasize, substitute memory and image for sensation, put a veil between yourself and your body.

I told her I used spit. She put her fingers to her tongue and wet them. She was businesslike, she was doing nothing to excite me, she was looking at her hand which glistened pinkly. Her legs lay apart like logs. All of this could have happened in a hospital bed. I couldn't see at first where she placed her fingers. All I could see was the movement of her wrist, flapping motions, rhythmic but not urgent. I began to hear her fingers slosh around then she brought them back to her mouth for more spit. I turned myself around so that I could see between her legs. She raised her knees up. Her labia were dilated and scarlet. She resumed stroking at the knot of their convergence. An easy enough thing to hold my eyes' attention, but could I remember to sense my arms and legs and to listen? Stop. Go back. Gently. Sense. I wasn't sexually aroused.

For a moment I wondered what Maisie must be feeling. Why did I wonder this and what business could it be of mine? I could not know. Maisie less than others. Comrades do not know one another, comrades have too much respect to penetrate the veil or was "comrade" one more excuse for my pitiful isolation?

What? Who says? Whose pitiful isolation? *Our* pitiful isolation. The world's pitiful isolation. Not me, Jack, don't count me in or out.

Her torso slightly arched now, tensed, like a bridge in the wind. Her jaw hard and her lips apart. I could see Maisie's tongue. What phenomena were these that I observed? How piece them together in a narrative of love?

I didn't ask. I declined to ask. Looking up at her from below, a landscape of hills and dales, nostrils of fire.

Different angles, Maisie, I see you from different angles, Maisie the tigress, Maisie the mountain, Maisie the *kore* lying where she fell, millennia ago, dreaming of her Buddha-boy.

When she made a noise, it was funny, really. The word closest to it being a squeak, Maisie squeaked like something you hear alive in the walls of an apartment, then her fingers went down like miners into their hole and stayed there and when they came out, slow and warm, she was as quiet as a vigil.

Her eyes settled on me without eros or even curiosity, but only as though to say: so what did you see? Her green eyes the eyes of a fish, quiet and ancient.

Are you, did you, I said and hesitated, not being very smart.

For a moment then, and I didn't know why, but my vision expanded until we were both in a picture from Delft or Rotterdam. "The Artist and His Model." "The Studio." "The Quiet Morning." A curl of satisfaction, as if after love, in the girl's smile?

For a moment there was so little to separate us.

And yet still I had no idea about her. All I had was a picture.

Your turn, Maisie said, as if I didn't know.

Portrait of the Artist as a Young Self-Pleasurer, though I was feeling no pleasure then, but rather the anxiety of performance before an audience of one.

Had I not always been a prude? Had I not always feared embarrassment? I remembered these accusations then, though not where they came from. Perhaps they came from nowhere.

Go back. Gently. Sense.

I mustn't let her steal my attention. I mustn't let my hand my eye my dick go to her.

Maisie in repose, her green eyes the eyes of a fish, so what will she see?

I did not want her approval.

Of course I wanted her approval.

But why did I want her approval?

I felt insane, a child's mind in a child's body in a world where people were supposed to have grown.

What happened to me? Why was I left behind?

Maisie help me kiss me adore me. No.

Stop. Go back.

She is here but so are the walls, so is the number five bus outside, its diesel heaves, its downtown passengers going up or maybe its uptown passengers going down, its bus driver with her ham sandwich in the bag behind her back.

Go back. Gently. Sense. Arms. Legs. The world.

Maisie a little light station in its midst but do not be blinded, do not cry, be a man.

Why jerk off?

Why not?

Go back. The wash of guilt. A wave and then it flattens on the beach.

A wave that recapitulates every wave that's gone before.

I put my fingers on both sides of my tongue, as if holding it, as if in command, as though it is more masculine for my fingers to take than my tongue to give, as though this choice of the greater masculine might stand in mitigation of the act. Spit on your fingers is for girls. Spit on your fingers is for sex.

Nevertheless my tongue summons up more of it, sucking on the front of my palate as if in a silent mating call.

My fingers smell of my shame.

Are you crazy? You've deep-ended now.

Go back. Sense.

My hand the center of the picture, pale and wet like Maisie's. Maisie in the room somewhere.

My hand grips my penis which is soft as a boy and cool. At first my hand senses it more than my penis senses my hand, but this changes, and as my penis coalesces in the slippery exchange of rhythms they start to dance with one another, they look equally into each other's eyes.

I bring more saliva to the party.

My penis, like a land creature returning to the sea, swims happily in it and is quiet.

I am beyond guilt's reach now. I've gone offshore, at least for a while. I look at the ceiling, looking for patterns of the ocean in the puddles and lines of the plaster fixes.

I refuse pictures of sexual enticement. Returned to sender, gone. In order to keep them out, my mind's voice counts. I take my breaths as the rhythm of my hand. In out in out up down up down four strokes for every in breath four strokes for every out.

Do not break ranks do not give in to tits and ass.

Tits and ass can watch from the side. Green eyes can watch from the side as we march past, in breath up and down up and down out breath up and down up and down.

How martial. How boring. No, how brave. I have an aim. I will not let sex intrude.

I sense the blood running in my arms and legs. I sense my neck and shoulders tighten. Relax. Go back. Let them go.

Now my blood slows? I think it does. And my nostrils relax and my jaw and my toes, which wriggle as I keep jerking off.

Whoever can jerk off and chew gum at the same time please stand up come forward for your prize.

Here I am. It's me. Remember me?

Little me?

I can jerk off and drop my blood pressure and chew gum

and relax my jaw and wriggle my toes even while I move my breath in and out in breath and out breath up and down in and out around and about.

My penis loves me now. My penis wants no other.

You narcissist, you devil.

In out in out in out in out. Breaths as clipped as a soldier's speech.

Maisie in my peripheral vision, a cheerleader, a friend, as neutral as the bed.

I can do this! I can fucking do this!

I sense my spine or try to. Is it there? Do I really have one?

My spine the bearer of my hopes, the old electric eel.

My body prepares. To see what will happen, like the men at Alamogordo in their concrete bunkers with their dark glasses but no, I'll stand up, I'll throw my glasses off I'll be part of the experiment I'll be neither subjective nor objective neither here nor there, in the center of it I sense my forehead.

O do not sense your cock. O do not sense your cock. Sense everything else and your cock will take care of itself I swear I'm not making this up.

Maisie. Quiet. Go back.

I see what help she is now. I remember her and I remember to go back, remember to sense. It's true what they say—the conscious keep each other alive.

Stop. Don't say this. Don't say anything don't think anything. Sense. Arms legs penis spine something in the middle of your head a little towards the front. What's this? What's its name? Don't ask its name. Go back. Sense. No words. Not even the words "no words."

And who shall choose the end of it? Shall my penis or shall "I" and who's "I" anyway?

Yes, "I." Yes, I.

That thing in the middle of my head a little bit towards the front that has so many names but no name at all that thing is it not like the bell at the county fair at the strong man's booth where you get a mallet and pound something on the ground and the something flies up on a pole and if you're really strong the something will fly so high on the pole it will ring the bell whereupon praise will befall you and grace and honor and the love of the carny girls.

The eternal return of the hero give me a break go back sense no words anything but words.

"I" decide I decide enough of this Maisie must be getting bored it's time to get on with the day all experiments must come to an end like good things go to heaven in out up down saliva enough for this slippery world my cock my love go for it faster yes no words.

I am lurking inside my head. "I" am lurking inside my head when the sparkling sweetness comes my way, the restorer of worlds. What has my cock to do with it, or "my" cock, is it not but a switch, a mechanical device? We're talking electricity here, we're talking the spark of life, immeasurable. Sweetness settles over my shoulders over my body like a cloak, power crowns me, or "me," or whoever.

It is all in your head, it is all in your mind. What you sense in your cock is but a pale reflection of what is.

I feel dissolved. "I" feel dissolved.

No words. Fire gone out.

Maisie's over there smiling her fish-eyed smile, *kore* girl carved in stone, waiting for her Buddha-boy.

There's come on my fingers, warm, overpainting such saliva as is left. She hands me my underpants to wipe myself off.

So there's that but it's the day before Christmas so there's also Christmas shopping to do. Back downtown, Canal Street, Mott, the Bowery. Because of the "event" after Christmas, I've taken the whole week off, Chinatown is thronged, with fifty dollars in my pocket I feel rich. Shopping for myself, shopping for ourselves, because this too is part of the work, to bathe ourselves in another kind of love, until the water of the bath is the same as our insides and when we get out we don't know we're gone. Jerk off and buy presents for yourself and defend yourself if attacked. That's the kindergarten course, the one that breaks everything down to its simples. Compassion is so much more advanced, helping others, fucking others. Heal thine selves, would-be physicians of the world. So in Chinatown I buy a cleaver for myself, smooth-grained handle and carbon blade, sufficient to chop the head off a chicken or anything else and I feel I've committed a metaphorical act; added an extension to my hand, a worthy gift, proper to Bobby's assistant in the galley, a workman who does not quarrel with his tools but rather cossets them and oils them, a cleaver such as Joe might have bought, and at seven dollars what a deal. I joke around with Maisie about getting it gift-wrapped. It would slice through the paper, slice through the box, get loose in New York like King Kong. Maisie in her olive coat on a day that looked like rain, seeming happy after our morning together though what the "together" part of it meant I wasn't sure. Lunch in the dim sum joint on Doyers. She's chirpy, we need to buy stuff for the "event," she says, they did five days nonstop in Somerville and everyone brought cushions for their ass and candy to sneak in here and there. You had to prepare for it, it was like a campaign, and what about kneepads for your knees? I said I dreaded the whole thing but she said it wasn't so bad, though seven days would be twice as bad as five. I said to her, not looking her way, that we were like Tristan and Iseult, only in a kind of weird and reversed way, we kept a sword between our emotions while our bodies did what they liked.

A cleaver, Maisie said, is that what you bought the cleaver for, to keep between our emotions?

I said I didn't know.

"It was all just a deception anyway, that Tristan thing?" she asked. "Wasn't it? The sword? Just to fool the king?"

And that's more or less when it started, when I had the inkling that if I looked at her once more, despite all the prohibitions and cleavers galore, I would begin to fall in love with her. I sat slantwise to our little table so that in the frame that my eyes most readily concocted she was little more than a hint out at the eastern border, but hint or no, there she was, her freckled face and know-it-all eyes, her red hair not fully grown, like a fledgling not quite ready to fly. On Bowery at the only store of the time, maybe anywhere in the country, that stocked goods from "Red China," Maisie bought toothpaste and soaps and a comb, and flimsy kneepads for both of us in case we wound up sanding the floor. I tagged along with a curious eagerness, as though watching her shop was like watching something more intimate by far than a couple hours before when her hands had found her vagina. I'd never seen her sister shop. I'd come to think, in an odd way, that rich girls never shopped, not for toothpaste anyway.

Though how long had it been since I even thought of Maisie as rich? Even in her parents' apartment, she seemed like a squatter, a beggar.

But now I did. Maisie bought a lamp for herself, a gaudy tinseled thing, antidote to everything she'd grown up with, something fabulous, wasn't it fabulous, she kept saying, a lamp, as it were, to go with Joe's Christmas tree, a Chinese outlier of it. We dodged and slipped our way through the last minute crush of humanity up Mott Street, then west on Canal, stopping to look at the fishmongers' wares. This rich girl who gave it up, this rich girl who moved on, to crazy and beyond.

Up Broadway a guy had books on a cart. We were walking by and I felt Maisie beside me, comrade Maisie who could walk fast and in step with me or I in step with her, and I must have glanced because I always glanced at what booksellers had to sell, an unbroken habit, a lust for the bargain, transformed, perhaps, into a search for the miraculous at three ninety-eight or less, but in all events there went my eyes, to a facsimile of Blake, the *Songs of Innocence and Experience*, with Blake's own engravings, printed probably in Hong Kong, black cover with drawing of Tyger Tyger burning bright, wrapped in cellophane as though it were Henry Miller.

How much, I said to the guy and the answer was eight dollars and I would have argued with him but Maisie hadn't seen me yet nor did I want her to she was a couple steps ahead, so I handed him even change and he put the Blake in a brown bag. Blake being someone from "before," somebody Joe never mentioned and might actually have thought was a crazy old coot, yet despite what I was already imagining as Joe's narrow-mindedness, wasn't Blake apropos? I felt if I gave this to Maisie now I would be giving her a piece of my whole life. I felt also I'd be doing a subversive thing, *ex parte*, private, playing a hunch. By then she was up the block, half turned towards me with her hands in her pocket, not really impatient but not patient either, and I thought she looked just fine. As soon as I caught up with her I gave her the bag. "Merry Christmas," I said, as flat as I could. Throwaway Christmas, throwaway gift, downplayed to death, yet there it was. She brought it out.

"What's this?"

"Just, uh, saw it. I don't know."

"Great, it looks great."

"Do you like Blake?"

"Sure. I mean, sure."

"Did I break a rule?"

"Which rule?"

"Buying you a present?"

"No."

She turned the book over. The back of the jacket was a sheet of black. She didn't take the cellophane off, but rather put it back in the bag and put the bag in the bigger bag with her lamp, and we walked along. Her smile went blocks ahead of us, distant and knowing, a smile I hadn't seen quite, but it had mystery and seeming courage.

"What possessed you, young man?"

"Affection."

"Whatever happened to the sword? Excuse me, the cleaver."

"Your esteemed self has caused me momentarily to fuhgeddaboudit."

"Uh-huh."

"Why 'uh-huh'?"

But she didn't say. Though of course I knew what she could have said. A tidy lecture on non-attachment or mom.

"I love Blake," she said instead.

"You're not angry?"

"Surprised."

"No big deal."

"Thanks, though."

"Nada... I just thought... I mean you were the one who said drive to the country. You're the one who reminded me of my other life."

"Other lives?"

"Probably... I don't know."

"If I say I like you, that's stealing your attention, right?"

"I don't know. Is it?"

"If I say 'I love you'... ?"

"Stop. Go back. Sense."

"I am. Maisie..."

"Hmm?"

"Forget I said any of it. An experiment."

It was like, I thought, when you try not to sense, there it is. When you try not to fall in love, there it is. Maisie who was all at once on Broadway as it began to rain, the one.

"A gift can be one-sided," I said.

"I have to go to the loft."

I was glad because she sounded rueful.

"What about our secret life?"

"What secret life? Which one?"

At Bleecker in the narrow alcove that smelled of rain and urine, backlit by the white buzzer with Joe's name on it, I kissed her. Her lips parted a little and I touched her hair. She pressed the buzzer.

"You know I don't really want the book," she said.

Still in its bag she removed it from her bigger bag.

"Oh?"

"Sorry?" Her shrug. "Do I have to explain?"

"Of course not... Okay, fuck it, who cares?"

I took it from her and threw it across Broadway, over the hedge of pedestrians narrowly missing a cab landing in the blotchy roadway most of the way across.

"Better?" I asked.

She shrugged again.

Someone was buzzing her up now. Probably Joe, from the length of the buzz.

"See you later," she said.

I nodded.

She went in and I turned my back on her as the elevator doors wiped her away.

Car after car, by now, their windshield wipers going, were running over the book. I could see it out there, as squooshed as any cat, small impediment to the city's flow.

I hated walking in that rain.

Life's an experiment, I said in words to myself, and told myself to shut up.

14

Love and related ethics. Troubadour Sufi Persian Arab Chinese Indian Song of Songs go hither and yon what will you learn about love?
 What will words provide?
 The Beloved. Neither this nor that nor anything else.
 In the grace of the Beloved's gaze.
 In the night of the Beloved's absence.
 Unsayable ecstasy unsayable sorrow.
 The Lover. You. We. I.
 What will the Beloved's face look like?

જ

Whereas I pitiful I pitiful you pitiful we, the poverty of our little scrawls.

જ

Distance.

જ

May we glimpse our own pathos, finally?

જ

The human face the metaphor of the Beloved's.
Is this deception?
Is this sacrilege?
Or, possibility?

✢

Drunkenness.

✢

A whiff of perfume.

✢

Madness.

✢

The scent of roses.

✢

The poet under his tree, in repose. . . is he asking or is he telling?

✢

Her number at her parents' apartment was a 2–8-8. BUtterfield 8. One of the old-time exchanges. O'Hara's novel. Liz Taylor in the role.

I phoned her. Feeling an unanticipated need to speak with my co-conspirator. I decided that's what I would call her, if I spoke with her, my co-conspirator. But I knew she wouldn't be there. I phoned the BUtterfield 8 number six or seven times, on each occasion feeling more compelled, as if I was beginning to lose my nerve. And what would I have said to my co-conspirator if she was there? Propose, with the stately, measured cadence of a conscious being, an early evening fuck? That would be nice. That sounded sweet. 2–8-8, BUtterfield 8, as if a telephone exchange could be endowed with sensuality. Despite all my best intentions, I was sorry Maisie wasn't there. It was only when I'd finally moved my attention off her, in favor of unwrapping my cleaver, oiling it, feeling its rough-hewn Chinese blade with my fingertip as if preparing for a life's work, that she called me.

"Hi."

"Hey."

"So. . ."

I never got to calling her my co-conspirator. Her voice had that sandpaper taste again.

"Something's wrong."

"What?"

"My glands are swollen."

"Are you sure?"

"Don't patronize me."

"Did you call the doctor?"

"I'm going to talk to Joe."

"But did you call the doctor?"

"Of course I called the doctor. He wasn't there."

"It's Christmas Eve."

"It is."

"Okay then I won't ask you about it."
"What could you ask?"
"Oh come on Maisie—are you okay?"

But her larger point was true enough. What I knew about Hodgkin's disease you could fit into two sentences. Something about stages. Maisie was Stage 2, which wasn't so bad, but the next stage if it came was.

She repeated that her glands were swollen and asked if I knew what that meant and I guessed that I did and said so and asked her which glands.

Her neck, she said, had I noticed her neck?

"I did, actually."
"Today?"
"Uh-huh."
"Because you were looking to see? Because something looked wrong?"
"No."
"You just liked my neck."
"Yes."
"You romantic."
"Maisie—"
"I'm not asking you to think about it, understand? I don't want you to think about it. That's why I never talk about it. I'm not even supposed to. It's bad for me. People like you. Treating me like a freak."
"Okay. Fine."
"Not that you are. I didn't say that you did. You don't."
"Can I come over now?"
"No."
"Are you sure?"
"I'm still at the loft."

"Will I see you later?"
"At Philip's."
"Maybe there's another doctor you can call."
"I don't think so."
"Well—"
"This is my business, okay? I'm sorry I called. Really. It was stupid of me."

And maybe it was, I thought, when she hung up. My co-conspirator.

I went over to the New Yorker bookstore then. Thank God for Jews and secularists, open on Christmas Eve. I wanted a book on Hodgkin's disease. I would read up and make myself useful to her or anyway know better who, or what, I was confronting. But I didn't think her glands were swollen. They hadn't looked swollen to me. I thought she was simply afraid.

15

Philip's party on Christmas Eve was from midnight to dawn. It was hardly billed as a party. More like a refuge for orphans, strays and insomniacs. People sat on the floor and played board games or read the Sufi books or quietly talked. Almost nobody stood around. Nobody milled. The single room of Philip's apartment held us in a kind of suspended elegance, as if it were a hatbox. It was a room seeded with his childhood—models of locomotives, train timetables, books on baseball, stamp albums and a Scott's catalog— but at the same time, with its frayed leather armchair and faded wall paint of indeterminate color, grayed further by the mysterious emanations of a negative ionizer, it breathed the composed disarray of a college room, say an American dream of Oxbridge. The archaeology, the layered cities, of a boy. As well, for me, it was the room where I'd first come to meet these people. It held the feeling, as much as anyplace, of home for me, despite we, the group, having come in and built Philip bunk beds and a redwood deck, spiffing the place up beyond the previously supposed boundaries of Philip's taste, even giving him an ostentatiously lordly perch over the backyards of 12th and 13th Streets. Two short birch logs burned innocuously, with steady indifference, in the fireplace. Philip greeted each guest with a glass of hundred-proof bourbon, which they didn't have to drink, nobody was making Russian toasts with it, but it was there anyway, part of a stash he'd acquired doing a Talk story on a New Yorker who'd become a master distiller in Louisville, offered now both as sacrament and sacrilege: all hurt feelings welcome here.

I sat down to play cards with Big Ronald, Matthew Fellner, Laura and Julie. Poker for pennies, the kind of game where the girls had a cheatsheet which they passed back and forth showing what beat what, which still didn't keep Julie from asking every ten minutes or less what a straight was or the difference between a straight and a flush. I liked Julie, in the old college phrase she was tough, lanky with a turned-up nose and nasally Five Towns accent. She and Matthew had been together for years, he was a rich kid from Great Neck, one step up the nouveau ladder from her, they drove a Suburban now but before the group they'd lived "alternatively" in Crested Butte, from which she'd brought back, like the proverbial pearl of great price, an amazing chocolate cake, succor for the long stoned Colorado winters, composed of every impure ingredient to be found in the local co-op, cake mix and instant chocolate pudding and Crisco and bags of chocolate chips and whatever else, an example of which she'd provided this night, to go with the card games and the bourbon. We all believed in sweets, as metaphor and remembrance. People who didn't believe in chocolate were afraid of being sweetened themselves. But what was I doing with Julie and Matthew? Were it not for the group, they'd never have been my friends. They were bland, their jobs were boring, they could do me little good, although Julie's tits were nice. The old analysis, the pre-group analysis, of the "power-mad rat" that had been me and was still me most of the time. The same with Big Ronald, the commodities trader from Okieland. Ronald was a rascal, he'd blown up bridges in the Peace Corps in the High Atlas, he cared about money, he actually had kids, a couple of them from a down-home marriage. I had no idea, really, what had brought Big Ronald to the group, but there must have been something in him, something unsatisfied, breathing through a straw, buried under the burlap twang and toothy smile. Or, he'd been going out with Laura. Maybe Laura had brought him. It was often that way. You came here on account of a squeeze and then you didn't want to leave. Laura'd been an office manager, until the job at Cowgirls East came up. Putting on his avuncular career counseling hat, Joe had said try it maybe you'll like it, and she had, and she did, the girl camaraderie, the guys with their hard-ons. She broke up with Big Ronald, who then screwed Liddie for awhile and after Liddie he said he was tying a rubber band around it. Were these my people? They were now. I was finding it easy to sense this night. Being with others who were sensing, doing nothing much. The room seemed to glow, as if we were in a set designer's gaslight. I was losing, as usual, at cards. No real fighting spirit, nor skill. Julie wanted to win and cheatsheet or no she was doing it, yelping less ironically than we cosmopolitans might have hoped for each time she hauled in a pot. Sense. Look. Listen. But as we played, the words in my head grew denser and more consistent, until eventually I could recognize in them a theme of surprised self-satisfaction. I was not unhappy to have Big Ronald, Matthew, Julie and Laura as my friends, I was not unhappy to be wasting my time playing cards with them. Wasting time, consciously wasting time, an unexpected badge of pride; worthless friends, consciously worthless, a badge of superiority. And what was this "worthless" shit? Worthless word, worthless words. Worthless workers of the world unite, save me from a world of ambition and snobbery. Escape from my falsest self. Here, family.

Here, friends. Here, the vain world is seen for what it is and we laugh. Even I laugh, who hadn't laughed enough. Sitting now in the card-playing embrace of the solid, the openhanded, the less deceived, the sort who might dedicate their lives to something and stick with it to the bitter end. For a few moments I saw Big Ronald and even Laura as I imagined Joe must see them. Good seed, good soil. Until with a kind of garish, urgent rush I recognized the pride I felt at being with them as no better than the pride that might have led me to ignore them, it was all pride, all the same, all of it keeping me from what is. Words. Hallucination. Go back. Gently. Sense.

All my bullshit schema. All my theories. All my self-criticism.

What did they get me?

Confusion.

Go back.

I drained the bottom of my cup of bourbon. Its warmth, the room's warmth, my friends' warmth.

All is forgiven.

How could it not be forgiven?

Forgiveness as organic, as what is.

Go back.

The sweetness of the bourbon. The sweetness of Philip, of his boyhood.

Laura's tits, Julie's tits. The sweetness of these too.

Where's Maisie? Where's Bobby?

But Maisie was supposed to be here.

Moments later I wasn't sure if I'd begun to think this last thought of Maisie before the doorbell rang or after.

Could my unconscious not hear the ring before my conscious mind?

Wasn't that how precognition worked?

It wasn't Maisie at the door, nor Bobby. I cranked my neck to see whoever Philip was greeting, a bundled shape smaller than himself. "You made it. Come in. Look who's here." Philip waving at me like a bandmaster, as the guy from Saint Vincent's took a couple steps across Philip's threshold, a little bit tentative, a little bit shivery, as if he was happy to be out of the cold but not sure if he'd really come to the right place. It was a quarter after one and for a second I took him for Santa Claus, the Santa of the old black-and-white movies anyway, the one that came in unusual guises.

Some patchy back-and-forth with Philip about his name, which was Joao, which Philip already had to know, since he'd called him to invite him. Philip offering him bourbon, offering him chocolate cake, taking his coat and still flagging me over, never chirpier than when he was gracious, like the kindest chipmunk on earth. When Philip threw a party he had a tendency to invite anyone he ran into for weeks in advance, but there were none outside the group who could be counted on to show up after one or two in the morning. What had Joao been doing? What did he imagine? It was a long ways from Sao Paulo. He had on a thin acrylic black sweater, he'd oiled his hair, and he held in his hand a small square box wrapped with a single dark-colored ribbon which he'd retrieved from his coat pocket before Philip whisked the coat away. Forthrightly, as though embarrassment wasn't part of his nature, Joao handed the box over and Philip fussed about it, opened it with quiet ceremony to find inside a key chain with a picture of Pelé set against the flapping green of the Brazilian flag. Philip poured Joao his ration of bourbon. Joao recognized me as soon as I got up. "Okay with girl now?" "No more girl. No more girl. Different girl." The pleasures of pidgin, allowing each side to think it's doing its best.

Philip asked Joao if he felt like talking about Saint Vincent's, because wasn't now as good a time as any, and Joao, who knew phrases, said why not. Why not, why not—why not me do the interviewing, Philip said, Louie could do the interviewing, if Joao didn't mind. Why not?

There was something about Joao that put him not out of place with us. Even I had discovered that in a room full of people trying to stay in the present the one who wasn't, who was clueless and flying all over, would stand out, as if he was fighting the room or oblivious to it. But Joao didn't stand out. Who knew, was it his faith-healing or his simple modesty or was he a secret Sufi saint? In a corner of the room, out of the way, I interviewed Joao. I was probably better off for having no preparation at all for it. My questions flowed freely and conversationally. Joao started telling me how much money he'd saved the City of New York. Helping the indigent, clearing out the ER, curing the hypochondriacal and otherwise. We started adding it all up. Eight thousand, twenty thousand, forty-seven thousand, a hundred and thirty-three thousand. The number growing with each retelling. I took a few notes. I began to be a little bit glad that Maisie was late. My nervous system alive with my big chance, to get something in the *New Yorker*, to get on with that part of my life, to be a writer after all. So that, actually, after a little while with Joao, whose English seemed strung together with oddly jagged phrases, as if he were composing ransom notes from words cut out of the newspaper, I found myself hardly sensing at all. Or rather, I didn't find myself. Forget "stop." Forget "go back." Forget "gently." I was swept up in the possibilities that my new gap-toothed friend was giving me. Not that he treated me as a friend. Plainly he would rather have been interviewed by Philip. Immigrant on the economic and cultural margins or no, he still knew where the butter was. "I tell this to Philip?" "Philip writes what magazine, *New York* magazine?"

Joao finished his bourbon. None the worse for it. But he didn't want another, he had professional principles, work to do, Christmas Eve, slow night, but there would be stabbings coming into the hospital for sure, Christmas Eve people still hurt each other and themselves. Joao's words, he could get rhetorical as hell, when it came to his mission.

Philip asked if I could go back to the hospital with him. Joao said could Philip come back, he could show Philip too many things. Philip said he couldn't get away, the party, people coming, but I could be his eyes and ears. In the end, with an averted gaze, Joao accepted me as Philip's eyes and ears. Some old disc from England of Noel Coward and Gertrude Lawrence was on the phonograph now. Philip had been, in a patch of moonlighting, some travel magazine's record critic for awhile and there were hundreds of records stacked in his closet, from which he'd plucked these reedy, ghostly voices, their sophistication weathered by the scratchy low fidelity. The music and the bourbon must have kicked in more or less at once on Joao, who before we left grabbed Philip around both arms the way he'd once laid hands on me at Saint Vincent's and began dancing him around the floor, by way of saying thank you for having him come here, no one could ask him for Christmas because he was far from Brazil, except Philip, who was his friend who did and now there would be this story and everyone will see how much money he saves New York which is very broke and so they will give him a green card. Philip backed off Joao's embrace as gingerly as he could. He was anyway as averse to dancing as I was.

Joao and I were tramping down the stairs just as Bobby climbed them. I imagined I saw something alike between the two, a slyness, or maybe just their size, or was it an elfin sensitivity that I'd become familiar with in Bobby but hadn't expected to see soon again. I introduced them. They didn't shake hands. We stood there a moment, Bobby taking off his woolen gloves.

"Seen Maisie?"

"No. Where are you going?"

"Over to Saint Vincent's. Do this story. On this guy."

"Great. Great."

Joao raising a hand.

The three of us standing there another moment with nothing to say.

"If Maisie shows up, would you tell her I'll be back?"

"I will."

Bobby raised his hand like Joao's and we went out.

'Twas Christmas in the Pest House. Bobby's favorite cartoon. But I didn't attach a vivid clarity to the memory until we got to the Saint Vincent's emergency. Just like Criminal Court AP-5, a good enough example of life's ongoingness. Something also about what purgatory must be about, in particular contrast to the cultivated warmth of Philip's apartment.

But here did they not save lives?

Indeed a slow night. Only half the plastic chairs filled. No wait to get a nurse to sign you up. It was Joao's practice to sign in with some ailment or other, then leave before his name was called. This, he felt, technically kept him from getting kicked out, kept the security guards off his case anyway. But it was all with a wink and a nod. Only the most newbie of the nurses didn't know who he was. The cute henna'd Puerto Rican girl on duty Christmas Eve seemed to like having him around.

Joao turned out to have a bit of regularized technique. The way he'd been with me a couple weeks before was how he behaved with everyone else. He would park himself a plastic chair or two away from a waiting patient and when things got slow strike up a conversation. This and that, the wait, the comparative charms of New York's different emergency rooms, the weather. Then, slowly coming around to it, he asked his questions, did his diagnosis, offered his services. People were always skeptical, but whether they chased him off or accepted him seemed to depend on a mysterious congeries of factors, impatience, poverty, trust or mistrust of who or what, who did you mistrust more. Also, a quality of receptivity? A slow night in the ER was even slower for Joao, because the less time people had to wait the less likely they were to put themselves in his hands. It occurred to me while we were waiting that I might ambush a resident and query him about Hodgkin's disease, the New Yorker having had nothing on its shelves, why not kill two birds? But Joao soon engaged a confused old woman in conversation. She thought she was back in Poland. She was a child and her hand had a booboo and where was her mother on Christmas? Or maybe I had some of this wrong, the woman's fuzzy chin tucked into the folds of her neck and her voice had a shrill, leaking air quality that made it difficult to follow what was already not very logical thought. But her hand plainly had been burned, from scalding water or maybe some pot she'd been cooking with, the entire back of it was red and blistering. I found it difficult to imagine what Joao could do for this woman. I even became fearful he was going to massage her arm or something equally ineffectual and tell her to go home and she'd leave and not get the care she needed and then what would our story be, non-medical malpractice by a scrawny *poseur*? Or would the story be conspiracy by an Assistant D.A. to promote unlawful professional practices? Joao's black eyes took her in, neither friendly nor unfriendly, not intense nor mild, more the seen-it-all eyes of the scientist I'd seen the other week. But when he took her hand it was as if she were a princess, he let her fat fingers drape over his like ripe fruit, and he kissed it. "You have beautiful hands," he said.

The woman's flesh-narrowed eyes widened. "I love you too."

Joao stood up. "Wait for help. You understand?"

"Wait for help," she repeated, and kissed her hand herself.

We left. I didn't ask.

So did I have here the Angel of Saint Vincent's or the Lothario of Saint Vincent's? He was keeping his secrets to himself now, his small, slightly rodential features in a kind of studied equipoise, as if his display of virtuosity was self-evident.

I resolved to go back when he wasn't around and ask everybody a ton of questions.

Then as we walked east, cold raindrops began to fall, fat and random, and as the little bullets of moisture began to bat us, I felt a subtle wave of elation, breathing in the cold rain, appraising my fresh success at being in the world but not of it. Gurdjieff said the worst position for a man was to be between two stools, but for the moment I was loving precisely this bifurcation, like a giant spreading his legs far apart, one foot in one world and one in another, each world serving as ballast, as collateral, for my forays into the other. And if I could write a story about Saint Vincent's, could I not follow it up with stories about the D.A.'s office? I could quit my job, I could churn them out, I could be ironic about the city and funny and charming like Philip and write sentences that ran like fresh water. My mind was full of plans, to the degree I very nearly forgot Joao with his pride and mystery walking right beside me. Stop. Go back. People could pass their whole lives and not remember that there was someone walking beside them. Joao interrupted our shared silence by tendering me his calculation that he'd just saved the City of New York eighty or ninety dollars. His Christmas present to the city. Joao split off from me at Sixth and 12th. He was taking the train to Brooklyn. We said good night. He said he would call Philip to see when this story would be coming.

I went on to 13th Street. Four o'clock or thereabouts. No muggers in sight. A car alarm somewhere. The rain abating. When you sense the nerves and sinews of your arms and legs more intensely, you feel something like you're walking on air. Not the musical comedy metaphor but something more specific and cognizable, as though your arms are propelling you along and you don't really need the ground as much as you thought. Or perhaps a closer metaphor would be the sense of swimming through air. I buzzed Philip's and was buzzed in. I climbed the stairs trying out various subvocalized formulations of how I should thank him. Stop. Go back. No words. I remembered "no words" just before I got to the door, then remembered that "no words" were already words. On and on. Nice try.

Coward and Lawrence had given way to Fred Astaire and Ginger Rogers on Philip's phonograph. Oh Rio, Rio by the sea, oh. Flying down to Rio where there's rhythm and rhyme. I heard it already in the hall, a siren song all the more seductive for being muffled and faint. Philip held the door open for me. I walked in and there were Joe and Maisie dancing cheek-to-cheek. Bobby was playing Clue and ignoring them. Maisie didn't even look my way. For a big man Joe was graceful on his feet and Maisie loved being twirled.

16

And so. And so. Really, is there more to be said about it?

☙

Though one thing that might be said is that Maisie's glands were not swollen. She'd simply been afraid.

☙

Let us turn our attention to jollier things, shall we?

☙

Current events. There's a good one. Always on the list, when a change of topic is desired. The late seventies, what a wonderful epoch, so much going on.

Disco whip inflation now Jimmy Carter Vegas Pintos homicides galore Abe Beame Church Commission Star Wars the movie not the missile defense recession stagflation peace.

All these came and went while we minded our own business.

Really, we didn't care. Made a few jokes. Joe flew a flag on Earth Day. The world would always be there, one thing or the other. Gurdjieff's group in Russia worked right through the Revolution, moving from here to there, staying a half-step ahead of history.

༄

An alternative formulation of why people came to the group. It had nothing to do with self-understanding. It had nothing to do with existential doubt. It may have had something to do with the temper of the times, what was permitted and what was still denied, the teetering of established frameworks, but mostly it had to do with power.

A boy grows with all kinds of dreams of taking on the world. He gets to a certain age and it looks like it's not going to happen. The socioeconomic cultural historical psychological biological "realities" begin to settle in. He's looking much smaller than his dreams. Someone holds a hand out. "Shut your eyes and come this way. All your difficulties will be removed." The boy follows, hoping to recoup, hoping to get it all after all.

The Faustian bargain all over again?

༄

But then, that might have been only one boy's story.

༄

My unhappy childhood, my father going away, my mother in disarray.

The point was, to get it out there so you could get past it. Treat it tenderly, so that you could get past it.

Kissing our hurt wings, so that each bird could fly.

༄

Or, on some other occasion, less politely put: "One more unhappy childhood. Big fucking deal."

☙

Bobby asked Joe once, years before, "Are you asking us to give up our minds, our conscious minds, the only ones we're aware of?"

"You'll have to tell me."

"I think you are. And if you are. . . don't our conscious minds . . . aren't they our moral factor, our conscience?"

"Your superego."

"My conscience. Which, if I give it up. . . I mean, that's not too responsible."

"Then don't give it up, if you don't want to."

"That's what the Germans did, with Hitler, gave up their rational minds, because Hitler said there was something deeper."

"The Germans were crazy."

"But. . . aren't we a little like that?"

"Do you think I'm Hitler?"

"I don't know who you are."

"That's honest, at least."

"On the other hand, I think, what if it's the only way to get from here to there? Getting rid of all the baggage. Sooner a camel passes through the eye of a needle. . ."

"Than?"

"A lot of American Tourister?"

"Guess you'll just have to leave your luggage in the hands of someone you trust. Use your conscious mind to try to determine if there's someone you can entrust your precious baggage to."

"I do. . ."

"And?"

"I don't think my conscious mind can ever reach a conclusion."

"I don't think so either."

"But can it give me hints?"

"Can it?"

"I think so."

"And if you let your unconscious instincts percolate through . . ."

"That isn't fair."

"Isn't it? Doesn't your conscious mind tell you it's necessary?"

"My conscious mind doesn't tell me anything for sure."

"It can't."

"I don't know if I can trust you."

"Then suffer."

One of a thousand snippets of inquiry, that ended with Joe's shrug.

༄

Who was Joe? Kike from Bensonhurst. Pratt. Head of the whole design department, didn't that mean something? In his field, then, a bit of a success. Skidmore Owings for awhile. The big time, in his telling of it, projects worth hundreds of millions. Which he would recall as if to certify his worth in the world, so that people wouldn't think he had a quarrel with it based on failure or resentment. Then India. Then the Old Painter. Then cancer. A divorce in there somewhere. What would the ex say? That he was angry, of course, that he'd gone off some deep end. Had the ex been a part of the Old Painter's group? Probably. I didn't know.

Was Joe kind? Perhaps. Funny? Perhaps. Shrewd? Perhaps. Perhaps perhaps perhaps.

More than most Joe defeated the urge of the Other to catalog and define, to place people in a box of their characteristics. Long live the fluidity of man!

Was he enlightened, however much he trashed the word?

Perhaps.

One step up the ladder from the rest of us?

Perhaps.

Deluded and sicko and dogmatic and small-minded and good with a slide rule but in the end without humanity?

Perhaps.

He was "on" all the time. That was the claim, and even what it seemed.

That he'd been "on" so long, it was actually natural now. What he'd discovered, what he'd changed into, was more "him" than anything he'd been before.

This seemed, generally, true. There was something very specific about Joe, even when you subtracted the teacher part.

Don't act out of negative emotions, he'd say, but then he'd act out whatever he seemed to want to act out and it wouldn't be "negative."

Or was it "negative" but it didn't matter because he was in a different place from us, with different rules, or no rules at all?

Playing with words? Hypocrisy?

Or lessons in the suppleness of life.

Could we see how the two were different, his emotions and ours? Was he watching his more subtly? Even, playing games with them, luxuriating in them, feeling further emotions, of nostalgia, of fond distance, on account of his awareness of his emotions?

Mostly, Joe seemed kind of brave. Jaunty and brave, like an actor who's overcome stage fright.

༄

The whole question of "help." The group seemed to be about "helping people." Joe was "helping" us, for which we paid him, but not, according to his occasional pronouncements, by way of an equal bargain, because the help he gave us couldn't be priced; rather, he asked to be paid, he said, because people valued something more if they had to pay for it; also it cost him money to run the group. Forty dollars a month per person. Cheap therapy, if that's what you thought it was. In turn Joe reminded us that most of us did little to help anybody else, for which we were not to blame because we were basically incapable of it. In this respect, masturbation was an apt enough metaphor, a wry, if cogent, example. We must clear our own minds before being able to see clearly the minds of others. And if we could see clearly the minds of others, would we know how to help them?

People in their confusion often wanted things that didn't help them.

But help them to do, or be, what, then?

Make a little more money get laid live life more intensely be healthy wealthy and wise? Jobs relationships parents bosses lovers the past the present the future sagging tits and migraines the nuts and bolts the stuff that therapists get paid for their meat and potatoes their bread and butter their clichés.

But what then, and who cared? When the person—as was the way of men?—was still dissatisfied?

Then and only then, the question might arise: were they suitable for the work?

Did they have a sincere desire to understand themselves?
Was that even the question?
Was that the one true help?
And which of us could provide it?
Joe?
Take nothing on faith.
No leaps of faith.
Was that possible?

༶

Cheek-to-cheek they danced. He dipped her as though they were at a high school prom. Maisie who'd never been to such a prom, who'd gone to boarding schools all the way.

Why wouldn't she look at me? Of course she wouldn't look at me.

She'd moved on, again.

And why shouldn't she, wasn't that a part of her magnificence?

What negative emotions did I feel? Let's catalog them.

Hatred. Bitterness. Envy. Anger. Fear. Humiliation. Shame.

Depression is anger, isn't depression anger?

And yet.

I also felt a numbing sadness, as though part of me had been washed out to sea.

Why had Maisie come to New York in the first place? Joe who'd had cancer too. Joe who it was said could help her.

Could I have helped her?

My gush of sentiment, my hauling up of ghosts, stirring her and us around, distractions, playing around, encouraging her own old ghosts.

I'd been hunting in the king's preserve all along.

17

Chopping away. Chop chop. Chop chop chop chop chop chop chop chop chop chop chop chop. How many times can I say it? How many times could I think it or hear it? Chop, which doesn't really sound very much like what it represents, and even less so in my mind's watery reverberations. Where is the thudding essence, where is the variety, the thwacking groans, the aches, the claps, the flat bangs, the breathy stretches of the blade? Instead of saying "chop" why don't I simply listen to the blade? Why must everything be interpreted, the world put in place? Stop. Go back. My new Chinese cleaver, my Christmas present to myself, its handle bright with shellac, its blade branded with two pictographs, like chicken feet, genuine, irreducible, of which I have no comprehension.

The slab of it, the weight, the way it pounces on the scallions, like a big guy who is also fast. Christmas morning in the loft. I've come down at nine o'clock to do some prep for later in the day and I've brought my cleaver with me. Scallions then bok choy then Chinese broccoli then whatever else Bobby's stuffed into the fridge as if getting ready to feed the Union Army. I let the blade fall mostly on its own. I flick my wrist lightly, a priest dispensing holy water. It is odd, perhaps, that having "given up" possessions, having professed nonattachment, I've never been prouder of the few things I own. A cleaver, a working tool, something that bears infinite inspection, for its evolution, its stately history written in steel, its blood sport, its necessity.

I chop like a madman, feeling what I feel must be the bright breath of a sleepy Christmas morning, sun's out, frost cusping my precious clean panes, feeling nothing at all really but wondering why I feel so good, as now the bok choy falls in a heap. Buckets of bok choy. It has a crunch when it dies. It is white and green like a distant morning. Iceland. Greenland. Is Joe still sleeping? Does the loft smell faintly of his farts? I wish he'd come out and see my cleaver.

Back in his bedroom. A folding screen instead of a door. Is Maisie there? Stirring now. A bit of rustling back there, creaks of the floor. My neck tenses. I chop with self-conscious intensity. Too much. Phony? Go back.

When Joe comes out, it's in his terry robe of many colors. Gray eyes still narrow in sleep, he almost looks Chinese. Mongolian, anyway, Siberian. One of those Jews who went to Birobidzhan? Hair mussed. He stretches his arms out lazily, fists balled up, like a round, quickly drawn figure in a Zen cartoon, or a shmoo. Good morning. Hi. He throws the switch on the coffeepot, comes over to see what I'm doing. Stands in back of me as if to drive me nuts but I don't turn around. "Maisie's still asleep," he says, and there's nothing I can say to that.

"Am I chopping too loud?"

"No."

And then:

"You buy that?"

"This? Uh-huh."

"Nice."

Chop chop. Chop chop chop chop chop.

"Maisie's head ... My head ... Maisie's head ... My head ... You would've made a great executioner. Monsieur Danton, let Louie do it. He knows how these newfangled machines of decapitation work."

I grin nervously or is it smile grimly, or was it both? Both and all of it, but I do not turn. Too cool to turn around or glare or catch his glance.

"Maisie's head... my head... mom's head... dad's head... my head... Maisie's head..."

I continue to grin nervously or smile grimly, as I hear the tease in his voice. Not mean, nothing really mean, but certain, his singing delight, as if he were yelling "Gotcha!"

He pours himself a mug of coffee. I can see his Joseph robe out of the corner of my eye. The Little King, who like everybody else before breakfast looks ten years older.

"Want some?" Of the coffee.

"No thanks. I'll finish this first."

He pours his half-and-half, casts a glance at my working profile, his Santa Claus glint on full display. "Get it?" Joe asks me. He wanders off as I say nothing and continue to chop. But get fucking what? Maisie's head? My father's head? My mother's head! This is precisely what I *do* get, yes I fucking get what I fucking get is precisely this ridiculous certainty, this simpleminded, paperback Freud on the cheap two-bit ignorant shit, this "one-way-or-another-I'm-me-so-I-must-be-right," this patronizing condescending self-righteous shit, but most of all this fucking "Get it?" grin. Get fucking what? Get laid, that's what. Jesus, the fatuity of it all.

And not even of it "all," not of Philip not of Bobby not of Maisie, but of Joe.

Maisie's head Joe's head, my father's head my mother's head. Oh now that's real profound.

That's going to get me across the river assuming I even want to get across some fucking river or whatever's the metaphor du jour.

I chop. Chop chop chop chop chop chop chop chop chop chop. Maisie's head. Joe's head.

Well, Joe's head at least.

Does it lighten my load to chop off his head?

Does it lead to my delight?

In five minutes I'm exhausted. I pour myself a cup of coffee and sit.

Maisie's up now. Joe owns a second coat-of-many-colors, for his guests, and Maisie's wearing it now. It works wildly with her red hair, all but bleeds it out.

But she's cheerful enough.

"Hi. . . I should explain." Breathy, throaty morning voice.

"No need."

She takes me at my word. She's not one to go where she isn't wanted. Wary of traps, plays the world like a battlefield.

Or was that the learned behavior of the group? Was it any longer possible for me to figure out what was there before and what came with the new territory?

"My glands weren't swollen. Sorry. False alarm," she says.

"I knew it," I say, and leave it at that.

I am on to the Chinese broccoli now. Having the job to do steadies me. What did I even think of Maisie?

When I saw her this morning I felt a sort of silly shame, as if I knew I couldn't touch her but couldn't remember exactly why.

Maisie, you devil.

Maisie, you doll.

Wandering around the loft now. Both of them wandering around, I wasn't sure doing what, like two planets loosed from their orbits.

While I chop. Choppity-chop, the greater resistance of the Chinese broccoli to my blade. I chop harder. I will not stand for resistance. I take control. I do what is needed. I am I, after all.

My rage begins to overtake me, begins to lighten my load. I am so angry my face must redden and I feel lightheaded and for a moment I notice it is all without words. Or almost without words, words getting as sparse as signs in a desert.

Have I ever been so mad and it is all about nothing? I pity my mother, who fell apart. I pity my father, who was so weak to run away. But I do not pity myself because I have no pity for myself it's an empty well gone dry gone fishing forget myself now. Haunt my rage. Inhabit it, come to know it. And the pity like soft moss growing in the dark beneath.

I do not know how long it is and all my food is chopped. Neat pieces of equal size, meet for stir-fry, job well-done.

I wipe my cleaver dry with a paper towel then oil it with vegetable oil. Is this how? How can it not be "how," it's my cleaver, my blade, my instrument. Whose head should it chop off next? Any that I decide but why should I decide. My rage is too much fun. It lightens too much of my load.

And just think, milady, it was down there all along, mucking about in the basement, fouling up the plumbing. We'll take care of it now, we'll get it all set to rights, air the place out, good as new.

Yes? No? Yes and no?

I feel like crying, for pity, for my mother, for my father.

What have they got to do with any of this?

Not to blame, not to blame.

Are we really well past Freud, or any number of steps behind? Or right on time?

All right on time.

No words.

Few words, anyway.

And yet, for a moment. I love words!

The hidden genius of humanity. Hiding in plain sight.

Yes? No? Yes and no?

I've never quite loved words before. Now that I'm giving them up.

A few seconds anyway, maybe more, maybe it's more now.

Rage, the cleansing genius.

In my peripheral vision Joe waddling around. Flicking on the lights of the Christmas tree. Their multicolored gleam, his multicolored robe.

Is color all right, after all?

Is the world all right, after all?

The shushing of the shower. The water tickling Maisie's back, bouncing off her flesh, her breasts, dripping her and stripping her. Down the drain with your sins, my love. We're all reborn. You too. So, fuhgeddaboudit.

Didn't I say that stupid thing to you one time?

Sing to me. Sing in the shower. I can't hear your voice but if you're singing I'll know that you are.

I put my vegetables in bowls and wax paper over the bowls and put the bowls in the fridge, my hands, my fingers, my arms, cool and calculated, no effort lost. Elegant I am. Necessary I am. Joe is pouring himself a second cup of coffee and asks again if I want some.

I sit with him. The coffee tastes of gold. The shower water ceases. She must be drying off but I do not think *she is drying off.* A medicine cabinet opens and shuts. The bathroom is actually quite far away, twenty feet or so. Joe looks like a tired

Buddha today, rings under his eyes, dark and planetary, and slightly gory with his biblical, his faux-biblical robe.

For once I am not afraid of him. Why should I be afraid? Naked citizens of the world, unite.

Joe renders me with a bloodless stare. I feel strung from head to toe. I feel joyous.

"Breakthrough?" Joe asks.

In that neutral tone, that I always thought was conscious and contrived but now I guess he can't even help. When the situation calls for it, it just comes out.

Could it be that Joe plans nothing at all? That he just reacts?

I think I hear him say "Breakthrough?" again, but it echoes, he only says it once.

I don't know.

But I am giddy.

I am speechless.

I believe Joe is a great man. Joe must know something. I am his partner, sidekick, amigo. I am here. This is enough. Fuck Maisie who cares tell her to go get us some more half-and-half. Which I sort of think and which when she comes out of the shower he actually does, he says, Maisie would you go get us some half-and-half?

Oh I am up on the world today.

But Maisie says she has a headache and she needs to lie down. She looks washed and pale. I hardly recognize her.

I sit for a while with Joe.

Everything subsides. Whatever "everything" was.

I leave around eleven. Joe's going to watch the football and I've got to get my things together for the week. My changes of clothes, my money, my candy, toothbrush, whatever more. Be prepared.

Motto of melancholy and springtime.

I walk to the train at Broadway-Lafayette. On the way uptown my car is laced with people going to church. I feel engaged. I feel grand. Who cares how I feel? It's not who you know but what you know but who you know, or is it? A big guy with his legs sprawled in the aisle of the train. Jews in their paperbacks. Guys off work, guys who worked Christmas Eve. Somewhere after 34th Street the train stops dead and the lights go off. The gloaming of the emergency power. All our faces in shadow. The engine cuts out. People breathe, people mind their own business, those who were hanging from straps still clutch them, as if they don't want to lose what they've got if the train starts again, or they don't want to be caught off guard. Guys sleeping with their noses in the *Daily News*. Headline at an angle about the Pope in Rome and midnight mass. Rustling among the pigtailed girls, the boys in suits, their mamas quick to hush. Suddenly all voices can be heard. There are few of them. People embarrassed to speak, to be known. The darkness, the shadows, the strange breaths. Who *are* all these people?

Why are we together? And it occurs to me, too, are we going to stay together? Have we always been and will we always be?

Who *says* this train's going to move?

Oh *sure*, it'll move. But when? After forever?

Because this is starting to feel like forever.

We all know that time can slow but did we know that it could slow among strangers underground in the dark and electric silence?

Come now, come now, calm down, take a breath no don't take a breath hold your breath didn't Joe say once if too much starts coming up just hold your breath and that will stop it all?

I hold my breath. It stops nothing. I hold my breath again. I am afraid of these angel children. I am afraid of the guy's sprawled legs. I am afraid of the crinkling newspapers and the silence and the cool that's entering the car because the engine's off, the noise is off, the heat is off, everything off. Is this what Joe calls a "breakthrough," is this what a "breakthrough" is? I'm going to die down here. I am going to die, anyway and sometime, but it seems it's going to be here. I'll go crazy I'll jump out on the tracks. Get me out of here. Claustrofucking-phobia a disorder in the *DSM*. I'll jump on the third rail. What have I gotten myself into?

It's this work, it's this exercise, it's this shutting these words out of my head and this sensing everything, how can I be sensing everything? I don't want to sense everything, I don't want to sense this car, this dark, this stuff, these breathing people, I am a freak, I've made a mistake, go back, no don't go back going back is what Joe says to do going back is part of it too, no, go forward, go forward, I don't want to understand myself and never did, it's alienated me from everybody turned me into a freak who will find me now who will penetrate who will ever know who will come get me. I am alone, and stuck down here. I am afraid.

18

Go forward, go forward. Which is what we eventually do, to the next station.

At the next station I got out and walked.

And as I walked did I "think" or did I think?

What is thought? What is hallucination? Is thought hallucination? Is "thought" hallucination?

I do not want to go crazy. I do not want to lose control. If I go crazy and lose control won't I kill myself, won't I do some powerful thing?

☙

Joe said don't use drugs, drugs are hallucination, drugs are distraction, from what is.

And drugs use up finer energy and when the drugs wear off it's gone.

And you haven't earned anything.

But at the moment, as I walk, the breeze from the river slapping my face awake, I think of things quite the other way: at least with drugs you'd know it would be over, you'd know it's not forever. You could tell yourself and wait it out.

But this? This, what, this terror? Which is. Which is what it is. Is without end, because what will end it?

Kill yourself. Kill yourself, that'll kill it, or will it?

One more dismal idea. Think you can escape just by death?

Hamlet come alive, at last.

Sententious phrases galore, come alive, at last.

Or at least I see what they were pointing their crabby arthritic fingers at.

Fear.

So there's something about what Joe's about, after all, and maybe it's subtle and fine and gentle in the end but for the moment it's bigger than a bomb. Blow me up anyway, blow up my world.

I feel small and stupid.

How dare I. . . what? Step clumsily on the hem of it all? Curse, be casual, ignore, pretend to a million false truths?

I am afraid enough of death and if there's more than death . . .

Who can stand this? Who is man enough?

And so have I not played a neat game of approach-avoidance?

It's an old game for me, but let's say, for argument's sake, that's true of us all, monkeys running at the fire, monkeys touching it or just feeling the heat, monkeys running away.

I pretend to myself I'm Birdman, I'm a venturer a seeker-after-something a careener through life on the lookout for what it's about, but if I get the smallest hint of what it's about I am so struck with awe and speechless I run I cry surrender make excuses regroup reconsider reconnoiter reinterpret every pledge and every word, every gesture.

I like reading about things at my house in my comfy chair in front of my comfy fire if I even had a fire. Armchair general, dreaming of battles that are far enough away. Yes or no? Me or not me?

Continue, please.

Continue.

☙

Maybe later I won't be so afraid. Later, when I'm again far enough away, or when I'm nestled anyway in the softness of Joe's voice, when others will be there to cheer or back up, there for each other or anyway stuck together, thirty birds on a journey to where.

☙

It's ignoble to be between two stools. It makes you two-faced.

But I'm comfortable that way, admit it. To the world, I say one thing. To this other world, another.

☙

I buy a paper at the newsstand at 86th Street. I continue to my apartment. I get my things together for the event. I watch a little of the football. The Jets are getting pasted.

By the second half my fear has retreated.

19

Bobby and I saw her with the same eyes that night, Maisie sitting cross-legged on the floor, hunched a little forward, between Laura and Joe, her impertinent hair like her entire biography saying she might be anywhere tomorrow. Her half-eaten meal between her legs, that Bobby had prepared, his secret gift to her, still close to her when he was not. Maisie didn't *act* like she was a blessing to wherever she happened to be, but either of us might have seen her that way. The only difference being that I saw Bobby looking as well, and he didn't see me. That's how I knew, or thought I knew, that for once I was the man and he was the boy. The night of Christmas, after both of us had looked at Maisie, Bobby and I went out to find some girls.

My idea entirely, like taking Junior to a whore, buck him up, back in the saddle. Both of us having been left. My gesture of friendship. For once, something I could do. And was it, as well, proof to myself of my own immunity? I am not attached to Maisie, I let Maisie roll off me, she can get Hodgkin's disease Stage 112 and die or so I tell myself and wonder why. The meeting after dinner lasted until almost ten. Talking about the "event," prepping for the "event," Joe's pep talk, follow your aim, hold your question, "Damn the torpedoes! Full speed ahead!"

Bobby looked so gloomy. Dead goldfish look, out on the street, on Broadway. Come on, let's do it. He didn't really know what I was talking about, the few girls in Bobby's life having either come to him or been there. Bobby wasn't a hunter, but it was my gesture to act as if he might be or anyway wouldn't it be fun for once, cheerful anyway, new way to kill a little time. Bobby when are we gonna cut the gloom shit out? What happened to the principle of nonattachment? Let it come and let it go. Don't censor but don't believe. Plenty of mermaids in the sea, just look at me, I didn't say; nor any of the rest of it. But I behaved as if it were so, and maybe to humor me he tried, with a skeptic's chilled bemusement, to go along. "It's pretty late."

"Who cares?"

"It's Christmas."

"Lonely hearts."

"I didn't know bars were open on Christmas." The kind of thing that Bobby wouldn't know.

Roget's on Broadway in the eighties might as well have been closed. The bartender looked at us every several minutes with a lingering purposefulness, as if maybe we'd leave and he could close up. I bought Bobby a drink and felt the lofty trajectory of my patronization despite the fact there wasn't a woman in sight. Bobby picked at the label of his beer. The place smelled of leftover cold cuts, wafted from a dreamtime steam table. I wondered with half-formed words how I had got to this position, where I could fall in love one day and say fuck her the next. Had I not been a sensitive child? Felt all the stings of rejection. Yet here I was, giving manly advice on John Suckling's subject; a kind of suspect miracle. And Bobby who was ahead of me in pretty much everything else was stuck.

Or was he?

Had I not become, on further reflection, rather a cold insensitive anesthetized bastard?

Go back. Gently. Fuck "further reflection," and furthermore "reflection."

Sense, look, listen.

But why bother if it turns us into automatons?

It doesn't turn us into automatons, it doesn't turn us *into* anything, it turns us *towards*. . . what?

How say it?

Bobby and I not saying any of this, but all of it alive between us, inchoate, at issue.

All the venerable travails of love, the doubt, the longing, the misery of absence, the aspiration and striving and proving, redirected away from breast and womb, warm blood and earthy lies, towards. . . dot dot dot again.

No, no. No, no, that's wrong. That's the propaganda. That's the ideal. In truth, I'm between two stools. I don't love anything now. I don't know what to love. Have I begun to love myself?

Joe? Love Joe? I don't love Joe. I don't "love" Joe. Does Bobby love Joe? Does Bobby "love" Joe?

We're so miserably lost.

Except that Bobby "loves" Maisie. What a throwback. What a disaster. How could Bobby feel so much for Maisie, that he sits here and peels his beer label like a boy? Maisie who must have been for him an image, a symbol, a hint, an embodiment but of what?

Or that other word they use, incarnation. Fuck incarnation. Fuck it all. Bobby come back. Stop. Sense. Look.

Is Bobby advanced or is he fallen by the road? All a race after all.

What a bore, to race through life. What a chore. A little of this, a little of that. A thousand "I's," a thousand Bobbies. But which one do we have here in Roget's on Christmas night? The one that loves Maisie or "loves" Maisie, that's mournful and alive with hate for Joe for taking her?

"Bobby, are you," I ask. "Bobby are you mad at him?"

He shrugs as would be expected and his thumb nubs at the remains of his label.

Don't tell me how life should be, don't tell me how to be. He seems to be saying?

Yes Bobby I was wrong about girls tonight, no lonely hearts, I say, more or less.

Close to him, rubbing shoulders with him. His narrow shoulders, his slender arms. Mine slender but not as slender as his.

"It doesn't matter at all," he says.

But it does, I almost say.

Bobby says, "If I was mad at Joe for being with Maisie wouldn't I be mad at you as well?"

"I guess you would."

"But I'm not," he says, "I'm not, I never was. And not because I 'let go' any feelings."

"Why, then?"

"Who knows."

"Girls are better at this than we are," I say.

And by "this" I think he'll know what I mean but maybe he won't. Bobby shrugs. Good enough. Warm-blooded anyway.

The way of the sly man, sitting in bars, a few others have passed in and out or lingered by now, and now a girl I met in here a couple months ago from South Dakota walks in.

How rude of me not to make up her name. Barbara.

Her name is Barbara. Barb, they say in Sioux Falls.

So Barb, this is my friend Bobby. Buy Barb a beer. Too cold

to go back to South Dakota or nobody to go back to. A little unclear with Barb. Her heavy frame, her sluggish good nature.

She may weigh twenty pounds more than Bobby.

She enters into our conversation, the one that we weren't really having.

What'd you do today and how've you been and is it starting to snow, what a trip it would be if it snowed. Barb like a lone lamppost on a block. She remembers me well, she's happy to see me, but now I have to do the good-guy-horseshit-thing-of-the-year, win that award for once I've got to pass Barb along to Bobby so I do the obvious things, I praise Bobby to considerable heights, I mention the *New Yorker*, did she see his Mister All Electric Kitchen, if she didn't (which she didn't and she too, *vox populi*, conflates the *New Yorker* with *New York*), she really must. I do not mention the group, I do not mention anything weird, we are in the world now and we play the world's games as well as anybody.

Bobby for his part has little to say, but his smile is strawberry jam. He was in South Dakota once. There's that. Mount Rushmore. He draws Mount Rushmore on a napkin. Our presidents funny, cockeyed, insane, their noses and hair too pointed and their eyes too close. Barb isn't quite amused though she looks like she thinks she ought to be. She seems a little afraid that Bobby might be the type to blow Mount Rushmore up. Wrong vibrations. Try again. Bobby as prospective bourgeois, steady job, praise from the top. Bobby as well-connected, Shaker Heights and all the rest of it. Bobby as poor slob on Christmas whose girl went away. Careful with mentioning the girl. Careful, careful, careful. But Bobby does it anyway because he doesn't know what to do. Our little naif, our shy, cunning Bobby. Mentioning Maisie was no good at all, I'd begun observing Barb's light mustache damp with beer and figured Bobby had too, things were not going well for Mister Fix-up, time for Plan B, plead illness upset stomach go home have to call Europe in the morning or maybe Kuala Lumpur all of it or some of it I forget which exactly but anyway I left them, rather abruptly. How cavalier, how dashing, how second-rate stud. As if the last thing to be done was whisper in Bobby's ear, *for me, Bobby, for me.*

But I didn't whisper that. I said to Barbara that Bobby might draw her on a napkin and one day it would be worth a mint, I said good night, left a well-calculated tip, and left.

On Broadway I found the phone booths calling out to me, singing to me like the Lorelei, streetwalkers one to a block, and what they were singing was BUtterfield 8.

No Maisie don't tempt me don't trick me again I walk up Broadway I'll not be detained not drop a dime in a phone when you won't be there anyway I know where you are.

Yet I'm shaken to think that I would even like to call her up. What a liar I am, what layers of self-deception, all that posing with Bobby. What a laugh, what a fake. And oddly or is it simply the way things always are, glorious in their banality, between men and women, between friendship and love: I know it for certain now, I like Bobby better than I like Maisie. As Marcel said of Albertine, all this and she wasn't even my type.

I do not dial 2–8-8. I go home and one way or another manage to notice on my hollow core door desk where I've scarcely sat for years my notes about Joao. For sure to spite them both, Maisie and Joe, to show them my dust and that I'm still alive, in an hour I sketch a story about the Angel of Saint Vincent's. It's full of blanks and strained and I have no magic to hide the lonesome "we" that every Talk story still in 1978 requires, but it's a start and when I'm done I want less to call BUtterfield 8.

Bobby phoned me around one when I was already in bed. He was home and he was alone. The gory details, just a few. Mildly apologetic. He'd drawn her on another napkin. She'd looked at herself, perplexed. Never mind the jaw too square the nose too long the eyes too beady. . . was that a mustache? Barb said that she too wasn't feeling well. Good Samaritan, good night. With the fewness of his words, Bobby sounded as if maybe he blamed me, for making a fool of him, or wasting his time.

20

Our silence.

We did not talk about the group with others. It wasn't in any of our biographies.

Unless someone asked, or sensed something, from the *Bird Guide* or Philip's Talk stories or the person's prior experience with Ichaza or Castaneda or somebody.

Girlfriends and boyfriends inevitably found out, and often they wound up coming to meetings.

Later they would throw off the girlfriend or boyfriend who brought them and then they would stay or not, or the girlfriend or boyfriend who brought them would stay or not.

You never knew. Who would stick, who would go.

There was something erotic about it all, or something that started as erotic.

The circle. The quiet lack of inhibition.

The poetry of love.

The bright paint on the window frames of Joe's apartment.

The roses on their shelves, under their lights.

༄

Our morality.

Once on a Tuesday evening:

Philip: Is morality conditioning?

Joe: Yes.

Philip: But do we need morality?
Joe: If people wised up, they wouldn't need it.
Philip: Ah.
Joe: In the meantime, that's why we've got cops.

☙

People struggling to believe.

☙

Whatever it is, struggling to believe.

☙

Not *believing*. Believing would be different, believing would be like a machine without friction. Struggling to believe.

☙

The "event."
  We'll be spiffing up the place. Painting the window frames, sanding the floors, painting the old tin ceiling. Making a nice little home for whatever it is in a loft on the tenth floor. For Joe. Let's be specific. A nice little home for Joe. *Mi casa, su casa.* Why not? Didn't the village always support the parson? Respect for wisdom, even in New York in 1978. Respect for ourselves, Joe would say. Our home. Most hours of the day, somebody coming or going. The once-and-future clubhouse; workshop, too, carpenters, making tables, Jesus wannabes. What a vision. What an alternative. Build a workshop in yourselves, build a

clubhouse in yourselves. The sort of things that Joe would say, we wouldn't even have to hear them, I wouldn't even have to hear them. Build a small place in yourselves, quiet and beautiful, where you can hear running water, and if the rest gets done, so much the better. Somewhere in the world, one place or the other, people have always done this work of cultivation. "We." "I." Whoever. The "event." On the eve of it Joe gives an example of an aim: "I/we/you will live or die trying." Tomorrow it starts.

21

Several of us sit across a patch of the floor like oil derricks in a desert, fiefdoms of enterprise, going about our business with a seeming perpetual automatism. We are assigned to sanding the floor. Years of wax and grime and urethane clog its pores and encrust it with a hardened atmosphere of discoloration, as if it were wearing a petrified coat of smog. I see this theoretically, with my mind's eye that I must never trust but that operates nonetheless, guessing, judging, and criticizing. I have not yet seen what the boards will look like when they're bare. Even to say "boards" would be a stretch, since my eyes work on one board only, one portion of one board, the part of it where it meets the next board in line like a passenger car in a train, my universe, my country, home to all my history and efforts, a section of the unredeemed world two inches wide and ten inches long, give or take the occasional incursions into neighboring territory by accident, the scuffs and scratches on adjacent boards as if they've suffered collateral damage. By ten o'clock my mind is imprinted with a new language, in which "60" and "80" and "100" and "150" all have utilitarian meaning, the language of sandpaper. My chosen sanding block rests in my hand, small and rectangular, like a bar of soap you might get in a not overly generous hotel. Number sixty sandpaper is wrapped around it. I've not come even close to using an eighty yet. Coarse, that's my speed, I've a long way to go, even on this tiniest patch of board, to get to medium coarse. I sand with many light strokes. Infinitesimal dust rises and clings to my sandpaper and fingers. I do not overdo it. I have a long way to go, I tell myself with words then banish the words, in the proverbial manner of closing the barn door after all sorts of creatures have fled.

I shift my legs. I am stiff from the waist down. I half-recline like a Jew at Passover but in this position I find too little weight in back of my arm. The sanding block brushes over the board like a whisper. I shift again. My ass hates the floor. My flat, skinny ass that's already had enough of this. Why doesn't he assign the fat-assed people to sand the floor? Look at Laura, she could sand all day. Perfectly balanced on her two majestic cheeks, the natural Buddha of floors. Go back. Slow down. Sand. The muscle in my forearm feels like a burnt coil. I relax my fingers on the block. I inspect the sandpaper to see if it's still got grist. With the side of my hand I plow the dust away from the board. I do this too often, I decide, I'm like a windshield wiper when it's barely raining. Who decides? Why decide? Go back. Look at the floor, look at my board. Its grain is like a hundred streams. It is perhaps a shade lighter than when I began, perhaps a shade lighter than the boards that adjoin it. It makes a mottled appearance, some regions of it lighter, others, gullies and ravines, darker and less explained. The whole still glows dully with old wax. My knees ache too. It is ten o'clock. I've taken my watch off but I steal a glance at Joe's forearm as he trundles by on one of his trips. He's wearing a short-sleeve shirt as usual. The stainless steel watchband snakes and glints on his thick forearm. The blond hairs of his forearm make a prairie. Where's he going? Who cares? Go back.

I take a break. I sit in Joe's captain's chair, my hands on the armrests, symmetrical and loose. All around me the others sand and paint and hammer. As busy as little bees, though their affect looks more like the Stepford wives, pushing carts with slow stares. Oh don't ask why. Oh don't ask why. I still love Lotte Lenya. The no bullshit cruelty of Brecht. What would the wily old kraut commie make of this? Go back. But I don't go back. One thing to another, Brecht to Germans to Jews, their toothbrushes cleaning the sidewalks of Berlin or was it Vienna? What an idea that one was. Teach the people of the book a thing or two about manual labor. The virtues of work, work makes free. Are we Nazis now? Are we following a Nazi path, is my sanding block so different from the toothbrush? Look. Listen. Sense. Who? Me or them? Go back. The Jews were being humiliated and we are not being humiliated. Or are we? The Jews were not free to go and we are. Or aren't we? We are, I am! The world with its lessons. Could the Jews in servitude have learned a lesson of freedom? Maybe they did, maybe some did. You can learn anything from anybody but that doesn't make everything the same. Joe is not some sitcom guard and we are not Stalag 17, nor even with my bomber jacket do I make William Holden. How'd I get on this? Who cares. My break's gone on too long. I sit in Joe's chair and daydream. It doesn't matter if I work or rest, everywhere I daydream. Hopelessness is all.

I go back to sanding. This is only the first day, the first morning of the first day. I work a little while, then take another break. I am falling in love with breaks. Why not, no one's watching. What a child. I long to go out. I long to go to the store, to buy more sandpaper. I change my sandpaper as often as I can. But still I have enough. When can I go outside, breathe the cool air, go to the store?

And it occurs to me as well: why don't we go rent a sander?

He wants the floor sanded, rent a sander. I long to go to the store to rent a sander.

No. Don't. Sense. Sand. My tired arm, my flat ass. The board as resistant as a stiff-necked Jew, as me myself and I. We are both encrusted, hardened, I see the comparison now, vividly, with pathos.

How could I have accumulated so much crud in thirty-two years?

It occurs to me this could be the same amount of time that's passed since the board's been sanded. What if it's been precisely thirty-two years, eight months, how many days, twenty-five days?

Not too bloody likely, but still.

Go back. Sense a *little bit*, anyway.

Yes I do. I sense my hand. I listen to the sibilant scratching of the paper against the floor. It's like a woman doing her nails. We'll never sand the whole floor like this.

To recapture the attention of my eyes or maybe out of boredom I look around. Maisie in jeans and a loose flannel shirt, cross-legged and shapeless, sorting papers out of a cardboard box, her red hair her emblem, like words that need never be said but if they could talk would say. . . what? Yes they would say "what," they would say "what" and then be still and intent and defiant, but right now she's not defiant, she's learning, she's young, or that's what it looks like anyway, she looks like a plant in the ground. And Philip and Cal washing windows, like a tag team, a comic duo, the sunshine boys as window washers, griping in silence, their lips not moving, Philip on one window, Cal the next, Cal's long arms, longer than mine, reaching up to the top window like Lamarque's giraffe to the top branches. Neither of them looking like they quite believe, having the postures of hypothesis and hope, their eyes, their hands, the glinting windows, all in mazy motion as if in Xanadu did Kubla Khan something or other decree, or in this case Kubla Kahn. Joe shaking his wrist, shaking his watchband, here and there the Little King the Little Kahn. A few words to Laura that I cannot hear, a few words to Ty, who's sanding too. I am doing a census now. I am checking everybody out, or at least those at this end of the loft, those this side of the galley, but the galley blocks my view of the rest. Joe bustles out of sight, towards the band saw. As he departs he leaves a wake, a fading contrail of attracted attention, a kind of evanescent evidence. Was he sensing? What was he sensing? The force of his wake, his one ball, his vitality. For a moment I like it. I like being part of a chance.

And Bobby in the galley, cooking alone. I long to move up. If I can't go to the store, at least I could be there. Like prisoners in the camps, again, hoping for minor improvements to their fates. As if everything depended on minor improvements, minor improvements like signs, or like moves on a chessboard, proof the game's still being played. You can leave! I chide myself, then chide myself for chiding myself, then chide myself for chiding myself about chiding myself. You can walk out anytime! There's that. Just test it. Go!

But if I went, what would I do with these friends I've made, these comrades of a long march? Really, I've gotten used to them. A world supplied. A world other than the one that is no more than it is, concrete image of itself, fetishized, commercial, world of indifferent betrayal. Something tender is here, or personal anyway.

Joe yells "Stop!" I hear the word penetrating my dream, I can almost see its force, a missile crashing down through my fantasy's atmosphere. Everyone holds whatever position they were in. My hand is tight, my neck muscles tense, my mouth hard and set. Flecks of dust on my fingers.

"Does anyone have anything they want to talk about?"

I steal a glance around. My neck gets tenser as my eyes move. Bobby with a spatula in the air, as if he were conducting an orchestra. Maisie hunched over, almost doubled up. Philip touching the connecting piece of his glasses, professorial, unsurprised, even relaxed. Is it possible he was really relaxed when Joe yelled "Stop?" Of course it is. There are things undreamt of in my philosophy, but I am beginning to dream them now.

Maybe I am, could it be that I am?

The only one with anything to say is hatchet-faced Phyl, previously notable for having been picked up for prostitution on the Bowery, to wit a French for twenty dollars U.S. currency said the officer, while Phyl told the group it was certainly her first time and only on account of an unexpected cash crunch, terrible luck; which I said nothing about but found hard to believe because with the efficiency of the New York vice squad as I knew it to be you'd have to have given eight or ten thousand blow jobs before the odds of a bust went against you. But anyway Phyl who I can't look at now without thinking of what a wide and tolerant assemblage we are, writers and Wall Streeters and D.A.'s and streetwalkers, a late twentieth-century urbanist's dream, says that when she heard Joe's voice it was like her mother waking her up in the morning.

Tears are in her eyes. She says, at the moment, she's feeling like she wants to hate her mother but she doesn't. Is this sentimentality or truth?

I think of the re-education camps for intellectuals, where they learn how to be as smart as the workers.

Is that, too, what we've got here?

Pol Pot. Mao.

Good for us. Good for them.

Though is there, was there, gentleness and attention to doubt in such camps? Like a bourgeois I rush to warn myself, "of course not, of course not." Though how do I know for sure?

"Stop." I hear the echoes of Joe's word. Go back. Sense.

My arm.

Back to work. While Bobby, sweet and sour, works in the galley. Is he scouring, is he oiling? I wonder about his mind. I wonder how it flies around. I feel guilty for having fucked Maisie. I feel crazy and in love with Bobby. My Talk story. Almost forgot. Philip. The three of us. Are we all queer?

Quick look at Laura's tits, do I get a hard-on? Yes.

Next case. Move on.

But I do have my friends, don't I?

Love is an action, let us not forget.

"Love" is bullshit. "Love" is pathology.

But "love" has always been pathology, in all the poems, Majnun and Laila and the troubadours. Denis de Rougemont, remember him, from college. Tristan and Iseult. All pathology, all "love," all something at least, worth hanging a life on, worth something.

Our circle of love.

Bullshit, bullshit, no. As much hate here as anywhere, and at least anger keeps it clean. Don't get mired in "love."

Or if you're going to get mired in "love," let it at least be for a "love" as pure as words can make it, a "love" of beauty itself, veiled and hinted at, that yes or no maybe or not held me in Philip Deschayne's apartment that first night I went.

Go back.

The wood. Another board.

A trip for sandpaper, across the room. Bend it to the block. Continue. Aching. No meal. The meal is late.

Midnight. Bobby still preparing the meal.

Baked potato. Caviar and sour cream.

We eat, we breathe, we are quiet, each little globe of salmon roe bursting as if in my brain like a bright orange balloon, then we talk.

The group talks. Various, but the sense of having only just begun. Familiar territory here. A man may do ten years in prison but be conscious for only seconds or minutes, adding up all the bits and pieces, the flashes and epiphanies. A way to look at it, anyway. So has each of us already done a five or ten year bit?

The plasticity of time, warped to our desires.

And space? What of it? Isn't there plenty of inner space to fly around in? If space is a really, really, really big box, or better yet those Russian nesting dolls, wouldn't there be space to fly around in one of those Russian nesting dolls?

Freedom from space. What a fine idea. Goes along with the other one, freedom from time, a boxed set.

What a lovely, thoughtful gift, thank you very much.

Go back. Come on. Come back. Give it all up. Sense.

My hand. Sand. Coffee. Fatigue.

By eight the sun has risen.

Carry on. The boards are my friend. I go inside one of their grooves, find a place for my mind to sleep. Cozy and warm, protected, the place for an animal, let winter go by, hibernate. Down here where my eyes see myself. Sawdust falling like snowflakes on my lair.

But when you wake up are you still in the *katzetlager*?

Eleven o'clock on the second day. Bad breath and Dunkin' Donuts. Take as many breaks as possible.

And now, what a bonanza. Joe calls a meeting to talk about how we're doing.

In the meeting I say all I'm glad about is this meeting. I say I'm at the point where being tired doesn't sand away my fantasies, it encourages them, my vigilance is gone. I feel like I'm showing off when I say this and I am.

Others also show off. Nearly everybody is showing off.

Except Bobby, who says nothing. Why is Bobby saying nothing? Joe asks. He asks it of Bobby, then of anyone else. Bobby looks glazed. His head is not down, he eyes Joe, he looks around the room, he smokes a cigarette, but he says nothing. Is he playing a game? Maybe he just doesn't want to show off, I say.

Or has he simply found a better way of showing off?

Bobby who knows how to make an entrance, who knows what a star turn is.

Joe asks Philip what he thinks. Philip with what sounds like a true believer's answer: "Probably he's angry."

"What do you feel?"

"He should wise up."

I hate that phrase, "wise up." Another of Joe's, dragged out from some '40s trunk, smelling of old celluloid and casual arrogance, I despair of Philip when he says such things, I cling to the hope that he says "wise up" only because he wants to hear what it sounds like in the air, wants to measure it and grade it and see how people react, even how Joe reacts and how he reacts to Joe; Philip as a holder of long questions, learning something or not.

Or is this my tattered fantasy, that my emotions continue to patch together, because he's my friend and if my friend doesn't fight and wonder like a Jew with God then what am I?

But what if Philip did fight, already, what if he did wonder once? He could have done it all in his deep, graceful mind and . . . satisfied himself?

Joe goes around the room. How to help Bobby. What to do with Bobby. Why don't we just leave him alone. Can't anyone just leave him alone?

Joe says we remind him of when he was a child, there was a kid who cried sometimes and the other kids could always make him cry, tears of rage, by telling him he was starting to cry even when he knew he was not, or wasn't anyway till they started on him.

I had a friend like that, too. I was almost that kid myself. I'm touched that Joe tells the story. It seems to be a story that condemns cruelty, or recognizes it anyway. Bobby stays quiet. As if he's unimpressed, as if he's gone deaf.

Joe shifts around who's doing what. I'm off the floor. I'm back to my beloved windows, which weren't really beloved until I spent a day sanding the floor. Windows that you can see through, windows that you can see an end of. Windows that put you out on the sill in the cold air. The dreams of the concentration camp, a slightly better job.

Who cares. Go back. Sense. The point of it all.

Will I make an "I" or won't I? Will "I" make an I or won't "I?"

When will all of this fall away? Nothing is falling away. I am secretly glad it's not falling away because if it all began to fall away I would be terrified and I myself would fall away. "I" myself would fall away.

The day is windy. Even at this height I am pelted by bits

of trash and soot. I wear a jacket. I nurture hopes that the window cleaner will run out so that I'll have to go to the store for more. But it doesn't run out and anyway I find another, larger, refill bottle in the closet. I wash windows until it is dark and then I go back to sanding the floor.

Sense. Stop. Something is beginning to change. Once I come back inside, once my flat ass sits again on the floor, whole seconds go by without words in my head. The quiet is as sweet as water, and the very word "sweetwater" means something to me I never imagined it could mean.

Sweetwater Clifton, sweetwater who.

Sweetwater. Quiet. Running in my head. Change. Joe used to talk about change all the time, change is hard, he'd say, change is rare, change is slow until it is not. People don't want to change. You have to want to change. Words in my head again. Go back. Silence for a little longer. Sweetwater in my mouth, my saliva. The world is bright and sweet. My peripheral vision expands more easily. I can see the whole damn loft at once. I am so touched, in ways I cannot say. My chest burns dully, as though coals burned inside, embers in a brazier. Something is building. The sweet water of anticipation. Shapes take on depths they always had. How could I never have noticed? Furniture, walls, people. The air itself has more depth.

Joe comes by. Usually I'm someone he ignores. I am certainly not someone he dotes on. I feel his eyes in back of my shoulder, I sense his weight, his hairy arms, I've heard the creak of the boards, the halting of the creak of the boards, announcing his approach. I continue to sand. I see the fissures of the board, I see the cracks in the piece of sandpaper where it's been folded and folded again, I see my hand gripped like a claw and let it go. "Don't let me disturb you," Joe says.

"You're trying to steal my attention," I say, without moving my eyes, though they feel rigid and cease to really see.

"You're letting me," he says.

"Always a pleasure," I say.

"Cheers," Joe says, and moves away, in his wake the scent of roses.

I go back to work. I feel my resistance breaking down. But resistance to what? Is this brainwashing, after all? Dr. Droid, Dr. Void, Dr. J. the evil eye commies with their comic book . . . **BRAINWASHING!** Turning ordinary good Americans who one day if left in peace would water their lawns into filthy reds overnight.

The aroma of Bobby's cooking a second day. The sweetness of scallions in the wok, the sesame and ginger. *It won't be long now.* Or will it, the way time goes now? The scallions and ginger as if beckoning. Overwhelming. I've never desired ginger so much.

Hints of a finer food? Impressions, they say, are finer food.

Impression of Bobby with his wok, sober. I begin to wonder again, what he is about, how things work through him or not. I am astonished by my lack of perception. I can't even guess. Why not? Is he not my friend?

Don't do it, I tell myself, don't let him steal my attention, don't let myself even say it's he who would steal my attention, whether he would or not the buck stops here, it's I or "I" who must not let my attention be stolen. Go back. Look at Bobby. Smell his food, his seduction.

But sense. Sand. No words in head, to describe Bobby or myself or argue or have an opinion or critique or anything else. If I have something to say, I will say it, I will not rehearse it. Sand. Work. Lightly. Harder. This board, too, shall be clean.

My arm is getting stronger. I work the sandpaper back and forth. The sawdust flies up. I am getting stronger. "I" am getting stronger. I remember that I yearn for something. A hint of the beautiful, my mouth full of sweet water. My yearning makes me stronger. Or keeps me going anyway. Sand the wax and grime of decades away. Turn the sandpaper around, rearrange it on the block. See the pockets of resistance on the board. I have sanded here, now I'll sand there. I'll get it all, someday.

And then it's dinner on the second day.

22

The pleasures of the work.

The waft of garlic.

Vodka.

The smoky atmosphere around the television, the men watching the football.

Even thinking of us as "men."

The easy sexual confidence.

The tingling spine of defiance.

The *Bird Guide*.

The aura if not the reality of effortless superiority, continued.

Poverty's spare, clean embrace.

The sense of mind triumphing over body and so the banishing of disease.

And the banishing of dying?

Don't be obscene. Don't go crazy.

That's where all of this falls down.

Not the banishing of death, but the shy dance with death.

The play of fancy ideas.

Neither the banishing of irony nor the shy dance with irony, but the growth, in bitter, disputed ground, that we till and cultivate as best we can, of a few simple flowers. Crocuses, maybe. Lilies of the valley. Roses that you can't kill with a stick, thorny bushes that go on forever, you find them by the roadside, neglected for years, and coax them back to life.

☙

The pleasure, too, of using the word "we." We did this. We felt that. As if "we" were not the greatest fiction of all.

☙

A king calls a competition. "We" and "I" are summoned. The competition is to decide which is the greater fiction.

They joust, they battle, they grimace at each other, they do all the stuff, play the lyre, spout poetry.

A long, long time has passed, and the winner is not yet known.

☙

Orphaned by the storm. So that Joe's apartment, and now this loft, become our orphanage.

☙

Be bold. Leap. Damn the torpedoes! Full speed ahead!

Brave phrases, that you couldn't, or wouldn't, say in public, for fear of being mocked, or found out, or denigrated, or misunderstood, or put in proper perspective. The sanctity of a space where Joe could say such things. "Don't fire till you see the whites of their eyes." Another of Joe's favorites, brave, silly, sincere. It was his silly sincerity that in my exhaustion I liked best about him. It seemed so against good taste, so against reasoned compromise, putting a claim directly on your heart: as if once in a lifetime certain things must be said.

❧

The pleasure, also, of the loft. It had the beauty, say, of the Brooklyn Bridge under construction, lithographs you see. The beauty of intention, imagining the whole of it from the part that hands and eyes have begun. The window frames being slowly painted their blues and greens. The relentless noise of the shop. Joe's particle board furniture, trimmed and clean, arranged around the big TV. The carpets with their image of prayer. Some day this place will be something, you say, it will be as bold as the man, and when it's finished he'll leave.

The pleasure of primary colors.

❧

On the morning of the third day, I slept a little while. I sat down on a register and my chin fell into my neck. I was asleep ten or fifteen minutes, and I dreamt the whole time of waking up, of being awakened. Yet I awakened only into more layers of dream.

Finally I started snoring and Big Ronald shook my shoulder.

The third day was like an hallucination.

Joe forbade anyone to go out, for fear they'd be hit by cars.

I completed sanding one line of boards, the entire width of the loft. It wasn't great but it was "good enough." My mind began running out of things to say about itself. It either kept quiet or it ran on like a fizzling balloon, incomprehensible. I wasn't even sure in what proportions it was one thing or the other. I stopped winding my watch. My breath tasted like damp sawdust. The others seemed to move slower and slower, and I must have as well even if I wasn't viscerally aware of it.

After awhile, I took a number of naps. Everyone did. Anytime anyone sat down, if they weren't smoking they were catching a few. Coffee more or less did its job. But we were trying to be two times awake, and our strength went fast.

"We," "our," fictions, but something like what it was. I have even fewer impressions of myself.

At meetings people mumbled.

Joe was staying awake, as well, because he said it was his responsibility, which when he said it and we were so tired made it seem as if he was blaming us, that it was our fault, our greedy need for supervision, that was causing him not to log his comfy eight or nine hours.

Bobby was quiet at every meeting, but in the galley he was a kind of maestro, furiously involved, turning out thirty plates of this, thirty plates of that. We ate off the dark blue plates every meal. Between meals Bobby washed them all, as if he really wanted to do it all, chief cook and bottle washer, master of beginning, middle, and end.

Meanwhile my frame of reference fell apart, a sea of peripheral vision flooded over it. It seemed to me that the whole loft and all its contents had become one big "we." The customary boundaries of "I" were there, but like broken lines, that on a map would indicate the most primitive sort of road, or a boundary between territories which no longer exist.

And then sometime on the morning of the fourth day, a sort of miracle. I began to feel stronger. This coincided with Joe asking me to help Bobby in the galley.

༺ༀ༻

The pleasure of exhaustion.

The pleasure of wondering what comes next.
The pleasure of cigarettes.
The pleasure of doing.

༺༻

The pleasure of standing beside Bobby, a little bit taller than he, a little bit jealous, listening to the creaks of the floorboards and the whispers of our blades as we slice through this or that.

23

Laura developed shooting pains in her leg so severe that she couldn't walk. Greg left with his fever at 106°. Nausea, nosebleeds, the severest sorts of migraines, symptoms you never heard of, anything that might get you out of there made an appearance. Mostly it was the simple exhaustion. Raoul gashed his hand in the service elevator doors. Others hallucinated and walked into walls. Almost as many took the week as a warning as took it for a challenge. By Sunday a third of us had left, and of those only a few returned. By comparison my "revival" made me feel jaunty. Maybe I wasn't so bad at this after all. Maybe I wasn't such a weakling worthless chicken coward. . . the words in my head were roughly formed, the words, really, of a boy. I was being boiled down. We all were. And all of us who made it from meeting to meeting expressed similar feelings of childish hope or pride. I started imagining myself a hero. Girls waving, parades. A phonograph record we found, in a stack of 78's, the day Joe took possession of the loft. Lucky Lindy, hero of the USA. Were "we" all, when you got down to it, eight-year-olds?

For Sunday dinner Bobby has decided on white asparagus. He has found them in Chinatown somewhere and must have paid a mint. Joe peeled off cash to pay for them. Joe was never cheap, or if he'd been cheap once, because his father had the dry cleaners and it was the way things were, he'd overcome it. People could change; the living proof being the guy with the hairy blond forearms in his Sears short-sleeve shirt.

But why had Joe changed?

Because he had more self-hatred than any of us, I propose to myself. The ritualized words of half-remembrance run roughshod over me. "Stop." "Go back." "Gently." I hear Joe's voice from the first Saturday afternoon in his apartment, baritone, inviting, unashamed. His words are in me and I can't stop them. I can't stop anything. And yet everything, if not stopping, is at least slowing down.

My thoughts of Joe are like a drunk's slurs. Are they thoughts or are they wishes?

I wash the asparagus. The tap water chills my fingers. I dry them with paper towels as though each piece of the paper towel is precious. In silence Bobby shows me how to snap the tough stalk off the tender part. He's like a mime, his gestures exaggerated and simple, as if he were talking to a foreigner, and he has the slender frame of a mime. The day has turned out blue and crisp. The sun glances through the loft's east windows teasing our exhaustion.

Come out and play. Come read the Sunday paper. A museum maybe? A walk in the park?

It is the duty of my mind to know where the stalks should be snapped. My mind, not my fingers, feels the bend in the stalk, the snapping point, the resistance, the point where living ends and dead begins. I mustn't waste an inch of stalk. I mustn't waste a quarter of an inch; less; infinitesimal, what my mind's eye alone can see. This is what I am looking for: my mind's eye, my mind's hand.

I put the saved stalks in a pan and the dead bits in a pile. For a moment I believe in myself, but Bobby turns from his sauce and looks my way laughing and then I believe nothing. "Is this all right?" I look—with a quivering forehead—but I do not say. "Good enough," Bobby looks—with bovine eyes, at the pan—but he does not say. He doesn't show me all over again how to do it, so it must be so.

The sorcerer's apprentice. Ah, there's a sweet phrase.

What about the sorcerer's apprentice's apprentice?

My mind is like a board sanded almost clean or anyway I would like to think so. I mock myself for thinking about boards at all. I mock myself for mocking myself. Maisie. How did it happen that now my eyes are following Maisie? She passes by. What's she doing? She's wearing a sweatshirt that says "Yale Crew." Where did that come in, what blast from the past? The sweatshirt gives a plumpy reassurance to her shape. Stage 1, Stage 2, Stage 3. Does Hodgkin's really go away? If I think about Hodgkin's am I trying to kill her? If I think "am I trying to kill her" am I trying to kill myself? We walk in mirrors, you and I, Maisie. But why do I say "you and I?" What's so special about "you and I?" Living a past that isn't passed. Fool's paradise, awash in sentimentality. Be real. Maisie in my peripheral vision going to the closet by the elevator, slowed, self-conscious, swimming in the air of the place. Maisie solid and unbowed, the back of her, her hair, the parts of Maisie that don't bother saying good-bye.

I am done with my asparagus. I am going to put them away. Stacking one paper towel on the other I become aware, as if from a suddenness in a still sky, a shooting star or was it, of the milky flash of her face. I allow myself to look her way, on the half-argued ground that if I'm consciously looking how can my attention be stolen? She's by the closet, paused, as if Joe had shouted "Stop!" looking directly at me with a blankness that could be fatuity or love or the sheer exhausted mistakenness of eyes that have to land somewhere. I look back at her as though it was more than luck. Our eyes hold. What's this? Her eyes like still green pools, her curiosity, our surprise, but before I begin to know what it is she looks away. A spell snapped or it was nothing to start with or she feels embarrassed for her lapse. I return perfunctorily to my paper towels, my asparagus, my job, my "self," but I feel like a sixth grader now, moony, all the eroticism in my world reduced to looking, to stares, to one set of eyes; as if it were she one more time or is this the last brightening ember? She brings a stepladder from the closet. She's indifferent to me again. Where's she going with the ladder, what's she doing with it now, carrying it in her arms as if it were an overgrown child? She doesn't look at me, I'm nowhere in her thoughts. The shame of my mistake suffuses me, but I'm also skewered by longing, as though these two strong emotions, having plotted my ambush, attack from opposite directions.

Go back. Gently. Give it a shot at least, let your longing take you where it will, feed the childish hunger in your eyes.

With what? Feed it with what, I ask, you ask, Joe's disembodied baritone asks, my father asks, my mother asks, like a mother whose cupboard is bare.

Learn to live with it then, let it drool and wonder. And Bobby? Consider Bobby, whisking his hollandaise or whatever he will call it right next to you. Has Maisie looked at him? I don't think so. Is Bobby aware? Of course he's aware. He whisks his sauce as if it were the stuff that dreams are made of. She walks past the galley and her breeze causes the muscles of his neck to ripple. We are all so tired. A little later there are tears in his eyes.

Maisie has brought out the stepladder so that she can paint the ceiling. Who told her to do this I cannot guess. Nobody else is painting the ceiling, yet it's in our plans, in our playbook. I imagine Maisie wants a moment when she can feel like she is reaching for the heavens, the happy feeling of the world looking upside down. I indulge myself with such fantasy, but do not look her way, not directly anyway. I arrange my chores so that she's enough in my line of sight that I remain aware of her, like Icarus falling from the sky in the Bruegel, unnoticed and noticed at once, the artist seeing what the world does not. A quart of paint sits on the top step of her ladder like a crown she's put aside. Her feet are on the third step and she's already, in her hair and on her sweatshirt, flecked with what looks like snow. Her brush is painting the sky, making it pure again. More paint droplets fall. She's put newspapers on the floor around her. Her hand with its brush waves slowly, her eyes wave slowly, she's aware of each mistake. Maisie stretched out thin so that her sweatshirt comes up and her torso is revealed, beige and taut, a prize in a box of candy. Bobby leaves the galley as if in a dream and walks over to her. She seems to pay him no mind. She dips her brush in the can and paints the tin heaven. Bobby stands beside the ladder looking up like a man who's seen something in a tree. Time passes. Maisie continues to ignore him. Her reach takes her on one journey then another, journeys to unpainted portions of tin. Is she becoming unbalanced? Bobby takes hold of the ladder to steady it, then lets go as if realizing his lie and his presumption. A gobbet of paint falls off her brush, splashing his hair and forehead and dribbles down.

I am aware that my own feelings for Maisie are gone forever. My co-conspirator who never was. But Bobby, what of him?

At two we eat in silence, the clatter of forks on plates competing only with the taxis and wind-rattled windows and whatever internal monologues our enfeebled minds are still capable of engendering. As usual after the meal we have a meeting to discuss whatever's come up. There isn't much now, people seem afraid to waste energy on speaking, a hoarding instinct is taking hold. Valerie mentions this. No one comments. No one seems interested in smartass remarks, or criticism. Big Ronald says he's had a nervous stomach for days but now has become thoroughly nauseated and suspects it's something he ate. A congenial topic at last, complaints about food and upset stomachs fly. The culprit is suspected to be the morning donuts from Ramon's, didn't the banana creams in particular have a sulfury smell about them and in addition they tasted off, a little bit sweet-and-sour. Big Ronald feels sicker just from people talking about it. For most of this discussion I'm feeling simply glad it's nothing I chopped up. When people are through speculating Joe weighs in. He speaks with the calibrated informality of someone accustomed to having the last word. He says what's going on with Ronald goes on of course all the time, people are always getting upset stomachs from the last meal they can remember or that's what they think, anyway, but actually it's all bullshit, it's all in their minds, chalk another one up for fantasyland, because he was just reading an article in *Scientific American* and the food you eat doesn't really get to your GI tract where all the trouble starts for twenty-four or thirty-six hours, so actually it really is all bullshit, how can you get an upset stomach from things that aren't even in your stomach yet? Joe loves finding out that things are bullshit. Big Ronald stirs his neck, his diagnostic grin settles out, he lights a Newport to get control of his breath. Others trim their sails accordingly. Val contributes her view that that was a really interesting article that Joe was talking about, it confirms other research she's read. A kind of bidding war is begun and now others as well remember that they've heard something confirming Joe's insight. Julie asks if it's a case of cognitive dissonance. Others think it isn't. This spurs Joe to start in about other studies he's read, about digestive medicines, which show that Tums are about as good as anything. "It's all bullshit, it's all in your mind—" He hesitates, "until it isn't." I hate the hesitation. I think of the Wizard of Oz. Yet I concede to myself that Joe doesn't really ram immensity down your throat. He actually has the minor gift of talking about trivialities without making them seem bigger than they are. He simply likes small things; gypsy music and minor keys. We then fall appreciatively, and exhaustedly, silent. For some reason I notice Bobby sitting with his hands in his lap and his legs nicely apart, as though he could sit this way discreetly protecting his private parts for a hundred years and no Buddha would complain. And as I watch him it's kind of crazy—is he doing it for my benefit?—Bobby's face crimsons and his eyes billow wide and round as if he's a balloon being blown up. "Asparagus pee," he says.

"What about it?" Joe senses the challenge in the choked fewness of Bobby's words, which come out barely bitten off.

Bobby harvests a breath. "What you're saying, I don't care who wrote it, it's wrong, or maybe you misunderstood it—two hours after you eat asparagus your piss smells like it."

The room titters uneasily, in nervous recognition. But Joe isn't amused. His eyes narrow in their Charlie Chan way. He taps a cigarette out of its packet. "It's different," he says, with such certainty one can almost feel it as wind.

"What's different? It's not different." Tears rim Bobby's eyes now. He's like a kid protesting a bad call in a game.

"One's a liquid," Joe reasons.

"It all goes in your stomach."

Joe shifts tactics, lightens up. "Is there a doctor in the house?" he calls.

"It's bullshit," Bobby says.

"Calm down. Take it easy."

"Asparagus piss!" Bobby shouts, like a kid again, one who's just discovered his big voice and is ready to shout down the world. "Asparagus piss!"

The others, including myself, know what this is about. We think we do, anyway, we think it's about right and wrong and hit and miss and denial and truth and while you're at it throw in faith and disbelief and trust and mistrust as well. And having a sense of humor about life, and is something happening to that too, is it dying in the dregs of these days? But no one says any of that. No one jumps in. No one takes sides.

It's possible that a kind of sadistic glee was taking hold of us then. Asparagus piss! It's true!

Philip, like one of the wise men holding up the world, takes it on himself to say something that to me sounds facetious but maybe is simply an exhausted mind trying to be helpful: "What Bobby's saying would only apply if you were asparagus positive, which of course not everybody is."

I feel as sorry for Philip now as when Diane's boyfriend was pounding on me and he stood there as helpless as a calf with the take-out coffee in his hand. My eyes canvas the room. Faces as blank as the proverbial *tabula rasa*. Are people sensing? Have they given up? Joe sits smoking his Newport with an air of purposeful distraction, as if remembering a movie where the natives had the white hunter in a pot, and the white hunter knew he mustn't show fear.

We return to work. I wash the dishes with Bobby. When the bubbles of the detergent start baptizing my hands, I know I've begun to go insane. The tears rimming Bobby's eyes remain, their gloss pink and inconsolable. When the dishes are done I go back to the floor. I sand with a rhythm that is mechanical and hypnotic, the way I'd learned to screw certain girls who were afraid of male feeling. Back and forth, back and forth, I suppose I could be jerking off as well, and get just as little pleasure. I am putting in time. Time meanwhile is doing its utmost not to cooperate. Joe shuffles around as though nothing has happened. He is wearing his slippers again. Five stepladders now dot the loft, oil rigs or Towers of Babel, take your pick. I lose track of Bobby again. I may even be watching the sway of Laura's swank ass on her ladder—for what more spiritual contemplation than that could one find on the afternoon of the fifth day?—when Bobby's voice, a little far off, breaks through the concerto of sandpaper and saws, like a patron making a fuss in a theater several rows away. As his voice comes closer, I turn. Why not? Steal my attention! Go ahead, take my wife, please! He is dogging Joe's steps, while Joe pretends with what seems like good-natured patronization that Bobby isn't even there. "Asparagus piss! Get it? Admit it! Why can't you admit one thing?"

People are stopping now, all over the loft, though I observe that Philip does not, he continues washing his window with grave sincerity. He looks like an athlete playing with pain. While Maisie seems bored with it all.

Joe puts on his trench coat and presses for the elevator. Bobby turns towards the rest of us. "Losers! Mediocrities! You all ought to be seeing shrinks! He doesn't have anything! What does he know? Asparagus pee!"

For a moment I can't figure out what he's doing but what it is is he's unzipping his fly and presently he starts pissing on a slab of the unredeemed floor. The pungent woody perfume of whatever's the acid in asparagus reaches at least as far as me. Bobby's pee puddles on the darkening boards. When the doors of the elevator open, Joe must have second thoughts about whatever his previous plan was and hauls Bobby, with a sweeping arm gesture that's like a vaudeville hook, inside the elevator with him. The doors shut. Shortly—how long? Thirty seconds? A minute?—they reopen as though someone's played a joke, as though the elevator has gone nowhere. Bobby emerges first, with his fly zipped. None of us know what if anything was said in the elevator, said or done or imagined. Joe takes his trench coat off, hangs it on a hook like a '40s detective back in the office. His features are bland now, and relaxed, as they get sometimes when he watches movies all night and his belly is finally full of them.

Bobby goes right to sanding the floor, on boards next to mine, his eyes still moist. Both of us begin to sand like demons. Or is "demon" the proper word? Does "demon" connote too much? "Go back." "Gently." To whatever you've got left of yourself, to your fear, your terror, sand your terror away. But how could either of us have arms so strong? I feel like I am coming irrevocably close to where I'd never wanted to be. How would I get back, Bobby? Bobby? Would you see me through? Everything feels too late, but I sand like a demon and so does he. The evening passes. We take no breaks. Our sections of board link together, then link up with others, continents of freshly sanded wood are coming into being. The world smells fresh. Our land is unadorned. The room shimmers. The others in it I begin to see as if I were wearing 3-D glasses. When they reach an arm in my direction I expect they're about to punch me. If their faces come my way I expect a kiss. Or do I really? "Really" is in short supply. Another night goes by. Cal puts a post-it on his shirt that reads "wake me if I pass out." I further my infatuation with sandpaper. It's the one-fifty I love now, its surface as smooth as skin. Yet what miracles it performs! It sands away sin! In its caress, the trampled upon, the ruined, the slicked and painted, are reborn. I feel the smallness of myself, reduced to the space between the windows and the galley. What relevance has bigness now? In smallness, in the country of the sanded boards, I shall find freedom or become very scared by its prospect. What if this is all I need?

I fall down on the floor at four o'clock. I do not even know I'm falling asleep. It seems like I'm simply talking to myself, telling myself to stop, telling myself to go back, telling myself to sense. When I wake up Bobby's head is on my shoulder. He's fallen asleep as well. Day has broken. There's rain in the eastern sky, rain or snow, the grayness of beginnings. Maisie is looking down at both of us. She's on her knees. "Open your eyes, sleepypeep," she says to Bobby. He lifts himself from my shoulder. He looks like he might say, like a boy in a myth, "Where am I?" For a second I imagine I know something about an angel.

Maisie gets up and goes back to work. Bobby and I sit there for awhile.

24

So we ran after the impossible and nothing happened. That's what it seemed like, anyway. But what does it mean when "nothing" happens, isn't that what we were looking for, "nothing" to happen? Isn't "nothing" the impossible?

I managed to say something like that to Joe at one of the meetings on the fifth day. He snorted and refolded his legs. "Suffer," was all he said.

Was Joe getting off easy? Those cryptic little remarks, that parodists could do shtick all day with. But Ty Duncan was a parodist, and he didn't laugh out loud or groan. It was one thing to make fun and another thing to be serious, and the premise of our life here was to know which went when. So Joe got a pass on "Suffer." Our minds bent around the word, searched for its cracks, emulated its strength. Such was the idea, anyway, though whether any of us had enough left to do it was an open question. And anyway, long, rolling, strenuous sentences on topics ineffable and unnamable were targets just as large if not larger. Say too much when nothing can be said. Or, say nothing at all and die.

At another of the meetings, Maisie said she finally realized what had made her sick. Sort of a showstopper; then she said, "Cancer."

"Funny, that's what I found out too," Joe said.

His voice like a deep well, with a surprise of feeling at the bottom. As if he was not only protecting her but leaving it obvious for once, the way an underappreciated uncle might. Had I misconstrued Joe? Only once had I seen Joe touch Maisie, the time they danced. Did he love her, in his fashion? Love her the way he loved everybody?

Sometimes those that are near. . .

Maisie came here so that Joe could help her: had I forgotten?

I'd forgotten nothing. Not just now, not on this subject anyway. But I wondered.

The tangling up of the personal with everything else.

Was Joe *sweet* on her?

He announced an interruption of the work, a New Year's Eve party. But it was hardly a real announcement because we were all already aware of it. Some of the Boston group were coming down. And there were going to be visitors from Berkeley, people we wouldn't know, but Joe was thinking of setting up a second group out there. This last was the real announcement. Maybe Philip knew something about this, maybe Maisie or Bobby or Liddie, but to most of us it was an utter surprise, like an only child considerably grown up hearing that his parents were having a baby. Joe went on to remind us that the event itself was continuing, just as war was the continuation of diplomacy by other means so we should consider the party a part of the event, a chance to observe our exhausted selves and others in a different context for a few hours. Use all the pig including the squeal.

He sent Bobby and I out for the booze. I hadn't been outside for a week, but it could as easily have been a month of Sundays for how unnerved I was by the rush of humanity. I felt like I'd be run over. I felt barely able to resist. How small I was, how small we were, Bobby and I, even with our secrets. The wind gusted. I swept my scarf across my face. Eighth Street with its usual mix of shoppers and hustlers, some of the latter of whom I was certain I'd seen before, lingering in the underlit corridors of the courts or standing beside second-rate lawyers to cop a plea, brought me up short: I suddenly felt like a released prisoner, like these guys I'd been putting in jail. I felt not so much a gush of empathy as what seemed a more useful reversal of fortunes. Why was I working at the D.A.'s office, aside from Joe's prodding, aside from all the explanations I supplied, the low pay, the Ivy League ease-of-access? So that I could have before me an image of what a prisoner was! I said this to Bobby in a rush. I told him to look around.

"Why'd you take a job, then, where you're locking people up?" Bobby asked.

It was a question I thought I'd already answered, but when he said it I wanted to cry.

It seemed like everyone in New York who'd got off work early was in Astor Liquor stocking up. The checkout lines stretched back into the liqueurs where Bobby and I sat as if stalled in rush hour traffic with our shopping cart full of everything Philip would need for another punch. Joe had peeled off two hundred dollar bills and I was feeling giddy again, with my fatigue, my freedom, the money in my pocket. But Bobby, since deflecting—that's really what it was, a deflection—my outburst on the street, had turned quiet. Normally it was he who was given to flourishes and I who taciturnly absorbed them. What had brought about the reversal?

A little later I thought I knew. While we waited in line a guy I knew from the courthouse came in. He was a court officer in one of the arraignment parts downstairs, kind of a large guy, big enough to be a cop, with a mustache that looked too small for him, that made his face look slightly squeezed. Dan something, good-natured enough, but I had no intention of more than nodding his way. I kept things proper downtown. I didn't go out and drink with anybody, except for Diane when there was Diane. And I had an aversion to mixing anything about my "inner" life with my job. Too much to explain. Impossible to explain. I wore my job like a cloak, to keep out the rain. Dan saw me, gave a little mock-salute which I answered with my nod, then seemed to settle himself, with a hand basket, in the aisle in back of the liqueurs. It was then Bobby said, "I'm learning how to fly."

I assumed he meant fly a plane, wondered for a moment where he was getting the money, but—conscious of not expressing negative emotions—I put enthusiasm rather than skepticism into my voice: "Great! Really? Where?"

"Nowhere," he said. "Inside myself."

"Oh. I thought you meant a plane."

"No. No plane. Me." He said it as though he'd been thinking about telling someone for awhile. His eyes went into the shopping cart. He picked up the Cointreau and peered at the label.

I felt uneasy on account of his seriousness. I attributed it, I supposed, to our lack of sleep. Perhaps I wasn't even hearing him right. But I hesitated before asking him to elaborate because I didn't want Dan in the next aisle to start picking up bits of this crazy conversation and hear my voice mixed up in it. I said nothing more. Bobby started peeling the label off the Cointreau before we'd even bought it. Nothing more was said about flying. I was so tired I half-forgot about it.

But at one point later, when I was sanding again and half-remembered, what passed through my mind like a verbal phantom was the title of Ouspensky's book about Gurdjieff, *In Search of the Miraculous*.

Had Bobby stumbled on a bit of the miraculous?

The party started around nine. Everyone went home and changed their clothes. The loft was half-painted and a quarter of its floor was sanded. Wherever we were at seven o'clock: "Stop!" "Good enough." It had started to snow shortly after dark and the snow made curtains on the windows and on Broadway the traffic went away. People trudged around. It would be a trudging-around New Year's Eve, snow in people's shoes and smiles on their faces. In the galley of the loft sat a pot of mulled wine, and a bowl with Philip's punch. Everything felt crystalline and fresh, life brought to a glow by blowing gently on it, holding out against the snowy dark encroachment.

The carload from Boston arrived. A little like country cousins, but there was a good looking guy with a razory smile, thin-lipped, short hair, who I was sure had slept with Maisie. He looked at her as though he'd never quite given up possession and she looked at him as though to say "what an asshole." The country cousins liked to dance. The green carpets were up. The thin-lipped guy danced with Maisie a couple of times and she didn't look at him much but their rhythms were the same and I wondered how much there might have been between them. Once Joe cut in, the Boston guy dropped away. At around ten the Berkeley contingent showed. And because a number of people from our group who'd dropped out of the "event" returned for the party, the loft began to fill up. Joe had commissioned Greg to make a dance tape for the occasion, and the result was punk not the Washboard Rhythm Kings, or punk and the Washboard Rhythm Kings. Conference of the Eclectics.

Philip had "cooked up another doozy." His phrase, again. Only Bobby and I, besides Philip, knew exactly what was in it, but many passed it by on spec as if it were Jim Jones' Kool-Aid. People were tired enough, giddy enough, without it. The room smelled of fresh clothes for the first time in a week. Our guests from Berkeley were mostly in their twenties, more athletic-looking than ourselves. I chatted up a pretty girl who turned out to be a dancer in an Oakland troupe, and she told me what some of the others did, they were carpenters and construction guys and mechanics and one guy with an idea for an outer space epoxy that he was cooking up in his garage. Not one was a Berkeley student. But I did recognize an older woman, maybe forty, lined face and a ponytail, eyes a little too bright. She had visited Joe once before, over the summer, a sort of mystery woman though Val, who knew so many people, knew her from somewhere; and now she was accompanied by a tall dark balding guy who from appearances in his younger days might have been a Pakistani cricket star but who wasn't Pakistani at all, his name was Rothenberg, he'd grown up in Minneapolis, and he was the left brain/right brain psychologist about whom Philip had written, the guy with the connection to the Sufis in London and Marrakech. This couple that wasn't really a couple hung back with Joe and Maisie and Philip as if they were the adults chaperoning the party. They drank Philip's punch and sat around, and it looked like the psychologist was telling stories, or gossiping. Some of the others from Berkeley paid deference to the woman as we paid deference to Joe, and from this accumulation of gestures it finally dawned on me what must be going on here: the woman, or the left brain/right brain guy, had invited Joe to come out and take over her group. It was as if at some point, maybe over the summer, the woman had acknowledged Joe's suzerainty, or anyway that she could learn something from him. Three cheers for the home team, we're number one, big index fingers stirring the air. But what would it mean if Joe started going out to Berkeley? What would happen to us? For a moment my mind raced through its Freudian archives in a kind of rushed defense of the realm, and what emerged was an unstable powder of separation anxiety and oedipal longings to murder.

People danced lethargically until they didn't, then everything was more or less frenzy. It was only we, the New York hosts, who hadn't rested all week. Not a few of us slept through all of it in the corners, curled up like dogs. Why not? We'd be back at work tomorrow. I couldn't imagine who would be adhering to Joe's dictum to keep sensing as if the event was continuing, maybe Bobby was; I sensed myself, but only because I'd got so used to doing it that I couldn't have stopped if I'd tried. That's how things were then.

I had never liked to dance, but I would dance if I thought it would get me laid. This seemed the case with the California girl, the girl in the Oakland troupe. In part I danced with her just to show Maisie I didn't care. How grown-up, how evolved. The girl, Austin, danced circles around me but she seemed to like my dour little gravitas, maybe she thought it was a New York thing. Or maybe it was the amount she drank. Neither of us was afraid of the punch. Bobby joined in and eventually, after midnight and nobody turned into a pumpkin or a saint, we went outside. Six or seven inches had fallen. We sat in the snow in the middle of Broadway. Strangers tromped around like pioneers. One group had plastic cups and a bottle of cheap champagne and they passed out drinks, to whomever, as they partied up the block. The traffic lights still worked, though they had nothing to direct, like the famous trees that fall in forests where no one hears. The snow still came down, light and steady, an airy benediction. Austin had never seen anything like it. Neither Bobby nor I had the heart to tell her we hadn't either. She shivered and loved it and I leaned over as we sat in the street as if I was about to kiss her but pushed snow down her neck instead. Children, children. Why not? It had been an awfully long week.

Bobby told us a story. He was sitting in the street as well. The story was too complicated for me to make sense of but it had knights in it and the Hundred Years' War and at a certain point I realized it was the story he'd drawn on the lamppost on Mount Auburn Street in Cambridge. In the story there was a jester, and whatever heads or tails I could make of all the other characters, their trappings, their comings and goings on the historical stage, I knew that in the very private Dungeons & Dragons of my friend's fevered mind the jester was the only good one. Bobby wasn't half-finished telling it when a bus came along, tires slashing for traction, wipers flailing, looming out of the north with one headlight on and one gone off, a lost Cyclops plodding its way to nowhere.

We hugged ourselves and hoped it would miss us and it did, but we didn't move.

In fact we didn't move till Joe came down. He had his trench coat on and Dr. Rothenberg with a striped scarf wound around him like an Oxford don and Maisie and Philip and the woman with the ponytail and too bright eyes. The grown-ups were going to look for something to eat. It was maybe two A.M. Rothenberg said something to Austin that had familiarity in it, and she got up and said she would like to get something to eat as well. Bobby and I also got up. Austin was too wise in the ways of things to ask us if we wanted to come. This she would leave to the nabobs, none of whom said anything to us, maybe

Joe was still pissed at Bobby from the day before, but anyway we stayed. They went off into the whiteness of the night. After half a block we couldn't see them.

Bobby said to me, "This sucks. He's eating us. I'm eaten. We're already dead."

"Not quite," I said.

"We're food for him," Bobby said. "My head's bitten off. I've got to escape."

"You won't get far if your head's bitten off," I said.

"We're already dead," he said.

25

Bobby and I walked up to Washington Square, where the drug dealers were having snowball fights, then we drifted, silently, back to the loft and back to the floor. In the hours between four and seven others trickled in as well, including Joe, who arrived with three plump ducks in a shopping bag that he was making a fuss about. Chinatown, somebody had ducks. Now Bobby could make Peking duck. Bobby looked sober and put the ducks in the refrigerator. Maisie was beside Joe with a bit of snow on her nose and in her hair. The heat of the elevator hadn't quite melted it off. They looked like a king and a queen. Indeed the thought arose in me, floated in half-formed words that I noted while chasing them off: is this what this group was all about, to satisfy our human longing for monarchs? What a joke that one would be. Maisie took off her coat and went behind the partition where Joe's bed lay. I followed Bobby's eyes that followed her then froze at the point of her inevitable disappearance.

Others cleaned up. I sanded. Which is to say I moved my arm back-and-forth, applied such-and-such pressure, listened to the hissing and shushing of the abrasive on the encrusted board, saw the dust grow on my fingers, contemplated this anti-habit as habit. What did you expect, if not the eternal return? I had lost weight and my stomach was in upheaval and my vision was mildly doubled and I loved every one of my symptoms. Proof I'd done something, anyway. Proof I hadn't just sat here and moved my arm.

But in the exhaustion of not only my body but my ambition, something peculiar developed on this last day. Emotions, strong emotions, I'd seldom felt, or not felt for a long time, arose in me. Joy then sadness then joy then sadness, in me who usually was neither a joyful nor a sad man, who was angry and fearful if anything; nor was there really any cause of these emotions excepting the "causes" that sat there everyday. Having said good-bye to my parents in more or less definitive terms, I now remembered them teaching me how to bike-ride, a summer day, their togetherness then, the buzzing of the bees, my cream-and-red Schwinn, my mother's hopefulness then. Joe's cancer, losing a ball, no words, Maisie's cancer. Sickness old age death the whole shot. Where had they been hiding? Let sadness go. Let gladness go. Sense. Look. Listen. And my sadness came back double, for Bobby who didn't get Maisie and watched her go with frozen eyes and Louie who didn't get her either and didn't even know what he'd missed; then my joy redoubled, too, just for my ability to feel redoubled sadness. A virtuous circle but why say "virtuous," why not "circle," why anything at all, why words? These three fat ducks, somehow, in Joe's imagining like the breaking of the atonement fast and so was he not a kike from Brooklyn after all, you can take the kike out of Bensonhurst, put him on a train Manhattan-bound, write a '20s song or a '30s song, but "kike from Brooklyn" will he remain. Joy and sadness.

All of it as if it had been hidden under canvas in the dark. In a box put away, like my grandmother's preserves.

Go back. Sense. Yeah, yeah, yeah. Like the Beatles' "yeah," or just yeah?

Bobby stayed sullen through the day. I blamed him for it, as if his sourpuss, or soberpuss, somehow threatened the excited cycling of my joy and sadness.

At four o'clock Joe called a last meeting, to see where we were winding up or if something might still be done. Greg had found a lamp in a niche, and this seemed to make Joe happy. Phyl said one thing she learned, she was never going to whore again, one more bullshit irrelevant saccharine lie which inexplicably made me want to cry. False hopes, odd dreams. A home for silliness. There should be such places. Refuges from the world's blind purpose. Or so it seemed, anyway, sitting there on the bench. The cruelties inflicted on people with flat asses. We knew nothing, but who did. Calm down. The end is near.

I thought I might say, might report upon, my adventures in joy and sadness, but then thought better of it—"showing off," "too rehearsed"—and then spoke anyway about trying not to speak. Joe looked at me as if I made life hard for myself. "What is it you really want to say?" he asked. I felt choked up. The room spun around. Joe's head seemed enormous, like the head of a jack-in-the-box, coming out of the sky. Nothing at all came to me to say. I who was so full of words. "Don't worry about it," he said. "Maybe next time."

Val spoke. Ty spoke. Liddie spoke. The preciousness of their voices. What of it? A week of this. Ugly breath in the room. Yet, the preciousness of their voices. I struggled to hear. Finally Bobby, who was dour still, said he'd spoiled the plum sauce. Joe reached into his corduroy pants in his silent movie way, as though the card would read "Money solves everything!" and snapped off a twenty from the fold of bills in his pocket and told me to go to Chinatown and buy plum sauce. He gave me an address of a place he was sure would be open, and I left.

☙

What happened in the hour or hour and a quarter that followed I pieced together from others. The meeting continued and there were words, that Philip described as a bit of urinary Olympics, between Bobby and Joe. Joe teased Bobby about spoiling the plum sauce, and Bobby went along with it awhile, teasing himself until it wasn't himself any longer that he was teasing but Joe for putting him in the galley in the first place. Was it another little gap in Joe's understanding that he'd thought Bobby could make plum sauce without screwing it up? Wasn't it Joe's responsibility to protect us from danger? Bobby said it all with smiles, Philip said. They would have been his first smiles of the day.

But Joe was not amused, and I suppose I thought, afterwards, why should he have been?

But shouldn't he have known what to say, or do?

Maybe he did.

Maybe he didn't.

Maybe there are some things no one knows.

Joe said to Bobby, "Sit still and eat your spinach."

"I already ate it," Bobby said.

"I don't know what to tell you then," Joe said, and that was the end of it.

People just wanted it to be over then. The week, the "event," all of it. They didn't care who won.

A little like the wisdom that soldiers get if they're on the losing side.

There are beauties in defeat.

There will be other days.

Giving up. Hands up. Submission. Freedom.

Did a cone of power arise then?

Did we become more than ourselves?

But how could I know?

And I wasn't there.

And anyway who talks about such things? Naifs and the brokenhearted.

Joe said, "We'll eat at seven," and in truth they did, they started without me because the store Joe sent me to was closed and I had to hustle around Mott and Bowery for another and in the meantime Bobby found a bit of old plum sauce in the refrigerator door, so there was that.

Everyone seemed so relaxed, Philip said later. Jokes about the floor, which now looked like somebody's skin rash. Ty would rent a sander tomorrow, even things out in no time. He smoked a pipe for the first time all week. A plate with the crisp skin of the duck, a bowl with the scallions, another plate with the pancakes, a cup of sauce. Bobby offered all of these as if proudly, and a little like a benediction. But no one praised the food because no one ever did, you were supposed to eat and breathe and sense and there was still time and the chance.

For what, Bobby?

He ate a pancake or two. Not bad if I say so myself.

That was his look, anyway. Mischievous, Philip said.

Enjoying a fine feedbag.

But where was Louie with the rest of the plum sauce? Joe was getting annoyed.

He praised the food.

Compliments to the chef.

Bobby said it, not Joe.

Or did he say it with a question mark?

Too much. Go back. Gently. Sense.

We would sleep well tonight.

The nightmare of life? Oh, please!

We are a garden that feeds our selves. We have gardens within us.

Joe got up to put the TV on. It was still New Year's, after all. Bowl games. The Orange Bowl was on, Oklahoma and Nebraska that year. The women looked bored, the men like silly stereotypes revived or pretending to be. No one really noticed—someone on the screen was completing a thirty yard pass—when Bobby made a run at the windows, or rather Big Ronald noticed because he was coming back from the toilet, but by then Bobby had flung the window up with such abandon that the old glass shattered and he was clambering onto the ledge as the shards rained down on him. Big Ronald shouted Bobby's name and ran his way. Bobby crouched like an actor playing a bug-boy in a film. Others stood and turned and started. Joe yelled "Stop!" Big Ronald lunged for one of his legs to grab hold of as Bobby sprang. Nobody saw his last expression.

I was returning up Bleecker Street with the plum sauce in my hand. A cab had let me off at Lafayette because Bleecker was badly plowed. I felt a whoosh that was like a dancer in the dark. I hadn't time to think. He landed on the sidewalk just ahead of me.

☙

The way he landed, the way he looked, I won't describe. Mostly because I won't get it right. I'll use too many words. But it was a mess.

And a hint of the obscene: there was something beautiful, as well. There always is.

The police came, not all that fast. The holiday, the storm. They took statements. I gave mine. I told the truth. Everybody did. What else was there to tell? Though everyone had trouble describing what the group was, what was going on upstairs. "Therapy," was what most said. A few said, "watching football," but then had to elaborate so the cops wouldn't think there was a contradiction. Each explanation seemed to me as close as the other; just coming from different angles.

Upstairs the shattered window was still thrown open. It was a window that I had washed. My window, my love. As clean, as clear, as starlight. The wind wound through the loft. The rest of the Peking duck sat on plates. No one touched the window frame or swept the broken glass until the cops said we could. Joe said little. He looked surprised. The only one weeping was Philip.

Letter from Bobby.

> To Whom It May Concern & You Know Who You Are:
> I wished there was a letter from Bobby.
> I wished there was something.

Sincerely yours.

But he did send me a dream. Maybe an arch way of putting it, but it's how it still seems.

In the dream I am Bobby. I-who-am-Bobby am getting ready to fly. I know how to fly. Or I think I know how to fly. I'm fairly sure. A chance.

I am in the loft. So are the others. They're having their meeting. Their backs to me, their cigarette smoke rising. Will they care, will they be amazed?

Neither rage nor defeat touch my soul. How can they, I am a fly-boy, tousle-haired and free.

But also, if I turn around and think about it, like Woody Allen with that big thing on from *Bananas*? That too, maybe. Vaudeville. Shtick.

But a worried look? Why?

I sense myself like crazy. I sense my brain, my spine, my wings.

Though don't go crazy, "wings." We'll wait on "wings." We'll see.

Will I not fall, like Icarus in the Brueghel, seen and unseen?

I-who-am-Bobby observe the window. I observe the night. I observe the building cornice across the street, and I observe myself observing these things.

My back is to the others now. I've served dinner, what more do they want? They've been well-fed, as they deserve to be. Burps and felicitations, my friends. Now we'll see. If what's what is what's what. I-who-am-Bobby will show them. . . that I can fly.

Sense, run, window, air, shouts, go, leap, go.

Nothing to it now that you're going. Because look, my friends, how time slows.

You thought I was doing this to shorten life, but see how life lengthens. Aren't you, aren't I, surprised?

The air on my hands and face. Calm down. Sense.

You're not really flying yet, you know, you're falling.

But oh so slow, who could really say?

Chilly air up here. Should've worn a scarf. Planning. Forgetful. Next time make a list.

A disputation on time as I-who-am-Bobby fall—or is it fly? And observe myself falling—or is it flying? Between the tenth floor and the ninth all of time in all the cosmogonies ever imagined passes by, I-who-am-Bobby experiences it all, the fires and the ice, the gold and the iron. And how will the time between the ninth and eighth beat that? Beat that, you sucker! Beat all the time that ever was! But somehow, there's even more time now, and more between the eighth and the seventh! Billions and billions of cosmogonies. Cosmogonies never thought.

Get the picture, get the dream? Still on the seventh floor. I long for a break in my fall. Why has the snow stopped falling? I long for a little snow in my face.

No fear. Why fear? When you see how much time you've really got.

On one floor all the animals troop by. It's like Noah, it's like creation. The garden, or excuse me, the Garden. I-who-am-Bobby take a peek. All these windows, some bright, many dark.

Million-stories-in-the-naked-city time. Million stories in the naked city got nothin' on me. Million stories, small potatoes.

What a dream he sent me.

And there's more. All for the $4.95 shipping and handling.

If I-who-am-Bobby wake up will I fall too fast? If I-who-am-Bobby wake up will I miss out?

But I want to wake up! I am here to wake up! Why else was I in this loft, why else am I in this sky, if not to wake up? How could I forget, when self-remembrance is all?

Sixth floor, lingerie. Fifth floor, hats.

I-who-am-Bobby have lived a hundred billion squillion-quadrillion light years already, I've lived as many light years as Scrooge McDuck's got money in his bin, and it's all petty cash. What a cartoon. What a story. Hear me out! I can fly!

And the sensation of it is just like life. Look around. Sense. Listen.

On the fourth floor my eyes go inside and the place is empty except for old sewing machines and junk and I go through a door and pretty soon I'm on a road that goes through galaxies of stars. Pretty nifty, no? Just one of the many opportunities. Just one of the things you're missing when you sit there like a lump.

Take a flyer! See the natural wonders! The Zambezi! Victoria Falls! Where space and time come together!

Third floor, colors. Second floor, shapes.

Or, third floor, fire. Second floor, water.

Or third floor, something else. Second floor, something else, a broken record maybe.

Suddenly I wouldn't mind a broken record, a broken record seems just the thing, because I-who-am-Bobby am running out of floors. It's the most awful thing in the world, really, to have lived a godzillion times a hundred billion squillionquadrillion light years and to realize it's almost up, to see the end looming up, rather fast really, like Louie on the sidewalk there, coming up the block.

He doesn't see me. How sad I feel that life is so short. No matter how long it is it's short. And no matter how many times you say that no matter how short it is it's long, when you get to the end of it, it's short.

This is what I-who-am-Bobby am thinking anyway, as I

prepare to abandon ship. Throw the switches. Hear the alarms. Dive! Dive! Dive! Get me out of here. I can't fall anymore, I'm finally going to have to fly.

Was it all a lie?

Wings? What about a rocket-powered booster out my ass? Wouldn't that work just as well? A methane-powered universe?

I sense my arms, I sense my wings, I sense my angel's breath. I am they, I am not this falling thing.

Was it all a lie?

I could still live, in a blink of an eye, more quattrobillion-squilliongodzillion light years than I've lived already, but what would be the point? There's still an end coming. There's always an end. I begin to feel totally exhausted, like I haven't slept, not really, in really quite a while. Why fight it? Why put off the inevitable? Let's go, let's move out, angel wings-or-rocket-powered-booster-out-my-ass-or-both-at-once don't fail me now, sense so dearly you sense light itself, become light itself, that will lift you away.

Huh? Say what again? I-who-am-Bobby do a bit of a wry, tragicomic doubletake, like a scientist in a cartoon when he realizes he's got something wrong, the formula's off, back to the drawing board, I-who-am-Bobby say to myself, there can't be so many subjects and objects, there's got to be just. . . dot dot dot. Quick, go with that then, dot dot dot, sense so deeply dot dot dot that dot dot dot . . . whoa, like the last words on a flight recorder before a crash.

Oh fuck.

Was it all a lie?

I woke up then.

26

Philip knew the parents a little bit. When they came to the city once, he'd shown them around the *New Yorker*. They liked Philip. He was low-key, friendly, didn't do that busy, obscure New York stuff; spent the time with them anyway. A demystifier. Philip was always a demystifier. He explained to them as best he could what had happened. They already knew about the group. Bobby, in a proselytizing moment, a moment of high confidence, even pride, or was it defiance, had told them a little. It frightened them, but they weren't surprised.

Bobby's father was one who tried to explain things, to himself, to his wife. She didn't want to hear.

All she wanted to hear was her music, Bach, she had a little cassette player, like a pre-Walkman, that she kept with her and played all the time, as if the Goldberg Variations would drown out the rest. That was the saddest part, Philip said. Even when he talked to them it was playing, though she turned it down a little. Her eyes were glassy. Philip didn't say to them, when the father asked who Joe was, that he was some weird guru Bobby had gotten mixed up with; because Philip didn't think it was so, and it wasn't. Not in my view, anyway. Not then; nor, really, now either.

☙

I'm trying very hard to remember if Philip really said "saddest."

I remember quite clearly where we had the conversation, at the coffee shop that used to be at Broadway and Canal that was known for its egg creams. It was some days later. "Sad," "saddest." Not words that Philip used, because to use them was to express negative emotions, to falsify, manipulate, attack. But I know he didn't say it was the "worst" part. Nor the "most difficult" part. Nor the "craziest" part. I'm pretty sure he said the saddest part.

✧

If this story could go one way or another, if it could nudge itself, say, in the direction of a movie sale, I suppose there could be a crisis now. Did he jump or was he pushed? Does our Assistant-D.A.-by-accident-or-design believe his friends or suspect them? Does he protect them or betray them? Does he get jammed up himself?

Figure the girl's in it up to her eyeballs.

And there'd have to be evil so that there could be good.

The kinds of movies Joe loved always had lots of both.

✧

But the story doesn't nudge itself. The only betrayals, as usual, are the writer's.

✧

The family made arrangements to take the body back to Cleveland. There was nothing in the *Times*. I didn't know then, and don't know now, if this was because such a death was not newsworthy on New Year's Day 1979, or because somebody hushed it up. Or it just fell through the cracks. The *Harvard Crimson* reported it. A short piece, that talked about the lamppost on Mount Auburn Street and his contributions to the various Harvard magazines and his successes in New York. Something I didn't know. He'd been invited into the startup of a new *Lampoon* radio show—the one that later lent so much (is this the polite way of putting it?) to the creation of *Saturday Night Live*.

☙

At the meeting on Thursday night, everyone came and a bowl of dates was passed. The twenty-nine birds. I got there early to get a seat on a bench. Others with more supple legs folded them on the green carpet. I noticed, beyond the galley, that the window had been fixed. Pristine dunes of white putty bordered glass as clear as rainwater. Otherwise I sensed the disorientation of being in a place that looked the same but was not. Joe made no speech, said nothing at all for awhile. He sat in his Eames chair and smoked his Newports. His face was hard to read, but it seemed maybe swollen, a fighter after a fight. His watery eyes did their usual dance around people's stares. But he didn't seem uncomposed. I surveyed the room. Most of the others were as regular and dispassionate as he. The work was continuing. Was it possible? That people were simply sensing, trying, in the shadow cast by this new development, the loss of someone they might have called their mascot, to deal with whatever might be "coming up" now? Working on themselves.

Was I working on myself?

What the fuck was going on?

It wasn't Joe alone. No one seemed ready to say anything. Ten minutes passed, perhaps more. I hated the crowding on the benches. I hated sensing the heat of others' arms. I told myself not to make words out of these. Sense the sweat of others if you must but why do you have to subvocalize it, lay everything up with illusion? Then told myself not even to tell myself this much, then told myself not to tell myself *that*.

The old joke. The old college try.

But overall, the words in my head may have been less then. Instead of words, snatches of songs. Maisie, Maisie, give me your answer true. I'm half-crazy. . . while Maisie sat there, on the bench to my right, her knees apart, her ashtray in her hand, her red hair like a one-man flag. Joe did not even say "Does anyone have anything they want to talk about?"

It seemed as though we might break up without one thing being said. It had happened two or three times over the course of things, meetings at which people sat there until Joe called it a night. I'd felt each time an embarrassed queasiness, as if open to accusations I could not quite hear, but my discomfort was clearer and fiercer now, and it had the sweaty oppressiveness of shame. Spade whom I wrote for so many hours would say something now. When your friend dies, aren't you supposed to? When your mascot dies. . .

I almost said those words exactly, shame, Spade, mascot. But no wind blew them out of my throat. Maisie, Maisie, give me your answer true.

Or give me anything, the world is out there longing to be kissed or at least seen.

"He said something," I said.

Surprising myself that these words were actually aloud.

As if I scarcely knew where they came from, my voice husky in a room that seemed to dim.

"Who did? Bobby did?"

Joe's radio baritone, easy, reassuring, skimmed over me as if my intention were deeper, buried in a bunker.

Was this really me, speaking so hoarsely, with scarcely a premeditated word in sight? "He said, yesterday, he could fly. . . He said he had to escape. . . I mean, he said them at different times. It wasn't like they were together. He started talking to me in the liquor store, about flying. I didn't. . . I let it drop, because there was a guy I knew standing near us, I didn't want him to hear. . ."

"So it's all your fault?"

"Is it? He also said. . . he told me we were food, we were already dead, our heads were bitten off."

"Oh? By who?"

"You," I said.

"So then it's my fault."

Which was the kind of thing Joe said often enough, and usually gleefully enough, as if it were child's play. But he was grim now, playing for keeps. His glance arced over our heads on the benches like a missile shot, which then, gathered back by gravity, landed somewhere on the flat neutrality of the elevator doors.

"I didn't mean it that way," I said.

"But it's not your fault, it's my fault," Joe insisted. "That's what you think."

"I don't know. . . if anyone's to blame."

"But you don't want it to be you."

"No."

The boundaries of my skin seemed to thin, so that, sensing

myself, I formed a mental image of myself larger than I was accustomed to think was me, I extended more out into the room. I sensed myself more deeply, until my skin seemed to melt into my sensing of it, the two were one and the same, and "I," released from my skin, reached out to the others on the benches, a little bit more, a little bit more, until I felt I could almost grab Joe and make him a part of "me." Later I imagined that what I felt might have been what a person who loses a limb feels, when he can see it isn't there but senses that it still is.

Then it simply ended. Joe was taking a moment, as if he'd won. Maybe he had. His cigarette parked on his lip.

"He almost hit you. He could have landed on you. You'd be dead. Don't you feel a little angry about that part?"

I didn't know what I felt, but I knew that it wasn't anger, and I said nothing.

"Who else thinks it's their fault?" Joe asked.

There coalesced in me then a distinct, even striking, expectation that others would chime in, explaining how it was their fault, it would be everybody's fault, kind of the reverse of the old Pete Seeger song where a boxer dies and everyone who knew him disclaims responsibility. A cheap, heroic Hollywood scene of indictment and catharsis from the black-and-white days when there was such a thing as "the people." My eyes tracked around the benches and I could almost hear what everyone would say. Philip would be chirpy, above the fray, but confess he had a crush on Bobby and had told him once and scared him. Cal would remember the time, when Bobby was complaining about something so trivial that Cal had long since forgotten what it was, that Cal had said to him, jokingly, to get him to shut up and stop "attacking" him with his little pity-inducing complaints, "Well, you can always jump." Ty would rue firing him off a magazine job, long ago, for being so late turning anything in. Liddie wouldn't go out with him. Phyl wouldn't give him a blowjob when he asked and why not because she gave everybody else. Val would remember dreams where Bobby was a devil. Raoul just plain didn't like him, for being a show-off, stealing attention. Greg would shed big sentimental tears for not having eaten Bobby's Peking duck, for having left it on the plate and Bobby had picked the plate up and stared at the uneaten portion. Big Ronald never listened to him, thought he was crazy, never trusted him for having been—no offense to present company—at Harvard. Julie told him what to do the whole time in the galley, castrated him left and right, when she worked with him before me. Laura didn't like his cartoons, they were so violent, Bobby could see her face twist up when she looked, this was just last week and she was surprised how hurt he looked. And so it would have gone, the confessions, if that's what they were, the contributions, as if people were tossing their bits and pieces on a pyre.

I imagined this scene but it didn't happen.

The only other one who spoke was Maisie.

All she really said was that he was sweet. "He wasn't a 'power-mad rat,' like some people said. He was sweet."

Her throaty voice, its smoke burying the dead.

She also said that when she dumped him, she gave all the "group" excuses. He was crazy, he was trouble. All the things people said about her.

But she'd been sick and she was here to see Joe, to help her get better, and she was supposed to not need trouble, trouble was supposed to be bad for her health. And so. . . and so. . . "He was sweet, Bobby was a sweet boy," she said.

Maisie, Maisie, all for the love of you.

When Maisie was done, Joe put a leg up and began to play with his toes. His feet were thick like his neck, I remember his black socks then, he rubbed his toes through his black socks as though he was massaging them, warming them up, and it seemed all so much like an act that I felt we were supposed to recognize it as such. Then he started to laugh. It was one of those freak storms that start more suddenly than you think a storm can, a big rolling laugh bouncing off us all, a squall of a laugh, his eyes wet and his belly quaking, a cliché and happy to be one. He let his foot go and stretched his arm out like a cartoon of a Zen master yawning, getting all the laugh that was in him out.

Joe didn't seem to care that no one laughed with him, that he was making a spectacle of himself. It was a laugh big enough that it could have irony in it and still not be ironic, rage in it and not be angry, it subsumed these, put them in their proper places, no more parts of his laugh than they were parts of life.

Joe never made a spectacle of himself but now he did. All of us looked at him with. . . how shall I say this without compounding the mystery of it? Reflections of ourselves? In my case it might have been fear. His laugh lasted more than a minute, it was like an episode, or a seizure, something that you could describe in medical terms. Nor was he laughing to himself. It felt like a code being sent out into the night. When he was done with it, the meeting was over.

As we left I observed Philip at the elevator, like the rest of us saying nothing, slipping on his shoes with what seemed now less like conscious attention, more like the slow weight of years.

༄

And what did the laugh mean? I had no idea, but Philip did. We met a second time in the coffee shop at Broadway and Canal, a few days following the Thursday meeting. He said he thought it had to do with, if you join an expedition and you know it's dangerous, then if something happens, if you were Bobby how would you want people to remember you, as a victim? It was sort of like one of those NO ONE UNDER 18 ADMITTED signs, no one under eighteen admitted, and no pity either.

"So we should honor Bobby in his strength, not his weakness?" I actually used such tall, ungainly words.

Philip didn't answer. He stirred his coffee and looked at me oddly. I remembered when I first met him and had observed that he was not afraid to stare at people. I thought maybe he was in a kind of trance. I was also quite sure, despite his words, that he was very angry at Joe.

The reason we met then was that I'd polished up my story about Joao. Philip read it through. When he was done all he said was, "Let's see. . ." He put his coffee aside, laid the five triple-spaced pages flat on the formica between us, and as if I weren't there went through them with the Mont Blanc pen, gilded with his initials, that had been his Christmas present to himself. After awhile there was hardly a phrase of mine that had not suffered at least collateral damage. The pages were crisscrossed with blue trails so ornately and densely patterned that I had hardly an idea what he had written. It took him forty-five minutes. When he was finished, he grinned slightly—a grin, I thought at the time, of grim satisfaction—and said, "Not bad." The way Joe always said it.

The story appeared the following week but by then the Angel of Saint Vincent's had disappeared. No one at the hospital knew what had become of him, though the Puerto Rican nurse who liked having him around thought it must have had to do with the law. I checked this out with Immigration and the NYC police, but neither of those had picked him up. He was simply gone. Did he ever see himself on a newsstand somewhere, or in a magazine left on a bus seat, or in a public library? I don't know.

I felt an odd pride for our story. I recognized in it a few things, for example, the sums that Joao and I had calculated he'd saved the city. Mostly I felt like a stranger to the very things that I'd uncovered. But hadn't I been present at the creation? I felt a little as I'd felt when I copied Hammett. I searched for the verbal formulation that might express the maximum sense of my achievement without outright lying. "I worked with Philip Deschayne on a Talk story." "Philip's been teaching me how to write Talk stories and we just had one in." But really I had no one to tell. This was Philip's world, finally. I thanked him for the way he'd involved me in it and he mumbled some version of "you're welcome," but all our words sounded a little stilted, as if there were echoes of Bobby in them, as though in wanting to make sure we didn't say too little, we were inevitably saying too much. He shared with me the five hundred dollars.

ം

It was the end of the group. In three months Joe moved to Berkeley. Some went with him, some stayed.

I stayed. So did the other "intellectuals," we who were there early, the Harvard-Yale types. But Liddie went with him, and Big Ronald and Greg, several of those who came to Joe through his ad in the *Voice*. Maisie returned to Boston.

I stopped doing the morning exercise. The first morning that I determined not to do it I felt "the terror of the situation," as if I'd lost my bearings in the world.

I stopped, also, fighting to "stay present to myself," to "remember myself," I stopped telling myself to "stop, go back, gently."

Yet I seemed to sense myself without telling myself to. A habit I didn't quite care to shake, a talisman maybe, a chip on the luck of life, or a deal brokered with my fear. I could hardly tell, in totality, whether after leaving the group I had more words in my head or less. I judged it all to be about the same. Maybe it had always been the same.

All the time that I was in the group, one strand of my free-floating fantasy had it that I'd liked Philip and Bobby better before there was a "group," that what I really liked about it all was the little literary "salon" at Philip's, the spare poetry of the stories read there, the *Bird Guide*, the *New Yorker*, the pretty pathway for my ambition. In this view, the group was like a fetter, but one necessary in order to enjoy the rest. Now that the bond was gone, it seemed as if life might be wide open, as if I would have everything and eat it too. I quit my job downtown. I went back to writing everyday. But the *Bird Guide* died for lack of a purpose, and Philip soon found himself in a fresh writer's block as big as all of 43rd Street between Fifth and Sixth. Despite the Angel of Saint Vincent's, the *New Yorker* seemed farther away. The battle for Shawn's succession had begun, at least the early skirmishes, and Philip himself began to have contempt for the place. Even the streets of the city, which I had thought would be all mine all the time for prowling and scoring, seemed mostly busy now. I spent a couple weeks on a sexual spree, then tired of it. I began to notice that I had little money.

A last straw of sorts was that the Old Painter started spreading rumors about Joe. Rumors or simply statements of misgiving. I heard these from Joe first. The Old Painter was saying Joe shouldn't have been teaching to start with, he didn't have his blessing to do it, he understood nothing, and Bobby Gelfand should still be alive. I wondered what Maisie had told him. He sounded like an old Jewish patriarch disowning his son.

&

I went out to Los Angeles, moved into an apartment in Ocean Park, and began writing scripts to send around. For twelve hundred dollars I bought an old Cutlass convertible. My tiny apartment had a sliver of an ocean view.

One weekend I drove the Cutlass up to Berkeley. Joe was living in a two story bungalow off Sacramento Street. An assortment of mostly older cars jammed the driveway and the parking places around his house. It was a Sunday morning in the fall. The air lacked any crispness but in distinction to Ocean Park, Berkeley had at least a brave cohort of trees whose leaves dared show their age and turn brown. I went inside the house. The walls were unfinished—or more likely, the sheet rock had been pulled off them—leaving the feeling of a cabin in the woods. Joe's Eames chair sat in the front room a bit regal for its surroundings and there was also a Franklin stove and a stack of futons and benches, the last parked against the wall studs. A familiar green carpet covered the floor. People with fresh, unfamiliar faces waxed the benches, cleared ashes from the stove. One person was washing the small, high-set windows. Everyone worked with self-conscious slowness. It was as if I were watching an old dance performed by a new troupe of players. None of these people appeared to notice me, or they did and refused to be distracted.

Presently Liddie walked in. She certainly did see me, but pretended she hadn't. It seemed to be her job to watch the others. She was acting as if either it was perfectly normal for me to be there or I was a non-person. I said nothing to her but smiled her way. This got me nowhere. She touched the arm of the girl who was sweeping out the stove, lightly, no doubt instructively, but I had no idea why.

I wandered through the bungalow. I noticed that no works of the Old Painter were on any of the walls. In the rustic kitchen all the pots and woks from New York were hung over a new galley stove. This transportation of Bobby's old preserve into a new setting that, as it were, owed him nothing, that could not be imagined even to hold a candle for him, was perhaps the most disorienting view of all. I came out through the kitchen onto a redwood deck that overlooked a backyard scarcely wider than the bungalow but deep. Bamboos filled the back of the yard. Three people were at work thinning the bamboos and raking in-between them. The rest of the yard appeared as a slow motion sculpture garden, figures clipping plants, mowing grass, turning a compost heap, planting what looked to be star jasmine by a trellis, pruning an orange tree that dripped with fruit. Big Ronald sat on the deck steps smoking a cigarette, his white legs sprouting out of shorts that must have been recently bought. When I saw him, I waved. I'd always liked Big Ronald. He looked past me as if I were deck furniture.

So it was true. Somebody must have seen me coming. I was being ignored. Or another way of putting it, I reminded myself, was that these people were working, I was interrupting, and they were trying not to be interrupted. I sensed myself like crazy then. I didn't want to be attacked. I wanted to figure out what was going on. My sense of it was that people were engaged in something more than maintaining their attention—even the most severe of us in New York, if an old friend arrived from across the country, might have nodded in greeting—and that they considered me some sort of deserter, or weakling or disappointment. Of course it was possible that I was. I wasn't in a mood to argue, even with myself.

Liddie came out. This time I wasn't ignored. She spoke to me quietly and with conscious neutrality: "If you want to see Joe, he's in his room." I followed her back inside. I felt like I was following a geisha. We walked up the stairs into a redwood-paneled hall at the end of which was a shut door. I could hear radio noise from within, which as we got closer I realized was football.

Liddie opened the door for me. Joe was sitting alone in front of his old Sony. He was in a butterfly chair which made him look a bit planted, like some overgrown species of melon. The room contained a queen-size bed but was otherwise sparsely appointed. A photo of the dancer from Oakland sat on top of the Sony, apparently something had developed in that department, as it always seemed to, quietly, for Joe.

"Pull up a chair," he said. He was so matter-of-fact I might have seen him yesterday. The 49ers were playing the Giants in New Jersey, so the game had already started.

I sat with Joe and watched. The Giants were ahead by a touchdown but Joe was rooting for them to die and be buried in an unmarked grave. No transplanted New Yorker residual sports team loyalty for Joe. He was for the Niners all the way. He cursed or cheered on every play, though it was all a bit of an act. He was simply enjoying himself, waiting for Montana to swing into action. "He never does anything till there's two minutes left," Joe assured me.

Liddie brought him up some food. He asked me if I wanted anything. I shared some take-out burrito with him. I was sensing myself without even trying, as had always happened when I was with Joe and afraid, but I wasn't really afraid now. Joe asked me if I liked his place and I said I did. He asked me if I liked Los Angeleeze, his old Bensonhurst way of saying it, and I said I didn't really but that might change if I ever found work. I told him I liked having the beach a couple blocks away. And I told him I found the way others were treating me today a little odd. Like I was a tax collector, or maybe an alien. "Separation anxiety, don't you think?" Joe said curtly. "You were one of their daddies and ran away."

Which made, I supposed, a certain sense; or anyway I flattered myself that it did. I found I still liked it when Joe psychologized, it felt reassuring, a safer port.

"So people haven't been trashing me, or us, in meetings?

"Don't be childish," Joe said.

But I wasn't sure.

Montana rallied his guys in the fourth quarter, completed about fourteen passes, and the Niners won going away. Joe put his leg up and played with his toes and looked self-satisfied. When the game ended, he shut off the set.

I thought maybe it was time for me to leave, but he sat back down.

"So." He pushed out a cigarette and lit it. "We've got people who live in Los Angeleeze who come up here on the weekends. It's not so bad a commute. . ."

"I don't think so," I said.

"If you were ever interested. . ." he continued. "You could probably get a ride. . ."

"Really, I don't think so," I said.

He was silent awhile then. "I've got to go down in a couple minutes. Meeting."

"Of course."

"*Told* you about Montana."

"Yeah."

More silence, more sitting there in the butterfly chairs that turned people into plants. I again got mentally prepared to leave.

"If you're ever in Los Angeles. . ."

"Why would I go to Los Angeleeze?"

I shrugged.

He looked my way with a softer expression. It was mostly in his eyes. They weren't so insistently open, for a moment they lacked that huge belief in themselves. Joe looked, quite possibly, rueful. "Whatever happened in the group," he said, "I hope it won't stop you from finding help somewhere else some day."

These seemed at just that moment the kindest words Joe ever spoke to me. The kindest in their intention, the most generous. Or maybe the only really kind words he ever spoke to me. He said them in his baritone, and they seemed so naked and truthful. Though it wasn't long before I started to wonder. What's "kind," what's "kindest."

I didn't answer him, I didn't think that an answer was called for.

Or perhaps I was made uneasy by his words and simply didn't know what to say.

A little while later I left, feeling cloudy.

In the ensuing months and years, I kept track of my old friends from the group, Philip particularly. I was good about calling. Philip got married, had two kids, finally left the *New Yorker* after Tina Brown started her rampage. When I went back I'd see Philip and Joe, and once in a while Ty and Valerie, who stayed together.

I sensed they all went back to versions of their earlier selves; either that, or in moving on, more of their old personalities reappeared. Philip resumed suffering writer's blocks and depressions and a scattered, make-do way with deadlines and money, but also a genuine gentleness in him reemerged, or grew stronger, less encumbered by the war on common feelings fought by the group. He seemed less self-consciously in command of himself or his world, but more genuine, and actually stronger. Philip, a father. Wonderful. Perfect. Seeing the others always made me wonder about myself, whether after the group I had regressed or gone forward. I was never sure. I wondered whether those were even the right words, whether there was an arrow pointed one way or the other that you could say ran through people. One thing I noticed for certain, the slightly preternatural sexual prowess I'd developed, the product, I supposed, of such close monitoring of my body combined with the battering my superego took, began to slip away.

I never asked Philip or Joe or anyone who left the group if they were continuing their spiritual pursuits in an organized way, if they'd joined something else, were following someone else. When I visited Philip in his new office at Columbia, I noticed he'd placed all his old Sufi books on reasonably prominent display behind his typewriter, and that some new ones seemed added to the mix. From these I guessed that he might have resumed his relations with the left brain/right brain guy. But I didn't ask. I didn't really want to know. On occasion he seemed bitter or bemused about Joe, he who'd been closest to Joe of all of us. He'd make a remark, in a sardonic tone, about some rumor he'd heard, some story from California. But he may simply have moved on.

For myself, I'm not much of a joiner and never was, despite what this story might suggest. I nibbled a few times. I'd go to hear Krishnamurti speak in Ojai, under the oak trees, sitting taller than a ninety-year-old had any right to sit, lambasting the gurus, disavowing "followers," offering people their own private chance. And I visited a Zen rabbi on LaBrea in Hollywood and found his cheery lox-and-bagel syncretism excruciating.

Instead I read books. Some of the usual suspects and some more obscure, trying to figure out not so much what I might do as what I had already done. Where was I? Where were any of us? When I read a book, say, by Suzuki, I tried to sense myself so deeply that the book would resonate in parts of myself that I scarcely knew were there. But how could I tell the imaginary from the real? An armchair general, some questions I was a little bit content not to be able to answer.

☙

It was in the early nineties that I received a letter from Joe. It was a form letter, xeroxed, addressed to "members of my old group." In it Joe said he wanted us to know that he had been wrong about many things in his teaching, chief among them the mixing of psychological concepts with ideas from a different plane of learning altogether, to the confusion of both. He apologized, asked our forgiveness, implied that his failings were due to the fact that the Old Painter hadn't instructed him properly, and requested that if any of us knew someone who had not received this letter, that we send it to him.

He also recommended a book, one I'd never heard of, if we wanted an exposition of certain ideas in keeping with what Joe now understood them to be.

I ordered the book from a secondhand shop and then let it sit on my shelf for a month. When I read it finally, I felt disappointed, even insulted. The book seemed so crude. It assumed the form of an objective description of self-observation and self-remembrance, but it was so larded with tall tales of quasi-miracles and small moments of simple improbability that the author came off as scheming and unreliable, as if he believed himself to be writing from such a lofty perch of spiritual superiority that it entitled him to con the poor peons who'd be reading him, supply them with whatever they might need in order to be impressed, all for the greater good, of course. I'd sometimes detected similar notes in Gurdjieff's own writings, and in the writings of his early followers, as if they were daring you to disbelieve, presenting lies so that you would experience what it is like to be lied to. But perhaps that assigns too great, or too mean, a motive to all of them. In all events, I was embarrassed that Joe had recommended the book.

And it infuriated me that someone in whom I had put so much trust could have slipped so badly. It reminded me of the thing I'd always most doubted about him: his taste. Yet what I remembered about Joe was so much better than the humorous drivel, the clumsy manipulations, of this book. Joe was a magnificent mongrel who took from here and there and didn't care. He was bold, of Brooklyn and America, he didn't kowtow to getting every dot and jot of some dead Armenian's theory right. "Wrong about many things" and proud of it—that was the Joe I remembered, who seemed so absent from his letter.

At the same time, I remembered Bobby's asparagus pee. As well, it's always flattering to be apologized to, especially when the apology comes from one who sometimes bullied you. For a while I was going to write him back, or go up to Berkeley, to tell him I liked the old Joe better, damn the torpedoes and full speed ahead, don't let the bastards get you down. But I didn't like the smell of what he was involved with now, it smelled musty, of texts and ghosts.

I had no one to forward Joe's letter to, Philip had received it and Cal had received it, and by now these were the only two from the group that I was in contact with, so I put it away in a drawer.

༄

I bought a house with a rose garden. The roses were of the old varieties, with names as heavily scented as their petals—Duchesse de Brabante, Souvenir de la Malmaison, La Reine Victoria—that have more recently made a return to fashion. Those were busy times for me, but I would try to make room for the roses. On Sunday afternoons you might see me out there, in a wool black-and-orange N.Y. Giants hat too hot for the sun, with a Swiss clippers not unlike Joe's that I doted on a bit, kept cleaned and oiled anyway, and kept indoors.

The woman I bought the house with, who would later be my wife, thought I was less than fastidious with the roses and in some respects this was true. I skimped on the heavy work, the garden always needed more weeding. But actually I liked it pleasantly overgrown.

What I did not tell my future wife, for fear it might be lost in the revelation, was the secret I brought to this amateur's work. As I clipped and shaped, removed deadheads, sprayed for aphids, I made a conscious effort, whenever I noticed there were words in my head, to stop, and go back, gently, to looking, to listening, and to sensing my arms and legs. For moments my mind would be still. I heard the groaning and heaving of the traffic stream on the nearby street, the tinkling of the pool fountain, the jostling songs of the finches at the feeder. I saw the hundreds of shades of rose, the aphids living their lives on the undersides of leaves, the dew, the magical forests of yellow stamens, the warlike plenitude of thorns, as if sufficient to defend whole worlds. I sensed my body so deeply it seemed to be not all of me, but a burning image of me. Peace. I sensed peace.

Inevitably I clipped a rose or bent it towards me and with a relaxed abdomen, from as deep a place as I could find, breathed slowly, unstintingly in, as if I'd discovered a thirst I never knew I had. The perfume of the rose, familiar but scarcely describable, transported me at once out of what seemed the anteroom of my life to the place and time when Bobby Gelfand was alive, we all were young, and eternity seemed possible. Live every minute, the old guy said, in the awareness that one day you will die. I'd hardly done that. I've hardly done that. Joe waddles around his apartment or the loft in his corduroy pants, squirting his miniature roses under their Gro-lites with water from his plastic bottle. We do our work. Bobby's at the stove, cooking something good. Sense. Look. Listen. Thirty birds set off to find the mighty Simurgh, whose name means thirty birds. And how many arrived?

THEME SONG FOR AN OLD SHOW

to my parents

In a cavern, in a canyon,
Excavating for a mine,
Dwelt a miner, forty-niner,
And his daughter Clementine.

Refrain:
Oh my darling, oh my darling,
Oh my darling Clementine,
You are lost and gone forever,
Dreadful sorry, Clementine.

California

My father had a friend named Gene Lang who went to California in the forties and became a composer for the movies. He lived in a house that had orange trees. You could walk outside and pick oranges off your own tree. I heard about this when I was young. Maybe my father told me about it or maybe he showed me a photograph that he had received. Either way, I formed a sunlit image of these trees with their large orange fruit within easy reach, in the backyard of a house. They were, I suppose, like the trees you might see in a Persian or Indian miniature, in pleasure gardens or gardens meant to represent perfection. Many years later I would put into a TV script that one of our show's main characters, a scruffy former police snitch from the East who's come to California to start over, buys an orange tree in a five-gallon pot on the street and then spends a majority of his time watering it and feeding it and pruning it and fretting when its leaves turn yellow, as though this tree embodied all his hopes for a sunny new beginning. A few years after Gene Lang, my father left my mother and our family and went to California with another woman to become a producer for television, and a little bit also, the movies. I was nine years old then. He moved almost three thousand miles away, which in those days seemed as far as I don't even know what would seem today. The gallery where I stored my dream images of California expanded to include a kidney-shaped pool in Bel Air, surrounded by the sorts of vegetation I'd only ever seen possibly in the bird house at the zoo, tall and weeping, dense and dark, guardians of an exotic life. The fact that the pool was kidney-shaped was particularly important. I wasn't sure what a kidney was shaped like, nor even what a kidney was exactly. If you'd asked me, from my photograph of my father's swimming pool, I might have called it peanut-shaped. But I knew, from magazines, from my mother's talk, that kidney-shaped pools were particularly precious and rare, as if the effort to make the pool's sides other than straight required expense a little beyond reason. No one in our neighborhood in Rochester, where my mother moved us after my father left, had a pool at all, except for the DeKovens and theirs wasn't even sunk in the ground. My father was also in the photograph, placed a little to the side of the pool, the way they place the owners of racehorses in photos of the horse in the winner's circle. He stared through thick-framed sunglasses at the camera, looking proprietary and self-confident. His striped swimming trunks appeared to be dry. He had a short-sleeve shirt on that looked to be made of the same stuff they made towels from—I'd never seen such a thing. But his hairy arms stuck out from the shirt, and these seemed familiar and friendly enough. His hairy arms and legs: when I saw these, I had the feeling of almost claiming him back. Beside him were Irene and her son. The new happy family. My mother didn't even know I had this photograph. I kept it between pages of my stamp album. The only other things I knew about California were from television. The white picket fences and white clapboard houses of the sitcoms, the priapic city hall on *Dragnet*, the Hollywood-and-Vine signs on some early variety show, oversized and preposterously cheerful, as if they deserved an exclamation point at the end of each of them. And somehow I also imagined: a convertible in every driveway. My father was a convertible man. We had convertibles even in New York. An Olds, then a Buick. The convertibles had names. Esmeralda. Esmeralda was lost in the divorce. Really lost, the registration papers got lost in some exchange of documents and nobody seemed able to find them or get them replaced and the car sat in a garage until it was towed for scrap. Or that was the story I was told anyway. Looking back, I'm not sure it makes sense. I didn't know what car my father drove in California, but I was sure it was a convertible, while we in Rochester drove the used '52 Chevy four door that my mother's father sometimes loaned us.

※

One song, too. "Oh My Darling Clementine." Where it entered my brain I never knew, never asked. I suppose everybody knew that song. The miner, the lost daughter, the mournful, sentimental, sappy emblem of the West. But it wasn't sappy to me then. It filled my mind. It was there when I took out the photograph of my father by his pool. It was there when I went to sleep at night dreaming of convertibles and driveways. It was a companion of my solitude.

※

Irene. Made-up name. Maybe not even a good made-up name. What about Phoebe? What about Liz? So many to choose from but I said Irene and I'll stick to it. Irene, so much like Eileen. Or is the "r" in it a little angrier? Irene had her moments of anger. She was rich, she was from New York, so my mother used to say as if that would explain pretty much all of it. "Park

Avenue, no less." Irene's father, I would learn one day, made his fortune in war profiteering. I'm not sure in which war, and I suppose it's not the polite way to put it. He supplied socks for the boys overseas. A Park Avenue apartment resulted, and a country place in Connecticut on a lake, and private schools for the girls. Irene went to Sweet Briar College in Virginia. I don't know how many Jewish girls from New York went to Sweet Briar in the late thirties but I imagine not too many. At Sweet Briar Irene played golf and tennis and rode a horse. She was tall enough to be athletic in a lanky way, she looked good in clothes, her face was long and her blue eyes pierced and pleaded as though to say I'm a complicated one and she may have had a nose job along the way. Or anyway her nose was as pretty and complicated as she was. She was "best friends" with my mother in Scarsdale, where we lived before the divorce. How this came about I was never sure, but my father and Irene's husband had been in college together, so it must have had to do with that. The four of them played bridge and golf and tennis. I struggle now to imagine my mother keeping up with all of this. She was a small woman who left home to go to nursing school in New York and met my father while a nurse at a camp in the Poconos and he was a counselor there. He had just finished his third year at Yale, young because he'd skipped grades in school. He rowed her on the lake. They were each other's first lover. My mother joined the Book-of-the-Month Club so she'd know what to say and think. And she acquired golf clubs and a tennis racquet and learned how to drive. And in truth she liked all of these things, but especially the books. She liked books more than my father did, who had gone to Yale but took things more for granted. But how to compete with Irene? I try to imagine my mother, four or five inches shorter than Irene and shy and socially uncertain, trying to drive a ball down the center of a Scarsdale fairway. She was left-handed too, but owned right-handed clubs, because she wanted to do things the way other people did them. After my father left with Irene, she hated them both with a hatred I'd never seen in anyone.

※

I made up an imaginary city from the name of my father's departed friend Gene Lang. The city was Langden and it was on the border of California and Oregon, across from its rival city of Jansen, against which it played in all sports in a thousand foot long stadium. Each was a city of two million. Patrup Langden was Langden's police chief and star pitcher. He won thousands of games each year. Everything in Langden was bigger than it was elsewhere, and more modern, and Langden nearly always beat Jansen. Though Jansen also had its virtues. It was named after a pitcher who won twenty-three games for the New York Giants in 1951. Then the Giants left too, for San Francisco. Everything good seemed to be in California, and for this opinion of mine, or perhaps it was more a feeling, I felt guilty. When Irene was still my mother's best friend, I had found her pretty. One day she came over with her son, who wasn't my friend, and for some reason, in the front yard of our house, she lifted him up and started shaking him and kissing him at the same time. I must have walked into this. I wasn't there when it started. I couldn't tell whether she was angry or happy with him, but I wished she would do that to me too. For this I also later felt guilty. My mother did not have an easy time of it, all of us living with her parents again. She got a modest job in a doctor's office. She made us breakfast and dinner. Privately she must have cursed herself and her trustfulness and the presumption of her leaving home to start with, to go to someplace like New York to nursing school. Who did she think she was? But she didn't say these things to my sister and me. Instead she cursed men.

And how could I really disagree with her? The facts looked pretty bad. Here we were with not enough money living in her parents' house and there he was out in California with her "best friend" and a kidney-shaped swimming pool. Even if all men weren't like this, wasn't I likely to be? Who was she training me up to be, the anti-*him*? I never thought things through quite that way. But I knew I didn't want to be against my father. It wasn't long before his name started appearing on television, at the ends of mysteries or westerns. Though, if she could, my mother would shut the set off before his name came on. But I knew it was there. I'd seen it a few times. And it was actually better, I thought, that she shut it off, because if she left it on it would give her another chance to curse him. When his check was late, which it often was, she cursed him. When it was too small, which it always was, she cursed him. Or she would be silent and bitter. And who was I to blame her, who had liked Irene when she tossed her son up and down and wished it were me being tossed and kissed? Where was my backbone, what sort of boy/man was I? There was a time for a person to take sides and say what was right. Which I would then do. I wrote him letters of reasoned complaint. We could use this, we could use that, surely he could see the reasonableness of my mother's position. He told me my mother was putting me up to things. He explained everything from his own point of view, and then that would seem reasonable too.

This would take place in phone conversations. The phone in my grandparents' house was on the stairs, in the middle of the house. The phone would ring and someone would call out "long distance," and life in the house would freeze, as if it were one of the games of red light/green light that my sister and I played outside and the person who was it had just shouted "red light." I felt every word I said on the phone was being heard by several sets of ears. And surely it was. I could barely get words out on the phone. I never said what I meant. I wondered what it was like at the other end of the line, in California.

Then, after a long enough time had passed, my chance. My father asked me if I would like to come to Los Angeles over my summer vacation. This, too, was said on the phone. I said I'd have to ask my mother. But I didn't know how to ask her. I didn't know how not to hurt her feelings. How could I explain to her that I *wanted* to go there? In my bed at night I would get clever about this. I would tell her that I would bring back things for everybody. I would tell her that I would argue with him on our behalf. I would tell her that I just wanted to see a Giants game. Yes, the Giants were in San Francisco, but they'd come down to Los Angeles some time, and that's the time I would choose to go, and come home right after. But I never said any of these things. I could hear what she would say back, or not say.

Time passed and my father called to say that I would have to decide. But still I couldn't, the whole question having become like a record needle stuck in a groove. I went around and around. I bicycled up to the drugstore and took my paper route change and called him from the pay phone so that I could talk without fear. But that was ridiculous because I was always afraid, of one thing or the other, one side of me or the other. My father said I shouldn't have to ask my mother, because this was something I could decide myself. I had never thought my father was unreasoning but I thought he was unreasoning then. Of course I *could* decide. But how could I say to him that I didn't want to hurt my mother's feelings because he had hurt them enough already and I didn't want to hurt them any more?

Or how could I say what I didn't quite understand, that I was doing part of his job for him? Not that it was his job anymore. He'd quit that job. This too I didn't quite understand. Especially since he seemed to think he was taking care of things as well as he ought to, given all the circumstances. Did he not call, did he not write, did he not send checks? I could protest, pick all these apart, but I would never win. Not when he was out by the kidney-shaped pool and I was not.

Three days before the day my father said I would have to decide, I told my mother whatever I could tell her. That I wanted to do this, that I would not be gone long, that another year my sister could go. Not about the Giants or any of that. I had this weird hope that if I was simply honest she would see there was nothing to fear and how much I loved her and wasn't deserting her and would reward me. She didn't seem surprised. Maybe she had read my mail, or things had been said on the phone on the stairs. Whatever. She said of course I could go; but if I went I shouldn't come back. I remember not being afraid of this. I remember thinking that I could do it, that is, go, and if she really meant it, not come back. I remember how small and undefended my mother seemed then. What made it impossible is that I knew she couldn't bully me, and what made it sad is that she knew this too. It was in the way she turned away, busily, busying herself with something, putting the dishes away. She had to busy herself, so that she wouldn't say more, so that the speech she had carefully prepared for herself, her position, the best she could do, as against absolutely everything, *him*, the whole world, wouldn't be lost. Later I bicycled up to the drugstore and put more of my paper route change in the pay phone and told my father thank you very much for the invitation but I couldn't this year, but maybe next year?

☙

Instead of going to California, I started writing him stories, set in the cities of Langden and Jansen. In Langden, this. In Jansen, that. They were often stories of calamities; shipwrecks, floods, big dams breaking. Though Patrup Langden, mayor, chief of police, announcer, pitcher, captain of all Langden teams, would occasionally come up with something to save the day. There were a couple my father seemed to like, where the quotient of catastrophe was less. Once he wrote me, "Keep it up." A boy writes stories to his father. Evidence that writers aren't really born, that something happens and then they are?

☙

Polio. A year or two before Dr. Salk produced his vaccine, I came down with a mild case. This was just before my father went away.

In fact I may have caught it on a two-week visit to my grandparents upstate, going to the Rochester beach every day with my mother, while my father was in New York putting the finishing touches on his affair with Irene. Returning to Scarsdale, I fell off my bicycle one day and went into a long sleep. I stayed in bed for six weeks. Only when I was recovered enough to be walking around did my parents tell me that I had had polio. A few weeks after that my father said he was leaving. My being sick must have delayed his plans. He said the usual things about how they'd not been getting along and so he would be staying in the city for a while and would call every night. The fact of Irene only came out days or weeks later, in my mother's screams and her collapsing on her bed. Later I came to believe, with a rare, even odd, certainty, as if the only thing I could ever truly trust again was my own intuition, that my contracting polio had to do with my father's affair, that it was my own desperate effort to save my parents' marriage, or a confession of guilt for the collapse that was coming. How could I have known? But on the other hand, how could I not have known, who was my father's son, and who had wanted Irene to shake and kiss me? When, fifty years later, the tsunami struck in Asia, it was easy for me to believe that the animals had sensed it in advance and sought higher ground.

Irene was the one, I decided. Without Irene none of this would have happened. Even if he'd left, which he wouldn't have, he would have called every night like he said he would, if it wasn't for Irene. He would have visited every weekend, if it wasn't for Irene, and on the phone he would have sounded like he cared more, like it was more important to him. He would maybe not even have left New York, if not for her. Though this last idea produced in me more complicated feelings. I couldn't quite begrudge my father California. It seemed too great for that. And the thought of us all going out there, packing up Esmeralda, making a trek like the pioneers, my parents sharing the driving, didn't quite seem real to me. I could imagine Irene out in California, driving my father's convertible, her golf clubs in the backseat, in a way that I could not imagine my mother doing the same.

I imagined Irene in beautiful clothes, the sun always shining, the convertible always washed, going here and there in a daytime that never quite ended. My father, in the strain of our now-rarer conversations, would tell me things about her as if catching me up on the news. Probably he didn't know what else to say, after the baseball and how I was doing in school and whether he was busy or not. "Irene's working at the museum." "Irene's taken up gardening." "Irene sends her love." But she never got on the phone herself. I was left to imagine a person who my father thought to be more or less perfect. Meanwhile my own life went along. I learned how to play tennis in the high school gym. I started playing golf on the public course with my mother's old clubs. My paper route gave me money to spend. Girls grew breasts in Rochester, as elsewhere, and boys' voices broke. And I began to see that I was a smart kid and that smart kids, even from Rochester, could begin to chart their own paths. Staking out some future position for myself, I began to buy Ivy League clothes. I could tell Gant shirts from others. And the roll of the collar of a Brooks Brothers shirt and how the Brooks shirts came without pockets. As if, with such knowledge as this, the world could be conquered. I must have told my father somewhere along the way that I had taken up tennis. He played tennis himself. I imagined him in white Lacoste shirts with alligators playing every weekend with Irene. His white socks, his white sneaks, his white shorts, all new and the best, and Irene playing with a visor. The kind of tennis that was advertised, tennis as it was meant to be, with something of the upper-class purity of a dream.

I am trying to get to something here. I am trying to lay the foundation. Gifts from California were another sort of tension in our house. My father was not great with gifts. He would be late with Christmas, late with birthdays, or he would forget altogether. Or perhaps he didn't forget. Perhaps I only assumed this. Perhaps, for some reason, he simply didn't want to. But if a box did come, it was best not to make a big deal of it. It was best not to open it with other things. I would take my box to my room and open it there and whatever was in the box I would leave there. A book about art. Probably there were others but I can't remember what they were, things that if they were brought out of my room would revive my mother's bitterness and spoil whatever else was out there. Until one day a box came with no reason. It came in July and my birthday was in March. So it was a surprise in a way, and I treated it as a surprise, I didn't take it at once to my room. My mother walked into the living room as I opened it, and I didn't walk away with it, I'm not sure why. I suppose it was too late for me just to walk away. I suppose I could still not imagine that my father was sending me a gift in July. Or maybe I had decided to take some sort of stand, full of goodwill and understanding, but nevertheless a stand, which I could even back up if necessary, by saying, here, you see, he's not so bad, he sent a gift for no reason at all. Anyway I opened it. It was a rectangular box, not deep, and about two feet long, the sort of box you might send a suit jacket in. My sister walked in as well, three years younger than me, whom I always meant to protect and sometimes did. I sliced the wrapping tape with a steak knife. I popped the corners of the box. There was a note from my father. I read it quickly, refolded it, and put it under the tissue. "Irene thought you would like these." Wrapped in the tissue were four cream-colored Banlon tennis shirts. They gave me a queasy feeling at once, as if I'd suddenly realized that something I was looking forward to had actually been meant for somebody else, the sender had accidentally put my name on the package instead of the right person. I lifted them up to show to the others. The smooth synthetic fabric clung to my open hand and draped over it, as if it had no life of its own. My mother said, "Well wasn't *that* nice and thoughtful," and went off. I expected her to add more, because she wasn't always pithy with her sarcasm, but this time she was.

As I took them to my room, it was as if I were trying to question these shirts. Who sent you and what do you want? They had no tags on them and I began to think that they were actually used shirts, or shirts that somebody had given them and they didn't want them. Because I could not imagine Irene having such bad taste in shirts. How could you play tennis in *Banlon? Cream-colored Banlon?* Even I, in Rochester, had a few old Lacoste shirts that a friend of mine had outgrown and his mother who was friends with my mother had passed along. And they were white and cotton and had alligators on them, or hanging half-off them by then, and they didn't cling to you as if they were dead. Is this how life was really lived in California? *Cream-colored Banlon?* I couldn't believe it. And yet I did, somehow. In a way, it was the beginning of my education. I never knew for sure whether Irene was sending me some things she thought were wonderful or passing off on me things she didn't really want. In a way, the second would have been better. It would have preserved something pristine in my mind. I duly sent a polite thank-you. I put the shirts in the bottom of my bottom drawer, underneath pants that were too small for me, and never wore them once.

☙

In a sense, I walked into my grandmother's death. I went to New York on some sort of scholarship sponsored by the Lions Club to study the United Nations and when I went to visit my grandparents on Eightieth Street she was in bed dying. Nobody had told me that she had breast cancer and was dying, just as no one had told me that ten years before she had had a first bout with breast cancer. She was my beloved grandmother, generous and vital, the sort of person my sister later became, and I could scarcely believe it when I saw her in bed, shriveled and weak-voiced and without makeup, her teeth not even in her mouth. As I understood it, she managed to stay alive an extra three days until my father could break free from work and arrive from California. I had not seen my father in eight years. He and Irene were staying at the Carlyle, which until then I had never heard of. The three of us, my father and Irene and I, were eating in the Schrafft's on Seventy-ninth Street when word came that my grandmother had died. Until then we had been conversing easily enough. I had found out from Irene, though I don't recollect precisely how, that the Carlyle was the best of hotels, and perhaps from my father that this was where executives of his company stayed. I felt buoyed by this, as if vicariously I was staying there too. The two of them seemed happy to see me then. They even felt like family, a special, seldom-heard-from branch of the family where life went on easily and people spoke politely and about things like art and stayed at the Carlyle when they came in from California; but family nonetheless. For a little while I lost the sense that it was us against them. I had never been on a family vacation, but this was like one, until the Schrafft's waitress came over and said there was a call for my father from the doctor.

They didn't want me to go to the "viewing." The Mets were new to New York that year and they sent me to the Polo Grounds to see a game. It wasn't like seeing the Giants but it was the next best thing. I got to see the Polo Grounds one last time, before they tore it down. Again, I felt that my father and Irene were being kind. I didn't know why I shouldn't attend the "viewing," but I liked it that they were thinking about me, and thinking about getting me out of something even if it wasn't clear what their reasoning was. And I liked it that they sent me to the Polo Grounds, as if they had to know that the very words of the place, "Polo Grounds," had a magical aura for me, a mixture of the gigantic and happier times and polar bears and Willie Mays. Though one thing was odd: my father had become a Dodgers fan. I asked him why and he said it was because he was living in Los Angeles now. And something also about the company getting tickets to the games. This still didn't seem to me sufficient. I felt that I had inherited from him the Giants blood that was in my veins. I finally decided sports weren't as important to him as they were to me. Or loyalty? But I scarcely dared think this. Things were going too nicely now. It was as if my grandmother in her death had placed a blessing over us.

Before they left town, my father asked me what I was thinking about for college. We were in a car going up to Irene's place in Connecticut on the lake. My father said that Berkeley was a good school. I said I had been thinking about Yale. If I could get in, that is. I didn't know if I could get in. My father said one or two more good things about Berkeley, it was in California and I could be a California resident and go almost for free. I got fearful because this sounded to me somehow like my father becoming a Dodgers fan, and like the Banlon tennis shirts. I didn't want to go to a public school. I wanted to go to the best. Why had he brought up the idea of almost going for free, when I felt that Yale blood flowed in my veins just like Giants blood, intermingled, my inheritance, my chance? I couldn't say all of this or even really think it, consciously anyway. Instead I said almost the same thing I had said already, with the words changed a little so that it wouldn't seem like I was repeating myself and being obnoxious about it. "I don't know, Yale's really good, I'm sure Berkeley is too, but I really like Yale, if I could get in, if it could work out. But my mother couldn't afford to send me," I added. We drove along. The inside of the car, its padded gray upholstery, seemed cosseting and protective. I was not afraid. I could hear my own voice, saying what I thought, the way I thought normal people said their thoughts. I was in the back. My father was driving. I could see his sunglasses in the rearview, and the back of Irene's short, frosted hair. He said if I got into Yale we'd figure out how I could go there, we'd make sure I could go there. Earnest and firm, sincere without being extravagant, it seemed like the most wonderful promise he could make me. He was treating me like a man. It was the happiest time I ever spent with my father and Irene.

༄

Before I applied to college, I had another conversation with my father, from the pay phone in the drug store. He hadn't said anything more about paying for Yale and I wanted to be sure.

"I'm applying."

"Great."

"They also sent some financial aid forms. Should I? . . . Do I? . . . I'm not sure if I should fill them out."

"Well won't you need a scholarship?"

"I thought. . . what we talked about. . . in New York. . ."

"What did I say? Tell me. Remind me."

"You said we'd make sure I could go to Yale if I got in."

"I do remember. But let's see if you get in first."

"I just need to know, about these forms."

"Financial aid? Of course. Apply. What I said in New York—I meant, after whatever scholarship you get, then whatever's left, we'll try to make up the difference, so you can go."

"But the financial aid is based on need."

"With your mother's income, you'll probably qualify."

"But it says, there's a line for your name, and they want to know your income."

"You have to explain. I'm sure there's a way to do that. You live with your mother. You put down your mother's income."

My father's voice, in all of this, was calm and friendly, as if he really was on my side of this and if I followed his advice, things would be alright.

I tried to imagine his position. He had a son who was Irene's son and a second young son that he'd had by Irene and then he had me and my sister and the checks he sent to my mother every month and a new life to build in California by the kidney-shaped pool, so why, if he had all this expense, would he not want to take advantage of the possibility of my qualifying for a scholarship by dint of living with my mother whom after all he supported, after a fashion? Especially since I was his Rochester son who wouldn't come visit him in California when invited and wanted to go to Yale instead of Berkeley, which, yes, was a public school but a good school, one of the glories of California, where college would almost be free. Maybe he even thought I was avoiding him again, but I don't think it was that. I think, I thought then, that it was the money.

I got into Yale and got financial aid because it was true they looked to what my mother had and not my father, or more accurately they looked to what *I* had, that is, what I would need if I was going to be able to go, and they got that right. My father filled in the cracks a little with checks twice a year and once in a while I bought clothes on sale at J. Press instead of the Co-op. I became infatuated with the rich, and some of that is in the book I wrote a couple before this one. But it was the old rich that allured me, not the new, not the rich who acted as if they had eaten a lot of money and choked on it. These new rich were in California and wore Banlon shirts. They visited me once in a while when my father was in New York on MCA's dime staying at the Carlyle. We would have dinner and be polite. Soon enough, my stepbrother joined me at Yale. *He* wasn't on scholarship. We still were not friends. And he didn't really get Yale. From time to time in college I felt as if I were participating in a scam, sent out to fleece Yale out of a scholarship like one of Fagin's boys sent out to fleece honest Londoners. I hated that feeling. The only way I could make it go away was to remember that I was not going to Yale as my father's son. I was going as not his son.

✧

Meanwhile they were flying around. They went to Europe every year and stayed in the apartment in a mews in Mayfair that MCA owned and my father did a day's business and then they went to museums and restaurants and at night my father gambled and after England they went to the other countries and more museums and restaurants. One summer they asked me along. Irene's son, whom my father had adopted by then, came too, and I got to know him better than I had. The whole time he wanted to be back in California with the girl he was in love with. To judge by Fred, California didn't seem that great a place to grow up. You grew up whiny and discontent and unable to cope with the world outside California, to judge by him. They sent Fred back after two weeks because he was so unhappy, and I traveled with them ten days more, to Munich, then to Paris, and I went with them to more museums and learned more about how things were done in a certain sphere, you had your hotel in Munich (the Vier Jahreszeiten) where you always stayed, and your hotel in Paris (the Bristol) where you always stayed, and you commented about the nice things about each specific hotel, for instance, the fantastic venison at the Vier Jahreszeiten, or some exiled prince of Spain in the elevator at the Bristol; and of course I learned how to leave my shoes out at night to be polished, and I learned what "Alte Pinakothek" meant. These things, actually, I loved to learn. Knowing them made me feel less like a bastard. Though I still felt like one sometimes, when I remembered my scholarship and my father's name nowhere on my Yale application.

In those couple of weeks in Munich and Paris, when we spoke, or more particularly when they spoke, it was with greater familiarity. My father confided that his own father had been a weak man, that my grandmother had been the boss and made the money and took a lover. Irene once noticed me clearing my navel of bellybutton lint and told me this was a masturbatory habit. This annoyed me to hear. Where had she heard that, and why was she saying it? I personally could find no connection between my navel and my masturbatory practice, but I've never forgotten it. Did Irene see a shrink, did she read books of pop psychology, did she know sophisticated things that I didn't? I came to see it as part of the whole picture, just as my picture of my father's father, punching an adding machine in the back of my grandparents' shop while my grandmother and her staff sold the dresses out front, now incorporated that he was "weak." My father particularly mentioned how for years in the Depression my grandfather had spent his time gardening in a house they had rented in the country while my grandmother worked for Saks and made important trips for the company to Europe and made a *friend* on one of the ships who eventually paid for part of my father's college. So was this why I was going to Yale as not my father's son, because he had gone as not *his* father's son? At the time, this never occurred to me.

The following winter they were back in New York on his business and took Fred and me both out to dinner. Another meal where their appetites were great, and mine, and Fred's, a little slack, as if we were looking at different movies. Later, in New Haven, Fred and I were walking back from the train when Fred got emotional and shouted that he hated Yale and hated his mother and hated my father. I felt oddly happy to hear this. I would have been happy for him to leave Yale and it reassured me that he had grown up *out there*, and with *them*, by the kidney-shaped pool, and look where he was now and where I was. The next day or the day after, I was never sure which, Fred flew back out to California to see his girl. This was sudden and he told no one. Things may have gone badly with the girl. My father called a couple days later to say that Fred was dead. He had been driving their Karmann Ghia convertible without sleep and gone off a mountain road.

I put him, I put all of it, in a distant corner of my mind. I felt guilty that Fred had sounded so bitter with me, which was surely a sign of trouble, but what should I have done? Called my father, snitched, caused trouble? There were other things Fred had said as well. "Oh, they're fine if you want to have a good time all the time!" He shouted this across the whole freshman campus after midnight as though he were a crier reporting the British were coming, after I had said something tepid in support of them, he shouldn't hate them, they meant well, something like that. So he left me with a delicate secret. If I confessed to them that I'd seen Fred in trouble and done nothing about it, I'd have also to tell them how, in his last days, he'd screamed that he hated them. Or maybe they would not have been surprised. When I visited them in Los Angeles the following Christmas, my first time in California, I summarized that evening by saying that Fred had been upset. They seemed as content as I was to leave the rest vague. And anyway the description they seem to have agreed to regarding Fred's death, at least for public consumption—that he had spent two days with the girl and left "upset"—dovetailed with mine of the last night I saw him. Upset and sleepless when he left the girl. Suicide was never mentioned, nor was it assumed.

It's absurd to say that Irene had gotten over it by the time, ten months later, that I went out there. She never got over Fred's death. But on the surface it was hard to tell. Maybe she was trying a little harder to be kind, to hold her tongue; or at other moments she seemed to be thinking, regarding anything and everything, that there was no time to waste. My heart warmed to her a little then. My own mother was far away. I spent my week in California going out to more restaurants or playing with their young kid Thomas who was shy and seven years old and seemed to need a lot of playing with then or driving their new Dodge convertible around, the substitute for the Karmann Ghia, as if the small, foreign, German car had been somehow to blame for Fred. My father even said this. No more small cars. He never owned one again. In the Dodge I spent most of the time dating the daughters of their friends and trying to make out. In this I had limited success. Either I simply pushed them too hard and too fast and was a little bit uncouth, or they hadn't the sophistication to see what they had here, a cool Yale guy from the East who knew a lot more than they did. I even knew about LSD, which none of them had ever heard of. The beach, the hills, the curves on Sunset, the Strip, the clubs, the studio in the Valley. They gave me money and I spent it. My conclusion after a week was that California was nice but a little bit inferior. Every minute I was there I felt as if I was taking Fred's place.

༒

I'm not sure when Irene and my father first moved back to New York. It must have been when I was in law school. But it began a period of their lives when they were unsettled and ping-ponged back and forth from coast to coast, uncertain where they should be. Irene now seemed to blame California, or Los Angeles anyway, for Fred's death. Or maybe it wasn't blame at all, maybe it was more a sense of not wanting to be so near the place of his wreck, his crack-up, her failure, whatever it was. They moved to Darien, then to Santa Barbara, then New York, then Los Angeles again, temporarily, when my father had his last show on, then to someplace out in the country near Chappaqua. At the time they first moved East, my father was near the height of his success in television. He had produced a dozen shows, many of them westerns with huge weekly audiences, *The Dooley Boys, The Outpost, Canyon Creek*, and could lay a decent claim to having pioneered a whole new form, the TV movie. A dozen other men, I'm sure, have laid claim to the exact same invention, but I believed my father when he told me that he went to the Universal head Lew Wasserman and sold him on the idea. And, oddly, I believe him to this day. What's true for sure is that he produced one of the first ones, a scary take on the Mafia taking over everything. Let others come with their claims.

My father's successes gave me courage in a way. As in: if he did this well, you won't do worse. Something like that, some combination of mythology and pride. Not that I knew what I would be in life. I had ideas to be a writer. But then there was this law school I was dragging myself through and I wasn't sure how being a writer would work. I suppose I assumed I would be a successful writer, because my father was a successful producer, and the word "successful," like a blank check, would cover it all. My father then made a U-turn on himself. It was the late sixties and the notion of self-actualization, of do-it-now, laid claim to him as to so many others. This and the fact that Fred was dead and Irene felt life was short, and the wholesale revulsion against the corporate that was in the culture. Normal run of stuff, but it wasn't everybody who gave up as much money as he did to become an independent film producer. I felt actually kind of flattered by him then, and fearful at the same time, as he reached to grab hold of a *zeitgeist* that was obviously more mine than his. He took an office in midtown Manhattan. I worked for him one summer, reading scripts and being really no help at all. I hadn't a clue as to what something "commercial" meant. My mind was far away from it. I couldn't even say what the "youth" wanted, because my Ivy League slice of the "youth" was pretty well severed from the rest. I believed in art. He, with reservations, did too. We were not a successful couple, and I slept on the rollaway couch in his office and seemed to provoke the resentment of his secretary, who had followed him over from Universal and would come in each morning to find me there. I sometimes wondered whether she had had an affair with my father, or had wanted to, so that my presence was more than an inconvenience, more a roadblock that for some reason he had placed in her way. She had a body that looked to have been pressed into a nice-enough shape.

Irene's troubles didn't end. She had minor abdominal surgery for something and peritonitis developed and she wound up with a catheter that she would have for the rest of her life. Does this make sense medically? It's what I remember, anyway. It came from a time in her life—and I suppose on reflection that was nearly all of it—when I wasn't paying close attention. And one good friend in particular didn't welcome her back to New York as Irene had expected and hoped for, and maybe even needed; instead, the friend seemed to imply that Irene had screwed up out in California and Fred's death was the proof of it. Or this was how Irene understood her friend's coolness, and it didn't help.

Meanwhile my father was headed for success or failure, depending how you chose to look at it, and I imagine he chose the rosy view one day and the dark glass the next. He got two movies made in New York. This was at a time when scarcely any movies were getting made in the city, it was considered impossible, too expensive, the unions, all of that, and to get two movies made without even a major studio in back of you could have been thought a minor miracle. On the other hand, they were both flops. A good review here and there, but no one in the theaters. One of them was for the "youth" market, or the twenty-something market anyway, and it starred a gay guy who was being directed by another gay guy and who was supposed to be playing a horny, mixed-up twenty-something not-gay guy and neither of the gay guys was experienced in film and the thing came off sexless, curdled, and campy. The other was a sci-fi thing about mind control and it was less embarrassing but boring.

Or these were the thoughts anyway, of me, in my twenties with my own hopes and pretensions, who either wanted my father to be king so that he could anoint me the prince or wanted him to stay clear of my turf altogether, leave the "youth" market for me to fail to understand. It lessened my own self-confidence when he failed. I suppose I believed in genes.

It was in these years when we were all living around New York that I noticed a subtle change in my father and Irene. They had always doted on one another, supported one another, shored up one another's jokes and shared their food in restaurants as if it were a daringly informal and intimate thing to do. But now they seemed so polite to one another. Please's and thank you's and taking extra care not to give each other offense, as if they were dancing minuets with their words. Where had that come from, or had it always been there and I'd never noticed? But I noticed it now and it had to have been big enough for me to notice. I brought blinders to them. There's no less shameful way to say it. Though is it half a defense to say that I was in my twenties then, and brought blinders, more or less, to pretty much everyone who was not? The proof that they were extra-polite to each other came from the fact that otherwise I would never have noticed it. But what did it mean? All I sensed really was that my father had reached the apogee of his life and had begun to decline. Or was it my perception of him that had reached its apogee and begun to decline?

It was about this time that my father began writing letters to the editor. So many problems with the country, so much to try and make right. I'd not even known before of his civic inclinations. Maybe it was only that he had a lot more time, as a movie producer in perpetual development rather than a TV producer in actual production, to see how the world was going. Mostly he sent them to the *New York Times*. They published a few. Every time they published one, he called me up to tell me. "They're publishing my Archie Cox." Remember the WIN buttons, Whip Inflation Now? He had one in on those. They titled it "Whip Ford Now." I suppose these could also be thought distractions from his life. But he seemed to believe he was making a difference, and he may have needed that for Irene as well. Her feet on the ground somewhere, however futile. Some response to outrage after outrage, to the dislocations of the times. Dirtying her hands with the world at last.

☙

I remember Calvin Trillin saying something like there should be a Dostoevsky Rule for writers and the Dostoevsky Rule should be this, that if you have the talent of Dostoevsky you can write anything you want about people you are close to but if you have less talent than Dostoevsky then you had better not. I like Calvin Trillin a lot, not least for suggesting that the shelf life of a book these days is somewhere between that of milk and yogurt, but I've found myself unable to abide by his rule. When I came back to writing fiction some years ago, I had in mind to write a kind of "meritocracy" series, novels that would chart the progress of my generation, or anyway the narrow slice of it that I knew well. The first book, in retrospect, came easily enough. Nothing ever comes easily, but I had a story to tell that was clear and seemed true enough, and I had feeling to put into it that had never gone away. It was the story of my hero in college, Harry Nolan, who might have been president of the country one day, and his wife Sascha Maclaren on whom I had a crush. My sixties book, so to speak. The sixties. The seventies. The eighties. The nineties. A book for each decade, a neat quartet, about the best and the brightest and what happened to them, or us. Something you weren't going to see on TV or in the movies. Something, I told myself, that you might not even read in somebody else's book. The novel as sociology? A dirty job but somebody's got to do it? Maybe so or maybe not. But also Forster's thing about if you had to choose between your country and your friends, would you have the courage to choose your friends? Not that in my case courage was involved. Rather, more, the imagination of courage: *if* I had to choose, which would it be? I feel even now maybe more loyal to my generation than to a generalized idea of "America," and more loyal still to a class that may never even have existed—it may all have been a fiction, the way some have said that romantic love is a fiction, or anyway a literary convention. In the second book, the characters come at the world from a different angle, seem for a little while to say good-bye to it. Probably that description reduces it too much. They join a group. They're looking for something. A sort of schema, then, in the sixties embracing the world as their natural inheritance and in the seventies feeling disinherited and seeking transcendence. Which was whatever it was, which left them wherever they were left. Still trying to come out on top, you could say that much anyway, and now in the eighties, if the scheme would hold, they would have to return to the world because where else was there to go? Change the world, change yourself, change nothing. Only accept.

But I had a terrible time with this third book, my eighties book. What I knew on the ground in the eighties was the same thing that I knew in dreams when I was young: California. I went out to Los Angeles, ostensibly, because where else would a writer in 1980s America go who wanted only to accept "what is?" I wanted to make a living. I didn't want to be poor anymore. Or things must have seemed that way, to myself, to others. What really was going on would be for the novel, the third book, to explore.

I started the book again and again. I will record for you what some of these beginnings were, the ones that I never got around to trashing.

> The way we used to do the show, we'd start every episode
> with a typewriter-like font in a corner of the screen:
> NIGHTSHIFT. Then the NIGHTSHIFT would fade out
> and the date would fade in. Then the show would start.

The idea I had then was that I would use the celebrated television show *Northie* that made my show business fortune and reputation such as they were as the formal basis for the book and the center of its interest. After all, were the eighties not all about business, and what place could be more archetypal of this than the place that made Reagan a star? Moreover it was not unusual in the eighties for pundits to write articles in the Sunday papers or *Vanity Fair* about how television drama would soon be replacing literature as the mirror and conscience of our age. The very form of the screenplay seemed compelling, for its concision, its no-bullshit approach. I intended to call this version of my book, *Notes for an Unproduced Teleplay*.

I never liked Zacky Kurtz much. He wore pressed jeans. I don't care what year it was, can you imagine such a thing, such a style? Can you imagine what went into making a guy who could think such a style was acceptable, who could stand there looking at his pressed jeans piled in his bottom drawer?

Or if they were pressed, would you if you were Zacky Kurtz eschew a drawer and hang them all on hangers? Zacky in his walk-in closet looking at his long row of pressed jeans on hangers, lined up like his equally long row of Houston Astro baseball hats. Two hundred dollar jeans, by the way. No Levi's, no Dockers here. Beverly Hills jeans.

Not that I know anything really about jeans. I haven't worn them since fourth or fifth grade—too tight on my skin or in the crotch or something. A baggy pants guy, all the way. Zacky gave me a pair of Nocona crocodile cowboy boots once, hardly used, right out of his closet. He probably thought he was spiffing me up, and maybe he was, but I hated the high heels, they made me feel phony. And they weren't even so high, they were high heels only compared to what you would find on ratted-out old loafers. But I guess that was me, baggy pants and ratted-out old loafers from Bean's. Incorrigible, in Zacky's view. And someone who'd squeeze a nickel till the buffalo crapped, in one of Zacky's occasional sage Texasisms, thrown off with an ironic flourish, as if to show he hadn't forgotten where he came from.

Thrifty, I liked to think. I who before 1981 had never had more than three thousand dollars in the bank. And I was a grown man then, close to forty years old. Not that Zacky hadn't once been poor, or felt he was poor. That was essential to him, that explained so much about him. Houston, the great, zoneless nowhere, father a Methodist minister who died penniless and young, as if Zacky had been born just too late for a thirties movie of upward mobility. But Zacky had never squeezed a nickel, not as long as I'd known him anyway. Get it and spend it, get it and spend it. That was his joy, or, as Zacky would have had it, who balanced his Texasisms with equally sardonic outbursts of Latin, his *delectatio*. He really wasn't cheap about anything, he was six feet four inches tall with broad shoulders and a long reach and he'd hug you with those great appendages of his if he hardly knew you, and it wasn't, all of it, anyway, a scam. If you were a help to him, he hugged you for real.

He also put an avuncular arm around people and squeezed their shoulder and kissed them, often with a bit of athletic elegance, as if reminding them or reminding himself that Columbia University had once brought him north to be their quarterback. Or maybe he was suggesting that he was somehow the entertainment industry's answer to Lyndon B. Johnston. Texas charm, Texas power? He presumed, I suppose. But why shouldn't he have? For most people who knew him he was the boss, or they aspired to have him be their boss, they angled to be on his team. He seemed to bring good luck; Zacky was a hit. And when he squeezed my shoulder, I, who had helped him a lot, felt a shiver, a twitch, something I could no more locate than deny.

In this version, as I now read it over, I must have thought to focus on the period when Zacky was my boss on *Northie*. He brought me along, he gave me my start, and later he was my partner. I've included as much of this second false start as I have because on reading it over it rings true, and Zacky remains an important figure in this story I'm telling now. Why write the same thing twice?

And here was a third beginning:

> It seemed like a good idea once. Maybe one day it will seem that way again, but today it does not. Today I wish I'd never told anybody that I was going to carry my tale into the eighties.

Speaks for itself, I guess. For the problems I was having, which if I could summarize went something like this: I would write forty, fifty, seventy pages, I would have an outline in hand, and I would begin to lose interest in what I was writing. Something seemed missing. I didn't think the problem was in the story. Enough had happened to me and I'd found my characters and a plot, I jiggled them here and there but mostly they were what they were. And the setting seemed to fit, the land without shadows.

Morning in America, the city on a hill, all that rubbish, or was it? Reagan brought the top tax bracket down to twenty-eight percent. Now wasn't *that* something to write about? The meritocrats were approaching middle age. In eras of less advanced medicine they'd already be old.

I was stymied. My feelings ran cold. And I suppose I could point out something about myself that of course must be true for others too, but that maybe I have a bit of a special gift for: things hiding from me in plain sight. A couple of Christmases ago I was given Amos Oz's wonderful book of growing up in Jerusalem, *A Tale of Love and Darkness*. Later I saw Oz on C-Span and he was joking about how his American publisher said he had to put the word "memoir" on the cover of the book because in America people wanted to know whether they were buying a fish or a chicken, and so Oz let them do it even though he knew that his book, partly about distant ancestors, contained the truths of imagination as well as memory. I loved this man when I saw him on television, his playfully narrowed eyes and the thick, proud emphases of his accented English, as if every sentence he spoke was a definitive affirmation of some hopeless contradiction that he was more than willing to call life. But I digress, maybe. Never mind love, maybe. The man gave me something. Later in his book he wrote about how he got started as a writer. He was stuck in a kibbutz in the middle of nowhere believing that if you were going to be a writer you had to live out in the wide world, "Paris, Madrid, New York, Monte Carlo, the African deserts or the Scandinavian forests," where real things happened. Romantic things, daring things, lonely brave things, scarcely known in the lives of those he lived with then, or in the lives of the people he had grown up with in a lower middle-class neighborhood in Jerusalem. Then one night he read Sherwood Anderson's *Winesburg, Ohio*, about a place he had scarcely ever heard of, where people were as "ordinary" as those he'd always known. And Anderson had found dignity and complexity and of course everything else in Winesburg's citizens, and Oz took this to heart and never after looked back. He realized, he said, that wherever a writer is, *that* is the center of his universe. And eventually he came to be writing about his family in this beautiful tale that I held in my hands until late in my own night in Los Angeles during the last days of the year 2004. What touched me most, really, was how honored he was when, decades later, someone asked him to write a blurb for a new edition of *Winesburg, Ohio*. I imagined someday someone asking me to write a blurb for *A Tale of Love and Darkness* and how dumbfounded I would be. I knew then that what was hiding in plain sight, vis-à-vis this book that I could not write, was my father.

I resisted at first. I was worried that putting my father into a book about my generation in the eighties would pull the book out of shape. I would of course have to start decades before. And what about my scheme, my best and brightest characters first embracing the world as their natural inheritance, then feeling disinherited and seeking transcendence, then in the third book returning to the world because where else was there to go? What had my father, my family, to do with that? Everything, I decided. What is coming back to the world about if it is not about coming back to our fathers? We never really leave our mothers, no matter where or what. And really, when I thought about it, I knew so many people like myself who came back to their fathers in the eighties. "Business." That, too. Going into "business," our fathers' world. It was a book that, finally, I felt I could write.

Los Angeles

When I arrived in Los Angeles in the spring of 1980, I found an apartment in a rent-controlled building two blocks from the beach in Ocean Park. The building had once been an Elks retirement home. Many of the people living there were on county assistance. My room had a sliver of an ocean view and my rent was one hundred seventy-six dollars a month.

On arriving there some guy on the boardwalk could have painted my picture and put the following caption on it: "Portrait of a Young Mystic, Recently Returned to the World."

That would be referencing the esoteric group that I had been a part of in New York and that I had left when my friend jumped out a window. I arrived in Ocean Park with enough attention mustered from five years in the group that I felt I could bust open brick walls. The world seemed bright and endlessly interesting, as it might to someone released after years in jail. I was broke and meant to do something about it, but this problem, if it was a problem at all, more often than not lacked immediacy. I ran off a succession of quick affairs. Sometimes I went in the ocean. I spent hours in the Rose Café, where there always seemed to be sand on the floor, reading the papers and trying to pick up still more girls, between bouts of turning out sample scripts to send around. Yes, I was looking for my chance, but if I didn't get it, then what? The prettiest girl I met the whole time was in the very building where I lived. Her name was Melissa and I met her in the laundry room and she had a bigger apartment than mine. She may have paid three hundred in rent.

The most vivid image I hold of Melissa from that time is not strictly from that time at all—I must have cobbled it together from things she said, places where we happened to be together, photographs. And although I can almost see her within a photograph's borders, and in the slightly hazed-over colors of an aging print, there is to my knowledge no photograph that has it all. A little bit younger than I ever knew her, almost in profile, a breeze scattering her hair across her cheek, in front of her pale green Cadillac. The Cadillac is so long it takes up the whole image, an old car but Melissa has waxed the paint so it shines. She wears a fitted, thin red sweater. A few of her dresses that she sells to shops from the back of her car are cradled over her joined arms. It's impossible to know what she's looking off at. It's possible that she's looking off at nothing, that the entire image is a pose. Her complexion is pale, as if she hadn't been in the sun, but it is a bright California day, the sun glints off her hair and the hood of the car. Her nose is a little long. She has the look of a swan. She's probably a bit too thin and her hair, cut shorter than when I ever knew her, so that one can see her neck's slender elongation, is the honey-est of blond. She seems to be in her late twenties. I would have met her a year or two later. I have no idea why this image stays with me. Maybe the courage of it. She seems to me brave in the picture, with her dresses, her sweater, her car. It's possible there was something like this image in her apartment, in a frame or an album, but I don't remember.

She was having an affair at the time, with someone who turned out to be Zacky Kurtz. I learned this only slowly.

Melissa was not free with information. Yet we became friends. Maybe this was because so many of the people in our building were old and on welfare and we must have stood out to each other. We would have coffee once in a while at the Rose. I must have told her about my intentions, how I was here to make some money writing scripts and then when I had a pile of it, say, a hundred thousand dollars, I would leave and rent a place in the Hamptons where rents were cheap in the winter and begin to write my books, or in all events, even if I didn't have a hundred thousand dollars, I would leave before the Olympics came in 1984. The Olympics would be my alarm clock, my last-ditch warning, the way that I could tie myself to the mast against the sirens. Though I didn't say "sirens" to her. Melissa would more than likely not have known much about where they came from, and I had the feeling even then that she was not somebody you could charm with clever allusions, that you could only hurt her feelings that way. Nor did she seem to have any "intentions" herself. Not the way I had them. Not that she would talk about, anyway. She had come to Los Angeles because she married a musician and when they had no money she made shirts for rock guys. The rock guys thought the shirts were beauties; it was said that Melissa could do anything with a sewing machine, that hers would fetch a bone if she wanted it to. Then her marriage to the musician ended and she was even broker than before and an old guy came along who gave her valuable watches and knew people in L.A.'s garment district and he set her up as a maker of dresses. This was before Zacky Kurtz. She designed everything as if she were going to wear it herself. She had reps in a few places, but she sold the dresses better herself, out of the old Cadillac's enormous trunk which she had lined with silk and rayon. Buyers and shop owners liked it when she came around. Her toothy smile, the big old Caddy, and she would be wearing one of her dresses and they looked great on Melissa. She was charming. She never really *sold* anything. She just showed up and the clothes were in her arms, and people would take them. She was too shy to sell—the secret of her success. Though if she was a success, it was a modest one. She paid the rent and bought a few things. People said that Melissa was so beautiful she should be a movie star. Local version of praise, replacing the national hopefulness of "could" with the more expectant and knowing "should," yet Melissa would have been even more shy to act than she was shy to sell. Lord knows her boyfriend Zacky could have made something out of her. But Melissa liked doing what she did, and it was something that no one else did, not the way she did it anyway.

Six or eight months passed from the time I got my apartment and when I got a call from my father that he and Irene were coming out, he had a couple meetings with people and they would stay a few days then go up to Santa Barbara, but when he was in Los Angeles would I like to have dinner? For some years previous I'd been almost out of touch with him, involved with my New York "group," in which it was often said that parents and conditioning and habits were the source of most of our difficulties. I took this lesson as far as it would take me and where it left me off, I imagined, was with my feelings about my father and growing up and my mother and divorce and California and Irene and kidney-shaped swimming pools exposed and worn away, so that I could begin to live my own life now. So that I could come to California aware that this was where my father and Irene had made their lives without me, but not because of it. I had my own reasons. I was a writer and

I needed the money and it was someplace I hadn't tried. And in fact my life in Los Angeles after I arrived was nothing like my images of what theirs had been. My life was Venice and the beach and the bungalows of Ocean Park and people who were passing through or just getting by. I never went to Bel Air, nor to a museum. I called up an agent or two who my father suggested might help me, but they didn't and I stopped calling. It was as if our two paths never crossed. In this, Melissa was like an archetype, of a Los Angeles unlike theirs, and when they invited me for dinner it seemed almost natural for me to invite her along.

We went to one of their old places in Beverly Hills. Unlike everything in Venice in those years, it wasn't painted white. And the food was old-fashioned too, veal in this or that. But tasty enough, in a way that reminded me of Europe, of them in Europe with their red guides and concierge tips; they would never go to a restaurant with bad food. As soon as we sat down, as if surprised by an inevitability, I began comparing Melissa to Irene. There were odd similarities, in height, in the blue metallic of their eyes, in their somewhat elongated slender noses and lanky frames. Irene had never been as blond as Melissa but she must have been a little bit blond once. And Melissa looked great in her clothes, and Irene maybe still did too, she who I used to imagine playing sports in just the right thing. Though I don't quite remember what Irene was wearing that night. Something roughly woven, a jacket? I'm not that good at this, remembering her, or clothes. What I do recall is that the politeness of Irene and my father to each other was out in full force. She told a flattering story about him playing chess with Ronnie Reagan in the Universal commissary and having to explain to Ronnie gently how if your pawn got to the end of the board you could get any piece you wanted back. He told a flattering story about her binding books with tactile covers for the blind in Tijuana. They were bragging, really. It's what it came down to when you subtracted out that she was talking about him and he was talking about her. But who were they trying to impress? Surely not me, the unemployed writer. It must have been Melissa, the beauty, my friend. They must have thought she was my girlfriend and were making sure she knew what worldly, accomplished, humane, and well-thought-of parents I had. I was afraid that Melissa would feel hurt by this, as she would have been hurt if they had started quizzing her on the capital of Delaware or South Dakota. What amazed me more than their name-dropping was that, far from retreating into a shell of resentment, Melissa could compete. For every name they dropped, she dropped one of equal or greater value. She didn't mind at all. It was like a contest to her—she wouldn't have started it but now that they'd started it—to see who was best. And younger people, more currently stylish people, were in her armory. I had neglected to calculate that even a clandestine affair with Zacky Kurtz would result in a slurry of celebrity acquaintances. Referred to obliquely, of course, the exact circumstances of each bit of her gossip or observation left nicely obscure. And before Zacky, all those rock guys she made shirts for. Though of course Irene and my father didn't know the rock guys, so mentioning those was like serving outside the lines, in a tennis match where it was two against one. I was the one who knew nobody. Not in person, anyway. Later I told Melissa I didn't know she had it in her. She said she didn't know what I was talking about. She had gone back to being quiet. I thought about it again and decided that Melissa, despite her shyness, and some other things, was a lot like Irene.

A short catalog of the kinds of things my father professed to have an opinion about. The show at the Met, the Baryshnikov this or that, the oil situation in the Emirates, the op-ed piece about the secretary of the treasury, the Booker Prize, the bestseller list, new advances in cloning, the Knicks, the Mets, the electric cars, the mayor's temper, the race situation here and in postcolonial Africa, communists, land mines, Academy Awards, Nobel Prizes, the U.N. and American intransigence about it, the decline of statesmanship, steroids in the Olympics, hormones in beef, child labor in developing countries, plundered Nazi art, Klee, Ernst, Pollack, whoever, Warhol, Schnabel, grand pianos.

༺༻

It was Melissa who introduced me to Zacky and Zacky who put me on what seemed like a magic carpet, something out of *The Thief of Baghdad*. Zacky at the time with his partner James Morton had one of the big new hits on television, a cop show set in the nighttime of an absurd ghetto world. Depending who you listened to, *Northie* was realistic, surrealistic, tragic, comic, tragicomic, or way over the top. Certainly it took a lot of chances. It did shows entirely from the criminals' point of view, where you hardly saw the cops at all, and then the same stories entirely from the victims' point of view, where you also hardly saw the cops at all. It did shows that took place in "real time," and shows where one hour covered an entire year. It did a silent movie hour complete with dialogue cards. It did black-and-white hours. It did one hour where the first act was in black-and-white and the second in color and so on. It did an entire hour shot with a stationary camera. It did an hour show entirely inside a police car. It did an hour where the actors switched their parts around.

And it was as energetic as it was risk-taking. There were other shows with bigger casts, *Northie* had only six regulars, but things were always bumping into other things or getting smashed up. Zacky took an interest in me because Melissa told him I was smart and because they wanted writers who hadn't been corrupted by writing for older shows and because I'd put in my time with the D.A.'s office in New York and seemed to know what I was talking about when it came to the mean streets. Then he read my scripts and laughed. He gave me an assignment, then another. My young mystic's training in self-abnegation resulted in scripts that were just like theirs. I had a gift for imitation. Which in a television series was a particularly good gift to have, since of all art forms the one a TV series most resembles is the skyscraper—ornamentation on the first few floors and on the top, but in between, seventy or ninety or a hundred floors that are just windows, as if it were true that a giraffe is just a horse that reached for the highest leaves.

And this was true even in shows that were daring. Within months of my joining the staff, in a year when shows from our rival MTM were favored to sweep the board, *Northie* won enough Emmys to stuff the trunk of Zacky and Morty's limo, and then came a string of other awards, and the magazines and entertainment shows, and the ratings, and more money. Though Morty was tired of it already, and there were rumors that he was angry at Zacky for hogging the publicity. Not that Morty wanted it himself, but he seemed to have contempt for anybody who would. The publicity and the credit: who would want such things? What kind of person? Morty had been a master printer before he was a writer and soon was thinking of going back to Oregon and a letterpress. Which seemed as if it would be fine with Zacky, who in the seventies had often been called the "King of TV," mostly on account of a wildly popular, easy-going detective show called *Darlington* and another called *Billie Rae*, and was hoping to ride *Northie* past those up-and-coming MTM guys to become reigning king once more. Both Zacky and James were soon grooming me to be Morty's successor. Or not a successor precisely, because Zacky didn't want another partner. He simply needed someone who could do the work that Morty did, which in Morty's view was more than his share, of the experimental work anyway, that had come from the fevered brain of a master printer and not been on television before, as opposed to the tropes of a veteran like Zacky. Zacky had been in TV his whole adult life, and he was forty-seven years old, nine years my senior, the year I joined *Northie*. And I was grateful to him.

But sardonic, bleak, and younger James Morton was closer to my style. I had complaints with even *Northie*'s television from the start. Until he left the show, Morty and I would go out to lunch and grouse. How manipulated most of it was, how calculated, a dollop of emotion here, a zinger of a joke there, as if the only point was to please. Yet in truth, I liked such grousing. It was something, for a writer who had been in his room, to come out and have others to grouse with. I liked the company, the free lunches, even the pleasure of reintegration into a society that I'd scarcely known was there. And having people say nice things about you all the time, even if they were lying, agents buttering you up for future commissions, actors buttering you up for better lines. As Zacky would put it, when Texas overcame him, it was like stepping in high cotton. I vaguely knew that I'd been lucky. But I put stock as well in another of Zacky's favorite bits of schoolboy Latin: *Fortuna est fortuna, sed labor omnia vincit.* And then too, the money coming in, like thunderstorms rolling over a desert that had been parched for years.

My father was maybe even prouder of me than he was shocked by my rapid progress, which must have seemed to him like an unexpected September run from a ball club previously struggling in the second division. After my first show was on, he called up of course. It seemed as if everybody I knew called up, as if everybody had seen. Most had just a few kind words. But my father said, "Very professional."

"Thanks."

"I had a little trouble hearing a few lines. I guess I'm getting old."

"All the crosstalk."

"Is that what they call it? When everybody talks at once?"

"I think so. I guess so."

"But she's marvelous. The girl."

"She is. . ."

"And the thing about the autistic kid who ran numbers was touching."

"It happens to be true. The kid's at Harvard now."

"Look, could I make one suggestion?"

"Why not?"

"Just a little one. . . Take the episode, make ten copies, I'll give you a list, you send them to the top ten agents in town."

"But I've got an agent."

"Now's your chance to get a better one."

"I like the one I've got."

"Just making a little suggestion."
"Thanks. Really. I'll consider it."
"This is your chance."
"I think I'm okay."
"It was a *marvelous* show. It really was."
"Thanks."
"Well if there's anything I can do. . . If you want that list of agents. . ."
"Let me think about it."
"Think about it."
"Good-night."
"Good-night."
"Thanks for the call."
"If I can be of any help. . ."

Only a producer, was pretty much my thought; as if the subtlest art of the producer was to noodge tenderly.

☙

The odd thing was, he didn't seem to know exactly how far I'd already come. Either that or he couldn't quite acknowledge it. Or couldn't quite believe it. As if it was as much a dream to him as it was to me.

Yet it wasn't a dream to me. It felt more like something natural, or expected, like an inheritance. I could do this because he had done it before me. Stepping into this world that I half-wanted and half-despised felt like stepping into a bath that was exactly my body temperature.

☙

Theme Song for an Old Show

One small miracle of *Northie*: that it really did feel like a northern, inner-city show, even though Zacky had Houston in his bones. And his co-creator, Morty, was from Eugene.

Zacky had come north only when Columbia gave him his scholarship. But he made up for lost time. He quit football after his freshman year. He spent the rest of his time, by his own account, "down the hill" in Harlem. Either in Harlem or at Rockefeller Center, where NBC had its headquarters, hoping for his break into show business.

For reasons known only to themselves, Zacky and Morty set their show in Boston, in what felt like Roxbury or Dorchester, but it never lost the rhythms and rhymes of Zacky's years spent close to that other great institution of learning called UCLA, the University on the Corner of Lenox Avenue.

☙

Another small miracle, not only of *Northie* but of all the breakthrough TV dramas of the eighties, in my opinion anyway: their zest. There was little about the demented, confused, heroic, preposterous, greedy, scatological, contemporary fairy tale of urban life in America in the eighties, in other words the life so many of us lived or would have lived if we could, that couldn't fit somehow into their maws. In many respects, we who were doing them just took our own lives and plastered them onto whatever world our show was set in. What a wrong thing to do, bad, bad, bad, except it worked. Maybe because everyone in the eighties had middle-class hopes.

Yet they were never entirely realistic shows, nor as far as I knew were they meant to be. That's where the critics, I thought, had it wrong. They thought what was good about

Northie, or for that matter the MTM shows or even *Cagney & Lacey* or *China Beach*, was their "realism," and whenever a new one came along where the toilets flushed louder they thought that was more realistic and better. I can only speak for *Northie*, but in our case the "realism" was only a tease. There were all our formal experiments, for one thing. And then there was that huge appetite, as if that night we were eternally playing in might gobble up the world. Surreal, vain, a little nuts, a little wrong. But the heart of it never broke. It had pity. It had mercy. It took its share of cheap shots and believed in everybody. When it was good, anyway. It had the bitter exuberance of the end of our youth.

༒

The next time the Emmys came around, I took my mother. Invited her out, put her up in a hotel, took her out shopping for a dress. I've heard the TV and movie stars have made mom night kind of a fashion recently, but she was the only one, or close to it, that year. People doted on her. Hagle, the star of our show who played the unflappable Lieutenant Donald D. O'Brien, kissed her hand, hugged her, and bored her for twenty minutes talking about his hiking experiences in the Carpathian Alps. Or "bored" is strictly my interpretation. I'd heard about his hiking experiences in the Carpathian Alps so many times and I felt she should be bored, but actually she was the ideal listener. Everything interested her, and as soon as she had the chance she returned his conversational favor, telling him all about her varied experience volunteering at the library back home. I had wondered how she would feel coming to the place where the one whose name she wouldn't even say unless it was absolutely necessary ran off with her best friend. But it didn't seem to faze her. It was as if she had waited a very long time to make her entrance, but when she made it, she made it in triumph. I was her triumph. In the limo back to Santa Monica she went through the goodies bag they give you at the dinner like a child with a Christmas stocking. It's weird how even the rich like these things, but my mother seemed not so much greedy as surprised. As in: how could they afford to give out all this for free? The companies must be going broke! It was my year that year and I placed the ungainly statue they'd given me in her lap. The statue had electric-like wings that were kind of sharp, and she rubbed her fingers over them. "A person could get cut," she said.

"So be careful."

"They should sand them down at least. This is terrible."

"They leave them that way so the envious can keep stabbing one another."

"Your father never won one of these."

She said it in such a way that I could imagine malice in her voice when it wasn't really there. No echo, no disappointment, nothing. As if she could have added: "Just an observation." But she got quiet, picked up some of the Revlon stuff they'd given her, the cleanser, the moisturizer, the whatever else, and looked at it all with a curiosity not so different from a child's.

It was at moments such as these that I least felt like I was living my own life, or rather that I had my own life but was loaning it out, to others' purposes and feelings. If it was me, I told myself, I'd have gotten right out of this limo. But I was happy enough for her to be in it and she wouldn't have been in it if I wasn't in it too. We drove along through rain-dampened streets with the dark windows making everything darker and the statue still in her lap and I took a kind of spiritual siesta. It's what it felt like, slipping off to a pied-à-terre of the mind where everything was more or less at rest. A pied-à-terre I kept just in case all of the rest of this didn't work out.

As I understand, or understood, what Krishna once told Arjuna, it is proper for people to spend their lives living out the societal roles that fate has given them. Then when those roles are fulfilled, a man may wander off. To the forest, wherever, in search of his soul.

℘

Now I read over what I wrote previously, and I ask myself: would I really have gotten right out of the limo?

Second thoughts. A book of second thoughts.

℘

My father became more collegial with me. One measure of which that I happened to notice was that he began to swear in my presence. Nothing terribly daring, no motherfucking motherfucker fucking cocksucking bitch whore cunts, just a smattering of shits and damns. But they were there, in the natural rhythms of his speech. As if we were both in the same business now, we both knew the same jokes.

He was still in New York and was trying to get shows on again because his movies had been flops. He knew he was getting older and he may have needed the money. I don't know how much money they had spent, on moving back and forth, on Europe, on art, on restaurants, on her catheter or whatever it was and the aftermath of Fred and on bringing up Thomas, whom after our few days together in Bel Air I hardly knew at all. I didn't seek him out. He went to private schools and then he went to Yale. We were seldom in the same city. I heard, from my father, from Irene, that he was a nice kid.

It was much harder for my father to get shows on now. He no longer had a big studio behind him. Then as now, television was not receptive to the old guys, unless the old guys were so rich they could hire the young guys to do their work for them. Instead he hired Irene. They were partners, after a fashion. They had an office on Thirty-eighth Street and tried to tap, as my father said, the tremendous talent of the Broadway playwrights for television. This was what he now had to sell, this and his track record, but his track record was from a ways back. And why Irene? Because she needed to work? Because it was keeping it all in the family, a mom-and-pop shop, no outside salaries to pay? Because of Fred and her bad dreams? Because it was a way of holding it all together, just as their politeness and their ping-ponging back and forth across the country and his letters to the editor and sharing their food in restaurants was a way of holding it all together? A sentence in which the "all" must refer to their marriage, their bet together—but anything else?

They would take the Broadway playwrights out to lunch. The fun part of the job. Irene learning what my father really did. And my father doing his determined best to be a man of his times, liberal and forward-thinking, making his wife his equal in all he did.

I'm not sure whether Irene had ever held a job in her life before. That must have been part of it too.

Irene reading scripts and answering the phone and having opinions, like a D-girl almost sixty. And why not? Brave enough.

Yet the odds seemed long. And being in New York didn't help, when most of the business wasn't. A quixotic thing in a way, a way of saying, to yourself or others, that you were keeping your hand in. He began to call me more frequently. To catch me up on what he was doing or tell me what I should be doing. Always polite, almost deferential, as if he wouldn't presume to tell me whatever it was he was about to tell me, but what the hell, he'd take a chance, he was my dad after all, and so what about this or what about that. I loved this. I think I loved it. I loved being treated like a colleague, which was different from being treated like an equal because with a colleague you didn't have to measure so precisely, who was up, who was down. It reminded me, a little, of when my father had told me at my grandmother's funeral that he would make sure I could go to Yale if I got in.

And so I was also wary, as if on the lookout for something unsaid. Was my father just buttering me up? Did he want something from me? And yet, if so, why not? Wasn't that what colleagues were for, to commiserate with each other and want things from each other? One day my father asked me if he could send me a script. He said it was something that he and Irene were both quite proud of, it was by E_____, the well-known, highly regarded Broadway playwright, and they were going to turn it in soon to CBS, but if I had any thoughts before they turned it in, that would be great. There were ways that I felt flattered by this. He was asking me to critique this well-known, highly regarded Broadway playwright, or to put my two cents in anyway. Or even more flattering: he seemed to be asking me for a pat on the back. Was I now someone he would like a pat on the back from? I was terrified that I would hate the script.

It was set in some future world where there was a pioneering civilization and then there were marauders and it was going to be an updated western, a sci-fi western, or that's how they pitched it anyway. Always make the pitch simple. Of course there'd not been a successful western on television in fifteen years, but that was exactly the point, bring 'em back, the classic formula for success, take an old, worn-out genre and give it a new lease on life. Wasn't that how shows like *Northie* succeeded? I remember my father asking me this, telling me most of this, when we were on the phone and he asked me if he could send out the script. He seemed to be trying out the point that his script and *Northie* were similar types of projects, revolutionary yet with a memory of hits past in their bones.

I did hate that script. I hated it so much that I wondered if I was fated to hate it, if no matter it had been written by Mark Twain and named *The Adventures of Huckleberry Finn* I would have hated it. It was sentimental and trite and labored and well-meaning and pathetically, falsely optimistic and the characters speechified and postured and each one was better than the last, except for the "baddies," of course, and the women were all gems and strong and the future didn't look so bad. Mostly I hated the well-known highly regarded Broadway playwright's patronization, as if he was going to use television to teach everybody something, as if people needed to be taught. Since I wasn't aware that such patronization was in his work on Broadway, I was afraid that my father and Irene in the do-gooding spirit that was taping them together had put him up to it, or at least had let him get away with it, get away with not understanding the medium at all. It was as if the well-known, highly regarded Broadway playwright had decided that he could only rationalize taking such big, easy bucks as these and stooping so low as to *do television* if he was being uplifting. Old-fashioned? Anyway, without nuance or laughs-in-the-middle-of-tragedy or sarcasm or absurdity or doubt. As if the broad American demographic wouldn't get such things. But I was in the process of making a small fortune precisely because America would, did, get such things.

Or was I wrong about it? It's what I feared. The arising of my unconscious, bopping my father over the head at the first opportunity? And the fact that I was doing one of these lucky, advanced, sophisticated shows. Wasn't most of television still not like this, didn't you have to be sentimental and trite, especially on CBS, with its audience in the "C" towns and "D" towns of middle America? I wasn't sure. I didn't watch the stuff. I was less of an expert than a hundred million Americans. And everybody else was telling him the script was great. It's what he told me, anyway. But wasn't that what people did? You tell your friend, your colleague, your whatever the script is great and wait for the network, or whoever's up the food chain, to shoot it down.

"Hi, Dad."

"Hi."

"I read the script."

"Oh?"

"Actually, I read it twice."

"Great."

"Have you turned it in yet?"

"Not yet. Friday. Unless, of course, you have things to suggest. I told E_____ my son was reading it."

"You did?"

"He knows your show."

"Oh. Good."

Theme Song for an Old Show

"I don't know if he actually *watches* it every week. . ."

"Well, whatever. Look, I don't have too much to say. A couple of things."

"Did I tell you, Mike Landrum called. He thought the script was *marvelous*."

"Great."

"People seem to like that it has, I don't know how else to put it, an old-fashioned feel, I guess. They feel like they're on solid ground. With a twist, of course."

"The future."

"The whole universe, that E_____ created, the whole *Star Trek* thing."

"But there isn't really too much science fiction in it, I mean, you know, special effects."

"It's not a special effects show. It's a character show. It's all about people, that's all. Just people."

"I think that's great. I mean, it's the right place to start."

"So tell me. . . You said you had a couple things."

"Nothing much. Just general. If there was one thing, I'd mess up the characters a little."

"Make them *quirkier*?"

"Not quirkier, necessarily. Quirky's a little creepy. To me, anyway. Just mess 'em up a little."

"I'm not sure what you mean, 'mess 'em up a little.'"

"Just… some of them . . . I guess I mean less one-dimensional."

"The characters are one-dimensional?"

"It's not that they *are*. It's they could be. . . *less so*? Am I making any sense? Less good guys and bad guys."

"There's always been good guys and bad guys."

"Of course. Of course."

"Look at *Star Trek*."

"Right. You're right... Though actually, I don't know you're right. I never saw *Star Trek*."

"You never saw *Star Trek*?"

"Bits. I've seen bits of one or two."

And so I guess I'd found my excuse. I didn't know television.

"Anything else?" my father asked.

"I don't know."

"You said you had a couple things."

"I guess I'd wait, I'd see what they say, the network. I mean, if they love it..."

"They love E_____. They couldn't have been more complimentary."

"I'd just wait then. When they have notes, I mean, if they even have any, maybe it'll be exactly what they want just the way it is right now, and I wouldn't want to say something, and E_____ changes it, and that's what they don't like... so if they have notes, then, if you want, we can talk some more."

"Sounds good. But basically you liked it?"

"I did."

"Great."

But CBS never gave him notes. They must have hated it so much, they didn't bother.

What my father and I never talked about was doing a project together. The assumption was always that I was busy with *Northie*, or busy with Zacky, or busy with something. I imagined he didn't want to presume on my success. I imagine he was being kind in not asking. But I think he would have liked to do a show with me then. I could add, "especially after the debacle with E_____."

But even if that hadn't been a disaster, I think he would have. For the pride of it, if nothing else. Though, if I could generalize, with a producer there's always something else. The enhanced chances for success, the fresh stories to tell your friends, the competition of it, ha ha, beat you at last, beat you with my own son. All of those and more. I would have liked to do a project with my father for the roundedness of it, and the warm bath of generosity I would swim in, but I feared it. Why work with him and have to argue against the sentimental and old and tell him that Irene would have to butt out of it because I couldn't listen to her as well as everybody else? I was on a roll. I had Zacky Kurtz or he had me. I was part of one of TV's big hits. I kept telling myself maybe. Time passed and we said nothing.

❧

And now a sort of forward movement of the plot. While my father got older, Zacky's wife, Maryanna, a black-haired Italian girl from South San Francisco who had some street fighter instincts in her, got an inkling about Zacky's affair with Melissa. Or maybe she didn't get an inkling, maybe Zacky only imagined she got an inkling, or maybe it wasn't even that, maybe he simply wanted to distract her so that she would never get an inkling. Or maybe he just felt guilty. In all events, Maryanna was an actress and she had a small, recurring role on *Northie* from the start of it, playing a police department nutritionist who would come around and complain about the food in the vending machines and try with little success to improve the cops' diets. Maryanna was brilliant in the role, funny and sharp, wistful and wry, and we liked having her come around. But now Zacky began to build up the part, so that soon there was a "Maryanna" plot in nearly every episode.

The problem was that on *Northie*, a show about cops, Maryanna wasn't playing a cop. Over at the network, there were grumblings that the show was losing its masculine edge, or more importantly, its male viewers. Which was fine by Zacky, who was content to explain it by saying that he was exploring his feminine side and who would add that people with paired X chromosomes watched television too. But it was really, I thought, about Melissa.

I would tactfully suggest to Zacky that even though I really loved Maryanna, we were beginning to overuse her. My reward was that when the network called to complain, Zacky would tell them the problem wasn't Maryanna or his desire to explore his feminine side, the problem was me. Time for recourse to one of the entertainment industry's most eternal clichés: no good deed goes unpunished. Then Maryanna found out about Melissa for sure and Zacky dropped Melissa and I was angry with him then, for the way he did it, over a weekend and not looking back, and even for the way he set Melissa up with an old shrink of his, as though mental health benefits were part of her severance package, or he was afraid she would kill herself and make a scene. I said something to him once. Innocuous enough, but it was something. I said, "Melissa doesn't need a shrink, she needs someone to take care of her." Taken out of context the words may seem harsh, but they were hedged when I said them, with "I don't know's" and "maybe's," and they were in answer to his question whether I knew how she was doing. But he hated me for saying it. He hated me for knowing. I felt like when I was little, writing my father or riding my bicycle to the drug store pay phone, in defense or explanation of my mother. Which I suppose, if we're talking about me, got close to the heart of it all. Zacky as another father figure. I'd had one in college, my friend Harry Nolan, who might have been president of the whole country one day and who I wrote about. Then I'd had another in Joe, the "group" leader who I also wrote about. Always looking for a father. As if: my own father was back, yet I still didn't quite believe that he was back, or it was too late for it now, even if my own father was kinder than Zacky, which he was. But Zacky was stronger than my father, depending on what you thought "strong" was. "Strong" in the way my father meant it when he said his own father was "weak?" All of this confused me. Zacky told me the shrink he set her up with had fallen in love with Melissa. So she would have someone to "take care of her," if that's what I meant. He said it with cold eyes.

And he would have gotten rid of me. My contract was coming up and he would have done something. I was pretty sure of it and my agent Sterner was pretty sure of it, he'd heard it at the network, and anyway it fit what Zacky did, according to Sterner anyway. There were lines you could cross with him and lines you couldn't. As there should be with men who would be king. Stifled finally, exhausted possibly, Morty had escaped by simply leaving. But what about me, who wasn't ready to leave?

I found an answer that had a name. Adam Bloch. If I were writing a script now, I would capitalize his name, so that the actor playing him would wake up and start reading. I had known Bloch at university. He played the most tragic part of all in the events I wrote about before. He was the one who drove us all, figuratively and all but literally, off a cliff. And I had never forgiven him. To paraphrase something I heard in a movie once, he was the kind of Jew you boiled down ten Jews in order to get. The adjectives I might apply won't barely cover him. Awkward, sincere, quiet, observant of a vast range of things and unobservant of a vast range of others. How he bore the guilt of the accident I'd never known, we'd never talked about it. What could I have said if I had been unwilling to forgive and what could he have said if he had been unable to forget? Or not "forget." "Forget" isn't right. If he'd been unable *not to obsess*? Adam went on from Yale to get his Ph.D. from Chicago in economics, taught someplace a couple of years, and, as if furtively, as if all his decisions were made at night, decided to chuck the academy and go into business. He never told anybody why. It must have seemed—to his parents, to whomever else, though there may have been nobody else, he was an only child—a more than small step backward on the ladder of assimilation when he took the output of a hippie cousin's barn in the hills of Pennsylvania, where the hippie cousin was dyeing old shirts in fresh colors, and opened a storefront in downtown New York to sell them by the armload. But this was the start for Adam in purveying stonewashed everything. He became the Ralph Lauren of stonewashed. He made a mint. He became, after Fred Smith who founded Federal Express, the most successful entrepreneur that our class at Yale produced. And with his winnings he went to Hollywood, in time to be my savior. Adam wanted to buy something, wanted to live in the sunshine at last. He called me and I took him around and introduced him to people, at my agency, at the network, wherever. The time came for my contract to be renewed and Zacky blocked it; or he didn't block it precisely, guys in Zacky's position seldom left their fingerprints on anything if they could help it, but he made sure conditions were attached that I would never accept. The way it was done. I felt a sort of dull dread, ubiquitous and clammy, what you might feel for something long awaited as inevitable that nevertheless, when time passed and it didn't happen, you finally dared believe it might not. But shmuck me once, shame on you; shmuck me twice, shame on me. Another of the industry's sagest clichés. I'd been left by one producer in my life and was damned if I'd be left by another. I went to Bloch. I told him of a company he could buy, if the money was really burning a hole. He did a short course in figures, he made the kind of offer that even a cliché couldn't refuse, and I am making a long business story much shorter in the interests of concision but anyway in a matter of months if not weeks he owned Cangaroo, the company that made *Northie*. It was Zacky who got fired and not me. Bloch didn't know enough about the business to know he couldn't do that, so he did. Or he didn't actually do it, he was about to do it, and the network was said to be backing him and I would become the boss. But then I myself intervened, out of loyalty and guilt. Not much of a scene. I just did it, made a few calls and it was done. Told Bloch, when all was said and done, he'd be making a mistake. Made out Zacky to be something like a designated hitter in the American League, an aging slugger who could still give you a big year. Zacky said, "Thanks, guy." We didn't talk about it more. We were partners after that.

~

I suppose a boy whose father left is later a man who is easily led. Or could almost the opposite be true, will he pick men to lead him who themselves will leave, and he knows it, and he will leave first if he can? Is betrayal his fate and his action? Is loyalty his curse?

☙

Despite the money coming in, I had never quite moved out of the Ocean Park Apartments. I liked the idea of a guy making big bucks keeping his rent-controlled apartment. Ed Koch, when he was mayor of New York and got Gracie Mansion to live in, had done the same. Everyone in New York seemed to know this at the time and it may have won him some votes, as it tended to prove what a true-blue New Yorker he was. Kept you in touch with your roots, anyway. Or maybe it was this that Zacky was referring to when he said I'd squeeze a nickel till the buffalo crapped. I just didn't want to be suburban, I didn't want to be like Zacky, who by the way had settled in Hancock Park instead of the Westside, as if to remind his cohorts in TV's upper echelons that he remained a Protestant in their midst. The big Spanish job with eighteen rooms on South Muirfield, the expanse of granite countertop in the kitchen, the stove that could roast whole babies, the three thousand dollar heated Japanese toilet that adjusted to your every contour like a seat in an expensive car and did many other wonderful things. To all of this I continued to say no. I continued to chat up the welfare cases in the lobby and use the coin-ops in the laundry room to wash my clothes and when I felt like it I'd go down to the second floor and see if Melissa was around. Or sometimes I would know that she was around because I could look out and see her big green gleaming Caddy in the parking lot.

One day I knocked on her door and there was no answer when I'd seen the big green Caddy and I touched the knob and was able to turn it, and the door came open in my hand. Stupid thing for me to do, she could have been in there fucking somebody, fucking the psychiatrist who'd fallen in love with her, or sleeping or anything else that was none of my business, though I was her friend. Anyway, the door fell open in my hand and I called her name, Melissa, Melissa, and when there was no answer I took a couple steps in. A beautiful place, by the way. One of those places where there were flowers on the windowsills and the lamplight had a pink cast and the refrigerator was mostly empty. I guess I'd had some sort of instinct. It wasn't anything I'd ever done before, go into some girl's place without a key. She was on the couch passed out and there were bottles of pills on the floor.

Sounds like a scene that enough guys have written but it was real enough then. She wasn't quite passed out, because when I sat beside her and said her name and shook her, she whispered my name back. I did this, we did this, a number of times. Her eyes slid almost open, then slid back again, and her breathing was soft. She was in a white bathrobe that made her look like a ghost and her hair was damp, so that I imagined she must have taken a shower and come out here to read the *People* magazine that was by the pills. There was also the core of an apple on a plate. The pills, whatever they were, were prescribed by Zacky's psychiatrist and I called his number that was on one of the bottles. He came over in twenty minutes, which is as fast as anybody gets anyplace in Los Angeles, and we got her to a sitting position so that she could swallow some other pills he gave her, and he did a few probes and tests and said a hospital wasn't necessary, so we waited. The psychiatrist was a short man with twinkly eyes and a pudgy face like a clown. A kindly man, by the look of it, formerly married to someone well-known in the business and for a long time a shrink to the stars. I asked him what had done this to Melissa and he said her medication for her "unstable condition." I said I didn't know Melissa had an unstable condition, and I'd never seen her unstable until now, but the psychiatrist—whom we may as well call Candleman, Kenneth Candleman, another name to put in capital letters for the script—assured me that he knew this. I began to feel contempt for him then. What was he doing telling me anything about her, when he'd fallen in love with his own damn patient and here she was passed out? What were these pills, anyway, I asked, and he said again that they were medication for her unstable condition. I asked him if she'd taken too many of them, and he said he didn't know. But there were still lots of them in each of the bottles. That, and the apple core, and the *People* magazine. So we sort of both of us ruled out a suicide attempt. Candleman made a point of telling me that as soon as he felt a "countertransference" with Melissa, he'd given her up as a patient. But then what was he doing prescribing her these pills? I asked him that. He said he'd prescribed them "before." After that, we were quiet, and after that, we talked about football. He'd gone to Michigan and they were good that fall. As I said, he seemed to be a kindly man, and at one point when he looked at Melissa there seemed to be tears in his eyes. Enough to change them from sparkly to watery, anyway.

Candleman didn't leave until she was awake. That was after three or four hours. Three hours and a half. She was groggy. She got up and took another shower. She said she didn't know what happened. Candleman asked her a few questions, had she been drinking, other medications. Yes, and yes. The night before anyway. And little sleep. He told her don't do any of those things anymore, not for now anyway, and then he left. I fixed her tea. It was dark by then. I went out to the pizza place and brought back pizza. She ate a little of it and I did too and then put it in the empty refrigerator. I told her I didn't think she should be taking those pills at all and also that if she suffered from anything it wasn't some mental disease *du jour* but rather a spiritual ailment that pills could hide but never cure. I felt full of a kind of certainty that I had seldom felt in my life. We made love for the first time that night.

The next day she went over to Candleman's and threw all her pills at him like they were buckshot and yelled at him that he had made her sick in order to control her and *he* was the sick fuck and why shouldn't she be mad, of course she was mad! She left with tears of righteous anger in her eyes. I imagined Candleman watching her get back in her car as if she were a Greek goddess returning to the woods. Later that day he left three messages on her machine. Melissa was there sewing curtains and never picked up the phone. In the first he was earnest and rational and said he had picked up the pills off the floor and would like to drop them by because as she could see from the rage she flew into, there was a reason for the pills. He was not trying to manipulate her, he was not trying for advantage, he was trying only. . . and there was no finish to that thought. In the second message he was pleading and admitting mistakes and saying again that he would like to come over. His voice was hoarse and he didn't mention pills or helping her or anything but, as she knew, his love of her. In the third he asked where she was and suspected that she was there and if she was there would she please pick up because it was important and he'd called before as she knew and if she didn't call soon he'd be coming over to check on her because he was afraid. She listened as if to lies, picking them out like nits, and made her curtains because she could do nothing else. I came back to her apartment after work. She told me about her day and about

Candleman's messages and I felt less certain than I had been. But I still felt like I could take over for the pills.

We made love that night and the next night. I stopped going to my apartment. On the fourth night she told me how Candleman had given her magazines to make her smarter like the *New Republic* that she didn't care about but she felt she should. Even though she hated him for it, I thought better about Candleman for that. Why shouldn't Melissa read such things and see what worthless gab was in them? Why shouldn't she have the chance not to feel bad about herself over nothing? I could imagine her quoting the *New Republic* about this and that, Reagan or the East Germans, I could imagine her getting away with it, as if sometimes a scam's the best thing for you. But I knew she didn't want to hear it, and she knew what I was thinking. The next day was a weekend and we took a walk in a park in Malibu, overlooking the ocean on a cloudy day. On the walk Melissa began to cry. She asked me to tell her the truth, was she too stupid for me? I could have given her the easy answer, because of course she wasn't stupid at all, but I knew what she was talking about. And that she was giving me a chance then to walk away. Every single thing that I could ever hate about her was right there asking to be hated. I could take my stand against self-pity, passive-aggression, lack of irony, humorlessness, narcissism, the need to control, latent hysteria, and ignorance. I felt a thousand miles away from her. She could have jumped off the nearest cliff and I wouldn't have seen. Or to put it another way, everything human about her that I had rejected and left in enough other women I could have rejected and left in Melissa just then, and yet for no reason at all, or what seemed like no reason at all, I didn't. I suppose it was because I had already saved her. Or imagined that I had, hoped that I had. The cruelest seduction of all or the cleverest anyway, you save someone and you're the one seduced. I told her she wasn't stupid at all, because of course she wasn't stupid at all, but I didn't add that she shouldn't have to be told. "Really?" Melissa asked, turning her head back from the ocean. It seemed as if she were trying to believe something, but I wasn't sure if it was what I'd said. Her eyes were as dark as the ocean was that day. Confusion in them, then something tentative, as if asking, or telling, *look where my life has brought me.* We kissed as if each was kissing the other's tender weakness, we walked out of the park, and we stayed with each other again.

༄

After that, the closest I ever came to leaving Melissa was when we went to see her parents in Seattle. Nothing against her parents. They were good, decent people, her father had worked at Boeing on the shop floor and worked his way up and her mother had religious faith. Artistic people, too, her mother beautified and her father could do or make anything. Their clapboard house in the far suburbs with the screened-in porch was filled with everything he had carved or painted, some of it kitsch but some of it not, some of it, like the hordes of World War I lead doughboys he'd painted all white so that they looked like an army of ghosts, you wondered, as you might wonder occasionally about artists in museums of the new, how he thought to do that. We went up there the Easter after we started being together. The evangelical church was fine, the relatives were fine, the rampant Republicanism was fine. What got me was going out to dinner at the Applebee's restaurant. Applebee's is a chain, as maybe you know. They had them in

Rochester, they had them outside Seattle. Big pictures of the food on the menu. Dinners at six or seven ninety-nine, or those were the prices then, and I ordered the ribs and Melissa a salad and her parents the surf-and-turf. And I felt so at home. Gentiles or no, across the country or no. I could have been out to dinner with my mother and my sister the way we'd go to the HoJo's on Saturday nights for fried clams, the big treat of the week, which was beautiful and sweet and sad, seeing my mother paying for anything at all, or remembering her paying for anything at all. It was as if the restaurant and her parents and the surf-and-turf and the pictures of the food on the menu had all conspired to betray Melissa, to reveal her as from my mother's world and not Irene's. The four of us sitting in the vinyl booth and Melissa with her iceberg lettuce salad so happy to be home with her parents or maybe even happy to have brought one home to her parents, and me thinking: she is happy now like my mother must have been once, and when she was happy was that not a sign for my father's betrayal to start? I felt starved and nourished by the Applebee's ribs and corn on the cob, that I could hardly eat, and then in a panic wolfed down, as if desperate not to reveal my mind. The others saying the sweet-enough, middle-of-the-country things you say when you're going out to dinner and it's a treat. How is it, delicious, they do a nice job in these places. And from Gil, her father: "Get enough to eat?"

Could I live my whole life at Applebee's and not run away? Or to put it otherwise, if I was going to betray Melissa someday, wouldn't it be best to leave now, before the dessert came? But because I'd saved her life once or imagined that I had, I decided to wait this one out. The chocolate pudding with the swirl of Reddi-wip was fantastic.

It wasn't until we had flown south to Los Angeles and were again in her rent-controlled apartment with the flowers on the sills and her mannequin pinned up with jagged shards of raw silk that soon enough would be something surprising and the soft light of her lamps, that I recalled fully, which is to say with a full heart, that Melissa was as self-made as I was, that we'd both run away and started over, and that it was this running away and starting over that had brought us both to the Ocean Park Apartments. She was my mother and she was not. She was Irene and she was not. And I was just plain lucky. To be able finally to be a sentimental slob once in a while.

❦

In Melissa's austerity, the erotic seemed to flow most excessively. Another of her paradoxes. She seemed to live by her paradoxes, as if jumping from puddle to puddle. Or do I mean jumping over the puddles, from one bit of dry land to the next? I'm not even sure, not even now. Her diets, the periods she went through when she wore only white, her susceptibility to every banal new fad, like Proust's maid and the *pneu*. Or you could say also, her embrace of the new, she wasn't afraid of the new. The erotic all bottled up in her, headaches, confusions, explosions. The erotic as a great engine of her being.

And another interesting fact about her: Melissa didn't like me all that much. Not after we became lovers, not after, as it were or as she thought, she could see me up close. And how could I disagree? There was so much that she observed. My holding back, my failure to speak my mind, my speaking my mind, my weird opinions, my obscure intuitions, my old "group" and whatever that was all about, my snobbery, my disbelief in fashions, gyms, and health, my grumpy dogmas about such things, my cocksureness, my doubting all the time, my doubting her, my saving whatever I was saving in order to write it down somewhere, my tendency to look at other women's tits if I could get away with it which I could but not quite with her, my laziness, my so-called Jewishness, my working all the time and ambition and need to get someplace that always remained obscure, my father and Irene, my irony, my ironic critiques of her, sneaking them in there as if she wouldn't notice, my own passive-aggression, my evident desire for money, my contempt for those who desired money, my trying to keep one step ahead of everybody which in practical terms meant trying to keep one step ahead of her and her opinions and beliefs with the result that she could hustle and bustle all day to keep up with me about one stupid thing or other that she didn't really care about anyway and as soon as she got there I'd be gone, my sarcasm, my liking for jokes as crude and mean as they come, my eagerness to *épater the bourgeoisie* which she wouldn't even know what it meant but she feared the bourgeoisie meant her, my tolerance for smokers, my cheapness just like Zacky said, my obsessive persistent obnoxious pathetic one-track-mind predictable demand for sex all the time, my fetishizing of her, my objectifying of her, my refusal to buy a new car, my old J. Press clothes, though a few of these she liked a little bit, my hesitation to get in the habit of taking a shower absolutely every day, my not caring that much if I got food on my clothes, my refusal to lose my temper unless goaded beyond all reason, the anger in my eyes, the stiffness in my neck which wasn't all the time but sometimes. It didn't take Melissa so long to accumulate such a list. A couple of months, maybe. On review I wish I could find some points on which she was wrong. But anyway, she didn't leave. Or rather, since we were staying at her place, she didn't kick me out.

And on another, perhaps not entirely unrelated, issue: Melissa's long roster of Jewish boyfriends. She had known no Jews at all when she grew up. There were maybe none in twenty miles, if by "none" you could mean only a few, the owner of the tailor shop or the stationery store. She only started meeting Jews when she was with the rock musician. They, we, must have seemed like part of her brave new world, the world that welcomed her or anyway was receptive to the possibility of her, when she ran away from everything she had known. And by now I was well down a list, of which the only recent exception had been Zacky, but that did include Candleman and the old guy who gave her the watches and a sitcom writer and a computer whiz and there were others before those, I was never certain how many, but at least one had been a so-called Zen rabbi who held forth and/or sat somewhere in Hollywood and who I knew about only because when I told Melissa she didn't have a mental disease *du jour* but rather a spiritual ailment that pills could cover up but never cure, she said this Zen rabbi had once told her the same thing. I eventually called up the Zen rabbi and found we had quite a lot in common. There could have been a couple lawyers, too. And a plastic surgeon, who promised her that if she ever wanted her tits done, he'd do a bang-up job. But there was nothing wrong with Melissa's tits. I was never sure about the plastic surgeon, whether he was a lover or just someone she met somewhere, like me, who became a friend.

Anyway, a good-sized sampling of the Jewish gene pool. Enough to make comparisons, enough to spot trends. And did there come a moment after one of them when she confided to a friend, "Never again. I'm off Jewish men." But she wasn't. Something in her of Portnoy's shikse goddess, who wanted a man who would give her a kid who read Kafka? Maybe. Or more likely, not so much. Melissa would have heard of Kafka but not been sure at first if you meant Kafka the dress designer or Kafka the writer. Yet she was surely looking for something she felt was missing in herself.

༜

More plot, more business. After the third season of *Northie*, James Morton had taken his winnings and enough of his printing apparatus as he needed and gone to France, St. Paul de Vence having won out over the backwoods of the American northwest in the contest for who would get his discontented soul. But after a year and a half he'd come back, on account of either being pissed off at the French or pissed off at a French-Italian woman in particular, and Adam Bloch on my advice made my pal a rich deal. It wasn't long before it was in *Daily Variety* that Morty was developing a new police show. This drove Zacky nuts. By now he and Morty were hardly speaking. If anyone was a bridge between them it was me, but even I didn't see Morty much since he disdained the studio and the drive to the Valley and got away with mostly working at home. To Zacky, the fact that Morty was developing a new cop show, even for a different network, suggested that Bloch or somebody somewhere was losing faith in *Northie*. And then the rumors began to flare again that it was Morty's talent and not Zacky's that had made *Northie* fresh to start with. Zacky and I had a shared series commitment with the network to produce a new show for them after *Northie*, but even this failed to mellow Zacky's qualms. It was enough that he had to worry about the younger guys over at MTM, Bochco and Paltrow and the others, but now his own erstwhile partner might be coming up with something to put *Northie* in the shade. On the morning of the debut of Morty's new show, Zacky's envy was so great that he avoided even opening his newspapers, as if it were a good case for mind over matter, if he never looked, then the reviews would not exist. But they did exist and they were glowing. "A genius of the small screen," said the guy in the *LA Times*. Maryanna didn't know about Zacky's approach/avoidance game with the papers and blew it by trying to commiserate, "Morty must have sucked Clarence's dick," she said, in reference to the *LA Times* reviewer, and in a bitter mood Zacky took her revelation as enmity, rubbing the salt of Morty's apotheosis in his wounds: Here, dear, let me be the first to tell you that you're officially second-rate. He who'd done so much yoga and t'ai chi he now confided in people only half-facetiously that he was L.A.'s most centered Gentile felt he knew uncentered aggression when he saw it. Riding over the hill in his beat-up Bronco to the Burbank studio he was still thinking how he ought to divorce the black widow (a reference to Maryanna's first husband, who died in a skiing accident), if it wouldn't be so damn expensive. I met with Zacky every morning to work on *Northie* stories, but we got no work done that day. Neither of us had seen Morty's show. I was waiting for it to air, as I always did with new shows; saw them, if I saw them at all, the way the audience would see them. We tossed the football back and forth. The ritual of all the writing teams in Hollywood, a football, a basketball, a whiffleball. Saying pretty much nothing, supposedly thinking, but thinking about what? And then Zacky said, "What about... *bare ass*?" He said it like he'd invented something big. The emphasis of it, the drama. I said I didn't know what he was talking about. "We go for. . . *bare ass*. Not on *Northie*. On the new show." I felt like a straight man in a bad joke.

"Why are we talking about the new show now? I thought we were talking about *Northie*."

But of course I knew why we were talking about the new show. Zacky's way to recoup, his way to reclaim his crown. It was all he cared about.

"Can we do that?" I asked.

"We don't have to get balls, we don't have to get shaved pussy—but a little cheek? Why not? You know other guys are going for it, you bet they are, it's the fucking Holy Grail if you could get it, if you were the first one to get it. . ."

I could exaggerate this, but I swear Zacky's blue eyes glazed over then. Thinking of being king forever, maybe, thinking of showing them all.

"Has this got to do with Morty?"

"Morty? What's it got to do with Morty?"

"Nothing. Of course. Nothing."

"Hey, in this business, you've got to be a *visionary*."

But when I got back from lunch that day, Zacky had something entirely else on his mind. I found him in a state. He looked at me with beseeching, puppy dog eyes. Whatever it was, I told myself I was not going to fall for it. Yet my words stumbled over his mooniness and I asked him anyway, "What is it?"

"Maryanna's filed for divorce."

I wasn't sure how I was supposed to take this. No more black widow? But Zacky was morose. And then, could he ask me if I'd do him a favor?

"No. You can't."

"Kind of a big favor."

"Certainly not."

"Would you go to the Sav-On and buy me some underpants?"

"Oh, Zack." I said something like that.

He looked sorry enough and what else was there to say? Remind him how often he'd expressed the wish to divorce her himself? Zacky reached for his wallet. I told him don't bother.

"I didn't shit on the wallet," he said.

So I didn't ask for the details, nor did he offer them. At the Sav-On, I spent a while contemplating whether Zacky would prefer the ones with baseballs and footballs or the ones with cows and cowboy hats. I finally chose the latter, reminded of another of Zacky's Texasisms, about some producer who was all hat and no cattle. I don't know if I hated him or thought he was fantastic then, for sending me on that errand. L.A.'s most centered Gentile, well, maybe. When I got back he was more distraught than when I left. The lawyer had called. Zacky was still behind his desk, his mooniness turned to stone disbelief. The only word that escaped his tongue as I handed him the drugstore bag with the underpants was "half." It was muttered like an oracle. Apparently California laws on divorce were going to apply even to the onetime King of Television. It was going to cost him half of all he had, even his points on *Northie*.

And then. And then. So much happened on this one day that it was why I first started thinking about putting all the action of my book on one day. Not this day, precisely, but this day combined with one or two others, so that the sum of it would be like a jam-packed night on the Roxbury streets. But it was this one day where I started, when Zacky was envious, and came up with "bare ass" as if he were Einstein, and Maryanna left him, and it was going to cost him half. The envy, that was the thing that kind of stuck. How could people so rich and famous still be so envious? How could it drive them, contort them, so? The facility even Zacky the most centered Gentile in Los Angeles had for comparing himself to his peers, as opposed to all the rest of humanity.

Later that day Zacky took a suite at the Bel Air and invited the head of the network over for a drink. I only heard exactly what happened some years later, when the network head, Jaworsky, happened to be passing through the village back east where I had a summer house, and we went out for our own drinks. Zacky had by then gone to a different network, there was some bitterness involved, and Jaworsky was not unhappy to tell me the tale. He'd showed up at the Bel Air and, like myself, found Zacky in a state. Zacky told him about the scene with his three girls where he had to tell them he was moving out, then he told him about coming to the hotel and calling all the escort services then hanging up every time a woman's voice answered, then he told him how he'd hated Maryanna and sworn to leave her this very day but now that she was gone he didn't want to live without her. And he told him how it was going to cost him half. Jaworsky told me how flattered he felt, that Zacky would confide all this to him, that Jaworsky was the man he would turn to in the hour of his distress. Then Zacky said to him, "This life goes fast, you know that, Jaw? You have to make things count. You have to dare and you have to believe. What's the point of half-measures, when you only go round once? Am I starting to sound like a beer commercial yet?" Zacky looked so droopy that Jaworsky hugged him then. And that's when Zacky proposed bare ass for the new show.

When Jaworsky told me this, we both laughed our asses off. I'd known that Zacky broached the subject that night, but not how. I suppose I was filled with awe for Zacky then, years after I'd last seen him, when I heard the story of him using the pathos of his own divorce to get bare cheeks on network television. Jaworsky told him he'd think about it.

But the day wasn't quite over yet. I went home and watched Morty's new show when it aired. It was so remarkably predictable that I could almost not believe Morty did it. It was like a *Northie* with all the experiments and emotions and absurdity left out, so that what you were left with was most of the production values but a plot structure going back to television's earliest days, to *Dragnet* or maybe even before. Just the facts, ma'am. Jesus, Morty—was this what happens when a guy does something he doesn't really want to do? It felt almost as if Morty was expiating all he had contributed to the rollicking embraces of *Northie*'s nights. I couldn't believe it was going to be a hit, but halfway through I knew I was wrong, or I knew what he was going for anyway: his main cop, his hero, slugged a wobbly prisoner because he didn't like his answers. Morty's hero was a bully. Morty was idealizing the authoritarian. Putting the pig back in the pigs, playing the conservative card, as if to say, haven't you noticed, this is the Reagan era. It felt almost as if he were pushing your face in it. And the critics didn't seem to care about the hero slugging a wobbly prisoner because he didn't like his answers. Unless it was that precisely that they were calling "daring," as if Morty at last was telling it like it is. And ah, the subtle performances, the terse writing, the production values, the *realism*, all in an old-fashioned no-nonsense cop show! However surprised I was at how little joy there was in it, I was more surprised that no one in the papers seemed to notice. Even before the end credits rolled, my mind filled with calculations as if it were a train station full of strangers. Were *Northie* and its kind finished? Had Morty stolen the future, or only seen it? Were all my gut instincts wrong? Was my lucky run over? Where would my next deal come from? Morty had always been my friend, and yet what I felt, actually, was envy.

∽

And later I saw him on the interview shows, doing the circuit, getting as complicated and high-flown as he could get about the police role in society, and violence and redemption and Dostoevsky and the criminal's need for punishment, and the interviewers fawning and lapping it up, and all I could see was a guy who didn't really want to be there. Envy. Envy that rubs your heart with salt.

Zacky told me he never watched any of these interviews. The prerequisites, the strategies, of envy and I who recently enough had had contempt for Zacky on account of his envy began to envy him for his excellent management of it. He knew how to avoid what he wanted to avoid.

∽

But was envy what I really wanted to write about? Envy or Hollywood or television or the new rich? As well as I can describe it, my self-hatred got wind of what was going on and said, "I thought you were writing about the meritocracy and the best and the brightest. What have *these* to do with that?" Or more particularly, writing so much about myself. "I" "I"

"I" "I" "I," like a lament in an old song of the Pale. People talk about self-loathing as if it were the Cracker Jack prize inside the box of suffering souls, but I don't think it's that. In my view it's more like they're all one and the same thing, the box, the candy, the prize. And is that really such a bad thing, a vigorous brushing of the back of self, as in a Russian bath? Doesn't self-hatred keep us honest, doesn't it lead us toward love?

The corollary to this being, perhaps, that if you talk about love all the time the crud accumulates on your skin and pretty soon you're not too healthy at all.

In all events, shortly after I conceived of keying my eighties book on envy and television and the new rich, I had a grave doubt and spun in the opposite direction and felt it should be all about my friend from Yale Teddy Redmond, who was in *Meritocracy: A Love Story* and who came out to Los Angeles in the mid-eighties. Teddy was a WASP if there ever was one, St. Paul's and Greenwich and Yale and for a long time a bit of an attitude that the world, if it didn't exactly owe him a living, was likely to hand him one anyway. But the years stripped a lot of that away. Working for Chase or Cravath and joining the Field Club were not what he had in mind from life. Teddy joined the Peace Corps, came first to believe and then to disbelieve in the Third World, bummed around in Spain, wound up finally in New York, became a writer after all. I didn't see him much in New York. He worked for *Newsday* for awhile. He moved to Brooklyn, lived with a girl, broke up with the girl. He had always been sarcastic, and over time his sarcasm seemed to harden and grow crusty. He became obsessed with the world situation, especially when under Reagan the Cold War resumed full bore. His sense of entitlement increasingly was buoyed by outrage. He felt the wisdom we as a nation had learned the hard way was being tossed heedlessly away. By the early eighties he had moved to New Orleans, lived with and broken up with another girl there, begun and abandoned a novel. He inherited a small amount of money and invested it, badly, in a private school scheme for inner-city kids. He was still good-looking and athletic, in a bony, trim way. He decided he was emotionally isolated and went into therapy. We had become friends, I once told him, either in spite of or because of his inherited anti-Semitism. Or mine, he shot back.

There was more about Teddy, that I'll get to later. All I want to say here is that I was desperate once for him to be the center of my book. I felt he spoke for "us" better than I ever could. "Us" being who, exactly? The meritocrats, the Yale and Harvard guys, the best and the brightest, the captains of a more-or-less liberal America whose ship by the eighties was sailing on a windless sea?

Though there was something else useful about Teddy: his hatred for Los Angeles, that was almost funny it was so comprehensive. You wouldn't want to get Teddy started on Los Angeles. The fake tits, the fake Spanish houses, the clean cars, the roads without potholes, the possibility of getting a ticket for jaywalking, the possibility of getting a ticket for not stopping at a crosswalk, the local news, the ignorance of the world, the bland faces, the bodies as overgrown as the vegetables, the landscapes that didn't belong there, the incessant hum of the boulevards that were too wide to cross, the lack of anyplace to walk to, the guys with their business, the girls who cared about the guys' business, the lack of appreciation of the Eastern type of person, the bland Okie speech, the silly Val girl speech, the moronic Watts guy speech, the perfidious

Dodgers, the perfidious Lakers, the lack of decent hamburgers combined with the local conviction that there were good hamburgers there, that it was right for a hamburger to be thin as a pancake and well-done and covered with mustard and mayonnaise instead of ketchup, the lack of ivy-covered towers, the lack of Sunoco stations, the dreamy reasoning, the self-satisfaction, the failure to produce any world-class serial killers lately, the anomie, the lack of family tie, the ease of getting laid that almost took the fun out of it, the surfer clothes, the bland politicians without an ethnic smell to them, the bland cops without an ethnic smell to them, and what the cops wore, those dark ties on dark shirts, even the chief wore one, the chief of police looked like a weenie or a fascist instead of just an ordinary Irish thug, the fact that it was the second biggest city in the country and it had only one newspaper left, the fact that nobody read a newspaper, the contentment with jobs, with capitalism, with status quo, the lack of political consciousness, the lack of literary consciousness, the lack of consciousness at all. No, you didn't want to get Teddy started on L.A.

So with Teddy there would be some jokes and some vestigial high church backbone and some political sense-of-the-world, and to boot a grand project he had in mind for years, a tragic seed, against which Hollywood and for that matter myself could be tested and found wanting or not. For years Teddy was obsessed with the story of Charlie Chamberlain, one of the postwar Ivy League adventurers of the early CIA, a guy who'd had a good war, parachuting behind enemy lines in France, once getting a whole German platoon single-handedly to surrender by shooting wildly and running around it until they thought they were surrounded; so good a war that when it was over he didn't want to be a banker and play squash and take the train home to Greenwich, and instead of that death-in-shades-of-gray joined Central Intelligence the year it was formed, and rose in it with more such inspired, slightly harebrained schemes as he'd come up with in the French village, some of which worked but more of which didn't, so that in the end, when the whole country turned its back after Vietnam, he had a fall from grace and came to see the world for what it was. Teddy himself being from Greenwich, it seemed that he would be telling something of his own life, with dashing, failed covert ops standing in for his own reckless dare as a writer. Not that Teddy had ever got shot at or shot anybody. But still. The upper class bravado that later got bent out of shape. Irony here or satire, something hard and irreducible? Learning the moral lessons of the world, finally not being so sure you were right. Being actually, finally, confused. And doing a kind of late twentieth-century American penance, working with ghetto kids on the streets of New Haven.

Perhaps even more than he loved Chamberlain's story, Teddy felt it must be his ticket out. He would sell it and be gone from this place of weenie cops and overstuffed, tasteless omelets. But a sale proved not so easy. He refined his story, rewrote it, pitched it, changed the title and pitched it again, and meanwhile the years slipped by. One got the feeling about Teddy that he'd come to Los Angeles with Charlie Chamberlain in his luggage and he wasn't going to leave until this great ghost was no longer there.

Although it was true that I sometimes felt, even after thirty years being his friend, that I didn't know enough about Teddy Redmond to make him the spine of my book, I probably would have done it, would have gone that way or tried, if I had not, as I wrote earlier, found Amos Oz's wonderful book in December of 2004 and come to believe that wherever a writer is, there is the center of his universe.

☙

If I had kept Teddy, I could also have kept Eve. Eve Merriman. Or I suppose I am keeping her, since I'm writing about her now, maybe not as much as I otherwise would have, but enough. She was Teddy's girlfriend when he came to Los Angeles. A Bennington girl, she had poise, brains, long brown hair, ambition, and she could run hot or cold. Eve fashioned herself a writer like the rest of us, only she didn't write much, she was better at getting into meetings than writing, and she got into meetings that maybe it would have been better for Teddy to have gotten into. After a while they split apart and then Eve called up everybody she could, including me, looking for work and not getting much. Eventually Zacky made a pass at her. This was after his separation. I never knew exactly what came of it, but it must have been something, because he got her a script to write.

But the chief reason to keep Eve in the story had less to do with Teddy or Zacky as the fact that she fulfilled every vestige of fantasy of an upper-class Protestant Katharine Hepburn–style woman that I still might have had. Eve could sail, ride, and think, she combined a Bennington girl's accommodating views on sex and politics with knowing what Abercrombie's used to be like, and though she couldn't cook worth a damn, she knew where the forks and spoons went. To boot, her family had a summer house on Mount Desert in Maine, like the family of my old crush Sascha Maclaren and her sister, my one-time lover Maisie. In a way, she was a last, slightly watered-down incarnation of these. She wasn't great and complicated like Sascha or big-hearted like Maisie but she had the looks and she knew the jokes and she was tough enough. And so, perhaps inevitably, she became a kind of dark alternative against which I placed my affair with Melissa. Dark because she embodied the world and its demands and weight the way that Melissa could not. Melissa was all about promise, Eve was about what was. And I knew, for a little while anyway, that I could have had her. When she called me up, after she left Teddy, it was in her voice. Talking about Teddy, talking about Maine, talking about some people maybe I should have known, as if there was no need for the conversation to end. Her voice itself a little flat and cattish like Hepburn's but so unaccented that you could not pin one thing on her. And her knowingness. Eve had knowingness. She knew what I was about. The only thing was, I could never save her life. It wasn't the kind of life that someone like me could save. It was as if that part had already been taken care of. Betty and Veronica and I chose Betty, because her heart was always broken? But the argument kept coming back. Wasn't Veronica the one you were supposed to choose? I even fashioned it once as a neoclassical plot. I would be with someone like Melissa and someone like Eve would come along and I would drop the someone like Melissa in favor of the someone like Eve and too late I would find that the someone like Eve either lacked a heart or had a witch's heart or hated me with such heart as she had in a way that left nothing to chance and no escape, except by waking from the nightmare and running all the way back without stopping once to the someone like Melissa, who would be either gone by then or not, but most probably she would be gone.

The chase at the end of the film? But beware, there'll be no film version at all if the someone like Melissa is utterly gone. She mustn't have her dignity, she mustn't have her freedom or her defiance or pride, or even her hurt, tragic confusion; the audience must be served its curdled dessert, its happy ending without end.

※

My father finally got a show on CBS, a half hour, a sitcom. This time he had not only a well-known, highly regarded Broadway playwright to write it, but a well-known, highly regarded Hollywood sitcom director who'd done the pilots for a string of hits to direct it, and the cute premise of a cooking show where they'd give out real recipes between the jokes. He also had a dame of the London stage to play the cooking show's big mama, and I thought, when I heard about it, *maybe*. Maybe, and why not, and it sounds as good as anything else, and the oldest weasel words of all, *nobody knows anything*.

I suppose I should put in here—remind you, really, since it must be very nearly universally known—that most new television shows fail. Although "fail" is in a way a phony word for it, a show gets too few viewers and it goes off the air and the actors and everybody else go on to other jobs if they can, but whether the show had a few decent laughs, or said something or other about something, or nothing about nothing, or was crazy different from anything that had ever gone on before, doesn't usually get recorded in the record books, any more than Jimmy Piersall's stunts in centerfield or Satch Paige pitching on no days' rest ever made it into the encyclopedia of baseball. I don't even know if the phrase "noble failure" has a place in the annals of television.

But maybe that's what *Big Lady* was. I didn't think so at the time. I thought the dame of the West End stage still sounded English when she was supposed to sound like Brooklyn, and the premise wasn't old-fashioned but the characters were. Big mama solves everything. I was embarrassed by it. I told no one at *Northie* that my father even had this show, or if I told anyone, it was only in passing. I knew even less about sitcoms than I knew about the rest, but I wasn't surprised when *Big Lady* failed.

I called my father when the show was canceled. I told him only things he already knew. I told him it's hard to get shows on. I told him it was even harder at his age, and if you left like he did and tried to come back, that had to be harder still. All the things that he could take pride in, and he said thank you.

But then he started to talk about money. "If I'd stayed at Universal, my stock options would have vested," he said. "I made a mistake."

But I didn't want to talk about money then, it made me even sadder than the rest of it, and it frightened me a little.

"You took your shot," I said. "You should feel lucky you got to take it."

"It wasn't a good show," he said.

"It had a few problems," I said.

"Of course the critics were flattering. They loved Dame Alna."

"Well so there's that then."

"She even got Brooklyn right."

"I didn't think so, but neither here nor there."

"You didn't? Really?"

"Neither here nor there."

"*The Times* thought she was marvelous. Even the *Post*. Three stars in the *Daily News*."

"I was just talking about her accent."
"You know how many times MCA's stock has doubled?"
"Is that a question?"
"It was a lot of money."
"The stock options."
"I made a mistake," he said.

❧

But even a show that has too few viewers only has too few compared to some dream of what some other show that would take its place might have, or too few compared to the show that came before it, or to the shows on the other stations. It was still millions. My father failed before millions, or in spite of millions.

And how many will ever read this book?

❧

Early on when I knew her, Melissa said something like, "I don't want to get pregnant. I don't want to get fat." I didn't believe her then or it made me sad or I thought it was a joke. She had to be kidding me or herself. But it made me think how much I wanted to make her pregnant. Every time I looked at her I thought I saw every tool that a mother ought to have, and she didn't seem to believe it. Another seduction? Was I just a simple guy who falls for such things? Anyway she changed her mind. After I knew her a couple years, she said, "I want to have a baby. Even if you don't."

The last part I could have lived without, because it was after all I who'd brought it up in the first place. But bringing things up in the first place never scored many points with Melissa. She needed to think she had done things by herself, or thought things by herself. She needed to come to her own conclusions and I suppose she still wasn't sure about me.

Or perhaps it was my dubious potential as a family man. I didn't much believe in nuclear families because my father ran away and because my mother became bitter about men and because of the "group" I was in where families and conditioning were said to be the problem and because of the times we lived in. What point in courting the most predictable of disasters? Live free or die, as they say on the license plates of New Hampshire. I suppose my cock put in a word or two as well. Its wish to roam.

None of which I hid from her, except for my cock's wish to roam, which I'd been reliably told by Zacky Kurtz, old Hollywood hand on the subject, that you never, ever, ever, ever, never, on pain of death-by-sliding-down-a-bannister-of-razor-blades-into-a-vat-of-boiling-sulphuric-acid told the woman you were with, and anyway when I was in Melissa's presence my cock never had that wish. I seldom trusted Zacky's wisdom on anything, but on this one I did. Melissa wanted to get knocked up and so we did that.

And next the question of the health insurance. Now you could say for a guy making millions you shouldn't predicate your whole future domestic life on extending your generous health insurance benefits to the girl you got knocked up and your unborn child, if everything else is saying no, no, no, and wait-just-a-gosh-darn-minute here. But waste not, want not. I'd learned that when I was poor. Melissa had no health insurance.

I was happy, in a way, that I now had a way to make good use of mine.

It was as if I might extend, to the whole nine yards of it, this fantasy of saving her life. Or still, maybe it wasn't fantasy, maybe it was the first real thing I'd ever done or might do.

I've previously written about how Melissa didn't always like me very much, and seemingly the less so, the closer we got. No use picking over those scabs again. No use adding to the list. She had her reasons, her distrust, her defiance. But the day I asked her to marry me, she didn't say no. She was a few months pregnant. The insurance would pay for the ultrasound.

❧

What did we sound like together? I realize I've written so little dialogue between us.

We sounded a lot like some old married couple.

❧

Melissa was never so much about the words. She could be painfully articulate when desperate or on the phone with one of her girlfriends, but you would never pick her out from her words. Her look that was a little bit ghost-like, her sure hands, the way she bounced back from sadness, something would happen she did not like and she would fret and take a shower and get dressed again and go back out, like a fighter in the late rounds.

❧

Now you can say there are a lot of different kinds of old married couples, so which kind did we sound like? It depended, on which day.

❧

The whole question, again, of leaving. I asked her to marry me and share my health insurance with me and still she did not leave. Even though I was too smart and got rich too easily, taking money out of the mouths of worthwhile gentiles? Melissa as Robin Hood, righting a kind of imbalance? She who said yes to giving her child a name other than hers and to redistributing the wealth in ways maybe not middle-American and Republican but anyway in ways other than mine.

Maid Melissa of Ocean Park.

❧

So we sounded like different kinds of old married couples depending on which day. But on the different days, which different kinds? The carping kind, the careful kind, the silent kind, the ruthless kind, the trying-hard-to-be-loving kind, the after dinner and maybe a glass of wine kind, the sexual kind, the Noel Coward amusing kind, the forgiving kind, the forgetting kind, the buy-things-to-get-past-problems kind, the articulate kind, the too-articulate kind, the little bit sad kind, the kind that wishes for revenge, the lying-around-reading-a-book-or-listening-to-the-heart-of-your-baby kind, the kind that just is for a little while. And we weren't even married yet.

❧

A conversation we had once.

"Are you just going to smother me because your own parents broke up?" she asked.

But it wasn't really a conversation, because I didn't have an answer.

※

To take possession by a kind of force. A coercion. To use the law and custom and money to get your way about something, to have something. Is even a proposal of marriage an action of unimaginable violence?

※

Melissa had her problems with my father and Irene. Though it's possible her problems with them were really her problems with me, her fears for me, how I might turn out some day. She did not identify with Irene at all. She almost seemed to feel, as if it were a battle over the pieces of who I was, that she must take my mother's part and root out or oppose everything that was not. She liked my mother. They sometimes talked on the phone. And of course she knew what my mother would have called "the whole story."

I would remind her once in a while that passion is an unruly beast; and that she herself had had her affairs with married men. This was not an effective line of argument. And why was I arguing at all? I didn't really disagree with her. Or I did disagree with her but I also agreed.

All I knew was that I wanted to hold no grudges against my father. I wanted to be too big for that, too old for that, even too spiritually evolved for that. The problem was that he would call up and he would patronize Melissa, and Irene would, or that's how Melissa saw it anyway. For sure they thought they were only ingratiating themselves. But they didn't know how to do it, nor was Melissa letting them in on the secret. Nor was I. I didn't know what the secret was. Their politeness, their microscopic concern with whatever she said, their endless praise of her dresses, even their offers to give them to some friend or other who turned out the deeper you got into the conversation to be someone terribly important. All the encounters we had seemed like subsequent impressions off the same block of our first dinner together in Beverly Hills.

Nor did the fact that Irene seemed to be doing badly excite much pity in Melissa. She was too afraid of her to have pity. She may not even have seen that Irene was doing badly. I would say so and it would end up in a fight, as if I were somehow betraying my mother all over again or revealing how I would some day betray Melissa herself. All of it made me wonder whether I had chosen Melissa as revenge against my father and Irene. Or perhaps it was a deep seeking of justice, finding the person who would treat them now as Irene had once treated my mother and me. Offhandedly, without real interest, as an inconvenience. Or as some sort of vague threat, guilt-inducing, our complaints and entreaties like people from the servants quarters popping their heads out when they weren't supposed to. Yet Melissa might have seen that Irene was doing badly, because Melissa had so often done badly herself. Or does similarity make us blind to the other? Irene's depressions, Melissa's depressions, Irene's insecurity, Melissa's insecurity, Irene's fussing with food in restaurants and Melissa's faddish diets, Irene's isolation, Melissa's isolation, none of them necessarily overlapping in time, but they had been there, in these same two people. Melissa was doing better now and Irene was doing worse.

As I say, none of this I wanted, or seemed to anyway. I wanted peace. I wanted the peace of the conqueror, where things weren't all my way but mostly were, and everyone would acknowledge that I had brought something off. And hadn't I? I was on speaking terms with everybody. We were living in a civilized world, more or less. There was money to patch things up. I had brought my mother out to the Emmys. And yet, my father and I drifted apart.

And none of it was his fault. None of it. If by "fault" you meant now, if by "fault" you meant the last conversations and present kindness and even expressions of love. I could not mistake this. The upcoming baby, the upcoming marriage. I was bringing fresh breezes into his life. For god's sake I was making him a grandfather at a time when Irene was only making him unhappy. I said to him once, "Let's do one together."

"A show?"

"Why not? Next season. Whenever. We'll come up with something."

"Marvelous. Really. That would be marvelous. Just let me know. Whenever you'd like to talk. When you have time, of course. I know you've got *Northie*."

But I never seemed to have the time. And he didn't bring it up again, I'm sure because he didn't want to be a pest. I didn't bring it up either.

&

There came a time when I made Teddy Redmond something of a project. Maybe this is in comparison to my father, or maybe it isn't. Friends are different from relatives, aren't they? Anyway, Teddy made the rounds with his story of Charlie Chamberlain, and when he got as far as he could go and it was nowhere, I offered to try to help him. My thinking was that maybe Adam Bloch could be persuaded to take an interest. We had all been classmates, after all, Yale sixty-six. Adam had known Teddy a little bit through Harry Nolan, and then there was the weekend of the crash. As I wrote earlier, I had never forgiven Adam for it, but with me at least it didn't seem to be something he expected. It was part of our past that was simply there, a story that came out the same way every time you looked at it. You could start to root for a different ending, but there never was one. This much we shared, and I suppose Adam's guilt, and my own for being unforgiving. But with Teddy I didn't know. Teddy had been the harshest of us all with Bloch, had blamed him the most, had seen the least excuse. And they hadn't spoken since, except a few words at a dinner I gave once in Los Angeles, but there were a lot of people there.

I didn't think I was trying to rewrite the past, I thought I was trying to help Teddy get his film done. His idea was to go to HBO with it. HBO was his mantra, HBO HBO HBO, HBO would have the taste and subtlety to film the story of Charlie Chamberlain. But Teddy had no track record as a producer, nor as a writer for that matter, and he needed a strong production company behind him to get in the door there. And so that's where I thought to bring Bloch in. Cangaroo wasn't a company that had ever made movies, its whole history was in series television, but could Adam be persuaded to break the mold for once?

Though it wouldn't have to be framed to him as "for once"—the company had from time to time financed the vanity projects of its producers, before Bloch's arrival. All the vanity projects had been disasters.

I invited them out for a drink, the old Yale guys, twenty years out, and look where we all were. In college Bloch had been a weenie but smart, and Teddy had been a preppie but fidgety, and I had been whatever I was, a little bit of neither of those, a little bit writerly maybe, but mostly pure aspiration. Or we had all been pure aspiration, the only difference being that Bloch and I knew it and Teddy then did not. It took years of losing for Teddy to realize that he secretly wanted to win. And then there had been this terrible accident where the one we all loved died, and most of us blamed Bloch, who'd been driving.

The place in Brentwood was dark and wood-paneled the way places in Los Angeles seldom are unless they want to suggest somewhere else. I was the only one who ordered anything but iced tea. Bloch had to go back to work afterward and Teddy was uneasy enough. He had first ignored Bloch in college, then patronized him.

Bloch with his millions, and still an isolate. He had come to California without even leaving a girl behind. No one knew exactly what his private life was like. The common suspicion, voiced by Zacky, was that he had none, that he went home and worked some more. But how could that be? Even mama's boys got to the point where they wanted a family, unless they were queer. Or that's what the sociology of the street said anyway, and Bloch wasn't queer. On this point everyone agreed. Maybe he devoted his private time to charity, a secret Mother Teresa, fulfilling the Talmud's mandate to keep your good deeds quiet. Maybe he just needed a little time to get used to things out here. Maybe he suspected people of being after his money. I had this recurring daydream of Bloch looking in the mirror each night and despising himself. He was compact, his hair was wiry, his nose a little bulbous, his complexion ruddy and rough as if he'd been recently under a sunlamp, and yet he wasn't really an ugly man. He was less ugly than when he was young. He was presentable, really, he dressed neatly in a manner to suggest the department stores and took care to give no offense, spoke softly to underlings, listened more than he spoke. There was a quiet anonymity to him. In an age of accountants, which we might have been in, he would fit. But he never blinked. He had never blinked, not much anyway, for as long as any of us had known him.

Our conversation drifted from Yale to New York to where we were. For awhile it seemed like we all might have been the best of friends. No feints, no exploratory jabs. Members of the same tribe fallen into enemy territory. Or maybe that's what happens. You don't have to have been the best of friends, if you're from the same tribe and in enemy lands, you start thinking you're the best of friends. You share a common perspective that was invisible before. L.A.'s shortcomings, Hollywood's shortcomings, Reagan's shortcomings. When Teddy changed the subject, the incredible thing was how awkward he was about it. Teddy had always been a little jumpy, but his jumps came with wit and they landed him on his feet. He knew how to handle people. He knew where their weaknesses were and he wasn't afraid. He wasn't the kind who'd start something with, "Not to change the subject or anything, but. . ." He wasn't one to get his forehead furrowed or fix some strange stare on you. That was what Bloch used to do, and didn't do so much anymore.

But now he said, "Adam, I don't know how to say this." He did something funny with his nose, scrunched it up. "I'm not sure I even thought I'd see you in my life again. I wanted this arranged so I could talk to you about a project. It's a good project. I think it could be good. But I can't talk to you without saying this other thing first."

And then it was like he couldn't say what that other thing was. He got as quiet as Bloch. I thought I should jump in and say something, keep the flow, whatever. But there was no flow.

All of us knew what the other thing had to be.

"I'm having a hard time remembering why it was your fault," Teddy said, about the thing that was long enough ago it seemed like a legend.

But then legends are always with us. Bloch put his iced tea down. "Because I was driving," he said, about the crash that killed Sascha Maclaren. We were at a table towards the back, where it was darker even than in the front of the faux-dark bar in Brentwood, and I was on the side of the table with Adam, and in the darkness I could see that he wasn't blinking. I could see the steady gleam of his nearer eye. "You thought I caused it by being a bad driver."

"You were a bad driver," Teddy said.

"I was," Bloch said.

"But even if you were," Teddy said.

"It was an accident," Bloch said. "I believe that. I always have. But she died. And there had to be somebody to blame."

"You were easy to blame," Teddy said.

Through all this I said nothing, as if I were listening in on the gods. Though why do I say that, "gods?" The most ordinary guys in the world, trying to figure something out, get past something that had long been there. And actually I felt a part of it too, by saying nothing, by letting it go.

I was the part of it that wasn't going to mess it up.

Though should there be exposition here? At the end of

summer in 1966 we were driving on a road late at night and Bloch was the only sober one and in the fog that came up he thought he saw a deer and he swerved to miss it and went off the road. And there was no deer.

"But if the rest of us hadn't been drunk," Teddy said, "then you wouldn't have had to drive. You were making up for us being fools."

"I said that then," Adam said.

"I remember," I said, and hated the sound of my voice, the way you hate the cold when you jump in the water.

"But I wanted to be the hero," Bloch said, and took his iced tea again, and had a very tiny sip of it. And then, sarcastic in a way he never was, "I learned it was better not to be helpful after that."

"We were cruel," I said.

"It's only because I was trying," Bloch said. "It's what happens when you try. That's when you get in trouble. When you have to try to be helpful."

"I'm sorry," Teddy said.

"So what can I do for you today?" Bloch said.

Bloch trying maybe to be witty, trying to put an end to something. As if he could take it all but Teddy saying he was sorry.

Of course Bloch was wrong to say that then. It wasn't what Teddy meant. Yet it was the most honest thing Adam could say, it came with feeling pushing it out.

Then that was pretty much the end of it. It had been a try. And there we still were, twenty years later, as if meeting in some bar in some foreign country, expats and their stories.

Thank god for the waitress. More iced tea, more whatever I had. We seemed to like being with each other after that.

Smaller and smaller talk, until we were down to gossip, who in our class had done this or that, been divorced three times, got a job in the Reagan administration, ran an investment house, farmed oysters in Indonesia, was CIA, was queer, died of AIDS, lived in Moscow, lived in Arizona with Tibetan Buddhists, grew pinot noir in the central coast, became a vet and pioneered an extraordinary technique for artificially inseminating sheep, fucked Sharon Stone or somebody who looked just like her at a resort where everybody was incognito. At the end of it Teddy told Adam about Charlie Chamberlain.

Adam didn't look surprised. But then, he never looked surprised. He didn't look interested or intrigued or eager or skeptical either. He was back to being his leaden self. You couldn't tell.

"Let me think about it," Bloch said, but he didn't blink.

We really didn't know.

The next day I called his office to see what he thought. His assistant said he was on a conference call. Now it happens there must have been a memo some years ago that went out to all the assistants in Los Angeles that the excuse you should make for your boss when an unwelcome call comes in is that he's on a conference call. The "conference" part of it is particularly key, it sounds important and precise, and lets you know that even though it's a lie you hear all over town, it's a lie that somebody took some care with. Hours later the assistant called back to say that Mr. Bloch had to go into a meeting but he wanted me to know that we could go ahead.

I still didn't know what he really thought. About any of it, really.

"What a screwed-up thing forgiveness is," I said to Teddy, thinking I was ironic or profound, then thinking I was anything but.

"Let's go to HBO," Teddy said.

☙

I didn't invite my father to the wedding, nor my mother. It got too complicated, the thought of who would sit next to who, and Irene. We made it a small wedding. Melissa didn't invite her parents either. A kind of wedding of our hopes, two people who had made themselves over. We had bought a house in Santa Monica canyon, a log cabin sort of thing, so that our baby wouldn't be born in a welfare hotel. The wedding was at the house. Teddy came, and Bloch and Zacky, and Morty, and Sterner, and a few of Melissa's friends, and a guy I knew from our old group in New York, Philip Deschayne, a *New Yorker* writer who happened to be in Los Angeles on a speaking tour the weekend of the wedding. For some reason we had a rabbi. Melissa's soft spot for rabbis.

The smallness of the occasion was mostly my idea, and Melissa interpreted it as also my fault in a certain way, in that if my parents didn't present such problems, there wouldn't be a problem at all. She was five months pregnant. "Log cabin" might not quite do justice to the house. It was bigger than my father's old house in Bel Air. It didn't have a kidney-shaped pool, but by the eighties kidney-shaped pools were *déclassé*. Anything but a lap pool was *déclassé*, and we were putting in one of those. All these facts I duly noted and wondered why I noted them. Then in the city where, so it's been said, everything is commoditized, we made the best of our little vows. No formal stuff, no made up stuff. The rabbi managed not to put in his cautionary little shtick about "mixed marriages." People felt Melissa's belly. She made her own dress. That night we didn't make love, because she was still mad about not having her parents there.

Whereas I had my parents there that night, in a dream that was once in a lifetime. In the dream I was my mother and I was invited to the wedding after all, and so was *he*. But the wedding is in the Poconos, not California, the "log cabin" is on a lake, and I see *him* first at breakfast, where we chat a bit. I am not frightened to see him. I am not *anything* to see him. He is a little older than I remembered. What's forty years in a dream? And just as my only son is observing this and thinking there couldn't be two people on earth less suited to one another and how did they ever get together in the first place . . . we're having another little conversation on the porch of the "log cabin," which the son can't hear but it's about him and would he be proud of us now, chatting so civilized, so mature, like in the movies, like strangers on a train. Which leads to a dinner in a restaurant in town. Irene is nowhere in sight. He takes me in an old car that is the only car he has now and is not even a convertible and is older than my own. He tells me he saw me at the Emmys—on TV of course, he wasn't *at* the Emmys, he saw me on TV. I register the simplicity of his car, the way the cocksureness of his life has been shed. I do not feel intimidated. And what does he feel? Charitable? Virtuous?

At the restaurant I order fried clams. Why not? It's my favorite. I am aware that it's slightly vulgar, or so he the big food snob might think, but I don't care. It's sustained me, my love of HoJo's fried clams. He talks more about seeing me at the Emmys— on TV, of course, he saw me on TV.

"Why did you do this, why did you come?" one of us asks, I'm not sure which, and the other of us replies, "To not let you have what you want."

Then one of us, I'm not sure which, says, "What do you want? To feel good about yourself, the final triumph of self?"

"Sorry about her death," I say, referencing Irene, realizing she's dead, or otherwise she'd be here.

He nods. "Don't have to say that," he says. "She ruined your life."

"It's true, I don't have to. I take it back," I say.

"I have a new friend," he says.

"I never had a *friend*," I say, at some point later, in indirect response.

"Blame me for that one," he says, referencing my lost trust in men.

"I did but I don't," I say. "What did you ever see in me?" And, when he doesn't answer right away, I become what I feel is very bold and say, "I remember what I saw in you. A way out. A handsome choice. Intense, but kind. Gone to Yale."

He couldn't remember when such kind words had been said to him, when even the word "kind" had been used.

I go on: "I know what you saw in me. Someone available. Someone to touch you."

"No!" he shouts, "No, no, no!"

Then it's the next day and he rows me in a boat. He is the only one who ever rowed me in a boat and his strokes are choppy and slow the way they weren't once long ago and the weeds are slow and the moonlight is as pale as skim milk and while he's rowing he tells me that he's sick, which somehow I already knew, a nurse's instinct or whatever that is. And now everything goes very fast, with the illness that will be fatal and he telling me again how he saw me at the Emmys and how happy he was to see me there, it was the right place for me to be and what a mistake his life has been, including this *friend* of his, he's giving up this *friend* of his. For which I am not prepared to give up in turn one bit of my bitterness and disdain and anger and resentment and hurt for all time, until all time is over and I am. I take pity on him then and will care for him for the rest of his days. Or that's the feeling anyway, the feeling that that's what I am going to do. The feeling, too, that he goes into remission from whatever illness it was, and I die shoveling snow because I always liked shoveling snow, I never liked California, I liked places where you could shovel snow, and he dies of a broken heart. That's his punishment. A broken heart.

༄

I neglected to mention: our house in Santa Monica Canyon, our log cabin, had an orange tree.

༄

They sent a piece of glass as a wedding present. I'm not sure what it looked like but it had a little tag that came with it and the tag said it was called "The Swan." I don't know. Maybe it looked like a swan. It didn't seem very personal. It came a couple of months after the wedding. It occurred to me they might have been angry that they weren't invited, or reached the arguably logical conclusion that if we didn't think it was an important enough event to invite our relations, then they didn't think it was important enough to think up a gift with personal feeling. It didn't occur to me that in those months Irene may have been too distracted to shop for wedding gifts and that my father didn't know how to shop for gifts. "The Swan" reminded me of the legendary fruitcake of Malibu, an ageless and inedible concoction that for years had been going from house to house, as a house gift at Christmas parties. Receiving the legendary fruitcake of Malibu came to be like a Chinese good omen, promising luck for the whole next year. Melissa wrote a thank-you note. "The Swan" was in the dining room for awhile. It was only weeks later that my father called to say that Irene had shot herself.

❦

The reasons for such a thing. There are always reasons and there are never reasons. People make up reasons but they diminish the act. The act has mystery to it. Even in the most pitiful circumstances, it embraces mystery. We step back from it. Perhaps we avert our eyes. There is so little to discuss, yet we discuss. Fred and Irene. Irene and Fred. She had acted as if life was short and so it was. I knew so little about either one of them.

❦

I went back to see my father. Melissa was due with the baby in a week. I drove a rental car from Kennedy up to the place in Connecticut on the lake that was still in Irene's family. It wasn't where they had lived, but it was where he would later wish to throw her ashes. She had left no note, expressed no preference, said no good-byes. Or perhaps she had and I just hadn't heard about them.

Something to my father, something to Thomas? There were things that were none of my business. Of course there were.

I had expected other people to be there. Thomas, at least;

but he wasn't, he'd been up the day before. The place itself I barely remembered. Small and clapboard, painted barn red. A dirt path down to the water. It was November and it felt like grief, like the season that takes people away. A few leaves clung to naked branches. Maybe you notice these things more if you live long enough in California. And then my father at the door of the place. It still had the screen door on. He held it open. I came in with my carry-on bag. We embraced, a little awkwardly, because the carry-on was still on my shoulder. I was taller than he was now. All my life, I thought, he had been a little taller than me.

He didn't want to be back in Chappaqua, where she had shot herself and the blood was still on the bathroom wall. He said that to me, more or less. His words weren't exactly those. I don't remember what they exactly were, they were less articulate, left more for me to fill in, as if the one thing I could do now was give him a hand with words.

But there wasn't really so much for either of us to say. Or of course there might have been a million things, but we didn't say them. It was as if we only wanted to say something that would change something. The main room of the house had many pictures of Irene and her brother. On the tables, on the walls. Irene with her horse in the hunt country of Virginia. Irene and her brother with the Duomo in the back of the frame. Irene and her brother and parents and grandparents and vacations and a school graduation, some private girls' school in New York, for the Jewish girls who couldn't go to Spence, but the school's gone now because Spence lets the Jewish girls in. Irene as a part of a family that seemed tightly knit and happy and rich, and that I had never known at all. Only a little short of an Old World family, with a patriarch who made things right.

But then what had gone so wrong? My eyes wandered over these pictures. Though I felt embarrassed to look too closely, as if why look so closely now when I never had in her life? But then, I'd never quite been invited to in her life. I'd been invited to look from a bit of a distance, and then later I didn't care. A few photos of Thomas as well, and of Fred, their bright Kodacolor, even when beginning to fade, like a garish intrusion on a settled world. While in my feelings I searched for one more image, of Irene in our front yard in Scarsdale shaking and kissing Fred, and me watching with a boy's astonishment.

Wishing it was me. Was that really what I had wished? I guess it was.

None of which I told my father, but maybe I could have then. Or maybe, just as I knew much about him, he knew much about me. We spent our afternoon mostly silent. They sometimes call such silences eloquent, but I don't know. My father in a checked sport shirt, tan pants, and a belt that was a little too long. Always neat, even today. Must have run a shaver over his face and looked in the mirror and seen what? Eyes as if they'd like an excuse not to look back, hooded by lids that were even heavier today. So little light in those eyes. A mottled complexion that had spent too many summers in the California sun. A long nose like an old companion, nothing to write home about but what can you do. That had been his feeling anyway, a feeling that his nose had never really interfered with his life. And now?

An old guy. But neither of us was young anymore. The same build, the same kind of pants more or less, receding hair though his was more gone than mine, and mine had more color and my eyes had more light. Yet it was as if someone in the silence could have said: just wait.

My father was so considerate that day. That was one thing he could still do, he could be polite and considerate and ask about my flight and Melissa and the show and whether it had been easy to get the rental car and find the way to the place in Connecticut and what was I thinking about for dinner, because there was nothing much in the fridge but we could go out to dinner later, there was either a sandwich shop nearby or a little farther away there was a place like an inn. These bits of conversation were like little sprinkles of rain in the desert of our silence.

They say, they're always making these films that say, that the desert has so much life in it. I have no opinion about this. I only report what they tell me. Thomas my half-brother whom I'd seen only rarely since he was a shy child by the kidney-shaped pool in Bel Air where we'd played when he lost his real older brother, was coming back up on Thursday. There would be a cremation, then a scattering of the ashes. Of course he didn't expect I would be there for these, with the baby coming. I did find some room sometime in the day to tell him a couple funny stories about Zacky. Zacky Kurtz as comic relief. A good thing, really. Though my father had a lot of time for Zacky, who had given his kid his job. And too, my father still had a kind of wary respect for people who were big in the business, as if you never knew who you still might want to pull a favor from someday. The 1970s "King of TV." My father liked to hear about the kings of the industry, even if he felt in his heart of hearts that in his day the kings were more royal and longer-lasting.

We went to the inn for dinner after all. My father felt the sandwich shop wouldn't be to my liking. I ordered the lamb chops and he ordered the chicken and he barely touched it. And

I felt so ashamed and sorry. All the times when he and Irene enjoyed their food and fussed and "shared" and put things on my plate or his or hers and talked out what they would order and read the menu half out loud and taught me how to send things back if they weren't right because the chef would want to know, and then the desserts, which were always "marvelous" and in the middle with many forks, all of which I had liked at first but came to feel embarrassed about, as if in some magical reversal it turned out it was they who didn't know quite how to behave and not me. And now my father barely touched his roast chicken and I wanted nothing more in the world than for him to have his appetite back and be hearty and love food and start over. I felt ashamed for having turned against him what was good about him, and why shouldn't he have enjoyed life? Why shouldn't he have been extravagant in the ways that he could be? And why shouldn't he have been thankful?

That's what seemed missing now. My father's thankfulness for life. We went back to the house and there was a tape of one of his old shows that he must have left there on a weekend and we put it in the VCR. He apologized for the bad reproduction, but I didn't think it was so bad. An old black-and-white western where you knew who the good guys were. *The Dooley Boys*. His most popular show, went eleven seasons, set in gold-rush country, the forty-niners, the wicked banker, the fallen doves, the sheriff and the new guy who comes into town with a dark stare and rumors around him. A surprise or two, it's not the new guy but the wicked banker who's the bad guy this week, and a flash of a young Clint Eastwood in the back of the bar somewhere, which my father pointed out, stopped the play, went back, froze, pointed out again, more animated than he had been all night. At the end, over the end credits,

"Oh My Darling Clementine." I had forgotten over so many years where my love of that song must have come from. Or did I come to my love of it independently, or could it have been another thing passed in our genes or secret minds? Some old-timer like Gabby Hayes sang that song with his banjo, you saw him for a flash just at the end of the credits, and silly tears were in our eyes, in the eyes of my father and me. There was a room with twin beds where my father had slept the night before and another with a bed unmade, and my father began to look for sheets to make up that unmade bed. "The twin beds are fine. I'll sleep in there," I said.

"But I play the radio to get to sleep. It'll keep you up."

"It's okay. Really."

"Are you sure?"

So we slept in the same room. My father had striped pajamas as he had when I was a boy. I remembered these. I was sure of that. And he had brought his pajamas with him. I had not and slept in my underwear. I went to sleep easily enough but he did not. I woke up at four and he was up, lying on his back listening to the WINS weather. I got up and kissed his forehead and got back into bed and went back to sleep.

☙

As in a late medieval allegory, Passion and Responsibility in their separate realms. Is *The Faerie Queene* late medieval? I forget. *Piers the Ploughman*? Stuff from college, not so much forgotten as back there somewhere, under other stuff. Waiting to be useful, hoping to be useful, as if you never knew, one day there might be the call and there they'd be, ready to dust themselves off, ready to explain the world. Passion with its one great ally Death. Responsibility with a whole host of them, Reason and Culture and Amity and Society and Life Itself but the lot of them were maybe not as strong as Death, which by the way had a beautiful child called Romance. The Courts of the Two Realms. Two Languages, and not a word of either language translated into the other. Oh sure, each had a word for Love, in fact it was the exact same word, but in each of the languages it meant something totally different.

All Passion and Responsibility could do was fight it out. The old ignorant armies clashing by night, blind to each other, uncomprehending, without words. And did God turn his back, or did he at last send his emissary, called Tragedy, to go and see what was going on and come back with a report?

This is not a bedtime story I ever told Melissa. Nor anyone else, until just now. But in my ongoing effort to understand and forgive, to be a man, and not a bigger man than my father was, but just a man, a little bit taller than he or a little bit shorter. . .

There are even occasionally sentences that begin and do not end.

☙

Our baby was born December 6, 1986. We called her Carolyn. Our second child, Stephen, was born four years later. I'm not really jumping ahead in the story, I just wanted you to know, that we stayed together. We tried to make a family.

Which was something, I think, for people like us, for people who came where we came from.

I told Melissa that I wanted to be married only once. I told her this a lot, actually. Or a few times. And she would be suitably impressed and blame it on my fucked-up family and my fear of being left all over again.

But she didn't leave. Still she didn't leave. I don't know much about marriage, I feel I could hardly write about it at all, the daily intricacies, the millions of moments, of angles, of looking at the two hearts. Modern marriage, I guess that's what it's called. Or is it called postmodern marriage by now? All I really know about it, for sure, is that she did not leave. Though to me that was kind of a miracle.

Why wouldn't she leave? Especially after a few years, after you could see what it was all about and there was still only one kid. You took your child and your half-the-money and your looks that were still great and your own ideas about the way things should be and your guts and your wish to go dancing and your aspiration to a better or at least more varied sex life where your soul would be either more exposed or less and you started over, because that's what the law and all the magazines and the TV and your friends who did it before you and the counselors who heard your complaints and the lawyer and good common late twentieth-century sense said you could do and even ought to do if a, b, or c went wrong or if you didn't want your spirit to get frumpy and staid or if you didn't want to wait until it was too late, by which they meant when your good looks would be gone. Get back in the pool, get back to the gym.

And yet, I still didn't believe in the thing myself. Not in the vows part, the "death-do-us-part" part. I believed in the day-to-day part, today I didn't want anybody to be left. I didn't want the tears, the lies, or the loss. I wanted to build something a brick at a time, even though most of the time the thing fell down and you had to start over. Or even that's not quite so. I thought it was a nice description of what was going on. I didn't mean it to be that way. I hadn't the will. I was too confused. I imagined that if Melissa left, or if I left, I would root around and find someone and there would be love again and it would all be the same again. Not in the details. Of course not the details. And of course it would not seem like "rooting around." It would seem like chance, it would seem like living a life. But the most unlikely thing in the world was that anything would really be better, and the most likely thing in the world was that it would be worse. A conservative view? A cynical view? When I said to Melissa I wanted to marry only one time, I did not mean that I would stay married. I just meant that I would not make the same mistake again. Maybe it's just that I was in love with her.

And of course if she didn't leave, like Maryanna, she would not take half. Good point. Can you go off and write your novel when half the money's gone and there are alimony payments to make and child support and second houses?

It was a miracle that she didn't leave. When we met, we were not even young. As if by accident, we undertook this strange project.

I always thought I'd saved her life, but with the birth of Carolyn did she save mine?

"You know what I hated about you most?" Melissa said one night when the baby was in her arms. "That I could never do anything for you, you always had everything, you were always giving me. Your money, your ideas, your advice. Or that's what you thought. How could you think that?"

"I didn't."

"You did."

"Maybe I did."

"You want to hold her?"

I did and she passed her over.

⁂

My father came out to see the baby in March. It was the first time he stayed in my house. My house, our house. I wasn't sure what to call it then, I'd never had a house at all, nor a bride. My father would lift Carolyn up, put his finger in her fingers, watch from a distance of respect while Melissa gave her a bath. We didn't talk about Irene, even in the evening, when he and I sat together. We talked about Carolyn, and when we exhausted that we talked about the business and the show and Zacky, and when we exhausted that we talked about sports. We talked as if the sun would rise as well as set. And wouldn't it? Why not? What else could we say about the past? I suppose I didn't want to hurt his feelings. I told him that in a matter of years I would take my winnings and quit and go write my books even if I had no idea yet what my books would be. I just thought, somehow, they must be there. When I was twenty I had wanted to write them. I had filled my drawers with drafts. My father didn't say anything, as if he couldn't decide whether to be cautionary or supportive.

The next day Melissa's parents arrived from Seattle. A full house. The possibilities for a comedy of manners. The Republicans from way out there, the old Jew with his letters to the editor and feelings about Reagan and now Bush and when would that part of it ever end. Gave him something to think about, anyway, something other than Irene. Everybody on their best behavior. Melissa's father not knowing quite what to talk about with mine, so he tried fishing. My father said he used to fish. He could remember when he would fish. Then my father asked him about Boeing and airplanes. That one actually worked out well. My father loved planes and Melissa's father knew all about them. And it gave my father a chance to talk about all the planes he'd flown on, and where he'd flown on them to, and to remember what all that had been like, which was the past but it was not a cruel past.

In the afternoon outside we did something for Carolyn that we called a "blessing" but we didn't really know what it was. Melissa's parents weren't going to get a baptism out of us, that's all we really knew for sure. Yet both of us possibly felt that we had brought Carolyn into a world where God was as likely as anything else and if not then we had better step in. Agnostics' roulette, why take a chance. Or as the young mystic who'd almost forgotten that's what he'd been might have put it, why not take a chance. Each of the grandfathers spoke. Melissa's father mentioned Jesus a few times. My father mentioned the United Nations. I must have winced a few times. An actor we knew who had a mail-order minister's license from the Universal Life Church read Blake and spritzed our child with a few drops of water. I may have winced again, but what the hell. When something's the best you can do, you do it. The truth of it is it made me proud. Though could I really say why?

Afterward my father decided to take a dip in the new pool. I loaned him some trunks and he wore his shirt. I don't think he really knew that lap pools were the only kind of pool that in Los Angeles in 1987 wasn't *déclassé*. He asked me why we didn't put in a bigger pool. I told him we didn't want the upkeep, Melissa only wanted to swim laps. He walked to the edge of the pool, to where the steps were. I was a little distance away, clipping my new old roses. I looked his way and was surprised by the skinniness of his legs. They seemed disproportionate to the rest of him, the way you look at certain features of reconstructed dinosaurs and wonder how they ever could have worked, and if the people who put all the bones together could have got it wrong. He walked down the steps into the pool, stood a few minutes with the water to his waist, splashed water on his face. He seemed like pictures you see of bathers in the Ganges. When he climbed back out, his dark wet hair clung to his legs, and they appeared even skinnier than before. I had an urge to feed him up. I had an urge to say, "My father was a bigger man than this." And to add, so that whoever the hearer was wouldn't take it wrong, "He had bigger bones than this." Where had he gone to, or had he always been that way?

Fathers and Sons

Time for the plot to find its final shape. The approach of a key date. At the point where I was going to put all my story into one day, so that it would be like a surreal night on *Northie*, the date I chose was November 9, 1989. I chose it in part because enough did happen close to me that day, and because there were some other things that could be made to fit, some of them things I've already written about. But also because November 9, 1989 was the day the Berlin Wall opened. There would be the symbol of this but also how the rumble of the distant storm played or did not play on my characters. It was like the end of the decade, but really it was more than that, it was the end of the Cold War that had thrown its shadows like an enormous hungry bird incessantly over our whole generation. Or it was close to the end, anyway, close enough to tell what was coming. But I could never quite fit my father into that one day scheme. It's most of why it always seemed false. After the day when I saw his skinny legs by the lap pool, he went back to New York and I began to think how I had to do something for him. A gesture anyway. Probably it wouldn't work, but a gesture. I had no time to start another new show. There was *Northie* and there was the series commitment with Zacky. But I could get him some money, maybe, and I could get him something to do. Or I thought I could, with a little creative budgeting from Bloch. In the eighth season of a big show, there ought to be room somewhere for a show-runner's dad who after all had been one of the industry's early guys. Yet I resisted the idea for weeks. I told myself he didn't really want to come back to California. I told myself he didn't want handouts. I told myself he would be embarrassed. None of these I believed. What I really believed is that I would be embarrassed, that his taste would be old and off, that he would introduce himself into places where he didn't belong, that he would somehow undermine my own authority or weaken people's belief in my own creativity or expose myself to the old joke that all a producer really produces is relatives. I didn't want him close enough to *noodge*. I didn't want to have to deal with him and Melissa all the time. I didn't want, in a sense, the unexpected. Things were going nicely enough. I didn't want to jinx them. After a month of knowing every reason why it was a bad idea, I got Bloch to hire my father on a five-thousand-dollar-an-episode consultancy. His job would be to submit a set of comments on each script. He could do this from either New York or California.

But he chose to come to California. He seemed reborn. He found a place in Santa Monica. He took walks in Palisades Park. He put on five pounds. He called up all his old friends and let them know he was back in the business. And his rich friends from London came and they didn't stay with him but he took them to the set. I didn't see him every day. More like once a week. He'd come over, see Carolyn, or we'd have lunch. His comments would come in on two single-spaced pages and I would read them and sometimes Zacky read them. They were invariably polite and cautious, maybe questioning the exact meaning of a line here, suggesting a snip there. I can't remember when they ever caused us to change even one thing. And he knew this. He didn't mind. He would say things like, "Can't hurt to have an extra pair of eyes on it." And this was true. He was happy for the checks every couple weeks and happy to keep in motion. He had no illusions; none that he himself couldn't see through when he wished to, anyway. And he got along famously with Zacky. One day the television academy came to interview him, they were interviewing all the old-timers left, and he talked for several hours. It was these stories that attracted Zacky. Since he felt himself to be a moment in television history, he was eager to know what had come before him, as if to place himself in the larger scheme. Stories of Wasserman and Schreiber and Desi Arnaz and Astaire and Hitchcock and Aubrey and Stanton and Gleason and Laughton and Reagan and the day Walter Wanger shot Jennings Lang in the balls. Some of the names you know and some of them you don't. It looked different from the inside. Zacky felt my father was a gentleman.

About four months after my father started his consultancy, we got one of those calls from the network that you only get when your show's reached the top of the hill and started on the road down. It had to do with a twenty-five share. We needed to have a twenty-five share. That is, if we didn't have twenty-five percent of the audience watching television during our time period by the end of the year, they'd think about canceling the show. But the company needed one more year of producing the show in order to make its profit. Bloch asked us to try to come up with something that would boost our ratings at the end of the season. This call came toward the end of October. The whole task was complicated by the fact that Zacky and I refused to do cliffhangers. They were stupid, they were beneath the dignity of *Northie*. Or to put it more crassly and in a way we hoped the suits at the network would understand, it would *undermine our brand.* What a phrase. Like calling everything that's done in the world "product." Another product of the eighties, calling everything done in the world "product." Anyway, Zacky and I put our heads together and came up with having our show's irredeemably bad cop, Schlessing, seem to get away with murdering his snitch. The snitch himself was a fairly popular character and we would do this in the last episode and it wouldn't be a cliffhanger because we wouldn't play it like a cliffhanger, it would be in the mix with everything else, only it would give the network suits something lurid to promote. It was my idea but it pleased Zacky especially, because it seemed to be answering the hardass approach of Morty's show tit-for-tat. Or hooter-for-hooter, as Zacky more likely would have said. Anyway, he wasn't going to be out-pigged by Morty, our pig could be piggier than his. In Zacky's mind the network would never have called if it hadn't been for Morty's new hit.

The two of us called up Jaworsky with our idea. Jaworsky said he was excited about it, which in industry-speak meant about the same as saying it didn't put him immediately to sleep, but then he had an *even better* idea. What if Schlessing doesn't quite get away with it—the crime's found out by Lieutenant O'Brien, and O'Brien in turn covers it up, saving Schlessing. "Now *there* would be a real cliffhanger," Jaworsky said.

"We don't do cliffhangers," Zacky and I said, in a discordant sort-of unison that should have been comical but wasn't.

We hung up more depressed than if we had never come up with the idea. We cursed network executives and their "even better" ideas with the usual curses, the fuck did they know, they weren't writers, they just took credit for what writers did. Zacky seemed to be one with me on this. It would tear the heart out of the show. Donald O'Brien stood for the decent man caught in impossible circumstances. Destroy his character and there was no show left. But then, wasn't that Jaworsky's point? It was an old show. Who would care if there was nothing left? Feed the wallboard into the fire and we'd stay warm a few minutes more. Tear out the floorboards and pull off the roof to feed the flames.

❧

Have I said enough how much my father liked his job? He would call me if his script was more than a few hours late. He would also call if after he got it he found typographical errors. These calls were not part of his "notes," they were his diligence. He banked his checks with his old broker, he put in calls to his old lawyer. He was fond of thinking, of saying if he could ever fit it in, that he was the only one from *The Dooley Boys* still working, "except for Clint, of course." He may even have had a few dates that I never heard about. Widows and divorcees, why not? He had things to talk about again, and money to go out to dinner. I told him he ought to be saving some, because *Northie* wasn't going to last forever. I didn't have to tell him this.

In the meantime Zacky and I had received the call from Jaworsky that wound up with his "even better idea" and we went to Bloch to complain and strategize. But Adam didn't see our point of view. "I'm not a writer."

"Of course you're not a writer. Adam. Listen. Please. Once O'Brien goes down as a character, there's nothing left to the show."

We were in his office and I was aware of doing all the talking. Maybe Zacky was thinking that I was the one who knew him better and I was the one he'd listen to, since he'd listened to me once before, when he bought the company and sacked Zacky. Or maybe Zacky was just lying low.

"You can't do something the next season?" Bloch asked.

"To excuse covering up a murder? To explain what? To redeem him?"

"All I need is one more year," Bloch said.

"Has Jaworsky called you?"

"Called? He calls every day."

"Fuck."

Maybe Zacky said "Fuck" as well. If he did, it was all he said. It was beginning to bother me. In the elevator down I said we should go see Hagle. The guy you'd think would have the most to lose, the former bit player who'd become *Northie*'s star by playing Donald O'Brien with a wry, surprised detachment, as if to ask was it a cosmic mistake that he wound up being a lieutenant of police. Surely Hagle would find some threat to his recently acquired lifestyle in having O'Brien reduced to a criminal. Get Hagle on our side and we'd have enough to say no, even without Bloch, I said to Zacky, or really I asked, because he was senior to me in everything that was political and I wanted him to know that I knew that. Zacky nodded that it was so. "You can't shoot if you don't have your star," he said. *"Nullum astrum, nullum spectaculum."* Well, really. Zacky said he couldn't go see Hagle because he had to get his hair cut. Which might have sounded lame coming from anybody else, but oddly not from Zacky, whose harmonious view of life seemed to depend on regularly getting his hair cut, his boots shined, and his end wet.

I went to see Flip Hagle alone. I found him in his trailer watching a soap, a pink-nosed, pink-cheeked Canadian from the prairies of Manitoba who looked as Irish as anybody. Or enough Irish to play Donald D. O'Brien anyway. I told him what was being planned for his character, expecting him to be shocked and outraged but instead he looked at me with the straight face of a pawn and said we'd come up with something brilliant.

"Are you crazy? Flip! Come on!"

He looked sheepishly back toward his soap opera on his thirteen-inch set. I was hoping it would remind him where he could still wind up, if this thing came to pass. Daytime soaps, Flip, remember those? That could be *you*! I didn't shout that but I could have. Maybe I should have. Instead it dawned on me that what I was telling him was no surprise.

"Somebody already talk to you about this?" I asked.

Flip shrugged. He was not a talented man at hiding his feelings. Neither am I, I suppose, nor probably a lot of people, but for an actor it seemed odd, as if the one thing you might have expected of him was an ability to fool you.

"The network?"

He shrugged again.

"The company?"

"I'm thinking about it," he said.

"Thinking about *what*? It's a disaster."

"I've got that situation."

"What situation?"

"You know. That situation."

Flip had the look of a sixth grader whose teacher just told him to get his hand out of his pocket. More rueful than embarrassed, really. I knew it all then. Six months before, during lunch hour, Flip had been arrested in his car on Ventura Boulevard and charged with soliciting. One of the grips had told him that if you didn't mention money or a specific sex act you could never get in trouble, but the undercover cop in a miniskirt that Flip pulled his Jag over for disagreed with the grip's interpretation of the law. *All I did was point down*, Hagle was heard to say, leaving out that his pants were unzipped at the time. Zacky had to call the chief of police to get the thing disappeared.

"So Zacky told you?"

Not even a shrug from Flip. Staring at the soap again, but the soap had gone to commercial. Flip was studying, with the concentration of a great master of his craft, an ad for Windex.

I waited for Zacky in his office. When he came back, he was proud of his hundred twenty dollar haircut. "Doreen knows hairs," he said. Zacky had a way, when he was feeling good, of kind of gliding along, of following some inner rhythm, like a bird more graceful in flight than at rest. And his haircut somehow seemed to amplify that impression. He had the look, especially after he was shorn, with his thinning blond-white hair like a crest atop his large square head, of some exotic, quite beautiful bird of prey.

"Did you talk to Hagle?" I asked.

"Me? Of course not. You were going to."

"Did you talk to his agent?"

"About what?"

"About this. About where Jaworsky wants to go with his character. And also about his arrest."

"I don't remember. Possibly. He called."

"Today?"

"I don't know. Yesterday. Hey, Mr. D.A. go back to the prosecutor's office. They've got lots of people you can interrogate there."

He was checking his phone messages, not paying me much mind.

"I thought you were against the idea," I said. "I thought you were with me on this."

"If you're saying I'm blackmailing Hagle to get him to accept Jaw's lame idea, when I don't even like Jaw's lame idea, you're quite wrong."

He was prioritizing his phone slips now, deciding who to call back first.

"But not entirely wrong," I said.

"You heard Bloch today. And he's your friend. Doing this show isn't a suicide pact."

"Why didn't you tell me you'd folded? You could have saved us a lot of trouble."

"I haven't folded. We'll just see. We'll wait things out."

When I didn't know what else to do or who else to commiserate with, I told my father. This had an unexpected result. He said nothing. Or rather, he seemed to say the equivalent of nothing, he said greeting card things, what a shame, get well soon, the network was too smart, it wouldn't let a good show be destroyed this way. It was the end of the run, I said. He said nothing then. We were walking in Palisades Park. It was a clear day of Santa Ana winds and you could see Catalina. He pointed it out. He said the smog seemed to be less these days.

It appears my father called Zacky himself. If I'd known about this, I would have been furious. He called to make sure that what I was saying was so. Zacky apparently told him that it was not so, that nothing had been decided. But my father understood otherwise. Old enough to hear between the words.

A few days later, he wrote a letter to Bloch and copied the network.

Dear Mr. Bloch,
I am resigning my consultancy position on Northie as of the next episode. I am doing so to protest the ill-advised destruction of the moral center of the show.

I have known Lieutenant O'Brien for the several years that my son has worked on Northie. It's obvious that that character would never cover up a murder committed by one of his men or by anybody else. What are you going to blame it on, amnesia? It's ridiculous.

You're taking a marvelous show and turning it over to all those who glorify the increasing brutality of our country, to those who cynically say it's okay for our police to get away with anything since everybody else does.

What you're doing is symptomatic of this era, but it's also worse than that. It's validating it, as only television in our culture can. Anything for money, anything for power. Call me an old fogy, but I want no more part of it.

Thank you for your kind support until now. I've been honored.

Sincerely yours.

Bloch called him, Zacky called him, even Jaworsky wrote him a note. "He sent me a very polite note." My father's own last dance with power. My guess was they were afraid that he'd go to the papers with it, that he'd copy the *New York Times*. Though what's the oldest thing they say about publicity, just get the names spelled right? Anyway, they all told him nothing had been decided yet, or, in Jaworsky's words, we were exploring options to keep this historic show viable. Bloch thanked him for his service. Zacky told him he was a great guy, and a brave guy.

We had dinner before he left Los Angeles. "I'm sorry if I caused you any trouble," he said. "It probably wasn't a good idea to start with."

"Hiring you as a consultant?"

"I just caused you trouble."

"It was one of the better ideas I ever had. Better than Schlessing killing his snitch anyway."

"Maybe they still won't do it."

"Maybe your letter will have some effect."

"Do you think so?"

"I don't know."

"It makes me so mad. That people can be so stupid."

"You don't have to resign, you know. You could still take it back."

He pressed his lips together. Then they softened and he sipped his wine. "Nice. A nice Pommard. And very reasonable."

☙

The day the Berlin Wall opened. November 9, 1989. If I had told the whole story that day, Zacky would have shat his pants and Melissa would have thrown her pills at her shrink and we would have made love and broken apart and come back together and Teddy would have despaired of L.A. and Jaworsky would have had his "even better idea" and Morty's new show would have come on and been a smash and Zacky would have blackmailed Hagle and plied Jaw with the pathos of his divorce in order to get from him "bare ass" and some other things would have happened, as well, that really did happen on that day, all of it crunched together the way shows like *Northie* crunched their worlds together. Time as the great organizer, or time as the great trickster. But in this scheme of time my father would have been left out. Left the country by then. Gone to London. It's where he went after Los Angeles.

Teddy Redmond got up that day and went to the Omelet Parlor on Main for breakfast and by then it was already on the news about Berlin. The nine-hour time difference. Teddy heard about it at breakfast and the rest of the morning was a struggle to focus on Charlie Chamberlain. We were having lunch that day, he and I, to plot our plans to take his story to HBO. He kept turning on CNN to see what was happening with the Wall. By noon Pacific Standard Time the gates were thrown open, the Easties in their plastic cars were pouring through the Wall like lemmings, strangers embraced in the street, couples fucked on top of the Wall. Teddy wished he could be joyful, and perhaps he almost was, but he also had darker intimations. He faulted himself for what he took to be a constitutional resistance to the sight of happy people. But then CNN found a right-wing commentator, a Soviet era scholar from Johns Hopkins, who predicted it all: the Cold War was over, communism was finished, even our war in Vietnam was redeemed, it was only a matter of time but *we had won*. Teddy recognized that this was what he had been sensing. Why wasn't he happier? He thought he knew why.

We met at a white box of a place on Ventura Boulevard for lunch. I was inexcusably late, but if I'd written the book all taking place on one day I would have been late because I would have been at the Sav-On for Zacky and the question of whether to buy him the drums and bugles or the cows and cowboy hats would have consumed me and caused me to forget for a little while my lunch with Teddy and been my lame excuse. The clatter of deals being made in every corner of the place was oppressive. It was one of those restaurants designed to let every sound bang around so that people will think it's lively. But it was near the studio, and Teddy didn't work and I did. By the time I arrived, Teddy's patience was plaintive, the way silence can be when it doesn't have the fight left in it to be accusatory. We talked about the Wall. I hadn't been paying it much attention, heard a few bits on the radio driving in to work, but of course the last weeks had been raising hopes. I was facile, reflexively optimistic, failed at first to catch Teddy's mood. He was worried that somehow the opening of the Wall would hurt his chances of selling a script about Charlie Chamberlain.

"Why the fuck couldn't they have waited a month?"

"You know they called me about the scheduling of it. Sorry. I didn't think."

"You should've gotten back to them," he said.

"The Communists don't listen to anybody," I said.

Trying to be sardonic, trying to play it through. Both of us were, but Teddy stumbled over what he really felt. "The world is full of bad luck," he said.

And I could see his point. The Cold War broke Charlie Chamberlain. And now that we'd apparently won, were we really going to be in the mood to hear about the martyrs, the complicated ones? I tried to cheer him up.

"Nothing's won yet," I said, "Nothing's clear cut yet."

But he didn't believe me, he'd been watching the joy at the Wall all morning and listening to the right-wing commentator.

"Well so, good, then," I said "I mean, isn't it a good thing?"

"Of course it's a good thing," Teddy said, but he was still miffed and he said again that the timing was bad.

I put on my producer's hat, as they call it, but really it was to buck him up that I said, "Maybe the timing could be just fine if we tweak the character a bit. Charlie Chamberlain as unabashed hero, wouldn't HBO go for that? Maybe even a network would go for that. He died thinking he was a pawn of history when it turned out he was one of its kings. Or better, what about this? Forget the whole drowning-in-the-Sound stuff, forget the suicide, have him live long enough to see his triumph, have him tell the story looking back from the opening of the Wall, couples fucking on top of the Wall."

But Teddy was still glum. "Charlie wouldn't believe any of that," he said, and then I was glum too.

He returned from our lunch thinking I'd gone over to the other side and maybe I had. Teddy was living in the Ocean Park Apartments by then, he'd gotten my old place when Melissa and I bought the house. Never give up a rent-controlled apartment, it's like an heirloom that you pass on through the generations if you can, just like rent control itself, the succor of hungry souls.

As soon as Teddy entered the lobby, he was accosted by Red, the building's self-appointed historian, who was gathering names for a petition of congratulations to the people of Berlin from the residents of what had formerly been known as the Brandenburg Apartments. Perhaps Teddy wasn't aware of that, that when the building was owned by the Elks it was called the Brandenburg?

Must have been some German Elks or something, Red speculated. Red was a retired member of the Screen Actors Guild, having had bit parts in westerns in the fifties, and I knew him, too, from my days in the building. Before I had work I'd sit around the lobby and listen to Red talk about the old days. The father figure for when all else failed?

Teddy signed Red's petition, unloaded on him the gripes of

his day. Mostly about me, actually, me in and for myself and me as stand-in for the world. So quick to adapt, so quick to forget, money rains on the world and people bathe in it. "Now the yahoos will do anything they want," Teddy complained. Communism not as a good thing but as a brake on our own worst instincts. And what role for the man in the middle, the ambassadors, the interlocutors, the men of reason? Put out to pasture? Inconvenient, like daffy aunts in the attic, when it comes to compiling new editions of the national myth. Let the plutocrats take it all, fuck 'em, then. Teddy said most of this and implied the rest. Red looked at him with the unfazed expression of a guy who'd heard crazier than this. "But it's a great day for America," he said. "It's a great day for freedom." Teddy told me all this later, in an apologetic mood. But I don't know that he had anything to apologize for. Then he and Red went upstairs and turned on CNN and began to drink.

Many hours later they had finished off Teddy's Bacardi and watched Ted Koppel. Teddy carried Red back to his apartment because it was the only way Red was going to get there. Teddy dumped him just inside Red's door, left, decided he'd been cheap, returned, lifted Red again, and carried him to Red's daybed where he put him down and put the covers over him and patted them smoothly across Red's chest, so that the bed seemed to have been made with Red in it. This last Teddy couldn't quite explain. Red was mumbling in his stupor about a pinko friend of his who'd had it all wrong according to Red and good riddance to him now, may the landlord evict him and may swallows eat him alive. Teddy was gone before he realized that it was probably Teddy himself that Red was mumbling about.

That same night I hardly thought about Teddy at all. I

watched a little of the reruns on the news from Berlin. I said to Melissa something about Teddy being a stubborn case. But she didn't seem interested and I let it pass. It must have been midnight when Zacky called.

"Hey. Sorry if I'm interrupting a conjugal visit. Give my regards to your long-suffering bride."

"What's up?"

"I just got off the phone with Jaworsky. He says we're not going to get *bare ass* on the new show if we don't do this thing with O'Brien."

"I thought we weren't going to get renewed if we didn't do this thing with O'Brien."

"We didn't respond. So he's upped the stakes."

"This is bullshit."

"Guy, it's *their* network. You can't rewrite that one."

"No, but you can go out with dignity. Or I don't know. I'm not saying I know. But there was a time we were together on this."

"That's why I'm calling you now."

"Let's call Bloch."

"I talked to Adam. He understands what's at stake."

"You talked to Adam? . . . You've been a busy guy, Zack."

"I understand what's at stake too."

"*Bare ass?*"

"It's historic."

"Watch the news. That's historic."

"Just write the scene, would you? If it sucks, that's another conversation."

"I thought nothing was decided yet, I thought we were playing for time."

"We were. Time's up."

In the middle of the night I woke up to the sort of conclusion that nights are for. Zacky was right about it all. He was the showman, he was the man who knew what the people wanted, he was the man who'd been around television his whole adult life and cared about it and endured the slings and arrows and fought back and connived because he had to or otherwise he'd long be dead, he'd been the king and kings had scars, and if he said "bare ass" was what television needed and he wanted to be the one to bring it off before his rivals did, who was I to say no? I who could not have cared less if you said fuck or piss or shit on TV, who thought it was all a joke, that people could still think it was daring or an advance or "free speech" or anything just to say dirty words to millions. Or to show a tit or two or a cheek of bare ass, when in France you could see guys blowing themselves on television. Now *there* would be something, a contortionist who could blow himself on TV. What a flat world we were living in. Weren't there real things to be daring about? My smart kid's attitude, my sophisticated cosmopolitan intellectual give-a-fuck attitude. Too good for it all, too good for TV, only got into it for the fast bucks so I could go off and be superior. Zacky would be there when I was long gone, still politicking with the network guys, still leaving no fingerprints, still trying to get his way and once again be called the king.

Fifteen years later, for what it's worth, I can say that some version of it came to pass. Zacky wasn't the first to get a bit of "bare ass" on television, Jaworsky bait-and-switched him and that honor went elsewhere, but Zacky did go on to three more sparkling hits—an hilarious comedy set in a morgue, a touching and remarkably candid show about a Methodist minister, and a reality show involving intercultural dating—and his star on various Walks of Fame and so much money that he forgot how much he gave to Maryanna. Maybe he never got shaved pussy on network TV, but he eventually got a few cheeks.

And who's to say that's not an affirmation of free speech? Why not? Zacky must have felt the whole world was kissing his ass. Though I haven't seen him in a while now.

That night I also wondered: superior to who? The answer was obvious enough but I turned it around and around. Because he too had left the business. He too had faulted its vulgarity and lying and cost to the larger culture. He too had wished to be superior. An uphill battle, then? Did Tantalus have a father? Probably, since we all do. Melissa slept beside me, her light pure downy beginnings of a snore, as if just enough to touch the air passing through her. Letting it know, letting the air know, that she was alive? I hoped so. And what about me, who had all these big ideas. It wasn't so much that I had a book to write as that I thought I ought to write one. I ought to quit lying. But Zacky wasn't lying. Or Zacky lied about a few things, but not about his work, in his work he thought he was telling the truth. "Bare ass" he thought was the truth. So why shouldn't he stay right where he was? It was only me for whom it was fatuous and lies and the slow death that comes from wasting all your time. The critics would love "bare ass." It would give them something to write about. And they would love O'Brien covering up murder for the same reasons. We were entering a new America. I didn't know why, but we were. Something about the Wall, something about the day just passed? But it had already been going on, it didn't just start today, as if prophecy and intimation were just as real as facts. One thing I believed, anyway.

The world goes slowly or the world goes fast. America quietly, unconsciously, toughening itself up for the day soon coming when it would not be embarrassed by the word "empire?" Or was that day today? I counted up all my money as I once used to count up all the girls I'd fucked. Then I counted up what I thought I'd need and doubled it in case Melissa one day left. Then I asked myself if it was enough to double it, if Melissa one day left. Then I asked myself if I was crazy. Then I got up and wrote the scene that Zacky and Jaworsky and Bloch wanted me to write. Not that Zacky couldn't have written it himself. He could have and he would have. A simple scene, really. They were just giving me the chance to come along.

I won't trouble you with all the details, what O'Brien said, what Schlessing said. Just the facts, ma'am. Or cut to the chase, or whatever.

```
INT. O'BRIEN'S OFFICE - NIGHT

Schlessing leaves the lieutenant's office, rattling the
door, not looking back. O'Brien looks after him. The
squad room is emptying out.


O'Brien flicks the blinds of his office. It's something
he's never done.


Will it attract suspicion? Will someone think he's
sick?


He opens his top desk drawer and stares into it.
```

A long BEAT, then he reaches into his back pocket
and withdraws a handkerchief and with it lifts the
piece out of the drawer. He puts the piece into his
briefcase.

He reveals nothing. His face is like a dreamer's face.

INT. SQUAD ROOM — NIGHT

O'Brien traversing the squad room with his briefcase,
saying his good-nights. Kovel, LaRocca, Williams,
McBride, the new desk officer Tommy. As he's exiting,
Weiss and Limestead wrestle in a speeded-up guy who
goes nuts when he sees where he's headed, breaks free,
bites Weiss, smashes the vending machine which topples
over in the ensuing melee, and O'Brien doesn't notice.
Or he doesn't turn back, anyway. His walk is like a
dreamer's walk.

From a corner of the squad room, like Iago, Schlessing
watches him go.

EXT. AN AVENUE NEAR THE WATER — NIGHT

O'Brien, on foot, crosses in front of a darkened
warehouse.

A COUPLE OF HOMELESS MEN

Asleep in the warehouse doorway under newspapers.
O'Brien passes them by, rounds a bend so they cannot see.

A sixteen-wheeler clatters along the cobblestone
avenue.

EXT. A DESERTED WHARF — NIGHT

O'Brien walks out onto the wharf.

When he's far enough away, so that it seems like
he's the only man left on earth, O'Brien goes to the
water's edge, opens his briefcase, reaches into it
with the handkerchief in his hand, removes the piece,
and throws it into Boston Harbor.

He rubs his hands with the handkerchief as though to
get the dirt out, then drops the handkerchief into his
briefcase.

He walks back up the wharf. We see the tears in his
eyes.

Then I also wrote, for Zacky's eyes only:

THE HOMELESS GUYS AGAIN

They're stirring. They've got a bottle of Night Train.
They salute O'Brien as he walks past.

O'Brien, to return the greeting, pulls the belt of his
pants, drops his trousers and underwear, and moons the
homeless men.

```
CLOSE — O'BRIEN'S CHEEKS

As he wiggles them and shakes them.

THE HOMELESS GUYS

Amused, toasting him back.

RESUME

O'Brien pulls his pants back up, cinches his belt, and
continues on.
```

Got to get your cheap laughs somewhere. Show you're a sport. Show you know how to behave. And why did O'Brien cover up for Schlessing? A case of amnesia? The good of the force? Someone told him to and he did what he was told? Somebody who had something on him, somebody who could squeeze him, somebody who would have the last word? In the end I decided it was better not to explain it at all. A mystery, wrapped in an absurdity? Somebody somewhere might buy that. Or a case of amnesia? Tune in next time. Wasn't that the point?

The next day I called Bloch and told him I wouldn't be coming back to *Northie* the next year. That is, if there was a next year. Bloch assured me now there would be.

☙

It was the only time I can remember that my father became angry with me. When there's a divorce, when you go away, I suppose that already diminishes your authority. What else can you threaten, what more can you do? I suppose my father had never been angry with me because he didn't think he had the right to be. Or anyway not to show it to my face. But he was angry when I called him in London to tell him I was quitting the show.

"You're only doing this because I did it! Are you crazy? You worked hard for this! You're not going to get another deal, you know. Not as good as this one. You're on top of a top show! You could ride that for another ten years. Think of Melissa! Have you talked to Melissa? What if you have more kids? You never know what's going to happen. And you're giving up the series commitment too? Series commitments are like gold, and you just throw it back in the creek?"

Funny thing for me to say, but I didn't know he could be so angry. Or of course I must have imagined it. But hearing it was different, hearing it was as if I was hearing *him*. The way my mother would put the word *him* into italics, in her voice, in her bitter sarcasm, whenever the subject was *him*.

"I think it's different between you and me," I said. "You were doing it more as a protest. Because the business was your life. I'm doing it more to save my life."

"Don't get melodramatic with me now!"

But his anger was already softening, turning more toward pleading.

"Have you asked yourself, if there are two hundred fifty million people in America, how many of them would be quick to change places with you?"

"And the starving children in China."

"And those too. Right. Those too."

"I'm an ingrate, I guess. I'm leaving food on my plate."

The line went dead then. It's what I'd always hated about

phones. The person at the other end of the line, my father at the end of the line, out in California in the sunshine, could just stop talking if he wanted to and I'd never know if he'd ever talk again. And yet my father had never actually done that, until now. I wished I could see his face. I wished I knew what was inside him.

"Dad?" Did I say that, "Dad?" In that pleading way that was like his own.

I thought I heard his voice break. "I caused this. I'm sorry. I caused this."

"I don't think you did," I said.

☙

All the chances in the world to change my mind. Or it seemed that way at first. Everybody assumed, that is, Zacky assumed, Bloch assumed, my agent and over at the network they assumed, that I was just playing hard to get. Or that I was planning to test my free agency, that I would shop myself all over town. I told them all it wasn't so. I told them I just wanted to go write my books. Didn't Morty leave to go print beautiful books, or chase French girls, or whatever that was? But Morty came back, everyone pointed out. Bloch even sent Morty to see me. His emissary, the guy I'd listen to if I had a brain left. There's an old axiom in Hollywood that the more you don't want them, the more they want you. But Morty cautioned me this could be taken too far. There would come a point where it was too much trouble, where I was too far out to sea, and they would turn and move on. They, whoever *they* were, were superstitious and insecure but they were not crazy. I told Morty one reason I was leaving was that I felt envy for him, and he was my friend. Morty laughed as if I was the crazy one. "Envy's part of the sport," he said.

"I just want to do this one thing with a friend of mine," I said, and I told him about Charlie Chamberlain and the Cold War and the ending of the Cold War and Teddy's problems.

Morty had no answer for that one. Then Zacky called Melissa, to tell her of the hole in the show that I would leave. Then the company called my agent to say more money could be found. Then Jaworsky called to say that my scene with O'Brien made him cry. Then Bloch called. I don't remember every word, but I remember where we got to. "The best thing you can do if you want to get Teddy's project going is stay on the show another year."

"Because you'll quit backing us if I leave?"

"Because you'll be so busy they'll think they're stealing you," Bloch said.

"I want to write my books," I said.

"Nobody reads books anymore," he said. "Or I don't anyway. I don't have the time."

The things you hear. The things that must be true, if enough people say them.

The power of the created universe in your hands, you shmuck, and you throw it all away.

Bloch stopped calling after that. The company stopped making better offers. Zacky was polite but acted betrayed, almost as if I'd gone over to Morty. "Just do what you have to do." He said that a few times. An act of disloyalty, I guess, to question his world.

And then Sterner the agent heard something funny, he heard Adam was mad at me about something, and it wasn't that I meant to leave.

"What was it then?"

"I don't know. Nobody knows. You've got history with him, don't you?"

Which had to mean what I'd thought likely enough when it happened, that Bloch hated Teddy's apology and hated me for scheming to set it up. As if it had been more than he could look at. Better a billionaire isolate than a billionaire chump.

But Teddy hadn't really tried to make him a chump. He had tried, from the disadvantageous position of a supplicant, to open something in Adam. I suppose I wondered, if Bloch didn't have his billion dollars, would it have been different; if he had no gilded cage to retreat to, could he have been brought back to life? Too grand a way to put it, maybe, but at the time it seemed true enough.

All the emissaries, all the seductions.

But nobody ever came to me and said, "We'll stop this whole business with O'Brien, we'll throw those scenes out, if you'll stay." Not that I would have wanted them to. If they had, it would have only caused me problems. They would be taking away my easy excuse.

❦

Not as simple a thing as maybe I've made it seem, by the way. To chuck it all, the attentions, the flatteries, the miracle money, your picture in the paper, NPR or the *Wall Street Journal* or *Playboy* calling up, the tickets to games, the easy awards, the assumption you know something about the culture or are even doing your little bit to make the culture, people knowing who you are. Addictive the way everything's addictive, after awhile it gives you no pleasure but it keeps you from feeling bad. You withdraw the way you withdraw from anything else. As if it were seasickness you're trying to get rid of, you keep your eyes on the horizon.

It didn't hurt that I had already written a lot of the same thing. It may even have been, if I'd kept at it, that one morning soon I'd have awakened with no more urban fairy tales to tell. Another mild observation of mine, or maybe it was Morty's: television would be better off if they didn't hire the same people over and over again to do it. Few guys have that much to say, or if they do it's their compulsion talking, recycling the same things over and over in ways they can't even hear. Though isn't that the point? Product, again. What do producers produce if not product? Twenty-odd hours a year. Thousands of pages of script. I say the people doing it now, the geniuses, the new kings, but only because PR guys get paid to call them that, should do the right thing and politely step aside. Why not? A one series limit, or maybe two, like the two-term limit on the presidency. Bring in the new blood. It's a big country and there's lots of people who'd like the dough. All this is very likely to happen tomorrow.

I went with Teddy to HBO. Teddy told the story of Charlie Chamberlain as he wanted it to be told. They listened and asked a few questions. Two weeks later one of their guys called and said they'd talked it over and Chamberlain was surely a fascinating and dashing figure and they were quite interested in him as a character but his story was sort of a downer for the times. But what if we could change it so he was more of an unalloyed hero, he fought the commies with all his heart and now we've won? Would we be interested in that? I gave Teddy every chance to say yes. He needed the money, he needed the job. Sure we could take it to Showtime or Turner or the movies.

But HBO had been his idea of heaven. We went out and got drunk on tequila and wine. We pieced together the way drunk guys do that I was a dancing bear in a gypsy bar. Dance a few clumsy steps with a leash around my neck then stumble off the stage. Or he was, or we both were. We were friends again. We said no.

A few years later Teddy got somebody, an independent producer in Boston, to put up the money for a script about Charlie Chamberlain along the lines of what Teddy believed. But the script languished. Someone else rewrote it. Teddy got the rights back. As far as I know, he's still trying to set it up today.

I became unemployed and started to write and still Melissa did not leave.

※

Alternative theories of why I quit TV. There aren't any. Leave space blank.

None that I want to put forward, anyway. None that I really believe.

Fun while it lasted.

※

At some point I went over to London to see my father. We'd spoken on the phone, we'd even exchanged letters once or twice, but somehow I had expected to find him not as I found him. I'd imagined he'd be more with his rich friends, taken up by them, maybe going out with one of the widows or divorcees. He was after all in a fairly enviable spot. *Northie* was big in Britain. He could rightly claim to have been a recent consultant, he could be out there voicing his complaints and arguments, he could be writing fresh letters to the editor. And maybe he was. But he would have told me if they'd been printed. I found him in a one-bedroom furnished flat off Baker Street. Hardly the high-rent district. He told me about the tennis court where he played every day. He pointed out to me the stack of pages that was the novel he had begun to write. This I said nothing about, but it seemed so odd to me, he had never been a writer, even as a producer he had only made notes, little suggestions, rearranged or complained, hired and fired, he was from before the time when writers took over TV, and yet here he was. . . imitating me? It was as if life had reversed itself entirely.

I took him to lunch at the Ivy. Got him dressed up, so to speak. He was in his element there, the West End types, whoever else. An old agent came up and shook his hand, didn't know he was living in London now. He ordered the biggest plate of fresh berries I'd ever seen. Bigger than you could get at Michael's in Los Angeles. It made his eyes big and cheerful and a little conspiratorial and he called the waiter for a second plate. "There! There we are!" I felt as if he were talking to a little boy. "Look at *those*!" With the back of his fork he plowed berries onto the smaller plate. But really he wasn't talking to a little boy, it was just his happy fussing, a little like Zacky's *delectatio*. It's not true, as I wrote once, that I didn't like Zacky Kurtz much. In a way, I loved him. He just reminded me too much of my father.

When I had my plate of berries, he asked me, "Do you mind that I'm writing? I'm much worse than you, don't worry. No competition from me. But there's a few little things I thought I wanted to say."

"How's it going?"
"Terrible. I may quit."
"Don't."
"I start. . . but I get so tired."
"Just do a very little bit every day."
"I'm trying that. I'll get back to it."

But I didn't think he would. I thought he would get a certain way and then I could hear it in his voice, how he would stop.

"Why don't you write about Irene?" Something I shouldn't have said.

He shrugged. "Maybe," he said.

I never saw anything he wrote. But I'm sure he didn't need my stupid suggestion. It must already have been about Irene. Something about Irene, and it got too painful.

Or probably such thoughts comforted me. I didn't really want him to turn out to be a writer. It could be like his last shows all over again, and then what would I say? And what would I feel about my own prospects, if I came from dry seed? Or what if he was really good, what if he out-wrote me, what if that was the point of it all? The spur to my father's writing, if that pipsqueak can do it, then surely I can. I was afraid, somehow, of losing something. One way or the other, losing something. But what? Was there absolutely nothing about me that couldn't be taken away?

Questions that go all the way back and never really have answers. Unless the answer, put forward by the same folks that brought you the late medieval allegory of Passion and Responsibility, is somehow, awkwardly, Love? Did I become my father's voice because he would not be that voice himself? The berries were a little sour, but I added sugar, then they were good.

From the Ivy that afternoon we walked over to the National Gallery. I hadn't been in the place since I was there with my father and Irene, half a lifetime gone by. When I'd been in London with Melissa or on business, the Tate and the galleries were more our speed. Or even the British Museum. I loved the invisible dust of the British Museum. But my father was a National Gallery man. The Titians, the Raphaels, the Rembrandts. The canon of the West. His bible, I guess. I walked from gallery to gallery with him, often a little behind, not moving to the next picture until he was ready, until he had his say. Usually just a few words. "Marvelous."

But in the room with the Rembrandts he said nothing at all. I thought it was maybe because like me he was slightly bored. I almost said it, that I was slightly bored, that I had a hard time looking into the pictures' darkness. But it was in his silence that I saw those Rembrandts. He sat down on one of the benches. His legs may have been tiring, or he simply stopped to look. His face was a Rembrandt face then, shadowed, enduring, aware. Almost all the light gone except what was left, and what was left was more than I had imagined. As if when you take almost everything away is when you can see what everything is.

We went to his tennis court after that. It could have been private or it could have been public but it was not a fancy place. My father played in white shorts because he always played in white, but hardly anybody else did. He had an old guys' doubles game. He hustled around and I heard someone say that his forehand was strong. Don't go by me, I wouldn't know, I've forgotten what tennis I ever knew. But he seemed limber enough, he looked pretty good. When he was done, he introduced me around. The way he did things, "a writer," and then a few minutes into it something about *Northie*, and then everyone with their questions and comments and nice things to say. Though it couldn't really have been a surprise. They all knew about his own connection to the show.

"Why did you move here?" I asked him a little later.

"I have friends here. I always loved London."

"But do you see your old friends?"

"Of course. From time to time," he said. "But you know I don't really have their kind of money. This city is so expensive. Sometimes you can feel like a nuisance."

"Do they think that about you?"

"It's not what *they* think that matters."

"So why did you move here? You must have known all that."

"I was mad at Ronnie. And now Bush. What they're doing to our country."

"I'm glad you still call him 'Ronnie,'" I said.

"Reagan? That's his name. Did I tell you when I played chess with him in the Universal commissary and he didn't know that if you got a pawn to the end of the board you got any piece you wanted back?"

The part of the conversation that made me feel better about it all. "Ronnie." Great. If he'd lost his gift for name-dropping, it would have been as bad as losing his appetite. We both ate well that night, in an Indian place in his neighborhood. In stops and starts he began to tell me an idea he'd had for a screenplay. He was almost embarrassed to tell me, like a boy bringing home a new girl. The story line was this: a Texan television producer like or unlike Zacky Kurtz does a show where the hero is a brutal guy who beats people up or shoots them and then feels occasionally bad about it. One day the producer is flying his new plane, runs out of gas, and crash lands in the desert. Even his clothes get burned up, and most particularly his wallet with all his identification. He makes his way over the desert in his underwear and when he finds a deserted shack he breaks in and goes to sleep. In the morning a sheriff is there and arrests him. The shack was the site of a murder. The sheriff is a bully, almost a copy of the producer's TV character, except that after he beats people up or shoots them he doesn't feel bad about it. He is certain the producer did the crime, disbelieves everything the producer says, and proceeds to torture him to get him to confess. Beatings, shocks, hooks. The producer keeps trying to get on the good side of the sheriff, uses all his self-vaunted charm, tells him about his show and his hero/cop who is in fact a role model to the sheriff. It makes the sheriff even madder to hear all these lies and blasphemies about his role model coming from this "killer." It goes on from there. The producer suffers a lot. He eventually confesses and that only makes matters worse. And is there redemption in the end? Does the producer do penance, does he see any sort of light, does he even survive? To be continued, to be figured out.

"Write *that*," I said. "Don't write about Irene."

"Maybe I will."

"You could probably sell it for a bundle."

"I'm not really a writer, you know," my father said. "Maybe you should do it."

"Maybe," I said.

My father picked up the check.

☙

I suppose I always imagined that if I wrote about him, he would forgive me. A producer, after all, is the one who does whatever it takes in order to get whatever it is done. Why else have producers? But would he understand my urgency to write it, the urgency of unsaid things? Dear father, I understood this urgency so late.

How powerfully I missed him in those early years. I laid a sort of trap for him. This book I wrote, dark flower with thorns of rage and betrayal, these books, would be worth less to me if he did not approve. You can say that's wrong, but you can't tell a reflex that it's wrong. Something so far in there that you dig, you excavate, you try to act like some accomplished surgeon of the soul, at your peril, at the peril of it all.

☙

Though something else, not unrelated. Somebody said to me once, in a fit of irony, "The Germans have never forgiven the Jews for Auschwitz." Was it possible my father never forgave me for his leaving?

☙

I flew back the next day. He died the following summer, playing tennis on a hot afternoon. The preferred way to go, I think, if you're a certain kind of guy. A Japanese eats *fugu* until it gets him or it doesn't and an old Jew who's mad at America plays tennis through a London hot spell. When I got the news I didn't cry, but what does that mean? I told Carolyn, we told Carolyn. I said a kind of silent prayer that also had no words. His ashes went into the lake in Connecticut with Irene's. Thomas took care of that one. Thomas and his new family, his wife and the two kids she came with. And my sister was there, who'd seen him only twice in her adult life, had stayed away from him at every chance. There was a memorial gathering a few months later in Beverly Hills, at the house of old friends. I went with Melissa. We were the youngest there and in a way we were like the stars. Doted on and introduced, Melissa especially. My father must have told them all about Melissa, must have bragged, must have said how much he adored her.

All the old friends reminded me a lot of my father and Irene. A couple of retired directors and a lawyer who wasn't retired yet and their wives and the people involved with the County Museum and a woman who owned a lot of property in Santa Barbara and in a wheelchair with Parkinson's Gene Lang the composer whom I'd named my imaginary city of Langden after and some others I didn't quite figure out. No clergy, no rabbi, no Unitarian minister. It impressed me how many people came. There were few at first, but they kept showing up. In the middle of it, Thomas arrived. Just off the plane. We chatted for a while. He was getting started with a software business and had to go from there up north. I kept thinking, every moment I talked with him, how much he looked like Irene. It was as if I took all the resemblances we shared for granted, the dark eyes that were his and mine and our father's, our lips, our hair, our whatever else, and what was left, looking at me with an expression that might have been critical or might have been tragic, was Irene.

It doesn't seem fair to say what people said about him. You could go to all the memorials there ever were and never hear anything really different. But I would say that people seemed to think my father, whose name was Bill, had a gift for friendship. A few wept. Several mentioned his letters to the editor. Thomas told me in London he had had a lady friend. Someone from the tennis club, a schoolteacher, forty-five years old. It must have gotten going only toward the end. I hadn't heard a word about it. Then they played an episode of *The Dooley Boys*. Gene Lang had brought a cassette. It wasn't the episode I'd seen in Connecticut but it might have been. The wicked banker again. And at the end, the old Gabby Hayes type, over the end credits, singing "Oh My Darling Clementine." Somebody told me that my father had liked that song. I'd never known that.

Then I had this silly producer's thought that the song must be out of copyright, or they couldn't have afforded to play it each week at the end of the show. My father's thought? Or no thought at all. But by the time Melissa and I left, I couldn't get its tune out of my mind. It was like that song at Disneyland, when you take your kid to the Small World ride and then you can't get rid of it for days. The first verse. The chorus. I'd never really known the rest. Something about the miner's daughter drowning because she went too close to the water.

It was driving me a little crazy. It was driving me to tears. It was driving me back to my childhood.

In the car, Melissa said, "Try singing it out loud."

"I can't carry a tune," I said.

"Just do it. It's like hiccups. It'll get rid of it."

So I sang as much as I knew of the song.

"In a canyon, in a cavern, excavating for a mine, dwelt a miner, forty-niner, and his daughter Clementine."

My voice as flat and hoarse, maybe, as that old miner's. I remembered that my father couldn't sing either, or he said he couldn't anyway. I had never heard him sing. Not that I could remember. Not even "The Star Spangled Banner" at a ballgame, nor a song in a children's book.

"Oh my darling, oh my darling, oh my darling Clementine, you are lost and gone forever, dreadful sorry, Clementine."

I sang in our car parked in the street in Beverly Hills in front of my father's friends' house. When I was done Melissa was weeping. I held her in my arms.

ADAM THE KING

to Gayle and Sarah

I

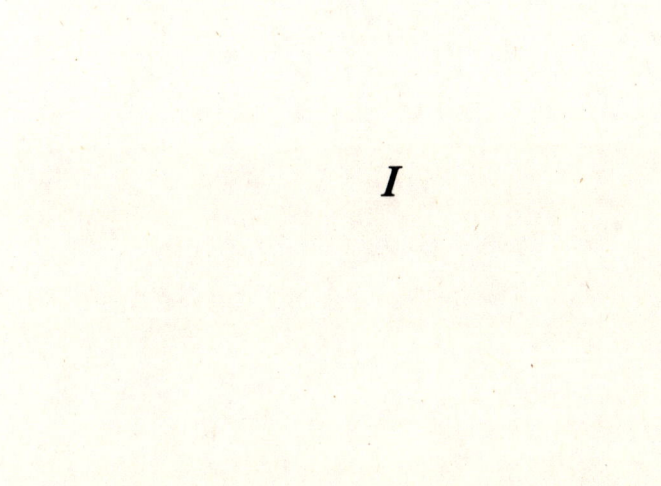

1

Adam and Maisie had the wedding of the year that year in Clement's Cove. And they were no longer young. He was in his fifties and never been married. She'd been married once, for about twenty minutes to a Navajo chief outside Taos and later she adopted two little Chinese girls, but mostly she had lived alone. They invited everybody as if it were once in a lifetime. Their families that hardly knew each other and probably never would, old friends, newer friends, an ecumenical crowd, those who got rich and those who didn't, those who invented something and those who played along, government guys, research guys, investment guys, TV guys, a few artists, a couple writers, doctors and lawyers and wives, ex-hippies who started country businesses and those whose best days were thirty years behind them. The meritocracy in all its multiform display. And they invited everyone in Clement's Cove, too. All the year-rounders, the people who weren't from away. A big tent, as the politicians used to say. And it was a very big tent. They had to clear trees to fit it on the land, a tent of Camelot or the Thousand and One Nights.

The caviar was flown in, the lobsters were rushed from Stonington, the rolls were baked that morning in Paris. Bloch paid for everything, though the Maclarens were still as rich as kings. It was his pleasure to pay. It was his desire. He attended to every detail, the flowers, the chairs, the valet parkers who came from Boston and had to be taught about the outcroppings of glacial ledge in the fields, the linens, the shuttles from the airport, even the weather, he would have fixed the weather if he could, he would have sent planes to seed the sky or do whatever they could do. But the weather report was bad and there was nothing that planes could do. In a way the wedding was an extension of the house that Bloch had built, the kind of place that people in places like Clement's Cove would once have called a folly, to build so outsized for the cove, and in the old shingle style, with a copper roof and a turret from which to see the sea in many directions and a flagpole like the mast of a ship and its porch wrapping around and around as if once you were on it you would never get off it. Bloch's Folly. He had built it all to surprise her. It was as if Maisie were a girl being blindfolded at her birthday party and couldn't take the blindfold off until somebody said "now" and the cake or the present would be there and she could like it or not. When she saw the house for the first time, all that I heard that she said about it was that it would be nice if it had a lap pool.

Maisie didn't care about the details of weddings, though she was happy enough that Bloch did. Somebody had to, so why not? She would be there and that was enough. What Maisie cared about were her two little girls, whether the day would be too much for them and if they would feel a little lost and who would take them for a walk. Whereas Bloch cared about Maisie as if the world boiled down to her. Maisie and her little girls and if he could do this one thing right.

All morning the catering trucks came and went, and the pickup trucks of the workmen, and the FedEx vans from the airport, like a parade in a children's book, the whole realm turning out with its tribute. The morning darkened as it went. The storm was coming from the south. It was the first weekend of September and there were remnants of hurricanes around and Bloch checked the sky and wondered.

I was one of the ushers that day, Cord and Teddy and I, and Maisie's brother and a few Maclarens I hardly knew. I watched the morning go gray and still from my own house across the cove. Most of the summer folk of Clement's Cove were gone but I had stayed on for this. Melissa was out in California packing for Berlin, where I had a fellowship and a book to write. Our own cottage in the cove could have fit into Bloch's garage. Cord's, which had been in his family since the twenties, was twice the size of ours and I had thought that was as it should be. I hadn't wanted to come in and buy a place larger than my old friend's. But Bloch had no such social thermostats to control him. Or perhaps he did but they were not reliable, they were prone to making mistakes, Bloch when he came to the moment of his life when he felt he was going to finally live it didn't know quite what to do. Maisie was his compass. Do it for Maisie. And if she didn't want it? Then back to the drawing board. Bloch was in a sense a purer creature than I. He had made all the money, for one thing. Billions. Bloch had made billions. The thing Americans did, make money, the thing that an American would do if he could. And all the time he had made it, he was storing himself up for the day when he would begin to live.

A tabula rasa, in a way. But if that's what he was, then how did you explain his terrible secret? When he was young, Bloch was the driver when Maisie's sister Sascha died in a crash. This happened when we were all staying at Cord's, just out of college, on a weekend in September when we were sending a friend off to war. How do you wind up close to a woman whose sister you killed in a crash? You are sincere with her as if you were standing naked before God. Or that's what I imagined anyway. Impossible for anyone to fathom. But then the crash had never been about it being Bloch's fault. It had been more about others, like Teddy and Cord and myself, needing someone to blame. And Maisie, who was wise in enough things, could probably see that, just as Harry Nolan, Sascha's husband, the friend we were seeing off to war, had seen it right away. It took many years for me, and even then I wasn't sure. Once in California Bloch saved me my job but I was never very grateful because he had been driving that car. And now he was marrying Maisie. And he had built this rich man's domain, that he could have built anywhere, but built it here, near where Sascha died. And he chose Cord and Teddy and me to stand up for him, who'd blamed him and probably tormented him and been slow to forgive. It was as if all his adult life, every moment he wasn't making money, Bloch had been quietly searching, in the same way other men search for a fountain of youth, for the antidote to tragedy, and now at last he had discovered, in a kind of mirror image of the past, burnished by time, something at least worth putting to the test.

On the coast of Maine the rich don't really believe in cars. They believe in boats more than they believe in cars. But they still have to get from here to there and only a few came by boat on this afternoon of glowering skies. By three o'clock the fields around the cove were spotted with BMWs and Volvos and the pickup trucks of the locals and the taxi shuttles from Bar Harbor airport where the private jets came in. Cord and Teddy still looked good in tails whereas I felt shoveled into mine. There were even rumors, courtesy of Cord, that Teddy had gotten lucky with a bridesmaid the night before. Teddy too old to grin in the old sheepish way when confronted with it, but there it was or there it wasn't. He who still led an anxious, disordered life, had given up writing in favor of a bicycle shop in Connecticut but more recently had careered around the country in one of those quests to screw one last time all your old lovers. If he was melancholy about it, he didn't say so. Cord, by contrast, the retired banker, who made a living helping out our classmate Fred Smith at Federal Express, was the first of us to retire to Clement's Cove year round and to lead what seemed the shorthand version of the good life, three great athletic kids who went to the public schools, charities, community involvements, wife out fighting the Wal-Mart coming in. Cord welcomed me to Clement's Cove, and welcomed Bloch in turn, when he bought the largest lot of all at the head of the cove.

Maisie still had her looks that day. She had endured Taos and Navajo tribal politics and gurus and throwing her money away and years alone and a second bout of Hodgkin's and still her red hair flew around in a perpetual tempest. They say red-haired people age less than others and it seemed true enough of Maisie. Her face was chubby, her green eyes still gave you hell on an instant's notice, and in her Vera Wang creation-of-the-day she somehow still looked like a virgin, albeit one who wouldn't last for long. Maisie had gotten used to money again. Bloch had allowed her to get used to it. And she had allowed him to get used to spending it, he who was the one who'd always turned the lights off when people left a room.

They stayed apart from one another before the wedding. A tradition here, a tradition there, pieced together like their lives. Bloch stayed in the house that had hardly been lived in and tilted his bowtie first one way then the other and pushed back his wiry hair so that no one could say he was hiding the receded hairline and rued his bulb of a nose that would not take a vacation for even a day and stared at his cello in live horror. Was he really going to play it? He had promised Maisie. She had made him promise. He had practiced for twelve years and no one had heard him yet.

A tradition here, a tradition there. A rabbi, a minister, each playing a part they were slightly unfamiliar with, polite to a fault, making it up a little as they went along, as if "Judeo-Christian" were a vaudeville act that could work out after all. Maisie's girls angelic with their flowers. The locals as dressed up as anybody else. The tent shuddering in the rising winds. The old aristocrats on the Maclarens' side, tall on average and a little stooped and if they were perplexed by anything, not showing it. Meanwhile we ushers seemed determined to look younger than we were. Cord's hair still seemed golden that day and Teddy's gaunt sunken look pretended to have mischief left and I sucked in my stomach.

And then the rain began. The minister recited Bloch's good deeds. The rabbi noted Maisie's courage. When Bloch kissed her, it was with lips so light they would not leave a mark on air, a phantom kiss, a kiss no one could see, you could see their lips approaching, you could see them almost touch. . . and then it was on to the music and the party and the next day it would be the lead wedding in the *Times*, the one where they show the couple in some happy, candid pose and tell little anecdotes about them to suggest how well they'll get along. In this case, the *Times* reported on the merciless storm that nearly blew down the tent and how the bride's father was among the guests who gripped the tent poles to keep them stable and how the storm began its howling in earnest just as the bridegroom, an amateur cello player, began regaling his guests with Saint-Saëns's "The Swan." The *Times* reported that Bloch played magnificently, undaunted by the storm, with a Nicolaus Kittel bow from 1853 that he had acquired in Budapest for ninety-one thousand dollars. In truth he played a little bit like a madman giving the performance of his life. Rain dripped down on him. Table ornaments flew around in the wind. People huddled under their jackets and in the dry spots and, as the paper reported, held onto the tent poles to keep the whole thing from folding up. And perhaps because Bloch played as if the howling storm were the counterpoint to his soul, no one left.

I didn't return to Clement's Cove for a year and a half. The book, the fellowship, the kids in schools and camps, a place we found for awhile far away where I could write and Melissa could paint. When I came back it was mostly to check up on things. It was early in May in a year when the mud season was slow to leave. Not even the black flies were out. I flew into Logan from Europe and drove directly to Clement's Cove on a bone damp afternoon. The road down to the cove twists back on itself in descent so that through the clearings you can see where you're going before you get there. I strained to see our own little house in its bed of trees and Cord's with its perpetually falling-down dock and several more, of the neighbors, all shuttered and stoic, like faithful servants in an old story waiting in silence for their master's return. I couldn't see Adam and Maisie's house because it was out at the head of the land, but when I turned into my own dirt drive and descended to the choppy gray water, there it was. Or rather, there was the burnt-out hulk of it.

I stopped the car, the way you do things, make certain gestures, just to prove to yourself the world's somehow changed. Adam and Maisie's house, Bloch's Folly, a burnt-out hulk. The walls stood, stained and scarred, but the windows were all broken and the porch roof collapsed and the copper roof was fallen in. It was worse than if it had been reduced to ashes. It was as if it had left a ghost behind.

A car was parked in the circular drive but I couldn't see a person around. I turned my own car around and drove over on the lip of road that hugged the cove. Some makeshift, temporary gates had been left open at a careless angle. I drove up between the poplar trees to the house. Another of Bloch's crazy gestures, because Maisie loved France he'd planted poplar trees, as if they were lining a straight road in the Ile de France, on the crooked coast of Maine. The trees looked young and a little clueless, as if they'd just been planted yesterday. I parked behind the green Explorer that I'd seen from across the water. The grounds still smelled of smoke and burnt things.

Whoever belonged to the car must have heard me coming. A small man came out with a smile. He had a yellow pad and had been making a list. Hi. How's it going? Not too bad.

"What happened here?" I asked.

"Not really for me to say. All they told me was to sell it."

"Like this? You're selling it like this?"

"As is. Correct. Why, you interested?"

"No. But I know these people."

"You're ahead of me then. They just told me to sell it. Terrible, huh? This was a beautiful place."

"It was."

"Terrible. A real beauty. You know, they imported seven tons of flagstone from Modena, Italy. A real tragedy. Of course, the flagstone's still intact. Can't burn flagstone... Well, if you'll excuse me..."

He went back inside. He left the door ajar and I could see him in the dark hall beginning to make more notes on his pad.

II

2

In the general store when they heard that Bloch had bought the head of land out to the Cove, Mac who owned the store said that what he heard was that he'd paid over three million just for the land and there was no way it was worth half that, because if you compared it to what Tim Hutchinson over in Orcutt paid for his, which wasn't that long ago, and Tim's piece had frontage too, four hundred feet of frontage, and he paid only a million for his, nine hundred fifty thousand to be exact, so compare the two, what Tim Hutchinson paid, what this Bloch fella paid, it just showed what some of these crazy people from away would do. Tom Benson the plumber said Bloch's was a nicer piece, it had views to Camden and a lot of Hutchinson's was mud at low, so you couldn't really compare. Ralph Audry who operated the transfer station said you could for sure compare three million to one million, and he added that generally speaking the prices were nuts over in Clement's.

Bonnie who was married to Mac and ran the store with him said it didn't matter to these people anyway what things cost, they had as much money as God and so who cared.

How much money *did* he have and who was this fella, Lewis Early who was retired from small engine repair and currently collected bottles and cans for redemption asked, and Mac said what he heard was two billion dollars and it was from dot com, and Carl Henry the lobsterman said he heard it was more like five and it was from owning a TV studio and Tunk Smith whose claim to fame was he was married four times said maybe twelve, he heard twelve and it was from playing the stock market and Bonnie said they were all wrong, this is how stories get blown out of proportion, what she heard was one billion, which was still a lot when you thought about it and it came from all of those things that were mentioned but in addition he invented something like tie-dyed, or not tie-dyed, stone-washed, it was like he invented stone-washed jeans or something and anyway who cared, he had as much money as God.

At about that point Verna Hubbard came in for her coffee. Verna cleaned houses and lived in a trailer over in Clement's on land that her father who was a fisherman had had and his father before him and Lew Early asked her what she'd heard and she asked him "Heard about what?" and he said about the big land deal out there to the Cove and if that property that the fella from away bought went for three million then what would hers be worth now? Verna said her whole property was the size of a three-cent stamp and the only view it had was trees and the propane tank and anyway she wasn't selling.

Yeah but they'll be raising your taxes soon enough, Ralph Audry said, who'd been a selectman and felt he was conversant with such things more than the average citizen was.

Verna said if they tried to do that she'd be over to Town Office the next morning and Burt Cummins would be hearing holy hell from her, but anyway she wasn't selling.

In the general store on the morning following the day when Bloch laid the foundation for his house, Con Stephens who was contractor for the stonework was in, but he wasn't talking. Ralph Audry said he'd seen the owner Mr. Bloch himself on the grounds the other day and he looked like an ordinary guy, kind of a short guy and he didn't wear a tie. Lew Early said what he heard was the guy had an architect up from New York and wherever this Mr. Bloch went, the architect from New York walked right along a half a step behind him, if they'd been any closer they would have been Siamese twins. This Mr. Bloch didn't say a whole helluva lot, but he seemed to know what he wanted.

Mac thought the fella better know what he wanted, if he was spending ten million dollars like that. Carl Henry asked who said it was ten million dollars. Mac said just figure it out for pity's sake, if the land cost three, the house was going to cost at least another six, so that would be right close to ten million dollars, by the time you had overruns and the like.

All these things they said were to get a rise out of Con Stephens, but Con sat there on his stool and drank his coffee and said nothing. Mac asked him how he could even drink that coffee, he was being so close-mouthed, but all Con did was grunt.

The talk turned to who was getting the work over there to the Cove and who was hoping to get work over there and Tom Benson the plumber observed that all the plumbing was coming from France so when it broke who was going to fix it. Tunk Smith, who was also caretaker of several properties in addition to having had four wives, said he had fixtures from France in one of his places and it didn't matter, France or Timbuktu, your basic toilet was your basic toilet.

Then Verna came in with Roy her boyfriend and what Roy heard, he said, was that this guy this Mr. Bloch was Jewish, he was a Jewish fella from New York, which finally got Con to say something, he said it didn't matter to him at all, whether the guy was Jewish or Buddhist or Hindu.

In the general store on the day Maisie came to Clement's Cove to see the house for the first time, Verna, who was herself overweight and wore jeans that didn't hide the situation, said that she'd seen her drive past and walking around the place with Mr. Bloch and she was a redhead who could use to put on a few pounds.

3

That thing about Maisie and the lap pool. There was more to it than appeared. In 1997 she had had her second bout with Hodgkin's disease. The chemo knocked her down and her recovery from it was slow. She who'd never believed in food fads or exercise fads or the whole nineties sense of "health" as a daily enterprise to substitute for prayer became a devotee of health food stores and gyms and anything that would give her a better chance. It wasn't that she'd changed her mind, it wasn't that she now believed in any of it, it was just she didn't know what else to do and now she had these little girls. The Hodgkin's had come six months after the little girls.

Bloch was part of that program too. Someone to take care of her, someone to take care of them all. She was harsh with herself when she thought of him that way, but she knew that enough of it was true. She knew, anyway, what he wasn't for her yet, and she doubted he ever would be. She didn't know. She didn't want to guess. He was there and that was enough. And for him, too, she thought. She could see his own needs. She didn't oppose them. In a way, she loved him for them. She felt grateful and lucky that he had needs and that her simply being there had something to do with them. A marriage of equals, then?

The house was part of his proposal. She had spent her childhood summers on the coast and had loved it as children will always love their one safe place, but when her parents divorced, the house on Mount Desert became empty and damp and she didn't want to go there. Clement's Cove was where the Elliots had gone forever and there was a piece for sale that was high and had views down almost to Rockland and she wanted a little pebbly beach for the girls and the Cove had such a beach. And so Bloch bought the land. He told her he bought the land. He showed her the plans, too, but she didn't want to see the house until it was built, she wanted the surprise.

Or really, she wanted Bloch to be able to give her that surprise, she wanted to be able to give him that much, she who hated the fact that otherwise she gave him too little. The day he took her up there, the day she saw it for the first time, the day she said it would be nice if it had a lap pool, was the day that he proposed.

But you have to understand, about the lap pool. Maisie loved the coast, the bay, the cove, but the cold water was hard on her now. Something about the chemo or something about the disease. Or something about just getting older. When she was young she'd swum like crazy in it, off Bartlett's or on Singing Beach, and left all the boys astounded. Fifty degrees, sixty degrees, who cared. The boys did, but not Maisie.

And now she needed to swim, for the exercise, for health, for the chance of it, for her two little girls, and anyway she'd always loved to swim, but if the water wasn't eighty-five degrees she'd shiver and feel faint and swimming more in it wouldn't warm her up. So the pool was for her health and for her spirit and for those she loved, and when she specified a lap pool it wasn't for fashion's sake, she simply thought a lap pool would be a smaller thing and would fit better on the rocky land and it was all she really needed.

On the day Bloch proposed, he tried to think things through

one more time. But which things? He wasn't even sure which things he should be thinking through. Whether she loved him enough or not or in what fashion or what love was or whether he loved her enough or was even capable of it or was his soul cold or if it was cold could it be warmed or what about this house, this ridiculous house he'd built and whether it was ridiculous or absurd or crazy or a folly like the locals used to say or a thing of beauty and comfort as he hoped that Maisie would say and whether it mattered what she would say, of course it would matter but would it be determinative and if so, determinative of what. The calisthenics of an agile mind. The one thing that Bloch had always had. But until he started dating Maisie, he never blinked.

How unfair, how untrue. Of course he blinked. He could remember blinking. But only once in a while. But after Maisie, after they ran into each other on a New York street and he managed to untie his tongue enough and she knew something about him, had read something about him, and so a dinner and then a lunch and then a dinner and then a weekend and there'd never been such a thing in his life before, Bloch blinked more. He'd read enough to know that someone like him was called an isolate by the world, and he was an isolate no more, because the one woman maybe in the world to whom he could explain the sickness of his soul and have it actually mean something, the sister of the woman he'd killed in a crash, he'd run into on a New York street.

Seventy-second Street and Madison, across from the Ralph Lauren. What was either of them doing there? They never said. Maisie was carrying a gym bag. Staying at her mother's old place. Bloch in town on business. This and that. One thing and the other. He who'd dated one starlet once, and been taken to the cleaners pretty good before she ran off with a day player with a drug habit, who'd otherwise never "dated" at all, who'd grown as rich as a tick on a dog in California and begun giving it away because he didn't know what else to do, who was fifty-four years old and an isolate who hardly ever blinked, became, with Maisie, a version of a happy man. Careful, reserved, courteous, undemonstrative, worried, precise, still too often on time for appointments, but no longer melancholy. When he proposed to her, he got down on his knees.

This was on the porch of the house in Clement's Cove and she was sitting on a French wicker chaise looking down the bay, and it was after she said whatever she said about the lap pool. Bloch the undaunted. Bloch the guy who took enough chances, when there was finally something he wanted.

He loved the kids. He moved back east. They made their plans. She got better. He fretted and stayed up nights reading the *New England Journal of Medicine,* so that if she wasn't better, if there were signs, he'd be the first to know. And he, too, began to love it on the coast, for all the reasons that people from away always loved the coast, but also for a few things he was almost afraid to say, even to himself, something about the way the land and sea were so intertwined, like lovers embraced. Their weekends there got longer. They stayed awhile. He began to know who people were in Clement's Cove and the people there began to know him, knew his face anyway, the sound of his voice with its traces of old Pittsburgh flatness, his neat appearance, not quite daring yet to be country, when he came in for his paper.

And Maisie, who was more a natural, who knew the coast, who sailed and gardened and cooked and took her kids around and who'd grown up so rich she'd almost forgotten about it, came and went like someone who belonged there, or as if she didn't care whether she belonged or not.

What she said to him once, what he said to her:

"You're the most awkward, funny, ill-at-ease, quiet, confused, dopey, clueless, smart one I've met yet."

"What does 'one' mean?"

"I don't know. I'm not sure. I'm just trying to say thank you."

4

What Bloch thought about his wedding, all in all: that he got through it, that she was his now, that all of this was his now, or hers now, that he was a fool to think such thoughts. That the rolls were good. That the lobster was good. That his playing was atrocious. That no one noticed that his playing was atrocious. That society, or what he'd always imagined society to be, or enough of it, was there, and wasn't that a kick too, and how could that have happened to Adam Bloch from Pittsburgh. That the rain was a gift of the gods. That the rain was really something. That she did not love him.

What Verna Hubbard thought about the wedding, all in all: that it was some to-do. That it was nice, it was the right thing, to invite everyone. That Mac and Bonnie were sure all dolled up. That the call from that lawyer in Bangor the other day, saying he represented Mr. Bloch on a matter and would like to talk to her about it at her earliest convenience, what was that all about? That whatever the musical instrument was that he was playing, Mr. Bloch did a nice job of it, it was beautiful, she liked it. That she didn't really like the idea of this big house going up next to her trailer, but if it had to be somebody, and it had to be, because it was in the nature of progress and how things were going these days, then it might as well be these Bloch people, and why shouldn't they be adopting little Chinese girls, nothing wrong with that, she'd do it herself if she had the money. That the bride could put on a few pounds. That he could have kissed her more. That it didn't matter about the storm, sure it was a storm but what did you expect, don't get married on the coast of Maine, go get married in Pasadena, California, if you don't want a storm. That he was playing a *cello*, of course, a cello, what was she thinking, the cello's the one that's that size, Donny Hendricks in Penobscot played one just like it, in the Baptist church, and Donny wasn't good at it at all, by comparison, when he played it was like a toothache. That whatever this lawyer for Mr. Bloch was calling her about, she'd listen politely, of course. That Roy could have come to the wedding with her, it wouldn't of done him a bit of harm, but that was a whole other story that she didn't want to think about or talk about.

What they thought, all in all, about the wedding in the general store: Bonnie thought it just showed what money could buy. Mac thought the lobsters would've been better if they got them right there in Bucks Harbor, Bucks Harbor Marine, what'd he go all the way over to Stonington for just for lobster? Ralph Audry thought, along similar lines, if they'd hired Pete Ellison over in Sedgwick for the band, Petey's got a helluva band, much better than these guys, wherever they were from, Petey's been playing at the Reef in Castine and all over, and he's good, wouldn't have been a poor choice at all, to go more local with that.

Lewis Early thought they should have postponed it on account of the weather.

Burt Cummins thought that was ridiculous.

Lewis thought it wasn't ridiculous at all, they postpone ballgames all the time, they could have done it just like a ballgame.

Burt Cummins said ballgames don't have out-of-town guests who just have a weekend to be someplace.

But so you postpone it a few hours, a rain delay, that's all, why not, Lew Early said, people get stuck in old ways of thinking and that's when you get rained on.

Carl Henry thought the bride, contrary to what Verna Hubbard was saying, didn't need to put on a few at all, she had a terrific figure for a gal of her years.

Tunk Smith estimated those years to be between forty-two and forty-five.

Carl Henry heard, *au contraire*, more like fifty-two, which was hard to believe but Bonnie said she could have had some work done, of course, and Lew Early said what kind of work and Bonnie asked what kind of planet Lew had been living on, if he didn't know what "getting work done" meant.

Con Stephens, who was still working for Mr. Bloch on the house, expressed no thoughts at all about the wedding, as he felt, given his contractual arrangements, it would not be seemly.

5

On their wedding night Adam and Maisie stayed in the house that he had built. In most of the rooms there were only sticks of furniture, the first pieces to arrive, outposts, like the occasional houses you find in old photographs of American cities, where whole blocks have been laid out with nothing on them except these lonely pioneers. Maisie fed the girls wedding cake for dinner that night and read them the story by Robert McCloskey set in Bucks Harbor about a girl who lost a tooth. Old favorite. Maisie's mother had read her the same story, in a year when that story was new.

They ate their cake in the half-empty kitchen and she read them the story in front of a fire. The living room's fireplace was so vast it looked like it could eat the room, but Maisie and her girls cuddled in front of it, lying on sleeping bags and pillows on the floor, like kittens all together. Maisie built the fire because she was the one, between her and Bloch, who knew how to build fires. She'd never been a girl scout but she'd put in her time outdoors. Bloch watched it all like an old dog of the house beholding its settled world. Not the usual thing with him. Then they all went upstairs.

Their bedroom was the one room of the house that was filled with furniture and things, as if it were a place for them to barricade themselves in, like the "safe rooms" the rich build in New York in case people came to rob or rape. Maisie's idea, to fill up this one room and make it livable right away. Bloch understood, but only in a secondhand way, that the emptiness of the rest could be intimidating. He'd only ever lived in apartments. He expected houses to be intimidating. He was doing all this for them, and the sooner the rest of the furniture arrived, the sooner Maisie picked it out, or somebody picked it out, or they just ordered a carload of it, the better, as far as he was concerned. For himself, he could have lived as a monk.

But didn't he want the world to know what he had done? Wasn't that how palaces and mansions and villas and Maine summer cottages in the old robber baron style got built? Bloch wasn't sure, as he wasn't sure about much, except that he wanted them all to be comfortable, and in this bedroom upstairs, and in the little annex next to it where the girls would sleep for now, and in front of the fireplace downstairs when the rest of the cavernous room was dark, and in the kitchen where you could stand up and eat cake in front of the Sub-Zero's open doors, all seemed comfortable, as if right with the world.

Maisie put the girls to sleep and Adam kissed their foreheads and then Maisie got undressed in the bathroom because she didn't like to get undressed in front of people, she liked walking naked but not getting undressed, it was something sexual and she didn't understand it. Not that she didn't understand about sex. She understood it about as much as anybody. But she had become humble about the parts she didn't understand, because it seemed more truthful to be that way than otherwise. She didn't mind Adam seeing her naked. In a way, there was nothing sexual about it. But getting undressed, she felt invaded and she didn't know why. Something about straddling two worlds, being caught between two worlds. She didn't want even his eyes, or especially his eyes, to invade her; and what Maisie wanted, Adam accepted, though he couldn't help but yearn.

Hers was a body that welcomed freckles. They were like ants on the picnic of her body, and there was something friendly about that too. She came out naked and walked around naked and Bloch looked mostly at her eyes and took his pants off and laid them on a chair because he always laid his pants, folded, on a chair, as though he were visiting a cheap whore, though that had never been Bloch's style. In his underpants, sitting on the edge of the bed, the flesh of his stomach fell over the waistband of the pants, yet Bloch was not a fat man. Nor was Maisie fat, though there wouldn't have been many like Verna who thought she should put on a few. Her shoulders were round, her unsuckled breasts still argued against gravity at least a little bit, her hips were broader than they'd been. A milkmaid's body, or so she thought, when she thought about it at all. Both of them were over fifty years old and they'd seen each other's skin.

She went to the window and put open the curtains and tried to see what she could see, across the cove or down the bay. Bloch shuddered when she did this, as if others could then see her naked. And then what? He didn't know, he couldn't imagine it, any more than he could imagine himself standing naked in a backlit window. It was night. The storm was passed and you could see for miles. But was anybody out there? He wasn't going to change her, she who teased him for his fears and his shyness and may even not have liked him on their account, so he said nothing and kept his shuddering to himself and Maisie cupped her hands to her eyes and pressed her nose to the glass so that she could see better and said, "Louie's watching TV."

"You can see over there?"

"I can see the TV's on. That horrible light."
"What's he watching?"
"I can't see that."
"Can you see him?"
"I can't. The room's dark."
"Can he see you?"
"Would you stop it, please?"

But because he said it, she stayed an extra minute by the window. She couldn't let him get away with that. When she finally came to the bed, he was under the covers with a section of newspaper two days old. She got in on her side as if they'd been married forever and he put the paper down.

"So."
"So..."
"It looks like we did it," he said.
"It looks like we did," she said.
"Do you regret it?" he said.
"I don't know yet," she said.
"I don't," he said, and his words felt lonely in his ears, it was as if he could hear them abandoned there.

Bloch wished to reach for her then, to reassure himself. But he didn't, because he had learned that when he reached for her to reassure himself she always turned him down. There must have been something in the reaching, an invisible strain of muscle or spirit, that showed through and warned her. It was impossible to fool her, impossible to be bold when he didn't feel bold, and so instead of reaching for her he said, when the room seemed quiet again, their small talk dispersed in the lighter air that had come in after the storm, "I spoke with Jackman the other day."

"Who's Jackman?"

"The lawyer in Bangor."

"About the pool?"

"He called the Hubbard woman. She hasn't phoned him back."

"Is that really the only way?"

"It's the only practical way. It's the way that makes sense."

"I hate her to have to move."

"Do you?"

"If she doesn't want to."

"If she doesn't want to, then I suppose she won't. But I think she will want to."

"Because of what you'll offer her? Just don't say 'people have their price,' okay? Just don't say that. I'll hate you."

"Well. We'll see."

"I hate money," Maisie said. "That's called ingratitude, right? That's what's called spoiled."

"You're hard on yourself," Bloch said.

"When would it be built?"

"The pool?"

"By spring?"

"I'd hope so. It depends."

For a moment Maisie imagined living in Verna Hubbard's trailer. She imagined cooking smells, cabbage and vinegar. She imagined the floor flexing when you walked on it. She took the clips out of her hair and lay them on the table next to the bed. She gave her hair a shake and rubbed her scalp a little.

"I don't feel like it tonight. Do you mind?"

"No," Bloch said. He tried to make the word sound solid, rounded, truthful.

And because he didn't like to lie to her, even if it was to keep the peace, even if it was to try to be a bigger man than he was, he told himself it was nearly the truth, because of course he minded, but he felt it was a part of life, for people to not feel like it, for people to mind when the other people didn't feel like it, and for the minding to begin to dissipate, like their words in the lighter air of the evening, when you thought about it that way.

She kissed him and moved away from him and they went to sleep.

Bloch dreamed of how lucky he was.

6

On Adam and Maisie's wedding night, Verna waited up for Roy. There was nothing on TV as usual Saturday night so she put in a tape of *Sleepless in Seattle* and ate a ninety-nine cent box of mints from the dollar store in Ellsworth. She watched the tape even though she knew the end and she ate the mints even though the chocolate on them didn't taste like chocolate and she wondered what Roy could be doing. He was out with Freddy. He said they had a job but Freddy was always saying he had a job. But on the other hand it was Saturday night and if you had a limo this would be the night to have a job. But what would he need Roy for?

She tried his cellphone but it was never on. That was another thing. She asked him to leave it on and how hard a thing was that? He said it wore the battery down but if somebody said to her to please leave hers on, she'd leave it on, if she didn't automatically anyway, which as it happened she did. Roy had his opinions about things. That was the polite way you could put it. Though along with his opinions also came ideas, Roy had enough ideas to stuff a car trunk, and that part about him she liked. Or anyway when they didn't get too crazy, which sometimes they did, in particular when Freddy was involved. But at least he didn't just sit there. Roy, she felt, had the chance of doing something for himself one day, and that was more than she could say for some others.

Not that there were a lot of others, by way of callers. Roy

was about it. So where the fuck was he, Verna wondered irritatedly, then worriedly, then more fondly, until it was twelve-thirty in the morning and the sheriff called to say where he was, which was in their custody, in Ellsworth. They put him on and she was so upset she put her hand over the phone so that it wouldn't make matters worse, Roy hearing her in a disordered state. He said on the phone, in a voice that sounded more intimidated than himself, that the situation over there was all a big mistake and he was going to fix it but in the meantime could she come over and be sure to bring her credit card.

By the time Verna got over to Ellsworth, Freddy's wife Marilyn had bailed out Freddy, so that Roy was alone. The sheriff's station was a place that had fluorescent lights everywhere, which in the middle of the night was especially disconcerting, it made you feel like you were in an experiment where they deprive you of sleep. Verna had been in the station before, but not often, and not for anything that you could call outright criminal on anybody's part. Her dad had been driving drunk once and once Roy was in a bar fight, where it definitely wasn't all his fault, but his big mouth had got him in more trouble than should have been the case. Now a sheriff's deputy brought him out after another deputy ran her credit card through the machine. Two hundred fifty dollars, which would, however, as the deputy explained to her, be eligible for a hundred percent refund unless Mr. Soames failed to appear when and as required. The deputy who brought Roy out didn't hold his arm or anything, Roy came out like a free man. He gave her a look like he wasn't going to say anything while in enemy territory and she oughtn't to either, and they walked out to her car.

Verna drove an older Celica that without the rust spots wouldn't be considered in too bad a shape. They were driving away from the station before either of them said anything. Then Roy said his car was still over in Bar Harbor but they could go get it tomorrow, it didn't have to be tonight. In a way it was unnecessary for him to say that, unless to remind Verna he was being contrite and a reasonable man, since Verna was already driving toward Clement's Cove, not Bar Harbor. Then Roy said, "Thanks for coming out for me," and after that they didn't say anything until they were more than halfway home.

Then he asked her if she wanted to hear what happened, because it was not too bad a story really, now that he was going back over it in his mind, he could laugh about it now. Verna didn't like it if Roy was going to make a joke of it, so she said, with considerable plainness, "Sure. What happened?"

So Roy told her, as follows. Freddy had been putting out some advertising where the cruise liners come in at Bar Harbor, for his limousine services. The people on these cruises, they're on vacation, they've only got a few hours, they want to see a few things, money's no object with them. So even though everybody had a good laugh when Freddy bought the old limo, in fact Freddy knows what he's doing sometimes. So these two ladies from Cleveland come up to him earlier tonight, and the only thing they want to see is where Francesca Romano the celebrated Food Channel chef lives, on account of the fact that on the cruise ship they'd been telling everybody the fact that Francesca Romano had recently bought a house and now lived over this way, and that was the one thing they were all atwitter about. They offer Freddy two hundred dollars just to take them where Francesca Romano lives. You wouldn't want to say no to that. So they all go, in the limo, over to Pretty Marsh, and these old ladies, they don't give a hang about all the Rockefellers, all they want to see is where the celebrated Food Channel chef lives. And he, Roy, was driving for some reason, though he has no idea where she lives, he was just going where Freddy said to go, turn here, turn there, all they've got over there, on Mount Desert, is a lot of high bushes anyway, you can't see anything, not even in daytime, and this wasn't daytime.

So after about twenty minutes or maybe a half hour Roy turns down this dirt road *per* Freddy's instructions, and it's totally unmarked, the ladies are starting to bother, but that's how these rich and famous people like it, Freddy says, their privacy, all of that, he's starting to sound like the guy who did that TV show about the lifestyles of the rich and famous, if she, Verna, happened to remember that.

Roy himself was beginning to have his doubts, along with the ladies, when up ahead, sure enough, there were lights on. So he drives up into this big circular road and there's this house about the size of what the guy from wherever he was from Mr. Bloch built over by her, and before the ladies could like even gasp and ooh and ah, Roy sees this woman with a housecoat coming out of the back of the house somewhere and running through the woods like a crazy person, like any second she was going to start running naked in the woods or something. And he could see she had a cellphone, she had her arm up to her ear like a cellphone, and that was weird too, and Roy didn't like it because, as Verna knew, crazy people were not exactly his type, but anyway the ladies were still going batshit about the house and how big it was and whether it was in good taste or not, considering that this was the Queen of Italian Cuisine's house, and Freddy was telling him, Roy, to cool it and calm down, because the customers were getting what they paid for and the customers called the shots, which Roy actually of course had to agree with in some sense.

But then, okay, they start to leave, because at the same time Freddy didn't want any trouble. So they were leaving, they were back on the dirt road, and suddenly in his headlights straight ahead Roy could see there were these big branches and logs across the road, it was like a big old beaver dam or something, and this woman in her housecoat, she was just piling things up, as fast as she could. And of course it turns out this was Francesca Romano herself. And there was no way around that roadblock, she was as good at building a roadblock as she was good at cooking up a lasagna. Like Freddy and himself the ladies also couldn't believe she could build that roadblock like that, but they were even more excited to be seeing Ms. Romano in person, and were just getting out of the limo so they could go over and introduce themselves and maybe get her autograph when the sheriff's cruiser pulled up. Francesca Romano had zero interest in meeting these ladies. She just wanted all of them arrested for trespass and some other things.

However the sheriff told her he couldn't arrest the ladies because they were just like the male suspects' captive audience or something and so she drops the charges against them but not against Freddy or himself. He and Freddy tried to explain how they just got lost and didn't know where they were but one of the ladies, real helpful, said they were all out looking for Francesca Romano's home but of course she and her friend didn't know it was illegal or anything because they just thought they'd drive by on the road, which was public of course. Jesus. So that was about it. The sheriff took Freddy and himself over to Ellsworth and impounded the limo and then he called her, but now that he's thinking about it, it's almost funny.

That Francesca Romano, that was the part that was almost funny, seeing her running around in her housecoat. And that roadblock she built. Just like a beaver dam. Verna listened to this whole story but didn't laugh at the funny parts the way Roy did. She laughed a little, but not too much, and when he was done the first thing she asked him was, "So how old were these ladies?"

"Ah, who knows. I mean, they weren't *old* old."

"Thirties?"

"Maybe. Who knows."

"Twenties?"

"Definitely not. Not twenties, for sure. Definitely."

"And they read Freddy's advertising, that's how they hired Freddy? Like, he's got brochures?"

"I guess so. Sure. Why not?"

"Because last time I saw Freddy, he was talking about doing up some brochures but he said no way did he have the money for it yet, he was talking all this stuff about cost-effective, whether it was cost-effective, he'd have to see."

"Well I don't know if he printed something up exactly yet. Hey, who cares, right? He got the customers."

"Yeah. How? And how come he needed you along?"

"What are you saying here, Verna? What are you suggesting?"

"Oh nothin', Roy. Nothin' at all. I'm not suggesting you two shitbags just picked up these girls off the cruise and were just driving them around in Freddy's shitbag limo trying to impress their pants off 'em. And this thing, you think I believe this stupid shit, this fucking story like I'm a moron, two "ladies," *ladies*, hire a limo after it's dark to go look for houses? And then I come bail you out? You call *me* to bail you out? Why didn't you call those whores from the cruise line, why didn't they bail you out?"

"This is a lie," Roy said. "You're getting yourself crazy for a lie."

"Am I?"

"Absolutely."

"Asshole. Dickhead."

By then they were pretty much back to Clement's Cove. Verna blamed herself more than she blamed Roy. When she got home she threw out what was left of the ninety-nine cent mints. She imagined the whores from the cruise ship were skinny.

Roy had to admire one thing about Verna, her capacity to figure certain things out. But he didn't tell her this. He promised to repay her the money. She said he didn't have to repay her the money, he just had to make his court appearances, and he'd need his money for a lawyer, so thank you very much and good-night. The last thing Roy told her was that he was going to fix this whole thing because it was a big mistake, so she shouldn't worry about that part of it.

Roy didn't go to sleep right away because Verna didn't want him in her bed, and while he was up he saw by the phone Verna's note to herself to call Mr. Bloch's lawyer in Bangor. As soon as he saw the note, Roy thought to himself maybe Mr. Bloch wanted to buy Verna out. Why wouldn't he? Her trailer was an eyesore. Even Roy could see that. Roy read the note again with considerable excitement. It made him remember that Verna was sitting on a gold mine.

7

The problem was the ledge. Almost all of the head of land that Bloch had bought was ledge. There was dirt on it and things grew on it but the dirt was thin and the things that grew on it had shallow roots and even the trees that grew for thirty years could blow over in the winter storms. It was a beautiful piece of land but it was fragile and obdurate at once.

Verna's father Everett had kept the softest piece for himself. He had sold off most of the rest in the fifties and then again in the sixties, but Dottie had wanted to keep her garden, which had peonies and unheard-of good tomatoes, and so he moved the trailer over close to her garden, which was on the one deep pocket of soil that was there. The land that was left for Bloch to acquire would need blasting out the ledge with dynamite if you even wanted to put a lap pool in, and you couldn't blast too close to the shore because there were the state laws against it, and in the spine of the land were the high trees that gave it its privacy and majesty so that the architect said for God's sake don't blast there, and if you put in a lap pool too close to the house, so you could see it from the house, the house would become like a California house, modern and convenient, which was the last thing you wanted on the coast of Maine. The lap pool would have to be hidden in the woods but there was no place to hide it in the woods.

And then there was Verna's land. Everett Hubbard had never owned the entire head of land, but if you went back in the deeds you would find more than a hundred years ago or even before the Civil War that the Hubbards and the Masons and the Clements held it all. They were mostly fishermen and the land wasn't good to farm and over time all three families sold off here a piece and there a piece, and by nineteen hundred the rest of the cove with its pretty views and safe water was being sold to the rusticators from Bangor or Boston or even farther away, but Everett Hubbard's father, William, became a kind of a holdout when even the other Hubbards sold, and Everett took after his father, selling when he felt he had to but never all of it.

And now Verna had the little piece where Dottie's garden had been and where Verna still grew a few tomatoes herself and where you could put in a lap pool or anything else if you wanted to because the ground was good for it and it was far enough away from where Bloch had built so as not to be seen. It was on the road coming into Bloch's place, but you could screen that off with trees.

What Bloch thought about all of this was that if she didn't want to sell, she wouldn't sell. It was as simple as that, really. He wasn't going to intimidate her, he wasn't going to scare her off her land, or build high fences around her land so that she'd be living in a prison, or anything else. If she didn't want to sell, she wouldn't, and then he'd think what to do next.

And in fact intimidating her was the opposite of what he wanted. What he wanted was to be accepted here, and he knew the locals were part of that. He wanted to go into the general store and buy his paper and have the people there say hello. After the anomie of California, after the rough and tumble of the various business worlds where he'd made his exceptional pile, after a life lived alone, he wanted finally to live somewhere. He wanted Maisie, he wanted her little girls, to live somewhere too. And of course there was New York, they would live in New York, they would do all the things you do or can do in New York, but he still wondered if New York was somewhere. "Somewhere" meaning that if you came back to a place half a lifetime later, what you remembered, or enough of it, would still be there. Or if the place itself remembered, if the place remembered you.

Bloch remembered more than enough of Clement's Cove. It had never left him, and it was far from happy what he could not forget, but he knew of no other place where he and Maisie had a chance. And she needed to swim and the sea water was too cold and so he hoped that whatever he offered to buy out Verna Hubbard, it would be enough so that she would want to sell.

So he offered her a half million dollars and in addition to move her trailer to wherever she wanted it moved to. He'd come to this figure after talking it over with Jackman, the lawyer in Bangor. Jackman said it was twice what that little landlocked postage stamp of land was really worth. Bloch wanted to offer her enough to be generous and to be seen by her to be generous but not so much that he'd seem like a fool, or someone who was coming in and throwing his weight around, or someone who was disrupting the way life was. He was already dimly, vaguely aware of what some people were saying about his house. When the house was about halfway done he'd overheard workmen talking at lunch and it had frightened him and almost discouraged him. He wanted Verna to be happy and not be mad at him and to tell others what a reasonable man he was.

What he would never say is Maisie made him do it. Or that he was doing it for her or her health or that it had anything really to do with her at all. It was always "we" who wished to acquire Miss Hubbard's land if we could, we who wanted a lap pool. And wasn't it so? He wanted to make her happy. Only to our old friend Cord would he even mention Maisie's name in connection with any of it.

Verna turned down Bloch's offer of half a million dollars. She called up Jackman the lawyer in the days following the wedding and Jackman explained what Bloch was proposing and conveyed the offer and Verna fussed inside herself at first because she'd never heard half a million dollars connected to her name in her life before and didn't know who to talk to about it. All she knew was that she didn't want to talk to Roy. She wanted to talk to somebody who wouldn't be overwhelmed by hearing a half a million dollars and who wouldn't have a prejudice, or something they were trying to get out of it for themselves.

Finally she decided she would ask Cord Elliot, Mr. Cord Elliot, because he was around for a couple of weeks now instead of traveling someplace all over the world like he usually did in September and because she cleaned house for Mrs. Denny Elliot once a week and because Verna's father in his retirement after he was done with fishing had been the prior generation Elliots' caretaker for a number of years and Everett always said all the Elliots were pretty good but this young one, this Cord fella, was particularly pretty good, which had been Verna's experience subsequently.

She knew that Cord Elliot was friendly with Mr. Bloch but not too much more about it than that. It was a chance but anyway she took it. After her half-day cleaning over there she sought him out in his study and told him about Mr. Bloch's offer and asked him what he thought and whether it was a good offer and what should she do.

Cord first had a good laugh because Mr. Bloch had apparently not said anything to him about it and he thought, he said, that it was a little cagey of old Mr. Bloch and wasn't he becoming the land baron of Clement's Cove. Verna said she figured he was. Then Cord asked Verna what it was she wanted to do, what was her gut instinct, as the people in business were always saying these days, and Verna said it was all so sudden, she didn't have any gut instinct, she could hardly think about it but a half a million dollars was quite a lot of money.

Cord asked her if she needed the money.

Verna, who tended to be understated about money because she felt that if she was understated people would believe she was more familiar with it than she was, said she didn't exactly need it but it couldn't do too much harm, that was one thing for sure. Verna said she didn't know what her father would have done. All the Hubbards had always fished out of Clement's and she still had her father's old boat out in the falling-down lean-to she called her "boathouse" and she didn't know about that either.

Cord said it sounded like she wasn't ready to make up her mind yet but if she said no he was fairly sure Mr. Bloch would come and offer her more money than half a million dollars and maybe that would help her decide. Verna couldn't believe at first that Mr. Bloch would offer her more money but Cord Elliot laughed and said again he was fairly sure of it and so she told Jackman the lawyer, politely, no, she wasn't going to sell. Bloch raised his offer to three quarters of a million and she said no and then he raised it to a million and she still said no. In the meantime she'd been thinking about her father's old boat in its lean-to and how Everett sold off bits and pieces but never sold off all and how she liked the little bit of woods her trailer sat in and the way her tomatoes grew strongly like her mother's had. And who knew what the whole place would be worth in another hundred years?

Bloch made his final offer at a million and a half dollars. Jackman told her it was his last and final offer. The way Bloch thought about it, he could offer her any amount of money but if she wouldn't take a million and a half, which was already so many times more than the property was worth, then she didn't want to sell at all. Verna thought about all the money so hard that for two nights she couldn't sleep and Roy wondered what was the matter with her. She visited Everett's boat, which he'd built himself in his last years, she sat in the lean-to with it as if asking her father's advice. It was a sleek little boat with a lap-strake construction and less of a prow than the ordinary lobster boat and Everett always said it was going to be his boat for pleasure, not for work, but he died before he ever got pleasure from it. Or that wasn't so. He had the pleasure of building it, the pleasure of coming out to look at it on winter nights, away from everybody else, sitting out there with a charcoal brazier and what he dreamed about. Verna remembered that, or some version of that. But he only put it in the water once, to test it out, and it didn't sink, and that was in autumn, and that winter he died. And she'd never put the boat in herself, she was afraid of it or too in awe of it. Verna didn't even like boats, but she had reverence for this one. She decided it was telling her it didn't want to be moved.

So she said no again, to one and a half million dollars, and Bloch and Jackman made one last try, despite the previous offer being Bloch's last and final offer, Jackman said Bloch would in addition pay for a new plot of land to put her trailer on, but it didn't change her mind.

The next time Adam ran into Cord, on the road going

around the cove, he said nothing about his negotiations with Verna Hubbard. They talked about the dolphins that had been coming into the cove recently and the weather and the Republicans and whatever and when they'd talked those through, a bit laconically, because Bloch was still not a big talker even with a friend, Cord decided to ask him about Verna and her piece of land. It was partially, but not entirely, a case of his instinct to tease someone who in his view could use a little teasing getting the better of his instinct for discretion.

"So I heard you've been expanding your real estate empire over there on the head."

"How'd you hear?"

"Confidential sources."

"Actually, she turned me down."

"Smart woman."

"You think?"

"What'd you offer her, a million?"

"More. More than that."

"I'm gonna sic Denny on you pretty soon. After she's through fighting off Wal-Mart."

"Maisie wants this pool," Bloch said.

"What? What kind of pool? A swimming pool?"

"Just a lap pool."

"She wants a swimming pool on the head? She wants a lap pool in Clement's Cove? I've got to talk to that girl. She better go back where she came from. Mount Desert Island, maybe they've got lap pools. Not in Clement's Cove."

"It's for her health," Bloch said. "She can't swim in cold water anymore. She's got to swim to build herself up."

"Can't you put it on your own land?"

"Not easily."

"Well can I tell you something, confidentially? You ought to try to put it on your own land."

"If I could. . ."

"So figure it out. Get that smarty-pants New York architect to figure it out."

"Why do you say that?"

"Don't go getting your undies in a bunch. Listen, Adam, it's none of my business, alright? But you offer someone like Verna Hubbard something crazy, what if she takes it finally? She's going to hate you for it. Sooner or later, one way or the other. And that gets around. That's all."

"You want her to stay."

"She's been here a long time."

What Bloch almost forgot while they spoke was that he'd already decided to give up on Verna and her land. But Cord's suggesting it to him made him wary. He felt criticized. He felt Cord, his friend, was telling him not to be gauche and pushy and to mind his manners. Cord with his plantation noblesse oblige, Bloch thought.

Then he rued even thinking it, because if he couldn't listen to Cord, who could he listen to?

"Or why doesn't she go somewhere where there's a pool, if she's got to swim," Cord went on, about Maisie again. "They've got a pool over in Castine. The Maritime Academy's got a pool."

"Isn't that a long drive?" Bloch said.

But what he really wanted to say, he hesitated to say. Until he said it anyway, because if Cord was really his friend, Bloch felt he should be able to say to him such things. "You want to know? This whole thing confuses me. People buy and sell things all the time. And that includes land. People have been moving from one place to another for the whole history of this country. A willing buyer, a willing seller. It's always been that way. So what am I doing wrong?"

"I'm not saying you're doing anything wrong. I'm just giving you my advice."

"That makes no sense, what you just said. You're only giving me advice because you think I'm doing something wrong."

"Suit yourself then."

"Anyway," Bloch said, "I already decided. I'm not pursuing that anymore. I'm not making any more offers to Verna Hubbard."

"So what were you being so stubborn about?"

"I don't know," Bloch said.

"You want me to talk to Maisie?"

Bloch shook his head that he didn't.

They'd been walking a few steps at a time, walking and stopping and looking around, the whole time they were talking, until they were at the top of the road where it sprung out of the woods for maybe twenty yards before the houses started again and it went down on the other side. It was a pretty little cove that lay out below them, with gray water and a little mud now that it was low tide and there were various docks that were in various states of disrepair, but no boats because it was October and they'd all been pulled. You could see across to various islands and over to Islesboro and Camden and farther down the bay and both men experienced versions of the thought that this was no place to be arguing.

But Bloch's version was darker. Cord thought, rather simply, though not too simply, that the manifest bounty of nature ought to be a reminder for men who were part of it to get along. Bloch still wondered, as he returned to his house down his road with his poplar trees past Verna Hubbard's trailer, if he was really a part of nature's bounty.

Of course he was, of course he was, but on the other hand what if he wasn't? Who decided such things or could you just think it through? Did Cord think such things? Bloch didn't even know. All he knew was that Cord didn't think and Bloch didn't think, neither of them thought, that Bloch should keep trying to buy Verna Hubbard out. And why was that?

8

After she refused Bloch's last and final offer, Verna tried to keep to herself what she had done. She figured she didn't need other people's opinions about it and she didn't want their admiration either. She didn't think she could stand the embarrassment if she walked into Mac and Debbie's and people started treating her like some crazy hero, like she was nuts but you had to admire it, that she said no to the billionaire from away. And, as well, if other people knew, then Roy would know. You couldn't tell Bonnie, for instance, and not have Roy find out.

So for days she felt giddy with her secret that she had no one to tell, and while she scrubbed other people's floors and brushed their toilets she thought of the million and a half dollars she'd turned down almost as if the money were actually hers, as if the very act of turning it down somehow made it so, or gave her bragging rights over it, anyway. To Verna, turning it down felt almost as good as she imagined having it would feel. Especially if you took in account all the people you could read about every day of the week or saw on television, for whom money that came to them out of the blue only caused trouble. Like lottery winners. Take lottery winners, for a perfect example. You always read about lottery winners where the guy says he's going to quit work, but then what has he got to do all day long, or then there's a family fight and divorce. Verna felt for a couple of weeks as if she had the best of all worlds, but then Roy found out her secret.

Apparently the lawyer Jackman had been out on the Bloch property at a time when workmen were still around and one of Con Stephens's boys overheard Jackman mention some figures and intentions and "the recalcitrance of the owner" on his cellphone back to his office and this percolated among the other workmen for awhile until Tom Benson put two and two together when he observed Mr. Bloch's architect from New York nosing around Verna's trailer one day. The various angles of this story made it to the general store and from there it was inevitable that Roy would learn of it.

In the general store they didn't have the details just right, but it was close enough, and when Roy heard it, it felt like he'd been shot out of the sky, because for weeks he'd been dreaming about that note that was by Verna's phone that said for her to call Mr. Bloch's lawyer in Bangor. His first thought when he heard Mac talking about Verna cold-shouldering the lawyer was that it couldn't be her final decision yet, if she hadn't mentioned any of it to him even once, and so there had to be a way to change her mind, if he could just not get all crazy and mad at her and cause a scene that would make her more resolute than she already was.

Roy's second thought was that this was just like Verna. She hadn't told him because she didn't want him to know and didn't trust him, and why was that? Roy thought he knew why that was. Because she was a bitch and a beast and a moron who had no appreciation of him or the ways he was good to her and protected her, that's why that was. Although Roy struggled to remind himself that this was no way to be approaching it. If he approached Verna with negativity, that was a sure way to fail. Instead he tried to imagine her as some kind of princess, with a crown made of two million dollars kind of lopsided on top of her head, like the crown of a carnival queen. Two million dollars was the figure that had made it to the general store. Somebody had been rounding up.

Roy didn't say anything to Verna right away. Nor did he even show much reaction when he heard it from Mac in the general store, he just nodded as if of course he knew all of that already and had only been keeping tight-lipped in accordance with Verna's wishes. Roy felt he would look like a real ding-a-ling if he was just about the last one to hear about Verna's fortune and Verna's no. But in fact that was the case, mostly because he didn't go in the store much, he spent most of his workdays off somewhere else, with Freddy, for instance, who wasn't from around this peninsula at all, who was from over on Mount Desert and a graduate of M.D.I. high school.

When he was with Verna for the next couple days, Roy acted like a guy with his pregnant girl. It was as if she were pregnant with gold. Verna noticed the difference, but while Roy was still figuring out what he'd say to her and how to lay the groundwork, Verna herself discovered that Bonnie and Mac knew her secret and that everybody in the general store knew it, they'd all been talking about it behind her back for days, and if she hadn't complained about the cost of the chocolate milk going up ten cents, so as to elicit from Mac one of his patented little remarks, concerning how she sure should be able to afford an extra dime these days, she'd still be in the dark.

So if they all knew, then Roy surely knew and was being cagey. Verna, like Roy, felt she had to take care now. After all, she had kept something from him. Something big, in a way, something that was all she could think about sometimes and that she thought about even more because she had kept it from him. That night, the way she decided to phrase it, being a bit cagey herself, or trying to be though she wasn't much for it, she said, "First of all, it wasn't two million dollars."

Roy was helping her with the dishes at just that moment and feeling fairly good about himself for pitching in. He wasn't prepared. He was still, as it were, laying his foundations. For a moment, when she said it, he even had hopes that if it wasn't two million, it might be even more. Though the way she said it, kind of critical-sounding of whoever mentioned that number in the first place, he would have to admit it wasn't likely. "How much are they offering then?" he asked.

"They're not offering anything. It's over," she said.

"It's not over till it's over. You know who said that?"

"It's over."

"So okay, it's over. So just for historical purposes, maybe you could fill me in as to exactly. . ."

"He offered one and a half million and to move the trailer to someplace else, which he'd also buy for me."

"So that's *almost* two million."

"It's not," Verna said. She'd thought about it a lot, and the last thing she wanted was people blowing things out of proportion.

Roy put the dishrag down, though Verna continued to wash. "Why'd you say no, Verna?"

She shrugged and made an extra effort to get the black off the bottom of the pot. Nor did she look at him.

"Why, Verna?"

"Things you wouldn't understand, Roy."

"I know I'm a dummy, I know I didn't go too much to school, but I understand two million dollars, Verna."

"It wasn't two million."

"It was damn close."

"Roy, keep your voice down when you talk to me."
"I was not yelling. I wasn't."
"You were. You were starting."
"Could we have a discussion about this?"
"What do you want to know?"
"If this is absolutely final, for one thing."
"It's how I want to do it."
"But is it final?"
"I don't know. Yeah. No. It's final."
"Well that's piss poor, you know that?"
"Roy, it's not your property. So when do you even get a vote?"
"I get to express an opinion, don't I? It's a piss poor decision, in my opinion."
"Thank you very much."

She scrubbed the bottom of the pot more obsessively, as if the black spot on it was the stubbornness of Roy's mind that she was trying to scrub clean.

"Verna, I'm thinking of your situation, that's all."
"Are you really?"
"Of course I am. Just let's, could we just think this through a second here?"
"Okay, Roy, be my guest."
"What's the property really worth?"
"I never asked."
"Well, what's the most anyone ever offered you before?"
"I don't know. Two hundred thousand, I think."
"That's my point! You got a place worth two hundred thousand!"
"It could be more now."
"Yeah, it could be more now, but basically two hundred thousand, and this guy's offering you, okay, not two, okay

Verna, not two million. See, I'm not a bully, I'm not exaggerating. One million seven hundred thousand, including if he buys you another place. That's profit! You could have a nice farm over on the river, you wouldn't have to live in this shitbox if you didn't want to. . ."

"It's not a shitbox. . ."

"For argument's sake, that's all, I'm just saying, no it's not a shitbox, Verna, it's not a shitbox, okay, but if you move you'd have all that money, you put that just in the bank making interest, that interest is more than you ever saw in your thirty-seven years of your life."

"So somebody else'll offer it. If I need the money."

"Nobody else is going to offer it! This is a special situation, it's special circumstances!"

"Would you keep your voice down?"

"I'm trying to get you to listen, Verna! This is your chance of a lifetime!"

"*Your* chance of a lifetime, maybe."

"You know, this is low. This is truly low."

"If I take that money, you going to marry me then, Roy? Have I got to bribe you to get you to be serious?"

"I'm talking about *you*, Verna."

"Yeah well I'm talking about us."

"We talked about all that."

"So okay, and now we've talked about all this. Now can we just change the subject?"

"Just tell me why."

"Why what?"

"Why what? Why what?!"

"Roy, they're going to hear you down the road, you keep yelling like that."

"Don't tell me to keep yelling, Verna, that's just changing the subject."

"I'm not telling you to keep yelling, I'm telling you to *quit* yelling."

"Just tell me why you fucking did this fucking stupidest thing of your life!"

"Because of my daddy, okay? Because he wouldn't want me to."

"Your daddy's dead."

"I knew what he'd be thinking."

"You think he wouldn't want you to be taking care of yourself?"

"This is the last piece, Roy!"

"You buy a farm on the river, you get a hundred acres, you start over, selling off this, selling off that, a hundred years you'll be down to nothing again."

"What's that supposed to mean?"

"This is how the big boys do it."

"The 'big boys.' What do you know about the 'big boys,' Roy?"

"Is that sarcastic? You being sarcastic with me, you bitch?"

"Well don't start trying to bully me then."

"I am, I *was,* trying to look out for you. Your daddy? Your daddy talk to you or something?"

"He did, in a way."

"This is too much."

"I was in with the boat and. . ."

"He talks from boats, does he, Everett does?"

"See, this is why I wouldn't tell you anything. Because you wouldn't understand."

"Fuck me. Fuck me, fuck me, fuck me."

"Oh shut up."

"Did you tell your daddy how much you were being offered? Old Everett would shit his pants, I bet."

"Don't talk about him like that."

"Did you?"

"Did I what?"

"Tell him how much."

Roy threw the dishrag across the room then and stomped around, so that, just as Maisie imagined, the floor of the trailer flexed and echoed. When he was done pacing the narrow kitchen, he said he was going out.

"Don't be mad at me, Roy," Verna said.

But he left anyway.

He went out to his truck where he kept a pint of vodka because Verna didn't want him drinking in her house and he drank enough of it and listened to CDs and tried to remember exactly how things went wrong here. He'd been caught unawares, he didn't have his proper foundations built, he lost his cool, and so you could blame it on that, but on the other hand you couldn't talk to Verna. Stubborn as a mule, just like she looked like, when you got right down to it. She hid from him, she lied to him, she had this thing about her daddy, and plus it was absolutely true how she looked if she didn't take extra efforts to fix herself up, she looked like a mule or a moron half the time, so what was he doing with her finally, Roy asked himself, he finally had to ask himself this question, of whether he couldn't do better than Verna. When he asked himself this question was when he got really mad, for all the time he'd wasted and the frustration of trying to talk to that person and be patient with her and be nice to her and what did it all get him, she says she's turning down two million dollars because her daddy who's dead told her to.

When he was drunk enough Roy went over to the lean-to thinking he'd have a little talk himself with the old man. The boat sat in its frame like it was some kind of throne it was sitting on, like it didn't have to talk to a peon at all. It pissed Roy off, he felt stupid and humiliated and like Verna had gotten the best of him and made a fool of him talking about how old Everett talks to her out of boats, and as if to right the situation or at least to quell it, to eliminate it from being a matter of concern, because sometimes you had to admit that the people you counted on were shit and fucked and morons, he gave the boat sitting on its frame a good shove. It didn't move. All he did was leave his handprints on the bright scarlet paint of the hull. The obstinacy of the boat, just like Verna, or whatever, pissed him off further, so he shoved it harder and when it didn't budge then, he yanked at the cradles and kicked them and yanked them some more until one came out and the boat fell forward on its prow like a dead man, and then from Everett's old tools he grabbed an ax to swing at the hull that had fallen. He managed to crack several planks and put ax holes in the foredeck and would have destroyed it all if Verna hadn't heard the clatter and seen the light on. She came over fearing the worst. She cried for him to stop and pulled at his arms and almost got axed herself yet she managed to pull him down and wrestle him and plead with him and finally he dropped the ax as if he had no idea how it got in his hands in the first place. Among other things he was disgusted and had had enough. He got out of her embrace, stood up and dusted himself off, and without another word he left.

9

There was no real consensus in the general store about any of this, except the boat part. Everyone agreed that Roy should not have harmed old Everett Hubbard's boat. Whether it could even be fixed or not was an open question. Tom Benson had seen it because he was out delivering propane to Verna and it looked to him like you could lay in a few new planks and get something to match up on the deck and maybe you'd be there, but he was the first to say he knew little about boats and probably it was more complicated than that. Several others put in, though they hadn't seen it, that just from what Tom was saying it had to be more complicated than that.

As for Roy, he was lying low. He hadn't been in the store at all. Burt Cummins said he was over in Bar Harbor, doing who knew what, whatever.

Verna came in, though. She looked pale and kind of like pudding and didn't talk about any of it. Bonnie stepped outside with her and they had a few words, but it was just between them and not for repeating.

When Verna wasn't around, the opinion in the store was pretty much fifty-fifty as to whether Roy was gone for good. Con Stephens said Roy had an eye for the skirts, and Tunk Smith opined there were enough of them over in Bar Harbor. Carl Henry said Verna had a heart of gold and you wouldn't find that every day in Bar Harbor. Ralph Audry said it wasn't a *heart* of gold that Roy was necessarily interested in. Bonnie said there was no way in any event Verna was ever taking that bastard back, and of course she spoke with the authority of having talked to Verna personally, even if she wasn't repeating any of the particulars of that. Mac said some people seemed to be forgetting that Roy smashed up Verna's *boat*, for Christ sake. Old Everett's boat, Lewis Early corrected. But opinion was still fairly evenly divided as to whether Roy was gone for good, because, as Burt Cummins put it, you never knew with lovebirds.

And of course the whole question was tied up with the other question of whether Verna should or should not have sold to Mr. Bloch and whether she could still change her mind or if she'd lost her last chance and the wisdom or damn foolhardiness of all of it. Ralph Audry remembered his father telling him about when the Hubbards had the largest spread on Clement's Cove. Mac said you couldn't go by that, if you went by that, then the Indians originally had the largest spread on Clement's, the Indians had the whole spread, for pity's sake. Ralph said he wasn't talking about the Indians. Mac said of course he wasn't talking about the Indians, that was just his point.

But Tom Benson and Tunk Smith kind of agreed with where Ralph was going with his opinion, it was kind of like honoring the past, what Verna was doing.

Carl Henry felt it was more about the money and Verna was just being shrewd to hold on and someday what she had would be worth a whole lot more even than two million dollars.

Burt Cummins firmly disagreed, he said you could look at a whole history of prices in the Town Hall and of course everything had gone up a ton and probably would continue to, but it would be years and years, maybe even after Verna's time, before prices caught up with what Mr. Bloch was offering for

Adam the King

that little tiny bit of Verna's. Since he worked over in Town Hall, Burt was listened to on this.

Nobody had much to say about Mr. Bloch or Mrs. Bloch, except that she wasn't apparently going by Mrs. Bloch, she was still Miss or Ms. Whatever-she'd-been-before, which Bonnie had heard on *Oprah* was getting to be a thing of the past. The assumption seemed to be that when people have that kind of money it's hard to know much about them. Nobody, at least not now, was condemning Mr. Bloch for making the offer. It was just a little weird, that's all, a little out of the shape of things. Though, as Ralph Audry put it, there were a lot of things out of shape these days.

Bonnie did come up with one confirming piece of fact. Mr. Bloch was indeed a Jewish fella. Not that that had anything to do with anything. It didn't, Mac said, but he sure had a lot of money.

10

Bloch went back to his New York architect. The New York architect brought up a team of landscape architects. The landscape architects brought in a geologist from Portland and soil experts from Camden and everyone brought their engineers and there was a pool designer too. More lawyers were hired to advise on the coastal laws. A plan came into being. The pool would be sunk in the high narrow spine of the land and it would run north and south as the land ran, and so that its scar on the land could not easily be seen, trees almost as big as those that would have to be removed for the construction would be brought in and planted when the construction was done. It was all tremendously expensive. They began blasting the ledge in November.

Once the decision was made, Bloch moved on. They were living in the city, in a loft on Greenwich Street north of the Trade Center that was as large and comfortable as the co-op apartment on Fifth Avenue that Maisie had grown up in. Maisie did the decor herself. She was afraid of decorators. Throughout the winter she took care of her girls, took them to museums and the little park by the river and entered them in "Mommy and Me," and the rest of her time she spent reading and throwing a few pots and taking classes and going to the gym, not so much to regain her strength any more, because she'd done that, but to keep herself strong. She still did a bit of yoga. She believed in nothing, she might say to you if you asked, but when she said it you might look at her and think she still believed, or once again believed, in the possibility that life was good.

I might put in here that Maisie had once been my lover. For a little while and in an odd circumstance. We were both members of a quasi-esoteric group, with a leader, in New York. In the late seventies, and I'd loved her like a comrade, and then she took up with the group's leader, and then it all fell apart. I've written about that part of our lives. After the group, we drifted apart, and Maisie went out to Taos and opened a breakfast restaurant, and had lovers and her twenty-minute marriage and more lovers but the years to have children went by, and then when she wanted to there were problems with conceiving, because of the Hodgkin's, the doctors said. So she adopted her two little girls from Hubei province, China, and gave them names from her family, Alexandra and Margaret, as if by doing it there could never be some dotty aunt who would question where they belonged, and then she met Adam Bloch on a New York street.

Bloch was done with business now, though if you made the billions yourself you're probably never really done with it. There are still managers to pay and papers to sign and reports to review and philanthropies to found, and you must be polite to people who are suitors for your money, who want it for this or that, to make more money with it or to give it away. Bloch allotted two hours of his day to his money. He still felt modest about it, really. He didn't live the way other billionaires lived, or the way he read about them living, anyway. He didn't really know. He didn't know other billionaires, except maybe a few from his various businesses, and those were about business and he didn't pursue their acquaintance anymore. He had never had many friends.

Now he played his cello every day. He gave it two hours, like his money. He took walks with Maisie and the girls or took the girls out for ice cream or went sometimes to the museums with all of them. Did that fill up his days? Not really. He tried to become interested in politics, but mostly failed, though he felt the impeachment of Clinton was an outrage and gave more money to the Democrats then. He built an art collection of contemporary pieces that he didn't entirely like, and was thinking of trading them all in for Mughal miniatures. Often he longed to be back in Maine, to sit on his oversized porch and watch the water or see how the construction of the pool was getting on or walk into the general store and have ordinary people say hello to him. He would call up somebody every couple days, the architect or the engineers, to see how the pool was coming. When there was news, he would tell Maisie.

A lot of their life was like that, telling each other little bits of news. They went to functions together. They spent their evenings together. They had sex, say, once every week or sometimes every two, and mostly in a desultory fashion. It was not a marriage of passion, he knew that from the start. Or what was he talking about? It was a marriage of *his* passion.

As for Maisie, she wondered, quite often, if this could last or how long it could last. She didn't consider this a disloyal question. She wasn't "bailing out." She just wondered, the way she imagined anyone would if they'd scarcely been married before and were in their fifties and life was exigent and complicated and possibly short. She liked Adam. She found his naïveté, his modesty, his instinct to do no harm, to try to leave the world no worse for his having been here, endearing. Especially because he had done harm, and he knew it. Harm to her, harm to everyone she loved, and even if he had done so inadvertently, it had left a stain. He was like a man doing a penance, and for some reason Maisie found this to be one of the acceptable ways of being in the world.

A simple conversation they had once:

"I'm sorry, Adam."

"For what?"

"I think you know for what."

But really he didn't. Not then, when she said it to him, when the girls were put to sleep and they were sitting quietly each with their books and their thoughts, in the library she'd insisted he build for himself, that had a window looking west, across the river and into the night.

Later it dawned on him that what she had said was like a template for a conversation that could have gone exactly the other way. He should have said, "I'm sorry, Maisie." And she could have said, "For what?" And he would have said, "I think you know for what."

Would that have made him feel better? Would that have been a better way of doing it?

Even falling in love, for Bloch, was something like a penance. He married the sister of the girl he killed. Though he would remind himself not to say it that way, not to place more blame than he could bear. The sister of the girl who died in the crash. There. Was that better? She came from the best of families. She was fiery in ways that he could never be. She filled in the missing pieces of himself. Her red hair flew around. She was or had been sick and needed taking care of. She wasn't intimidated by all the money. She knew a million things he didn't and she had a million graces he lacked, so many that she could throw them away, profligately. She had lived a life without nets, had even cut the ones she was born with. She was a little crazy, and he was surely not, he longed for the champagne of madness. She was the sister of the girl he killed, marked out to him like a blazing star by fate.

They stopped work on the lap pool in January on account of the freezing conditions but they resumed in March and Verna saw again the stream of trucks and trailers going up and down Bloch's road. Bloch was told there had been delays. The weather, the frozen ground. Now they were shooting for the end of the summer. Bloch was a patient man himself, but to his knowledge Maisie wasn't. Reluctantly he became a boss again, he asked questions and where he found the answers silly or implausible he fired a few people, just to show the rest that such a thing was possible. He put off telling Maisie but finally he did, he told her that the pool wouldn't be ready until fall. She shrugged as if for a moment she'd forgotten it was being built at all. "There must be a YMCA up there somewhere," she said.

11

Roy came to regret what he had done. He argued with himself about it, because he was always regretting things he had done, Roy recognized this as a pattern in himself, do something one week, regret it the next, and then sometimes he would act on his regrets, and things, instead of getting corrected, would go from bad to worse. But regarding Verna there was no way he couldn't see how he'd screwed up. For one thing there weren't a whole lot of other girls coming into his life. Freddy had all kinds of girls on the side but Roy didn't have any on one side or the other. You could see the difference between him and Freddy when sometimes Freddy would pick up two girls for them and both the girls would pay attention to Freddy. Roy couldn't figure it but there it was, sometimes you just had to face the ugly facts. Freddy just had a way with the skirts, it was like he could always think of something funny to say, whereas Roy could think of things to say but they usually weren't funny. Secondly, concerning Verna, there was no way he should have busted up her daddy's boat, that boat meant a hell of a lot to Verna and it was just a mean drunk thing to do. And Verna wasn't a bad old girl, to boot. The one thing that had nothing to do with Roy's weighing process, as he saw it, was all the money Verna was supposed to get for her land, since after all she wasn't getting it. Roy decided the first thing he'd say to her, if they ever got back together, was that he respected her decision vis-à-vis Mr. Bloch, and that would be the end of that discussion so far as he was concerned right there.

Roy felt actually it would be a considerable sacrifice on his part to say this, since at the moment there was no question that he could use the money. The thing with the Queen of Italian Cuisine had finally gone to court and wound up costing him fifteen hundred dollars, once you added the lawyer's fee on. But more than that, Freddy was about to launch an expanded operation that had an excellent chance for success. Royce Gilmore, who owned the largest limousine operation in the eastern part of the state, had passed on in February and his daughter who got the business had decided to slim down operations and was selling off a portion of their vehicles. Freddy knew the owner of the lot in Ellsworth where they were being consigned and had negotiated a knock-down price for all of them sold together, which he was offering Roy a fifty-fifty percentage piece of, provided Roy could come up with the proper funding. Roy was flat busted himself, the only thing he owned was his pickup truck that was five years old with a hundred ten thousand miles that he still owed the bank on. But he wasn't going to tell Verna any of this. If it came out later, fine. The one thing he wanted to communicate to her in the first place, and he would do this in no uncertain terms, was the fact he was sorry.

Verna took Roy's apology under advisement. He just came over one day and told her how he'd screwed up. The weirdest thing. She heard an engine sound outside that sounded like his truck, but she'd been mistaken so many times about that on account of all the trucks going up to Mr. Bloch's place that she wasn't even going to look. She took a peek through the curtains anyway, because she always took a peek whether she wanted to or not, and there it was. Roy told her how he'd screwed up and was sorry and would make efforts never to fly off like that again or go drinking to excess, and also how he respected her decision vis-à-vis Mr. Bloch and that it was the end of that discussion as far as he was concerned.

Roy certainly *looked* sorry enough. He brought over a dozen and a half carnations from the Tradewinds and his eyes didn't dart around like they sometimes did, like they were eager to be out of a situation – this time they either looked straight at her or at the floor. She told him that what she worried about was compliance, i.e. if he'd do what he said. He said he could only do what he could do. Verna couldn't argue with that. Roy could see things were going in his direction just by the way she couldn't find the next words she wanted, it was like she was in the process of changing her mind but hadn't thought up the words to do it yet. He figured to close the deal by telling her how messing up Everett's boat was something that if he personally ever wound up being God, he'd for sure send himself to hell for. He hated to say that but it was true. It was the worst thing you could do to a man's memory and his daughter, but he intended to fix the boat like new.

"I don't believe you can," Verna said.

"You think I don't have skills, Verna?"

"I think you've got skills, Roy. But I don't believe you can."

"Then we'll just have to see."

Roy had a toothy smile, a little lopsided as well, that could seem brave sometimes. He was defying her doubts now, and she remembered that about him. Roy had a certain kind of confidence, which Verna so far lacked that when she saw it in someone else, even if it seemed more stupid than brave, and likely as not to wind up like a busted dream, she couldn't quite ignore.

This time Roy moved in. He'd never moved in before, though

he'd spent any number of nights a week there. He brought his clothes over in a box. That was about it. His tools he kept in his truck. He quit paying rent on the place over in Sedgwick, and that was surely a help. A portion of what he used to pay over in Sedgwick, he gave to Verna for his share, and that was also a help, in terms of keeping things on an even keel with her.

Most evenings Roy spent over in the lean-to with old Everett's boat. He decided it wasn't in as bad a shape as he remembered. He spent a lot of time looking at what needed to be done and then he set to work. Measure twice, cut once – everybody said it, but you couldn't deny it. Then he consulted with various persons, Tom Benson in particular, about the best way of getting the new planks bent to shape and certain other aspects. He'd once helped his own daddy build a boat, smaller than this one, more a dinghy, but it had been lapstrake too, and that's what he was otherwise going on, his memories of that. That was his ace in the hole which gave him the confidence to say anything to Verna in the first place. It had been the choicest time he could remember with his father. They took a whole summer and when the old man wasn't fishing they built that dinghy.

Verna watched Roy's progress with interest. Tom Benson came over to look at the progress sometimes and Tom was saying it was a helluva job. What Verna noticed mostly was that when Roy was through for the evening, he'd come over and be in the sweetest mood. He must have been proud of himself or something. It used to be that nights he'd spend a lot of his time complaining, about the various things you could of course complain about, the weather and money and people from away and what the state was telling you you had to do or couldn't do now and the way they made it hard on people with any initiative or ideas and what somebody or other said or was said to have said, about himself or about something; or he'd be scheming, coming up with his ideas and already upset because they were going nowhere. Now he'd come back to the trailer and have one beer and they'd watch the news and the sports and more often than before, before they went to sleep, he'd be in the mood for a little more.

Things went on this way through the mud season, and Verna began to hope she had a new man on her hands. She began to hope he'd never finish his project of rebuilding her daddy's boat. In the meantime there had been delays with the limousine deal that Freddy had negotiated. It was an on-again, off-again thing, one week Royce Gilmore's daughter wanted to slim down operations, the next week she didn't. But by the middle of May she'd finally made her mind up. Freddy was salivating. That's how good a deal it was, fifty percent off blue book. Finally it was putting pressure on Roy: in or out. Of course his answer would have to be out, as things currently stood, but he was still hoping for some version of a miracle. One night when they were particularly getting on, he decided he ought to at least mention the deal to Verna, just to see what she would say. He picked up some lobsters from the Marine and an oversized bottle of wine and when they were done with a hands-down outstandingly delicious meal he broached it with her.

Roy's eyes radiated the purring excitement he felt when this whole issue came up in his mind. They were little boy's eyes. He didn't know how else to put it, he said. He felt she should just be aware. But if people were going to make something of themselves in this part of the world, they had to take their chances where they could get it.

"You mean, Freddy." Verna, as expected, did not think highly of Roy's prospective business partner.

"I know you don't think he's too high class an individual."

"He's proved that," Verna said.

"He's just a real character," Roy said.

"So what is it this time exactly?"

"You know if you're going to have an attitude going in, what's even the point of me telling you anything?"

"Tell me, Roy. Really. I want to hear."

So Roy told her about Royce Gilmore and his daughter and the slimming down of their fleet and the limos halfway below blue book and the deal Freddy had negotiated with Peterson's Cadillac in Ellsworth and the whole idea of a fifty-fifty split, which would give Roy something in the world at last. He laid particular emphasis on the market research that Freddy had carried out to make sure there'd be demand for all these limos. His market research showed there'd be plenty of demand, there was pent-up demand, it was a case of if you build it, they'll come.

"What kind of market research?" Verna asked.

"What do you mean, what kind?"

"I mean, did he hire somebody, or what? He just go ask strangers in the street, would they like a limo ride?"

"Why're you being so cynical, right from the jump here?"

"Well you said, 'market research.'"

"I don't know exactly what kind, okay? Okay?"

"Okay. Fine. Then how much money would you have to put up?"

"Forty thousand dollars."

"Forty thousand dollars?"

"Forty thousand dollars, what's wrong with that, that's peanuts, for a half share in six limos? Fifty percent off blue book, you could take 'em down to New York and just sell 'em for a profit that way, if nothing else worked out."

"You don't have forty thousand dollars, Roy."

"That's correct. I don't."

"Well then. . ."

"I just thought you should be aware. I didn't say I was going to do it. See, this is a perfect example, you're always telling me I don't tell you stuff. And right here, here's stuff. Don't seem to make you any happier, if I tell you everything."

"I'm happy you told me, Roy."

"Are you, Verna?"

"Well it's good for me to know what you're thinking about, isn't it?"

"It's why I told you. I wasn't asking you to put up the money yourself."

"I don't have forty thousand dollars, Roy."

"I meant, making that deal with Mr. Bloch over there."

"You're still thinking about that, aren't you, Roy?"

"I'm not *thinking* about it, Verna. It's not like I'm *thinking* about it. But it's a hard thing to put out of your mind totally, you'd have to say that."

"I still think about it," Verna said.

"Do you. Is that so?"

"It's like you said. It's not like I *think* about it. But it's kind of hard not to."

"All I meant, if you wanted to do something. If you wanted to be in on this deal yourself, by any chance."

"I don't."

"Of course. Absolutely. I didn't think so. But if you did. See, I wasn't thinking any more like you'd sell your piece. It's more like, you go to the bank, you say this Mr. So-and-So offered me this for my property, so I guess that's what it's worth now, so you get a loan out on it. That's all I was talking about. One of those home loans. Not even a mortgage, just one of those home loans they got now. Not that you'd want to. I'm not saying you should."

"I already got a loan out, Roy."

"Is that right? I didn't know."

"So I couldn't take out more."

"If your place was worth more, because of this Bloch guy."

"They're going to know, just like you said, it was a one-time thing."

"Well anyway it don't matter, since I'm not getting you involved in this."

"It's not a question of *me* getting involved. It's a question of *you* getting involved in some knucklehead idea which wouldn't be the first of Freddy Belliveau's knucklehead ideas that turned out to have a joker in it someplace. Just think, Roy. Just think. Why would the daughter be selling off the limos, if there was a demand for them out there?"

"Why didn't Royce Gilmore sell 'em off then? He's the one knew his business, and he didn't sell 'em, he just dropped dead, he couldn't help himself."

"I still say, she's got the established business. You're going up against that. What if she takes your money and goes out and buys three new limos? Then where'd you be? She's got the superior cars *and* the established business."

"You know you're thinking like a business person here, Verna."

"No way. It's just common sense."

"I mean, with that kind of business acumen you're showing here, I'd go fifty-fifty with you myself."

"You're bad, Roy."

"But let me just answer this question, okay? Because it's a good question, it's a smart question. And actually it was the first thing I happened to ask Freddy and he went and we asked and the answer is, she's pulling out of Mount Desert Island altogether. She's living over in Old Town, it's too far for her to Mount Desert, that's why she's slimming her operations down. Mount Desert's going to be free territory."

"She gonna put that in writing?"

"Aw, Verna. Jesus. Expect the Almighty to bow down to you, expect assurances about every single thing. You got to take some things on chance, that's just life, Verna. You never believe anything, where are you?"

"Well. . . one thing I would say. . . there's plenty of rich folks on Mount Desert Island."

"Of course there are. Of course there are. You got the Rockefellers, you got a million people. Hey, Freddy's not exactly going broke over there, and he's only got one vehicle."

"I'll tell you what I do think, Roy. Every person should have one chance one day. It's only right."

Verna got up to put the lobster shells in the trash and get out the ice cream. Roy was curious about those last words of hers, but he chose to say nothing. He'd learned enough about Verna to leave some things alone. You get as close as you can get to something, and then you don't press it, you don't blow it. It was a rule he was trying out, anyway. It was something Freddy had told him. Freddy had read a number of books about management.

In the days that followed Verna did some online research concerning limousines and the demographics of Mount Desert Island and the overall economic conditions of that part of the county and she made some discreet inquiries of a few of the folks she cleaned house for as well, and in particular Mr. Elliot, who'd been in banking and all of that prior to retiring to Clement's Cove. But Mr. Elliot didn't know much about limousines. He never took them himself. He said he figured the summer folk over there, if they were anything like around here, which maybe they weren't, but if they were, a limousine service might be a little bit spiffy and a little too like the cities they left. On the other hand, there was all the traffic at the airport and they'd have a superior product to the Bar Harbor taxis, and maybe if they converted a couple of the limos so they'd be more like touring vehicles, bright colors, et cetera, take out the smoked windows, lemonade in the minibar instead of hard liquor, there could be a whole second line of business, a fun way for people to see the coast. Or join up with one of the steamboat operators, a half day of that, a half day in the limos, which Verna interpreted as a kind of surf-and-turf of tourism.

She had a lot to think about. Late in the afternoons, when she was done cleaning but Roy wasn't home yet, she'd go over to the lean-to to consult with her daddy's boat. It wasn't speaking to her now. It sat there like a boat. It was starting to look the way it used to look before Roy bashed it all up. He was at the point of sanding the whole hull down and starting over with the paint, and it looked kind of like a naked version of itself, like Verna almost wanted to wrap it in a blanket. But it made Verna happy that Roy was working on something her father had worked on, even if the reason for all that work she'd rather have forgotten. It showed how even a catastrophe could in proper conditions turn into a good thing. It showed God's working, in a way. Or maybe it did. Verna wasn't sure, but she had hopes in that area, as she had hopes now that when Roy was finished working on the boat it would be what she had not believed possible, it would be just as it was the day that Everett died.

And as for the trailer and the land and the money and Mr. Bloch's offer, Verna began to recall how close she'd come to taking it in the first place. It was only that scruple about her father's wishes that had stopped her, and she couldn't hear that scruple now. Now she thought about how, if she sold her land to Mr. Bloch, the money that Roy would need would be only a tiny, minuscule portion of what she would receive. She would hardly notice it was gone. She could help Roy and it wouldn't hurt her at all. He could even blow it all and it would be a disaster and he'd feel terrible and admit that Freddy was a jackass and someone he would never listen to again, but she could forgive him. Easily she could forgive him. She could tell him that it was the right thing for everyone to have one chance one day. The only dread she felt about any of it now was what if she was too late? Or, no, of course she was too late, the trucks were going up and down every day, what did Mr. Bloch need with her land now? Unless he simply wanted her land. Unless it would make a tidy package for him. Or maybe, and this was just a vain hope, she'd heard about the delays they were having. The delays might mean trouble. The delays might mean Verna still had her chance.

12

When Bloch heard that Verna had changed her mind and now wanted to sell him her property, he was faintly annoyed. He had gone far out of his way and made choices he hadn't wanted to make when she said no in the first place. He had spent as much time as he wanted to spend on the question. He was happy that things were now proceeding on an even keel and that when he and Maisie returned to Clement's Cove on Memorial Day he could go over and check up and be like the sidewalk engineer that a few times long ago with his father in downtown Pittsburgh, like a boy in a *New Yorker* cartoon, he'd thrilled to be. There had been delays, but they seemed past now. And anyway, the delays made him only more reluctant to change his course. If he dropped what he was doing now, after so much effort and so many delays, people would only think he was a fool times two. They'd call him money-crazy. They'd call him indecisive or neurotic or worse. Bloch wondered if they ever called people neurotic in Clement's Cove. It didn't seem quite right. It didn't seem like what they would say. But it would be what they meant.

Of course there was the alternative of leaving the pool where it was and just acquiring Verna's plot as a kind of mopping-up operation. There was even a certain rationale to it, to buy the last bit of land on the head that wasn't already his. He of course wouldn't pay her what he had offered her before. That was past. And it had anyway been a moment of childish desperation.

Bloch could see such things in retrospect. He got crazy because of Maisie. He would become crazy again for her, he knew that much about himself, he would do crazy things as many times as were necessary. But they weren't necessary now. He didn't even mention Verna's change of heart to Maisie. He felt it would only upset her. He was afraid at any moment she would throw off Clement's Cove and all of it, and then where would he be? Maisie was volatile. This was an article of Bloch's faith. Everything he had done here was to tether her to the earth, or really to him, as if he came along as part of the bargain, Adam as part of the earth.

It was a straightforward business proposition, really. When Adam was at sea, his instinct was to revert to the thing he was good at. He might be clumsy with feelings and dull of speech and he blinked too seldom and his mouth could go dry with longing or regret, but he could make sense out of things from a business point of view. The money, in absolute terms, meant little to him. *Monopoly* money, really. But he felt he must at least try to make it mean something to him, just as he must at least try to shut off lights when he walked out of a room, not out of compulsion, or for nostalgia's sake, but in order to keep life in a proportion he could recognize. His business sense told him that Verna had a powerful motive to sell now. It also told him that her land was worth a quarter million dollars at most and that he could get it for half that, he could get it for almost anything he wanted to pay, but he oughtn't to pay too little because that was not how business worked. Business, if you were a man like Bloch, meant cultivating a reputation for fairness. Take the last dime out of a situation and you might be a princeling today but you were a dead man tomorrow. Act as though there were honor to the whole thing, clothe the wretched beast in velvet, and the world won't run away. Bloch the honest broker. It was shtick, but it had always worked. Having a head for figures wasn't a bad thing, either. Bloch remembered, with an embarrassed regret, that he still liked to play *Monopoly*. But these days he was careful not to play to win.

He went so far as to talk it over with Jackman the lawyer. What to offer. How to phrase it. Whether to move her trailer for her or buy another plot for her. The things that had been in the air before, when he needed it and was crazy. And Bloch might have gone through with it, might have made Verna a tidy little offer for her land, but for the fact he got a flat tire driving home from the lawyer's office in Bangor. He didn't even know where he was, except that he was north of Route 1. It was a landscape of marshy springtime fields and rolling hills and a stream meandered through the fields and Bloch remarked to himself there could be worse places to be stuck without cellphone service. He stood in the road and waited for passersby and waved at the first pickup truck to come by. His was a slightly rueful wave, as if he felt foolish to be in this situation and sorry to put anyone to the trouble. But the truck pulled over anyway.

The driver was bulky with a reddish beard and small eyes set like peas in a ruddy face and he wore a T-shirt that made a joke about black flies. He asked Bloch if he had a spare. Bloch said he wasn't sure. Bloch offered him twenty dollars if he'd change his tire. The guy said he wasn't going to be changing anything if Bloch didn't have a spare. He rooted around in Bloch's trunk and came up with a half-sized tire that he showed considerable contempt for, as being what the car companies believed they could get away with these days. Bloch nodded and watched the guy work. The guy kept up a patter about various subjects both related and unrelated to what he was doing, the nail that got Bloch's tire, the prevalence of nails and such on roads where there'd recently been construction, the piss-poor cellphone service north of Route 1 generally speaking, and what it would have cost Bloch if he'd had to call a tow truck, which he explained to Bloch as, "They'd of got you by the shorties, my friend. They'd of jew'd you pretty good."

When he was done the guy repacked Bloch's jack neatly where it went and dumped the flat in the trunk and Bloch paid him the twenty dollars and the two men went on their ways. Bloch was grateful for the guy's stopping and for the good-natured part of him and the honest way he'd worked, and all these made it harder for Bloch to forget the guy's opinion as to how the towtruck operator would have treated him if the tow truck had got there first. "Jew'd you pretty good." Bloch told himself the guy wouldn't know a Jew if a Jew foreclosed on him.

Yet he would drive a couple of miles and the remark would come back, like a road sign around a bend. Bloch hated himself for letting such a thing turn his eye. Remember the blacks, the Jews' old rallying cry, meant if for nothing else to put things in perspective. And all the rest, the AIDS victims, the gays, the transgenders, the lesbians, the Puerto Ricans, the Mexicans, every minority you could name, as if lined up in a silent army, like the terra cotta soldiers of Xian. This country was good to the Jews. "Jew'd you pretty good," unconscious, almost sweet, in the ordinary course of things. Yet Bloch found himself crossing Route 1 as if hoping for a return to friendly territory. And when it didn't work, and he still remembered? Vaguely, Bloch sensed himself on the wrong side of a bright divide, with the guy in the pickup and Verna and most everyone he knew around here, even Hayward Jackman the lawyer, even Cord, even Maisie, on the other side.

The desire to be a victim or the yearning not to be. The push and pull of every man's life. The shadows, the echoes, of the millennia. Did people believe in ghosts? Bloch resented being played this way, or playing himself this way, or whatever it really was. He who didn't believe in ghosts, who believed, still, in the possibility of reason.

He remembered what Cord had said about Verna. The Hubbards had been around a long time. And it didn't matter the circumstances, some day she, or her child if she ever had one, or somebody, or everybody, would hate him for buying her out. He couldn't chance that. He didn't even think it was right to chance it. He could see that now. He was on the wrong side of a bright divide, but every bet he had made assumed the opposite. Or at least the possibility of the opposite. He would act as if it were all true. He would be the champion of Verna Hubbard's land. He would protect it even when she in a weak moment wouldn't. He would prove something even if he couldn't say what it was. He would never buy Verna out.

13

Verna didn't want to tell Roy the bad news. It was the worst part of the bad news, really, having to tell it to Roy. She couldn't even get herself to cook a meal to make it softer. He came home and it plopped out of her like an egg.

Roy sat in the Naugahyde lounger that had been Everett's with his knees apart and a beer. He'd not been anticipating this. He'd told Freddy good things were cooking. But now that he heard it from Verna's lips, he wasn't surprised at all. Not one bit surprised. The only thing warring in him was why he wasn't surprised. On the one hand, there was the fact that every time one fucking stinking half-assed opportunity to give him half a leg up in life came along, it turned immediately or soon enough to shit. Roy tugged at his beer and considered this to be God's truth. Almost thirty-five and he was never going to catch a break if he lived to be a hundred and six. That's how some people just were born, their lives stank, and no amount of perfume or sweat or ideas or anything they did in their whole fucking existence was going to change the outcome of that one iota. On the other hand was the possibility that this was all Verna's fault. After a couple of beers, while she sat there with him in the half-dark with neither of them saying much, he decided maybe it was the second thing.

Finally he said to her, with some circumspection, "So. Did you come back to him with some kind of lower offer?"

He'd been silent so long, Verna was caught unawares. "What offer?"

"Didn't you make an offer in the first place?"

"I just told the lawyer I changed my mind. I told him I'd sell."

"Jesus, Verna. You got to make some kind of concrete offer with these things. You can't just leave it in limbo."

"It wasn't up to me to offer. He's the one offered, in the first place."

"Yeah, but you're coming back to him now. You got to show you mean business."

"Roy, he just said no. I'm sorry. But he did. He said no. It's not my fault."

"I'm just talking tactics. You got to have tactics. For instance, okay? I thought of this. I'm not saying you do this. I just thought of this. But let's just say he says no. What kind of cards you got to play, Verna? You've still got cards. You're not tapped out. By any means. And this is just what I thought, for instance. He's got a nice place there. He's got millions in, rich people coming and going, right? Right by your own place, which they can see. So say he says no. The next thing, just for instance, you start messing up your yard a little. Why do you have to have the neatest mobile home in Hancock County? Obviously, you don't. You leave stuff out. You leave the garbage can out. You forget to mow the grass. Any number of stuff. You make your place an eyesore."

"Roy, that's horrible. You're crazy."

"It's just tactics, Verna. I'm not saying forever. It's just tactics. If he's going to say no, you do something back."

"I'm not making my place an eyesore."

"It was just for instance, okay? The point is, you don't just take this lying down."

"I'm not taking anything lying down."

"Of course you are. What do you call it, then, what you're doing?"

"I'm not aggressive, that's all. It's no point."

"How do you know, if you haven't tried?"

"You want to call the lawyer, Roy? Go ahead. See what he says. You call him."

"Well maybe I will."

"Be my guest then. Just don't go telling him you're going to trash my place."

So Roy took over the negotiation. The next day he called Jackman and left a message that he would now be representing Miss Hubbard in the possible sale of her land.

Two days later Jackman called him back, on Roy's cellphone line, and said his client wasn't interested at this time but he would get back to him some time in the future if his plans changed.

Roy hated this formality of tone. He took another tack and said that Miss Hubbard understood Mr. Bloch's position, going ahead with the pool and all, but surely there were other considerations regarding the possible value of the land to Mr. Bloch, and Miss Hubbard was prepared to be reasonable and understanding in terms of price. She wasn't out to make a killing, she just wanted fair value.

Jackman expressed appreciation for Miss Hubbard's reasonableness, but repeated that his client's interests were focused elsewhere at this time.

Roy thought Jackman was a fucking asshole by then. He decided to go specific, just like he'd advised Verna, and said her property could be had for a half million dollars cash.

Jackman said thank you and that he had another call coming in, and hung up.

Roy called back two days later, but Jackman didn't return his call.

Roy decided he'd at least try this thing of trashing Verna's yard. He left a bag of garbage by the road one night and the raccoons got it and then the crows and the garbage was all over. Verna went to pick it up but Roy stopped her. She said he was a fool. He said, okay, he was a fool, but he was in charge of this negotiation now and she at least had to give him a fair chance, he'd clean up the garbage himself later but just let it sit there for now.

Verna got teary and said she'd rather not sell at all. Roy said he could understand how she felt, and if she truly felt that way he'd desist as of now, but it would be the end of his dream. Verna hated him for saying that, but the garbage stayed in the road. Somebody from Bloch's place came down and shoveled it up.

The next night Roy put out more garbage and left his truck up close to the road instead of down the driveway and since it wasn't supposed to rain he put his tools out all around Verna's yard, as if he planned to plant them or something. The next day he put her old barbecue out in the driveway and a blue plastic beach float that had a hole in it and some other stuff that even a garage sale would be ashamed of. Verna had given him five days to make this work. On the fifth day he called Jackman again. When Jackman picked up the phone, Roy felt his tactics must be having their intended effect. He was almost giddy with expectation. He wasn't going to give in too easily. He was going to get Verna good money for her land.

But all Jackman had to say was that his client intended to call the Town Hall if in the near future Miss Hubbard didn't come into compliance with the local zoning on refuse, unless there was some excuse, such as illness or being away, that his client was unaware of.

Roy said he was unaware of any problems or of Miss Hubbard being out of compliance. But maybe there was an alternative compromise that could be worked out, Roy said. If Mr. Bloch truly didn't want Miss Hubbard's land anymore, still he might want an expansion of his right-of-way on the road so that he could plant trees and never have to see Miss Hubbard's trailer again.

Jackman laughed and said his client liked seeing Miss Hubbard's trailer.

Roy refused to believe this. He said that for only eighty thousand dollars Mr. Bloch could have the expanded right-of-way and a screen of trees and never have to worry about Miss Hubbard's refuse problems again.

Jackman promised that he'd relay the new offer to his client. He felt duty-bound, he said, to convey new offers to him. Roy took heart in this. He told Freddy things were coming together. He took Verna out to Deer Isle to dinner. Two days later Jackman called back and said no. Roy reduced his offer to sixty thousand, then to fifty, then to forty, but Jackman still said no. His client just wasn't interested.

Verna fixed up the front of her trailer so that it was prim and decent again. Roy hated her for doing it because it reminded him of his defeat. But then, if she'd left it all untidy, that too would have reminded him of his defeat and he would have hated her for that too. He recognized this. He was a man who could recognize things in himself, for good or bad. He was ashamed of himself for blaming Verna for everything and vowed on the day that one fucking thing, like even the smallest tiny fucking thing in the universe, turned out right for him, he wouldn't blame her anymore.

14

In the general store the feeling prevailed that Verna should never have waited so long if she wanted to sell her land. Strike while the iron's hot, somebody said. A bird in the hand, Carl Henry said. A case of don't count your chickens, Tunk Smith said, but it turned out he was ribbing the others on account of their clichés. In general, people blamed Roy. It continued to be a wonder to Bonnie that Verna took him back in the first place. But Tom Benson said he was doing a nice job on the boat. People forgot that about Roy, he said, he was a fella who could do things when he put his mind to it.

"What mind?" Bonnie cackled, and there were a couple of other people's guffaws that trailed along with her. But no, seriously, she said, it was good for Verna to hold on out there, it was the guts thing to do and it was only Roy who had talked her out of it to start with. Roy with his big ideas and that criminal friend of his Freddy Belliveau.

Lewis Early asked why was she calling Fred Belliveau criminal and Mac said you just don't go calling people criminal with no evidence.

But Bonnie stuck to her guns, pointing out the incident with Francesca Romano and what she heard from a friend in Southwest, namely, that during the eighties Freddy smuggled marijuana over there.

If he never got caught, then it's only suspicion, said Tunk Smith, who'd had similar suspicions raised about himself in the past concerning his ability to support his ex-wives. Allegations only, Carl Henry said.

And anyway who cared, Con Stephens said, none of it had beans to do with Roy anymore, because Freddy had gone out and got himself a new investor. This was what Tom Benson heard, too, straight from the horse's mouth, Roy himself told him that Freddy was romancing some summer person over in Northeast Harbor to invest fifty thousand dollars. That was last week he told him, and Roy had seemed pretty upset.

But he shouldn't be, Burt Cummins said, Freddy was doing him the favor of his life, not to get him involved in such a shaky scheme as that one.

You never knew, Mac said, with a business proposition you never knew.

He knew, Burt Cummins said, Freddy and his limos were a loser, and in fact if you went to New York City these days, they hardly even used limousines any more, they got these *town cars*, that's what people wanted now, *town cars*, it just showed how little Freddy or Roy knew about anything.

Bonnie said her feeling still was that Verna ought to kick Roy's butt back over to Sedgwick. Who'd she go out with then, Ralph Audry asked, did Bonnie have any bright ideas, considering she was so quick to be busting up people's relationships. Bonnie had to admit that at present she didn't. So that's the whole story in a nutshell right there, Lew Early said. Tunk Smith, who for some reason was considering himself the cliché police today, said nobody better say that beggars can't be choosers. As for Mr. Bloch, it was no surprise to anybody that he no longer wanted Verna's land. It just made sense. He'd gone in another direction. The consensus in the general store, as expressed by Mac, was that Mr. Bloch was more worthy of respect for not buying Verna's land than he would have been if he bought it. It showed he wasn't interested in coming here and just buying everything up.

15

Most of the summer people came back to Clement's Cove for the Fourth of July. They came to air out their houses, see friends, relax, and act a little silly, or nostalgic, or unsophisticated, or immature. They came to make sure their children had the childhoods they remembered or had never had. The parade, the fireworks, the tug-of-war and three-legged races, the burnt cheap hot dogs from the Tradewinds, the odd phenomenon of seeing grown men and neighbors walking around in red, white, and blue pants and top hats, the party at the beach. It was the start of the summer. Coming back to Clement's Cove for the Fourth of July was like standing up for the kickoff at the Harvard–Yale game.

Maisie had a vicious migraine, so it was left to Bloch to take the girls to the beach. He took them by their hands and they walked down the road. Bloch felt like an ersatz patriarch, a father in disguise. Could this really be him, with those little hands in his, holding on with the excitement of dear life itself? When he had first met Maisie's girls, he could hardly tell them apart. Now he could tell you hundreds of things about each of them. Alexandra was sturdy and tall and impulsive and she learned how to swim the first time she touched water and screamed when the TV went off and liked artichoke leaves and broccoli and was starting to read and loved any animals that were larger than herself but not the little ones so much. Margaret had delicate bones and coughed every winter and drew perfect little drawings of the things in her world, she concentrated and scrunched her forehead up and when she was done there was a purple flower or a bunk bed that looked just like a purple flower or the brand-new bunk bed and she never complained about anything, even about her sister who could try to boss her but couldn't really, because Margaret was too busy and careful and inward to be bossed. Hundreds of things more, at least. Go on. Let him bore you. Let him start taking out the pictures from his wallet.

Sascha. Maisie sometimes called Alexandra "Sascha." Maisie's sister's name, her sister Alexandra, whom everyone had called Sascha. Bloch walked down to the beach with Alexandra and Margaret gripping his fingers and he felt honored even by their names. The life he had chosen to live or the life that had chosen him. Sascha. One day, perhaps, he would call Alexandra "Sascha." For a few minutes they stopped by the road so that all three of them could pick berries.

One odd thing about the party at the beach was that Bloch knew more of the Mainers than he knew the summer people. By their faces, anyway, or by their nods, alternately wary or deferential or matter-of-fact, when they saw him coming into the store or the post office or walking along the roads. There was Verna, of course, and Mac and Bonnie, and Burton Cummins from Town Hall and Con Stephens the contractor and Thomas Benson the plumber and then all the others who'd worked on the house or the pool in one fashion or another, so that Bloch was embarrassed to think he might have been the employer of people he didn't even recognize. Not that that meant a helluva lot in Clement's Cove, to be the boss. People did the work they did, which was the best that they could do, and if you didn't like it you could find somebody else and see if they'd do it any better. Bloch liked it that way. He liked Clement's Cove. But still it felt odd how few of the summer people he could even nod to. Melissa and I were away. Cord was around, but he was dishing out hot dogs like a Southern carnie tout and didn't have time to talk, beyond shouting out the girls' names and giving them the fattest dogs he could find on the grill. Or that's what he said he was doing anyway. To Bloch they looked all the same size.

And anyway it hardly mattered to Bloch, on this day that seemed to propose country innocence, whom he knew and didn't know. The point was for Alexandra and Margaret to make friends. The three of them wandered by races that Bloch had never seen before and didn't quite understand. They hung out by the cotton candy. They went back to see how Cord was doing. But Cord's kids were all grown. High school, college. One at Yale. Maisie's girls, even Alexandra, seemed a little shy today.

And then the boat came in. Something unexpected, not only for Bloch but everyone else. Roy had put old Everett's boat in the water to test it and when she tested good he decided to put her to decent use giving the kiddies rides on the Fourth. Everett used to do it himself on the Fourth, not in this boat but in his old boat that he fished in, so Roy was just carrying on a tradition. He figured if nothing else it would win him some points with Verna, and it did. It made him seem to her as if he liked children. And who knew, maybe he did, and he just didn't know it before.

Roy very nearly beached the boat. He brought it in so close that kids could climb aboard just by taking off their sneakers and socks. He shouted he was giving free rides and every kid who wanted one should just line up. Pretty soon there was a fat line of little kids and big kids, summer folks and locals, that snaked up the beach above the tide line. Roy was a hit. With its scarlet paint so fresh, the boat looked almost like a toy put in the water by some local giant for its amusement. And Everett's old sixty-horse Mercury, that Roy had declined to send over to Danny Creighton for a rehab in favor of working on it himself, surely sounded enough old and cranky, but on the other hand Roy had got it going, which was believed to be something of a feat unto itself.

Bloch watched the ragged lineup of shorts and baseball caps from a little distance away. Alexandra asked if they could go on the boat. She said she wanted to, but for her part Margaret wasn't sure. "Let's watch it go first," Bloch said. And so they stood their little distance away, on a patch of ooze and mussels, and Bloch was relieved when the girls for a few moments turned their attention to the gathering of shells. Bloch wanted to see if it was all a legitimate and safe operation, Roy and his boat and his renovation. He wanted to see as an ersatz parent whether this was something he should be permitting.

The depth of Bloch's ambivalence surprised him. To go in this boat or not. To risk Maisie's girls or not. To trust the world or not. It began to feel as if his whole new life was at stake, and if he failed he would be back where he had been, back somewhere he could hardly any longer remember. Roy was passing out life jackets now, but they were old, bleached, flimsy things, the kind that once upon a time had been bought at a discount store or an auto parts store, the kind you'd get if you thought life jackets were a silly thing to start with. Though Bloch corrected himself, criticized himself: they were also what you'd buy if you had little money. Still, they looked flimsy, and he saw Roy putting one on a girl who was Margaret's size and it was so big on her it could have floated off her. Everett Hubbard's old life jackets, probably. Bloch knew little about life jackets, but he didn't like the look of these.

He knew little about the water, either, but he could see beyond the cove and it was not yet noon and the froth of late afternoon was already out there. Bloch didn't know. He wasn't sure. He let the girls look for shells while he continued to watch the little bright red toy of a boat.

Roy must have filled it with so many kids because the line was long and he didn't know how else they'd all get a chance. Ten kids, a parent or two, and Roy, so that they all wound up standing up or sitting on the little foredeck or the rails. Verna pushed them off. The Mercury labored under its load and the boat meandered out of the cove as if seized with half-heartedness. But then that must have been a ploy on Roy's part, to save a thrill or two for down the line, because as soon as he cleared the head, he gave the Mercury full throttle and Bloch could hear its sharper groaning and see the toy boat banging itself against the waves and then it disappeared.

He wasn't sure how long it was gone. He didn't check a watch. The girls tired of gathering shells and Alexandra still wanted a boat ride, so in the end they got in line. But it was still a very long line and they wouldn't be getting to the front of it anytime soon. Bloch was concerned now with the boat's repair. He had heard how Roy had smashed up Everett's boat and how he'd built it back together, but had anyone checked to see he'd done it well? As far as Bloch knew this was its maiden run or its next-to-maiden run and he could see the whitecaps out there, and whether the work Roy had done was good enough in a battering sea was another version of the question that was turning Bloch this way and that as if he were already in the waves.

Just a question, he didn't know, nor did he know who to ask. And he didn't want to be made fun of, either. The flimsy jackets, the froth, the overload of human cargo, the maiden voyage, the repair, the groaning old Mercury motor. Bloch wondered what Maisie would do. It was a clear day and Bloch could see no fog anywhere, but thirty years ago on the weekend that Maisie's sister Sascha died in the crash he'd gone out with his friends in a boat from Clement's Cove and there was no fog then, either, but the fog had come up quickly and surprised them. Roy's boat was gone for what seemed like a very long time. He was probably taking them all the way to Cape Rosier and the open bay. What would Maisie do?

She would tell him to decide for himself, of course. She would tell him to use his judgment. She would assume he knew what to do. She might even assume or hope that if the boat got in trouble, if it capsized or hit a rock or the engine failed or a wave swept somebody off the rail that Bloch would have some clue as to what to do. But why would she assume or hope that? Who did she imagine he was? It was another factor to consider.

In fifteen minutes the little scarlet boat came around the head and again into view. When it reached the shore there was laughter and chatter and the people on the shore observed and remarked that nearly everyone on the boat was soaked. The flimsy life jackets were exchanged. Another load piled aboard. Roy couldn't get the engine restarted. He yanked at it and tweaked it and took the cover off and tweaked a few things more. Bloch watched his frustration grow, until it reminded him of the phone calls that Jackman had received regarding Verna Hubbard's trailer from this same Roy Soames. They had seemed so pathetic, in Jackman's telling of them, that Bloch had almost given in. But Roy was a whiner, Bloch decided, and he didn't trust whiners.

Finally, Tom Benson took off his shoes and waded to the stern of the boat and gave Roy some suggestion, and whatever the suggestion was, it got the old Mercury going again. By then Bloch had decided to take the girls home. He told them the line was too long and that Maisie would be wanting them home for lunch, so they left.

"Why, though? That's what I don't understand." Maisie was recovered from her migraine. It was later in the afternoon. The girls in their room napping, Maisie and Adam on the porch, in fleece jackets with their hands in their pockets because the fog had just come in. Light on its feet and stealthy, it slipped over the porch rails like a burglar and blew in whispers down the porch.

Bloch stared at her, unable to blink. He wasn't sure if he'd done wrong or been done wrong. He wasn't even sure if he could get out words. "It was that combination of things," he managed to say.

"But the whole point was take them over so they could see some kids, meet some other kids. They've got to do the things kids do here. They can't be like freaks out here."

"I know that, Maisie."

"I mean, we've got this enormous house, for four little people, it's ridiculous, I grew up like this, I don't need this, don't you get that?"

"Isn't that another subject?"

"I just want them to have a normal life here. *I* want to have a normal life here. And if you're going to be scared of every little thing, if you're going to act like a person can't catch a cold because it'll be the death of them or whatever that stupid thing was people used to say, when maybe it would be the death of them back then, but it wouldn't be now. You're just so scared of everything, Adam. Where does that come from? You're going to drive all of us crazy."

"It was just a judgment call. Really. I'm sorry. But if you'd seen that boat. . ."

"I have seen that boat."

"And?"

"I don't know. It floats, doesn't it? It didn't sink, did it? I mean, people around here know about these things. Believe it or not, they're scared of the water. A lot of these people, especially the old ones, they don't even swim. They know if a boat's not safe."

"You're probably right. I probably should have just done what they did. . . But the fog did come in."

"Jesus. Jesus. Yes. Now it's in. How many hours later?"

"I was just trying to do what I thought you'd do. And I still think, if you'd seen what I saw. . ."

"Wrong. No. Wrong."

"What about when. . ."

"Don't start with examples from the past, alright? Don't start with stupid examples from the past, because, you know, you're so logical, you think you can just be totally logical and that's all life is, just figure everything out, in that little mind there. You know what you're like? If somebody bashed you in the head, a lot of clock parts would come out."

"Thank you."

"Don't thank me, even sarcastically."

"Well what do you want me to say, Maisie? I already said I'm sorry."

"I just. . . I don't want to be a freak. I don't want my girls to be freaks. You brought us here. We didn't have to come here. But now that we're here. . ."

"I thought this would be a good home for you."

"Yes, yes, okay, I like it here, okay? But I don't want to be a freak."

"You're the one wanted the lap pool."

"What in Christ sake has that got to do with it? Oh for God's sake! It's only a lap pool. Is that such a big deal? Okay, forget it, tear it out, don't finish it. I'll go to the Y."

"There is no Y."

"You know what I'm saying."

"I'm sorry what I said about the lap pool."

They were quiet after that. But everything Maisie said had been building up in her. She had said all of it before in different ways. But it had built up again. Now she wondered if it was not, in fact, a little freakish on her own part, a little contributing to the delinquency of a timid rich guy, to want a lap pool dug in solid ledge on the coast of Maine.

But what Bloch said slowed her down anyway. "It's my joy for you to have what you need."

They were quiet again. Bloch rued sounding so eloquent. It sounded stupid to him, the sound of his hoarse words seemed to linger in the damp air of the fog.

Like a lie? Was that the miasmic shape his mind made in the mist?

If so, Maisie didn't seem to notice, and Bloch asked himself, further, if he had gotten away with one, if he had talked her into something that even he didn't believe.

"You know what this fog reminds me of?" she said.

"What?"

"When Sascha died. That was in the fog, wasn't it?"
"It was."
"I think that's what you're afraid of. I think you're afraid of . . ."
"Repeating it? Doing the same thing again? Killing somebody?"
"Am I wrong?"
"I can't . . ."
Suddenly Bloch felt as if he were choking. He looked away. He stared into the fog's blankness.
"What?"
"This is a problem. This is my problem, you see."
"What's wrong with you? Are you okay? Adam, look at me."
"Why?"
"Why? Look at me! Jesus."
So he did. He looked at her and again he didn't blink.
"I'm sorry."
"You can't be sorry all the time."
"But I am."
"You'll kill us all then."
"There was fog, yes. There was fog. The night Sascha died. Am I speaking clearly enough now? That night, there was fog."
"Adam, you're not scaring me, you know that, don't you? You're just being a shit now. Just come back here. Come back here."
"I'm here," Bloch said.

16

Maisie wanted her lap pool to be plain. She didn't want a spa or a fountain or waterfall or rock formations or black tiles or a vanishing edge. She wanted it to be as unadorned as the chlorine-faded tank suits that she swam in. That was her aesthetic. That was her choice. If she was going to scar the land, she wanted the scar to be as honest as possible. She wanted a mark simple and geometric and severe. She didn't want it to blend in. She wouldn't have believed it if it blended in. She didn't want to swim in fantasy.

Bloch had a bit of a time conveying this idea to the builders and designers. They'd keep to it for awhile, but then have some idea that this or that adornment would be a nice touch, or an interesting highlight, or just something that an expensive pool shouldn't be without. They couldn't quite accept the idea that something so expensive might not look it. It was beyond being conservative, it was beyond tasteful restraint, it was just plain, and it irritated them and even made them think that others, future customers, would think that Bloch had been overcharged. How could you put so plain a pool on your Web site? In truth, Bloch wasn't unsympathetic to the idea of having a few flourishes of observable luxury. Did the tiles from Saragossa that each cost as much as a caviar tin really have to be the color of sand? But they were what Maisie wanted. Bloch felt that she could see things that he couldn't.

The summer went along. The last summer of the millennium,

by some calculations, the second-to-last according to others. Bloch, being a rational man, was inclined to be in the second-to-last camp, but who was he to argue with the popular mood? It was a time that seemed peaceful enough. Presidential blowjobs still at the top of the national agenda, stock markets going nuts, a country struck dumb with its overall good luck. Maisie put the girls in a "pre-day camp" and went every day with them to make sure they didn't cry. For herself she found a heated public pool in Castine and drove over there in the late afternoons. The house began to be a little more lived in. They expanded the frontiers of what they used. When she thought of it, Maisie even bought stuff. And the Elliots would come over or they would go to the Elliots, and they met others over there. Women who were fighting the Wal-Mart with Denny, sailing buddies of Cord's. Clement's Cove was sweetly boring and quiet, so that you could hear yourselves think or laugh. Maisie read a biography of Tolstoy. Bloch read Gibbon. Both of them read to the girls.

Like a watchdog Bloch kept track of it all. Maisie's moods, the girls' moods, the progress of the pool. He wanted it done by Labor Day. They were promising that it would be and by August he began to believe it. Extra crews arrived. Crates with tiles and filter equipment and heater parts arrived. It was all coming together.

And perhaps it was only because it was all coming together that Bloch's darker imagination began to sense Maisie's indifference to it all. She made remarks about how she liked driving over to Castine, the pool was cold there but she was getting used to it, she liked getting out of the house. They had babysitters by then. Phalanxes of babysitters, and for next year Maisie was thinking of an *au pair* from Hungary or Slovakia, or maybe a pair of *au pairs*. Bloch liked it that she was even thinking of next year. But her indifference, if that's what it was, to the lap pool annoyed him. The fickleness of women, all of that. Bloch was not immune, he realized, to feeling the chronic complaints of men. The age-old complaints of men.

It became a subject he didn't discuss with her. He just wanted the damn thing done. It made him anxious wondering if she'd like it or not or if his darker imagination was betraying him or not. August could be anything in Clement's Cove but this one was warm. On the long dry days the workmen raced toward their finish line. On the eighteenth of August the general contractor knocked on the door and told Bloch that the heater and filter were hooked up in test mode. The tile work wasn't done and the coping needed its finishing grout, but the pool was full of ninety-degree water and if anyone wanted to try the thing out they should make themselves feel free. Bloch hesitated to tell Maisie. It was late afternoon and she'd just come from her swim in Castine. And he wanted this to be perfect now. He wanted the pool to have its best chance with her. She who, Bloch believed, believed in first impressions. Although, if that were entirely so, how had she wound up with him? *Pecunia omnia vincit?* Maisie came out of the kitchen and asked him who had been at the door and Bloch told her it was Falsey the contractor and the pool was heated to ninety degrees.

He let her go up the path herself in a terrycloth robe so that he could watch her disappear into the woods. In Bloch's modest understanding of it, Greek goddesses were always disappearing into woods, and he liked considering Maisie that way, an eternal something in a terrycloth robe. Nor did he want to seem to be following her around, or to be on the scene as if waiting for instant praise. Instead he sat on the porch. Whatever would be, would be. Silly thoughts, boyish thoughts.

Maisie threw off her terrycloth robe and took the plunge. The pool was so warm she thought she would have to tell Bloch to turn it down. It had to be ninety-five degrees. Adam had a way of going overboard, she thought, as she swam her laps. She was a little tired from having just swum an hour before, but the water, as usual, gave her its own good reasons to keep going. Her life was this now. Her life was swimming laps. Until she was done, and floated on her back, and saw the spruce rise everywhere around her like giant blades of dark grass and the sun glinting through. Maybe not a sacred glade, but close enough. The plainness of the pool was to her liking. It was there because men had come in and put it there.

In an hour she came back down the path in her terrycloth robe, her damp hair stringy and dark with chlorine in a way that seemed happy and used, and reported to Bloch that everything was terrific, except the water was a little too warm.

Bloch smiled reservedly, the way he'd learned to smile, in good news and bad, afraid he'd seem a fool to show how happy he really was. As soon as she was gone inside, he ran all the way to the pool himself, threw off his clothes down to his underpants, and in a moment of astonished joy, jumped in.

17

Something more about Maisie. She liked to get to the bottom of things. She didn't stand on ceremony, didn't keep her mouth shut. But Bloch was not so easy. That talk on the Fourth of July. The fog, his fear. It was not that she thought she was telling him anything new.

Crazy girl. Talking therapy. Labels that didn't apply. All her life, it seemed.

In her own humble opinion, winding up as sane as anybody else. And maybe saner, so go fuck yourself. Life had made her sane. As best she could figure it out, anyway. And occasionally keeping her eyes open.

She felt, or sometimes hoped, that she rounded out Bloch's life with sincerity. She didn't lie to him. Not much, anyway.

Had she married him because it was easy? No real answer to that one, except if there were fools around who thought any marriage was easy. But then the question wasn't whether marriage was easy but whether marrying him had been easy, and what if it was, but there were other things as well?

Had she tried to tell him that the reasons for his self-contempt were not real? Of course she had. She had *told* him. As if telling were the same as living.

The girls. The girls, the girls.

If she prayed for anything, Maisie prayed for time.

18

Things hadn't been going Roy's way. His fallback position was going to be that when Freddy closed the deal with the summer person from Northeast Harbor and got his expanded fleet of limos going, Roy could at least drive for him. A bitter pill, considering that until recently Roy had been hoping to be Freddy's partner in the business with a full half share of the profits. But at least the tips would be pretty good if you drove a limo on Mount Desert Island and the hours would be to his liking and he'd be away from the Clement's Cove area where in his opinion people had gotten into the habit of scrutinizing him a little too much. And now that wasn't working out, either.

The summer person from Northeast had backed out of the deal. Freddy wasn't getting his expanded fleet after all. He was in almost as bad a shape as Roy was.

Roy did odd labor around, for Con Stephens and Tom Benson among others, and some of that labor was even for Mr. Bloch himself, as an employee of Con Stephens he'd done some hauling away of pool debris. The whole thing galled him. Getting paid so much less than Con Stephens and Tom Benson galled him, when he was every bit as smart as they were and wound up doing the heavy lifting for them. But more than that, this whole thing with Mr. Bloch and his pool and his house and his wife and all the people working for them in various ways and everyone saying he was a nice enough fella and a fair enough individual to work for while Roy for his part could put two and two together. For instance, why couldn't Mr. Bloch come up with this lousy forty thousand dollars to protect his view from Verna's trailer? It was a fair deal, you couldn't say it wasn't a fair deal, Roy wasn't trying to gouge him. And he could sure afford it. And it could have solved all Roy's problems.

Not that Roy expected a stranger to solve his problems. Roy wasn't that crazy. But still. There was something Roy couldn't put his finger on but he knew he didn't like it. The money. For safety's sake, just call it the money. If you had so much of it you probably couldn't even count it, why be so fucking careful with it? Although, of course, the simple answer to that, what everybody said, was that's how you got to have more money than you could count, by being careful about it. There. That was it, that was what he was trying to put his finger on, that was what Roy didn't like. He felt this person ought to be freer with himself.

And the swimming pool, too. Nobody'd ever built a swimming pool in Clement's Cove before, nobody'd ever felt the need to, and least of all in the middle of a pile of rock. Days when he wasn't working Roy would be out in Verna's yard, splitting wood or fooling around with Everett's boat, and he'd watch the trucks go up and down the road and he'd think to himself, God almighty, what a fuss over nothing. Hadn't grown men got better things to do with themselves? He even made a bet to himself, that Bloch wouldn't swim in it once himself. He didn't look like the swimming type. He told Verna. He told her he'd bet her, too, but she didn't like to bet.

So Roy didn't take it well the night Verna suggested to him he ought to go work for Mr. Bloch.

"Why don't *you* go work for him then?" Roy said.

"I'm not the one needs regular work, Roy."

"I got work," he said.

They were watching the antiques show on the public station, which Roy couldn't stand, but which Verna got a kick from every time somebody that looked like herself found something in their departed aunt's attic and it turned out to be something like Abraham Lincoln's walking stick. She liked the way they all cried a little or covered their mouths when they found out what it was worth.

"Look at that thing. What is that thing?" Roy in his transparent change-the-subject mode, almost making fun of himself for changing the subject, because it looked like Verna was starting on a tear. "Looks like a dildo to me."

"It's an old pencil sharpener, Roy."

"They have dildos back then? Sure looks like a dildo."

"Jesus. Roy. Could I have that please?"

She reached across him and the lounger for the channel changer and muted the sound.

"I thought you liked this crap."

"I'm talking to you about something."

"I told you, I got work."

"You're standing around here two-three days a week. That's not work. You call putting little tiny dabs of paint on Dad's boat work?"

"No, that's not work. That's leisure. That's my leisure time."

"Suit yourself then."

"Well I am. I'm waiting on a number of situations."

"In the meantime, you sit around complaining, Con Stephens is ripping you off, everybody's ripping you off. I happen to know because Marla told me, Jimmy Phillips was getting twenty an hour up there for general labor, just general labor. Because he was working for Mr. Bloch instead of those blockheads. No middleman, Roy. It just makes sense."

"Why'd you mute the sound out?"

"So I could talk to you."

Roy again looked disgusted at the TV screen.

"What's *that* thing?"

"What's it look like, it's a picture. In a frame."

"Yeah, of what?"

"Roy."

"You go up there, Verna. You add a client."

"I don't have room for another client. Believe me, if I did, I'd be up there."

Roy pretended once more to be interested in the antiques show. After awhile he muttered, "Shit."

"It was just a suggestion, Roy. Don't be mad. Would you not be mad, please?"

"Shit."

It didn't occur to either Verna or Roy that Bloch might not hire Roy because he didn't like him or had already formed a negative impression of him. If anything, Roy felt, Mr. Bloch would have recognized at least his entrepreneurial spirit. Three days later, after enough time had passed so that Verna couldn't think he was doing it in response to her nagging, and because, as Roy put it, a few of the situations he was waiting on appeared as though they might not pan out, Roy went up to Bloch's place to apply for work. Or he didn't apply exactly. Roy made himself available. He went right to the front door and knocked. The wife came to the door. Maisie. Roy introduced himself, said he was living down the road, cited the variety of his skills, and said if they had anything for him he'd be happy to consider it.

Maisie liked Roy's looks. The gappy smile, the shock of hair, the lanky athleticism, even the bad country complexion. He looked like he could do what he said he could do. She needed help around the garden anyway, and there were some other things that Adam was talking about, handyman kind of things, and it was still summer when help was hard to find. So she said, "We'll hire you." Roy wasn't going to bring up the subject of compensation because it seemed tacky to him at this moment and he felt he'd be in a better position to negotiate once they saw him on the job, but she asked him what he wanted, so he had no choice but to say his normal rate was twenty dollars an hour. Maisie said that would be okay.

Later she told Adam what she had done. He connected the dots for her as to who Roy was exactly. Maisie couldn't see anything wrong with any of it. Adam said he didn't really care for the guy but on the other hand he didn't actually know him, and if Maisie wanted to give him a try, why not.

19

Things had always been a balancing act with Roy. Everything had its good parts and its bad parts. For instance in the case of working for the Blochs, the money was good and you could save on gas because it was right up the road and it only took two seconds to get there. That cut your workday by an hour or an hour and a half right there. On the other hand, there was Mr. Bloch himself. Mrs. Bloch wasn't too bad. Mrs. Bloch, Ms. Maclaren, whatever she wanted to be called. Maisie. She said Maisie was fine. Roy was warming up to that. He'd called her Maisie a few times already. Mr. Bloch, the same way, said to call him Adam, but Roy didn't feel he truly meant it. It was more like something he thought he should say to prove he was a regular guy or something. But Roy felt he wasn't exactly. He held himself too aloof. It was like the identical case with his money, in fact it was the same thing. Maybe he meant otherwise, but it wound up so you never just forgot who was the boss.

Which of course it wasn't right to complain about, since he *was* the boss. But on the other hand it led to, or was combined with, the other thing, which was that even though he was the boss, you could never tell exactly what he wanted. He was so fucking polite all the time, it was like he was afraid to tell you. And when he did finally tell you, it could be so fucking stupid and clueless you'd wish he'd never told you in the first place. Verna was learning not to get Roy started on this.

Though there was one case he must have told her about twenty times. After Roy was done getting Maisie's garden ready for the fall, the next thing they wanted was Mr. Bloch had a big pile of videos and DVDs and television scripts, obviously from when he'd owned a whole TV company in California, and he wanted Roy to dispose of them. That was the exact word he used, *dispose* of them. There were boxes of them. They nearly filled the bed of Roy's pickup. Roy didn't even know what they were exactly until he drove them out to the transfer station. In fact it was Ralph Audry out there who was the first to see what Roy had and suggested there could be something of value there. So instead of throwing all the tapes and DVDs in a dumpster, they stacked them up in Ralph's shed out at the transfer station. All the current hit programs were included in these tapes and a lot of movies Roy had never heard of, but then he wasn't one to keep up-to-the-minute regarding such things. They decided Ralph would sell them off at fifty cents or a dollar and the two of them would split the proceeds.

Then Callie Cummins bought a couple of these from Ralph and was in the general store with them and Mr. Bloch came in and apparently he could tell what they were because they were all marked "FOR YOUR VIEWER CONSIDERATION" or something of that nature. So now he came back to Roy and said, "I thought I asked you to dispose of those things."

"Which things?" Roy said.

"Those boxes of papers and videotapes."

"I did. I did that exactly, I disposed of them."

"Well I saw somebody in the store with some of them. Did you take them to the dump?"

"Absolutely. Took 'em to the transfer station and disposed of them."

"Well I don't know how, but I guess they didn't all get destroyed."

"Sir, Mr. Bloch, with all due respect, you didn't say *destroyed*."
"I didn't?"
"No sir."
"Well could we possibly destroy them?"

If that wasn't the stupidest thing. Even there, he didn't say "destroy them." He said, "could we possibly?"

Of course "we could possibly."

But anyway Roy destroyed them. What a waste.

That's how Roy concluded the story, each time he told it to Verna. What a waste. Verna teased Roy at first about how he wasn't going to get to be Mr. Bloch's caretaker with that level of communication. But she found it wasn't a matter to tease him about. Roy didn't aspire to be a caretaker. Looking after damn fools, that's all it amounted to. To which Verna took exception, reminding him that Everett her father had been a caretaker fifteen years, after his retirement. Roy grumbled and said it wasn't for him, that's all he meant. He was going to start a proper business, as soon as circumstances allowed. It was the only way to get out of this situation.

It was past Labor Day now. A lot of the summer people had left. Adam and Maisie stayed on, but even they weren't there as much as they had been. Or she wasn't, anyway. She had doctors appointments in New York. She and the girls flew back and forth. While they were gone, Bloch found another job for Roy. Past Verna's place, as Bloch's road wound up toward the big house, there was a bend and it came out of the trees and there was a magnificent view to the south and west. The bay, the Camden hills, the islands. People had been going up there for that view when there was hardly a road. Now cars were coming up there all the time, which Bloch wouldn't have minded but the problem was that once they were up there they couldn't get out, there was no room to turn around and so all they could do was drive on up to Bloch's house and turn around in the circular drive, which meant cars were coming right to his front door at all hours of the day and night. Not a *huge* number, Bloch said, he didn't want to exaggerate, but enough to be annoying and a problem. "You have any ideas, Roy, how to solve that?" he asked.

"Let me think on it," Roy allowed, but by that same afternoon he was hard at work. He dug up a number of large rocks, of which there was no shortage in the neighborhood of Verna's trailer, and lifted them into his truck and drove up to where the magnificent view was and placed the rocks at three foot intervals all along there, so that cars coming up wouldn't even have place to pull off the road.

He was very nearly expecting a raise from Mr. Bloch on account of his fast work. He didn't see him for a couple of days. He had some brush-clearing to do and went at it.

On the third day Bloch found him by the giant brush pile that he'd collected. "I saw the rocks you put out there," Bloch said. "On the road."

"You like that?" Roy said. "Nobody'll be parking there anymore, I'd estimate. The message'll be getting out."

"Well but here's a concern I have. The way it is now, if people stop anyway, they'll have to stay in the middle of the road, and there's that bend just past it going back into the woods. I'm just afraid it's going to cause an accident."

"If you're a fool enough to stop in the middle of the road, serves you right, I guess."

"I don't want an accident," Bloch said. "I don't want anybody getting hurt."

"Not too likely, I shouldn't think."

"Likely or not," Bloch said. "Have you got any other ideas?"

So Roy went back at it. He removed all the rocks from the side of the road and rolled them into the ravine. He went on to what he considered the next best obvious idea, putting up a gate. Not a big gate, not so delivery trucks and such couldn't get past. But enough gate to give people pause. He again set to work. He took measurements and began digging post holes for where he felt the gate ought to be. On his second day of working at it, he again observed Mr. Bloch strolling down from his house. He had a look of curiosity, like he just was wondering what was happening here. "Hello, Roy."

"Mr. Bloch."

"Really. Adam."

"'You say so."

"Look, Roy, what are you doing here exactly?"

"Laying the foundations. See if a gate can go here. Wouldn't do anything without your final permission, of course. And then too, you'll want to make your choice of gates, whether it's locked or not, whether it's one of these remotes or not, like a garage door opener in your car."

"Roy. I think I don't want a gate here."

"You think, or you don't want?"

"I don't want a gate here, Roy."

"Then how're you going to keep people out of your place? You said you wanted to keep people out of your place."

"I just don't want a gate. It's too, I don't, too something. . . too much."

"You're the boss."

"What about a sign?"

"I don't know if signs'll do the job."

"Well could we try it?"

So Roy went to the builder's place in Blue Hill and came back with an array of NO TRESPASSING and KEEP OUT and PRIVATE DRIVE signs in bright colors that would reflect at night. He staked them in the ground where Bloch's road began and further along the way as the road went up.

But Bloch didn't like these either.

"You know what they remind me of? Burma Shave signs."

"Why's that?" Roy asked.

"I suppose. . . there's so many of them."

"They don't say Burma Shave. They say keep out."

"And they're a little bright, the colors. And a little big."

"You said you didn't want people going up there."

"Couldn't we try something a little smaller? You know, plain wood, stained wood, or something. Just to remind people. I'd like to be polite about it."

"For pity's sake. You know what, Mr. Bloch? You don't know what you want."

Bloch smiled weakly. "Well I suppose there could be some truth to that."

"*Some* truth? That *is* the truth. I've done every damn thing but put a stoplight up here, and nothing's right, nothing's good for you. I don't know how to please you because I don't think you know how to please yourself, and that's the Lord's truth, Mr. Bloch. And don't say 'Adam.' Just don't say, 'Call me Adam.' I'm getting a little sick of this stuff. I'm getting a little bit fed up to here. You don't know what you want. And you don't know when people are steering you correctly. I'm afraid I can't help you any more, Mr. Bloch."

To make his point emphatic, Roy grabbed the nearest NO TRESPASSING sign that he'd staked in the ground, ripped it out and threw it down. "And by the way, you don't have to pay me for these signs or work on the gate or lifting all those fucking rocks. We're even."

Roy walked back down the road toward Verna's trailer, thinking this had been long overdue in coming.

When Maisie got back and he told her that Roy had quit, she was quiet about it. She didn't ask a lot of questions. Though in not asking a lot of questions, Bloch felt that Maisie was somehow taking Roy's side. As if Bloch had somehow provoked him. As if Roy was the one who lived around here and knew how things were done around here. As if Roy was somehow more of a man, younger and more full of life and a stabbing energy. She didn't say any of these things, but Bloch felt them in her silence. He might have been wrong, about her feelings, but he felt he wasn't wrong.

They began packing so that all of them would return to New York. She had too many doctor's appointments to keep going back and forth. And the girls' preschool would start in the middle of October.

The pool was finished now and Maisie swam in it every day.

Bloch solved the problem of the road and the unwanted visitors by posting a small wooden sign on a tree by the road on which was written, in letters that might sparkle a little at night but were otherwise undemonstrative, "Please Respect Our Privacy." Some paid it attention and some didn't, but overall the problem was less.

He slept not as well now. He would wake up after two or three hours of sleep and stare over at Maisie, who was curled away from him. He knew that if he moved toward her or touched her, she would not want it. She would hold still or whisper that she was sleeping or that she needed to sleep.

Cord Elliot had taken up hang-gliding and one day when Teddy Redmond was up from Connecticut, he invited Bloch to go with them over to Schoodic where there was a hang-gliding school. Cord and Denny had just returned from ten days in Marrakesh, Cord never having been one to sit around. Teddy had no intentions of going hang gliding himself, he had a foot afflicted with a touch of gout and anyway he simply wouldn't. He wasn't crazy like Cord. He would enjoy watching Cord fly around in the sky in a contraption that looked about as flimsy as some women's underwear. That would be enough thrills for him.

And when Bloch heard Teddy's intentions, he figured he could follow along in Teddy's wake, even if he had no touch of gout himself. Cord and Teddy were the ones, along with myself, who had turned on Adam after Sascha's death, who had been slow to forgive him and in some sense never could. These were facts on the ground, to Bloch and all of us, but also facts on the ground were the thirty-odd years that had intervened, and Bloch's generosity toward us all, and our mellowing, our ability to see around the corners of things better. The result being that we were all shocked and amazed yet on the whole happy enough, in a you-never-know-in-this-world sort of way, when it got around that Bloch had run into Maisie on a New York street and they had started dating; and felt more of the same when we heard they were to be married; and Cord welcomed them to Clement's Cove and so did I; and we stood up for him at his wedding, as if thirty-odd years had never intervened, as if once and for all we had become men. Always a tenuous proposition, always a test of faith.

Now Bloch was driving over with Teddy and Cord to Schoodic to watch Cord jump off a cliff, and Bloch was still a little afraid, as if there was something in him of the imposter, which in moments of sincerity, such as seemed called for by old friends, was in danger of being found out. The imposter that was in him, the imposter that was him, the imposter that was not him. Though he was content enough to be away for the day. Maisie was always going away, for a day here, a day there. She kept busy and she kept the girls busy. Bloch felt somehow that by going away he was lifting a bit of burden off her.

It was a familiar morning on the coast, that began with slashes of color and promise and soon clouded over with something more like the truth. A front coming in from somewhere. By nine the sky was gray and tense, as if the air was awaiting further instructions. Bloch sat on the hood of the car with Teddy and watched their friend float and loop around and rise in funnels of wind they could only imagine. He was like a birdman, like a guy with a crazy idea, distant, doing it, a speck suspended from blue-green wings between the hungry gray ocean and the bare glacial rises of the point. For a little while Bloch didn't think of Maisie. Cord as if representing them all, but what did he represent exactly? Their coming to the point in their lives where every solution was private. Get your money, fly your plane, build your house, get your kids into good colleges and if possible the same one you went to. And so it would go on, maybe. A matter of maintenance. But here was Cord, so high up in the air he looked like a little boy or a fool or a surprise. Being brave, in that private way. His friends had come along as if to keep the old days going, whatever those old days were, but Cord would have been there whether they were or not. Not a stunning victory. Maybe not even a victory at all. But something more than what Teddy's swollen foot or Bloch's skinny legs felt like as they dangled from the hood of the car.

He came down out of the white sky like a messenger, slow and circling, landing in a burnt-over blueberry field. Somebody who had turned out well and did it make a bit of difference to the world?

Though, in the preceding paragraph, wherever I wrote *their*, I could as easily have written *our*. Our friend, our coming to the point of our lives, Cord representing us all. I could have been there, but I wasn't.

Although in another sense, I was. My understanding later was that through much of lunch they talked about me. Why the fuck *wasn't* I there? Where the fuck was I and who the fuck did I think I was, "going émigré" as if it were something akin to going postal. Good-natured enough. And Adam wouldn't have said any of that. Teddy and Cord, the ones that I was easy with. Bloch would have stayed silent. Though later when they wondered what I was writing and why I didn't e-mail and whatever else you could say about a guy who pulled up stakes for awhile, he might have put in a word or two. No hyperbole from Bloch. He could still sit and look like a rock.

Then they were all packed up and driving home and it was quiet except for the radio that Teddy kept fooling with, finding little that he liked. Bloch was in the back with Cord's harness poking around his ears. Most of the way Cord and Teddy argued about Bush, who was then a presidential candidate, and Bloch kept quiet. Cord seemed to be of the opinion that because Bush went to Yale with us and Gore who was sure to be the Democrats' candidate went to Harvard, that he would feel compelled to vote for George. After awhile he half-convinced the others that really, *really*, he was joking, but Teddy still suspected that if it ever came down to it Cord would vote for Bush. Bush had once nicknamed Cord "Third String," on account of Cord being Yale's third-string quarterback at the time when Bush was a cheerleader, and the year before I myself had been with Cord when Bush called up out of the blue asking for "Third String's" opinion about a businessman from Memphis who wanted some key post organizing for them in Tennessee. This was part of what made Teddy suspicious. And Cord saying that Bush was a "pretty good guy." He harangued Cord awhile about how it wasn't enough to be a "pretty good guy," if you were president you had to think of the world or for that matter they did too. It wasn't enough for anybody anymore just to be a "good guy." Obviously a cut at Cord, but what had Teddy done to save the world? Open a bike shop in Fairfield, Connecticut? Fail to get a script made or a book done in fifteen or twenty years? Things Cord didn't say, but Bloch the ever-neutral one at least thought them. Cord himself was still a good guy, and good guys didn't say such things to their friends, or if they did, it was with friendly sarcasm. Two roads diverging, but whose was the less traveled? Cord changed the subject.

Changing the subject was about as angry as Cord got. He asked Adam how things were going with Maisie.

Adam being in the back, his friends couldn't see that he didn't blink.

The question reduced itself to the stone that was inside him. He didn't know what to say, so he said fine.

"You packing up pretty soon?"

"Maisie's got some appointments in New York next week. More doctors."

"Anything going on?"

"Not as far as we know. Just checkups."

"That girl's brave."

"I think she is."

"We've got to have you over to the house before you leave."

"Good. That would be good."

Teddy hadn't had a word in, so over his shoulder he said, "Hey Adam, Mister Confirmed Former Bachelor, if I could ask as someone who's a little risk-averse himself, what's it like?"

"It's fine."

"That's it? It's fucking fine?"

"I guess."

"You know, you're a fine commercial for conjugal bliss, you fuck," Teddy said.

"Well. But it is."

"Maisie's one of the great ones. You got one of the great ones. And I've done some sampling."

"I know you have," Bloch said.

"Are you happy or not?" Cord asked. "That's all it boils down to." He'd become a little annoyed with Teddy's needling tone.

Bloch held his head up and looked forward between the seats, as if he had a bad seat at the movies. His neck felt stiff. *Was he happy?* His fear grew that he might do or say something unmanly. He who believed that once before in his life, and with these two men, he had done something unmanly.

Yet there was something matter-of-fact in Cord's tone, different from Teddy's bantering, that sounded like it might bear the weight of Bloch's soul. He began to feel the urge to answer. He asked himself, as if it were a question that could be put to him equally by an angel or a devil, what were friends for, after all. A cliché, a conundrum, maybe even a verbal sleight-of-hand. Bloch didn't really know what friends were for. They might have been for a lot of things. The one thing he knew was that he didn't want to lose the ones he had.

Although maybe it wasn't possible to lose friends. Maybe that was the thing about them, that they were impossible to lose. Bloch didn't believe that. It sounded to him like cheap propaganda.

Cord's simple question floated in his mind. *Was he happy?* Bloch felt like a sleepwalker and someone in the next room was calling to him, trying to wake him up.

"I'm happy," he said. His voice was hoarse, the way it got. Then he choked back quiet tears, which the others saw but said nothing about.

20

Things that Bloch might have said to Cord and Teddy.

That there were moments when he hated her.

That he had done no wrong.

That this whole thing with Roy and the signs and the gate and the pool and the house and buying and not buying and Clement's Cove was a conundrum.

That being rich was also a conundrum.

That he must remember to be grateful, that he must struggle to be grateful.

That it was worth the remembrance, that it was worth the fight.

That he was embarrassed.

That there were too few Jews in Clement's Cove, for a Jew like him, who was too much a Jew.

That you could scratch that last thought.

That Maisie was well, thank you, that the girls were well, thank you, that he was well, thank you.

That he hoped it would be seen one day who he really was. That even he would see it.

Or maybe it was all in his unblinking wet eyes.

21

A dream of Maisie's.

She comes out of the house. Roy is working in her garden and looks up at her with disdain or complaint. He stands up and says, "This disease won't grow." He repeats himself. "This disease won't grow in this soil."

Concerned, she asks, "Is there something wrong with the soil? If there's something wrong with the soil. . ."

She comes closer, to see what's wrong, what he's talking about.

"You're going to have to do something," he says, "you can't go on like this."

But when she leans down to look, it looks just like soil and she wonders why disease won't grow in it.

He smells like sweat and fertilizer.

She looks down at the soil and feels his fingers on her chin, lifting her face until she can see his gappy, happy, friendly smile, his hungry smile, his floppy, dirty, happy, hungry hair, and he says, "Sorry, ma'am, but my breath smells like fertilizer," and then his rough lips kiss hers.

A dream, of course, that she might not have had. But I believe she did. Some version of it, anyway.

22

After Roy quit working for Mr. Bloch, the first problem that he knew he'd have to confront was how to tell Verna. He decided the best thing would be to get another job before he said anything to her. He even took the trouble of not looking for work around Clement's Cove, because word would get around. Instead he went over to Mount Desert. Unfortunately Freddy's situation over there had deteriorated from not too bad to worse.

Not only had the summer person from Northeast pulled out of the purchase deal on Royce Gilmore's limousines, but Freddy's alternate driver had driven over some rough terrain and screwed up both the air conditioning and the transmission on Freddy's own vehicle. A big bill, in consequence of which Freddy was doing all the driving himself these days. And it was out of season now. Less demand for car service. Roy went a week without finding anything.

In the meantime he plied Verna with some nice gifts. More flowers from the Tradewinds, a nice little book on knitting that he saw lying around over on Mount Desert. Verna liked to knit. She'd knitted him a scarf once, which he'd appreciated and told her so. Though he also told her, at a certain point, that he didn't really wear a scarf too much, which had caused tears and her promise never to knit him one fucking thing ever again.

So in a sense the book was a little joke between them, or an apology of sorts, it was a present that had some thought behind it. And he also brought home half a side of beef one night. All this he considered to be laying the groundwork for telling her and softening the blow. But he knew he couldn't delay too long, because even though Verna left early for her appointments, she would sometimes stop back home during the day and Roy would soon be running out of excuses as to why his truck was never around or why she never saw him going to or from Mr. Bloch's anymore. And of course he'd be running short of money pretty soon.

He decided he'd have to broach the subject without having found new work. It seemed to him that over dinner, when they were enjoying a couple steaks that came off the half a side of beef, was as good a time as any. He began by reminding her once again of the stories that suggested how ridiculous a person this Mr. Bloch could be to work for. The videotapes and all of that. His analysis of Mr. Bloch was as follows: he must have been damn lucky to make all that money he had, because he sure didn't know how to make up his mind about anything, and in a business situation, decisiveness is the first thing that's necessary, you could read that anywhere, and in fact it just made common sense. So either he was just damn lucky or he used to have some decent sense and getting all that money just rotted out his mind and instincts, so that he was complete mush now.

Plus he was pussy-whipped. Totally pussy-whipped, in Roy's opinion, in fact, in back of it all, you could probably explain everything that way. Or the two went together. He had to ask *her* the difference between his ass and his elbow, and if she wasn't ever around to ask, he was in deep, deep shit.

"So you must be developing a lot of patience and tolerance to be dealing with all that," Verna finally said.

"I was. I definitely was."

"That's pretty good, Roy. I mean, that wasn't, that didn't used to be a strength of yours."

"But I mean, anybody, anybody at all, they've got their limits. Am I right? You can't work in a dehumanized environment forever."

"Now what's that mean? Dehumanized environment?"

"I'm saying, the man's an asshole."

"Oh, Roy."

"Roy what?"

"I hear you say things like that. . ."

"It's only the truth. The man's impossible."

Verna hesitated. Roy, perhaps, could see what she would ask next.

"Did he fire you?"

"Not exactly."

"What exactly then?"

"Verna, you knew this was always a short-term deal. To tide me over. Am I correct? That you knew that?"

"I couldn't but hope otherwise, could I?"

"That's very touching, the way you just said that."

"Are you being sarcastic?"

But his voice didn't have a sarcastic tone. Not then.

"You told him to fuck himself, didn't you? Or equivalent," Verna said.

"It wasn't like that."

"Oh no? Then what was it like? Tell me. I'd be interested."

"The man called me a stupid fuck."

"I don't believe you, Roy."

"That's your problem then."

"When did this happen?"

"When did what happen? It just happened."

"I just want to know, did it *just* happen or have you been hiding it from me all this time and being nice and everything, talking so nice all the time, and it was all bullshit again, all just more fucking lies, because you had something hard to tell me? You going to quit your contribution now?"

"To what? To the expenses? I swear, no."

"So you got new work, Roy? I haven't heard of you asking around."

"Well you know you could show some sympathy here, too. I'm the one's out of a job here."

"Did he fire you? That's what I want to know, Roy. Did he fire you? Or did you quit because you're such a big shot and know-it-all?"

"I'm not a big shot. I'm not a know-it-all. But I've got my pride, Verna. There's a big difference. Maybe you don't recognize that."

"Oh, bullshit! Bullshit, Roy! You quit ten days ago, didn't you?"

"As a matter of fact I did."

"I know you think I'm stupid. And I am stupid, okay? It was just blind stupid fucking bad luck, I was over to the Elliots' and Denny Elliot's on the phone with Mr. Bloch and she calls over to Cord that Mr. Bloch wants to know if Bill Mason's a good overall worker since he's looking for a permanent caretaker and Roy Soames just quit on him out of the blue. That was a week ago, Roy. So I've just been having a fine time since then, haven't I, listening all week to your lies. What a blast, figuring how you're going to get out of this one, which lie are you going to tell me next."

"That's nice, Verna. That's real nice, that's exceptional. See, you were just doing the same thing. Not telling me what *you* knew, that's just like lying. We're in the same boat, Verna, so get off your high horse, would you?"

"Fuck you."

She pushed away from the table so hard that Roy's plate landed in his lap. She didn't exactly mean to do it, but she didn't exactly mean it to not happen either. For a second, when the plate tipped off the table edge and Roy yelped, she felt her fear and satisfaction in equilibrium.

She went into her room at the end of the trailer. As soon as he put the plate back on the table and wiped his pants off, Roy followed her there to say he was sorry.

"Don't say that."

"I just did."

"Well don't."

"Verna, I've got plans, I've got dreams."

"You know you sound like the TV. 'I've got hopes, I've got dreams.' What are you, going to be in a stockbroker ad now? You going to be the truck driver who bought the dot com stock and now he owns the whole island? 'We can help you with your dreams.' All you've got are lies, Roy."

By then she was turned away from him, adjusting the photographs on top of her dresser, straightening them up a little. Frames three inches or six inches, her father, her mother, her sister and her sister's husband, her niece. None of herself, however. Verna noticed it, and it seemed odd, like a jigsaw puzzle with one piece missing, and why hadn't she noticed it before? She had such photographs, in a box in the closet, of herself with her father and mother, of herself with her sister, with everybody. They just weren't up there. Instead of thinking of Roy and where he was exactly, somewhere in back of her,

Verna told herself that she should get some of those photographs out.

"What do you want me to do, Verna?" Roy said.

"Leave. Please."

"For what? For lying to you? For trying to soften the blow?"

"For being no good for me, Roy. I'm sure you'll be fine for yourself. I'm sure with your plans, all that'll be great for you. But as many times as you come back, you'll only be no good for me more."

Roy considered the possibility of coming up on her from behind then and kissing the back of her neck. It had worked before, in a variety of situations, but he felt that it wouldn't work this time. And that realization, in truth, wounded him.

"You think I'm just no good. Even for myself."

"I just said the opposite."

"That's just to get rid of me, right?"

"No."

"Of course it is. I see that now."

"Go be sarcastic on your own time, Roy."

"What's sarcastic about that?"

"Go screw up every chance you ever get on your own time."

"You don't believe in me. That's the key here."

"Oh for pity's sake!" She turned to face him. Roy thought to himself that she'd never had a pretty face, even to start with. It had always been too big, and now that it was upset and glistening, it looked ever bigger. It looked to Roy like grief. "No," she said. "No, I don't, Roy."

He packed up and left.

Verna thought afterward that it hadn't made too much sense, what she'd said and done, she could even understand why Roy wouldn't understand it. It was an overreaction, in a way, because of all the times before when she'd underreacted. She viewed Roy, basically, as irreplaceable. That is, she didn't expect another to come along soon. But that was just how things were. She got out a few pictures that had herself in with the rest of her family, because it had seemed so odd to her that there were none out, and she got some more three-inch and six-inch frames the next time she was in Ellsworth, and put those up on her dresser along with the others. There was one of them where they were all in Everett's old boat. Not his red boat, but his old boat. Some kind of holiday. She missed Roy all the time, but felt she had to see this through.

23

Because Maisie had to be in New York they missed the Blue Hill fair, but there was another fair in another county that Bloch wanted to take the girls to. A country experience. The cows being led around by 4-H boys and girls, the prize bunnies in their cages, the petting zoo, the cotton candy. The previous year, just before they were married, Bloch and Maisie had taken the girls to Blue Hill and it had been their peak summer experience, the one that might still occupy a happy patch of memory forty years on, and they had clamored and lobbied, as well as four-year-olds might, to go again. The only problem with the second fair, in Windsor, was that Adam and Maisie had decided to leave Clement's Cove for the season a couple of days before it began. More of her infernal tests. Getting the girls ready for preschool, getting their outfits together. Bloch decided to make Maisie a bold proposal. Bold only in this, that the one thing Maisie wanted complete and utter control of in her life was her girls. Yes, she knew it wouldn't go on forever. Yes, she was prepared, sort of, for the time when it wouldn't go on forever. But for now, they were her project. And Bloch had never spent a night with them when Maisie wasn't there. He had taken them to movies, he had taken them to concerts. Now what he wanted to propose to her was that she go back to New York and have her tests and he would stay on with the girls in Clement's Cove and take them to the fair in Windsor and they would join Maisie in New York two days later.

He was expecting she would simply say no. Or say something about how she needed the time with them to shop. Or even, if the going got rough, make some insinuations about how Bloch really knew little about children and wasn't prepared to deal with them for two days straight. He was expecting, in other words, to be disappointed, and to feel, as well, an absurdity in his disappointment. Here he was, a man who in business had directed hundreds if not thousands of people's lives, who had made or broken careers, whose every word was listened to, especially when his words were few. And Maisie would be telling him she didn't trust him with her four-year-olds. And that he wouldn't know what to do. Of course he would know what to do. He'd been around them all summer long. But she would not *trust* him. And the most absurd part: he would accept what she had to say, he cared deeply what she would say. He couldn't shuck it off. He couldn't say to himself he had another life to go back to.

Or of course, Bloch wasn't only anticipating such sentiments, he was already feeling them. He girded himself before he talked to Maisie about it. He felt his mouth go dry.

But it all came out the opposite of what he had imagined. Which just showed, when it came to certain people, and those people were women, the smarter you tried to be about something, the more likely you were to be wrong. Somebody had told Bloch that. Maybe Zacky Kurtz, the old producer of *Northie*. It wasn't something Bloch would have thought of on his own. His mind didn't work that way. Although maybe, he hoped, it was starting to. He at least remembered such things now, as if they were oddities he was beginning to collect from the human junk shop. He was becoming more normal, wasn't he? Such that when Maisie said sure, why not, and what a good idea that was, and she'd arrange for Joni the babysitter to come and help out, Bloch did not forget to blink.

This is why he loved her, he thought. Maisie could still be like sunshine itself. Her red hair and smile. Two older folks from very different places, but you cannot know where life will wind you up.

A sentiment Maisie might have concurred with. One day she felt like she was living with a stranger and another with a good friend, and yet he was the same all the time. So it had to be Maisie who changed. But if she changed, was it for better or worse? Was she just impossible to live with? Maisie tried to chart what she felt, after all, were glacial changes in Bloch. A growing confidence, a growing ease, a growing trust? When he proposed that he stay on with the girls and go to the fair, she had her misgivings but thought life had to be chanced. For once she was betting on him. It seemed only fair. Just as it seemed only fair, given that he was fair all the time, that she should be fair at least once in a while.

That night Bloch had a great misgiving. It didn't start as a misgiving, but then it was. Maisie was asleep beside him. A night unusually warm for the second week of October, so that she had put the windows open and you could hear the rush of the tide. Bloch lay on his back and thought of the brake light on his car. Or rather, into whatever he was thinking just before that, its flickering red light intruded, like one of those sudden interruptions you sometimes got on the radio, static and a booming voice, from the "emergency preparedness system," or whatever that thing was called. A reminder, doubtless, that a couple weeks before, on one or two occasions, the brake light of the Mercedes had flickered on and off. He'd had the brake fluid checked and possibly filled, but now lying in bed at midnight with the rush of tide in his ears he couldn't remember, if the fluid had actually been low, if at the service station they'd filled it. And what if it wasn't the brake fluid? Bloch struggled to think what else it could be. Rotors, brake pads, discs, as if words from a dialect other than his own. Bloch didn't know a lot about cars.

This was ridiculous, he told himself. Two weeks had passed. The light hadn't come on again. He'd had the fluid checked right away. He was driving himself crazy with false concerns, and only because Maisie had said he could keep the girls with him and take them to the fair. Bloch wanted to run this particular film in reverse, as in screening rooms when he hadn't liked something or hadn't understood something he could just tell the projectionist to go back. He wanted to go back to whatever he'd been thinking just before the red light came on in his mind's eye. It must have been something delightful, something about taking the girls. A petting zoo? A beautiful black-and-white cow with a prize medal around its neck? But he had no projectionist to buzz anymore, he was alone in this room with the windows open and he couldn't remember what it was. What it wasn't, for sure, was what he thought of now, which was the Blue Hill fair, not of the preceding fall when he and Maisie took the girls, but the fair as it had been at the end of the summer of 1966, when he had come to Clement's Cove with me and Cord and Teddy and our friend and hero Harry Nolan who we all thought would be president one day and who was going in the Army. And Sascha, who was Harry's bride, and my first, secret love, and Bloch's. We all loved Sascha. We went to the Blue Hill fair and from the fair we went and got drunk, all but Bloch who became the designated driver, and then there was fog on the road and he thought he saw a deer and swerved and that was when Sascha died.

It was enough for Bloch to think of the fair to think of all the rest of it now. It terrified him. Nor had he ever felt human after that. That's what it came down to, or that's what he was feeling now, or that's what he was telling himself now. Why should he get a chance with Maisie's girls, why should they drive with him in a car, why should he impose on them his guilt, his fault, or his evil luck if that's all it was? He would have to protect them from himself. As always, he would have to make plans, take extra care, not put them in a situation. His courtesy was his shield. It stood between him and the disaster of those he loved. Lying in bed beside Maisie, Bloch felt a cool breeze come in on the tide and he cringed. The next day he said to Maisie there should be a change of plans. He would drive her to the airport and Bill Mason would follow them up and, after dropping Maisie, Bloch would leave the car at the Mercedes place and Bill Mason would drive him home.

"But how will you get to the fair?" Maisie asked. "I thought that was the whole idea."

"Maybe the car will be ready tomorrow. If not, Bill can drive us."

"But what if you need a car tonight?"

"I'll make sure that Bill's on call."

"Can't you rent a car?"

"It'll be easier just with Bill."

To Maisie it sounded contorted and more complicated than it needed to be, but it also sounded like Adam's care.

"The car really has to go in now?" she asked.

"It would be better if it went in when I was still around," he said. "Really, I didn't think of the brakes until last night."

He sounded so certain of it that she didn't question it further.

That night Bloch read to the girls from another of the McCloskey books that were all set near Clement's Cove. Then Maisie called and Alexandra and Margaret each got on a phone and the three of them talked as if the girls were off on the adventure of their lives. They both referred to Adam as "Daddy," which was as true and as normal as it could be, but still pleased him to hear, "Daddy" in the third person. He who'd been afraid he might never have a child. The girls slept in the rooms down the hall from his, each in her own bed. Maisie had wanted them to have their own rooms, had spent much of the summer getting the rooms finished.

In the morning Bloch called the Mercedes place in Bangor. They had found nothing wrong with the brakes but Bloch told them to keep the car and winterize it and go over it all. He told them he didn't need it right away. He'd have it picked up after he was gone. Bill Mason drove them to the fair, which was at first disappointing to Bloch, because it turned out to be a hippie fair, more that way than the Blue Hill Fair, anyway, and there was no cotton candy. But there were pigs and cows and sheep and guys on stilts with big noses and flashy pants, and the girls were happy. They even liked the soy dogs.

Maisie had Joni come over to make them dinner and make sure the girls were all packed up. Maisie had done most of the packing before she left but there were still toothbrushes and the clothes of the last couple days. Maisie surprised herself with these bursts of organization. She had never been organized before. She had been the crazy one, who didn't quite care. But now she cared about every detail. She talked to the girls another long time. She told them she'd see them tomorrow afternoon, she'd be at the airport, and was there anything special they wanted for dinner. Soy dogs, Margaret said.

Joni left and Bloch read to the girls again, the rest of the book from the night before, about girls who were going home after a long summer on an island. Then he put each to bed and kissed their foreheads and packed his own things to leave and thought of how wise he'd been to leave the car at the Mercedes place, it was better all around, and went to sleep.

24

There was a ratty cot and a gas heater in the garage where Freddy kept his limo and Freddy let Roy stay there. Having given up his place in Sedgwick, and being between employments, Roy had no other place. Freddy chided him about how a single male should not be quick to give up his own place, a lesson Freddy had learned on one occasion or another. Of course it was different once you were hitched, as was the case with himself and Marilyn, in that case there was no real alternative. But a single male had to look out for himself these days. The women had the power. The women made the rules. Freddy would have let Roy sleep in the limo itself, which would have been more comfortable than the ratty cot, but he was concerned that air freshener might not entirely remove the resultant smell. In a business that catered to the well-off, you had to attend to all the details.

It wasn't correct to say that Roy missed Verna. It was more correct to say how much worse his life was now, even after you subtracted out what a pain in the ass she had been. For this worsening of his circumstances, Roy came to blame Bloch more than he blamed Verna. He could see Verna's point of view. He could see how she'd think he was a screw-up. But what had brought her to that conclusion? Mainly, if you could put it in a category, it was Roy's interactions with this Mr. Bloch. Roy felt he had not been a hothead in quitting. The man was arrogant when all was said and done, he didn't know the depths of his own ignorance, and how do you work for someone like that, and anyway it was a dead-end situation. Roy continued to feel his life was worth more than dead-end situations.

And as further proof of all of it was Mr. Bloch's refusal to negotiate in any way, shape or manner concerning Verna's property, when Roy was flexible as hell, when he was even offering the man a bargain. There was something fishy there that Roy had never figured out. It was as if the man had some secret reason, so that he didn't act the way a normal rich guy would when offered what amounted to a steal. And Verna'd bought into all that, hook, line, and sinker. How she'd talk about him! What a decent fella he seemed to be! What nice neighbors to have! It just showed about rich people, no different from anybody else! It was almost like she wound up liking the guy more than she liked Roy.

It even got to the point, a couple of times, in Roy's thinking, where he imagined it wasn't beyond the realm of possibility that this Mr. Bloch had had his way with Verna. You never knew with these shy-looking guys. A lot of times that was exactly how they snuck in there, with that shy kind of look. And, too, there was Mrs. Bloch's tendency to be away with those kids quite a lot. Of course the one part of it that didn't make sense was the established fact this Mr. Bloch had owned a whole TV company, and if he wanted to spread his seed around there must have been some real beauties out there. Verna was nothing to look at. Even Roy had to admit to himself, that part put a hole in his theory.

One night Freddy and Marilyn had one of their once-every-other-week fights and Freddy came looking to find Roy for a bit of company. Roy had been spending more evenings than not at a tavern in Bar Harbor and they went over there together. In the course of commiserating and getting plastered, Freddy allowed how this last brawl might finally be the one that finished it for him and Marilyn. *Que sera, sera*, Freddy said, and then sang the translation off-key, while looking around the room to see if any women had walked in. It was a night of slim pickings, just like most of the others. The Bruins were playing on the television. Freddy said it would be a damn different story with Marilyn if he could have closed that deal for the limos. She was a woman who respected success. That's what it came down to. As he himself respected it. That's where they were alike.

Roy was feeling grateful toward Freddy and a little hopeful they might soon be in the same boat and he commiserated along. "These women don't have any faith," he said. "With them it's all got to be black-and-white, it's all got to be a done deal. Absolutely. You're absolutely right."

"Now you know I'm not one to criticize," Freddy said, "but you gave up with that New York fucker a little quick."

"You're referring to. . ."

"The New Yorker guy, the guy."

"Mr. Bloch?"

"The hell is this 'mister' shit?"

"You're right. No, you're right. I don't know why I say that. It's like copying Verna everything she says."

"You gave up on him a little too quick."

"You think I shouldn't of quit that job?"

"Hell, no. Quit. Absolutely right you quit. You weren't gonna go anywhere with that, getting paid by the hour to cut the guy's toenails. No, I'm talking about getting the man to buy her out. You'd've gotten that done, we'd be sitting pretty now. Both of us. Plus Verna. That's the point she didn't understand, correct? She didn't understand it would be *plus* Verna.

She'd be among the first to benefit. And believe me, there's still plenty of opportunity."

"How so?"

"My friend, lest you forget, I'm still in business over here."

"Royce's daughter didn't sell his cars yet?"

"No, she sold his cars. She sold 'em, alright. To someone in *New Jersey*. You know what that means, don't you? Less competition around here. Less fleet chasing more business."

"So you're still looking to expand?"

"Absolutely. That Alice Gilmore didn't have the corner on previously owned limos. There's plenty around. You look online, they're all over."

"Well, if I could come up with the money, could I still be a part of the business?"

"The seat's still open at the table, partner."

It was the charm of that last word that warmed Roy up. If Freddy could still talk that way, could use the word "partner" and it didn't even sound sarcastic, then the last days and weeks of trouble might not all be a loss.

"'Course I don't have a clue where I could get that kind of money," Roy said.

"I know exactly where you could've. And you could still do it," Freddy said.

"You think? Cause the way I look at it, I'm fucked."

"Hell no. Your only problem, you gave up too quick. You didn't give the man enough hints."

"Hints. What hints?"

"Hints. Hints. Encouragements."

"I *gave* him hints. What about the garbage?"

"The garbage, yes. You put out garbage. Why should he give a fuck? He thinks you're a punk."

"Verna didn't want any more of that anyways."

"Verna's not part of it now, is she? Is Verna sitting here with us? Absolutely not."

"I thought of coyote piss once." Roy smiled easily in remembering it. "Put coyote piss on his porch."

"Oh that would be real effective. That would be tremendously effective."

"You know you can be a sarcastic fuck, Freddy."

"Listen to me." Freddy lowered his voice, almost like they were in a movie, almost like he really thought the barkeep, who was about halfway down the bar, would be listening. "Listen to me and shut up a second. The point is, not to get him to buy now. He's proved he's not gonna buy. So you got to get him to *sell*."

"Got it. Got it. You mean, because if he sold, then the next guy. . ."

"Whoever that is. Whoever that next guy is. Absolutely. You think the next guy's going to want that fucking trailer looking at his property? Anybody at all, anybody with a brain, once he's got that money invested, he's going to want Verna out of there. Which is good for all of us, right? Good for all of us, even her."

"Absolutely," Roy said. "Absolutely positively good for her." Roy tugged at his beer. "But just say, just say it was you who decided, what would *you* do, Freddy, to get him to sell?"

"What would I do? It's pretty obvious, isn't it? You don't do half measures. You don't act like a punk. First of all, you wait till he's gone, you wait till he's closed up for the season. . ."

"But he is gone."

"You told me he stayed on late."

"Yeah, but I happened to be by there. You know, just kind of checking. . ."

"On Verna? You are a pathetic individual."

"But his car's gone. Their car's gone."

"Oh, that's really *great*. The car's gone. What if they're out to a movie, fuckbrain?"

"Actually, okay. You want to know? I actually saw. . . I spoke to her."

"Verna?"

"And she told me the Blochs were gone. She saw them driving to the airport."

"Then, uh, the fuck are we waiting for?"

"Waiting for what?"

"There's only one thing ever got a man to think in a concentrated fashion about selling out. Lightning strikes his place. On a night when there's no lightning."

The number of beers they'd had, their desperation for any sort of success. These things put a hazy cloud of assent over what otherwise might have seemed a shaky proposition. As well, Roy sort of worshipped Freddy. Probably that was also a part of it. He aspired to be Freddy's partner in something.

As a result they never asked themselves, for instance, if Verna who would be the immediate beneficiary of all their plans would ever let Roy back into her life so that Roy and Freddy could benefit too. Nor did they reflect on the fact that Freddy knew little about arson, other than that his brother had burned down somebody's boathouse when he was seventeen and gotten caught for it. Nor did they think about where suspicion might fall if Bloch's house burned down. Or actually, the last they thought about a little bit. Freddy assured Roy that in cases like this the sheriff assumed it was an accident, because summer houses were always burning down, and a lot of times it was an insurance scam, but everybody looked the other way because they didn't want to get into legal hassles with rich people from away, and anyway the insurance premiums were too high, so there was some basic sympathy with the individual right there to start with. Roy did manage to ask, if everybody would believe it was an accident or an insurance scam, what there would be to persuade Mr. Bloch to sell out. But Freddy was thinking just then of the money that would be coming circuitously his way, and he forgot to answer and Roy forgot to ask again. It was a midnight adventure. It felt like taking back their world.

Freddy kept five gallon cans of gasoline in the garage where Roy was staying. They went back to get two of those first, and more beer and little bottles of vodka out of the minibar in the limo. They almost drove over in the limo itself, but Roy felt it might call too much attention to themselves, whereas if they took Roy's truck, just in case anybody saw them in Clement's Cove after midnight, it would seem only natural. Neither of them really questioned that reasoning either. A moonlit night and no one on the roads. From Bar Harbor to Clement's Cove, a distance of fifty miles, they passed only seven cars.

When they got to Bloch's road they parked at the bottom of it, so that the truck motor would not wake up Verna. They trudged up the road with the cans of gasoline and a few rags and such. They had continued to drink in the truck and that had quelled Roy's few doubts, that were anyway more like wispy contrails of his soul than anything that would really have stopped him. There was no car in the driveway of Bloch's house. Roy peered through the window panes of the garage to make sure there was none there either. The house was so dark that the moonlight shone brightly on it. Even Freddy could see that it was a damn pretty house and that all kinds of money had gone into it. A shame, in a way, but what could you do? Business was business. Something like that. No one else around. No one around at all, or so it seemed. A quiet lapping of the waves below them. Roy followed Freddy around, carrying the second can, while Freddy spilled gasoline here, there, and elsewhere. When he lit it there was no explosion, but quickly a ring of flame around the house. Roy and Freddy ran back down the road. They felt like freedom fighters. Fighting for their own freedom, anyway. They were gone quickly. Once they were out of Clement's Cove, they turned the radio up loud.

25

The first thing Bloch did when he heard the smoke alarms screeching was grab for his bathrobe and put it on. He didn't want the girls to see him in his underpants. It was a silk robe he'd bought in Beverly Hills, one of the few things he ever bought for himself until he began to court Maisie, and he kept it on a chair by his bed as if you never knew what might happen suddenly in life. An old earthquake habit from California, perhaps. But when he awoke from a dream of whatever it was, he wasn't in California, he was on the coast of Maine and whatever might happen suddenly in life was happening then. Smoke poured up the stairs that he could see from his open door. He began to cough. He shouted the girls' names. He ran out into the hall.

Flames licked up under the smoke. They were consuming the carpet on the stairs and now the banisters caught fire. In bare feet Bloch ran around the fire, shouting the girls' names. More smoke alarms went off. They were screeching everywhere.

He ran into Margaret's room. She was sitting up in bed, crying for help, for Maisie. The flames were leaping outside her windows. Bloch lifted her up and kissed her forehead and ran with her through the connecting door to Alexandra's room.

Alexandra wasn't in her bed. Bloch put Margaret on Alexandra's bed and ran into her bathroom but she wasn't there either. He shouted her name. "Alexandra! Alexandra! Sascha!" It was the first time he'd ever called her Sascha. The smoke began to choke and blind him. He turned in the haze, this way and that. "Alexandra! Where are you? Sascha! Alexandra!"

He found her in the back of her closet, underneath her hanging party dresses, sitting on the floor with her knees up as if they alone would keep away the fire. He brought her back to where Margaret was. He got them to lie on the floor because the smoke was less there. He took one fraction of a second to thank God for Maisie who had put a phone in each of the girls' rooms because she spent so much time there and dialed the operator because Clement's Cove had no 9-1-1 and reported the fire. The operator was someplace a hundred miles away and had to look up wherever Clement's Cove was and then said she'd forward it right away.

Bloch would have waited then, because of the smoke and fire in the hall and out the windows, he would have waited for help and wet the blankets in the bathroom and lain close to the floor with the girls and wrapped the wet blankets around them all so they could breathe and put towels in the cracks of the doors, the way they were always instructing you in hotels in the event of fire. He was lucid then. His mind that had often thought clearly thought as clearly as it ever had. But then the fire burst open Alexandra's door and plaster fell and there was little left between them all and the flames that came in the door.

He herded the crying girls back through the connecting door. He grabbed the blankets from Margaret's bed and took them into Margaret's bathroom and soaked them in the tub and wrapped both the girls into both the blankets so they were like one big wet roll.

The fire in Alexandra's room burned through the connecting door into Margaret's. Bloch raced to the door opposite, which led back into the hall. He opened it to a curtain of fire. The knob was so hot it scorched his hand. He came back and grabbed up the big, wet roll that was Margaret and Alexandra. It didn't feel heavy, it felt almost light, and the cool touch of the soaking blankets was comforting. Still barefoot, in his silk bathrobe, with the bundle of the girls in his arms, Bloch felt, for once in his life, not exhilarated, but certain.

He walked as quickly as he could but didn't run, because he was afraid of dropping the girls. The flames were like all the accusers of his life. He would face them down, he would show them they weren't true, he would purify himself by being more than he had ever been. Or really, he couldn't help himself. He was lucid yet didn't know what he was doing. All he knew was that he was doing it. He was walking through the flames that were the accusers of his life as if they weren't even there. His rage would be greater than theirs. His rage, his sorrow, his revenge, would be greater. He would show them. Bloch who'd killed Maisie's sister. Bloch who didn't blink. Bloch with his guilt or fault or evil luck or whatever it was, who accused himself and took steps to protect the innocent of the world from himself. Bloch who'd once gotten lost in the fog and now it was as if that fog had turned suffocating and acrid and caught on fire. He would show them but show them what? Was Bloch not human, did he not bleed, did he not blink?

He walked through the hall, where the flames were huge, and down the stairs, where by now the flames were less. His feet were scorched. His robe caught fire. His hair caught fire. His flesh was burnt.

The one thing for certain he never thought was that this small, rather unprepossessing, older, wiry-haired man with a small pot belly and a wife he was lucky to have was doing anything like those things they were always doing in the movies. He had made such movies, or paid for them anyway. He had known guys who played such parts and they were different from himself.

He didn't even think he was redeeming his life. He would never have used those words.

And he didn't really know that he was afraid. He should have known, but he didn't. It was like something that in all the commotion got overlooked. The way Bloch's mother might once have put it, "in all the commotion."

Once down the stairs, he finally ran. In the thick darkness of the smoke, across the long entry hall of the house or what was left of it, dodging fallen charred beams, out the door, into air you could breathe, across the porch that was also burning, down the stone stairs, and into the night grass.

Verna, who had awakened to see the flames up the road, arrived to find the two girls in the grass, still wrapped together in their blankets like one of those sandwiches the Tradewinds made with the Lebanese bread, their faces smudged but their bodies unharmed. Scratches and bruises, seemed to be nothing more. They were whimpering softly. Margaret seemed on the verge of falling back asleep. Verna kissed them both, and untangled them a little from each other. Bloch was a little distance away, where he had rolled in the moist grass, in order to put the fire of his flesh out. He was still in his silk bathrobe, the charred shreds of it anyway. At points, at his shoulders in particular, the silk seemed to have fused with his flesh. He was unconscious. Verna gasped for how terrible he looked. The siren to call the volunteer firemen out of their beds began to wail.

III

26

A chapter on me and Bloch, my alter ego.

I had always confused myself with Adam Bloch. This went all the way back, to when I met him in college. Then he had been like the nerd, the flamer as we used to say. The maladroit one, the one who never had the right thing to say, the kid who couldn't blink, the Jew who gave Jews a bad name. And it further pissed me off that the friend whom I then very nearly worshiped, Harry Nolan, the guy we all thought would be president one day, was fond of Bloch as well.

Then Bloch was driving the car and I was in the backseat and Harry and his bride Sascha were in the front and Cord and Teddy Redmond were there too, and you already know the rest of that story.

The dark stain of Bloch. It's how I thought of it, never sure whether that dark stain was really myself.

We were the two outsiders, the two Jews, the two with our hidden ambitions, or whatever you would say.

Maybe I imagined that we looked too much alike, though we didn't really look much alike at all. I was taller, thinner, he had wiry hair. Bloch was always compact, just shy of pudgy, he looked like someone who would be hard to move if he didn't want to be. He had a stubborn look about him, always. Bloch looked a bit like my soul, perhaps, or what I imagined my soul to be, but not particularly like the guy who walked around and was called by my name.

Our lives crossed too many times. Yale. Harry. Sascha. When he was already rich, I brought him to California and helped him buy the company I worked for and he saved me my job. And there was Maisie too.

My one-time lover. Bloch's bride. Clement's Cove. Bloch knew that I'd struggled to forgive him and maybe never had.

Not for Sascha's death, finally, but for the fact that he himself lived on. It was as if his very ability to survive anything seemed to make him what he was. Incapable of a broken heart?

Another thing, as the years passed, that I accused myself of. Being incapable of a broken heart. Or maybe it was simply that both our hearts, Bloch's and mine, had been broken so long ago and had never healed up. Hearts deep in waiting, watchful, injured, but alive. What is a heart if it's not that thing that's most deeply hidden? You could almost say that was a definition, find the most hidden thing and call it a heart. A definition for some of us, anyway.

Although, can you have a definition if it's not good for all? Bloch and I: he became the version of me I was most afraid to tell myself.

Then when he went and made all the money and saved me my job and was kind and started up with Maisie and came to Clement's Cove as if it were his project to become a human being at last, I came to see another version of me as him. For all those years of his ascendance it had been taking shape, but it crystallized, I think, at the wedding. Bloch playing his cello in the storm. Me if I'd gone all the way. Me if my own broken heart had been as large as his, if I'd suffered the same catastrophe.

I went off on my fellowship to Europe. Bloch stayed behind, in this place where we'd been thrown together in tragedy thirty-odd years before. I've of course had to imagine a lot of what he said or thought or exactly how he did things. But you see, I knew him well. Or I thought I did. I thought he was almost me. It turned out he wasn't. Not at all.

27

Something about Bloch and money.

He scored 800 on his math College Board, in the days before they inflated the scores. He could do columns of figures in his head, multiplications and long divisions in his head.

He liked to win. But he was not a sore loser. He simply resolved to win the next time.

His memory was good.

He was good at *Monopoly*.

He made his first fortune in stone-washed jeans and then a larger one in network TV and a still larger one in cable TV and then he was the only one of the Hollywood guys, or the only one I heard of, anyway, to see the potential of the Internet early. The rest of them just sat there and choked on the envy of it all when the kids up north made their piles. And then sometime early in 1999 Bloch sold out of the Internet too. None of us knew at the time that this was a smart thing to do. We thought only that he'd fallen for Maisie and didn't care about the rest anymore.

Later he was fond of quoting Bernard Baruch, who apparently told people the secret of his fortune was that he sold too soon. Bloch must have thought he was a little like Bernard Baruch then. He must have read a book about him.

It was something he could do, make money, when there were so many simpler things that he couldn't do. He would wonder sometimes why people marveled at his gift, or knack, or developed skill, or whatever it was. He never valued it especially highly. But he knew it was what he had to work with. He was not blind to what money could do.

He was generous with his money. Not flashy, but generous and orderly and even slyly sweet. Not one to put his name on hospital wards or museum wings, to want to know where the name would go before he wrote the check. He simply wrote the check. Bloch was not a scholar, but somewhere he had heard of a Talmudic teaching that the highest acts of charity were those done in secret.

Once a year he counted his money, or estimated it anyway, ballparked it on a piece of paper. But the year he married Maisie, he forgot.

And then there were the times when he hated it.

Because it wore him like a suit rather than the other way around.

Because it wouldn't go away when he told it to.

Because he couldn't even hate it without feeling ungrateful.

Because it had a way of insinuating that it was all that he was.

But his hating it was only a low-grade fever, really.

Mostly he got along. Mostly he played the cards that he was dealt.

28

Something about Verna's family.

Clement's Cove from its earliest days had been a good safe harbor to go fishing from. The founding family were the Clements, or as some have had it, the Clementses, who came down the coast from the vicinity of York sometime after the Revolution. Soon after them came the Masons and the Hubbards. Edward Hubbard moved his family from Newburyport, Massachusetts for the promise of cheap land and a fresh start in what was then a forested and isolated place.

By then the Indians were gone. The wars with the French had all but eliminated them from the coast.

Edward and his sons and grandsons fished for mackerel and cod. They didn't have to go far to find them. They fished "on shares," which meant that the catch of the whole boat was divided equally among all the fishermen aboard. No one was labor, no one was boss.

In the Civil War, five Hubbards fought. Horace Hubbard, age twenty-two, was killed at Gettysburg. William Hubbard, age twenty, died of typhus in a Confederate prison.

After the war, the canning plants came to the coast. John Hubbard and Clarence Hubbard and the first Everett Hubbard fished for herring that went to the plants and came out as sardines.

For twelve years or so there were weirs on Clement's Cove, so that the fish were caught right there.

A couple of the women in the family, Sarah Hubbard and Dorothy Morris, became schoolteachers. The others stayed close to Clement's Cove, or went over to Deer Isle or Sedgwick, and raised their families. The Hubbards became intermarried with the Morrises, the Audrys, the Cumminses, the Earlys, the Hutchinsons, and a few others, but never with the Clements. The two families didn't get on. It may have been they were too close neighbors.

The Masons and the Clements sold their land off to rusticators starting around 1880, and the Hubbards sold some off, too, since it wasn't worth a damn for farming, but John Hubbard was the first of the Hubbards to hesitate about doing so. He didn't believe in selling land off.

Summer houses were built, around but not on, the Hubbards' land.

Frederick Hubbard, age twenty-four, died when the *USS Maine* exploded. He was one of six Mainers killed aboard that ship.

John Hubbard Junior went out to Alaska to seek his fortune in the gold fields, and there were those who said he found one there. But he never came back. No one knew for sure what happened to him.

James Hubbard, age twenty, died in the Argonne forest. Another Edward Hubbard, age eighteen, died at the Second Battle of the Marne.

In 1923, Franklin Hubbard put a motor on his boat for the first time. By then the fish were farther from shore than they had been. In that same year, 1923, the Elliot family from Tennessee built their first shingle cottage on the cove.

In 1926, Millicent Hubbard, Franklin's second daughter, won a scholarship to go to Bates College in Lewiston.

During the Depression, Franklin Hubbard sold off more of the family land than he would have liked to do.

Daniel Hubbard, age twenty, died in the Battle of Monte Cassino.

By the nineteen seventies, the fish were nearly gone. William Hubbard and his son Everett Hubbard turned to lobstering, and a certain Hubbard whose name was not often mentioned, to protect the innocent, was said to have turned to marijuana smuggling.

In 1971, Janice Hubbard, a first cousin of Verna's, age twenty-four, died when the C-130 she was flying in crashed on a supply mission en route to TanSonNhat Airport, Republic of Vietnam.

In 1994, Everett Hubbard died, and Verna was left the last Hubbard living on Clement's Cove.

29

Something about Bloch and justice.

    I read this once, I'm not even sure it's true: that the measure of a just man is not how he yearns for justice when he is oppressed, but whether he still yearns for it when he is no longer oppressed.

30

A dream of Roy's.

She tells him to get in the pool with her.

He tells her, "It's too damn hot, you get in your own damn pool," which is just teasing, because he gets in with her.

It's like Verna's lost twenty pounds, he's about to tell her, "You lost twenty pounds," when it's not Verna at all, it's Maisie, she said to call her Maisie, so he says, "You lost twenty years."

And she says, "Thank you very much. I feel like I did."

In the pool they get so close they're rubbing against each other and for sure, he thinks, this'll cost him his job, but instead she says, "This'll cost Mr. Bloch his job."

Roy grabs her breasts then and she grabs him and they go at it for several seconds till all the water's drained out of the pool.

31

A letter was waiting for me at the post office. It had been there more than two weeks and Arnie Simmons, who was postmaster, was beginning to wonder what to do with it. He would have returned it to sender, he said, but the sender was someplace in Shanghai, China and he wasn't sure what the postal authorities in China did with letters stamped "return to sender." One of those dilemmas you faced in mail delivery, damned if you do and damned if you didn't. Arnie was glad to see me. What had it been? A year and a half? The way it worked, you only get one year of forwarding. So that, too, had made him uncertain what to do. Can't just turn off the hearing aid to regulations entirely.

The letter was from Maisie. It was on hotel stationery. One of the chains, Four Seasons, I think. I read it in the post office parking lot, halfway to my rental car, on that bone-damp afternoon of my arrival back in Clement's Cove. It began:

> Old friend. I'm not sure how much of this you know. Or, of course, if you'll even receive this. But I thought I ought to try. You know you could cease being a jerk about it and get e-mail by now. Have you, maybe? Let me know if you have. Though I'm not sure I would wish to put this in an e-mail.
>
> Adam is dead. I suppose that's the first thing I should

say. He died on October 29, 2000, in Jerusalem, Israel. How he got there, why he got there, I'm not even sure I can say.

She then related to me the facts of the matter regarding Bloch's staying on with the girls when she went back to New York, and the fire, and the fact it was arson, and what Adam did to save the girls. Pretty much as I've written them.

The letter went on:

> It was almost a miracle he survived at all. It's what the doctors said. Third-degree burns, seventy percent of his body. The trauma, the chances of infection. They flew him to Boston, to Mass General. They sedated him, kept him unconscious. I came up. It was this almost unbelievably schizophrenic experience, because I was so relieved about the girls, and so horrified about him. I almost couldn't balance it. They wouldn't even let me get close to him. He was in one of these tents. The infection danger. Also, they had to cool his body. It was so burnt, any heat alone could have killed him. If I'm perfectly, totally honest, I suppose there was something merciful in my being unable even to see him well then. I'm afraid I would have averted my eyes. And if I had, I would never have forgiven myself. Never, not ever. Yet I wanted to kiss him. Kiss his lips, I think. Be balm for his lips.
>
> But I think his lips. . . what's the point of even saying?
>
> I returned to the city. There was a plan to bring him

by air ambulance to New York Hospital. I approved it. I thought it was a good idea. Then the day before we were going to move him, I got word that he'd regained consciousness. They'd lessened the sedation.

I was going to fly up right away. But they said don't, he's still in his tent, by the time I got there he'd probably be asleep again. It was only one night. I said okay.

The next day he didn't show up. I was at the hospital waiting. We called Newark Airport. We called the air ambulance company. They said I'd have to speak to one of the directors. I was going crazy. I thought he must have died en route. You know the way, if a plane crashes, they put on the board, "see agent."

But it wasn't that. I was told there'd been a change of itinerary, at the patient's express request. I said well could they possibly explain to me the wife what the fucking change of itinerary was? They said they couldn't because it was a matter of patient confidentiality.

I said fine but I was the goddamn wife and my husband's life was in danger and if they didn't tell me I'd sue their ass into the Hudson River by sunset. They said they were sorry but it was a question of confidentiality, at the express request of the patient.

I went ballistic. I know, it sounds like I'd already gone ballistic, but then I went really ballistic. I screamed and threatened and probably called up everything I'd ever learned at McLean's about going crazy, and finally the guy said he could understand my distress but he would have to get back to me and he hung up. So I did, I called up Debevoise and we sued them the next day. Sued Mass General, too, when they weren't cooperative either. They said they knew nothing about it, it wasn't their business, the patient was released. Finally, one of the doctors, who we also sued, said, just as a matter of rumor, something he'd heard indirectly, so he didn't think it would be violating doctor–patient privilege, but something about going to Israel.

I called up every hospital in Israel that had a trauma center in it. And it was unbelievable, but I found him. He was in Hadassah Hospital, Jerusalem, registered under his own name. It was a place that had an international reputation for trauma, and it allowed me for a few seconds to imagine he'd chosen it for its excellence of care, that's why he'd snuck away from us all, he was going for the excellent treatment and as soon as he was better he would come back. But it wasn't that, of course. Whatever it was, it wasn't that. Among other things, you can't get much more excellent than Mass General or New York Hospital. I flew out that night. I wanted to surprise him. Or I imagined all sorts of things, him refusing to see me, him engineering another escape. But by the time I got there, he was gone. He'd died early in the morning. The doctors' fear of an overwhelming infection had been realized.

I've spent more time than I could ever admit wondering

what made him run away, and in such a perilous, awful
condition. You know the facts now as I know them,
so, dear Louie, you may have as good a guess as mine.
Maybe better. Maybe I'm too close to it. But what I
imagine, what I think. . . pretty basic, I guess, pretty
dumb of me. . . but I imagine he felt guilty. About me,
about all of it.

And asking himself all those "if's," replaying the trauma
of Sascha. I imagine he didn't feel like a hero at all. I
imagine he thought that single, selfless act of his was
normal, the least you could expect of a person. Or no,
not a person. A person who'd screwed so much up. A
person who was never out of debt, no matter how much
money he had. I imagine – and this is the worst part
of it for me – that he even felt guilty for being the one
who said he'd like the girls to stay so he could take them
to the fair.

So maybe he ran away because he couldn't face us? Felt
he didn't deserve us?

Embarrassment, the silent killer. Do you think so,
Louie? Please. I'm not telling you. I'm asking you. He
was my husband and I feel I knew nothing. Worse, that
I didn't try hard enough to know, when he was alive.

And going to Israel. Why Israel? All the time I'd known
him, he'd never made anything of being Jewish. Not to
me, anyway. But then, maybe he wouldn't. What about
to you? Did he ever to you? Tell me if I'm wrong. But

then I thought, Israel's supposed to be that place where
a Jew can go when nobody else wants him.

I even imagined he'd made arrangements, if he died to
be buried on Mount Scopus, or wherever that cemetery
is, I'm not sure I've got this right, but I've read it, a lot
of Jews, from all over the world, they decide they want
to be buried there. Talk about feeling like an outsider.
Me trying to have a coherent thought about that.
Me trying to imagine a place where you can go when
nobody else wants you.

My life's been too lucky. I've had this shitty disease, but
my life's been too lucky.

But he hadn't made any such arrangements. Or at least
the hospital wasn't aware of them. They gave me his
remains and I felt like one of those Army guys who
has to bring the bodies home. His parents were gone.
There was no one to consult. I had him cremated,
then spent weeks thinking about what to do with the
ashes. Selfish, probably, nothing but selfish, but over
Christmas, on Mount Desert, you know some piece of
our family always goes up there for Christmas, I put the
ashes in the family plot. By Sascha's grave, and Harry's,
and where maybe mine will be one day. The ground
wasn't quite frozen, but it was still a hell of a job. I loved
digging that hole. One thing I could do, dig that hole.

So there. End of story? I doubt it. I don't know what
I'll be feeling about any of it a year from now. I myself

am well, by the way. Physically, I mean. Clear on
all the latest batch of tests. The girls, also well. They
miss Adam. They don't understand. They really were
charmed by him, finally. They loved that fair he took
them to.

Probably you've heard this, if you've heard anything at
all, but the state police caught two men for the crime.
One was very briefly our caretaker, maybe you know
him, Roy Soames, who lived with that woman in the
trailer for awhile. I always thought he was cute. Isn't
that terrible? Adam thought he was trouble from the
start. I can't even think about that part.

Or yes, I can. I was unkind to Adam. I was unfair to
him. I didn't see him, for God's sake.

Roy and his friend, a guy from Mount Desert, are
charged with murder. The truth is, I feel horrid for
them too. They didn't mean murder.

But beyond that. There are nights, like the nights Adam
must have lived, when I'm certain it was all my fault, I
started it all, like the Helen of Clement's Cove. It's just
how it was.

I've brought the girls here, to Shanghai, so that they
could be in a place where most of the faces look more
like theirs. Probably not necessary, but anyway, we're
here. Shanghai, as you've probably read, is exploding.
We've been living in a hotel up to now, which means

the girls have been getting to live like little Eloises. I've made a few friends. The kids go to a bilingual school and are starting to learn Chinese. I've even talked to people about starting the kind of breakfast joint I had in Taos. There are plenty of ex-pats who would likely appreciate it. But most probably we'll come home after not too long.

About Adam Bloch. My husband. My friend. My lover, too. You know, we were lovers, sometimes it didn't seem like it, but we were. The one thing that keeps me sleepless and brings tears to my eyes is my fear that he died feeling unloved. Please, Louie, tell me if you can, that it was otherwise. But I don't think you can.

Maisie

IV

32

In the general store there was a difference of opinion as to what some said was a key piece of evidence. Lewis Early maintained that the fact Roy checked out the garage before they set the fire showed an intent to do no bodily harm. Tom Benson, who was more Roy's pal than some of the others, concurred that it meant Roy was not too bad a fella, really, kind of a weak sister was all it was, he just got his head turned around by a set of bad circumstances and unfortunate company from over to Bar Harbor, but it wasn't his nature to injure or kill. Tom added that it would be just like Roy, to look in that garage first and make sure it was empty. On the other side of the argument was chiefly Burt Cummins, whose main point was that felony murder was felony murder. According to Burt, you didn't have to intend to kill or even maim, all you had to do was intend to commit a certain felony, in this case arson, and if a death resulted, that was it, you were guilty of felony murder. Mac, Bonnie, and a few others deferred to Burt's apparent expertise on this subject. But Tom Benson said, all well and good, but that didn't mean it was right, to convict a man of murder in these circumstances. Go take it up with the geniuses in Augusta, Burt Cummins said. You could usually score a few points in the general store by referring anything back to the geniuses in Augusta. Another point of discussion was whether Mr. Bloch's death could properly be attributable to anything Roy did, including the arson. The point here, Lew Early said, was that nobody really knew the suspicious circumstances in which Mr. Bloch died. If it was okay for him to fly all the way over to Jerusalem, Israel, he couldn't've been in too bad health, could he now? Lew admitted he didn't know as much law as Burt Cummins, but for instance if those doctors over there messed something up and that's why he died, then you couldn't pin that back on old Roy, could you? And that whole thing about going over there, said Tunk Smith, to Israel when you're sick like that, what was that all about? Mr. Bloch ought to take some responsibility here, Roy oughtn't to bear all of it, Tunk said.

Although, according to Ralph Audry, Verna felt he should. Verna, according to Ralph, felt that Roy deserved whatever he got, which according to rumor and the best estimates anybody could come up with, would probably be about seven years in the penitentiary. Tom Benson said you had to take in account Verna's position here. Of course she wasn't going to go light on Roy, he said, it didn't make sense, after all he'd put her through.

But Ralph said her feelings had more to do with the fact it was evil what was done to Mr. Bloch. That was the strong word she was using, the evil done to him, Ralph said. According to Verna, it wasn't every man, no matter what they would say when they weren't personally involved, who would have got himself all burned up to the point of dying to save two little girls. Some would, sure, but a lot wouldn't. A lot would go only halfway, or get burned only a little and that would be it. Bonnie said she'd heard Verna express opinions similar to these. Verna felt Mr. Bloch was a very decent man, according to Bonnie.

Everyone could agree with that, Mac said, nobody was disputing that part, Mr. Bloch was a great performer in that fire.

And Roy was a numbnuts for sure. But the whole thing was a tragedy. That's all you could really say about it.

I was there for that discussion. I asked how Verna was doing. Bonnie said she was doing pretty good, she took a couple weeks off to go see her sister in Vermont, but she was back now and cleaning houses. Then I told the others I'd received a letter from Bloch's widow and that she and her little girls were in Shanghai, China. Tunk Smith wanted to know what she was doing there and I said I didn't really know for sure. Was it for one of those eastern medical treatments, Carl Henry asked, and I said no, she was well now. And I added that I imagined she just wanted to be away. Then Con Stephens asked me if I happened to know how much she was wanting for that property of hers. I said I didn't know that, either.

Then Mac asked me how well I really knew this Mr. Bloch. I said I knew him a long time.

33

That summer the wreckers and bulldozers came and they tore down what was left of Bloch's Folly. A lot of salvage, a lot of Italian flagstone, they said. Even the foundations were dug out, so that the new owners, Goldman Sachs people from New Canaan, Connecticut, could start over. They had a different idea for their house on the coast. More windows, more light. Making the most of the view. A house more like the Hamptons, unafraid of glass and steel. And Maisie's lap pool was not enough for them. They wanted a spa and an invisible edge and black tiles and a waterfall, everything the previous owners had disdained. It was all going to cost a fortune.

Verna watched the same workmen come and go. The new owners' attorneys called and made her offers. She was still not selling.